THE WO
GREATEST
SHORT STORIES

THE WORLD'S GREATEST SHORT STORIES

JAICO PUBLISHING HOUSE

Ahmedabad Bangalore Bhopal Bhubaneswar Chennai
Delhi Hyderabad Kolkata Lucknow Mumbai

Published by Jaico Publishing House
A-2 Jash Chambers, 7-A Sir Phirozshah Mehta Road
Fort, Mumbai - 400 001
jaicopub@jaicobooks.com
www.jaicobooks.com

THE WORLD'S GREATEST SHORT STORIES
ISBN 81-7224-058-9

First Jaico Impression: 1989
Thirtieth Jaico Impression: 2014

Printed by
Kadambari Printers Pvt. Ltd.
19, Ansari Road, Darya Ganj
New Delhi - 110 002

CONTENTS

ENGLAND

PAGE

The Celestial Omnibus . . . *E. M. Forster* 9
Dusk . . . . . . *"Saki"* 24
The Nap . . . . . *Walter de la Mare* 28
The Case of Miss Lomas . . . *H. E. Bates* 45
The Black Mate . . . *Joseph Conrad* 54
Before the Party . . . *W. Somerset Maugham* 79

SCOTLAND

At Sanchidrian . . . *R. B. Cunninghame Graham* 102
Story of the Physician and the Saratoga Trunk
R. L. Stevenson 109

WALES

Martha . . . . . . *Richard Hughes* 131

IRELAND

Two or Three Witnesses . . . *C. E. Montague* 145
Where the Tides Ebb and Flow *Lord Dunsany* 167
His First Flight . . . . *Liam O'Flaherty* 172

INDIA

The Lost Child . . . . *Mulk Raj Anand* 175

SOUTH AFRICA

The Buddhist Priest's Wife . . *Olive Schreiner* 180

NEW ZEALAND

PAGE

Taking the Veil . . . *Katherine Mansfield* 190

CANADA

The Moose and Rusty Jones *Sir Charles G. D. Roberts* 195

AUSTRALIA

The Birthday . . . . *Vance Palmer* 202

FRANCE

The Necklace . . . *Guy de Maupassant* 209

The Procurator of Judæa . *Anatole France* 217
Translated G. Morgan

Torture by Hope . . *Villiers de L'Isle Adam* 228
Translated C. D. Heriot

GERMANY

Adam Urbas . . . . *Jacob Wassermann* 233

Leiningen *versus* the Ants . . *Carl Stephenson* 253
Translated F. A. Beaumont

AUSTRIA

Dead Gabriel . . . . *Arthur Schnitzler* 273

The Invisible Collection . . *Stefan Zweig* 284

CZECHOSLOVAKIA

The Shirts . . . . *Karel Čapek* 295

HUNGARY

The Tale of a Child . . . *Josef Bard* 302

RUSSIA

How Much Land does a Man Require? *Leo Tolstoy* 318

The Kiss . . . . . *Anton Chehov* 332

The Pistol Shot . . . *Alexander Pushkin* 348
Translated J. S. Beckett

Twenty-Six Men and a Girl . *Maxim Gorky* 360
Translated J. S. Beckett

DENMARK

PAGE

THE LITTLE MERMAID . *Hans Christian Andersen* 374

SWEDEN

THE HONEYMOON . . . . *Per Hallström* 393

NORWAY

THE BROTHERS . . . *Björnstjerne Björnson* 405
SIMONSEN . . . . . *Sigrid Undset* 411

HOLLAND

THE FAIR-LOVER . . *Maarten Maartens* 439
TWO PAIRS OF TWINS . . . *Louis Couperus* 457

SPAIN

A SERBIAN NIGHT . . *V. Blasco Ibañez* 463
THE HISTORY OF ISABELLA CASTRUCCIO *Miguel Cervantes* 468

ITALY

THE POT OF BASIL . . . *Giovanni Boccaccio* 476
CLOSE FRIENDS . . . . *Luigi Pirandello* 479

PERSIA

LAYLÁ AND MAJNÚN . . . . *Nizāmī* 487

ARABIA

THE STORY OF THE MAGIC HORSE . *Traditional* 502

CHINA

THE PRINCESS LILY . . . *P'u Sung-Ling* 521
Adapted from the translation of H. A. Giles

JAPAN

THE TONGUE-CUT SPARROW . . *Traditional* 526

		PAGE
Pomegranate Seed . . .	*Edith Wharton*	529
Perfectly Independent . . .	*Edna Ferber*	557
A Story by Angela Poe .	*Stephen Vincent Benet*	574
Schools and Schools . . .	*O. Henry*	589
The Mystery of Marie Rogêt .	*Edgar Allan Poe*	599
In Another Country . . .	*Ernest Hemingway*	635

EDWARD MORGAN FORSTER

THE CELESTIAL OMNIBUS

I

THE boy who resided at Agathox Lodge, 28 Buckingham Park Road, Surbiton, had often been puzzled by the old sign-post that stood almost opposite. He asked his mother about it, and she replied that it was a joke, and not a very nice one, which had been made many years back by some naughty young men, and that the police ought to remove it. For there were two strange things about this sign-post: firstly, it pointed up a blank alley, and, secondly, it had painted on it, in faded characters, the words "To Heaven."

"What kind of young men were they?" he asked.

"I think your father told me that one of them wrote verses, and was expelled from the University and came to grief in other ways. Still, it was a long time ago. You must ask your father about it. He will say the same as I do, that it was put up as a joke."

"So it doesn't mean anything at all?"

She sent him upstairs to put on his best things, for the Bonses were coming to tea, and he was to hand the cake-stand.

It struck him, as he wrenched on his tightening trousers, that he might do worse than ask Mr. Bons about the sign-post. His father, though very kind, always laughed at him—shrieked with laughter whenever he or any other child asked a question or spoke. But Mr. Bons was serious as well as kind. He had a beautiful house and lent one books, he was a churchwarden, and a candidate for the County Council; he had donated to the Free Library enormously, he presided over the Literary Society, and had Members of Parliament to stop with him—in short, he was probably the wisest person alive.

Yet even Mr. Bons could only say that the sign-post was a joke—the joke of a person named Shelley.

"Of course!" cried the mother; "I told you so, dear. That was the name."

A 2

"Had you never heard of Shelley?" asked Mr. Bons.

"No," said the boy, and hung his head.

"But is there no Shelley in the house?"

"Why, yes!" exclaimed the lady, in much agitation. "Dear Mr. Bons, we aren't such Philistines as that. Two at the least. One a wedding present, and the other, smaller print, in one of the spare rooms."

"I believe we have seven Shelleys," said Mr. Bons, with a slow smile. Then he brushed the cake-crumbs off his stomach, and, together with his daughter, rose to go.

The boy, obeying a wink from his mother, saw them all the way to the garden gate, and when they had gone he did not at once return to the house, but gazed for a little up and down Buckingham Park Road.

His parents lived at the right end of it. After No. 39 the quality of the houses dropped very suddenly, and 64 had not even a separate servants' entrance. But at the present moment the whole road looked rather pretty, for the sun had just set in splendour, and the inequalities of rent were drowned in a saffron afterglow. Small birds twittered, and the bread-winners' train shrieked musically down through the cutting—that wonderful cutting which has drawn to itself the whole beauty out of Surbiton, and clad itself, like any Alpine valley, with the glory of the fir and the silver birch and the primrose. It was this cutting that had first stirred desires within the boy—desires for something just a little different, he knew not what, desires that would return whenever things were sunlit, as they were this evening, running up and down inside him, up and down, up and down, till he would feel quite unusual all over, and as likely as not would want to cry. This evening he was even sillier, for he slipped across the road towards the sign-post and began to run up the blank alley.

The alley runs between high walls—the walls of the gardens of "Ivanhoe" and "Belle Vista" respectively. It smells a little all the way, and is scarcely twenty yards long, including the turn at the end. So not unnaturally the boy soon came to a standstill. "I'd like to kick that Shelley," he exclaimed, and glanced idly at a piece of paper which was pasted on the wall. Rather an odd piece of paper, and he read it carefully before he turned back. This is what he read:

S. and C. R. C. C.

Alteration in Service.

Owing to lack of patronage the Company are regretfully

compelled to suspend the hourly service, and to retain only the

Sunrise and Sunset Omnibuses,

which will run as usual. It is to be hoped that the public will patronise an arrangement which is intended for their convenience. As an extra inducement, the Company will, for the first time, now issue

Return Tickets!

(available one day only), which may be obtained of the driver. Passengers are again reminded that *no tickets are issued at the other end*, and that no complaints in this connection will receive consideration from the Company. Nor will the Company be responsible for any negligence or stupidity on the part of Passengers, nor for Hailstorms, Lightning, Loss of Tickets, nor for any Act of God.

For the Direction.

Now, he had never seen this notice before, nor could he imagine where the omnibus went to. S. of course was for Surbiton, and R.C.C. meant Road Car Company. But what was the meaning of the other C.? Coombe and Malden, perhaps, or possibly "City." Yet it could not hope to compete with the South-Western. The whole thing, the boy reflected, was run on hopelessly unbusiness-like lines. Why no tickets from the other end! And what an hour to start! Then he realised that unless the notice was a hoax, an omnibus must have been starting just as he was wishing the Bonses good-bye. He peered at the ground through the gathering dusk, and there he saw what might or might not be the marks of wheels. Yet nothing had come out of the alley. And he had never seen an omnibus at any time in the Buckingham Park Road. No: it must be a hoax, like the sign-posts, like the fairy tales, like the dreams upon which he would wake suddenly in the night. And with a sigh he stepped from the alley—right into the arms of his father.

Oh, how his father laughed! "Poor, poor Popsey!" he cried. "Diddums! Diddums! Diddums think he'd walky-palky up to Evvink!" And his mother, also convulsed with laughter, appeared on the steps of Agathox Lodge. "Don't, Bob!" she gasped. "Don't be so naughty! Oh, you'll kill me! Oh, leave the boy alone!"

But all that evening the joke was kept up. The father implored to be taken, too. Was it a very tiring walk? Need one wipe one's shoes on the door-mat? And the boy went to bed feeling faint and sore, and thankful for only one thing—that he had not said a word about the omnibus. It was a hoax, yet through his dreams it grew more and more real, and the streets of Surbiton, through which he saw it driving, seemed instead to become hoaxes and shadows. And very early in the morning he woke with a cry, for he had had a glimpse of its destination.

He struck a match, and its light fell not only on his watch, but also on his calendar, so that he knew it to be half an hour to sunrise. It was pitch dark, for the fog had come down from London in the night, and all Surbiton was wrapped in its embraces. Yet he sprang out and dressed himself, for he was determined to settle once for all which was real: the omnibus or the streets. "I shall be a fool one way or the other," he thought, "until I know." Soon he was shivering in the road under the gas-lamp that guarded the entrance to the alley.

To enter the alley itself required some courage. Not only was it horribly dark, but he now realised that it was an impossible terminus for an omnibus. If it had not been for a policeman, whom he heard approaching through the fog, he would never have made the attempt. The next moment he had made the attempt and failed. Nothing. Nothing but a blank alley and a very silly boy gaping at its dirty floor. It *was* a hoax. "I'll tell papa and mamma," he decided. "I deserve it. I deserve that they should know. I am too silly to be alive." And he went back to the gate of Agathox Lodge.

There he remembered that his watch was fast. The sun was not risen; it would not rise for two minutes. "Give the bus every chance," he thought cynically, and returned into the alley.

But the omnibus was there.

II

It had two horses, whose sides were still smoking from their journey, and its two great lamps shone through the fog against the alley's walls, changing their cobwebs and moss into tissues of fairyland. The driver was huddled up in a cape. He faced the blank wall, and how he had managed to drive in so neatly and so silently was one of the many things that the boy never discovered. Nor could he imagine how ever he would drive out.

"Please," his voice quavered through the foul brown air, "please, is that an omnibus?"

"Omnibus est," said the driver, without turning round.

There was a moment's silence. The policeman passed, coughing, by the entrance of the alley. The boy crouched in the shadow, for he did not want to be found out. He was pretty sure, too, that it was a Pirate; nothing else, he reasoned, would go from such odd places and at such odd hours.

"About when do you start?" He tried to sound nonchalant.

"At sunrise."

"How far do you go?"

"The whole way."

"And can I have a return ticket which will bring me all the way back?"

"You can."

"Do you know, I half think I'll come." The driver made no answer. The sun must have risen, for he unhitched the brake. And scarcely had the boy jumped in before the omnibus was off.

How? Did it turn? There was no room. Did it go forward? There was a blank wall. Yet it was moving—moving at a stately pace through the fog, which had turned from brown to yellow. The thought of warm bed and warmer breakfast made the boy feel faint. He wished he had not come. His parents would not have approved. He would have gone back to them if the weather had not made it impossible. The solitude was terrible; he was the only passenger. And the omnibus, though well-built, was cold and somewhat musty. He drew his coat round him, and in so doing chanced to feel his pocket. It was empty. He had forgotten his purse.

"Stop!" he shouted. "Stop!" And then, being of a polite disposition, he glanced up at the painted notice-board so that he might call the driver by name. "Mr. Browne! stop; Oh, do please stop!"

Mr. Browne did not stop, but he opened a little window and looked in at the boy. His face was a surprise, so kind it was and modest.

"Mr. Browne, I've left my purse behind. I've not got a penny. I can't pay for the ticket. Will you take my watch, please? I am in the most awful hole."

"Tickets on this line," said the driver, "whether single or return, can be purchased by coinage from no terrene mint. And a chronometer, though it had solaced the vigils of Charlemagne, or measured the slumbers of Laura, can acquire by no mutation the double-cake that charms the fangless Cerberus of Heaven!" So saying, he handed in the necessary ticket, and, while the boy said "Thank you," continued:

"Titular pretensions, I know it well, are vanity. Yet they merit no censure when uttered on a laughing lip, and in an homonymous world are in some sort useful, since they do serve to distinguish one Jack from his fellow. Remember me, therefore, as Sir Thomas Browne."

"Are you a Sir? Oh, sorry!" He had heard of these gentlemen drivers. "It *is* good of you about the ticket. But if you go on at this rate, however does your bus pay?"

"It does not pay. It was not intended to pay. Many are the faults of my equipage; it is compounded too curiously of foreign woods; its cushions tickle erudition rather than promote repose; and my horses are nourished not on the evergreen pastures of the moment, but on the dried bents and clovers of Latinity. But that it pays!—that error at all events was never intended and never attained."

"Sorry again," said the boy rather hopelessly. Sir Thomas looked sad, fearing that, even for a moment, he had been the cause of sadness. He invited the boy to come up and sit beside him on the box, and together they journeyed on through the fog, which was now changing from yellow to white. There were no houses by the road; so it must be either Putney Heath or Wimbledon Common.

"Have you been a driver always?"

"I was a physician once."

"But why did you stop? Weren't you good?"

"As a healer of bodies I had scant success, and several score of my patients preceded me. But as a healer of the spirit I have succeeded beyond my hopes and my deserts. For though my draughts were not better nor subtler than those of other men, yet, by reason of the cunning goblets wherein I offered them, the queasy soul was oft-times tempted to sip and be refreshed."

"The queasy soul," he murmured; "if the sun sets with trees in front of it, and you suddenly come strange all over, is that a queasy soul?"

"Have you felt that?"

"Why yes."

After a pause he told the boy a little, a very little, about the journey's end. But they did not chatter much, for the boy, when he liked a person, would as soon sit silent in his company as speak, and this, he discovered, was also the mind of Sir Thomas Browne and of many others with whom he was to be acquainted. He heard, however, about the young man Shelley, who was now quite a famous person, with a carriage of his own, and about some of the other drivers who are in the service of the Company. Meanwhile the light grew stronger, though the fog did not disperse. It was now more like mist than fog, and at times would travel quickly across them, as if it were part of a cloud. They had been ascending, too, in a most puzzling way; for over two hours the horses had been pulling against the collar, and even if it were Richmond Hill they ought to have been at the top long ago. Perhaps it was Epsom, or even the North Downs; yet the air seemed keener than that which blows on either. And as to the name of their destination, Sir Thomas Browne was silent.

Crash!

"Thunder, by Jove!" said the boy, "and not so far off either. Listen to the echoes! It's more like mountains."

He thought, not very vividly, of his father and mother. He saw them sitting down to sausages and listening to the storm. He saw his own empty place. Then there would be questions, alarms, theories, jokes, consolations. They would expect him back at lunch. To lunch he would not come, nor to tea, but he would be in for dinner, and so his day's truancy would be over. If he had had his purse he would have bought them presents—not that he should have known what to get them.

Crash!

The peal and the lightning came together. The cloud quivered as if it were alive, and torn streamers of mist rushed past. "Are you afraid?" asked Sir Thomas Browne.

"What is there to be afraid of? Is it much farther?"

The horses of the omnibus stopped just as a ball of fire burst up and exploded with a ringing noise that was deafening but clear, like the noise of a blacksmith's forge. All the cloud was shattered.

"Oh, listen, Sir Thomas Browne! No, I mean look; we shall get a view at last. No, I mean listen; that sounds like a rainbow!"

The noise had died into the faintest murmur, beneath which another murmur grew, spreading stealthily, steadily, in a curve that widened but did not vary. And in widening curves a rainbow was spreading from the horses' feet into the dissolving mists.

"But how beautiful! What colours! Where will it stop? It is more like the rainbows you can tread on. More like dreams."

The colour and the sound grew together. The rainbow spanned an enormous gulf. Clouds rushed under it and were pierced by it, and still it grew, reaching forward, conquering the darkness, until it touched something that seemed more solid than a cloud.

The boy stood up. "What is that out there?" he called. "What does it rest on, out at that other end?"

In the morning sunshine a precipice shone forth beyond the gulf. A precipice—or was it a castle? The horses moved. They set their feet upon the rainbow.

"Oh, look!" the boy shouted. "Oh, listen! Those caves—or are they gateways? Oh, look between those cliffs at those ledges. I see people! I see trees!"

"Look also below," whispered Sir Thomas. "Neglect not the diviner Acheron."

The boy looked below, past the flames of the rainbow that licked against their wheels. The gulf also had cleared, and in its depths there flowed an everlasting river. One sunbeam entered and struck a green pool, and as they passed over he saw three maidens rise to the surface of the pool, singing, and playing with something that glistened like a ring.

"You down in the water——" he called.

They answered, "You up on the bridge——" There was a burst of music. "You up on the bridge, good luck to you. Truth in the depth, truth on the height."

"You down in the water, what are you doing?"

Sir Thomas Browne replied: "They sport in the mancipiary possession of their gold"; and the omnibus arrived.

III

The boy was in disgrace. He sat locked up in the nursery of Agathox Lodge, learning poetry for a punishment. His father had said, "My boy! I can pardon anything but untruthfulness," and had caned him, saying at each stroke, "There is *no* omnibus, *no* driver, *no* bridge, *no* mountain; you are a *truant*, a *gutter snipe*, a *liar*." His father could be very stern at times. His mother had begged him to say he was sorry. But he could not say that. It was the greatest day of his life, in spite of the caning and the poetry at the end of it.

He had returned punctually at sunset—driven not by Sir Thomas Browne, but by a maiden lady who was full of quiet fun. They had talked of omnibuses and also of barouche landaus. How far away her gentle voice seemed now! Yet it was scarcely three hours since he had left her up the alley.

His mother called through the door. "Dear, you are to come down and to bring your poetry with you."

He came down, and found that Mr. Bons was in the smoking-room with his father. It had been a dinner party.

"Here is the great traveller!" said his father grimly. "Here is the young gentleman who drives in an omnibus over rainbows, while young ladies sing to him." Pleased with his wit, he laughed.

"After all," said Mr. Bons, smiling, "there is something a little like it in Wagner. It is odd how, in quite illiterate minds, you will find glimmers of Artistic Truth. The case interests me. Let me plead for the culprit. We have all romanced in our time, haven't we?"

"Hear how kind Mr. Bons is," said his mother, while his father said, "Very well. Let him say his Poem, and that will do. He is going away to my sister on Tuesday, and *she* will cure him of this alley-slopering." (Laughter.) "Say your Poem."

The boy began. "'Standing aloof in giant ignorance.'"

His father laughed again—roared. "One for you, my son! 'Standing aloof in giant ignorance!' I never knew these poets talked sense. Just describes you. Here, Bons, you go in for poetry. Put him through it, will you, while I fetch up the whisky?"

"Yes, give me the Keats," said Mr. Bons. "Let him say his Keats to me."

So for a few moments the wise man and the ignorant boy were left alone in the smoking-room.

"'Standing aloof in giant ignorance, of thee I dream and of the Cyclades, as one who sits ashore and longs perchance to visit——'"

"Quite right. To visit what?"

"'To visit dolphin coral in deep seas,'" said the boy, and burst into tears.

"Come, come! why do you cry?"

"Because—because all these words that only rhymed before, now that I've come back they're me."

Mr. Bons laid the Keats down. The case was more interesting than he had expected. "*You?*" he exclaimed. "This sonnet, *you*?"

"Yes—and look farther on: 'Aye, on the shores of darkness there is light, and precipices show untrodden green.' It *is* so, sir. All these things are true."

"I never doubted it," said Mr. Bons, with closed eyes.

"You—then you believe me? You believe in the omnibus and the driver and the storm and that return ticket I got for nothing and——"

"Tut, tut! No more of your yarns, my boy. I meant that I never doubted the essential truth of Poetry. Some day, when you have read more, you will understand what I mean."

"But Mr. Bons, it *is* so. There *is* light upon the shores of darkness. I have seen it coming. Light and a wind."

"Nonsense," said Mr. Bons.

"If I had stopped! They tempted me. They told me to give up my ticket—for you cannot come back if you lose your ticket. They called from the river for it, and indeed I was tempted, for I have never been so happy as among those precipices. But I thought of my mother and father, and that I must fetch them. Yet they will not come, though the road starts opposite our house. It has all happened as the people up there warned me, and Mr. Bons has disbelieved me like everyone else. I have been caned. I shall never see that mountain again."

"What's that about me?" said Mr. Bons, sitting up in his chair very suddenly.

"I told them about you, and how clever you were, and how many books you had, and they said, 'Mr. Bons will certainly disbelieve you.'"

"Stuff and nonsense, my young friend. You grow impertinent. I—well—I will settle the matter. Not a word to your father. I will cure you. To-morrow evening I will myself call here to take you for a walk, and at sunset we will go up this alley opposite and hunt for your omnibus, you silly little boy."

His face grew serious, for the boy was not disconcerted, but leapt about the room singing, "Joy! joy! I told them you would believe me. We will drive together over the rainbow. I told them that you would come." After all, could there be anything in the story? Wagner? Keats? Shelley? Sir Thomas Browne? Certainly the case was interesting.

And on the morrow evening, though it was pouring with rain, Mr. Bons did not omit to call at Agathox Lodge.

The boy was ready, bubbling with excitement, and skipping about in a way that rather vexed the President of the Literary Society. They took a turn down Buckingham Park Road, and then—having seen that no one was watching them—slipped up the alley. Naturally enough (for the sun was setting) they ran straight against the omnibus.

"Good heavens!" exclaimed Mr. Bons. "Good gracious heavens!"

It was not the omnibus in which the boy had driven first, nor yet that in which he had returned. There were three horses—black, grey, and white, the grey being the finest. The driver, who turned round at the mention of goodness and of heaven, was a sallow man with terrifying jaws and sunken eyes. Mr. Bons, on seeing him, gave a cry as if of recognition, and began to tremble violently.

The boy jumped in.

"Is it possible?" cried Mr. Bons. "Is the impossible possible?"

"Sir; come in, sir. It is such a fine omnibus. Oh, here is his name—Dan some one."

Mr. Bons sprang in too. A blast of wind immediately slammed the omnibus door, and the shock jerked down all the omnibus blinds, which were very weak on their springs.

"Dan . . . Show me. Good gracious heavens! we're moving."

"Hooray!" said the boy.

Mr. Bons became flustered. He had not intended to be kidnapped. He could not find the door-handle, nor push up the blinds. The omnibus was quite dark, and by the time he had struck a match, night had come on outside also They were moving rapidly.

"A strange, a memorable adventure," he said, surveying the interior of the omnibus, which was large, roomy, and constructed with extreme regularity, every part exactly answering to every other part. Over the door (the handle of which was outside) was written, "Lasciate ogni baldanza voi che entrate"—at least, that was what was written, but Mr. Bons said that it was Lashy arty something, and that baldanza was a mistake for speranza. His voice sounded as if he was in church. Meanwhile, the boy called to the cadaverous driver for two return tickets. They were handed in without a word. Mr. Bons covered his face with his hand and again trembled. "Do you know who that is!" he whispered, when the little window had shut upon them. "It is the impossible."

"Well, I don't like him as much as Sir Thomas Browne, though I shouldn't be surprised if he had even more in him."

"More in him?" He stamped irritably. "By accident you have made the greatest discovery of the century, and all you can say is that there is more in this man. Do you remember those vellum books in my library, stamped with red lilies? This—sit still, I bring you stupendous news!—*this is the man who wrote them.*"

The boy sat quite still. "I wonder if we shall see Mrs. Gamp?" he asked, after a civil pause.

"Mrs.——?"

"Mrs. Gamp and Mrs. Harris. I like Mrs. Harris. I came upon them quite suddenly. Mrs. Gamp's bandboxes have moved over the rainbow so badly. All the bottoms have fallen out, and two of the pippins off her bedstead tumbled into the stream."

"Out there sits the man who wrote my vellum books!"

thundered Mr. Bons, " and you talk to me of Dickens and of Mrs. Gamp? "

" I know Mrs. Gamp so well," he apologised. " I could not help being glad to see her. I recognised her voice. She was telling Mrs. Harris about Mrs. Prig."

" Did you spend the whole day in her elevating company? "

" Oh, no. I raced. I met a man who took me out beyond to a race-course. You run, and there are dolphins out at sea."

" Indeed. Do you remember the man's name? "

" Achilles. No; he was later. Tom Jones."

Mr. Bons sighed heavily. " Well, my lad, you have made a miserable mess of it. Think of a cultured person with your opportunities! A cultured person would have known all these characters and known what to have said to each. He would not have wasted his time with a Mrs. Gamp or a Tom Jones. The creations of Homer, of Shakespeare, and of Him who drives us now, would alone have contented him. He would not have raced. He would have asked intelligent questions."

" But, Mr. Bons," said the boy humbly, " you will be a cultured person. I told them so."

" True, true, and I beg you not to disgrace me when we arrive. No gossiping. No running. Keep close to my side, and never speak to these Immortals unless they speak to you. Yes, and give me the return tickets. You will be losing them."

The boy surrendered the tickets, but felt a little sore. After all, he had found the way to this place. It was hard first to be disbelieved and then to be lectured. Meanwhile, the rain had stopped, and moonlight crept into the omnibus through the cracks in the blinds.

" But how is there to be a rainbow? " cried the boy.

" You distract me," snapped Mr. Bons. " I wish to meditate on beauty. I wish to goodness I was with a reverent and sympathetic person."

The lad bit his lip. He made a hundred good resolutions. He would imitate Mr. Bons all the visit. He would not laugh, or run, or sing, or do any of the vulgar things that must have disgusted his new friends last time. He would be very careful to pronounce their names properly, and to remember who knew whom. Achilles did not know Tom Jones—at least, so Mr. Bons said. The Duchess of Malfi was older than Mrs. Gamp—at least, so Mr. Bons said. He would be self-conscious, reticent, and prim. He would never say he liked anyone. Yet, when the blind flew up at a chance touch of his head, all these good resolutions went to the winds, for the omnibus had reached the summit of a moonlit hill, and there was the chasm, and there, across it, stood the old precipices, dreaming, with their feet in the everlasting river. He exclaimed, " The mountain! Listen to the new tune in the water! Look at the camp fires in the ravines," and Mr. Bons, after a hasty glance, retorted, " Water? Camp fires? Ridiculous rubbish. Hold your tongue. There is nothing at all."

Yet, under his eyes, a rainbow formed, compounded not of sunlight and storm, but of moonlight and the spray of the river. The three horses put their feet upon it. He thought it the finest rainbow he had seen, but did not dare to say so, since Mr. Bons said that nothing was there. He leant out—the window had opened—and sang the tune that rose from the sleeping waters.

" The prelude to Rhinegold? " said Mr. Bons suddenly. " Who taught you these *leit motifs*? " He, too, looked out of the window. Then he behaved very oddly. He gave a choking cry, and fell back on to the omnibus floor. He writhed and kicked. His face was green.

" Does the bridge make you dizzy? " the boy asked.

" Dizzy ! " gasped Mr. Bons. " I want to go back. Tell the driver."

But the driver shook his head.

" We are nearly there," said the boy. " They are asleep. Shall I call? They will be so pleased to see you, for I have prepared them."

Mr. Bons moaned. They moved over the lunar rainbow, which ever and ever broke away behind their wheels. How still the night was! Who would be sentry at the Gate?

" I am coming," he shouted, again forgetting the hundred resolutions. " I am returning—I, the boy."

" The boy is returning," cried a voice to other voices, who repeated, " The boy is returning."

" I am bringing Mr. Bons with me."

Silence.

" I should have said Mr. Bons is bringing me with him."

Profound silence.

" Who stands sentry? "

" Achilles."

And on the rocky causeway, close to the springing of the rainbow bridge, he saw a young man who carried a wonderful shield.

" Mr. Bons, it is Achilles, armed."

" I want to go back," said Mr. Bons.

The last fragment of the rainbow melted, the wheels sang upon the living rock, the door of the omnibus burst open. Out leapt the boy—he could not resist—and sprang to meet the warrior, who, stooping suddenly, caught him on his shield.

"Achilles!" he cried, "let me get down, for I am ignorant and vulgar, and I must wait for that Mr. Bons of whom I told you yesterday."

But Achilles raised him aloft. He crouched on the wonderful shield, on heroes and burning cities, on vineyards graven in gold, on every dear passion, every joy, on the entire image of the Mountain that he had discovered, encircled, like it, with an everlasting stream. "No, no," he protested, "I am not worthy. It is Mr. Bons who must be up here."

But Mr. Bons was whimpering, and Achilles trumpeted and cried, "Stand upright upon my shield!"

"Sir, I did not mean to stand! Something made me stand. Sir, why do you delay? Here is only the great Achilles, whom you knew."

Mr. Bons screamed, "I see no one. I see nothing. I want to go back." Then he cried to the driver, "Save me! Let me stop in your chariot. I have honoured you. I have quoted you. I have bound you in vellum. Take me back to my world."

The driver replied, "I am the means and not the end. I am the food and not the life. Stand by yourself, as that boy has stood. I cannot save you. For poetry is a spirit; and they that would worship it must worship in spirit and in truth."

Mr. Bons—he could not resist—crawled out of the beautiful omnibus. His face appeared, gaping horribly. His hands followed, one gripping the step, the other beating the air. Now his shoulders emerged, his chest, his stomach. With a shriek of "I see London," he fell—fell against the hard, moonlit rock, fell into it as if it were water, fell through it, vanished, and was seen by the boy no more.

"Where have you fallen to, Mr. Bons? Here is a procession arriving to honour you with music and torches. Here come the men and women whose names you know. The mountain is awake, the river is awake, over the race-course the sea is awaking those dolphins, and it is all for you. They want you——"

There was the touch of fresh leaves on his forehead. Someone had crowned him.

ΤΕΛΟΣ

. . . . .

From the *Kingston Gazette*, *Surbiton Times*, and *Raynes Park Observer*.

The body of Mr. Septimus Bons has been found in a shockingly mutilated condition in the vicinity of the Bermondsey gas-works. The deceased's pockets contained a sovereign-purse, a silver cigar-case, a bijou pronouncing dictionary, and a couple of omnibus tickets. The unfortunate gentleman had apparently been hurled from a considerable height. Foul play is suspected, and a thorough investigation is pending by the authorities.

"SAKI" (H. H. MUNRO)

DUSK

NORMAN GORTSBY sat on a bench in the Park, with his back to a strip of bush-planted sward, fenced by the park railings, and the Row fronting him across a wide stretch of carriage drive. Hyde Park Corner, with its rattle and hoot of traffic, lay immediately to his right. It was some thirty minutes past six on an early March evening, and dusk had fallen heavily over the scene, dusk mitigated by some faint moonlight and many street lamps. There was a wide emptiness over road and sidewalk, and yet there were many unconsidered figures moving silently through the half-light or dotted unobtrusively on bench and chair, scarcely to be distinguished from the shadowed gloom in which they sat.

The scene pleased Gortsby and harmonised with his present mood. Dusk, to his mind, was the hour of the defeated. Men and women, who had fought and lost, who hid their fallen fortunes and dead hopes as far as possible from the scrutiny of the curious, came forth in this hour of gloaming, when their shabby clothes and bowed shoulders and unhappy eyes might pass unnoticed, or, at any rate, unrecognised.

> A king that is conquered must see strange looks,
> So bitter a thing is the heart of man.

The wanderers in the dusk did not choose to have strange looks fasten on them, therefore they came out in this bat-fashion, taking their pleasure sadly in a pleasure-ground that had emptied of its rightful occupants. Beyond the sheltering screen of bushes and palings came a realm of brilliant lights and noisy, rushing traffic. A blazing, many-tiered stretch of windows shone through the dusk and almost dispersed it, marking the haunts of those other people, who held their own in life's struggle, or at any rate had not had to admit failure. So Gortsby's imagination pictured things as he sat on his bench in the almost deserted walk. He was in the mood to count himself among the defeated. Money troubles did not press on him; had he so wished he could have strolled into the thoroughfares of light and noise, and taken his place among the jostling ranks of those who enjoyed prosperity or struggled for it. He had failed in a more subtle ambition, and for the moment he was heart sore and disillusionised, and not disinclined to take a certain cynical pleasure in observing and labelling his fellow wanderers as they went their ways in the dark stretches between the lamp-lights.

On the bench by his side sat an elderly gentleman with a drooping air of defiance that was probably the remaining vestige of self-respect in an individual who had ceased to defy successfully anybody or anything. His clothes could scarcely be called shabby, at least they passed muster in the half-light, but one's imagination could not have pictured the wearer embarking on the purchase of a half-crown box of chocolates or laying out ninepence on a carnation buttonhole. He belonged unmistakably to that forlorn orchestra to whose piping no one dances; he was one of the world's lamenters who induces no responsive weeping. As he rose to go Gortsby imagined him returning to a home circle where he was snubbed and of no account, or to some bleak lodging where his ability to pay a weekly bill was the beginning and end of the interest he inspired. His retreating figure vanished slowly into the shadows, and his place on the bench was taken almost immediately by a young man, fairly well dressed but scarcely more cheerful of mein than his predecessor. As if to emphasise the fact that the world went badly with him the newcomer unburdened himself of an angry and very audible expletive as he flung himself into the seat.

"You don't seem in a very good temper," said Gortsby, judging that he was expected to take due notice of the demonstration.

The young man turned to him with a look of disarming frankness which put him instantly on his guard.

"You wouldn't be in a good temper if you were in the fix I'm in," he said; "I've done the silliest thing I've ever done in my life."

"Yes?" said Gortsby dispassionately.

"Came up this afternoon, meaning to stay at the Patagonian Hotel in Berkshire Square," continued the young man; "when I got there I found that it had been pulled down some weeks ago and a cinema theatre run up on the site. The taxi driver recommended me to another hotel some way off and I went there. I just sent a letter to my people, giving them the address, and then I went out to buy some soap—I'd forgotten to pack any and I hate using hotel soap. Then I strolled about a bit, had a drink at a bar and looked at the shops, and when I came to turn my steps back to the hotel I suddenly realised that I didn't remember its name or even what street it was in. There's a nice predicament for a fellow who hasn't any friends or connections in London! Of course I can wire to my people for the address, but they won't have got my letter till to-morrow; meantime I'm without any money, came out with about a shilling on me, which went in buying the soap and getting the drink, and here I am, wandering about with twopence in my pocket and nowhere to go for the night."

There was an eloquent pause after the story had been told. "I suppose you think I've spun you rather an impossible yarn," said the young man presently, with a suggestion of resentment in his voice.

"Not at all impossible," said Gortsby judicially; "I remember doing exactly the same thing once in a foreign capital, and on that occasion there were two of us, which made it more remarkable. Luckily we remembered that the hotel was on a sort of canal, and when we struck the canal we were able to find our way back to the hotel."

The youth brightened at the reminiscence. "In a foreign city I wouldn't mind so much," he said; "one could go to one's Consul and get the requisite help from him. Here in one's own land one is far more derelict if one gets into a fix. Unless I can find some decent chap to swallow my story and lend me some money I seem likely to spend the night on the Embankment. I'm glad, anyhow, that you don't think the story outrageously improbable."

He threw a good deal of warmth into the last remark, as though perhaps to indicate his hope that Gortsby did not fall far short of the requisite decency.

"Of course," said Gortsby slowly, "the weak point of your story is that you can't produce the soap."

The young man sat forward hurriedly, felt rapidly in the pockets of his overcoat, and then jumped to his feet.

"I must have lost it," he muttered angrily.

"To lose an hotel and a cake of soap on one afternoon suggests wilful carelessness," said Gortsby, but the young man scarcely waited to hear the end of the remark. He flitted away down the path, his head held high, with an air of somewhat jaded jauntiness.

"It was a pity," mused Gortsby; "the going out to get one's own soap was the one convincing touch in the whole story, and yet it was just that little detail that brought him to grief. If he had had the brilliant forethought to provide himself with a cake of soap, wrapped and sealed with all the solicitude of the chemist's counter, he would have been a genius in his particular line. In his particular line genius certainly consists of an infinite capacity for taking precautions."

With that reflection Gortsby rose to go; as he did so an exclamation of concern escaped him. Lying on the ground by the side of the bench was a small oval packet, wrapped and sealed with the solicitude of a chemist's counter. It could be nothing else but a cake of soap, and it had evidently fallen out of the youth's overcoat pocket when he flung himself down on the seat. In another moment Gortsby was scudding along the dusk-shrouded path in anxious quest for a youthful figure in a light overcoat. He had nearly given up the search when he caught sight of the object of his pursuit standing irresolutely on the border of the carriage drive, evidently uncertain whether to strike across the Park or make for the bustling pavements of Knightsbridge. He turned round sharply with an air of defensive hostility when he found Gortsby hailing him.

"The important witness to the genuineness of your story has turned up," said Gortsby, holding out the cake of soap; "it must have slid out of your overcoat pocket when you sat down on the seat. I saw it on the ground after you left. You must excuse my disbelief, but appearances were really rather against you, and now, as I appealed to the testimony of the soap, I think I ought to abide by its verdict. If the loan of a sovereign is any good to you——"

The young man hastily removed all doubt on the subject by pocketing the coin.

"Here is my card with my address," continued Gortsby; "any day this week will do for returning the money, and here is the soap—don't lose it again; it's been a good friend to you."

"Lucky thing your finding it," said the youth, and then, with a catch in his voice, he blurted out a word or two of thanks and fled headlong in the direction of Knightsbridge.

"Poor boy, he as nearly as possible broke down," said Gortsby to himself. "I don't wonder either; the relief from his quandary must have been acute. It's a lesson to me not to be too clever in judging by circumstances."

As Gortsby retraced his steps past the seat where the little drama had taken place he saw an elderly gentleman poking and peering beneath it and on all sides of it, and recognised his earlier fellow occupant.

"Have you lost anything, sir?" he asked.

"Yes, sir, a cake of soap."

WALTER DE LA MARE

THE NAP

THE autumnal afternoon was creeping steadily on towards night; the sun after the morning's rain was now—from behind thinning clouds—glinting down on the chimney-pots and slate roofs of Mr. Thripp's suburb. And the day being a Saturday, across Europe, across England, an immense multitudinous stirring of humanity was in progress. It had begun in remote Australia, and would presently sweep across the Atlantic into vast America, resembling the rustling of an ant-heap in a pinewood in sunny June. The Christian world, that is, was preparing for its weekly half-holiday; and Mr. Thripp was taking his share.

As if time were of unusual importance to him, two clocks stood on his kitchen mantelpiece: one, gay as a peepshow in the middle, in a stained-wood case with red and blue flowers on the glass front; the other an " alarum "—which, though it was made of tin, had a voice and an appearance little short of the brazen. Above them, as if entirely oblivious to their ranting, a glazed King Edward VII stared stolidly out of a Christmas lithograph, with his Orders on his royal breast.

Mr. Thripp's kitchen table was at this moment disordered with the remains of a meal, straggling over a table-cloth that had now gallantly completed its full week's service. Like all Saturday dinners in his household, this had been a hugger-mugger dinner—one of vehement relays. Mr. Thripp himself had returned home from his office at a quarter to two—five minutes after his daughter, Millie, and Mrs. Thripp had already begun. Charlie Thripp had made his appearance a little before the hour; and James—who, somehow, had never become Jim or Jimmie—arrived soon afterwards. To each his due, kept warm.

But the hasty feeding was now over. Mr. Thripp, in his shirt sleeves, and with his silver watch-chain disposed upon his front, had returned once more from the scullery with his empty tray. He was breathing heavily, for he inclined nowadays, as he would sometimes confess, to the *ongbongpong*. He had remarkably muscular arms for a man of his sedentary profession, that of ledger-clerk in Messrs. Bailey, Bailey and Company's counting-house. His small eyes, usually half-hidden by their plump lids, were of a bright, clear blue. His round head was covered with close-cut hair; he had fullish lips, and his ample jowl always appeared as if it had been freshly shaved—even on Saturday afternoons.

Mr. Thripp delighted in Saturday afternoons. He delighted in housework. Though he never confessed it to a living soul (and even though it annoyed Tilda to hear him), he delighted, too, in imitating the waitresses in the tea-shops, and rattled the plates and dishes together as if they were made of a material unshatterable and everlasting. When alone at the sink he would hiss like a groom currying a full-grown mare. He packed the tray full of dirty dishes once more, and returned into the steam of the scullery.

"You get along now, Tilda," he said to his wife, who was drying up. "We shall have that Mrs. Brown knocking every minute, and that only flusters you."

Mrs. Thripp looked more ill-tempered than she really was—with her angular face and chin, pitch-dark eyes, and dark, straight hair. With long, damp fingers she drew back a limp strand of hair that had straggled over her forehead.

"What beats me is, you never take a bit of enjoyment yourself," she replied. "It isn't fair to *us*. I slave away, morning, noon and night; but that's just as things are. But other husbands get out and about; why not you? *Let* her knock! She's got too much money to waste; that's what's the matter with *her*. I don't know what you wouldn't take her for in that new get-up she's got."

Then what the devil do you go about with her for? were the words that entered Mr. Thripp's mind. And as for slaving, haven't I just *asked* you to give over? Have reason, woman! But he didn't utter them. "That'll be all right," he said instead, in his absurd genial way. "You get on along off, Tilda; I'll see to all this. I enjoy myself my own way, don't you fear. Did you never hear of the selfish sex? Well, that's me!"

"Oh, yes, I know all about that," said his wife sententiously: "a pinch of salt on a bird's tail! But there's no need for sarcasms. Now do be careful with that dish, there. It don't belong to us, but to next door. She gave me one of her pan-cakes on it—and nothing better than a shapeless bit of leather, either. Just to show she was once in service as a cook-general, I suppose; though she never owns to it."

A spiteful old mischief-maker, if you ask me, was Mr.

Thripp's inward comment. But " Oh, well, Tilda, she means all right," he said soothingly. " Don't you worry. Now get along off with you; it's a hard day, Saturday, but you won't know yourself when you come down again." As if forced into a line of conduct she deprecated and despised, Tilda flung her wet tea-cloth over a chair, and, with heart beating gaily beneath her shrunken breast, hastened away.

Mr. Thripp began to whistle under his breath as he turned on the hot-water tap again. It was the one thing he insisted on —a lavish supply of hot water. He was no musician, and only himself knew the tune he was in search of; but it kept him going as vigorously as a company of grenadiers on the march, and he invariably did his household jobs against time. It indulged a sort of gambling instinct in him; and the more he hated his job, the louder he whistled. So as a small boy he had met the challenge of the terrors of the dark. " Keep going," he would say. " Don't let things mess over. That's waste! "

At that moment his elder son, James, appeared in the scullery doorway. James took after his mother's side of the family. In his navy-blue serge suit, light-brown shoes, mauve socks and spotted tie, he showed what careful dressing can do for a man. A cigarette sagged from his lower lip. His head was oblong, and flat-sided, and his eyes had a damp and vacant look. He thrust his face an inch or two into the succulent steam beyond the doorway.

" Well, dad, I'm off," he said.

Oh, my God! thought his father. If only you'd drop those infernal fags. Smoke, smoke, smoke, morning to night; and you that pasty-looking I can't imagine what the girl sees in you, with your nice superior ways. " Right you are, my son," he said aloud. " I won't ask you to take a hand! But slow and steady does it. Where might *you* be bound for this afternoon? "

" Oh, tea with Ivy's people," said James magnanimously. " Pretty dull going, I can tell you."

" But it won't be tea all the evening, I suppose?" said his father, pushing a steaming plate into the plate-rack.

" Oh, I dare say we shall loaf off to a revoo or something," said James. He tossed his cigarette-end into the sink, but missed the refuse-strainer. Mr. Thripp picked it up with a fork and put it into the receptacle it was intended for, while James " lit up " again.

" Well, so long," said his father; " don't spoil that Sunday-go-to-meeting suit of yours with all this steam. And by the way, James, I owe you five shillings for that little carpentering job you did for me. It's on the sitting-room shelf."

"Right-ho. Thanks, dad," said James. "I thought it was six. But never mind."

His father flashed a glance at his son—a glance like the smouldering of a coal. "That so? Well, make it six, then," he said. "And I'm much obliged."

"Oh, that's nothing," replied James graciously. "Cheerio; don't overdo it, dad."

Mr. Thripp returned to his washing-up. He was thinking rapidly with an extraordinary medley of feeling—as if he were not one Mr. Thripp, but many. None the less, his whistling broke out anew, as though, like a canary, in rivalry with the gushing of the tap. After loading up his tray with crockery for the last time, he put its contents away in the cupboard and on the kitchen dresser, cleansed the drain, swabbed up the sink, swabbed up the cracked cement floor, hung up his dish-clout, rinsed his hands, and returned into the kitchen.

Millie, in a neat, tailor-made costume which had that week marvellously survived dyeing, was now posed before the little cracked square of kitchen looking-glass. She was a pale, slim thing. Her smooth hair, of a lightish brown streaked with gold and parted in the middle, resembled a gilded frame surrounding her mild, angelic face—a face such as the mediæval sculptors in France delighted to carve on their altar-pieces. Whatever she wore became her—even her skimpy old pale-blue flannel dressing-gown.

She turned her narrow, pretty face sidelong under her hat and looked at her father. She looked at every human being like that—even at her own reflection in a shop-window, even at a flower in a glass. She spent her whole life subtly, instinctively, wordlessly courting. She had as many young men as the White Queen has pawns: though not all of them remained long in her service.

It's all very well to be preening yourself in that mirror, my girl, her father was thinking, but you'd be far better off in the long run if you did a bit more to help your mother, even though you do earn a fraction of your living. More thinking and less face, I say. And all that—But, "Why, I never see such a girl as you, Millie," he greeted her incredulously, "for looking your best! And such a best, too, my dear. Which young spark is it to be *this* afternoon? Eh?"

"Sparks! Dad, how you do talk! Why, I don't hardly know, dad. Sparks!" Millie's voice almost invariably ran down the scale like the notes of a dulcimer muted with velvet. "I wasn't thinking of anybody in particular," she went on, continuing to watch her moving mouth in the glass, "but I promised Nellie Gibbs I . . . One thing, I am not going to stay out long on a day like this!"

"What's the matter with the day?" Mr. Thripp inquired.

"The matter! Why, look at it! It's a fair filthy mug of a day." The words slipped off her pretty curved lips like pearls over satin. A delicious anguish seemed to have arched the corners of her eyelids.

"Well, ain't there such a thing as a mackintosh in the house, then?" inquired her father briskly.

"Mackintosh! Over this! Oh, isn't that just like a man! I should look a perfect guy." She stood gazing at him, like a gazelle startled by the flurry of its drinking-pool.

Now see you here, my girl, that see-saw voice inside her father was expostulating once more, what's the good of them fine silly airs? I take you for an honest man's daughter, with not a ha'penny to spare on fal-lals and monkey-traps. *That* won't get you a husband. But Mr. Thripp once more ignored its interruption. He smiled almost roguishly out of his bright blue eyes at his daughter. "Ask *me* what I take you for, my dear? Why, I take you for a nice, well-meaning, though remarkably plain young woman. Eh? But there, there, don't worry. What I say is, make sure of the best (and the best that's *inside*), and let the other young fellows go."

He swept the last clean fork on the table into the drawer and folded up the table-cloth.

"Oh, dad, how you do go on!" said Millie. "It's always fellows you're thinking of. As if fellows made any difference." Her glance roamed a little startledly round the room. "What I can't understand," she added quickly, "is why we never have a clean table-cloth. How can anybody ask a friend home to their own place if that's the kind of thing they are going to eat off of?"

. . . . .

A cataract of invective coursed through the channels of Mr. Thripp's mind. He paused an instant to give the soiled table-cloth another twist and the table another prolonged sweep of that formidable right arm which for twenty-three years had never once been lifted in chastisement of a single one of his three offspring. Then he turned and glanced at the fire.

"I wouldn't," he said, seizing the shovel—"I wouldn't let mother hear that, my dear. We all have a good many things to put up with. And what I say is, all in good time. You bring that Mr. Right along, and I can promise him not only a clean table-cloth, but something appetising to eat off of it. A bit of a fire in the sitting-room, too, for that matter."

"You're a good sort, dad," said Millie, putting up her face

to be kissed—in complete confidence that the tiny powder-puff in her vanity-bag would soon adjust any possible mishap to the tip of her small nose. " But I don't believe you ever think I think of anything."

" Good-bye, my dear," said Mr. Thripp. " Don't kiss me; I am all of a smother with the washing-up."

" Toodle-loo, ma," Millie shrilled, as her father followed her out into the passage. He drew open the front door, secreting his shirt-sleeves well behind it in case of curious passers-by.

He returned into the house, and at once confronted his younger son, Charlie, who was at that moment descending the stairs. As a matter of fact, he was descending the stairs like fifteen Charlies, and nothing so much exasperated his father as to feel the whole house rock on its foundations at each fresh impact.

" Off to your match, my boy? " he cried. " Some day I expect you will be taking a hand in the game yourself. Better share than watch! "

Every single Saturday afternoon during the football season Mr. Thripp ventured to express some such optimistic sentiment as this. But Charlie had no objection; not at all.

" Not me, dad," he assured him good-humouredly. " I'd sooner pay a bob to see other fellows crocked up. You couldn't lend me one, I suppose? "

" Lend you what? "

" Two tanners; four frippenies; a twelfth of a gross of coppers! "

Good God! yelled Mr. Thripp's inward monitor. Am I *never* to have a minute's rest or relief? But it yelled in vain.

" Right you are, my son," he said instead, and thrusting his fleshy hand into his tight-fitting trouser-pocket, he brought out a fistful of silver and pence. " And there," he added, " there's an extra sixpence free, *gratis*, and for nothing, for the *table d'hôte*. All I say is, Charlie, better say ' give ' when there isn't much chance of keeping to the ' lend.' I don't want to preach, but that's always been *my* rule, and kept it, too, as well as I could."

Charles counted the coins in his hand, and looked at his father. He grinned companionably. He invariably found his father a little funny to look at. He seemed somehow to be so remote from anything you could mean by things as they are, and things as they are now. He wasn't so much old-fashioned as just a Gone-by. He was his father, of course, just as a jug is a jug, and now and then Charlie was uncommonly fond of him, longed for his company, and remembered being a little boy, walking with him in the Recreation Ground. But he wished he wouldn't be always giving advice, and especially the kind of advice which he had himself assiduously practised.

"Ta, dad," he said; "that's doing me proud. I'll buy you a box of Havanas with what's over from the *table d'hôte*. And now we're square. Good-bye, dad." He paused as he turned to go. "Honour bright," he added, "I hope I shall be earning a bit more soon, and then I shan't have to ask you for anything."

A curious shine came into Mr. Thripp's small, lively eyes; it seemed almost to spill over on to his plump cheeks. It looked as if those cheeks had even paled a little.

"Why, that's all right, Charlie, my boy," he mumbled. "I'd give you the skin of me body if it would be of any use. That's all right. Don't stand about too long, but just keep going. What I can't abide is these young fellows that swallow down their enjoyments like so much black draught. But we are not that kind of a family, I'm thankful to say."

"Not me!" said Charles with a grimace like a good-humoured marmoset, and off he went to his soccer match.

Hardly had the sound of his footsteps ceased—and Mr. Thripp stayed there in the passage, as if to listen till they were for ever out of hearing—when there came a muffled, secretive tap on the panel of the door. At sound of it the genial, podgy face blurred and blackened.

Oh, it's you, you cringing Jezebel, is it? the thought scurried through his mind like a mangy animal. Mr. Thripp, indeed, was no lover of the ultra-feminine. He either feared it or hated it, or both feared and hated it. It disturbed his even tenor. It was a thorn in the side of the Mr. Thripp that not only believed second thoughts were best, but systematically refused to give utterance to first. Any sensible person, he would say, ought to know when he's a bit overtaxed, and act according.

The gloved fingers, Delilah-like, had tapped again. Mr. Thripp tiptoed back into the kitchen, put on his coat, and opened the door.

"Oh, it's you, Mrs. Brown," he said. "Tilda won't be a moment. She's upstairs titivating. Come in and take a seat."

His eyes meanwhile were informing that inward censor of his precisely how many inches thick the mauvish face-powder lay on Mrs. Brown's cheek, the liver-coloured lip-stick on her mouth, and the dye on her loaded eyelashes. Those naturally delicate lashes swept down in a gentle fringe upon her cheek as she smiled in reply. She was a graceful thing, too, but practised; and far more feline, far, far more body-conscious than Millie. No longer in the blush of youth, either, though still mistress of the gift that never leaves its predestined owner—the impulse and power to fascinate mere man. Still, there were limitations even to Mrs. Brown's orbit of attraction, and Mr. Thripp might have been Neptune itself, he kept himself so far out in the cold.

He paused a moment at the entrance to the sitting-room, until his visitor had seated herself. He was eyeing her Frenchified silk scarf, her demure new hat, her smart, high-heeled, patent-leather shoes, but his eyes dropped like stones when he discovered her own dark, languishing ones surveying him from under that hat's beguiling brim.

" Nice afternoon after the rain," he remarked instantly. " Going to the pictures, I suppose? As for meself, these days make me want to be out and in at the same time. It's the musty, fusty, smoky dark of them places I can't stand."

Mrs. Brown rarely raised her voice much above a whisper. Indeed, it appeared to be a physical effort to her to speak at all. She turned her face a little sidelong, her glance on the carpet. " Why, it's the dark I enjoy, Mr. Thripp," she said. " It "—and she raised her own—" it rests the eyes so."

For an instant Mr. Thripp's memory returned to Millie, but he made no comment.

" Here's Mrs. Brown, Tilda," he called up the staircase. Good heavens, the woman might as well be the real thing, the voice within was declaring. But the words that immediately followed up this piece of news were merely, " You'll be mighty surprised to hear, Tilda, Mrs. Brown's got a new hat." A faint cat-call of merriment descended the stairs.

" Oh, now, Mr. Thripp, listen to that!" whispered the peculiar voice from out of the little airless sitting-room. " You always did make fun of me, Mr. Thripp. Do I deserve it, now?"

A gentle wave of heat coursed over Mr. Thripp as he covertly listened to these accents, but he was out of sight.

" Fun, Mrs. Brown? Never," he retorted gallantly; " it's only my little way." And then, to his immense relief, on lifting his eyes, discovered Tilda already descending the stairs.

He saw the pair of them off. Being restored to his coat, he could watch them clean down the drying street from his gatepost. Astonishing, he thought, what a difference there can be in two women's backs! Tilda's straight, angular, and respectable, as you might say; and that other—sinuous, seductive, as if it were as crafty a means of expression as the very smile and long-lashed languishments upon its owner's face. " What can the old woman see in her?" he muttered to himself. " Damned if I know!" On this problem Mr.

Thripp firmly shut his front door. Having shut it, he stooped to pick up a tiny white feather on the linoleum; and stooping, sighed.

At last his longed-for hour had come—the hour for which his very soul pined throughout each workaday week. Not that it was always his happy fate to be left completely alone like this. At times, indeed, he had for company far too much housework to leave him any leisure. But to-day the dinner-things were cleared away, the washing-up was over, the tables fair as a baker's board, the kitchen spick and span, the house empty. He would just have to look round his own and Tilda's bedroom (and, maybe, the boys' and Millie's). And then the chair by the fire; the simmering kettle on the hearth; and the soft, tardy, autumnal dusk fading quietly into night beyond the window.

It was a curious thing that a man who loved his family so much, who was as desperately loyal to every member of it as a she-wolf is to her cubs, should yet find this few minutes' weekly solitude a luxury such as only Paradise, one would suppose, would ever be able to provide.

Mr. Thripp went upstairs and not only tidied up his own and Tilda's bedroom, and went on to Millie's and the boys', but even gave a sloosh to the bath, slid the soap out of the basin where Charles had abandoned it, and hung up the draggled towels again in the tiny bathroom. What a place looks like when you come back to it from your little enjoyments—it's *that* makes all the difference to a home. These small chores done, Mr. Thripp put on an old tweed coat with frayed sleeves, and returned to the kitchen. In a quarter of an hour that, too, more than ever resembled a new pin.

Then he glanced up at the clocks; between them the time was a quarter to four. He was amazed. He laid the tea, took out of his little old leather bag a pot of jam which he had bought for a surprise on his way home, and arranged a bunch of violets in a small jar beside Tilda's plate. But apart from these family preparations, Mr. Thripp was now depositing a demure little glossy brown teapot all by itself on the kitchen range. This was his Eureka. This was practically the only sensual *secret* luxury Mr. Thripp had ever allowed himself since he became a family man. Tilda's cooking was good enough for him, provided that the others had their little dainties now and then. He enjoyed his beer, and could do a bit of supper occasionally with a friend. But the ritual of these solitary Saturday afternoons reached its climax in this small pot of tea. First the nap, sweet as nirvana, in his easy-chair, then the tea, and then the still, profound quarter-of-an-hour's musing before the door-knocker began again.

. . . . .

Having pulled down the blind a little in order to prevent any chance of draught, Mr. Thripp eased his bootlaces, sat himself in his chair, his cheek turned a little away from the window, his feet on the box that usually lay under the table, and with fingers clasped over his stomach, composed himself to sleep. The eyelids closed; the lips set; the thumbs twitched now and again. He breathed deep, and the kettle began a whispered anthem—as if a myriad voices were singing on and on without need of pause or rest, a thousand, thousand leagues away.

But now there was none to listen; and beyond quiet hung thick in the little house. Only the scarce-perceptible hum of the traffic at the end of the narrow side street was audible on the air. Within, the two clocks on the chimney-piece quarrelled furiously over the fleeting moments, attaining unanimity only in one of many ticks. Ever and again a tiny scutter of dying ashes rejoined those that had gone before in the pan beneath the fire. Soon even these faint stirrings became inaudible, and in a few moments Mr. Thripp's spirit would have wafted itself completely free awhile from its earthly tenement, if, suddenly, the image of Millie—more vivid than even the actual sight of her a few minutes before—had not floated up into the narrow darkness of her father's tight-shut eyes.

But this was not the image of Millie as her father usually saw her. A pathetic, earthly melancholy lay over the fair, angelic features. The young cheek was sunken in; the eye was faded, dejected, downcast; and her cheek was stubbornly turned away from her father, as if she resented or was afraid of his scrutiny.

At this vision a headlong anxiety darted across Mr. Thripp's half-slumbering mind. His heart began heavily beating: and then a pulse in his forehead. Where was she now? What forecast, what warning was this? Millie was no fool. Millie knew her way about. And her mother, if anything, was perhaps a little too censorious of the ways of this wicked world. If you keep on talking at a girl, hinting of things that might otherwise not enter her head—that in itself is dangerous. Love itself even must edge in warily. The tight-shut lids blinked anxiously. But where was Millie now? Somewhere indoors, but where? Who with?

Mr. Thripp saw her first in a teashop, sitting opposite a horrid young man with his hair greased back over his low, round head, and a sham pin in his tie. His elbows were on the marble-top table, and he was looking at Millie very much as a young but experienced pig looks at his wash-trough. Perhaps she was at the pictures? Dulcet accents echoed into the half-dreaming mind—" But I enjoy the dark, Mr. Thripp

. . . it rests the eyes." Why did the woman talk as if she had never more than half a breath to spare? Rest her eyes! She never, at any rate, wanted to rest the eyes of any fool in trousers who happened to be within glimpse of her own. It was almost unnaturally dark in the cinema of Mr. Thripp's fancy at this moment; yet he could now see his Millie, with her pale, harmless, youthful face, as plainly as if she were the "close-up" of some star from Los Angeles on the screen. And now the young man in her company was almost as fair as herself, with a long-chinned, sheepish face and bolting eyes; and the two of them were amorously hand in hand.

For the moment Mr. Thripp sat immovable, as if a bugle had sounded in his ear. Then he deliberately opened his eyes and glanced about him. The November daylight was already beginning to fade. Yes, he would have a word with Millie—but not when she came home that evening. It is always wiser to let the actual coming-home be pleasant and welcoming. To-morrow morning, perhaps; that is, if her mother was not goading at her for being late down and lackadaisical when there was so much to be done. Nevertheless, all in good time he would have a quiet little word with her. He would say only what he would not afterwards regret having said. He had meant to do that ages ago; but you mustn't flood a house with water when it's not on fire. She was but a mere slip of a thing—like a flower: not a wild flower, but one of those sweet, waxen flowers you see blooming in a florist's window—which you must be careful with, and not just expose anywhere.

And yet how his own little place here could be compared with anything in the nature of a hot-house he could not for the life of him understand. Delicate-looking. Everybody said that. God bless me, perhaps her very lackadaisicalness was a symptom of some as yet hidden malady. Good God, supposing! . . . He would take her round to see the doctor as soon as he could. But the worst of it was you had to do these things on your own responsibility. And though Mr. Thripp was now a man close on fifty, sometimes he felt as if he couldn't endure to brood over them as he was sometimes wont to do. If he did, he would snap. People *looked* old; but nobody was really old inside: not old, at least, in the sense that troubles were any the lighter, or forebodings any the more easily puffed away; or tongues easier to keep still; or tempers to control.

And talking of tempers reminded him of Charlie. What on earth was going to be done with Charlie? There was no difficulty in conjuring up, in seeing Charlie—that is, if he really did go every Saturday to a football match. But Charlie was now of an age when he might think it a fine manly thing to be loafing about the counter of a pub talking to some flaxen barmaid, with a tuppenny cigar between his teeth. Still, Mr. Thripp refused to entertain more than a glimpse of this possibility. He saw him at this moment as clearly as if in a peep-show, packed in with their check caps and their "fags," and their staring eyes revolving in consort, as if they were all attached to one wire, while that idiotic ball in the middle of the arena coursed on its helpless way from muddy boot to muddy boot.

Heaven knows, Mr. Thripp himself was nothing much better than a football! You had precious small chance in this life of choosing which boot should give you the next kick. And what about that smug, new, creeping accountant at the office, with his upstart airs and newfangled book-keeping methods!

Mr. Thripp's mouth opened in a yawn, but managed only to achieve a fraction of it. He rubbed his face; his eyes now shut again. It was not as if any of your children were of much practical help. Why should they be, when they could never understand that what you pined for, what you really needed was not only practical help, but some inward grace and clearness of mind wherewith they could slip in under your own thoughts, and so share your point of view without all that endless terrifying argumentation? He didn't *always* give advice to suit his own ends; and yet whenever he uttered a word to James, tactfully suggesting that in a world like this—however competent a man may be and however sure of himself—you *had* to push your way, you had to make your weight felt, James always looked at him as if he were a superannuated orang-outang in a cage—an orang-outang with queer and not particularly engaging habits.

He wouldn't mind even that so much if only James would take his cigarette out of his mouth when he talked. To see that bit of stained paper attached to his son's lower lip wagging up and down, beneath that complacent smile and those dark, helpless-looking eyes, all but sent Mr. Thripp stark staring mad at times. Once, indeed, he had actually given vent to the appalling mass of emotion hoarded up like water in a reservoir in his mind. The remembrance of the scene that followed made him even at this moment tremble in his chair. Thank God, thank God, he hadn't often lost control like that.

Well, James would be married by this time next year, he supposed. And what a nice dainty pickle he was concocting for himself! Mr. Thripp knew that type of young woman, with the compressed lips and the thin, dry hair, and the narrow hips. She'd be a "good manager," right enough, but there's a point in married life where good managing is little short of being in a lunatic asylum between two iron-faced nurses and yourself in a strait waistcoat. The truth of it was, with all his fine airs and neat finish, James hadn't much common sense. He had a fair share of brains; but brains are no good if you are merely self-opinionated and contemptuous on principle. James was not like anybody in Mr. Thripp's own family. He was a Simpkins.

And then suddenly it was as if some forgotten creature in Mr. Thripp's mind or heart had burst out crying; and the loving look he thereupon cast on his elder son's face in his mind was almost maudlin in its sentimentality. He would do anything for James within reason: anything. But, then, it would have to be within James's reason—not his own. He knew that. Why, he would himself marry the young woman and exult in being a bigamist if only he could keep his son out of her way. And yet, and yet; maybe there were worse women in the world than your stubborn, petulant, niggardly, half-sexed nagger. Mr. Thripp knew a nagger of old. His brother's wife, Fanny, had been a nagger. She was dead now, and George was a free man—but drinking far too much.

Well, as soon as he could get a chance, Mr. Thripp, sitting there in his chair decided, he would have another good think; but that probably wouldn't be until next Saturday, if then. You can't think to much purpose—except in a worried, disjointed fashion—when you are in the noise of an office or keeping yourself from saying things you have no wish to say. The worst of it was it was not much good discussing these matters with Tilda. Like most women, she always went off at a tangent. And when you came down to it, and wanted to be reasonable, there was so little left to discuss. Besides, Tilda had worries enough of her own.

At this moment Mr. Thripp once more opened his eyes wide. The small kitchen loomed beatifically rosy and still in the glow of the fire. Evening had so far edged on its way now that he could hardly see the hands of his two clocks. He could but just detect the brass pendulum—imperturbably chopping up eternity into fragments of time. He craned forward; in five minutes he ought to be brewing his little private pot of tea. Even if he nodded off now, he would be able to wake in time, but five minutes doesn't leave much margin for dropping off. He shifted a little on his chair, and once more shut his eyes. And in a moment or two his mind went completely blank.

He seemed to have been suddenly hauled up helpless with horror into an enormous vacancy—to be dangling unconfined and motionless in space. A scene of wild, sandy hills and spiky trees—an illimitable desert—came riding towards him out of nothingness. He hung motionless, and was yet sweeping rapidly forward, but for what purpose and to what goal there was not the smallest inkling. The wilderness before him grew ever more desolate and menacing. He began to be deadly afraid; groaned; stirred—and found himself sitting bolt upright in his chair. And the hands of the clock looked to be by a hair's breadth precisely in the same position as when he had started on that ghastly journey. His face blanched. He sat appalled, listening to an outrageous wauling of voices. It was as though a thousand demons lay in wait for him beneath his window and were summoning him to his doom.

And all this nightmare horror of mind was due solely to a wailing of cats! And yet even as, with flesh still creeping, he listened on to this clamour, it was so human in effect that it might be multitudinous shades of the unborn that were thronging about the glass of his window. Mr. Thripp rose from his chair, his face transfigured with rage and desire for revenge. He went out into the scullery, opened the back door, and at sound of him the caterwauling instantly ceased.

And almost as instantly his fury died out in him. The cold evening air fanned his forehead. He smiled quixotically, and looked about him. There came a furtive rustle in the bushes. "Ah, there you are!" he sang out gently into the dark. "Have your play while you can, my fine gentlemen! Take it like your betters, for it's—a sight too soon over."

Above the one cramped, leafless elder-tree in his yard a star was pricking the sky. A ground-mist, too, was rising, already smelling a little stale. Great London and its suburbs appeared to be in for one of its autumnal fogs. A few of the upper windows opposite loomed dim with light. Mr. Thripp's neighbours, it seemed, were also preparing to be off to the pictures or the music-halls. It was very still, and the air was damp and clammy.

As he stood silent there in the obscurity, a deepening melancholy crept over his mind, though he was unaware into what gloomy folds and sags his face had fallen. He suddenly remembered that his rates would have to be paid next week. He remembered that Christmas would soon be coming, and that he was getting too old to enter into the fun of the thing as he used to do. His eyes rolled a little in their sockets. What the . . . ! his old friend within began to suggest. But Mr. Thripp himself did not even enunciate the missing "hell." Instead, he vigorously rubbed his face with his stout, capable hand. "Well, fog, anyhow, don't bring rain," he muttered to himself.

And as if at a signal, his own cat and his next-door neighbour's cat and Mrs. Brown's cat, and the cat of the painter and decorator whose back garden abutted his own, together with the ginger-and-white cat from a newsvendor's beyond, with one consent broke out once more into their Sabbath-eve quintette. The many-stranded strains of it mounted up into the heavens like the yells of demented worshippers of Baal.

"And, as I say, I don't blame ye, neether," Mr. Thripp retorted, with a grim smile. "If you knew, my friends, how narrowly you some of you escaped a bucket of cold water when you couldn't even see out of your young eyes, you'd sing twice as loud."

He shut the door and returned to his fireside. No more hope of sleep that afternoon. He laughed to himself for sheer amusement at his disappointment. What kids men were! He stirred the fire; it leapt brightly, as if intent to please him. He pushed the kettle on, put on the light, warmed his little privy teapot, and fetched out a small private supply of the richest Ceylon from behind some pots in the saucepan cupboard.

Puffs of steam were now vapouring out of the spout of the kettle with majestic pomposity. Mr. Thripp lifted it off the coals and balanced it over his teapot. And at that very instant the electric bell—which a year or two ago, in a moment of the strangest caprice, Charles had fixed up in the corner—began jangling like a fire-alarm. Mr. Thripp hesitated. If this was one of the family, he was caught. Caught, that is, unless he was mighty quick in concealing these secret preparations. If it was Tilda—well, valour was the better part of discretion. He poured the water into the pot, replaced the lid, and put it on to the oven-top to stew. With a glance of satisfaction at the spinster-like tidiness of the room, he went out and opened the door.

"Why, it's Millie!" he said, looking out at the slim-shouldered creature standing alone there under the porch. "You don't mean to say it's you, my dear?"

Millie made no reply. Her father couldn't see her face. She pushed furtively past him without a word, her head stooping out of the light.

Oh, my God, what's wrong now? yelled her father's inward monstrous monitor, frenziedly clanging the fetters on wrist and ankle. "Come right in, my pretty dear," said Mr. Thripp seductively; "this *is* a pleasant surprise. And, what's more, between you and me and the gatepost, I have just been making myself a cup of tea. Not a word to mother; it's *our* little secret. We'll have it together before the others come in."

"Lor', what a glare you are in, pa!" she said in a small,

muffled voice. She turned the light down so low that in an instant or two the flame flickered and expired, and she seated herself in her father's chair by the fire. But the flamelight showed her face now. It was paler even than usual. A strand of her gilded, pale-brown hair had streaked itself over her blue-veined temple. She looked as if she had been crying. Her father, his hands hanging down beside him as uselessly as the front paws of a performing bear, watched her in an appalling trepidation of spirit. This, then, was the secret of his nightmares; for this the Cats of Fate had chorused!

"What's wrong, Millie love? Are you over-tired, my girl? There! Don't say nothing for a minute or two. See, here's my little pot just meant for you and me!"

Millie began to cry again, pushing her ridiculous little handkerchief close to her eyes, Mr. Thripp's hand hovered awkwardly above her dainty hat and then gently fumbled, as if to stroke her hair beneath. He knelt down beside her chair.

For Heaven's sake! For Heaven's sake! For Heaven's sake! a secret voice was gabbling frenziedly in his ear. "Tell your old dad, lovey," he murmured out loud, softly as the crooning of a wood pigeon.

Millie tilted back her pretty hat and dropped her fair head on his shoulder.

"It's nothing, dad," she said. "It's only that they are all the same."

"What are all the same?"

"Oh, fellows, dad."

"Which one, precious?" Mr. Thripp lulled wooingly. God strike him dead! muttered his monster.

"Oh, only young Arthur. Like a fool, I waited half-an-hour for him, and then saw him with—with that Westcliff girl."

A sigh as voluminous as the suspiration of Niagara swept over Mr. Thripp; but it made no sound. Half a dozen miraculous words of reassurance were storming his mind in a frenzy of relief. He paused an instant, and accepted the seventh.

"What's all that, my precious?" he was murmuring. "Why, when I was courting your mother I saw just the same thing happen. She was a mighty pretty young thing, too, as a girl, though not quite so trim and neat in the figure as you. I felt I could throttle him where he stood. But no, I just took no notice, trusting in my own charms!"

"That's all very well," sobbed Millie, "but you were a man, and *we* have to fight without seeming to. Not that I care a fig for him; he can go. But——"

"Lord, Millie!" Mr. Thripp interrupted, smoothing her

cheek with his squat forefinger. " You'd beat twenty of them Westcliffs, with a cast in both eyes and your hands behind your back. Don't you grieve no more, my dear; he'll come back safe and sound, or he's less of a—of a nice young feller than I take him for."

For a moment Mr. Thripp caught a glimpse of the detestable creature with the goggling eyes and the suede shoes, but he dismissed him sternly from view.

" There, now," he said, " give your poor old dad a kiss. What's disappointments, Millie? they soon pass away. And now, just take a sip or two of this extra-strong Bohay! I was hoping I shouldn't have to put up with a lonely cup and not a soul to keep me company. But mind, my precious, not a word to your ma."

So there they sat, father and daughter, comforter and comforted, while Mr. Thripp worked miracles for two out of a teapot for one. And while Millie, with heart comforted, was musing on that other young fellow she had noticed boldly watching her while she was waiting for her Arthur, Mr. Thripp was wondering when it would be safe and discreet to disturb her solacing day-dream so that he might be busying himself over the supper.

It's one damn neck-and-neck worry and trouble after another, his voice was assuring him. But meanwhile, his plain, square face was serene and gentle as a nestful of halcyons, as he sat sipping his hot water and patting his pensive Millie's hand.

H. E. BATES

THE CASE OF MISS LOMAS

I

IN the dining-room of the Bellevue Boarding House Miss Lomas and Mr. Sanderson ate their fish in silence. They sat at separate tables. They were the only guests. Miss Lomas was somewhere between thirty-five and forty: a woman of medium height with pale brown hair and a reserved, almost apologetic manner, who looked as though keeping to the medium, even the unhappy medium, had been her life's most constant ambition. She had a habit, never varied, of staring out to sea as she ate. To-day the rain was coming down in thin curtains between great islands of cloud shadow and vast blue storms lying over the coast of France. It was already late October, and it looked as if the weather were breaking up at last.

Mr. Sanderson felt that he might say so. He had been at the Bellevue, now, for three days, but Miss Lomas, except to say "Good morning," or "Good afternoon," had not spoken to him. She had not even got so far as saying "Good night." She looked in some way pre-occupied with melancholy, with herself, with some indefinable and perhaps even unmentionable grievance or difficulty. He himself was not feeling too cheerful either; he had lost his wife, he had not been overgrand all summer. He was rather an upright, handsome man of fifty-two, though he felt, if anything, a little older. Nor was the Bellevue too cheerful. The smell of stale food was so thick and almost sickening everywhere that it was like an anæsthetic. It was perhaps hardly the place, after all, to put him on his feet again.

At last he spoke. "Well," he said, in a deliberate voice, "I rather think . . ."

He got no further. The maid, at that moment, came in to clear the fish plates. He sat silent, playing with the salt. The girl took Miss Lomas's plate. She came over to take his own. It was just then that he made up his mind to say to her what he had wanted to say to Miss Lomas.

"Well," he said, "I rather think it looks as if the weather has broken."

"Oh! you never know," the girl said. "The autumn goes on a long time here."

She spoke in a friendly voice, and Mr. Sanderson felt cheered. She was not much more than a girl. He watched her go out of the dining-room, eyes fixed on her slim legs.

She came back with plates of boiled mutton, and then dishes of potatoes and cabbage. All the time Miss Lomas gazed out of the window. They both ate in silence. Miss Lomas's mouth, while she ate, was a mouth with no expression of emotion on it at all—no hunger, no pleasure, no distaste, no annoyance, no weariness, nothing. It seemed to express a personality that was at once upright and negative. So that Mr. Sanderson could not help wondering about her. What was she, what was she doing, why was she so standoffish? She was negative almost to a point of mystery.

And then the pudding came. Before he had realised it Miss Lomas had refused it. Her only sign of refusal was to walk out. She was gone before he could make a gesture.

It began to rain before the girl brought in the coffee. The sea was turned by rain into a stormy expanse of steel, and the afternoon seemed suddenly almost dark, with rain sweeping along in dark gusts that splintered white on the deserted promenade.

"Nice how-d'ye-do," he said.

"Were you going out?" the girl said.

"Well, I was and I wasn't. I didn't really know what to do. What can I do? You know more about this place than I do."

"Go to the pictures. Or if it clears up you could walk over to the Flats. It's grand out there. I love it. It's always so grand and windy out there."

Somehow that didn't seem like a waitress. She spoke nicely, easily, with some sort of refinement.

"Been in service long?" he said.

She stood and grinned at him, openly, almost pulling a face. "Me? I'm Mrs. Harrap's daughter."

"Well, I'm blowed."

"I left school at August. I'm waiting to get a job."

"Well." He looked at her. She was pretty, with short yellow hair cut straight, and strong bare arms, and rather a fine high forehead. "Now I'm come to look at you, you're like your mother."

She laughed; and Mr. Sanderson, less depressed, laughed too, and they were intimate.

" Like being a waitress? "

She just grinned. " Would you? "

" Don't you get out? "

" Oh! yes. But what can you do in a place like this? "

" That's what I want to know."

He drank his coffee. The girl watched the rain. Suddenly he thought " Oh! damn it, why not? " and said:

" If I went to the pictures would you come with me? "

" I would. I'd love it."

" Good." He felt suddenly light-hearted. " That's more than I dare have asked Miss Lomas. Even at my age."

" She wouldn't come if you asked her."

" Why not? "

" I don't think she believes in it. In relationships, I mean—man and woman. Even if it's platonic. I think she lives it all in books." Then suddenly she said: " If I'm coming with you I'd better fly. I'll meet you at the cinema, shall I? We needn't broadcast it from the house-tops that we're going together."

" I don't know that we need," he said.

When he went to get his mackintosh Miss Lomas was just going across the hall and into the drawing-room, with a novel in her hands. She did not speak. She carried herself with the same upright negation as ever. Looking straight before her, she seemed to be looking always towards some kind of spiritual but empty horizon. Her medium, spiritless brown eyes had some sort of subdued pain in them. " Perhaps she suffers from indigestion," he thought.

Later he said this to the girl. When they met at the cinema the rain had ceased. It was windy, with sudden acres of blue sky and, under the shelter of the white boarding houses on the promenade, an almost hot sun. " It seems too good to go to the pictures," she said, and he agreed. " Let's walk over to the Flats instead."

" All right," he said, and they walked eastwards out of the town, into a gusty, bright afternoon. As they walked, the wind and sun cleared the sky above the sea until the air shone with a kind of lofty radiance. And then, beyond the town, the marshland stretched out, yellowish green, the grass still summer-dried, in places almost white with salt. Tufts of sea-pink, half seed, half flower, were still blooming in the drifts of shingle. The girl walked fast. She had no hat, and her hair blew all about her face. She talked a lot, exuberantly, girlishly. She would stop sometimes and point out headlands along the coast, or sea-birds, or churches beyond the rim of marshland. " I adore it," she would say. It was her favourite word. And she seemed to carry him along on a succession of flights of adoration.

And then they talked of Miss Lomas. " She has indigestion," he said. " That's her trouble."

" I don't know," the girl said. " She comes to us every winter. This is the fourth winter. She comes when the summer people have gone, and stops till Easter."

" Is that all? "

" Yes. She just sits and reads, that's all. That's all I ever saw her do."

" I still think it's indigestion," he said.

After that, they forgot her. Mr. Sanderson walked along with a great sense of exhilaration. At home he was a draper. It was fine to feel free, to smell sun and sea instead of serge and calico. " This walk is doing me good," he said. And then: " By the way, you never told me your name? "

" Freda," she said.

" And what's Miss Lomas's name? "

" I never heard it," she said.

In the late afternoon they rested. They sat down on the very edge of the shore, where hollows of sand were fringed with thin dune-grass and still blue sea-thistle. The girl lay down. He half sat beside her, resting on one elbow. Her hair was almost the colour of the sand. She lay with arms stretched out, her dress tight across her body, her eyes opening and shutting in what seemed to be an ecstasy of mental drowsiness. She seemed to lie there in deliberate invitation to him, so that he felt some kind of stupid eagerness, almost an ache, grow up in him. By that time the afternoon was going quickly. The tide was coming up and the sea losing its light. For two or three minutes he lay and watched the vague passage of ships. Then he turned and looked at the girl again. She looked back, straight, with a frankness of invitation that made him feel almost shocked.

" You're slow," she said.

Rather stupidly he bent down then and she put her arm up to him. He felt in some way passive, impelled by her. In the end he kissed her, not very well and with a feeling of being out of practice, with consequent stupidity. " Come on," she said softly. " Again. Better than that. A long one. A real one." She held her lips still and slightly apart and shut her eyes.

All the way back across the marshland in the sudden twilight, he was troubled by a constant notion that he ought to be careful. " She's only a kid," he would think. All the way he walked with his arm round her, closely. It was she who had put it there.

And then, in the town, they separated. He felt rather old and a little tired. Walking in that strong air, with intervals of unexpected passion, had been almost too much for him. He was glad to get back to Bellevue and have a bath and a rest before dinner.

And at dinner only Miss Lomas, as usual, was there; and, as usual, she did not speak. To his disappointment, also, there was no sight of Freda. Mrs. Harrap, a jolly, rather assertive woman with ear-rings, brought in the dishes herself. Even for her Miss Lomas had no conversation. And now, since she could not look out to sea, she looked at the venetian blinds, drawn down over the window. There was no difference in her manner. If the horizon itself had been shut out, the spiritual horizon remained, to be everlastingly affixed by her medium brown eyes, with their air of spiritless martyrdom.

He did not see Freda until much later. Miss Lomas had gone to bed and he was in the hall, reading the amusement guide before going himself. The girl came in as he stood there. The house was very quiet and for some moments she did not speak. She stood and smiled and then opened the door of the drawing-room and they went inside. It all happened without a word. It was dark and she put her arms about him and kissed him. It was literally she who kissed him. He stood passive, holding her tightly. "Again," she would say. "Tighter, hold me tighter. Please. Tighter." And he held her and kissed with something of the old feeling of inadequacy, rather stupidly, feeling somehow that he was no match for her.

Then, as they came out of the dark drawing-room, they heard a sound on the stairs above. It was as though someone had moved suddenly away.

"What's that?" he said. "Somebody watching?"

"It's nothing. What does it matter, anyway?"

After another moment, they said good night. The girl seemed careless, impish. And then, going upstairs, he saw that the door of Miss Lomas's room was ajar.

II

It was not until two days later that Miss Lomas spoke to him. In the interval he had twice taken the girl out again, once to the cinema, in the afternoon, and once to the pier, late in the evening. Coming out of the cinema, he had been surprised to see Miss Lomas. With umbrella and mackintosh on her arm, she had been walking rapidly along the promenade, as though in a great hurry to get somewhere. He got ready to raise his hat. And then, suddenly she crossed the street and did not see them at all.

Then, the following day, she spoke to him. He was sitting in the drawing-room, after lunch, reading the paper. He was feeling better in health. He could read and lose himself in what he was reading. And it was pleasant to think of flirting with the girl after all. Suddenly, there was Miss Lomas. She was standing in front of him, ready to speak.

Then, before she spoke, he noticed an odd thing. Her hands were tightly clenched. And she seemed to be looking beyond him. She seemed extraordinarily nervous, and it made him nervous. As he got up he kicked the chair-leg and dropped his newspaper and then hurriedly took off his reading glasses.

" I would like to speak to you," she said.

" Oh! yes, Miss Lomas," he said. " Oh! yes. Good. What was it? "

She was silent. He waited. And then she said, with a kind of righteous, almost comic abruptness:

" I saw you out with that girl."

He got ready to reply. She went on at once:

" I don't think it right. Secretly. She's only a girl." She repeated it, as though to convince him. " I don't think it's right. Your meeting her like that, secretly. It's not right."

" You mean you don't think it's right.

" It's the same thing. I don't think it's right."

" What do you want me to do? " he said.

For a moment she stood still, silent. She was breathing fast, in agitation. There was some kind of explosive dignity about her. Her eyes were no longer in any way medium. They were passionately, almost comically indignant. She was a little short-sighted and it was as though her eyes were not strong enough to sustain any such ferocity of emotion. Then suddenly she burst out. " Do you expect me to tell you what to do? " and went out.

The whole thing made him feel perverse. He was not more than momentarily angry. That afternoon he went out with the girl again, arranging it deliberately. He told her about Miss Lomas. " Interfering old cat," she said, and they had a good laugh about it together.

Then, after dinner that evening, something else happened. He took the evening paper into the drawing-room, prepared and even anxious for trouble. Miss Lomas sat there with her eternal book. He had hardly sat down when she got up and did an extraordinary thing. She apologised.

" I'm sorry about this afternoon," she said.

He could think of nothing to say. She was very earnest and it was almost comic. He simply stood still and listened while she made efforts, by repetition, as she had done earlier, to convince him.

" I shouldn't have said what I did. I'm very sorry. It was not my business."

Then he did feel, for the first and only time, momentarily angry with her.

" If it was not your business why did you do it? There's no need to spy on people."

She just stood silent, as though it were true and as though she accepted it. Her eyes did not change their look of medium stupidity. Except that now it was painful. He could not look at her.

After that there seemed nothing he could say and he left the room and got his mackintosh and went for a walk along the promenade. It was a squally, cold evening, with a sharp wind off the sea, and when he got back to the boarding house the drawing-room was empty and he rang for some coffee. Freda brought it.

" I must tell you about Miss Lomas," he said. " By the way, where is she? Gone to bed? "

" She went up some time after eight."

" I must tell you about her. She apologised to-night."

They went on to talk about it and they had another laugh about her.

" She's not a bad sort," he said. " She just suffers from indigestion, that's all."

" She's all right," the girl said. " Why don't you ask her to the cinema—just to see what happens. Just to see how she takes it."

" I thought you said she didn't believe in it? "

" Well, ask her. Just for fun. For a joke," she said. " Ask her for fun."

He put it to Miss Lomas on the following day, casually, rather off-hand. Very much to his astonishment she accepted, and they went in the evening, after dinner. On the way he said something about life being short and there being no reason why they should not be good friends and she said yes, she agreed except that sometimes life seemed rather long. He thought it an odd remark, but after that they did not speak much. She had dressed up a little for the occasion: a brown and mauve hat and, underneath her coat, a mauve silk dress. In the cinema she took off her coat and he could see her flat, unbecoming chest that had no shape about it at all. It was a cold evening, but once or twice during the performance she said how hot it was. He thought she seemed restless and afterwards at the boarding-house he said so.

"Oh! I'm like that," she said. "It was really wonderful."

And then, as she shook hands before going upstairs to bed, he was amazed to find out how really hot she was. Her hand was damp with sweat. It was as though it had been a kind of exquisite ordeal for her.

And when, after lunch on the following day, Freda wanted to know all about it, he said, joking: "I think it was a bit too much for her. She got all hot and bothered."

"She fell for you," the girl said. "That's all. You made a hit. She thinks you're Valentino. Very nice."

They were in the dining-room alone. The girl took a quick look round.

"Kiss me," she said. "Now. Quickly." She kissed him, rapturously, with devilry, and then said: "And tell me something. Valentino or no Valentino, that's the last time? Or else *I* shall get jealous."

"Don't worry," he said. "Once with Miss Lomas is enough for a lifetime."

Almost before he had said it he felt curiously uneasy. He turned quickly round and looked at the doorway. Miss Lomas was standing there. Caught in the very act of listening, she did not move or speak. She made no kind of protest, and after a moment she turned and went quickly back to the drawing-room.

"That's the limit!" the girl said. "That *is* the limit. That shows what she is."

"Yes, that finishes it," he said.

From that day until he left, a fortnight later, Miss Lomas did not speak to him. It was even, sometimes, as though he did not exist. She lived constantly in that medium spiritless brown world in which he had first found her, looking out to sea as she ate, reading eternal novels, gazing at her spiritual horizon beyond the drawn venetian blinds in the evenings. He saw a change only once. Looking up from his paper, unexpectedly, one evening, in the drawing-room, he caught her looking at him. She was looking at him with the oddest conflict of emotions: hatred and doubt and despair and what he felt was also a kind of religious devotion. It was as though she were trying to hypnotise him. It filled her ordinarily emotionless eyes with a painful complexity of tenderness and jealousy.

Two days later he left. He said good-bye to Freda on the previous evening. She took it badly. The weather had turned warm, with real soft autumnal humidity, and they lay in the dark beach and kissed a lot until, at last, the girl cried. "It'll be rotten when you've gone," she said. "What shall I do? Why don't you stay? Oh! I'll drown myself or something."

"Look here, don't talk silly."

"I will. It'll be so rotten. Why do you have to go?"

"I work for my living. I've got a business. I'll come back. I'll see you again."

"You won't. You'll forget me."

"I won't. I'll come. Now be a good girl and kiss me and promise you won't do anything silly."

There was passion in her kisses, but no promise. All the way home in the train he was worried by stupid fears. She was a dynamic girl and he felt as though he had left her in suspense. Over-charged with passion, she might very well go off into some tragic explosion. Girls did silly things and even, sometimes, killed themselves. He felt, all along, that he had been something of a fool.

A week later he got a letter. It was from the girl herself. It was a long letter, and she enclosed a cutting from a newspaper.

It was Miss Lomas, not she, who had killed herself. It was an awful thing, the girl said, and she did not understand it.

Nor did he understand it himself.

JOSEPH CONRAD

THE BLACK MATE

A GOOD many years ago there were several ships loading at the Jetty, London Dock. I am speaking here of the 'eighties of the last century, of the time when London had plenty of fine ships in the docks, though not so many fine buildings in its streets.

The ships at the Jetty were fine enough; they lay one behind the other; and the *Sapphire*, third from the end, was as good as the rest of them, and nothing more. Each ship at the Jetty had, of course, her chief officer on board. So had every other ship in dock.

The policeman at the gates knew them all by sight, without being able to say at once, without thinking, to what ship any particular man belonged. As a matter of fact, the mates of the ships then lying in the London Dock were like the majority of officers in the Merchant Service—a steady, hard-working, staunch, unromantic-looking set of men, belonging to various classes of society, but with the professional stamp obliterating the personal characteristics, which were not very marked, anyhow.

This last was true of them all, with the exception of the mate of the *Sapphire*. Of him the policeman could not be in doubt. This one had a presence.

He was noticeable to them in the street from a great distance; and when in the morning he strode down the Jetty to his ship, the lumpers and the dock labourers rolling the bales and trundling the cases of cargo on their hand-trucks would remark to each other:

" Here's the black mate coming along."

That was the name they gave him, being a gross lot, who could have no appreciation of the man's dignified bearing. And to call him black was the superficial impressionism of the ignorant.

Of course, Mr. Bunter, the mate of the *Sapphire*, was not black. He was no more black than you or I, and certainly as white as any chief mate of a ship in the whole of the Port of London. His complexion was of the sort that did not take the tan easily; and I happen to know that the poor fellow had had a month's illness just before he joined the *Sapphire*.

From this you will perceive that I knew Bunter. Of course I knew him. And, what's more, I knew his secret at the time, this secret which—never mind just now. Returning to Bunter's personal appearance, it was nothing but ignorant prejudice on the part of the foreman stevedore to say, as he did in my hearing: "I bet he's a furriner of some sort." A man may have black hair without being set down for a Dago. I have known a West-country sailor, boatswain of a fine ship, who looked more Spanish than any Spaniard afloat I've ever met. He looked like a Spaniard in a picture.

Competent authorities tell us that this earth is to be finally the inheritance of men with dark hair and brown eyes. It seems that already the great majority of mankind is dark-haired in various shades. But it is only when you meet one that you notice how men with really black hair, black as ebony, are rare. Bunter's hair was absolutely black, black as a raven's wing. He wore, too, all his beard (clipped, but a good length all the same), and his eyebrows were thick and bushy. Add to this steely-blue eyes, which in a fair-haired man would have been nothing so extraordinary, but in that sombre framing made a startling contrast, and you will easily understand that Bunter was noticeable enough. If it had not been for the quietness of his movements, for the general soberness of his demeanour, one would have given him credit for a fiercely passionate nature.

Of course, he was not in his first youth; but if the expression "in the force of his age" has any meaning, he realised it completely. He was a tall man, too, though rather spare. Seeing him from his poop indefatigably busy with his duties, Captain Ashton, of the clipper ship *Elsinore*, lying just ahead of the *Sapphire*, remarked once to a friend that "Johns has got somebody there to hustle his ship along for him."

Captain Johns, master of the *Sapphire*, having commanded ships for many years, was well known, without being much respected or liked. In the company of his fellows he was either neglected or chaffed. The chaffing was generally undertaken by Captain Ashton, a cynical and teasing sort of man. It was Captain Ashton who permitted himself the unpleasant joke of proclaiming once in company that "Johns is of the opinion that every sailor above forty years of age ought to be poisoned—shipmasters in actual command excepted."

It was in a City restaurant, where several well-known shipmasters were having lunch together. There was Captain Ashton, florid and jovial, in a large white waistcoat and with a yellow rose in his buttonhole; Captain Sellers in a sack-coat, thin and pale-faced, with his iron-grey hair tucked behind his ears, and, but for the absence of spectacles, looking like an ascetical mild man of books; Captain Bell, a bluff sea-dog with hairy fingers, in blue serge and a black felt hat pushed far back off his crimson forehead. There was also a very young shipmaster, with a little fair moustache and serious eyes, who said nothing, and only smiled faintly from time to time.

Captain Johns, very much startled, raised his perplexed and credulous glance, which, together with a low and horizontally wrinkled brow, did not make a very intellectual *ensemble*. This impression was by no means mended by the slightly pointed form of his bald head.

Everybody laughed outright, and, thus guided, Captain Johns ended by smiling rather sourly, and attempted to defend himself. It was all very well to joke, but nowadays, when ships, to pay anything at all, had to be driven hard on the passage and in harbour, the sea was no place for elderly men. Only young men and men in their prime were equal to modern conditions of push and hurry. Look at the great firms: almost every single one of them was getting rid of men showing any signs of age. He, for one, didn't want any oldsters on board his ship.

And, indeed, in this opinion Captain Johns was not singular. There was at that time a lot of seamen, with nothing against them but that they were grizzled, wearing out the soles of their last pair of boots on the pavements of the City in the heart-breaking search for a berth.

Captain Johns added with a sort of ill-humoured innocence that from holding that opinion to thinking of poisoning people was a very long step.

This seemed final, but Captain Ashton would not let go his joke.

"Oh, yes. I am sure you would. You said distinctly 'of no use.' What's to be done with men who are 'of no use'? You are a kind-hearted fellow, Johns. I am sure that if only you thought it over carefully you would consent to have them poisoned in some painless manner."

Captain Sellers twitched his thin, sinuous lips.

"Make ghosts of them," he suggested pointedly.

At the mention of ghosts Captain Johns became shy, in his perplexed, sly and unlovely manner.

Captain Ashton winked.

"Yes. And then perhaps you would get a chance to have a communication with the world of spirits. Surely the ghosts of seamen should haunt ships. Some of them would be sure to call on an old shipmate."

Captain Sellers remarked drily:

"Don't raise his hopes like this; it's cruel. He won't see anything. You know, Johns, that nobody has ever seen a ghost."

At this intolerable provocation Captain Johns came out of his reserve. With no perplexity whatever, but with a positive passion of credulity giving momentary lustre to his dull little eyes, he brought up a lot of authenticated instances. There were books and books full of instances. It was merest ignorance to deny supernatural apparitions. Cases were published every month in a special newspaper. Professor Cranks saw ghosts daily. And Professor Cranks was no small potatoes either. One of the biggest scientific men living. And there was that newspaper fellow—what's his name?—who had a girl-ghost visitor. He printed in his paper things she said to him. And to say there were no ghosts after that!

"Why, they have been photographed! What more proof do you want?"

Captain Johns was indignant. Captain Bell's lips twitched, but Captain Ashton protested now.

"For goodness' sake don't keep him going with that. And by the by, Johns, who's that hairy pirate you've got for your new mate? Nobody in the Dock seems to have seen him before."

Captain Johns, pacified by the change of subject, answered simply that Willy, the tobacconist at the corner of Fenchurch Street, had sent him along.

Willy, his shop, and the very house in Fenchurch Street, I believe, are gone now. In his time, wearing a careworn, absent-minded look on his pasty face, Willy served with tobacco many southern-going ships out of the Port of London. At certain times of the day the shop would be full of shipmasters. They sat on casks, they lounged against the counter.

Many a youngster found his first lift in life there: many a man got a sorely needed berth by simply dropping in for four pennyworth of birds'-eye at an auspicious moment. Even Willy's assistant, a red-headed, uninterested, delicate-looking young fellow, would hand you across the counter sometimes a bit of valuable intelligence with your box of cigarettes, in a whisper, lips hardly moving, thus: "The *Bellona*, South

Dock. Second officer wanted. You may be in time for it if you hurry up."

And didn't one just fly!

"Oh, Willy sent him," said Captain Ashton. "He's a very striking man. If you were to put a red sash round his waist and a red handkerchief round his head, he would look exactly like one of them buccaneering chaps that made men walk the plank and carried women off into captivity. Look out, Johns, he don't cut your throat for you and run off with the *Sapphire*. What ship has he come out of last?"

Captain Johns, after looking up credulously as usual, wrinkled his brow, and said placidly that the man had seen better days. His name was Bunter.

"He's had command of a Liverpool ship, the *Samaria*, some years ago. He lost her in the Indian Ocean, and had his certificate suspended for a year. Ever since then he has not been able to get another command. He's been knocking about in the Western Ocean trade lately."

"That accounts for him being a stranger to everybody about the Docks," Captain Ashton concluded as they rose from table.

Captain Johns walked down to the Dock after lunch. He was short of stature and slightly bandy. His appearance did not inspire the generality of mankind with esteem; but it must have been otherwise with his employers. He had the reputation of being an uncomfortable commander, meticulous in trifles, always nursing a grievance of some sort and incessantly nagging. He was not a man to kick up a row with you and be done with it, but to say nasty things in a whining voice; a man capable of making one's life a perfect misery if he took a dislike to an officer.

That very evening I went to see Bunter on board, and sympathised with him on his prospects for the voyage. He was subdued. I suppose a man with a secret locked up in his breast loses his buoyancy. And there was another reason why I could not expect Bunter to show a great elasticity of spirits. For one thing, he had been very seedy lately, and besides—but of that later.

Captain Johns had been on board that afternoon, and had loitered and dodged about his chief mate in a manner which had annoyed Bunter exceedingly.

"What could he mean?" he asked with calm exasperation. "One would think he suspected I had stolen something and tried to see in what pocket I had stowed it away; or that somebody told him I had a tail and he wanted to find out how I managed to conceal it. I don't like to be approached from behind several times in one afternoon in that creepy way and then to be looked up at suddenly in front from under my elbow. Is it a new sort of peep-bo game? It doesn't amuse me. I am no longer a baby."

I assured him that if anyone were to tell Captain Johns that he—Bunter—had a tail, Johns would manage to get himself to believe the story in some mysterious manner. He would. He was suspicious and credulous to an inconceivable degree. He would believe any silly tale, suspect any man of anything, and crawl about with it and ruminate the stuff, and turn it over and over in his mind in the most miserable, inwardly whining perplexity. He would take the meanest possible view in the end, and discover the meanest possible course of action by a sort of natural genius for that sort of thing.

Bunter also told me that the mean creature had crept all over the ship on his little, bandy legs, taking him along to grumble and whine to about a lot of trifles. Crept about the decks like a wretched insect—like a cockroach, only not so lively.

Thus did the self-possessed Bunter express himself with great disgust. Then, going on with his usual stately deliberation, made sinister by the frown of his jet-black eyebrows:

" And the fellow is mad, too. He tried to be sociable for a bit, and could find nothing else but to make big eyes at me, and ask me if I believed ' in communication beyond the grave.' Communication beyond—I didn't know what he meant at first. I didn't know what to say. ' A very solemn subject, Mr. Bunter,' says he. ' I've given a great deal of study to it.' "

Had Johns lived on shore he would have been the predestined prey of fraudulent mediums; or even if he had had any decent opportunities between the voyages. Luckily for him, when in England he lived somewhere far away in Leytonstone, with a maiden sister ten years older than himself, a fearsome virago twice his size, before whom he trembled. It was said she bullied him terribly in general; and in the particular instance of his spiritualistic leanings she had her own views.

These leanings were to her simply satanic. She was reported as having declared that, " With God's help, she would prevent that fool from giving himself up to the Devils." It was beyond doubt that Johns' secret ambition was to get into personal communication with the spirits of the dead—if only his sister would let him. But she was adamant. I was told that while in London he had to account to her for every penny of the money he took with him in the morning, and for every hour of his time. And she kept the bankbook, too.

Bunter (he had been a wild youngster, but he was well connected; had ancestors; there was a family tomb somewhere in the home counties)—Bunter was indignant, perhaps on account of his own dead. Those steely-blue eyes of his flashed with positive ferocity out of that black-bearded face. He impressed me—there was so much dark passion in his leisurely contempt.

"The cheek of the fellow! Enter into relations with . . . A mean little cad like this! It would be an impudent intrusion. He wants to enter? . . . What is it? A new sort of snobbishness, or what?"

I laughed outright at this original view of spiritism—or whatever the ghost craze is called. Even Bunter himself condescended to smile. But it was an austere, quickly vanished smile. A man in his almost, I may say, tragic position couldn't be expected—you understand. He was really worried. He was ready eventually to put up with any dirty trick in the course of the voyage. A man could not expect much consideration should he find himself at the mercy of a fellow like Johns. A misfortune is a misfortune, and there's an end of it. But to be bored by mean, low-spirited, inane ghost stories in the Johns' style, all the way out to Calcutta and back again, was an intolerable apprehension to be under. Spiritism was indeed a solemn subject to think about in that light. Dreadful, even!

Poor fellow! Little we both thought that before very long he himself . . . However, I could give him no comfort. I was rather appalled myself.

Bunter had also another annoyance that day. A confounded berthing master came on board on some pretence or other, but in reality, Bunter thought, simply impelled by an inconvenient curiosity—inconvenient to Bunter, that is. After some beating about the bush, that man suddenly said:

"I can't help thinking I've seen you before somewhere, Mr. Mate. If I heard your name, perhaps——"

Bunter—that's the worst of a life with a mystery in it—was much alarmed. It was very likely that the man had seen him before—worse luck to his excellent memory. Bunter himself could not be expected to remember every casual dock-walloper he might have had to do with. Bunter brazened it out by turning upon the man, making use of that impressive, black-as-night sternness of expression his unusual hair furnished him with:

"My name's Bunter, sir. Does that enlighten your inquisitive intellect? And I don't ask what your name may be. I don't want to know. I've no use for it, sir. An individual who calmly tells me to my face that he is *not sure* if he has seen me before, either means to be impudent or is no better than a worm, sir. Yes, I said a worm—a blind worm!"

Brave Bunter. That was the line to take. He fairly drove the beggar out of the ship, as if every word had been a blow. But the pertinacity of that brass-bound Paul Pry was astonishing. He cleared out of the ship, of course, before Bunter's ire, not saying anything, and only trying to cover up his retreat by a sickly smile. But once on the Jetty he turned deliberately round, and set himself to stare in dead earnest at the ship. He remained planted there like a mooring-post, absolutely motionless, and with his stupid eyes winking no more than a pair of cabin portholes.

What could Bunter do? It was awkward for him, you know. He could not go and put his head into the bread-locker. What he did was to take up a position abaft the mizzen-rigging, and stare back as unwinking as the other. So they remained, and I don't know which of them grew giddy first; but the man on the Jetty, not having the advantage of something to hold on to, got tired the soonest, flung his arm, giving the contest up, as it were, and went away at last.

Bunter told me he was glad the *Sapphire*, "that gem amongst ships" as he alluded to her sacastically, was going to sea next day. He had had enough of the Dock. I understood his impatience. He had steeled himself against any possible worry the voyage might bring, though it is clear enough now that he was not prepared for the extraordinary experience that was awaiting him already, and in no other part of the world than the Indian Ocean itself: the very part of the world where the poor fellow had lost his ship and had broken his luck, as it seemed for good and all, at the same time.

As to his remorse in regard to a certain secret action of his life, well, I understand that a man of Bunter's fine character would suffer not a little. Still, between ourselves, and without the slightest wish to be cynical, it cannot be denied that with the noblest of us the fear of being found out enters for some considerable part into the composition of remorse. I didn't say this in so many words to Bunter, but, as the poor fellow harped a bit on it, I told him that there were skeletons in a good many honest cupboards, and that, as to his own particular guilt, it wasn't writ large on his face for everybody to see—so he needn't worry as to that. And besides, he would be gone to sea in about twelve hours from now.

He said there was some comfort in that thought, and went off then to spend his last evening for many months with his wife. For all his wildness, Bunter had made no mistake in his marrying. He had married a lady. A perfect lady. She was a dear little woman, too. As to her pluck, I, who know what times they had to go through, I cannot admire her enough for it. Real, hard-wearing every day and day after day pluck that only a woman is capable of when she is of the right sort—the undismayed sort I would call it.

The black mate felt this parting with his wife more than any of the previous ones in all the years of bad luck. But she was of the undismayed kind, and showed less trouble in her gentle face than the black-haired, buccaneer-like, but dignified mate of the *Sapphire*. It may be that her conscience was less disturbed than her husband's. Of course, his life had no secret places for her; but a woman's conscience is somewhat more resourceful in finding good and valid excuses. It depends greatly on the person that needs them, too.

They had agreed that she should not come down to the Dock to see him off. "I wonder you care to look at me at all," said the sensitive man. And she did not laugh.

Bunter was very sensitive; he left her rather brusquely at the last. He got on board in good time, and produced the usual impression on the mud-pilot in the broken-down straw hat who took the *Sapphire* out of dock. The river-man was very polite to the dignified, striking-looking chief mate. "The fine-inch manilla for the check-rope, Mr.—Bunter, thank you—Mr. Bunter, please." The sea-pilot who left the "gem of ships" heading comfortably down Channel off Dover told some of his friends that, this voyage, the *Sapphire* had for chief mate a man who seemed a jolly sight too good for old Johns. "Bunter's his name. I wonder where he's sprung from? Never seen him before in any ship I piloted in or out all these years. He's the sort of man who don't forget. You couldn't. A thorough good sailor, too. And won't old Johns just worry his head off! Unless the old fool should take fright at him—for he does not seem the sort of man that would let himself be put upon without letting you know what he thinks of you. And that's exactly what old Johns would be more afraid of than of anything else."

As this is really meant to be the record of a spiritualistic experience which came, if not precisely to Captain Johns himself, at any rate to his ship, there is no use in recording the other events of the passage out. It was an ordinary passage; the crew was an ordinary crew, the weather was of the usual kind. The black mate's quiet, sedate method of going to work had given a sober tone to the life of the ship. Even in gales of wind everything went on quietly somehow.

There was only one severe blow which made things fairly lively for all hands for full four-and-twenty hours. That was off the coast of Africa, after passing the Cape of Good Hope. At the very height of it several heavy seas were shipped with no serious results, but there was a considerable smashing of breakable objects in the pantry and in the staterooms. Mr. Bunter, who was so greatly respected on board, found himself treated scurvily by the Southern Ocean, which, bursting open the door of his room like a ruffianly burglar, carried off several useful things, and made all the others extremely wet.

Later, on the same day, the Southern Ocean caused the *Sapphire* to lurch over in such an unrestrained fashion that the two drawers fitted under Mr. Bunter's sleeping-berth flew out altogether, spilling all their contents. They ought, of course, to have been locked, and Mr. Bunter had only to thank himself for what had happened. He ought to have turned the key on each before going out on deck.

His consternation was very great. The steward, who was paddling about all the time with swabs, trying to dry out the flooded cuddy, heard him exclaim "Hallo!" in a startled and dismayed tone. In the midst of his work the steward felt a sympathetic concern for the mate's distress.

Captain Johns was secretly glad when he heard of the damage. He was indeed afraid of his chief mate, as the sea-pilot had ventured to foretell, and afraid of him for the very reason the sea-pilot had put forward as likely.

Captain Johns, therefore, would have liked very much to hold that black mate of his at his mercy in some way or other. But the man was irreproachable, as near absolute perfection as could be. And Captain Johns was much annoyed, and at the same time congratulated himself on his chief officer's efficiency.

He made a great show of living sociably with him, on the principle that the more friendly you are with a man the more easily you may catch him tripping; and also for the reason that he wanted to have somebody who would listen to his stories of manifestations, apparitions, ghosts, and all the rest of the imbecile spook-lore. He had it all at his fingers' ends; and he spun those ghostly yarns in a persistent, colourless voice, giving them a futile turn peculiarly his own.

"I like to converse with my officers," he used to say. "There are masters that hardly ever open their mouths from beginning to end of a passage for fear of losing their dignity. What's that, after all—this bit of position a man holds!"

His sociability was most to be dreaded in the second dog-watch, because he was one of those men who grow lively towards the evening, and the officer on duty was unable then to find excuses for leaving the poop. Captain Johns would pop up the companion suddenly, and, sidling up in his creeping way to poor Bunter, as he walked up and down, would fire into him some spiritualistic proposition, such as:

"Spirits, male and female, show a good deal of refinement in a general way, don't they?"

To which Bunter, holding his black-whiskered head high, would mutter:

"I don't know."

"Ah! that's because you don't want to. You are the most obstinate, prejudiced man I've ever met, Mr. Bunter. I told you you may have any book out of my bookcase. You may just go into my state-room, and help yourself to any volume."

And if Bunter protested that he was too tired in his watches below to spare any time for reading, Captain Johns would smile nastily behind his back, and remark that of course some people needed more sleep than others to keep themselves fit for their work. If Mr. Bunter was afraid of not keeping properly awake when on duty at night, that was another matter.

"But I think you borrowed a novel to read from the second mate the other day—a trashy pack of lies," Captain Johns sighed. "I am afraid you are not a spiritually minded man, Mr. Bunter. That's what's the matter."

Sometimes he would appear on deck in the middle of the night, looking very grotesque and bandy-legged in his sleeping-suit. At that sight the persecuted Bunter would wring his hands stealthily, and break out into moisture all over his forehead. After standing sleepily by the binnacle, scratching himself in an unpleasant manner, Captain Johns was sure to start on some aspect or other of his only topic.

He would, for instance, discourse on the improvement of morality to be expected from the establishment of general and close intercourse with the spirits of the departed. The spirits, Captain Johns thought, would consent to associate familiarly with the living if it were not for the unbelief of the great mass of mankind. He himself would not care to have anything to do with a crowd that would not believe in his—Captain Johns'—existence. Then why should a spirit? This was asking too much.

He went on breathing hard by the binnacle and trying to

reach round his shoulder-blades; then, with a thick, drowsy severity, declared:

"Incredulity, sir, is the evil of the age!"

It rejected the evidence of Professor Cranks and of the journalist chap. It resisted the production of photographs.

For Captain Johns believed firmly that certain spirits had been photographed. He had read something of it in the papers. And the idea of it having been done had got a tremendous hold on him, because his mind was not critical. Bunter said afterwards that nothing could be more weird than this little man, swathed in a sleeping-suit three sizes too large for him, shuffling with excitement in the moonlight near the wheel, and shaking his fist at the serene sea.

"Photographs! photographs!" he would repeat, in a voice as creaky as a rusty hinge.

The very helmsman just behind him got uneasy at that performance, not being capable of understanding exactly what the "old man was kicking up a row with the mate about."

Then Johns, after calming down a bit, would begin again.

"Then sensitised plate can't lie. No, sir."

Nothing could be more funny than this ridiculous little man's conviction—his dogmatic tone. Bunter would go on swinging up and down the poop like a deliberate, dignified pendulum. He said not a word. But the poor fellow had not a trifle on his conscience, as you know; and to have imbecile ghosts rammed down his throat like this on top of his own worry nearly drove him crazy. He knew that on many occasions he was on the verge of lunacy, because he could not help indulging in half-delirious visions of Captain Johns being picked up by the scruff of the neck and dropped over the taffrail into the ship's wake—the sort of thing no sane sailorman would think of doing to a cat or any other animal, anyhow. He imagined him bobbing up—a tiny black speck left far astern on the moonlit ocean.

I don't think that even at the worst moments Bunter really desired to drown Captain Johns. I fancy that all his disordered imagination longed for was merely to stop the ghostly inanity of the skipper's talk.

But, all the same, it was a dangerous form of self-indulgence. Just picture to yourself that ship in the Indian Ocean, on a clear, tropical night, with her sails full and still, the watch on deck stowed away out of sight; and on her poop, flooded with moonlight, the stately black mate walking up and down with measured, dignified steps, preserving an awful silence and that grotesquely mean little figure in striped flannelette alternately creaking and droning of "personal intercourse beyond the grave."

It makes me creepy all over to think of. And sometimes, the folly of Captain Johns would appear clothed in a sort of weird utilitarianism. How useful it would be if the spirits of the departed could be induced to take a practical interest in the affairs of the living! What a help, say, to the police, for instance, in the detection of crime! The number of murders, at any rate, would be considerably reduced, he guessed, with an air of great sagacity. Then he would give way to grotesque discouragement.

Where was the use of trying to communicate with people that had no faith, and more likely than not would scorn the offered information? Spirits had their feelings. They were *all* feelings in a way. But he was surprised at the forbearance shown towards murderers by their victims. That was the sort of apparition that no guilty man would dare to pooh-pooh. And perhaps the undiscovered murderers—whether believing or not—were haunted. They wouldn't be likely to boast about it, would they?

"For myself," he pursued, in a sort of vindictive, malevolent whine, "if anybody murdered me I would not let him forget it. I would wither him up—I would terrify him to death."

The idea of his skipper's ghost terrifying anyone was so ludicrous that the black mate, little disposed to mirth as he was, could not help giving vent to a weary laugh. And this laugh, the only acknowledgment of a long and earnest discourse, offended Captain Johns.

"What's there to laugh at in this conceited manner, Mr. Bunter?" he snarled. "Supernatural visitations have terrified better men than you. Don't you allow me enough soul to make a ghost of?"

I think it was the nasty tone that caused Bunter to stop short and turn about.

"I shouldn't wonder," went on the angry fanatic of spiritism, "if you weren't one of them people that take no more account of a man than if he were a beast. You would be capable, I don't doubt, to deny the possession of an immortal soul to your own father."

And then Bunter, being bored beyond endurance, and also exasperated by the private worry, lost his self-possession.

He walked up suddenly to Captain Johns, and, stooping a little to look close into his face, said, in a low, even tone:

"You don't know what a man like me is capable of."

Captain Johns threw his head back, but was too astonished

to budge. Bunter resumed his walk; and for a long time his measured footsteps and the low wash of the water alongside were the only sounds which troubled the silence brooding over the great waters. Then Captain Johns cleared his throat uneasily, and, after sidling away towards the companion for greater safety, plucked up enough to retreat under an act of authority:

"Raise the starboard clew of the mainsail, and lay the yards dead square, Mr. Bunter. Don't you see the wind is nearly right aft?"

Bunter at once answered "Ay, ay, sir," though there was not the slightest necessity to touch the yards, and the wind was well out on the quarter. While he was executing the order Captain Johns hung on the companion-steps, growling to himself: "Walk this poop like an admiral, and don't even notice when the yards want trimming!"—loud enough for the helmsman to overhear. Then he sank slowly backwards out of the man's sight; and when he reached the bottom of the stairs he stood still and thought.

"He's an awful ruffian, with all his gentlemanly airs. No more gentleman mates for me."

Two nights afterwards he was slumbering peacefully in his berth, when a heavy thumping just above his head (a well-understood signal that he was wanted on deck) made him leap out of bed, broad awake in a moment.

"What's up?" he muttered, running out barefooted. On passing through the cabin he glanced at the clock. It was the middle watch. "What on earth can the mate want me for?" he thought.

Bolting out of the companion, he found a clear, dewy, moonlit night and a strong, steady breeze. He looked around wildly. There was no one on the poop except the helmsman, who addressed him at once.

"It was me, sir. I let go the wheel for a second to stamp over your head. I am afraid there's something wrong with the mate."

"Where's he got to?" asked the captain sharply.

The man, who was obviously nervous, said:

"The last I saw of him was as he fell down the port poop-ladder."

"Fell down the poop-ladder! What did he do that for? What made him?"

"I don't know, sir. He was walking the port side. Then just as he turned towards me to come aft . . ."

"You saw him?" interrupted the captain.

"I did. I was looking at him. And I heard the crash,

too—something awful. Like the mainmast going overboard. It was as if something had struck him."

Captain Johns became very uneasy and alarmed.

"Come," he said sharply. "Did anybody strike him? What did you see?"

"Nothing, sir, so help me! There was nothing to see. He just gave a little sort of hallo! threw his hands before him, and over he went—crash. I couldn't hear anything more, so I just let go the wheel for a second to call you up."

"You're scared!" said Captain Johns.

"I am, sir, straight!"

Captain Johns stared at him. The silence of his ship driving on her way seemed to contain a danger—a mystery. He was reluctant to go and look for his mate himself, in the shadows of the main-deck, so quiet, so still.

All he did was to advance to the break of the poop, and call for the watch. As the sleepy men came trooping aft, he shouted to them fiercely.

"Look at the foot of the port poop-ladder, some of you! See the mate lying there?"

Their startled exclamations told him immediately that they did see him. Somebody even screeched out emotionally·

"He's dead!"

Mr. Bunter was laid in his bunk, and when the lamp in his room was lit he looked indeed as if he were dead, but it was obvious also that he was breathing yet. The steward had been roused out, the second mate called and sent on deck to look after the ship, and for an hour or so Captain Johns devoted himself silently to the restoring of consciousness. Mr. Bunter at last opened his eyes, but he could not speak. He was dazed and inert. The steward bandaged a nasty scalp-wound while Captain Johns held an additional light. They had to cut away a lot of Mr. Bunter's jet-black hair to make a good dressing. This done, and after gazing for a while at their patient, the two left the cabin.

"A rum go, this, steward," said Captain Johns in the passage.

"Yessir."

"A sober man that's right in his head does not fall down a poop-ladder like a sack of potatoes. The ship's as steady as a church."

"Yessir. Fit of some kind, I shouldn't wonder."

"Well, I should. He doesn't look as if he were subject to fits and giddiness. Why, the man's in the prime of life. I wouldn't have another kind of mate—not if I knew it. You don't think he has a private store of liquor, do you, eh? He seemed to me a bit strange in his manner several times lately. Off his feed too a bit, I noticed."

"Well, sir, if he ever had a bottle or two of grog in his cabin, that must have gone a long time ago. I saw him throw some broken glass overboard after the last gale we had; but that didn't amount to anything. Anyway, sir, you couldn't call Mr. Bunter a drinking man."

"No," conceded the captain reflectively. And the steward, locking the pantry door, tried to escape out of the passage, thinking he could manage to snatch another hour of sleep before it was time for him to turn out for the day.

Captain Johns shook his head.

"There's some mystery there."

"There's special Providence that he didn't crack his head like an eggshell on the quarter-deck mooring-bits, sir. The men tell me he couldn't have missed them by more than an inch."

And the steward vanished skilfully.

Captain Johns spent the rest of the night and the whole of the ensuing day between his own room and that of the mate.

In his own room he sat with his open hands reposing on his knees, his lips pursed up, and the horizontal furrows on his forehead marked very heavily. Now and then, raising his arm by a slow, as if cautious movement, he scratched lightly the top of his bald head. In the mate's room he stood for long periods of time with his hand to his lips, gazing at the half-conscious man.

For three days Mr. Bunter did not say a single word. He looked at people sensibly enough, but did not seem to be able to hear any questions put to him. They cut off some more of his hair and swathed his head in wet cloths. He took some nourishment, and was made as comfortable as possible. At dinner on the third day the second mate remarked to the captain, in connection with the affair:

"These half-round brass plates on the steps of the poop-ladders are beastly dangerous things!"

"Are they?" retorted Captain Johns sourly. "It takes more than a brass plate to account for an able-bodied man crashing down in this fashion like a felled ox."

The second mate was impressed by that view. There was something in that, he thought.

"And the weather fine, everything dry, and the ship going along as steady as a church!" pursued Captain Johns gruffly.

As Captain Johns continued to look extremely sour, the second mate did not open his lips any more during the dinner. Captain Johns was annoyed and hurt by an innocent remark, because the fitting of the aforesaid brass plates had been done at his suggestion only the voyage before, in order to smarten up the appearance of the poop-ladders.

On the fourth day Mr. Bunter looked decidedly better; very languid yet, of course, but he heard and understood what was said to him, and even could say a few words in a feeble voice.

Captain Johns, coming in, contemplated him attentively, without much visible sympathy.

" Well, can you give us your account of this accident, Mr. Bunter? "

Bunter moved slightly his bandaged head, and fixed his cold, blue stare on Captain John's face, as if taking stock and appraising the value of every feature; the perplexed forehead, the credulous eyes, the inane droop of the mouth. And he gazed so long that Captain Johns grew restive, and looked over his shoulder at the door.

" No accident," breathed out Bunter, in a peculiar tone.

" You don't mean to say you've got the falling sickness," said Captain Johns. " How would you call it signing as chief mate of a clipper ship with a thing like that on you? "

Bunter answered him only by a sinister look. The skipper shuffled his feet a little.

" Well, what made you have that tumble, then? "

Bunter raised himself a little, and, looking straight into Captain Johns' eyes, said, in a very distinct whisper:

" You—were—right! "

He fell back and closed his eyes. Not a word more could Captain Johns get out of him; and, the steward coming into the cabin, the skipper withdrew.

But that very night, unobserved, Captain Johns, opening the door cautiously, entered again the mate's cabin. He could wait no longer. The suppressed eagerness, the excitement expressed in all his mean, creeping little person, did not escape the chief mate, who was lying awake, looking frightfully pulled down and perfectly impassive.

" You are coming to gloat over me, I suppose," said Bunter, without moving and yet making a palpable hit.

" Bless my soul! " exclaimed Captain Johns with a start, and assuming a sobered demeanour. " There's a thing to say! "

" Well, gloat then! You and your ghosts, you've managed to get over a live man."

This was said by Bunter without stirring, in a low voice, and with not much expression.

" Do you mean to say," inquired Captain Johns, in an awe-struck whisper, "that you had a supernatural experience that night? You saw an apparition, then, on board my ship?"

Reluctance, shame, disgust, would have been visible on poor Bunter's countenance if the great part of it had not been swathed up in cottonwool and bandages. His ebony eyebrows, more sinister than ever amongst all that lot of white linen, came together in a frown as he made a mighty effort to say:

"Yes, I have seen."

The wretchedness in his eyes would have awakened the compassion of any other man than Captain Johns. But Captain Johns was all agog with triumphant excitement. He was just a little bit frightened too. He looked at that unbelieving scoffer laid low, and did not even dimly guess at his profound, humiliating distress. He was not generally capable of taking much part in the anguish of his fellow-creatures. This time, moreover, he was excessively anxious to know what had happened. Fixing his credulous eyes on the bandaged head, he asked, trembling slightly:

"And did it—did it knock you down?"

"Come! am I the sort of man to be knocked down by a ghost?" protested Bunter in a little stronger tone. "Don't you remember what you said yourself the other night? Better men than me—— Ha! you'll have to look a long time before you find a better man for a mate of your ship."

Captain Johns pointed a solemn finger at Bunter's bedplace.

"You've been terrified," he said. "That's what's the matter. You've been terrified. Why, even the man at the wheel was scared, though he couldn't see anything. He *felt* the supernatural. You are punished for your incredulity, Mr. Bunter. You were terrified."

"And suppose I was," said Bunter. "Do you know what I had seen? Can you conceive the sort of ghost that would haunt a man like me? Do you think it was a ladyish, afternoon-call, another-cup-of-tea-please apparition that visits your Professor Cranks and that journalist chap you are always talking about? No; I can't tell you what it was like. Every man has his own ghosts. You couldn't conceive . . ."

Bunter stopped, out of breath; and Captain Johns remarked, with the glow of inward satisfaction reflected in his tone:

"I've always thought you were the sort of man that was ready for anything: from pitch-and-toss to wilful murder, as the saying goes. Well, well! So you were terrified."

"I stepped back," said Bunter curtly. "I don't remember anything else."

"The man at the wheel told me you went backwards as if something had hit you."

"It was a sort of inward blow," explained Bunter. "Something too deep for you, Captain Johns, to understand. Your life and mine haven't been the same. Aren't you satisfied to see me converted?"

"And you can't tell me any more?" asked Captain Johns anxiously.

"No, I can't. I wouldn't. It would be no use if I did. That sort of experience must be gone through. Say I am being punished. Well, I take my punishment, but talk of it I won't."

"Very well," said Captain Johns; "you won't. But, mind, I can draw my own conclusions from that."

"Draw what you like; but be careful what you say, sir. You don't terrify me. *You* aren't a ghost."

"One word. Has it any connection with what you said to me on that last night, when we had a talk together on spiritualism?"

Bunter looked weary and puzzled.

"What did I say?"

"You told me that I couldn't know what a man like you was capable of."

"Yes, yes. Enough!"

"Very good. I am fixed, then," remarked Captain Johns. "All I say is that I am jolly glad not to be you, though I would have given almost anything for the privilege of personal communication with the world of spirits. Yes, sir, but not in that way."

Poor Bunter moaned pitifully.

"It has made me feel twenty years older."

Captain Johns retired quietly. He was delighted to observe this over-bearing ruffian humbled to the dust by the moralising agency of the spirits. The whole occurrence was a source of pride and gratification; and he began to feel a sort of regard for his chief mate. It is true that in further interviews Bunter showed himself very mild and deferential. He seemed to cling to his captain for spiritual protection. He used to send for him, and say, "I feel so nervous," and Captain Johns would stay patiently for hours in the hot little cabin, and feel proud of the call.

For Mr. Bunter was ill, and could not leave his berth for a good many days. He became a convinced spiritualist, not enthusiastically—that could hardly have been expected from him—but in a grim, unshakable way. He could not be called exactly friendly to the disembodied inhabitants of our globe, as Captain Johns was. But he was not a firm, if gloomy, recruit of spiritualism.

One afternoon, as the ship was already well to the north in the Gulf of Bengal, the steward knocked at the door of the captain's cabin, and said, without opening it:

"The mate asks if you could spare him a moment, sir. He seems to be in a state in there."

Captain Johns jumped up from the couch at once.

"Yes. Tell him I am coming."

He thought: Could it be possible there had been another spiritual manifestation—in the daytime, too!

He revelled in the hope. It was not exactly that, however. Still, Bunter, whom he saw sitting collapsed in a chair—he had been up for several days, but not on deck as yet—poor Bunter had something startling enough to communicate. His hands covered his face. His legs were stretched straight out, dismally.

"What's the news now?" croaked Captain Johns, not unkindly, because in truth it always pleased him to see Bunter—as he expressed it—tamed.

"News!" exclaimed the crushed sceptic through his hands. "Ay, news enough, Captain Johns. Who will be able to deny the awfulness, the genuineness? Another man would have dropped dead. You want to know what I had seen. All I can tell you is that since I've seen it my hair is turning white."

Bunter detached his hands from his face, and they hung on each side of his chair as if dead. He looked broken in the dusky cabin.

"You don't say!" stammered out Captain Johns. "Turned white! Hold on a bit! I'll light the lamp!"

When the lamp was lit, the startling phenomenon could be seen plainly enough. As if the dread, the horror, the anguish of the supernatural were being exhaled through the pores of his skin, a sort of silvery mist seemed to cling to the cheeks and the head of the mate. His short beard, his cropped hair, were growing not black, but grey—almost white.

When Mr. Bunter, thin-faced and shaky, came on deck for duty, he was clean-shaven, and his head was white. The hands were awe-struck. "Another man," they whispered to each other. It was generally and mysteriously agreed that the mate had "seen something," with the exception of the man at the wheel at the time, who maintained that the mate was "struck by something."

This distinction hardly amounted to a difference. On the other hand, everybody admitted that, after he picked up his strength a bit, he seemed even smarter in his movements than before.

One day in Calcutta, Captain Johns, pointing out to a visitor his white-headed chief mate standing by the main-hatch, was heard to say oracularly:

"That man's in the prime of life."

Of course, while Bunter was away, I called regularly on Mrs. Bunter every Saturday, just to see whether she had any use for my services. It was understood I would do that. She had just his half-pay to live on—it amounted to about a pound a week. She had taken one room in a quiet little square in the East End.

And this was affluence to what I had heard that the couple were reduced to for a time after Bunter had to give up the Western Ocean trade—he used to go as mate of all sorts of hard packets after he lost his ship and his luck together—it was affluence to that time when Bunter would start at seven o'clock in the morning with but a glass of hot water and a crust of dry bread.

It won't stand thinking about, especially for those who know Mrs. Bunter. I have seen something of them, too, at that time; and it just makes me shudder to remember what that born lady had to put up with. Enough!

Dear Mrs. Bunter used to worry a good deal after the *Sapphire* left for Calcutta. She would say to me: "It must be so awful for poor Winston"—Winston is Bunter's name—and I tried to comfort her the best I could. Afterwards, she got some small children to teach in a family, and was half the day with them, and the occupation was good for her.

In the very first letter she had from Calcutta, Bunter told her he had had a fall down the poop-ladder, and cut his head, but no bones broken, thank God. That was all. Of course, she had other letters from him, but that vagabond Bunter never gave me a scratch of the pen the solid eleven months. I supposed, naturally, that everything was going on all right. Who could imagine what was happening?

Then one day dear Mrs. Bunter got a letter from a legal firm in the City, advising her that her uncle was dead—her old curmudgeon of an uncle—a retired stockbroker, a heartless, petrified antiquity that had lasted on and on. He was nearly ninety, I believe; and if I were to meet his venerable ghost this minute, I would try to take him by the throat and strangle him.

The old beast would never forgive his niece for marrying Bunter; and years afterwards, when people made a point of letting him know that she was in London, pretty nearly starving at forty years of age, he only said: " Serve the little fool right! " I believe he meant her to starve. And, lo and behold, the old cannibal died intestate, with no other relatives but that very identical little fool. The Bunters were wealthy people now.

Of course, Mrs. Bunter wept as if her heart would break. In any other woman it would have been mere hypocrisy. Naturally, too, she wanted to cable the news to her Winston in Calcutta, but I showed her, " Gazette " in hand, that the ship was on the homeward-bound list for more than a week already. So we sat down to wait, and talked meantime of dear old Winston every day. There were just one hundred such days before the *Sapphire* got reported " All well," in the chops of the Channel by an incoming mailboat.

" I am going to Dunkirk to meet him," says she. The *Sapphire* had a cargo of jute for Dunkirk. Of course, I had to escort the dear lady in the quality of her " ingenious friend." She calls me " our ingenious friend " to this day; and I've observed some people—strangers—looking hard at me, for the signs of the ingenuity, I suppose.

After settling Mrs. Bunter in a good hotel in Dunkirk, I walked down to the docks—late afternoon it was—and what was my surprise to see the ship actually fast alongside. Either Johns or Bunter, or both, must have been driving her hard up Channel. Anyway, she had been in since the day before last, and her crew was already paid off. I met two of her apprenticed boys going off home on leave with their dunnage on a Frenchman's barrow, as happy as larks, and I asked them if the mate was on board.

" There he is, on the quay, looking at the moorings," says one of the youngsters as he skipped past me.

You may imagine the shock to my feelings when I beheld his white head. I could only manage to tell him that his wife was at an hotel in town. He left me at once, to go and get his hat on board. I was mightily surprised by the smartness of his movements as he hurried up the gangway.

Whereas the black mate struck people as deliberate, and strangely stately in his gait for a man in the prime of life, this white-headed chap seemed the most wonderfully alert of old men. I don't suppose Bunter was any quicker on his pins than before. It was the colour of the hair that made all the difference in one's judgment.

The same with his eyes. Those eyes, that looked at you so steely, so fierce, and so fascinating out of a bush of a buccaneer's black hair, now had an innocent, almost boyish expression in their good-humoured brightness under those white eyebrows.

I led him without any delay into Mrs. Bunter's private sitting-room. After she had dropped a tear over the late cannibal, given a hug to her Winston, and told him that he must grow his moustache again, the dear lady tucked her feet upon the sofa, and I got out of Bunter's way.

He started at once to pace the room, waving his long arms. He worked himself into a regular frenzy, and tore Johns limb from limb many times over that evening.

"Fell down? Of course I fell down, by slipping backwards on that fool's patent brass plates. 'Pon my word, I had been walking that poop in charge of the ship, and I didn't know whether I was in the Indian Ocean or in the moon. I was crazy. My head spun round and round with sheer worry. I had made my last application of your chemist's wonderful stuff." (This to me.) "All the store of bottles you gave me got smashed when those drawers fell out in the last gale. I had been getting some dry things to change, when I heard the cry: 'All hands on deck!' and made one jump of it, without even pushing them in properly. Ass! When I came back and saw the broken glass and the mess, I felt ready to faint.

"No; look here—deception is bad; but not to be able to keep it up after one has been forced into it. You know that since I've been squeezed out of the Western Ocean packets by younger men, just on account of my grizzled muzzle—you know how much chance I had to ever get a ship. And not a soul to turn to. We have been a lonely couple, we two—she threw away everything for me—and to see her want a piece of dry bread——"

He banged with his fist fit to split the Frenchman's table in two.

"I would have turned a sanguinary pirate for her, let alone cheating my way into a berth by dyeing my hair. So when you came to me with your chemist's wonderful stuff——"

He checked himself.

"By the by, that fellow's got a fortune when he likes to pick it up. It is a wonderful stuff—you tell him salt water can do nothing to it. It stays on as long as your hair will."

"All right," I said. "Go on."

Thereupon he went for Johns again with a fury that frightened his wife, and made me laugh till I cried.

"Just you try to think what it would have meant to be at the mercy of the meanest creature that ever commanded a ship! Just fancy what a life that crawling Johns would have led me! And I knew that in a week or so the white hair would begin to show. And the crew. Did you ever think of that? To be shown up as a low fraud before all hands.

What a life for me till we got to Calcutta! And once there—kicked out, of course. Half-pay stopped. Annie here alone, without a penny—starving; and I on the other side of the earth, ditto. You see?

"I thought of shaving twice a day. But could I shave my head, too? No way—no way at all. Unless I dropped Johns overboard; and even then—— Do you wonder now that with all these things boiling in my head I didn't know where I was putting down my foot that night? I just felt myself falling—then crash, and all dark.

"When I came to myself that bang on the head seemed to have steadied my wits somehow. I was so sick of everything that for two days I wouldn't speak to anyone. They thought it was a slight concussion of the brain. Then the idea dawned upon me as I was looking at that ghost-ridden, wretched fool: 'Ah, you love ghosts,' I thought. 'Well, you shall have something from beyond the grave.'

"I didn't even trouble to invent a story. I couldn't imagine a ghost if I wanted to. I wasn't fit to lie connectedly if I had tried. I just bulled him on to it. Do you know, he got, quite by himself, a notion that at some time or other I had done somebody to death in some way, and that——"

"Oh, the horrible man!" cried Mrs. Bunter from the sofa. There was a silence.

"And didn't he bore my head off on the home passage!" began Bunter again in a weary voice. "He loved me. He was proud of me. I was converted. I had had a manifestation. Do you know what he was after? He wanted me and him 'to make a *séance*,' in his own words, and to try to call up that ghost (the one that had turned my hair white—the ghost of my supposed victim), and, as he said, talk it over with him—the ghost—in a friendly way.

"'Or else, Bunter', he says, 'you may get another manifestation when you least expect it, and tumble overboard perhaps, or something. You ain't really safe till we pacify the spirit-world in some way.'

"Can you conceive a lunatic like that? No—say?"

I said nothing. But Mrs. Bunter did, in a very decided tone.

"Winston, I don't want you to go on board that ship again any more."

"My dear," says he, "I have all my things on board yet."

"You don't want the things. Don't go near that ship at all."

He stood still; then, dropping his eyes with a faint smile, said slowly, in a dreamy voice:

"The haunted ship."

"And your last," I added.

We carried him off, as he stood, by the night train. He was very quiet; but crossing the Channel, as we two had a smoke on deck, he turned to me suddenly, and, grinding his teeth, whispered:

"He'll never know how near he was being dropped overboard!"

He meant Captain Johns. I said nothing.

But Captain Johns, I understand, made a great to-do about the disappearance of his chief mate. He set the French police scouring the country for the body. In the end, I fancy he got word from his owners' office to drop all this fuss—that it was all right. I don't suppose he ever understood anything of that mysterious occurrence.

To this day he tries at times (he's retired now, and his conversation is not very coherent), he tries to tell the story of a black mate he once had, "a murderous, gentlemanly ruffian, with raven-black hair which turned white all at once in consequence of a manifestation from beyond the grave." An avenging apparition. What with reference to black and white hair, to poop-ladders, and to his own feelings and views, it is difficult to make head or tail of it. If his sister (she's very vigorous still) should be present she cuts all this short—peremptorily:

"Don't you mind what he says. He's got devils on the brain."

W. SOMERSET MAUGHAM

BEFORE THE PARTY

MRS. SKINNER liked to be in good time. She was already dressed, in black silk as befitted her age and the mourning she wore for her son-in-law, and now she put on her toque. She was a little uncertain about it, since the egrets' feathers which adorned it might very well arouse in some of the friends she would certainly meet at the party acid expostulations; and of course it was shocking to kill those beautiful white birds, in the mating season too, for the sake of their feathers; but there they were, so pretty and stylish, and it would have been silly to refuse them, and it would have hurt her son-in-law's feelings. He had brought them all the way from Borneo and he expected her to be so pleased with them. Kathleen had made herself rather unpleasant about them, she must wish she hadn't now, after what had happened, but Kathleen had never really liked Harold. Mrs. Skinner, standing at her dressing-table, placed the toque on her head, it was after all the only nice hat she had, and put in a pin with a large jet knob. If anybody spoke to her about the ospreys she had her answer.

"I know it's dreadful," she would say, "and I wouldn't dream of buying them, but my poor son-in-law brought them back the last time he was home on leave."

That would explain her possession of them and excuse their use. Everyone had been very kind. Mrs. Skinner took a clean handkerchief from a drawer and sprinkled a little eau-de-Cologne on it. She never used scent, and she had always thought it rather fast, but eau-de-Colonge was so refreshing. She was very nearly ready now, and her eyes wandered out of the window behind her looking-glass. Canon Heywood had a beautiful day for his garden-party. It was warm and the sky was blue; the trees had not yet lost the fresh green of the spring. She smiled as she saw her little granddaughter in the strip of garden behind the house busily raking her very own flower-bed. Mrs. Skinner wished Joan were not quite so pale, it was a mistake to have kept her so long in the tropics;

and she was so grave for her age, you never saw her run about; she played quiet games of her own invention and watered her garden. Mrs. Skinner gave the front of her dress a little pat, took up her gloves, and went downstairs.

Kathleen was at the writing-table in the window busy with lists she was making, for she was Honorary Secretary of the Ladies' Golf Club, and when there were competitions had a good deal to do. But she too was ready for the party.

"I see you've put on your jumper after all," said Mrs. Skinner.

They had discussed at luncheon whether Kathleen should wear her jumper or her black chiffon. The jumper was black and white, and Kathleen thought it rather smart, but it was hardly mourning. Millicent, however, was in favour of it.

"There's no reason why we should all look as if we'd just come from a funeral," she said. "Harold's been dead eight months."

To Mrs. Skinner it seemed rather unfeeling to talk like that. Millicent was strange since her return from Borneo.

"You're not going to leave off your weeds yet, darling?" she asked.

Millicent did not give a direct answer.

"People don't wear mourning in the way they used," she said. She paused a little, and when she went on there was a tone in her voice which Mrs. Skinner thought quite peculiar. It was plain that Kathleen noticed it too, for she gave her sister a curious look. "I'm sure Harold wouldn't wish me to wear mourning for him indefinitely."

"I dressed early because I wanted to say something to Millicent," said Kathleen in reply to her mother's observation.

"Oh?"

Kathleen did not explain. But she put her lists aside and with knitted brows read for the second time a letter from a lady who complained that the committee had most unfairly marked down her handicap from twenty-four to eighteen. It requires a good deal of tact to be honorary secretary to a ladies' golf club. Mrs. Skinner began to put on her new gloves. The sun-blinds kept the room cool and dark. She looked at the great wooden hornbill, gaily painted, which Harold had left in her safekeeping; and it seemed a little odd and barbaric to her, but he had set much store on it. It had some religious significance and Canon Heywood had been greatly struck by it. On the wall, over the sofa, were Malay weapons, she forgot what they were called, and here and there on occasional tables pieces of silver and brass which Harold at various times had sent to them. She had liked Harold, and involuntarily her eyes sought his photograph which stood on the piano with photographs of her two daughters, her grandchild, her sister and her sister's son.

"Why, Kathleen, where's Harold's photograph?" she asked.

Kathleen looked round. It no longer stood in its place.

"Someone's taken it away," said Kathleen.

Surprised and puzzled, she got up and went over to the piano. The photographs had been rearranged so that no gap should show.

"Perhaps Millicent wanted to have it in her bedroom," said Mrs. Skinner.

"I should have noticed it. Besides, Millicent has several photographs of Harold. She keeps them locked up."

Mrs. Skinner had thought it very peculiar that her daughter should have no photographs of Harold in her room. Indeed she had spoken of it once, but Millicent had made no reply. Millicent had been strangely silent since she came back from Borneo, and had not encouraged the sympathy Mrs. Skinner would have been so willing to show her. She seemed unwilling to speak of her great loss. Sorrow took people in different ways. Her husband had said the best thing was to leave her alone. The thought of him turned her ideas to the party they were going to.

"Father asked if I thought he ought to wear a top-hat," she said. "I said I thought it was just as well to be on the safe side."

It was going to be quite a grand affair. They were having ices, strawberry and vanilla, from Boddy, the confectioner, but the Heywoods were making the iced coffee at home. Everyone would be there. They had been asked to meet the Bishop of Hong-Kong, who was staying with the Canon, an old college friend of his, and he was going to speak on the Chinese missions. Mrs. Skinner, whose daughter had lived in the East for eight years and whose son-in-law had been Resident of a district in Borneo, was in a flutter of interest. Naturally it meant more to her than to people who had never had anything to do with the Colonies and that sort of thing.

"What can they know of England who only England know?" as Mr. Skinner said.

He came into the room at that moment. He was a lawyer, as his father had been before him, and he had offices in Lincoln's Inn Fields. He went up to London every morning and came down every evening. He was only able to accompany his wife and daughters to the Canon's garden-party because the Canon had very wisely chosen a Saturday to have it on. Mr. Skinner looked very well in his tail-coat and pepper-and-salt trousers. He was not exactly dressy, but he was neat. He looked like a respectable family solicitor, which indeed he was; his firm never touched work that was not perfectly above board, and if a client went to him with some trouble that was not quite nice, Mr. Skinner would look grave.

"I don't think this is the sort of case that we very much care to undertake," he said. "I think you'd do better to go elsewhere."

He drew towards him his writing-block and scribbled a name and address on it. He tore off a sheet of paper and handed it to his client.

"If I were you I think I would go and see these people. If you mention my name I believe they'll do anything they can for you."

Mr. Skinner was clean-shaven and very bald. His pale lips were tight and thin, but his blue eyes were shy. He had no colour in his cheeks and his face was much lined.

"I see you've put on your new trousers," said Mrs. Skinner.

"I thought it would be a good opportunity," he answered. "I was wondering if I should wear a buttonhole."

"I wouldn't, father," said Kathleen. "I don't think it's awfully good form."

"A lot of people will be wearing them," said Mrs. Skinner.

"Only clerks and people like that," said Kathleen. "The Heywoods have had to ask everybody, you know. And besides, we are in mourning."

"I wonder if there'll be a collection after the Bishop's address," said Mr. Skinner.

"I should hardly think so," said Mrs. Skinner.

"I think it would be rather bad form," agreed Kathleen.

"It's as well to be on the safe side," said Mr. Skinner. "I'll give for all of us. I was wondering if ten shillings would be enough or if I must give a pound."

"If you give anything I think you ought to give a pound, father," said Kathleen.

"I'll see when the time comes. I don't want to give less than anyone else, but on the other hand I see no reason to give more than I need."

Kathleen put away her papers in the drawer of the writing-table and stood up. She looked at her wrist-watch.

"Is Millicent ready?" asked Mrs. Skinner.

"There's plenty of time. We're only asked at four, and I don't think we ought to arrive much before half-past. I told Davis to bring the car round at four-fifteen."

Generally Kathleen drove the car, but on grand occasions, like this, Davis, who was the gardener, put on his uniform and acted as chauffeur. It looked better when you drove up, and naturally Kathleen didn't much want to drive herself when she was wearing her new jumper. The sight of her mother forcing her fingers one by one into her new gloves reminded her that she must put on her own. She smelt them to see if any odour of the cleaning still clung to them. It was very slight. She didn't believe anyone would notice.

At last the door opened and Millicent came in. She wore her widow's weeds. Mrs. Skinner never could get used to them, but of course she knew that Millicent must wear them for a year. It was a pity they didn't suit her; they suited some people. She had tried on Millicent's bonnet once, with its white band and long veil, and thought she looked very well in it. Of course she hoped dear Alfred would survive her, but if he didn't she would never go out of weeds. Queen Victoria never had. It was different for Millicent; Millicent was a much younger woman; she was only thirty-six: it was very sad to be a widow at thirty-six. And there wasn't much chance of her marrying again. Kathleen wasn't very likely to marry now, she was thirty-five; last time Millicent and Harold had come home she had suggested that they should have Kathleen to stay with them; Harold had seemed willing enough, but Millicent said it wouldn't do. Mrs. Skinner didn't know why not. It would give her a chance Of course they didn't want to get rid of her, but a girl ought to marry, and somehow all the men they knew at home were married already. Millicent said the climate was trying. It was true she was a bad colour. No one would think now that Millicent had been the prettier of the two. Kathleen had fined down as she grew older; of course some people said she was too thin, but now that she had cut her hair, with her cheeks red from playing golf in all weathers, Mrs. Skinner thought her quite pretty. No one could say that of poor Millicent; she had lost her figure completely; she had never been tall, and now that she had filled out she looked stocky. She was a good deal too fat; Mrs. Skinner supposed it was due to the tropical heat that prevented her from taking exercise. Her skin was sallow and muddy; and her blue eyes, which had been her best feature, had gone quite pale.

"She ought to do something about her neck," Mrs. Skinner reflected. "She's becoming dreadfully jowly."

She had spoken of it once or twice to her husband. He remarked that Millicent wasn't as young as she was; that might be, but she needn't let herself go altogether. Mrs. Skinner made up her mind to talk to her daughter seriously, but of course she must respect her grief, and she would wait till the year was up. She was just as glad to have this reason to put off a conversation the thought of which made her slightly nervous. For Millicent was certainly changed. There was something sullen in her face which made her mother not quite at home with her. Mrs. Skinner liked to say aloud all the thoughts that passed through her head, but Millicent when you made a remark (just to say something, you know) had an awkward habit of not answering, so that you wondered whether she had heard. Sometimes Mrs. Skinner found it so irritating, that not to be quite sharp with Millicent she had to remind herself that poor Harold had only been dead eight months.

The light from the window fell on the widow's heavy face as she advanced silently, but Kathleen stood with her back to it. She watched her sister for a moment.

"Millicent, there's something I want to say to you," she said. "I was playing golf with Gladys Heywood this morning."

"Did you beat her?" asked Millicent.

Gladys Heywood was the Canon's only unmarried daughter.

"She told me something about you which I think you ought to know."

Millicent's eyes passed beyond her sister to the little girl watering flowers in the garden.

"Have you told Annie to give Joan her tea in the kitchen, mother?" she said.

"Yes, she'll have it when the servants have theirs."

Kathleen looked at her sister coolly.

"The Bishop spent two or three days at Singapore on his way home," she went on. "He's very fond of travelling. He's been to Borneo, and he knows a good many of the people that you know."

"He'll be interested to see you, dear?" said Mrs. Skinner. "Did he know poor Harold?"

"Yes, he met him at Kuala Solor. He remembers him very well. He says he was shocked to hear of his death."

Millicent sat down and began to put on her black gloves. It seemed strange to Mrs. Skinner that she received these remarks with complete silence.

"Oh, Millicent," she said, "Harold's photo has disappeared. Have you taken it?"

"Yes, I put it away."

"I should have thought you'd like to have it out."

Once more Millicent said nothing. It really was an exasperating habit.

Kathleen turned slightly in order to face her sister.

"Millicent, why did you tell us that Harold died of fever?"

The widow made no gesture, she looked at Kathleen with

steady eyes, but her sallow skin darkened with a flush. She did not reply.

"What *do* you mean, Kathleen?" asked Mr. Skinner, with surprise.

"The Bishop says that Harold committed suicide."

Mrs. Skinner gave a startled cry, but her husband put out a deprecating hand.

"Is it true, Millicent?"

"It is."

"But why didn't you tell us?"

Millicent paused for an instant. She fingered idly a piece of Brunei brass which stood on the table by her side. That too had been a present from Harold.

"I thought it better for Joan that her father should be thought to have died of fever. I didn't want her to know anything about it."

"You've put us in an awfully awkward position," said Kathleen, frowning a little. "Gladys Heywood said she thought it rather nasty of me not to have told her the truth. I had the greatest difficulty in getting her to believe that I knew absolutely nothing about it. She said her father was rather put out. He says, after all the years we've known one another, and considering that he married you, and the terms we've been on, and all that, he does think we might have had confidence in him. And at all events, if we didn't want to tell him the truth we needn't have told him a lie."

"I must say I sympathise with him there," said Mr. Skinner, acidly.

"Of course I told Gladys that we weren't to blame. We only told them what you told us."

"I hope it didn't put you off your game," said Millicent.

"Really, my dear, I think that is a most improper observation," exclaimed her father.

He rose from his chair, walked over to the empty fireplace, and from force of habit stood in front of it with parted coat-tails.

"It was my business," said Millicent, "and if I chose to keep it to myself I didn't see why I shouldn't."

"It doesn't look as if you had any affection for your mother if you didn't even tell her," said Mrs. Skinner.

Millicent shrugged her shoulders.

"You might have known it was bound to come out," said Kathleen.

"Why? I didn't expect that two gossiping old parsons would have nothing else to talk about than me."

"When the Bishop said he'd been to Borneo it's only natural that the Heywoods should ask him if he knew you and Harold."

"All that's neither here nor there," said Mr. Skinner. "I think you should certainly have told us the truth, and we could have decided what was the best thing to do. As a solicitor I can tell you that in the long run it only makes things worse if you attempt to hide them."

"Poor Harold!" said Mrs. Skinner, and the tears began to trickle down her raddled cheeks. "It seems dreadful. He was always a good son-in-law to me. Whatever induced him to do such a dreadful thing?"

"The climate."

"I think you'd better give us all the facts, Millicent," said her father.

"Kathleen will tell you."

Kathleen hesitated. What she had to say really was rather dreadful. It seemed terrible that such things should happen to a family like theirs.

"The Bishop says he cut his throat."

Mrs. Skinner gasped and she went impulsively up to her bereaved daughter. She wanted to fold her in her arms.

"My poor child," she sobbed.

But Millicent withdrew herself.

"Please don't fuss me, mother. I really can't stand being mauled about."

"Really, Millicent," said Mr. Skinner, with a frown.

He did not think she was behaving very nicely.

Mrs. Skinner dabbed her eyes carefully with her handkerchief and with a sigh and a little shake of the head returned to her chair. Kathleen fidgeted with the long chain she wore round her neck.

"It does seem rather absurd that I should have to be told the details of my brother-in-law's death by a friend. It makes us all look such fools. The Bishop wants very much to see you, Millicent; he wants to tell you how much he feels for you." She paused, but Millicent did not speak. "He says that Millicent had been away with Joan and when she came back she found poor Harold lying dead on his bed."

"It must have been a great shock," said Mr. Skinner.

Mrs. Skinner began to cry again, but Kathleen put her hand gently on her shoulder.

"Don't cry, mother," she said. "It'll make your eyes red and people will think it so funny."

They were all silent while Mrs. Skinner, drying her eyes, made a successful effort to control herself. It seemed very strange to her that at this very moment she should be wearing in her toque the ospreys that poor Harold had given her.

"There's something else I ought to tell you," said Kathleen.

Millicent looked at her sister again, without haste, and her eyes were steady, but watchful. She had the look of a person who is waiting for a sound which he is afraid of missing.

"I don't want to say anything to wound you, dear," Kathleen went on, "but there's something else, and I think you ought to know it. The Bishop says that Harold drank."

"Oh, my dear, how dreadful!" cried Mrs. Skinner. "What a shocking thing to say! Did Gladys Heywood tell you? What did you say?"

"I said it was entirely untrue."

"This is what comes of making secrets of things," said Mr. Skinner, irritably. "It's always the same. If you try and hush a thing up, all sorts of rumours get about which are ten times worse than the truth."

"They told the Bishop in Singapore that Harold had killed himself while he was suffering from delirium tremens. I think for all our sakes you ought to deny that, Millicent."

"It's such a dreadful thing to have said about anyone who's dead," said Mrs. Skinner. "And it'll be so bad for Joan when she grows up."

"But what is the foundation of this story, Millicent?" asked her father. "Harold was always very abstemious."

"Here," said the widow.

"Did he drink?"

"Like a fish."

The answer was so unexpected, and the tone so sardonic, that all three of them were startled.

"Millicent, how can you talk like that of your husband when he's dead?" cried her mother, clasping her neatly gloved hands. "I can't understand you. You've been so strange since you came back. I could never have believed that a girl of mine could take her husband's death like that."

"Never mind about that, mother," said Mr. Skinner. "We can go into all that later."

He walked to the window and looked out at the sunny little garden, and then walked back into the room. He took his pince-nez out of his pocket and, though he had no intention of putting them on, wiped them with his handkerchief. Millicent looked at him, and in her eyes, unmistakably, was a look of irony which was quite cynical. Mr. Skinner was vexed. He had finished his week's work and he was a free man till Monday morning. Though he had told his wife that this garden-party was a great nuisance and he would much sooner have tea quietly in his own garden, he had been looking forward to it. He did not care very much about Chinese missions, but it would be interesting to meet the Bishop. And now this!

It was not the kind of thing he cared to be mixed up in; it was most unpleasant to be told on a sudden that his son-in-law was a drunkard and a suicide. Millicent was thoughtfully smoothing her white cuffs. Her coolness irritated him; but instead of addressing her he spoke to his younger daughter.

" Why don't you sit down, Kathleen? Surely there are plenty of chairs in the room."

Kathleen drew forward a chair and without a word seated herself. Mr. Skinner stopped in front of Millicent and faced her.

" Of course I see why you told us Harold had died of fever. I think it was a mistake, because that sort of thing is bound to come out sooner or later. I don't know how far what the Bishop has told the Heywoods coincides with the facts, but if you will take my advice you will tell us everything as circumstantially as you can, then we can see. We can't hope that it will go no further now that Canon Heywood and Gladys know. In a place like this people are bound to talk. It will make it easier for all of us if we at all events know the exact truth."

Mrs. Skinner and Kathleen thought he put the matter very well. They waited for Millicent's reply. She had listened with an impassive face; that sudden flush had disappeared and it was once more, as usual, pasty and sallow.

" I don't think you'll much like the truth if I tell it you," she said.

" You must know that you can count on our sympathy and understanding," said Kathleen gravely.

Millicent gave her a glance and the shadow of a smile flickered across her set mouth. She looked slowly at the three of them. Mrs. Skinner had an uneasy impression that she looked at them as though they were mannequins at a dressmaker's. She seemed to live in a different world from theirs and to have no connection with them.

" You know I wasn't in love with Harold when I married him," she said reflectively.

Mrs. Skinner was on the point of making an exclamation when a rapid gesture of her husband, barely indicated, but after so many years of married life perfectly significant, stopped her. Millicent went on. She spoke with a level voice, slowly, and there was little change of expression in her tone.

" I was twenty-seven, and no one else seemed to want to marry me. It's true he was forty-four, and it seemed rather old, but he had a very good position, hadn't he? I wasn't likely to get a better chance."

Mrs. Skinner felt inclined to cry again, but she remembered the party.

" Of course I see now why you took his photograph away," she said dolefully.

" Don't, mother," exclaimed Kathleen.

It had been taken when he was engaged to Millicent, and was a very good photograph of Harold. Mrs. Skinner had always thought him quite a fine man. He was heavily built, tall and perhaps a little too fat, but he held himself well, and his presence was imposing. He was inclined to be bald, even then, but men did go bald very early nowadays, and he said that topees—sun-helmets, you know—were very bad for the hair. He had a small dark moustache, and his face was deeply burned by the sun. Of course his best feature was his eyes; they were brown and large, like Joan's. His conversation was interesting. Kathleen said he was pompous, but Mrs. Skinner didn't think him so, she didn't mind it if a man laid down the law; and when she saw, as she very soon did, that he was attracted by Millicent, she began to like him very much. He was always very attentive to Mrs. Skinner, and she listened as though she were really interested when he spoke of his district, and told her of the big game he had killed. Kathleen said he had a pretty good opinion of himself, but Mrs. Skinner came of a generation which accepted without question the good opinion that men had of themselves. Millicent saw very soon which way the wind blew, and though she said nothing to her mother, her mother knew that if Harold asked her she was going to accept him.

Harold was staying with some people who had been thirty years in Borneo, and they spoke well of the country. There was no reason why a woman shouldn't live there comfortably; of course the children had to come home when they were seven; but Mrs. Skinner thought it unnecessary to trouble about that yet. She asked Harold to dine, and she told him they were always in to tea. He seemed to be at a loose end, and when his visit to his old friends was drawing to a close, she told him they would be very much pleased if he would come and spend a fortnight with them. It was towards the end of this that Harold and Millicent became engaged. They had a very pretty wedding, they went to Venice for their honeymoon, and then they started for the East. Millicent wrote from various ports at which the ship touched. She seemed happy.

" People were very nice to me at Kuala Solor," she said. Kuala Solor was the chief town of the state of Sembulu. " We stayed with the Resident and everyone asked us to dinner. Once or twice I heard men ask Harold to have a drink, but he refused; he said he had turned over a new leaf now he was a married man. I didn't know why they laughed. Mrs. Gray, the Resident's wife, told me they were all so glad Harold was married. She said it was dreadfully lonely for a bachelor on one of the outstations. When we left Kuala Solor Mrs. Gray said good-bye to me so funnily that I was quite surprised. It was as if she was solemnly putting Harold in my charge."

They listened to her in silence. Kathleen never took her eyes off her sister's impassive face; but Mr. Skinner stared straight in front of him at the Malay arms, krises and parangs, which hung on the wall above the sofa on which his wife sat.

"It wasn't till I went back to Kuala Solor a year and a half later, that I found out why their manner had seemed so odd." Millicent gave a queer little sound like the echo of a scornful laugh. "I knew then a good deal that I hadn't known before. Harold came to England that time in order to marry. He didn't much mind who it was. Do you remember how we spread ourselves out to catch him, mother? We needn't have taken so much trouble."

"I don't know what you mean, Millicent," said Mrs. Skinner, not without acerbity, for the insinuation of scheming did not please her. "I saw he was attracted by you."

Millicent shrugged her heavy shoulders.

"He was a confirmed drunkard. He used to go to bed every night with a bottle of whisky and empty it before morning. The Chief Secretary told him he'd have to resign unless he stopped drinking. He said he'd give him one more chance. He could take his leave then and go to England. He advised him to marry so that when he got back he'd have someone to look after him. Harold married me because he wanted a keeper. They took bets in Kuala Solor on how long I'd make him stay sober."

"But he was in love with you," Mrs. Skinner interrupted. "You don't know how he used to speak to me about you, and at the time you're speaking of, when you went to Kuala Solor to have Joan, he wrote me such a charming letter about you."

Millicent looked at her mother again and a deep colour dyed her sallow skin. Her hands, lying on her lap, began to tremble a little. She thought of those first months of her married life. The Government launch took them to the mouth of the river, and they spent the night at the bungalow which Harold said jokingly was their seaside residence. Next day they went up-steam in a prahu. From the novels she had read she expected the rivers of Borneo to be dark and strangely sinister, but the sky was blue, dappled with little white clouds, and the green of the mangroves and the nipahs, washed by the flowing water, glistened in the sun. On each side stretched the pathless jungle, and in the distance, silhouetted against the sky, was the rugged outline of a mountain. The air in the early morning was fresh and buoyant. She seemed to enter upon a friendly, fertile land, and she had a sense of spacious freedom. They watched the banks for monkeys sitting on the branches of the tangled trees, and once Harold pointed out something that looked like a log and said it was a crocodile. The Assistant Resident, in ducks and a topee, was at the landing-stage to meet them, and a dozen trim little soldiers were lined up to do them honour. The Assistant Resident was introduced to her. His name was Simpson.

"By Jove, sir," he said to Harold, "I'm glad to see you back. It's been deuced lonely without you."

The Resident's bungalow, surrounded by a garden in which grew wildly all manner of gay flowers, stood on the top of a low hill. It was a trifle shabby and the furniture was sparse, but the rooms were cool and of generous size.

"The kampong is down there," said Harold, pointing.

Her eyes followed his gesture, and from among the coconut trees rose the beating of a gong. It gave her a queer little sensation in the heart.

Though she had nothing much to do the days passed easily enough. At dawn a boy brought them their tea and they lounged about the verandah, enjoying the fragrance of the morning (Harold in a singlet and a sarong, she in a dressing-gown) till it was time to dress for breakfast. Then Harold went to his office and she spent an hour or two learning Malay. After tiffin he went back to his office while she slept. A cup of tea revived them both, and they went for a walk or played golf on the nine-hole links which Harold had made on a level piece of cleared jungle below the bungalow. Night fell at six and Mr. Simpson came along to have a drink. They chatted till their late dinner hour, and sometimes Harold and Mr. Simpson played chess. The balmy evenings were enchanting. The fireflies turned the bushes just below the verandah into coldly sparkling tremulous beacons, and flowering trees scented the air with sweet odours. After dinner they read the papers which had left London six weeks before and presently went to bed. Millicent enjoyed being a married woman, with a house of her own, and she was pleased with the native servants, in their gay sarongs, who went about the bungalow, with bare feet, silent but friendly. It gave her a pleasant sense of importance to be the wife of the Resident. Harold impressed her by the fluency with which he spoke the language, by his air of command, and by his dignity. She went into the court-house now and then to hear him try cases. The multifariousness of his duties and the competent way in which he performed them aroused her respect. Mr. Simpson told her that Harold understood the natives as well as any man in the country. He had the combination of firmness, tact and good humour, which was essential in dealing with that timid, revengeful and suspicious race. Millicent began to feel a certain admiration for her husband.

They had been married nearly a year when two English naturalists came to stay with them for a few days on their way to the interior. They brought a pressing recommendation from the Governor, and Harold said he wanted to do them proud. Their arrival was an agreeable change. Millicent asked Mr. Simpson to dinner (he lived at the Fort and only dined with them on Sunday nights) and after dinner the men sat down to play bridge. Millicent left them presently and went to bed, but they were so noisy that for some time she could not get to sleep. She did not know at what hour she was awakened by Harold staggering into the room. She kept silent. He made up his mind to have a bath before getting into bed; the bath-house was just below their room, and he went down the steps that led to it. Apparently he slipped, for there was a great clatter, and he began to swear. Then he was violently sick. She heard him sluice the buckets of water over himself and in a little while, walking very cautiously this time, he crawled up the stairs and slipped into bed. Millicent pretended to be asleep. She was disgusted. Harold was drunk. She made up her mind to speak about it to him in the morning. What would the naturalists think of him? But in the morning Harold was so dignified that she hadn't quite the determination to refer to the matter. At eight Harold and she, with their two guests, sat down to breakfast. Harold looked round the table.

"Porridge," he said. "Millicent, your guests might manage a little Worcester Sauce for breakfast, but I don't think they'll much fancy anything else. Personally I shall content myself with a whisky and soda."

The naturalists laughed, but shamefacedly.

"Your husband's a terror," said one of them.

"I should not think I had properly performed the duties of hospitality if I sent you sober to bed on the first night of your visit," said Harold, with his round, stately way of putting things.

Millicent, smiling acidly, was relieved to think that her guests had been as drunk as her husband. The next evening she sat up with them and the party broke up at a reasonable hour. But she was glad when the strangers went on with their journey. Their life resumed its placid course. Some months later Harold went on a tour of inspection of his district and came back with a bad attack of malaria. This was the first time she had seen the disease of which she had heard so much, and when he recovered it did not seem strange to her that Harold was very shaky. She found his manner peculiar. He would come back from the office and stare at her with glazed eyes; he would stand on the verandah, swaying slightly, but still dignified, and make long harangues about the political situation in England; losing the thread of his discourse, he would look at her with an archness which his natural stateliness made somewhat disconcerting and say:

"Pulls you down dreadfully, this confounded malaria. Ah, little woman, you little know the strain it puts upon a man to be an empire-builder."

She thought that Mr. Simpson began to look worried, and once or twice when they were alone, he seemed on the point of saying something to her which his shyness at the last moment prevented. The feeling grew so strong that it made her nervous, and one evening when Harold, she knew not why, had remained later than usual at the office she tackled him.

"What have you got to say to me, Mr. Simpson?" she broke out suddenly.

He blushed and hesitated.

"Nothing. What makes you think I have anything in particular to say to you?"

Mr. Simpson was a thin, weedy youth of four-and-twenty, with a fine head of waving hair which he took great pains to plaster down very flat. His wrists were swollen and scarred with mosquito bites. Millicent looked at him steadily.

"If it's something to do with Harold don't you think it would be kinder to tell me frankly?"

He grew scarlet now. He shuffled uneasily on his rattan chair. She insisted.

"I'm afraid you'll think it awful cheek," he said at last. "It's rotten of me to say anything about my chief behind his back. Malaria's a rotten thing, and after one's had a bout of it one feels awfully down and out."

He hesitated again. The corners of his mouth sagged as if he were going to cry. To Millicent he seemed like a little boy.

"I'll be as silent as the grave," she said with a smile, trying to conceal her apprehension. "Do tell me."

"I think it's a pity your husband keeps a bottle of whisky at the office. He's apt to take a nip more often than he otherwise would."

Mr. Simpson's voice was hoarse with agitation. Millicent felt a sudden coldness shiver through her. She controlled herself, for she knew that she must not frighten the boy if she were to get out of him all there was to tell. He was unwilling to speak. She pressed him, wheedling, appealing to his sense of duty, and at last she began to cry. Then he told her that Harold had been drunk more or less for the last fortnight, the natives were talking about it, and they said that soon he would be as bad as he had been before his marriage. He had been in the habit of drinking a good deal too much then, but details of that time, notwithstanding all her attempts, Mr. Simpson resolutely declined to give her.

"Do you think he's drinking now?" she asked.

"I don't know."

Millicent felt herself on a sudden hot with shame and anger. The Fort, as it was called because the rifles and the ammunition were kept there, was also the court-house. It stood opposite the Resident's bungalow in a garden of its own. The sun was just about to set and she did not need a hat. She got up and walked across. She found Harold sitting in the office behind the large hall in which he administered justice. There was a bottle of whisky in front of him. He was smoking cigarettes and talking to three or four Malays who stood in front of him listening with obsequious and at the same time scornful smiles. His face was red.

The natives vanished.

"I came to see what you were doing," she said.

He rose, for he always treated her with elaborate politeness, and lurched. Feeling himself unsteady he assumed an elaborate stateliness of demeanour.

"Take a seat, my dear, take a seat. I was detained by press of work."

She looked at him with angry eyes.

"You're drunk," she said.

He stared at her, his eyes bulging a little, and a haughty look gradually traversed his large and fleshy face.

"I haven't the remotest idea what you mean," he said.

She had been ready with a flow of wrathful expostulation, but suddenly she burst into tears. She sank into a chair and hid her face. Harold looked at her for an instant, then the tears began to trickle down his own cheeks; he came towards her with outstretched arms and fell heavily on his knees. Sobbing, he clasped her to him.

"Forgive me, forgive me," he said. "I promise you it shall not happen again. It was that damned malaria."

"It's so humiliating," she moaned.

He wept like a child. There was something very touching in the self-abasement of that big dignified man. Presently Millicent looked up. His eyes, appealing and contrite, sought hers.

" Will you give me your word of honour that you'll never touch liquor again? "

" Yes, yes. I hate it."

It was then she told him that she was with child. He was overjoyed.

" That is the one thing I wanted. That'll keep me straight."

They went back to the bungalow. Harold bathed himself and had a nap. After dinner they talked long and quietly. He admitted that before he married her he had occasionally drunk more than was good for him; in outstations it was easy to fall into bad habits. He agreed to everything that Millicent asked. And during the months before it was necessary for her to go to Kuala Solor for her confinement, Harold was an excellent husband, tender, thoughtful, proud and affectionate; he was irreproachable. A launch came to fetch her, she was to leave him for six weeks, and he promised faithfully to drink nothing during her absence. He put his hands on her shoulders.

" I never break a promise," he said in his dignified way. " But even without it, can you imagine that while you are going through so much, I should do anything to increase your troubles? "

Joan was born. Millicent stayed at the Resident's and Mrs. Gray, his wife, a kindly creature of middle age, was very good to her. The two women had little to do during the long hours they were alone but to talk, and in course of time Millicent learnt everything there was to know of her husband's alcoholic past. The fact which she found most difficult to reconcile herself to, was that Harold had been told that the only condition upon which he would be allowed to keep his post was that he should bring back a wife. It caused in her a dull feeling of resentment. And when she discovered what a persistent drunkard he had been, she felt vaguely uneasy. She had a horrid fear that during her absence he would not have been able to resist the craving. She went home with her baby and a nurse. She spent a night at the mouth of the river and sent a messenger in a canoe to announce her arrival. She scanned the landing-stage anxiously as the launch approached it. Harold and Mr. Simpson were standing there The trim little soldiers were lined up. Her heart sank, for Harold was swaying slightly, like a man who seeks to keep his balance on a rolling ship, and she knew he was drunk.

It wasn't a very pleasant home-coming. She had almost

forgotten her mother and father and her sister who sat there silently listening to her. Now she roused herself and became once more aware of their presence. All that she spoke of seemed very far away.

"I knew that I hated him then," she said. "I could have killed him."

"Oh, Millicent, don't say that," cried her mother. "Don't forget that he's dead, poor man."

Millicent looked at her mother, and for a moment a scowl darkened her impassive face. Mr. Skinner moved uneasily.

"Go on," said Kathleen.

"When he found out that I knew all about him he didn't bother very much more. In three months he had another attack of d.t.'s."

"Why didn't you leave him?" said Kathleen.

"What would have been the good of that? He would have been dismissed from the service in a fortnight. Who was to keep me and Joan? I had to stay. And when he was sober I had nothing to complain of. He wasn't in the least in love with me, but he was fond of me; I hadn't married him because I was in love with him, but because I wanted to be married. I did everything I could to keep liquor from him; I managed to get Mr. Gray to prevent whisky being sent from Kuala Solor, but he got it from the Chinese. I watched him as a cat watches a mouse. He was too cunning for me. In a little while he had another outbreak. He neglected his duties. I was afraid complaints would be made. We were two days from Kuala Solor and that was our safeguard but I suppose something was said, for Mr. Gray wrote a private letter of warning to me. I showed it to Harold. He stormed and blustered, but I saw he was frightened, and for two or three months he was quite sober. Then he began again. And so it went on till our leave became due.

"Before we came to stay here I begged and prayed him to be careful. I didn't want any of you to know what sort of a man I had married. All the time he was in England he was all right and before we sailed I warned him. He'd grown to be very fond of Joan, and very proud of her, and she was devoted to him. She always liked him better than she liked me. I asked him if he wanted to have his child grow up, knowing that he was a drunkard, and I found out that at last I'd got a hold on him. The thought terrified him. I told him that *I* wouldn't allow it, and if he ever let Joan see him drunk I'd take her away from him at once. Do you know, he grew quite pale when I said it. I fell on my knees that night and thanked God, because I'd found a way of saving my husband.

" He told me that if I would stand by him he would have another try. We made up our minds to fight the thing together. And he tried so hard. When he felt as though he *must* drink he came to me. You know he was inclined to be rather pompous; with me he was so humble, he was like a child; he depended on me. Perhaps he didn't love me when he married me, but he loved me then, me and Joan. I'd hated him, because of the humiliation, because when he was drunk and tried to be dignified and impressive he was loathsome; but now I got a strange feeling in my heart. It wasn't love, but it was a queer, shy tenderness. He was something more than my husband, he was like a child that I'd carried under my heart for long and weary months. He was so proud of me and, you know, I was proud too. His long speeches didn't irritate me any more, and I only thought his stately ways rather funny and charming. At last we won. For two years he never touched a drop. He lost his craving entirely. He was even able to joke about it.

" Mr. Simpson had left us then and we had another young man called Francis.

" 'I'm a reformed drunkard, you know, Francis,' Harold said to him once. 'If it hadn't been for my wife I'd have been sacked long ago. I've got the best wife in the world, Francis.'

" You don't know what it meant to me to hear him say that. I felt that all I'd gone through was worth while. I was so happy."

She was silent. She thought of the broad, yellow and turbid river on whose banks she had lived so long. The egrets, white and gleaming in the tremulous sunset, flew down the stream in a flock, flew low and swift, and scattered. They were like a ripple of snowy notes, sweet and pure and spring-like, which an unseen hand drew forth, a divine arpeggio, from an unseen harp. They fluttered along between the green banks, wrapped in the shadows of evening, like the happy thoughts of a contented mind.

" Then Joan fell ill. For three weeks we were very anxious. There was no doctor nearer than Kuala Solor and we had to put up with the treatment of a native dispenser. When she grew well again I took her down to the mouth of the river in order to give her a breath of sea air. We stayed there a week. It was the first time I had been separated from Harold since I went away to have Joan. There was a fishing village, on piles, not far from us, but really we were quite alone. I thought a great deal about Harold, so tenderly, and all at once I knew that I loved him. I was so glad when the prahu came to fetch us back, because I wanted to tell him. I thought it would mean a good deal to him. I can't tell you how happy I was. As we rowed up-stream the head-man told me that Mr. Francis had had to go up-country to arrest a woman who had murdered her husband. He had been gone a couple of days.

"I was surprised that Harold was not on the landing-stage to meet me; he was always very punctilious about that sort of thing; he used to say that husband and wife should treat one another as politely as they treated acquaintances; and I could not imagine what business had prevented him. I walked up the little hill on which the bungalow stood. The ayah brought Joan behind me. The bungalow was strangely silent. There seemed to be no servants about, and I could not make it out; I wondered if Harold hadn't expected me so soon and was out. I went up the steps. Joan was thirsty and the ayah took her to the servants' quarters to give her something to drink. Harold was not in the sitting-room. I called him, but there was no answer. I was disappointed, because I should have liked him to be there. I went into our bedroom. Harold wasn't out after all; he was lying on the bed asleep. I was really very much amused, because he always pretended he never slept in the afternoon. He said it was an unnecessary habit that we white people got into. I went up to the bed softly. I thought I would have a joke with him. I opened the mosquito curtains. He was lying on his back, with nothing on but a sarong, and there was an empty whisky bottle by his side. He was drunk.

"It had begun again. All my struggles for so many years were wasted. My dream was shattered. It was all hopeless. I was seized with rage."

Millicent's face grew once again darkly red and she clenched the arms of the chair she sat in.

"I took him by the shoulders and shook him with all my might. 'You beast,' I cried, 'you beast.' I was so angry I don't know what I did, I don't know what I said. I kept on shaking him. You don't know how loathsome he looked, that large fat man, half naked; he hadn't shaved for days, and his face was bloated and purple. He was breathing heavily. I shouted at him, but he took no notice. I tried to drag him out of bed, but he was too heavy. He lay there like a log. 'Open your eyes,' I screamed. I shook him again. I hated him. I hated him all the more because for a week I'd loved him with all my heart. He'd let me down. He'd let me down. I wanted to tell him what a filthy beast he was. I could make no impression on him. 'You shall open your eyes,' I cried. I was determined to make him look at me."

The widow licked her dry lips. Her breath seemed hurried. She was silent.

" If he was in that state I should have thought it best to have let him go on sleeping," said Kathleen.

" There was a parang on the wall by the side of the bed. You know how fond Harold was of curios."

" What's a parang? " said Mrs. Skinner.

" Don't be silly, mother," her husband replied irritably. " There's one on the wall immediately behind you."

He pointed to the Malay sword on which for some reason his eyes had been unconsciously resting. Mrs. Skinner drew quickly into the corner of the sofa, with a little frightened gesture, as though she had been told that a snake lay curled up beside her.

" Suddenly the blood spurted out from Harold's throat. There was a great red gash right across it."

" Millicent," cried Kathleen, springing up and almost leaping towards her, " what in God's name do you mean? "

Mrs. Skinner stood staring at her with wide startled eyes, her mouth open.

" The parang wasn't on the wall any more. It was on the bed. Then Harold opened his eyes. They were just like Joan's."

" I don't understand," said Mr. Skinner. " How could he have committed suicide if he was in the state you describe? "

Kathleen took her sister's arm and shook her angrily.

" Millicent, for God's sake explain."

Millicent released herself.

" The parang was on the wall, I told you. I don't know what happened. There was all the blood, and Harold opened his eyes. He died almost at once. He never spoke, but he gave a sort of gasp."

At last Mr. Skinner found his voice.

" But, you wretched woman, it was murder."

Millicent, her face mottled with red, gave him such a look of scornful hatred that he shrank back. Mrs. Skinner cried out:

" Millicent, you didn't do it, did you? "

Then Millicent did something that made them all feel as though their blood were turned to ice in their veins. She chuckled.

" I don't know who else did," she said.

" My God," muttered Mr. Skinner.

Kathleen had been standing bolt upright, with her hands to her heart, as though its beating were intolerable.

" And what happened then? " she said.

" I screamed. I went to the window and flung it open.

I called for the ayah. She came across the compound with Joan. 'Not Joan,' I cried. 'Don't let her come.' She called the cook and told him to take the child. I cried to her to hurry. And when she came I showed her Harold. 'The Tuan's killed himself!' I cried. She gave a scream and ran out of the house.

"No one would come near. They were all frightened out of their wits. I wrote a letter to Mr. Francis, telling him what had happened and asking him to come at once."

"How do you mean you told him what had happened?"

"I said, on my return from the mouth of the river, I'd found Harold with his throat cut. You know, in the tropics you have to bury people quickly. I got a Chinese coffin, and the soldiers dug a grave behind the Fort. When Mr. Francis came, Harold had been buried for nearly two days. He was only a boy. I could do anything I wanted with him. I told him I'd found the parang in Harold's hand and there was no doubt he'd killed himself in an attack of delirium tremens. I showed him the empty bottle. The servants said he'd been drinking hard ever since I left to go to the sea. I told the same story at Kuala Solor. Everyone was very kind to me, and the Government granted me a pension."

For a little while nobody spoke. At last, Mr. Skinner gathered himself together.

"I am a member of the legal profession. I'm a solicitor. I have certain duties. We've always had a most respectable practice. You've put me in a monstrous position."

He fumbled, searching for the phrases that played at hide and seek in his scattered wits. Millicent looked at him with scorn.

"What are you going to do about it?"

"It was murder, that's what it was; do you think I can possibly connive at it?"

"Don't talk nonsense, father," said Kathleen sharply. "You can't give up your own daughter."

"You've put me in a monstrous position," he repeated.

Millicent shrugged her shoulders again.

"You made me tell you. And I've borne it long enough by myself. It was time that all of you bore it too."

At the moment the door was opened by the maid.

"Davis has brought the car round, sir," she said.

Kathleen had the presence of mind to say something, and the maid withdrew.

"We'd better be starting," said Millicent.

"I can't go to the party now," cried Mrs. Skinner, with horror. "I'm far too upset. How can we face the Heywoods? And the Bishop will want to be introduced to you."

Millicent made a gesture of indifference. Her eyes held their ironical expression.

"We must go, mother," said Kathleen. "It would look so funny if we stayed away." She turned on Millicent furiously. "Oh, I think the whole thing is such frightfully bad form."

Mrs. Skinner looked helplessly at her husband. He went to her and gave her his hand to help her up from the sofa.

"I'm afraid we must go, mother," he said.

"And me with the ospreys in my toque that Harold gave me with his own hands," she moaned.

He led her out of the room, Kathleen followed close on their heels, and a step or two behind came Millicent.

"You'll get used to it, you know," she said quietly. "At first I thought of it all the time, but now I forget it for two or three days together. It's not as if there was any danger."

They did not answer. They walked through the hall and out of the front door. The three ladies got into the back of the car and Mr. Skinner seated himself beside the driver. They had no self-starter; it was an old car, and Davis went to the bonnet to crank it up. Mr. Skinner turned round and looked petulantly at Millicent.

"I ought never to have been told," he said. "I think it was most selfish of you."

Davis took his seat and they drove off to the Canon's garden-party.

ROBERT BONTINE CUNNINGHAME GRAHAM

AT SANCHIDRIAN

IT was full harvest-time throughout Castile. The corn, short in the stalk and light, as is all corn that ripens early, stood ready to be reaped. In places it had been already cut, and lay in sheaves upon the ground. In others it was cut and carried, and again, between some patches, carts loaded high were creaking through the fields, if the word field can be applied to ground that has no hedges or divisions visible to any other eyes than those accustomed from their birth to the brown plains. Across the dusty, calcined steppe the Sud-Express had crawled since daybreak, stopping at every wayside station, jolting and creaking like a bullock wagon. The passengers had long ceased to look out, and sat perspiring in their darkened berths, for the Castilian plain in summer is not for eyes accustomed to see beauty only in places where even nature puts on a sort of easy, meretricious dress, and decked in pine woods, set with hills and waterfalls, seems to invite the applause of travelling photographers. Castile only reveals itself to those who know it under every aspect, wind-swept and drear in winter, sun-baked in summer, and at all times adust and stern, a mere wide steppe bounded by distant clearly cut hills, from which nothing is to be expected but strange effects of light.

On every side, right up to where it joined the distant hills, stretched the brown plain. The sun had scorched the very trunks of the trees till they appeared to suffer and to be about to burst, just as they crack and suffer in a frost. The only flowers left alive were a few yellow thistles and some clumps of artemisia, which reared their heads, as it were, in defiance of the sun. Long lines of men mounted on donkeys crossed between the fields of stubble and of corn. The Castilian summer had turned them black as Arabs, and their sad, high-pitched songs, as they kept on their way indomitably in the fiery heat, seemed to complete the likeness to the men from whom they had inherited all that they knew of agriculture.

Over the steppe, the narrow line of railway formed the connecting link with the outside world, the world of newspapers, of motor-cars, of aviation, and of telephones. Glistening bright in the sun, like a steel ribbon, ran the line. It passed by little tile-roofed towns, each clustering round its church, brown and remote—towns where a sandy, unpaved street ran out until it lost itself in the great plain; towns only joined to one another by a narrow track meandering through the corn fields, or the sparse round-topped pine woods, tracks that avoided all the obstacles, passing round, stony hills and following watercourses till they came on a shallow place to cross. Often the towns were only visible like ships hull down, the church towers seemingly hung in the air without foundations, they were so far off from the line. The train jogged on, passing by Ataquines, Palacios de Goda, Arévalo, Adanero and other little stations, where no one possibly could have got in or out since first the line was laid. It entered them and stopped under some dust-laden acacias or China-trees. A man emerged and called the station's name, adding "a minute" or "two minutes" as the case might be, although the train was just as likely to stop ten minutes or a quarter of an hour, whilst the electric bell twittered so faintly that at times one was not sure if it was really an electric bell that sounded or only crickets in the sand chirping metallically. Sometimes a horse stood blinking in the sun tied to a post, a gun upon the heavy old-world saddle and a brown blanket hanging from the pommel, almost to the ground; sometimes some charcoal-burners' mules stood waiting to be unloaded, and generally some ragged-looking fowls, half buried in the sand, were squatted at the lee-side of the round, mud-topped oven, striving to dodge the heat. Occasionally a half-dressed woman peeped from a window, her blue-black hair wild as a pony's mane, holding the blind between her teeth as she looked out upon the train. Such were the stations, mere islands in a sea of brown; each one the faithful copy of the other, and every one of them cheaply constructed and sun-bleached till they had all become as much a part and parcel of the landscape as the mud houses with their red-tiled eaves.

So from one little, ill-built point of contact with the world, to the next, as ill-built as the last, the train crept on, the heat increasing and the subtile air becoming more diaphanous, so that the distant mountains almost appeared to be transparent, and the dead haulms of fennel and of mullein to stand out so clearly that they looked like trees.

Herds of black cattle stood by dried-up water-holes, occasionally a bullock licked the earth where it appeared almost like china, polished and glazed as it had dried and baked, and then stamping and bellowing, slowly walked back into the herd.

Brown shepherds stood immovable as posts, their shadows forming a refuge for their dogs, their flocks all huddled in a ring, with their heads crouched low upon the ground, to escape their enemy, the sun. Nature stood silent in the violet haze, and as the train rattled across the ill-closed catch-points outside another little station, a porter called out in a long-drawn melody, " Sanchidrian, five minutes," and the express came alongside the platform, the engine throbbing as if it were something living and glad to be at rest. A goods train standing just outside the station bore the inscription, written with a piece of chalk, " No water in Velayos," and the whole plain looked parched and suffering as if the rain of fire that fell from heaven upon it had burned into its heart. No passengers stood waiting, even the little groups of country people that generally throng Spanish stations, making the platform a public promenade, were missing, for Sanchidrian itself was distant from the line.

The weary stationmaster in his gold-laced cap and uniform frock-coat was, with the porter who had called the station's name, the only living thing except two nearly naked children, sitting by the draw-well, and a lean yellow dog. The five minutes that the train ought to have remained might just as well have been abridged to one, or, on the other hand, drawn out to twenty, and no one would have cared, had not, emerging from a cloud of dust, a rider come up to the hitching-post, dismounted hurriedly, and holding in his hand his saddle-bags, walked quickly to the open door, at which the cooks and waiters of the dining-car stood trying to catch a little air. " Friends," he said, taking off his hat and passing his brown hand across his forehead, " have you any ice? " They stared at him as he stood in his short black jacket edged with imitation astrakhan, his tight, grey trousers strapped inside the leg with the same cloth from which they had been made, his black serge sash showing beneath his waistcoat with its silver buckles, and his red-worsted saddle-bags, tasselled and fringed, thrown over his right shoulder and hanging down his back.

" Ice, why of course we have it," said the waiter. " Who in this heat could live without it shut in the hot train? " answered the conductor, interested and glad to have the opportunity of a chance word with anyone outside his little world.

The horseman, who looked anxiously at the somnolent train out of the corner of his eye as if it were a colt that might spring forward at any minute and leave him in the lurch, began again: " You could not live without ice here in this train, you say, eh? My father cannot die without it. For days the fever has consumed him, and in the night, listening to every hour the watchman calls, he says 'Miguel,' that is my name—Miguel Martinez, at your service—'I could die easier if I had some ice . . . a little ice to put upon my forehead and between my lips.' Ice in Sanchidrian! As well go out to gather artichokes at sea. To-day he seemed just going, and the priest said to me, 'Miguel, saddle the Jerezano and go down and meet the train; there they have ice, for certainly those who travel by it must drink cool.' So I have come; say, can you spare me a lump of ice, for what I spoke about?"

The electric bell stopped twittering, and the porter called "Passengers aboard," but still the train stood at the platform, although the engine-driver had clambered slowly to his post. He whistled, and the couplings tightened with a jerk, just as a waiter holding a lump of ice about as big as a large loaf came to the door, wrapping it, as he walked, in straw. He gave it to the horseman, who stood waiting in the sun. "A thousand thanks," he said. "A son thanks you in his father's name. What is the value of this piece of ice?" The man who gave it, and the little knot of cooks and waiters standing at the open door of the long dining-car as the train began to move, looked at each other, and one said, "Friend, we do not sell our ice, it is not ours to sell. Moreover, may it relieve your father." Miguel, now walking swiftly by the moving train, said, "Once again, a thousand thanks; take, then, this packet of cigars," and handed to the last man he could reach one of those bundles of ill-rolled salitrose-looking parcels of cigars sold in the *estancos* of small Spanish towns.

The train swung on and rumbled past him, leaving him standing for a moment in the heat, waving his hand to the white-clad cooks and waiters grouped on the platform of the dining-car. Miguel stood waiting till it had cleared the station, and then, walking outside to where his horse stood waiting, unhitched him and threw the saddle-bags across the saddle, then gathering his reins in his left hand he mounted in one motion, and settling himself, drew out an olive switch which he had left sticking between the pommel and his horse's back; then having felt the lump of ice with his right hand, touched his horse with the spur and set his face towards his home. Putting the butt-end of his cigarette behind his ear, Miguel struck out into the road. The thick, white dust lay on the narrow track like snow, dulling the horse's footfalls and giving him the look of shuffling in his gait, although Miguel, holding his reins high and a little to the near side of the high pommel, and with his spurs dangling behind the cinch, kept him up to the full stretch of the Castilian pace.

His olive face, under his broad-brimmed, grey, felt hat with its straight brim, looked anxiously ahead, and when his little, nervous horse had got well warmed and the dried sweat melted again upon the skin, Miguel, pressing him with his legs, put him to a slow gallop, now and again putting his hand behind the saddle to feel how the precious lump of ice was standing the fierce sun.

A constant dripping through the worsted saddle-bags warned him to hurry, so he pressed on, passing long lines of mules laden with charcoal or with great nets of straw, and men on donkeys, who looked at him with wonder as he flew past them at three-quarter speed upon the road. Some of them merely said "Adios," and others shouted inquiries as to his haste, but he in every case answered with a wave of his hand and pressed his spurs into the cinch. He passed through groves of olive trees, silvery, gnarled and secular, under whose scanty shade men sat, eating their mid-day meal, their broad-brimmed hats lying beside them on the ground, their close-shaved heads wrapped in old-fashioned, blue-checked handkerchiefs, tied in a knot behind.

As he passed in a cloud of dust, pointing to their olives and their bread and to their leathern skins of wines, they made the gesture of inviting him to eat, and he returned their courtesy by a movement of his hand, taking a pull upon his horse as the track grew steeper and stonier, as it ran through an aromatic waste of cistus and wild thyme. His heavy Arab stirrups brushed through the sticky cistus which grew on each side of the narrow, sandy path till they became all coated with their gum and everything stuck to them as if they had been smeared with birdlime.

Butterflies hovered over the great white flowers, and lizards ran up tree-trunks, pausing and looking round just before they disappeared from view. From the recesses of the waste came an incessant hum of insects, and now and then a flight of locusts shot across the path, and plunged into the bushes, just as a school of flying fish sinks into a wave.

The hot half-hour between the bushes, struggling through the sand, had told its tale upon the gallant little horse, whose heaving flanks, distended nostrils and protruding eyes showed that he had almost had enough. When they emerged again into the plain and saw the little brown-roofed town, only a short league away, Miguel dismounted for a moment, and after slackening his cinch anxiously secured his saddle-bags, from which large drops of moisture fell upon the ground.

Tightening his girth again, he mounted, and the Jerezana, who had stood head to wind, responding to the spur, struck into a short gallop, his rider holding him together and pressing him with both legs into his bit.

They passed a threshing-floor, on which a troop of mares was being driven round to thresh the corn, followed by a man seated upon a hurdle laid on a heavy stone. The floor itself was white and shiny, and seemed as hard as marble, trodden by the horses' feet. Near it some sun-burned men threw grain into the air with wooden spades to winnow it, and as Miguel passed by upon the road they called out to him, giving him the time of day and asking how his father was; but to them all he only waved his hand and pressed his spurs into his horse's sides, which now were red with blood.

Outside the town the track passed through the bed of a dry stream, and came out on the other bank on a paved causeway set with pebble-stones that led into the town. A heavy stumble on the stones showed him his horse was failing, and he pulled him back into a trot. Passing the straggling cottages, each with its corral for goats, he came into the little street, and as he rode by the church door he touched his hat and crossed himself as his horse slithered on the stones. Turning out of an angle of the dusty *plaza* with its stucco seats and dwarfed acacias, he came into a street in which the houses seemed of a richer sort of folk, his horse now beaten to a walk. As he neared one which had a roughly sculptured coat of arms over the doorway a sound of wailing fell upon his ears. He stopped, and getting off his horse, he threw the reins mechanically on the ground. A priest came out to meet him. "Miguel," he said, "your father, may God have pardoned him, has left this vale of tears more than an hour ago. The Lord in his great mercy, for the fever burned like fire in his veins, was pleased to make his parting easy, and for an hour before he died he murmured now and then, 'How cool the ice is! It stills the throbbing of my forehead and slakes my thirst—my son Miguel rode for it to the train.'"

Miguel turned to his horse, and taking from the saddle-bags the lump of ice, now little bigger than an apple, followed the priest into the great bare room, where on his bed his father's body lay. Round it stood weeping women, and the children in a corner of the room holding each other's hands gazed stolidly at the brown face that looked like walnut-wood against the linen of the bed.

Falling upon his knees, Miguel kissed the thin hands crossed on the chest, and then after a prayer he rose and put the precious lump of ice first on his father's forehead and then upon his lips. He crossed himself, and after having said some words of consolation to the women, went out again to where in the hot sandy street his horse stood waiting, with his legs stretched a little forward and his head hanging to the ground. The sweat had made a little pattern in the sand as it dropped from his belly and his flanks. Miguel slowly undid the girths, and taking off the bridle, led the horse into the stable, and after throwing hay upon the manger, went back into the room.

The priest was praying, and the sobbing of the women sounded like surf upon a beach, whilst from outside the crickets' chirping filled the air with its wild melody. Far to the south the Sud-Express still crept along its narrow ribbon of bright rails towards Madrid.

ROBERT LOUIS STEVENSON

STORY OF THE PHYSICIAN AND THE SARATOGA TRUNK

MR. SILAS Q. SCUDDAMORE was a young American of a simple and harmless disposition, which was the more to his credit as he came from New England—a quarter of the New World not precisely famous for those qualities. Although he was exceedingly rich, he kept a note of all his expenses in a little paper pocket-book; and he had chosen to study the attractions of Paris from the seventh storey of what is called a furnished hotel, in the Latin Quarter. There was a great deal of habit in his penuriousness; and his virtue, which was very remarkable among his associates, was principally founded upon diffidence and youth.

The next room to his was inhabited by a lady, very attractive in her air and very elegant in toilette, whom, on his first arrival, he had taken for a countess. In course of time he had learned that she was known by the name of Madame Zephyrine, and that whatever station she occupied in life it was not that of a person of title. Madame Zéphyrine, probably in the hope of enchanting the young American, used to flaunt by him on the stairs with a civil inclination, a word of course, and a knock-down look out of her black eyes, and disappear in a rustle of silk, and with the revelation of an admirable foot and ankle. But these advances, so far from encouraging Mr. Scuddamore, plunged him into the depths of depression and bashfulness. She had come to him several times for a light, or to apologise for the imaginary depredations of her poodle; but his mouth was closed in the presence of so superior a being, his French promptly left him, and he could only stare and stammer until she was gone. The slenderness of their intercourse did not prevent him from throwing out insinuations of a very glorious order when he was safely alone with a few males.

The room on the other side of the American's—for there were three rooms on a floor in the hotel—was tenanted by an old English physician of rather doubtful reputation. Dr. Noel, for that was his name, had been forced to leave London, where he enjoyed a large and increasing practice; and it was hinted that the police had been the instigators of this change of scene. At least he, who had made something of a figure in earlier life, now dwelt in the Latin Quarter in great simplicity and solitude, and devoted much of his time to study. Mr. Scuddamore had made his acquaintance, and the pair would now and then dine together frugally in a restaurant across the street.

Silas Q. Scuddamore had many little vices of the more respectable order, and was not restrained by delicacy from indulging them in many rather doubtful ways. Chief among his foibles stood curiosity. He was a born gossip; and life, and especially those parts of it in which he had no experience, interested him to the degree of passion. He was a pert, invincible questioner, pushing his inquiries with equal pertinacity and indiscretion: he had been observed, when he took a letter to the post, to weigh it in his hand, to turn it over and over, and study the address with care; and when he found a flaw in the partition between his room and Madame Zéphyrine's, instead of filling it up, he enlarged and improved the opening, and made use of it as a spy-hole on his neighbour's affairs.

One day, in the end of March, his curiosity growing as it was indulged, he enlarged the hole a little further, so that he might command another corner of the room. That evening, when he went as usual to inspect Madame Zéphryine's movements, he was astonished to find the aperture obscured in an odd manner on the other side, and still more abashed when the obstacle was suddenly withdrawn and a titter of laughter reached his ears. Some of the plaster had evidently betrayed the secret of his spy-hole, and his neighbour had been returning the compliment in kind. Mr. Scuddamore was moved to a very acute feeling of annoyance; he condemned Madame Zéphyrine unmercifully; he even blamed himself; but when he found, next day, that she had taken no means to baulk him of his favourite pastime, he continued to profit by her carelessness, and gratify his idle curiosity.

The next day Madame Zéphyrine received a long visit from a tall, loosely built man of fifty or upwards, whom Silas had not hitherto seen. His tweed suit and coloured shirt, no less than his shaggy side-whiskers, identified him as a Britisher, and his dull grey eye affected Silas with a sense of cold. He kept screwing his mouth from side to side and round and round during the whole colloquy, which was carried on in whispers. More than once it seemed to the young New Englander as if their gestures indicated his own apartment; but the only thing definite he could gather by the most scrupulous attention was this remark made by the Englishman in a somewhat higher key, as if in answer to some reluctance or opposition:

"I have studied his taste to a nicety, and I tell you again and again you are the only woman of the sort that I can lay my hands on."

In answer to this, Madame Zéphyrine sighed, and appeared by a gesture to resign herself, like one yielding to unqualified authority.

That afternoon the observatory was finally blinded, a wardrobe having been drawn in front of it upon the other side; and while Silas was still lamenting over this misfortune, which he attributed to the Britisher's malign suggestion, the concierge brought him up a letter in a female handwriting. It was conceived in French of no very rigorous orthography, bore no signature, and in the most encouraging terms invited the young American to be present in a certain part of the Bullier Ball at eleven o'clock that night. Curiosity and timidity fought a long battle in his heart; sometimes he was all virtue, sometimes all fire and daring; and the result of it was that, long before ten, Mr. Silas Q. Scuddamore presented himself in unimpeachable attire at the door of the Bullier Ball Rooms, and paid his entry money with a sense of reckless devilry that was not without its charm.

It was Carnival time, and the Ball was very full and noisy. The lights and the crowd at first rather abashed our young adventurer, and then, mounting to his brain with a sort of intoxication, put him in possession of more than his own share of manhood. He felt ready to face the devil, and strutted in the ballroom, with the swagger of a cavalier. While he was thus parading, he became aware of Madame Zéphyrine and her Britisher in conference behind a pillar. The cat-like spirit of eavesdropping overcame him at once. He stole nearer and nearer on the couple from behind until he was within earshot.

"That is the man," the Britisher was saying; "there—with the long blond hair—speaking to a girl in green."

Silas identified a very handsome young fellow of small stature, who was plainly the object of this designation.

"It is well," said Madame Zéphyrine. "I shall do my utmost. But, remember, the best of us may fail in such a matter."

"Tut!" returned her companion; "I answer for the result.

Have I not chosen you from thirty? Go; but be wary of the Prince. I cannot think what cursed accident has brought him here to-night. As if there were not a dozen balls in Paris better worth his notice than this riot of students and counter-jumpers! See him where he sits, more like a reigning Emperor at home than a Prince upon his holidays."

Silas was again lucky. He observed a person of rather a full build, strikingly handsome, and a very stately and courteous demeanour, seated at table with another handsome young man, several years his junior, who addressed him with conspicuous deference. The name of Prince struck gratefully on Silas's Republican hearing, and the aspect of the person to whom that name was applied exercised its usual charm upon his mind. He left Madame Zéphyrine and her Englishman to take care of each other, and threading his way through the assembly, approached the table which the Prince and his confidant had honoured with their choice.

"I tell you, Geraldine," the former was saying, "the action is madness. Yourself (I am glad to remember it) chose your brother for this perilous service, and you are bound in duty to have a guard upon his conduct. He has consented to delay so many days in Paris; that was already an imprudence, considering the character of the man he has to deal with; but now, when he is within eight-and-forty hours of his departure, when he is within two or three days of the decisive trial, I ask you, is this a place for him to spend his time? He should be in a gallery at practice; he should be sleeping long hours and taking moderate exercise on foot; he should be on a rigorous diet, without white wines or brandy. Does the dog imagine we are all playing comedy? The thing is deadly earnest, Geraldine."

"I know the lad too well to interfere," replied Colonel Geraldine, "and well enough not to be alarmed. He is more cautious than you fancy, and of an indomitable spirit. If it had been a woman I should not say so much, but I trust the President to him and the two valets without an instant's apprehension."

"I am gratified to hear you say so," replied the Prince, "but my mind is not at rest. These servants are well-trained spies, and already has not this miscreant succeeded three times in eluding their observation and spending several hours on end in private, and most likely dangerous, affairs? An amateur might have lost him by accident, but if Rudolph and Jérome were thrown off the scent, it must have been done on purpose, and by a man who had a cogent reason and exceptional resources."

"I believe the question is now one between my brother and myself," replied Geraldine, with a shade of offence in his tone.

"I permit it to be so, Colonel Geraldine," returned Prince Florizel. "Perhaps, for that very reason, you should be all the more ready to accept my counsels. But enough. That girl in yellow dances well."

And the talk veered into the ordinary topics of a Paris ballroom in the Carnival.

Silas remembered where he was, and that the hour was already near at hand when he ought to be upon the scene of his assignation. The more he reflected the less he liked the prospect, and as at that moment an eddy in the crowd began to draw him in the direction of the door, he suffered it to carry him away without resistance. The eddy stranded him in a corner under the gallery, where his ear was immediately struck with the voice of Madame Zéphyrine. She was speaking in French with the young man of the blond locks who had been pointed out by the strange Britisher not half an hour before.

"I have a character at stake," she said, "or I would put no other condition than my heart recommends. But you have only to say so much to the porter, and he will let you go by without a word."

"But why this talk of debt?" objected her companion.

"Heavens!" said she, "do you think I do not understand my own hotel?"

And she went by, clinging affectionately to her companion's arm.

This put Silas in mind of his billet.

"Ten minutes hence," thought he, "and I may be walking with as beautiful a woman as that, and even better dressed—perhaps a real lady, possibly a woman of title."

And then he remembered the spelling, and was a little downcast.

"But it may have been written by her maid," he imagined.

The clock was only a few minutes from the hour, and this immediate proximity set his heart beating at a curious and rather disagreeable speed. He reflected with relief that he was in no way bound to put in an appearance. Virtue and cowardice were together, and he made once more for the door, but this time of his own accord, and battling against the stream of people which was now moving in a contrary direction. Perhaps this prolonged resistance wearied him, or perhaps he was in that frame of mind when merely to continue in the same determination for a certain number of minutes produces a reaction and a different purpose. Certainly, at least, he wheeled about for a third time, and did not stop until he had found a place of concealment within a few yards of the appointed place.

Here he went through an agony of spirit, in which he several times prayed to God for help, for Silas had been devoutly educated. He had now not the least inclination for the meeting; nothing kept him from flight but a silly fear lest he should be thought unmanly; but this was so powerful that it kept head against all other motives; and although it could not decide him to advance, prevented him from definitely running away. At last the clock indicated ten minutes past the hour. Young Scuddamore's spirit began to rise; he peered round the corner and saw no one at the place of meeting; doubtless his unknown correspondent had wearied and gone away. He became as bold as he had been formerly timid. It seemed to him that if he came at all to the appointment, however late, he was clear from the charge of cowardice. Nay, now he began to suspect a hoax, and actually complimented himself on his shrewdness in having suspected and out-manœuvred his mystifiers. So very idle a thing is a boy's mind!

Armed with these reflections, he advanced boldly from his corner; but he had not taken above a couple of steps before a hand was laid upon his arm. He turned and beheld a lady cast in a very large mould and with somewhat stately features, but bearing no mark of severity in her looks.

"I see that you are a very self-confident lady-killer," said she; "for you make yourself expected. But I was determined to meet you. When a woman has once so far forgotten herself as to make the first advance, she has long ago left behind her all considerations of petty pride."

Silas was overwhelmed by the size and attractions of his correspondent and the suddenness with which she had fallen upon him. But she soon set him at his ease. She was very towardly and lenient in her behaviour; she led him on to make pleasantries, and then applauded him to the echo; and in a very short time, between blandishments and a liberal exhibition of warm brandy, she had not only induced him to fancy himself in love, but to declare his passion with the greatest vehemence.

"Alas!" she said; "I do not know whether I ought not to deplore this moment, great as is the pleasure you give me by your words. Hitherto I was alone to suffer; now, poor boy, there will be two. I am not my own mistress. I dare not ask you to visit me at my own house, for I am watched by jealous eyes. Let me see," she added; "I am older than you, although so much weaker; and while I trust in your courage and determination, I must employ my own knowledge of the world for our mutual benefit. Where do you live? "

He told her that he lodged in a furnished hotel, and named the street and number.

She seemed to reflect for some minutes, with an effort of mind.

" I see," she said at last. " You will be faithful and obedient, will you not? "

Silas assured her eagerly of his fidelity.

" To-morrow night, then," she continued, with an encouraging smile, " you must remain at home all the evening; and if any friends should visit you, dismiss them at once on any pretext that most readily presents itself. Your door is probably shut by ten? " she asked.

" By eleven," answered Silas.

" At a quarter-past eleven," pursued the lady, " leave the house. Merely cry for the door to be opened, and be sure you fall into no talk with the porter, as that might ruin everything. Go straight to the corner where the Luxembourg Gardens join the Boulevard; there you will find me waiting you. I trust you to follow my advice from point to point: and remember, if you fail me in only one particular, you will bring the sharpest trouble on a woman whose only fault is to have seen and loved you."

" I cannot see the use of all these instructions," said Silas.

" I believe you are already beginning to treat me as a master," she cried, tapping him with her fan upon the arm. " Patience, patience! that should come in time. A woman loves to be obeyed at first, although afterwards she finds her pleasure in obeying. Do as I ask you, for Heaven's sake, or I will answer for nothing. Indeed, now I think of it," she added, with the manner of one who has just seen further into a difficulty, " I find a better plan of keeping importunate visitors away. Tell the porter to admit no one for you, except a person who may come that night to claim a debt; and speak with some feeling, as though you feared the interview, so that he may take your words in earnest."

" I think you may trust me to protect myself against intruders," he said, not without a little pique.

" That is how I should prefer the thing arranged," she answered coldly. " I know you men; you think nothing of a woman's reputation."

Silas blushed and somewhat hung his head; for the scheme he had in view had involved a little vain-glorying before his acquaintances.

"Above all," she added, "do not speak to the porter as you come out."

"And why?" said he. "Of all your instructions, that seems to me the least important."

"You at first doubted the wisdom of some of the others, which you now see to be very necessary," she replied. "Believe me, this also has its uses; in time you will see them; and what am I to think of your affection, if you refuse me such trifles at our first interview?"

Silas confounded himself in explanations and apologies; in the middle of these she looked up at the clock and clapped her hands together with a suppressed scream.

"Heavens!" she cried, "is it so late? I have not an instant to lose. Alas, we poor women, what slaves we are! What have I not risked for you already?"

And after repeating her directions, which she artfully combined with caresses and the most abandoned looks, she bade him farewell and disappeared among the crowd.

The whole of the next day Silas was filled with a sense of great importance; he was now sure she was a countess; and when evening came he minutely obeyed her orders and was at the corner of the Luxembourg Gardens by the hour appointed. No one was there. He waited nearly half an hour, looking in the face of every one who passed or loitered near the spot, he even visited the neighbouring corners of the Boulevard and made a complete circuit of the garden railings; but there was no beautiful countess to throw herself into his arms. At last, and most reluctantly, he bagan to retrace his steps towards his hotel. On the way he remembered the words he had heard pass between Madame Zéphyrine and the blond young man, and they gave him an indefinite uneasiness.

"It appears," he reflected, "that every one has to tell lies to our porter."

He rang the bell, the door opened before him, and the porter in his bed-clothes came to offer him a light.

"Has he gone?" inquired the porter.

"He? Whom do you mean?" asked Silas, somewhat sharply, for he was irritated by his disappointment.

"I did not notice him go out," continued the porter, "but I trust you paid him. We do not care, in this house, to have lodgers who cannot meet their liabilities."

"What the devil do you mean?" demanded Silas rudely. "I cannot understand a word of this farrago."

"The short, blond young man who came for his debt," returned the other. "Him it is I mean. Who else should it be, when I heard your orders to admit no one else?"

"Why, good God, of course he never came," retorted Silas.

"I believe what I believe," returned the porter, putting his tongue into his cheek with a most roguish air.

"You are an insolent scoundrel," cried Silas, and, feeling that he had made a ridiculous exhibition of asperity, and at the same time bewildered by a dozen alarms, he turned and began to run upstairs.

"Do you not want a light then?" cried the porter.

But Silas only hurried the faster, and did not pause until he had reached the seventh landing and stood in front of his own door. There he waited a moment to recover his breath, assailed by the worst forebodings and almost dreading to enter the room.

When at last he did so he was relieved to find it dark and, to all appearance, untenanted. He drew a long breath. Here he was, home again in safety, and this should be his last folly as certainly as it had been his first. The matches stood on a little table by the bed, and he began to grope his way in that direction. As he moved, his apprehensions grew upon him once more, and he was pleased, when his foot encountered an obstacle, to find it nothing more alarming than a chair. At last he touched curtains. From the position of the window, which was faintly visible, he knew he must be at the foot of the bed, and had only to feel his way along it in order to reach the table in question.

He lowered his hand, but what it touched was not simply a counterpane—it was a counterpane with something underneath it like the outline of a human leg. Silas withdrew his arm and stood a moment petrified.

"What, what," he thought, "can this betoken?"

He listened intently, but there was no sound of breathing. Once more, with a great effort, he reached out the end of his finger to the spot he had already touched; but this time he leaped back half a yard, and stood shivering and fixed with terror. There was something in his bed. What it was he knew not, but there was something there.

It was some seconds before he could move. Then, guided by an instinct, he fell straight upon the matches, and keeping his back towards the bed lighted a candle. As soon as the flame had kindled, he turned slowly round and looked for what he feared to see. Sure enough, there was the worst of his imaginations realised. The coverlid was drawn carefully up over the pillow, but it moulded the outline of a human body lying motionless; and when he dashed forward and flung aside the sheets, he beheld the blond young man whom he had seen in the Bullier Ball the night before, his eyes open and without speculation, his face swollen and blackened, and a thin stream of blood trickling from his nostrils.

Silas uttered a long, tremulous wail, dropped the candle, and fell on his knees beside the bed.

Silas was awakened from the stupor into which his terrible discovery had plunged him by a prolonged but discreet tapping at the door. It took him some seconds to remember his position; and when he hastened to prevent any one from entering it was already too late. Dr. Noel, in a tall nightcap, carrying a lamp which lighted up his long white countenance, sidling in his gait, and peering and cocking his head like some sort of bird, pushed the door slowly open, and advanced into the middle of the room.

"I thought I heard a cry," began the Doctor, "and fearing you might be unwell I did not hesitate to offer this intrusion."

Silas, with a flushed face and a fearful beating heart, kept between the Doctor and the bed; but he found no voice to answer.

"You are in the dark," pursued the Doctor; "and yet you have not even begun to prepare for rest. You will not easily persuade me against my own eyesight; and your face declares most eloquently that you require either a friend or a physician—which is it to be? Let me feel your pulse, for that is often a just reporter of the heart."

He advanced to Silas, who still retreated before him backwards, and sought to take him by the wrist; but the strain on the young American's nerves had become too great for endurance. He avoided the Doctor with a febrile movement, and, throwing himself upon the floor, burst into a flood of weeping.

As soon as Dr. Noel perceived the dead man in the bed his face darkened; and hurrying back to the door, which he had left ajar, he hastily closed and double-locked it.

"Up!" he cried, addressing Silas in strident tones; "this is no time for weeping. What have you done? How came this body in your room? Speak freely to one who may be helpful. Do you imagine I would ruin you? Do you think this piece of dead flesh on your pillow can alter in any degree the sympathy with which you have inspired me? Credulous youth, the horror with which blind and unjust law regards an action never attaches to the doer in the eyes of those who love him; and if I saw the friend of my heart return to me out of seas of blood he would be in no way changed in my affection. Raise yourself," he said; "good and ill are a chimera; there is naught in life except destiny, and however you may be circumstanced there is one at your side who will help you to the last."

Thus encouraged, Silas gathered himself together, and in a broken voice, and helped out by the Doctor's interrogations, contrived at last to put him in possession of the facts. But the conversation between the Prince and Geraldine he altogether omitted, as he had understood little of its purport, and had no idea that it was in any way related to his own misadventure.

"Alas!" cried Dr. Noel, "I am much abused, or you have fallen innocently into the most dangerous hands in Europe. Poor boy, what a pit has been dug for your simplicity! into what a deadly peril have your unwary feet been conducted! This man," he said, "this Englishman, whom you twice saw, and whom I suspect to be the soul of the contrivance, can you describe him? Was he young or old? tall or short?"

But Silas, who, for all his curiosity, had not a seeing eye in his head, was able to supply nothing but meagre generalities, which it was impossible to recognise.

"I would have it a piece of education in all schools!" cried the Doctor angrily. "Where is the use of eyesight and articulate speech if a man cannot observe and recollect the features of his enemy? I, who know all the gangs of Europe, might have identified him, and gained new weapons for your defence. Cultivate this art in future, my poor boy; you may find it of momentous service."

"The future!" repeated Silas. "What future is there left for me except the gallows?"

"Youth is but a cowardly season," returned the Doctor; "and a man's own troubles look blacker than they are. I am old, and yet I never despair."

"Can I tell such a story to the police?" demanded Silas.

"Assuredly not," replied the Doctor. "From what I see already of the machination in which you have been involved, your case is desperate upon that side; and for the narrow eye of the authorities you are infallibly the guilty person. And remember that we only know a portion of the plot; and the same infamous contrivers have doubtless arranged many other circumstances which would be elicited by a police inquiry, and help to fix the guilt more certainly upon your innocence."

"I am then lost, indeed!" cried Silas.

"I have not said so," answered Dr. Noel, "for I am a cautious man."

"But look at this!" objected Silas, pointing to the body.

"Here is this object in my bed; not to be explained, not to be disposed of, not to be regarded without horror."

"Horror!" replied the Doctor. "No. When this sort of clock has run down, it is no more to me than an ingenious piece of mechanism, to be investigated with the bistoury. When blood is once cold and stagnant, it is no longer human blood; when flesh is once dead, it is no longer that flesh which we desire in our lovers and respect in our friends. The grace, the attraction, the terror, have all gone from it with the animating spirit. Accustom yourself to look upon it with composure; for if my scheme is practicable you will have to live some days in constant proximity to that which now so greatly horrifies you."

"Your scheme?" cried Silas. "What is that? Tell me speedily, Doctor; for I have scarcely courage enough to continue to exist."

Without replying, Dr. Noel turned towards the bed, and proceeded to examine the corpse.

"Quite dead," he murmured. "Yes, as I had supposed, the pockets empty. Yes, and the name cut off the shirt. Their work has been done thoroughly and well. Fortunately, he is of small stature."

Silas followed these words with an extreme anxiety. At last the Doctor, his autopsy completed, took a chair and addressed the young American with a smile.

"Since I came into your room," said he, "although my ears and my tongue have been so busy, I have not suffered my eyes to remain idle. I noted a little while ago that you have there, in the corner, one of those monstrous constructions which your fellow-countrymen carry with them into all quarters of the globe—in a word, a Saratoga trunk. Until this moment I have never been able to conceive the utility of these erections; but then I began to have a glimmer. Whether it was for convenience in the slave trade, or to obviate the results of too ready an employment of the bowie-knife, I cannot bring myself to decide. But one thing I see plainly—the object of such a box is to contain a human body."

"Surely," cried Silas, "surely this is not a time for jesting."

"Although I may express myself with some degree of pleasantry," replied the Doctor, "the purport of my words is entirely serious. And the first thing we have to do, my young friend, is to empty your coffer of all that it contains."

Silas, obeying the authority of Dr. Noel, put himself at his disposition. The Saratoga trunk was soon gutted of its contents, which made a considerable litter on the floor; and then—Silas taking the heels and the Doctor supporting the shoulders—the body of the murdered man was carried from the bed, and, after some difficulty, doubled up and inserted whole into the empty box. With an effort on the part of both, the lid was forced down upon this unusual baggage, and the trunk was locked and corded by the Doctor's own hand, while Silas disposed of what had been taken out between the closet and a chest of drawers.

"Now," said the Doctor, "the first step has been taken on the way to your deliverance. To-morrow, or rather to-day, it must be your task to allay the suspicions of your porter, paying him all that you owe; while you may trust me to make the arrangements necessary to a safe conclusion. Meantime, follow me to my room, where I shall give you a safe and powerful opiate; for, whatever you do, you must have rest."

The next day was the longest in Silas's memory; it seemed as if it would never be done. He denied himself to his friends, and sat in a corner with his eyes fixed upon the Saratoga trunk in dismal contemplation. His own former indiscretions were now returned upon him in kind; for the observatory had been once more opened, and he was conscious of an almost continual study from Madame Zéphyrine's apartment. So distressing did this become, that he was at last obliged to block up the spy-hole from his own side; and when he was thus secured from observation he spent a considerable portion of his time in contrite tears and prayer.

Late in the evening Dr. Noel entered the room carrying in his hand a pair of sealed envelopes without address, one somewhat bulky, and the other so slim as to seem without enclosure.

"Silas," he said, seating himself at the table, "the time has now come for me to explain my plan for your salvation. To-morrow morning, at an early hour, Prince Florizel of Bohemia returns to London, after having diverted himself for a few days with the Parisian Carnival. It was my fortune, a good while ago, to do Colonel Geraldine, his Master of the Horse, one of those services, so common in my profession, which are never forgotten upon either side. I have no need to explain to you the nature of the obligation under which he was laid; suffice it to say that I knew him ready to serve me in any practicable manner. Now, it was necessary for you to gain London with your trunk unopened. To this the Custom House seemed to oppose a fatal difficulty; but I bethought me that the baggage of so considerable a personal as the Prince, is, as a matter of courtesy, passed without examination by the officers of Custom. I applied to Colonel Geraldine, and succeeded in obtaining a favourable answer.

To-morrow, if you go before six to the hotel where the Prince lodges, your baggage will be passed over as a part of his, and you yourself will make the journey as a member of his suite."

"It seems to me, as you speak, that I have already seen both the Prince and Colonel Geraldine; I even overheard some of their conversation the other evening at the Bullier Ball."

"It is probable enough; for the Prince loves to mix with all societies," replied the Doctor. "Once arrived in London," he pursued, "your task is nearly ended. In this more bulky envelope I have given you a letter which I dare not address; but in the other you will find the designation of the house to which you must carry it along with your box, which will there be taken from you and not trouble you any more."

"Alas!" said Silas, "I have every wish to believe you; but how is it possible? You open up to me a bright prospect, but, I ask you, is my mind capable of receiving so unlikely a solution? Be more generous, and let me further understand your meaning."

The Doctor seemed painfully impressed.

"Boy," he answered, "you do not know how hard a thing you ask of me. But be it so. I am now inured to humiliation; and it would be strange if I refused you this, after having granted you so much. Know then, that although I now make so quiet an appearance—frugal, solitary, addicted to study—when I was younger my name was once a rallying-cry among the most astute and dangerous spirits of London; and while I was outwardly an object for respect and consideration, my true power resided in the most secret, terrible, and criminal relations. It is to one of the persons who then obeyed me that I now address myself to deliver you from your burden. They were men of many different nations and dexterities, all bound together by a formidable oath, and working to the same purpose; the trade of the association was in murder; and I who speak to you, innocent as I appear, was the chieftain of this redoubtable crew."

"What?" cried Silas. "A murderer? And one with whom murder was a trade? Can I take your hand? Ought I so much as to accept your services? Dark and criminal old man, would you make an accomplice of my youth and my distress?"

The Doctor bitterly laughed.

"You are difficult to please, Mr. Scuddamore," said he; "but I now offer you your choice of company between the murdered man and the murderer. If your conscience is too nice to accept my aid, say so, and I will immediately leave you. Thenceforward you can deal with your trunk and its belongings as best suits your upright conscience."

"I own myself wrong," replied Silas. "I should have remembered how generously you offered to shield me, even before I had convinced you of my innocence, and I continue to listen to your counsels with gratitude."

"That is well," returned the Doctor; "and I perceive you are beginning to learn some of the lessons of experience."

"At the same time," resumed the New Englander, "as you confess yourself accustomed to this tragical business, and the people to whom you recommend me are your own former associates and friends, could you not yourself undertake the transport of the box, and rid me at once of its detested presence?"

"Upon my word," replied the Doctor, "I admire you cordially. If you do not think I have already meddled sufficiently in your concerns, believe me, from my heart I think the contrary. Take or leave my services as I offer them; and trouble me with no more words of gratitude, for I value your consideration even more lightly than I do your intellect. A time will come, if you should be spared to see a number of years in health of mind, when you will think differently of all this, and blush for your to-night's behaviour."

So saying, the Doctor arose from his chair, repeated his directions briefly and clearly, and departed from the room without permitting Silas any time to answer.

The next morning Silas presented himself at the hotel, where he was politely received by Colonel Geraldine, and relieved, from that moment, of all immediate alarm about his trunk and its grisly contents. The journey passed over without much incident, although the young man was horrified to overhear the sailors and railway porters complaining among themselves about the unusual weight of the Prince's baggage. Silas travelled in a carriage with the valets, for Prince Florizel chose to be alone with his Master of the Horse. On board the steamer, however, Silas attracted his Highness's attention by the melancholy of his air and attitude as he stood gazing at the pile of baggage; for he was still full of disquietude about the future.

"There is a young man," observed the Prince, "who must have some cause for sorrow."

"That," replied Geraldine, "is the American for whom I obtained permission to travel with your suite."

"You remind me that I have been remiss in courtesy," said Prince Florizel, and advancing to Silas, he addressed him with the most exquisite condescension in these words:

"I was charmed, young sir, to be able to gratify the desire you made known to me through Colonel Geraldine. Remember, if you please, that I shall be glad at any future time to lay you under a more serious obligation."

And he then put some questions as to the political condition of America, which Silas answered with sense and propriety.

"You are still a young man," said the Prince; "but I observe you to be very serious for your years. Perhaps you allow your attention to be too much occupied with grave studies. But perhaps, on the other hand, I am myself indiscreet and touch upon a painful subject."

"I have certainly cause to be the most miserable of men," said Silas; "never has a more innocent person been more dismally abused."

"I will not ask you for your confidence," returned Prince Florizel. "But do not forget that Colonel Geraldine's recommendation is an unfailing passport; and that I am not only willing, but possibly more able than many others, to do you a service."

Silas was delighted with the amiability of this great personage; but his mind soon returned upon its gloomy preoccupations; for not even the favour of a Prince to a Republican can discharge a brooding spirit of its cares.

The train arrived at Charing Cross, where the officers of the Revenue respected the baggage of Prince Florizel in the usual manner. The most elegant equipages were in waiting; and Silas was driven, along with the rest, to the Prince's residence. There Colonel Geraldine sought him out, and expressed himself pleased to have been of any service to a friend of the physician's, for whom he professed a great consideration.

"I hope," he added, "that you will find none of your porcelain injured. Special orders were given along the line to deal tenderly with the Prince's effects."

And then, directing the servants to place one of the carriages at the young gentleman's disposal, and at once to charge the Saratoga trunk upon the dickey, the Colonel shook hands and excused himself on account of his occupations in the princely household.

Silas now broke the seal of the envelope containing the address, and directed the stately footman to drive him to Box Court, opening off the Strand. It seemed as if the place were not at all unknown to the man, for he looked startled and begged a repetition of the order. It was with a heart full of alarms, that Silas mounted into the luxurious vehicle, and was driven to his destination. The entrance to Box

Court was too narrow for the passage of a coach; it was a mere footway between railings, with a post at either end. On one of these posts was seated a man, who at once jumped down and exchanged a friendly sign with the driver, while the footman opened the door and inquired of Silas whether he should take down the Saratoga trunk, and to what number it should be carried.

"If you please," said Silas. "To number three."

The footman and the man who had been sitting on the post, even with the aid of Silas himself, had hard work to carry in the trunk; and before it was deposited at the door of the house in question, the young American was horrified to find a score of loiterers looking on. But he knocked with as good a countenance as he could muster up, and presented the other envelope to him who opened.

"He is not at home," said he, "but if you will leave your letter and return to-morrow early, I shall be able to inform you whether and when he can receive your visit. Would you like to leave your box?" he added.

"Dearly," cried Silas; and the next moment he repented his precipitation, and declared, with equal emphasis, that he would rather carry the box along with him to the hotel.

The crowd jeered at his indecision and followed him to the carriage with insulting remarks; and Silas, covered with shame and terror, implored the servants to conduct him to some quiet and comfortable house of entertainment in the immediate neighbourhood.

The Prince's equipage deposited Silas at the Craven Hotel in Craven Street, and immediately drove away, leaving him alone with the servants of the inn. The only vacant room, it appeared, was a little den up four pairs of stairs, and looking towards the back. To this hermitage, with infinite trouble and complaint, a pair of stout porters carried the Saratoga trunk. It is needless to mention that Silas kept closely at their heels throughout the ascent, and had his heart in his mouth at every corner. A single false step, he reflected, and the box might go over the banisters and land its fatal contents, plainly discovered, on the pavement of the hall.

Arrived in the room, he sat down on the edge of his bed to recover from the agony that he had just endured; but he had hardly taken his position when he was recalled to a sense of his peril by the action of the boots, who had knelt beside the trunk, and was proceeding officiously to undo its elaborate fastenings.

"Let it be!" cried Silas. "I shall want nothing from it while I stay here."

"You might have let it lie in the hall, then," growled the man; "a thing as big and heavy as a church. What you have inside I cannot fancy. If it is all money, you are a richer man than me."

"Money?" repeated Silas, in a sudden perturbation. "What do you mean by money? I have no money, and you are speaking like a fool."

"All right, captain," retorted the boots with a wink. "There's nobody will touch your lordship's money. I'm as safe as the bank," he added; "but as the box is heavy, I shouldn't mind drinking something to your lordship's health."

Silas pressed two Napoleons upon his acceptance, apologising, at the same time, for being obliged to trouble him with foreign money, and pleading his recent arrival for excuse. And the man, grumbling with even greater fervour and looking contemptuously from the money in his hand to the Saratoga trunk and back again from the one to the other, at last consented to withdraw.

For nearly two days the dead body had been packed into Silas's box; and as soon as he was alone the unfortunate New Englander nosed all the cracks and openings with the most passionate attention. But the weather was cool, and the trunk still managed to contain his shocking secret.

He took a chair beside it, and buried his face in his hands, and his mind in the most profound reflection. If he were not speedily relieved, no question but he must be speedily discovered. Alone in a strange city, without friends or accomplices, if the Doctor's introduction failed him, he was indubitably a lost New Englander. He reflected pathetically over his ambitious designs for the future; he should not now become the hero and spokesman of his native place of Bangor, Maine; he should not, as he had fondly anticipated, move on from office to office, from honour to honour; he might as well divest himself at once of all hope of being acclaimed President of the United States, and leaving behind him a statue, in the worst possible style of art, to adorn the Capitol at Washington. Here he was, chained to a dead Englishman doubled up inside a Saratoga trunk; whom he must get rid of, or perish from the rolls of national glory!

I should be afraid to chronicle the language employed by this young man to the Doctor, to the murdered man, to Madame Zéphyrine, to the boots of the hotel, to the Prince's servants, and, in a word, to all who had been ever so remotely connected with his horrible misfortune.

He slunk down to dinner about seven at night; but the yellow coffee-room appalled him, the eyes of the other diners seemed to rest on his with suspicion, and his mind remained upstairs with the Saratoga trunk. When the waiter came to offer him cheese, his nerves were already so much on edge that he leaped half-way out of his chair and upset the remainder of a pint of ale upon the table-cloth.

The fellow offered to show him to the smoking-room when he had done, and although he would have much preferred to return at once to his perilous treasure, he had not the courage to refuse, and was shown downstairs to the black, gas-lit cellar, which formed, and possibly still forms, the divan of the Craven Hotel.

Two very sad betting men were playing billiards, attended by a moist, consumptive marker; and for the moment Silas imagined that these were the only occupants of the apartment. But at the next glance his eye fell upon a person smoking in the farthest corner, with lowered eyes and a most respectable and modest aspect. He knew at once that he had seen the face before; and, in spite of the entire change of clothes, recognised the man whom he had found seated on a post at the entrance to Box Court, and who had helped him to carry the trunk to and from the carriage. The New Englander simply turned and ran, nor did he pause until he had locked and bolted himself into his bedroom.

There, all night long, a prey to the most terrible imaginations, he watched beside the fatal boxful of dead flesh. The suggestion of the boots that his trunk was full of gold inspired him with all manner of new terrors, if he so much as dared to close an eye; and the presence in the smoking-room, and under an obvious disguise, of the loiterer from Box Court convinced him that he was once more the centre of obscure machinations.

Midnight had sounded some time, when, impelled by uneasy suspicions, Silas opened his bedroom door and peered into the passage. It was dimly illuminated by a single jet of gas; and some distance off he perceived a man sleeping on the floor in the costume of an hotel under-servant. Silas drew near the man on tiptoe. He lay partly on his back, partly on his side, and his right forearm concealed his face from recognition. Suddenly, while the American was still bending over him, the sleeper removed his arm and opened his eyes, and Silas found himself once more face to face with the loiterer of Box Court.

"Good night, sir," said the man pleasantly.

But Silas was too profoundy moved to find an answer, and regained his room in silence.

Towards morning, worn out by apprehension, he fell asleep on his chair, with his head forward on the trunk. In spite of so constrained an attitude and such a grisly pillow, his slumber was sound and prolonged, and he was only awakened at a late hour by a sharp tapping at the door.

He hurried to open, and found the boots without.

"You are the gentleman who called yesterday at Box Court?" he asked.

Silas, with a quiver, admitted that he had done so.

"Then this note is for you," added the servant, proffering a sealed envelope.

Silas tore it open, and found inside the words: "Twelve o'clock."

He was punctual to the hour; the trunk was carried before him by several stout servants; and he was himself ushered into a room, where a man sat warming himself before the fire with his back towards the door. The sound of so many persons entering and leaving, and the scraping of the trunk as it was deposited upon the bare boards, were alike unable to attract the notice of the occupant; and Silas stood waiting, in an agony of fear, until he should deign to recognise his presence.

Perhaps five minutes had elapsed before the man turned leisurely about, and disclosed the features of Prince Florizel of Bohemia.

"So, sir," he said, with great severity, "this is the manner in which you abuse my politeness. You join yourself to persons of condition, I perceive, for no other purpose than to escape the consequences of your crimes; and I can readily understand your embarrassment when I addressed myself to you yesterday."

"Indeed," cried Silas, "I am innocent of everything except misfortune."

And in a hurried voice, and with the greatest ingenuousness, he recounted to the Prince the whole history of his calamity.

"I see I have been mistaken" said his Highness, when he had heard him to an end. "You are no other than a victim, and since I am not to punish you may be sure I shall do my utmost to help. And now," he continued, "to business. Open your box at once, and let me see what it contains."

Silas changed colour.

"I almost fear to look upon it," he exclaimed.

"Nay," replied the Prince, "have you not looked at it already? This is a form of sentimentality to be resisted. The sight of a sick man, whom we can still help, should appeal more directly to the feelings than that of a dead man who is equally beyond help or harm, love or hatred. Nerve yourself, Mr. Scuddamore," and then, seeing that Silas still hesitated,

"I do not desire to give another name to my request," he added.

The young American awoke as if out of a dream, and with a shiver of repugnance addressed himself to loose the straps and open the lock of the Saratoga trunk. The Prince stood by, watching with a composed countenance and his hands behind his back. The body was quite stiff, and it cost Silas a great effort, both moral and physical, to dislodge it from its position, and discover the face.

Prince Florizel started back with an exclamation of painful surprise.

"Alas," he cried, "you little know, Mr. Scuddamore, what a cruel gift you have brought me. This is a young man of my own suite, the brother of my trusted friend; and it was upon matters of my own service that he has thus perished at the hands of violent and treacherous men. Poor Geraldine," he went on, as if to himself, "in what words am I to tell you of your brother's fate? How can I excuse myself in your eyes, or in the eyes of God, for the presumptuous schemes that led him to this bloody and unnatural death? Ah, Florizel! Florizel! when will you learn the discretion that suits mortal life, and be no longer dazzled with the image of power at your disposal? Power!" he cried; "who is more powerless? I look upon this young man whom I have sacrificed, Mr. Scuddamore, and feel how small a thing it is to be a Prince."

Silas was moved at the sight of his emotion. He tried to murmur some consolatory words, and burst into tears. The Prince, touched by his obvious intention, came up to him and took him by the hand.

"Command yourself," said he. "We have both much to learn, and we shall both be better men for to-day's meeting."

Silas thanked him in silence with an affectionate look.

"Write me the address of Dr. Noel on this piece of paper," continued the Prince, leading him towards the table; "and let me recommend you, when you are again in Paris, to avoid the society of that dangerous man. He has acted in this matter on a generous inspiration—that I must believe; had he been privy to young Geraldine's death he would never have dispatched the body to the care of the actual criminal."

"The actual criminal!" repeated Silas in astonishment.

"Even so," returned the Prince. "This letter, which the disposition of Almighty Providence has so strangely delivered into my hands, was addressed to no less a person than the criminal himself, the infamous President of the Suicide Club. Seek to pry no further in these perilous affairs, but content yourself with your own miraculous escape, and leave this house at once. I have pressing affairs, and must arrange at once about this poor clay, which was so lately a gallant and handsome youth."

Silas took a grateful and submissive leave of Prince Florizel, but he lingered in Box Court until he saw him depart in a splendid carriage on a visit to Colonel Henderson of the police. Republican as he was, the young American took off his hat with almost a sentiment of devotion to the retreating carriage. And the same night he started by rail on his return to Paris.

Here (observes my Arabian author) *is the end of the* HISTORY OF THE PHYSICIAN AND THE SARATOGA TRUNK. *Omitting some reflections on the power of Providence, highly pertinent in the original, but little suited to our occidental taste, I shall only add that Mr. Scuddamore has already begun to mount the ladder of political fame, and by last advices was the Sheriff of his native town.*

RICHARD HUGHES

MARTHA

I

THERE are not many streets turning off Limehouse Causeway, but there are more of them than you would think; or see, unless you looked carefully. One of these is called Bird Court. It is a queer cobbled alley that crawls on its stomach under a low arch, and finally runs its head against the blank dock-wall. The bead-hung windows of Messrs Ti Fung & Co. look upon this court. Their doors open upon the West India Dock Road, but the Chinese in these parts never have windows opening upon the same street as the door does: for quite good reasons of their own. If the houses are so built, they board up the windows, or frost them over.

Upon one side of the door in the Dock Road there is written, in large white letters, " Ti Fung & Co., English and Chinese Restaurant." On the other side is a sign in Chinese. Once inside, you will see no door upon the ground floor: only steep deal stairs. At the top of these stairs is the long, low room whose windows look on Bird Court; it is divided up by a few bead curtains and fringes of bits of painted glass. Other doors open off this room, but the signs upon them are all Chinese; and the ostensible business of the restaurant is carried on here at rows and rows of marble-top tables, where parties of young sailors sit eating curry-and-rice and other dishes that are not easy to diagnose. They are surprising, these young Chinamen, with their quiet, well-cut lounge suits and sleek black hair. You will hardly see better-dressed men in Piccadilly.

Lottie was a waitress at Messrs. Ti Fung; for all the waitresses there are English. She was a tall, blonde creature, with peroxided and scented hair, and covered in powder from head to foot. As she came down the gangway between the tables the Chinamen would one and all reach out and claw at her dress, trying to hold her back. Sometimes she would slap their hands; sometimes she stopped to laugh and talk, sitting generally on the table, while the Chinks would hold the ends of her apron-strings, stroking them or pressing them to their cheeks; and some would stroke the line of her arm with an approving finger. Lottie was a favourite among the Chinese, but the few Europeans who came here for their meals would never look at her. Wonderful creature! She had "waited" at Ti Fung's now for ten years, and had never once lost her temper. It was not her business to lose her temper.

Presently she went out for an order for Chicken-chestnuts and Tea, and came back with a steaming dish in one hand, and with the other led Martha. Martha solemnly carried a small cracked tray, with the teapot and the little handleless cups. She was a very solemn child, with a thin wisp of dull, black, crinkly hair that was tied in a stiff pig-tail with a twist of striped flannelette. Otherwise she wore black satin, like her mother; a frock very short, and cotton-topped silk stockings full of holes and ladders. They had been meant for a longer skirt than Martha's, for the cotton began well below the knee: and they had been meant for rounder legs. Her face was thin, too, with high cheek-bones, and large mouth, and narrow almond eyes that betrayed her paternity. Her expression was slow and seldom changed, though her movements were quick. Children in the East End do not shrink under a blow: either they fling themselves upon their attackers, biting and scratching like desperate things, or they wriggle like eels; and Martha's home-life had taught her a very great deal.

She had come with her mother to Ti Fung's ever since she could remember: and before that too, when she used to ride in on her mother's shoulder and the Chinamen would beg to be allowed to dandle her in their arms for a minute: and brought her toys, and later would teach her strange little songs to dance to on the table-tops. When she appeared with the tea it was strange to see these Chinks change, to see the inscrutable, dreamy look that Lottie had banished come back into their eyes: they bowed gravely to her, and ordered preserved ginger and lychees for her, and talked to her with all their politeness. And yet no one would have said the poor wizened little thing was an attractive child. She seemed listless, hardly to understand what they were saying. She made no response to their gentleness: even when some reeling Scandinavian blundered by, and they crooked their arms to prevent him brushing against her clothes, she did not seem to notice it. But it was not necessary: enough that she was a child: more, that half her blood was yellow. Her mother, who understood Chinamen, was satisfied. When they gave her flowers, she would smile slowly, and let them try to stick them in her hair: but there was hardly enough to hold the stalks.

But she always began before long to beg for paper; and the yellow men, who understood her whim, used to save old sheets of it for her, folded in their pockets. When her pencil was all worn away, one of them brought her a whole stick of Chinese ink, with a little brush, and showed her how to mix it in a saucer: and she used it up so incredibly fast that she was always begging for more sticks of ink. A great deal of it got on her face, or on the floor, and there were always black splashes on the walls. A number of mothers would have condemned the practice as "messy"; but Lottie was one of those large-minded people who do not object to dirt. Their room would have been filthy anyhow. But Lottie did object, on other grounds: she thought it "queer."

"'Tain't 's if," she used to confide to her cronies,—"'tain't 's if the kid could draw for nuts: she can't. Carlo's Lotta, now——"

Carlo's Lotta was certainly an amazing child: at a very early age she had shown a wonderful power for caricature, and by the time she was fourteen she earned enough money to keep Carlo and his wife in a state of drunkenness. She made it by going to all the prize-fights and drawing crude sketches for the sporting papers. But Martha couldn't do this: she very seldom drew people, and when she did there was never a shadow of likeness in her drawings: mainly she would pile up odd bundles of rubbish on a table, and draw them: beer-bottles, onions, and such-like: or she would draw things from unexpected angles, or make up things out of her head. As Lottie said, it was "queer."

But Lottie soon gave in, for she decided that Martha was altogether a bit "queer": there was, therefore, nothing to be done, provided that the child did not become expensive, but to teach her to shop and fetch the beer, and rub plates round with newspaper. That, to Lottie, comprised the art of house-keeping: otherwise, if the child kept the Chinks amused, why, it did her no harm, and was good for business.

So presently Martha began as usual to beg for paper, and young Shan Ting delightedly pulled out a whole wad that he had kept for her: some of it back-sheets of letters, paper bags—anything he could get. Martha smiled impersonally at the sight of it, without any attempt at thanks; but Shan Ting was able to produce a pencil too, so Martha soon squatted down with the pieces on the floor and began to cover them over with her strange scrawls. The curious thing about her was that she hoarded her paper like gold until it was used; but in her drawings, once done, she took no interest whatever. Generally she left them, crumpled, wherever she happened to have done with them. But Shan Ting and his friends crowded round her, for there was an Eastern quality in her notions of design that appealed to them rather than to Lottie; and yet her conventions were not in any strict sense Chinese, because her design was not entirely in the flat, but advanced and receded in a way they could not understand.

Lottie flitted on to other tables, leaving Martha to entertain the group: which she presently did in her quiet way, saying little and smiling little. She was one of those difficult people who seem entirely oblivious whether they are caressed or beaten, but treat all folk alike with a complete detachedness.

It was not usual for Europeans to take any interest in her: but presently one rose from the table where he was sitting over Ti Fung's wonderful tea and sponge-cakes, and joined the group. Wal Henderson was a tall fellow, youngish, and shabbily dressed, like all the Europeans of the quarter, wearing a tight " choker " round his unshaven throat. He had the sullen look of most East-enders, beaten yet provocative: it would not have been easy to recognise the Art Student of a few years back, so completely had he gone under. He elbowed the Chinks aside like a true Britisher, stood scowling down at Martha: but she drew on wholly absorbed, entirely oblivious that anything out of the ordinary was happening. Presently he picked up one of the discarded drawings, looked at it almost with a sort of rage and thrust it into the pocket of his coat. Then he sat down again and lit a cigarette. Lottie came back and bore Martha away, and the group broke up.

II

Lottie usually lay abed till late in the morning, fed by Martha on tea and kippers. She was surprised, therefore, to hear a bang at her door at about ten o'clock.

" 'Oo's that? " she screamed.

Something was answered in a bass voice.

" Well, yer can't come in," she called again, and added in an undertone: " Go and see what the blighter wants, Martha, there's a dearie."

So Martha slipped out of the door, and found herself face to face with a sullen-looking man. Inquisitive young heads were peering at them from the stairs below.

" Wodjer wornt? " she drawled, one hand on the door-knob for quick retreat.

" Want your ma," the man growled out.

Martha half opened the door to shout this information through.

Lottie, recognising the inevitable, poked out a head bristling with curling-pins.

It did not take Wal Henderson long to explain what he wanted: an ordinary enough request—someone to do for him. He lived in the next block of tenements, and thought Lottie might have time to come round and " swep up " before going to Ti Fung's.

Lottie thought otherwise. She was too fond of her bed. But she stopped to gossip.

" 'Ow's Liz? " she asked.

Wal shook his head slowly. " Gorn," he said. " Las' monf."

" Well, I never," commented Lottie.

Wal threw his head back, sucking noisily, like one with a bottle. " In the 'Firmary."

" Well, I never," repeated Lottie; " it did 'er quick."

" Merciful quick. But she was at it a long time afore *I* knew."

Lottie wiped away a sentimental tear.

" A nice girl, your Liz: pity she drank."

Wal felt something choking in his throat, and exclaimed fiercely: " I'm bloomin' well aht of it.—But I ain't got no one to do for me now: that's why I looked you up. Well, so long, miss."

Lottie stopped him with a gesture.

" 'Ere," she said, " 'alf a mo'. What about the kid? "

" Martha? " said Wal, looking up at her suddenly, but hiding his cunning.

" Yes."

" She ain't got no sense," said Wal.

" She's more sense nor you think! " cried Lottie hotly. " She'd do you all right."

Wal appeared to ruminate.

" She might," he admitted presently.

And so it was fixed up that Martha should do for Wal Henderson for eighteen-pence a week.

Wal did not smile to himself as he went back to his room, because he had long given up the habit of smiling. But he felt a certain satisfaction.

Presently he went to the chest of drawers that stood in the corner on one leg, like a naughty child, leaning against the wall. With a knife he opened the handleless top drawer and fished out various bits of paper, pieces of charcoal, and pencils: he walked thoughtfully about the room putting them here and there: stood back to watch the effect, and then went out.

When Martha arrived in the morning she knew pretty well

what to do. Wal was still asleep, breathing stertorously, his lower lip drooping. Martha hunted around for the tin teapot, found it half full of stale tea, so put it on the gas-ring to heat up. There were some kippers wrapped up in newspaper; but she could not cook them till the tea was hot: and she did the tea first because she could see Henderson had been drinking the night before.

Meanwhile there was nothing to do. Martha looked round and saw paper and pencil within reach. Almost without thinking she began to draw: a vague sea of melancholy Chinese faces, a memory of Ti Fung's. Starting from the front, she drew them, one by one, growing smaller and more expressionless in the distance. If you had asked her why they were melancholy, she could not have told you. It did not matter to her, once they were drawn, whether they had laughed or cried. Wal's snoring had suddenly ceased: but she was too absorbed to notice it. Presently she began to frame the faces round with a heavy black line.

"'Ere!" Wal shouted out. "Drop that and get on with it!"

Martha jumped towards the ring: the tea had been boiling some time. A cup of it strangely seemed to improve Wal's temper—or perhaps it was the smell of the frying kippers. But while he was drinking it she managed to finish the framing-line unnoticed.

Wal had a damp cloth for "washing up" instead of using newspaper: so Martha rubbed the cup and kipper-plate both with it, and left hurriedly to clean up her mother's breakfast. When she was gone, Wal carefully drew his legs out of bed, and ran a judicious thumb down his shins. They were rather badly bruised. Presently he lit his pipe, and then pulled on his trousers: tied his "choker," tightened the canvas belt round his waist, and put on his waistcoat. Before putting on his boots he looked long and carefully at the drawing, and presently hid it away in a chest under his bed.

So things went on for several weeks, and the pile of drawings in the chest under the bed grew. Once, when Martha had gone, Wal took paper and pencil and made a series of neat little sketches. Every now and then he stopped to admire his work, and then went on. When they were finished, he got out Martha's latest drawing, a straggling and unfinished design of house-tops, and set it beside them, scowling more and more at the comparison. The first thing he did was to scribble all across his own work; and the next was to feel a sort of jealousy, an absurd wish for revenge; and to take out the little pile from the chest. He screwed the top one into a ball and flung it into the corner. But he repented and went after it. He flattened it out carefully, then damped it and went over the back with a hot iron, and put it back safely in the pile.

Next day when Martha came she found him already up, and his breakfast eaten. Instead of setting her to clean up, he told her to sit on the edge of the bed, and made a rapid and very flattering drawing of her profile on canvas. (This canvas had been an old landscape of his; but he had scraped it and covered it over days ago with ground-white, ready for this.) Before beginning to use any colour he called Martha over to see it, and asked her if she liked it.

She shook her head.

Wal clenched his fists, but kept his voice in control. "Ain't it pretty enough for you?"

Martha said it wasn't that.

"You just don't like it?"

"That's right," said Martha.

"Why don't you like it?"

"Dunno."

Wal felt she was right, but his jealousy grew quite out of control, and he beat her soundly with a soft leather strap. She rushed to the door, but he was before her: finding retreat cut off, to his surprise she remained quite passive, hardly making a sound while he hit her: his jealous fit vanished, and left him in an abyss of misery.

The rest of the morning he spent teaching her the use of oil-paints. She got herself covered in paint from head to foot, just like any other student. During the afternoon he took out all his stack of pictures from the bottom drawer, and in a sort of sublime melancholy set himself to scraping the canvases and cleaning them and preparing them afresh. This was a very hard thing for Wal to do.

The first hard thing that he had done in his life was coming to live in Poplar: but that was not so hard as he had expected. He came for two reasons. The first was that there was no other place where he could afford to live and devote himself to his art. The second was that Liz was a barmaid when he first met her, and that she would be happier there than among his friends. His love for Liz died slowly, and by the time that it was gone he was absolutely absorbed in the life of the quarter, and neither could nor wished to leave it.

The second hard thing that he had done was after he discovered that Liz had another husband, and that she drank. His love was by this time nearly gone. But he kept her with him and nursed her almost until she died. The daily battle with the disgustingness of life wore away the finer side of his nature, hardened the vulgar side that had first admired Liz. Presently he realised that it was impossible for him ever to be the artist he had dreamed of being, and that it was impossible for him to leave the life he was living.

These were two hard things for Wal Henderson to swallow: especially as the latter had come about through doing what he thought to be right, and through sticking to Liz.

The third hard thing was when he destroyed his own paintings in order that Martha might paint on the canvases.

Martha knew nothing of this, and used the materials he gave her without thought. She worked all day and worked hard at her painting. In the evening she murmured " S'long " in a conventional way, and slipped out.

" She's all brain and no heart," said Wal to himself. " I've thrashed her till she was sick, and I've given her a chance she has never had in her life before—and she doesn't care for me either way, more than a doorpost."

" S'long ! " she had said: just the same as the first day that she had fried his kippers.

But meanwhile his sullen face danced before her all the way home, and she beat her clenched fists together to stop herself from crying.

Wal began to dream of the day when he should take a few of her drawings to a gallery, and an exhibition should be arranged, and the whole world should go mad about this pearl he had found in the gutter. He saw himself in the rôle of her guardian and protector—and, incidentally, her business manager.

He saw the honours due to a discoverer paid to him. And the memory of Martha's " s'long " interrupted him. She would throw him away like a worn shoe when she had no more need of him, he felt: but his queerly devotional attitude to art rose up to comfort him. The latent passionateness and sensitiveness of his nature were in strange contrast to her impassivity. It was the merely artistic temperament in contrast to the temperament of a real artist, he decided.

He took her canvases and set them carefully by the window to dry.

III

One night Wal came home more drunk than usual. He had met an old friend of the days when he had first begun to draw. They had but the vaguest memory of each other, for Wal had never been to an art school: they had only met occasionally in odd Bohemian attics, where penniless fellows talked wonderfully of the pictures they were going to paint some day: and then had come soon the time when Wal went under, and his friends saw him no more. But the fellow had resisted all Wal's attempts to escape him, and borne him off to a disreputable and so-called Bohemian gathering, where his own appearance was in no way out of place. There they had made Wal very drunk, chiefly on Crême de Menthe: and when he stumbled into his bed the whole world seemed suddenly to reel out of his ken, and he slept like a log. He did not wake till very late: Martha was sitting by him with a cup of tea, watching him. When he woke she put down the tea and mixed him some salts. He drank them, and, because his head was so painful, cursed her: and she hurried away without doing any painting that day. Wal went to sleep again and slept until midday.

At midday he woke a second time, and felt in his pockets for his pipe—for he was fully dressed—wanting badly to smoke. But instead of it his fingers closed on a bit of pasteboard. He drew it out and examined it half-consciously:

"*Edward Macyntire, The Surrey Galleries.*"

Vague memories of the night before elbowed and jostled each other in his mind. Who was Macyntire? He must have been that fair Jew fellow, with the weak moustache. They had been drinking port when the man arrived, but he had asked for beer: and so they had all had a pint to keep him company, and then a gin to settle it before going on to the Crême de Menthe. The others had got noisy during the evening, but Macyntire had sat quiet, and it was not till the party broke up that he had shown how very drunk he was. He had been sitting on a sofa, one arm hung caressingly over the end, apparently talking to himself: when he tried to stand his legs gave way, and he sat in the middle of the floor, laughing weakly. They bore him off; and Wal, who could still stand and had a few wits left, offered to see him home in a cab.

Macyntire had insisted on giving him his card before they parted, someone having mentioned that Wal was an artist.

Now he staggered out of bed and tried to collect his wits; could not, and spent a miserable afternoon loafing along the docks in the cool air. In the evening he came back and varnished some pictures. He took the pasteboard carefully out of his pocket, cleaned it with india-rubber, and set it under a tobacco-box. The next day he felt more capable of dealing with things.

He said nothing to Martha when she came; but after she had wiped the breakfast-things, told her that he was going to take her out of doors to paint. She made no objection, and he found her a quiet corner where she could sketch unmolested, a corner overlooking the Pool. In the foreground was a

Norwegian timber vessel, and the little police-boats were fussing in and out of the shipping. To his surprise, she steadily refused to draw. He was furious. He had found her a subject and taken all the trouble of bringing her there—but no, she would not: and, recognising the truth of the proverb about the horse and the water, he did not even hit her.

Presently she moved a few yards, the obstinate little wretch, and sat down quite contentedly with her notebook to draw something else.

As soon as she was thus settled, Wal went home and took the packet of drawings from under his bed: chose out the best of the oils and did them up in a parcel together. He put on his collar and took a bus for Oxford Street: stopped at the Surrey Galleries, and gave Macyntire's card to the man at the door, with his own name scrawled across the back. The man looked at him doubtfully, but took the card: and presently Wal Henderson found himself talking to Edward Macyntire, saying he hardly knew what.

And so it was arranged that there should be an exhibition of drawings and paintings by *Walter Henderson* at the Surrey Galleries in the following January.

IV

Wal staggered out into the sunshine, still slightly dazed from the night before the last. How had it happened? He did not know. Macyntire had taken it for granted that this was his own work: and, of course, Martha never bothered to sign things. It would not occur to her. Nor did she ever bother to inquire what became of her drawings after they were done.

Wal went home and found she had been making a careful drawing of a blind puppy, almost in one line; but neither a touch wasted nor a touch lacking; and there was no background whatever. Wal wrote "W.H." in the corner: leaded his thumb, and set its mark above. Then he went through all the drawings and paintings, signing them with his initials and his thumb-mark. The final step was taken: he was surprised to find how easy it was: when a thing had happened half by accident, the very idea of which in cold blood he would have dismissed, he felt no remorse whatever, no inclination to go back to Macyntire and explain his mistake. Fate gave him a shove and he slid smoothly.

It was not long before Wal managed to get a cheque from Macyntire on account, and took to shaving again every day and wearing a collar. It was not long, either, before Lottie began to get restive, and wonder that Martha should be absent all day, and never come with her to Ti Fung's, as she used. Young Shan Ting and his friends used to inqure after her; and when she still did not appear, neither did they come to Ti Fung's so often: for Lottie's own popularity was waning. It did not occur to her that anything might be amiss: for, after all, Martha was barely twelve years old. It was only that she thought Henderson was getting more than eighteen-pence worth of work out of her in the week: as, indeed, he was. But when she questioned the child, and Martha told her that Henderson let her sit in his room and draw, she grumbled at it as "queer," but did not think much more about the matter.

A few days after that Mr. Ti Fung summoned her to his office: and she wondered why. He loomed in front of her threateningly: a great dark mountain of a Chink, girt always with a blue baize apron.

"I hear," said he slowly, "that you are eensolent."

Lottie did not protest. She knew it to be his invariable formula; that protest was hopeless.

"People do not stan' eensolence. You are dismiss'!"

But Lottie hardly heard him. "*You are old,*" were the words ringing in her head as she crept out again.

She was badly shaken, but a little crude rum made her feel better. She began to think things over dispassionately, and yet found it hard to admit that she was old. And yet it was true that her ascendancy over the Chinese had gone: she had to recognise that. Things were not the same as in the old days when Martha used to come with her to Ti Fung's. Her mind clung to this explanation in despair: she hated to admit that she was old: she would not admit it, and put it all down absurdly to Martha.

Lottie paid for her drink in a dazed fashion and stumbled home in her high-heeled, over-trodden shoes. When Martha came in she flung a torrent of abuse at her, of which Martha understood not one jot, blaming her for all the misfortunes that had ever befallen them. Then she ended up saying that she should go to Henderson's no more; and that Martha understood: but said nothing.

Lottie went to bed debating in her mind whether to send Martha to a factory or to try and find some other more lucrative job for her. For Lottie had no intention of entering a factory herself. Presently she decided to try the factory, and then fell asleep. But when she awoke Martha was already dressed and gone.

Gone? Lottie was in a griping rage. Gone without even getting her breakfast: *that* was a dutiful child. And when she had spent half the night scheming for her future, too!

Lottie jumped out of bed earlier than usual, and hurried through her toilet, preparatory to learning them both.

Wal had been out late the night before, and slept late. He had been dining with Macyntire, and they discussed the exhibition, which was just about to open. Macyntire had made him feel a little uncomfortable. Macyntire was a master of the art of Boom, whereas of the other arts he was only a very shrewd critic. During the last month he had given many quiet dinners to really good fellows: fellows who edited papers, or wrote art criticisms, or were well known as collectors. Then, over the port, he would quite casually bring out a few of Wal's sketches, and ask their opinion of them; generally adding that they were never likely to be popular, of course . . . but—he would spread his hands with a shrug, implying that one had sometimes to run an unpopular exhibition for art's sake, showing that *he* was a Good Fellow also. All the real people, of course, would recognise their genius; and probably run the show down, so as to buy Henderson's work cheap. Then the other good fellows would protest, and say that they at least would stand by him, and expose any such wickedness. All through December, therefore, there were veiled references to the coming exhibition in the papers: dark hints about its excellences, darker hints about the characters of any who should dare to traduce it.

All this Macyntire, contrary to his use, told Wal; for he was surprised to find him more sensible than the average Unknown Genius: a man after his own heart. And he ended up by saying, half laughing: " The only pity, Henderson, is that you aren't an Infant as well as a Genius. If you were a young gutter-snipe, now, it would just account for those queer immaturities and unintentional crudities that I'm afraid of people falling foul of."

Wal, who was drinking his third glass of port, spilt it.

And so he had come home late, and feeling a little uncomfortable, and did not wake till he heard a terrific banging on the door. Martha was standing close by his pillow, pale and frightened, clutching hold of his blanket; and the door was locked.

" Who's there? " he shouted, and recognised Lottie's voice in the words that followed. He jumped out of bed and pulled on his trousers: then opened the door, nearly as angry as Lottie herself. Martha ran behind him and flung her arms tight round his waist.

" Come along out of that, you little devil, you! Didn't I tell you you wasn't comin' here any mo-er? "

Wal could feel the child sobbing against the small of his back, and his veins ran with a queer pride.

"What you been doin' to the kid?" he clamoured.

"What've *you* been doin' to her?" cried Lottie. "That's what I want to know. Ain't I 'er mother?"

"Fat lot of mother, you. What you been doin' to 'er? I'll get you lock-up, I will, chasin' the poor little thing till she thinks you're ready to murder 'er!"

Lottie answered slowly and dramatically.

"'Oo's 'er mother, you or me? Tell me that, Mr. Henderson."

"Who feeds her? Who looks after her all day? Who does she *love*?" he added triumphantly, bending back an arm to touch the child's shoulder.

Lottie stared weakly.

"Who's been father and mother to her both all this last month, while you were bluing yourself at Ti Fung's. Tell me *that*, miss. You say you're her mother: who was her father, then? Some sawny Chink? Tell me *that*, before you go hollering about your mother's rights!"

"Martha," said Lottie impressively, "I been a good mother to yer."

Martha sobbed louder.

"Ain't you comin' along of your *mother*?"

Lottie clung to the word desperately, like a talisman. She wanted the child: according to her lights, she was a good mother.

Martha clung tighter.

"No, she ain't," said Wal. "I don't know what you been doin' to make a kid leave its own mar; but that's what you done, and I guess it must 'ave been something terrible 'ard. Ain't you afraid of Hell for doin' the dirty on a kid, you devil?"

"She ain't done nothin'," said Martha. "On'y she said I wasn't coming 'ere any mo-er," she wailed.

Lottie stood limply and pathetically, like a dog unreasonably beaten.

"Fur Gawd's sake," she whispered, "let me 'ave 'er back!"

"No, I won't," said Wal. He felt so completely in the right, such a disinterested champion of defenceless childhood.

Lottie sprang forward, babbling furiously.

"What you want 'er for? What you been doin' to 'er, you lousy, you? I tell you it ain't right for a kid of 'er age to be away from 'er mar."

"I ain't done nothin'," he said slowly, "and I ain't a-goin' to do nothin', 'xcep' I ain't a-goin' to turn away a kid what comes to me for help: I ain't that sort of fellow. What you think I can get out of 'er? Why, nothin'! Only, I ain't a-goin' to let 'er back to be bullied by you, not if it costs me every penny I got to feed 'er!"

"You mean it?"

"That's right."

"Martha, are you comin' along o' me, or along o' Wal?"

For reply Martha pressed her streaked face harder in Wal's coat.

Lottie rubbed desperately at her eyes, tottered a few steps towards them, then turned and began to stumble down the stairs.

"Oh, Gawd," she was muttering.

Martha relaxed her hold, and sank on to the bed, hiccoughing from her long sobbing, her eyes red and puffed. She lay there longing for Wal's comfort, but he stood motionless in the middle of the floor, hating himself. Bit by bit things broke loose in his brain, each with a sudden sledge-hammer blow. Memories of the early past: then memories of all he had meant to do for Martha. Then the thought of that exhibition of pictures by Walter Henderson. Then the memory of Lottie stumbling, childless, blindly out on to the stairs. All the pains of Judas took hold of him. He writhed as if he was caught in a net of cords, struggling to escape from what he had done. Suddenly he turned on Martha, and his face was livid as with rage.

"Get out of this!" he screamed. "Out of it! Out of it!"

Martha sprang to her feet in terror. "Out of it, damn you!" he cried. "Go to your mother! You can't stay here, I tell you! Out of it, curse you!"

He took her by the shoulders and half threw her out of the door, so that she fell all aspread on the landing.

"Hurry," he was saying, "get a move on, you little devil! And take all this truck along of you!" He bundled up paints and brushes in a bit of sacking and flung them after her.

She lay huddled and ungainly and pathetic on the landing, not even sobbing, the paints spilt all around her, and he half kicked her across to the top of the stairs.

He slammed the door. "She's free of me now," he thought, "for ever." Things had come to such a pass that he could wish her nothing better.

C. E. MONTAGUE

TWO OR THREE WITNESSES

THANKS to our spirited Press, the eyes and the ears of the English nation are everywhere. Still, there may be, at any one time, more of these organs on one patch of ground than another. In all Connaught there were, at the time I am telling of, only four pairs of each. They were set in the heads of four London journalists, now taking their ease in their inn, at the small town of Callow, after the labours of the day.

These labours had ended at six. They had had to. The travelling Assistant Press Censor from Dublin had ordered it so: devil a word, he had said, would he take for the wire a moment later than six, and it Christmas Day in a week's time, and the girl at the post office having a long way to walk to her home in the darkness of the night.

The doyen of the four correspondents was Pellatt, who wrote for the "Day." Pellatt liked to be called the doyen. His paper, he said, was the doyen of papers. When first he had heard of that absurd six o'clock rule Pellatt had taken pity upon its author—had gone at once to see him alone and let him know what was what. The whole of the great world, as Pellat explained, all the people who counted, read the "Day." If any parcel of a country's history did not duly impinge at the time on the consciousness of the world, that parcel of history could hardly be said to exist: at most it had only the shadowy, problematic existence of some orchid that might, or might not, have bloomed in some unexplored equatorial forest, with no one to see. Had the assistant censor no love of his country?

At any rate, he had no vision. His mind was provincial. Weren't there four of them in it, he asked, and not Pellatt only? Every dog had his "Day." Once give a favour and soon there'd be copy pouring into the place till God knew what hour, whereas any post-office clerk that you'd see was a human creature the like of ourselves. So six o'clock it had been on this the first day of the four pressmen's labours at Callow.

It would be six to-morrow, as well. This was graver—to-morrow was going to be a big day. Thomas Curtayne, greatest of Irishmen, was to be buried in homely state at his birthplace, Kilmullen, a village some twenty miles off. Here was a sob-story chance, manifestly. The London papers were wanting to "feature" the rite: Curtayne's historic manner of giving old England a fugitive dig, now in the back and now in the stomach, during the pre-Treaty years had caught the fancy of our dispassionate nation of amateurs of the ring. Every correspondent would have to be there. And then he would have to be copious and vivid, crisp and magnanimous, right up to six.

Still, for the moment the four were at ease. Or three of them were. The fourth, Fane, the raw hand, was better off than at ease: his spirits were in a heavenly whirl. This was his first biggish job, and he thrilled with delight at everything that it brought; every hurry or makeshift or jar or rebuff was adventure; merely to sit there and hear the tremendous shop talked by the three middle-aged men, who knew all, was initiation; it gave him the raptures of swift conscious growth.

They were humane to him. Dinner, which they had allowed to be sound in the vital matters of claret and game, had been followed by bridge. "Not bad bridge either, considering——" Pellatt admitted after the last trick had fallen, while casting a disciplinary look at Fane from under his ponderous brows. Fane's failings were clearly the considerations referred to. Morris, his partner, had snubbed Fane's admissions and pleas, after each ill-starred flutter of their common cause, with repetitions of the formula "Correct mistakes and carry on," in tones of firm resignation. Fane felt that he had played like a conscript. But then he had been one—had only wanted, for his part, to look around Callow, to gorge himself with its quaint queerness. Still, everyone else's escape from an evening of pain had seemed to depend on his cutting in.

So he had played. But now, while Morris and Bute totted up, he would give himself without shame to the amusement of eyeing the room, so much more purely and deeply mid-Victorian in every colour and curve of its fittings and furniture than any room now to be easily found in fashion-following England. Odd that on rebel Ireland an older England should stamp her most durable image. Savoursome Tudor idioms were constantly piquing one's ear in the rustic speech of these wilds. One never heard them now in England. And those ghost-like "leaders" in Irish newspapers: up and down the badly printed columns walked the spectre of good Georgian London wit; here subsisted the ironies, coquetries, breeding and ease lost to England long since, when writers grew flustered and polysyllabic and shrill and forgot how it bit when Steele was most quiet. Ah, but of course we had character still! Our oaken English uprightness was not put away, out of use, in any lavendered drawer of this still-room in Ireland. Rugged integrity—that suit, at least, we were strong in.

We must be, for Pellatt was saying it now. When Pellatt, with his short-curled grizzled hair and Jovian eyebrows and his frown, a very Elijah of Handel, positively said "'Tis so" Fane could see it no otherwise. Pellatt was quoting some great person who had said that all our bother in Ireland had come of the desperate attempt of an honest and slow-witted race to govern a race of quick-witted scamps. "I'm not so sure," Pellatt judicially added, "about the 'slow-witted.'"

The fleeting hour was genial—no hour in which to set bounds to the great love a man bears to country and self. On the three curvilinear waistcoats before him Fane counted eight buttons undone; it gave him an intimate joy; he was in at the spot where greatness unbent. Within the three middle-aged bosoms subjacent to those straining waistcoats a similar process of kindly expansion advanced at no meaner pace. The three seasoned vessels began to confess, each after his kind, the severe morality of their professional conduct. Men are prone to do that when their bodies are deeply at ease; in that mellow condition the thought of the stern hold that you keep on yourself could move you to tears. In straight-flung words and few the handsome Bute acknowledged his creed—"Don't let your paper down, ever—that's good enough law and prophets for me." Bute bit his lip on the last word, with a manly control of emotion—Fane saw it and looked away for a moment, respecting it. Bute was a dear; Fane had already seen that; Bute's extremely kind and shy eyes, that dodged you behind shiny glasses, were always credentials enough to gain your goodwill. But now Bute the gentle concurrer with everyone else's movements, Bute the averter of all jolts and jars in your mind, the smoother of conversational ways and avoider of clashes and gloom, shone forth as more than a dear. And of course he was right: he had the key—Fane perceived it: have some one loyalty; be true to any one thing; all the rest follows.

And now Morris found tongue. Morris the rough diamond,

the "sound practical journalist" of "the old school," the man who, when cross, would complain of Pellatt's "racuous" voice and of Bute's "baynal" old gobbets of Latin; Morris, who said a few minutes ago that the assistant press censor was clearly "a total stranger to the amnities of life." Yet Morris surely knew a thing or two: he must. Morris worked for no single paper. He was the great News Agency man; his messages went to all papers, morning and evening; Morris's stuff would be used by any paper that had no man of its own on the spot. Now he broke forth, as well as he could at this hour, about "the brotherhood of the craft"; journalists ought to be comrades faithful and true; news ought to be pooled; "scoops" and "beats" and any dog's trick of the kind ought to be barred; any brother-craftsman attacked by the outer world ought to be backed to the death by the rest. "I mean to say, simply, the craft! Stick together, and stick to the craft!" As evenings wore on, Morris's speech came more and more to be composed of many "I mean to say's," each followed by some new essay in verbal expression less effective than the last. He bulged with rich meaning, rather than uttered it. Still, Fane understood. A man might have honour and grit though he did not carry his drink to perfection. Burns, no doubt, was like that of an evening. Sheridan too.

"Oh, I'm absolutely with you there," Bute was saying to Morris cordially. Pellatt was eyeing the weaker vessel with somewhat Olympian disdain, but Bute would not fail at doing the merciful thing.

"Well," said Bute, in the first pause that came, "*Cras*, I suppose, *ingens iterabimus aequor*." Bute had been a classical scholar at Corpus and seemed unashamed of the fact. "Time I crept into my narrow bed."

Morris, as soon as the door had closed upon Bute, proved how fast events had been marching within him. "Good ol' Butey!" he gurgled. "Mean t'shay, shafety first. Minnight oil, y'know. Mean t'shay, got to pump two'r three gallonsh—fill up spare tank before starting, y'know. Mean t'shay, good ol' wise virgin, ol' Butey, 's what *I* mean."

It was cryptic to Fane. Pellatt was simpler. "He might have waited a little," said Pellatt, austerely. Bute had not left him a moment to sum the case up and put the thing in the right light. All that Pellatt did now, with so meagre an audience to awe, was just to impart, in brief, what it was that had always kept him up to the mark. Just the one simple reflection: "Mind, he who writes for the 'Day' writes history. He who writes history makes it."

Pellatt took care to risk no anti-climax to this high-toned aphorism. He rose, and finished his glass. And Fane was equally willing to go and sleep on all the inspiring things he had heard.

Lanterns were gleaming about the inn yard when the yawning waiter brought in their unloved early breakfast. Unconfirmed rumour had given out that their man would be buried at 10-30. Unconfirmed rumour! "Good God!" Pellatt groaned, as he dourly and doggedly ate, "is there any other country in Europe would leave you in doubt?"

So, to make safe, and to get a look at Kilmullen first, they must start a good deal before eight. All motors and petrol had lately been commandeered by the State: nothing for it but horsed jaunting-cars; so each of the four had chartered one of these for himself, to secure individual liberty. Just as they finished their eggs the scrape and slipping of hoofs on the rounded stones of the yard, as the first horse was led out of its stall, roused Pellatt once more: "Horsed cars for the Press! What a country! Savagery! Absolute savagery!"

"*You* needn't grouse," Morris snarled. "*You've* not got to be back in this hole at 1-30 to wire your story for evening papers."

"I've got to write a story fit to live," Pellatt growled.

Bute rushed in to create a pacific diversion. He playfully wailed "*Quel métier! Quel métier!* Up early, down late. Wise man, old Chaucer—'Flee from the Presse and hold by Steadfastnesse.'"

It seemed that laments were the fashion. So Fane did not let on how he inwardly chuckled and grinned with delight. The voices and flitting lights in the yard, the big day's work afoot, with Charles's Wain still bright above a darkling gable, the sweet or sour tempers of men already in play before dawn—full of delicious differences—this was life, full-flavoured: the cup had strong wine in it. Heavenly, too, was the drive out from Callow; first through the murky pallor of failing night, growing haggard, and then the realist light of a cloud-covered dawn, dreary, circumstantially blank. Frost quickens fires, and darkness gives beauty to flame: that bald, aghast oncome of day, without colour or stir, seemed to brace the delighted spirit in Fane to rally its stout garrison of inward cheer for a defiance to all enveloping forces of torpor and glumness. On each of the three cars ahead, back to back with its driver, was seated a stolid, immobile figure, immense with greatcoats. Fane figured each of the three as a symbol of domination over investing armies of circumstance; each was a lamp amid gloom, a fortress exultantly held, a hut with a great fire in it and all the Arctic without. These and other picturesque images visited Fane's virgin mind all the way to Kilmullen.

All Kilmullen is built round "the Square"—an open quadrangle of turf, mangy-looking with wear. Each of its sides is about a hundred yards long. The high road from Callow passes along one of these sides. The church stands on the opposide side, near its centre. Next to the church, the priest's house is on one side, the school on the other. No post office exists. Next to the high road, at the corner nearest to Callow, a grocer's and general shop enjoys the blessing of a licence for beer and porter. Near it stands an old police barracks, now used by State troops. The rest of the village is white-washed mud cottages.

The four drivers made for the grocer's large stable yard: there a man of infinite leisure came to receive the horses, and Pellatt was first to get out the question next to all hearts. Was 10-30 really the hour?

"Tin-thirty! The funer'l!" The leisurely man invigorated himself to give what was almost a hoot of derision. "Tut! Not at all. Wan o'clock, or wan-thirty. An' early at that, with His Grace the Archbishop driving a good twinty miles from Clong to this place."

Pellatt's face could be read like a book at that moment—a black-letter book. The Irish again! The untrustworthy Irish! The Irish all over!

"That does it," Morris said firmly. He turned to his driver: "You needn't take that horse out. I'm going back now."

The driver pleaded the frailty of horseflesh.

"Well"—Morris relented so far—"give him a snack while I look at the church. In ten minutes we'll start." He hurried off to the church, where the man of leisure said the coffin was lying now on the tallest bier that ever you saw.

The rest followed more slowly. They would have time to look round, in all conscience, between now and one—"or one-thirty." Three hours wasted, out of the five in which they might have been writing their masterpieces at Callow, in front of a good bedroom fire apiece! Now—well, with luck, they might get to their writing by four instead of at one. Fane had to admit to himself that the cause had come a bit of a cropper. But Morris's fate was the worst. Poor old Morris would see just nothing at all. "Why"—his thoughts broke out into speech—"Morris's old evening papers won't get a word about the whole thing."

"No. Not if his horse falls down dead on the road," Pellatt savagely grunted.

Fane stared. " Oh, of course he could say how the place looked beforehand," said Fane.

Bute murmured, " *O sancta simplicitas!* "—goodness knew why.

Morris was speeding out of the church as they neared it. " So long," he said, valedictively. " Back to my post. Fool I was ever to leave it."

" The post office, you mean? " Pellatt jibed, with a stony glint in his eye.

" Absolutely," said Morris. " You one-paper artists may gad about, sniffing for atmospheres. I've got the whole of the Press to keep posted up on the facts, and I can't play the fool any more. So—c'rect mistakes and carry on." He sped off towards the grocer's.

" O these agency men! " Bute murmured mildly. At those ribald words about one-paper artists Pellatt had turned his back on the blasphemer. Fane marvelled. All was not clear.

When the three had taken a good look at the inside of the church they trailed out into the square and strolled on its grass and presently sat and smoked on the low tubular rail that ran about it, and Pellatt and Bute sank into melancholy, crabbed or sympathetic—and so the vacant morning dragged on. It was now that Pellatt's variety first struck Fane as being less infinite than Cleopatra's. Pellatt returned on himself. In what other country on God's earth, he acidly asked of Bute, could you not find out to-day the hour fixed for the chief public event of to-morrow? Spaniards, Arabs, Hindoos, Kaffirs were all people of system, compared with this feckless breed. The Irish were " natives " really—just natives—could never get on without some firm, upright ruler above them, someone who did not babble but did get things done and knew his own mind and told the truth and stuck to it.

Bute chimed obligingly in with the other's mood of the moment. Bute recalled the saying of some clever person: ask a Greek a question and he will give the answer most likely to profit himself; ask an Arab, and he will give the answer that runs to the fewest words; ask an Irishman, and he will give you for answer whatever might give you most pleasure. But Pellatt—first letting Bute know that all this was a chestnut—did not seem quite so sure about that disinterested desire to please. Anyhow, what an Irishman said was not evidence. " Give me, for God's sake, a country where people—at any rate, men like ourselves—are brought up to feel that lying is simply a thing that's not done."

Fane felt he was idling; he ought to be marking the words

of the two senior experts in observation of life. But Fane was young: pleasure distracted him. It was delicious just to sit there and see the things that went on, the personal life of the place, all its tranquil molecular movement, not hidden but only softeningly swathed in the light mist of that dull day. A tiny ass, drawing a tiny cart laden with peat, pensively picked its way, a wavy enigmatic way, along the road bounding one side of the square, its frail shanks and delicate feet moving daintily: near its head, but not intruding word or blow on the thoughts of the ass, an aged man meandered pensively too. Hither and thither over the turf of the square three mongrel dogs prosecuted together their race's old pursuits of love, war, and the chase, checked only when some lapse into pitched battle, or else a frenzied attempt to dig a rat out of the turfy bosom of the square, brought a shouted curse from a cottage door to remind the passionate creatures of the sovereignty of law. Presently children surged out of the school-house, plunging with shrill cries of joy into the lessonless outer air as into a bath, and, this first ecstasy being spent, began to play soldiers and marched up and down, banging tin cans with extreme gravity.

Oh, it was great, the low rhythm of this rustic world, like the pulse and breath of babies asleep, awaiting great days to come and amassing strength for them! Here in the castaway farms and the tiny towns with no street lamps—here was the forest in youth, the soil storing up richness for some such unpredictable sowing of seed as impregnated Assisi and Stratford. Winter held hushed in rest-giving arms the landscape that rose beyond the low roofs; in every hedge they had passed on the road the drugged sap slept its hardest, collecting in that semi-death the power to leap up straight at the sun and break into honeysuckle and rose. And here was a place kind as winter—really the noblest of seasons, the quiet creator with forward-looking eyes.

Carried down the full stream of this reverie, Fane did not notice that Pellatt had now said all the things which the English commonly say of the Irish, when cross, except those which had been added in pure good nature by Bute, to keep Pellatt going. Fane was not disturbed at his revelling till Bute's voice made itself felt like the touch of a child's propitiatory finger on a reading elder's arm:

> "Mon dieu, mon dieu, la vie est la
> Douce et tranquille."

Bute softly purred the much-quoted lines. All lines that Bute quoted were much-quoted lines. And then Fane saw a thing clearly—that Bute's mind, released from the call to play up to Pellatt's, instinctively sidled up to his, Fane's. To play up, to chime in, was Bute's way. But not to understand everything. Bute, like Fane, was now gazing gravely out at the life of Kilmullen; but Bute was audibly bored, and assumed that Fane was. Verlaine had been quoted with irony. "Yes, *mon dieu!*" Bute continued, "*tranquille à vous faire mourir*. Imagine living in this sort of a hole—if it *could* be called life!"

Fane did his best to be bored. He felt ashamed of his privy delight—if he knew better, if he were complete, if he had mastered his craft of observation, no doubt he would see nothing but tedium and commonplace now. He honestly tried. But nature is stubborn. Behold! Kilmullen was all very good, incorrigibly good; he could not pump enjoyment out of his mind as fast as that unseaworthy vessel allowed the stuff to pour in. "Where's Pellatt?" he asked. He had to say something, and now he noticed that Pellatt was gone.

Bute shrugged, without any harsh innuendo. "Gone to find somebody lettered enough to be moved at the notion of having the 'Day' in the place—should you think?"

Fane laughed. Yes, their thunderous doyen had that little failing—quite amiable. So was Bute's gentle touch on it.

Noon struck on the village clock's cheap tinny bell. They heard the strokes out, refilled pipes, and loafed again over the green. During the next half-hour momentous events did not abound. One of the mongrels, then sitting up on his haunches and quaffing the air with uplifted nose, suddenly turned his head round and saw with indignation a shiny black-beetle in the act of treading on his tail. The mongrel whipped round to avenge; the beetle hung on—an event, as events go in these haunts of peace, had come into the life of the place. Nobody else was in sight, yet Fane felt that the whirl of self-baffling pursuit which ensued was converting all Kilmullen's front windows into so many convergent eyes. Like a battalion formed in hollow square, Kilmullen gazed in on its centre. Fane felt its four frontages stir as the reeds round a pond wave very slightly whenever you throw a stone into its middle; the slow ripples presently break on the stems of the reeds and they stir and then stand still again.

Eventlessness had re-settled thoroughly down on the place by 12-29. Tired with active bliss, the three mongrels slept on the turf. The increased smoke that harbingers dinner was streaming up peacefully straight from many chimneys. Suddenly Fane felt a convulsion run through the reeds round the pond. A man, red with haste and looking important and heavily fraught, arrived on a muddy push-bicycle out of the great world without.

The stranger rode straight to the priest's dwelling-house; he propped his clogged and spattered mount against the hedge and entered. During the minutes that followed Fane felt that the very smoke from the chimneys stood still to watch the priest's door. One of the mongrels came to life, rose, sniffed, and gazed expectantly towards the same quarter, his flicking nostrils closely interrogating the intervening air. Of a sudden he flopped an ear forward; the tip of his tail wagged a note of satisfaction. The priest had come out of his door. Behind him came Pellatt.

"Downy old fox!" Bute chuckled, admiringly.

The priest walked quickly across to the old barracks. He dropped a few words on the way to each of two men who came eagerly out from houses to intercept him. When he had spoken, each of the men fell away with an air, as Fane thought, of remitted tension; some strain of intent expectation was off for the moment. O horror!

Pellatt was walking across to them. Fane hardly needed to know what was coming as soon as Pellatt should speak. "We're for it!" said Pellatt. "It's put off again!"

"My God! Till what hour?" said Bute.

"Three o'clock. The archbishop's shay has gone phut on the road. A crazy horsed landau, in this year of grace! The worship of saints is modern beside it. Good God! What a Church!"

"You've made friends with the padre?" said Bute unreproachfully.

Pellatt looked at him sharply. "I felt he would like," Pellatt said, "to know that the 'Day' would have a man here." This may have seemed to leave the two others cold. Pellatt added: "Besides, I thought we might all be the better for knowing the order of the service. Do you people want it?"

The two took down a few notes that he gave from his book. "I really don't think that it would have done," Pellatt explained, "to have us all trooping in. He isn't the easiest man to get on with. It takes the utmost tact to get anything from him at all."

Bute speculated aloud, in his sociable way. "Three o'clock. Finish 3-30. Beat the horse all the way back to his stable, to get in by six. Means—not a moment to write in."

Pellatt looked at him hard. "The time has been," Pellatt sturdily said, "when a man could write on a car."

Bute looked at Pellatt as hard as such gentle eyes could.

"Nothing like pressure," said Bute, "for squeezing the best work out of a man."

Their gallantry rendered Fane almost glad that the blow had fallen. Here was adventure made yet more adventurous; faced, too, along with stout comrades. What more could you want?

The tinny tinkle of the clock had just tolled one; the priest had reimmersed himself in his house; dinner-time had wholly depopulated the green; even the dogs had legged off to see what their several quartermasters could do. "Anyhow, let us lunch," said Pellatt, still in that tone of robust fortitude.

There was no real inn to give meals. But life could just be sustained at the grocer's on biscuits and stout. The shop had a cavernous further end, dim, smoky, and malty. Here, on two chairs and an up-ended barrel, the three ate and drank and two of them talked of the stern joys of duty done against odds, and the sunshine filling the mind that will do the dirty on nobody. Pipes and a further treatment of these topics followed the soldierly meal. Now and again one or another would step out to see that no novel turn of affairs was making history in the square.

At 1-50 Pellatt went out in his turn. At 1-55 he had not returned. Bute looked at his watch and jumped up, looking appalled. "My God!" he said, "has he made a bolt for his stable?" He ran out. Half-way to the door he turned round and said compunctiously: "Sorry, but if Pellatt goes I must go. It's a bad world. Look out for yourself." And then he was gone.

Fane, seated on his up-ended barrel, was not much perturbed. Still, he marvelled. First Morris had fled from the diamond mine, empty-handed. Then Bute was in terror lest Pellatt should rob himself too. If he did, it seemed Bute would feel bound in horror to add the wreck of his own day's job to those of the two others. Really, these points of professional honour were rather fine-drawn. Would he, Fane, be expected also to post back to Callow and wire to tell his paper that he had not stayed for the show and so could say nothing about it? A little thick, that. But Oh! good! here was Bute coming back.

The first consternation was gone from Bute's face. It was a worried face, though. "He's not gone," said Bute. "His car's there. No doubt he'll turn up at the time, but I *do* wish he wouldn't fade into the landscape so freely." Fane had never seen Bute so critical.

"Oh, he'll be buying a dog," Fane jocosely suggested.

"It won't be a pup," said Bute, almost grimly. He sat

down again and relaxed, or seemed to be trying to. Business permitting, the grocer would drift aft into the cavernous snuggery, drink a gift glass of his own merchandise, and fraternise warily with the alien. Borne by customers, news from the great world without would trickle at intervals into the shop, some of it overheard by Fane and his friend, some of it carried back to their lair by the grocer upon his next visitation. At 2-10 someone big and proud with poignant tidings came to buy starch and to tell the terrible shock it had given His Grace when the landau foundered, and he an old, aged man: but His Grace was the man with the courage, and he after fainting and shaken almost to bits; nothing would do him but get a new axle at Strones and then on to Kilmullen before the darkness of night.

In truth it was darkening already. Midwinter days droop young if a monstrous wainscot of massy black cloud in the west be making a false horizon half-way up the sky. A cellarly gloom had begun to invest the snuggery, never well lit. Voices heard in it now were acquiring, for Fane, the romantic tone of all voices lifted in obscurity. Two-thirty arrived, and an elderly woman dead to the world, a true priest's housekeeper, came to buy candles. Of this errand it seemed she was no whit enamoured. In sombre tones she explained its occasion to the grocer. Someone unnamed had invaded the house of the priest, "Aye, like a wolf on the fold or a pack of locusts itself, taking all, and then ringing the bell for more to destroy." She etched—like other etchers, not without acid—a portrait of this Tamburlaine of our days. "A brindle-haired man, and not a line on his face but it was the depth of a ditch, and a black scowl upon him would give you a right to engage he's a judge." Fane, in the semi-darkness, saw the profile of Bute go sharply round to attend. The artist's indignation was waxing as she went on with her picture. "He to be sitting beyond in the parlour, poking the fire as bold as how-are-you, and writing the Divvil knows what on a packet of telegraph forms he'll have stolen, I seriously think, from Callow post office. And nothing to do him at last but complain of the light of the beautiful lamp that we have and ask for a candle besides from his rev'rence, that right soon would be begging his bread with resisting not evil if I wasn't there." She snorted amain as she walked away with the auxiliary illuminants so reluctantly sought.

It was growing too dim for Fane to see Bute's expression. And yet Fane knew what it was. The cock of the head, the strain of the neck may tell a good deal: we are all cats, more or less; we can tell in the dark. Yes, Pellatt was living well on the country, and Bute's gentler spirit was taking off its hat to that robust and exacting domination. Pellatt was writing. Why, of course, he was describing the long wait, the atmosphere of Kilmullen, the lovely and wonderful things in which Fane had only wallowed or basked otiosely, all the fitting prelude to the dramatic poignancy of the coming event. Fool, fool that Fane had been, not to work too while yet it was light! Could he start still? Too late—it was two-forty now. "Shall we stroll round?" said Bute, with some anxiety in his voice, but not consternation. Good old Bute, he was the man to be with; they were the two wise men of legend, at sea in a bowl, but the senior sage was not downhearted—only wary.

In the square the premature twilight was bringing a few lamp-lit windows into distinction. To one of these lighted panes, an uncurtained one in the house of the priest, the two men were drawn, moth-like. As they gazed, the light was strengthened within: an unshaded candle, borne in some unseen hand, crossed the square of yellow radiance and came to rest close to the head of one seated. He looked up. Yes, Pellatt, of course, and his face not genially grateful, so far as they saw. Bute chuckled; "He thinks they ought to have put a shade on the candle. Hullo!"

A faint stir in another part of the square had diverted their eyes. The cyclist, visibly armed with the prestige of one on whom much hung, was just setting off up the main road. Oh, of course, to sight the archbishop's carriage and bring back the tip for the priest's humble procession to turn out and meet the great man at the skirts of Kilmullen.

The tin-voiced timepiece of the place never spoke without first clearing its throat: four or five minutes before striking an hour it rumbled or creaked and got ready. This hum-ing and ha-ing had scarcely begun when the cyclist scorched back to the square, and the priest with his decent train of assistants set forth on foot for the rencounter.

Now that he did come, God's viceroy on this patch of the earth was as punctual as a secular king. The voice of tin had not been thrice uplifted before the ancient prelate rose in the halted landau and shook out his travel-creased robes. But your men of eld cannot be rushed, least of all when eld has been pretty well shaken as well as wearied and cramped with a long, chilly drive. Foot after foot must be lowered, painful inch by inch, to the ground, with stalwart aid from a domestic chaplain. And entries of state, to court or hamlet, have to be decently made. It was 3-8 before the first homage was paid and the first blessing given. Only at 3-14 did the churchward procession set out.

As all the eyes and ears of England marched abreast among the lay details of this procession Fane noticed Pellatt's eyes fixed on a watch at his wrist, to the apparent neglect of all other objects of interest, sacred or profane. Pellatt was like a man timing a race. Fane glanced at Bute, and found Bute's gaze fastened on Pellatt's face as fixedly as Pellatt's on the watch. But Fane could not look at them long. There was too much to see.

At 3-20 the head of the little procession, marching in column of fours, arrived at the church. To file through the door they had to form two deep: Fane and Bute were now abreast; Pellatt had fallen back into the next file. Another two minutes, and Fane and Bute were kneeling side by side in a pew, Bute next to the gangway. During the next three minutes Fane knew, with a different order of certitude from most of his cognitions of other people, that Bute, as well as he, had lost hold upon everything else, flooded out by the inrushing sense of living fellowship in the presence of the strange event of death. It was unprofessional. Still, it does happen.

The first full force of this may have passed as they rose to their feet with the rest. And then, through the door that lay open behind them, there came, clear in the deep outer stillness of the windless afternoon in the dispeopled square the sounds of a cart put sharply in motion—the whipped horse's scraping clutch at the ground, and the brutal scrunch of wheels on rough cobbles. In the seconds that followed the beat of hoofs grew rhythmic and swiftly diminished; and Bute, coming back to the world and glancing quickly about him, whispered to Fane, "Stolen away, by the Lord—the old fox!" And then, in another second, "Young un, I'm going. Ain't you?"

The first tremendous hum of some droneful chant was just rolling out cumulus clouds of mystical awe from the altar blent with the sensuous drug of the rolling incense. "Gosh, no!" Fane whispered back. "We'd miss the whole thing."

"*Magnifique*," he half heard Bute protesting, and then "*n'est pas la guerre*, *n'est pas la guerre*, God help you!" And then he was aware of a vacant place at his side and of reverent slow steps suddenly breaking into a run on the flags outside the open church door.

But a greater event was to dwarf even this. The fugitive steps had not long passed out of hearing, the sounds of a second car at some distance starting and driving away had only just passed, when, with a shock and a sudden effect of raw edges, the service broke off: first the chanting voices, then the fortifying instrument—everything. Voices rose which did not seem to belong to that place. One, collected and clear, asked aloud, " Is there anny doctor here? " And then, " Is there anny trained nurse? "; and a sturdy young woman who looked like business slipped out of a pew and ran up straight towards the altar. Other voices, escapes for helpless emotion, squealed or bleated lamentations and random futilities: " Hold him up, now, the way he can breathe "; " Not at all. Lay His Grace on his back till you get the wine to him "; " The Lord God help us all—is he dead? "

Fane caught a glimpse of a limp bundle of archiepiscopal vestments carried out to a door at one side of the chancel. The nurse followed, to minister. Then the dismayed congregation just waited, minute by minute, the scene a tragic counterpart to that interlude, comically empty, which comes while bridal parties sign in the vestry. Fane looked at his watch when the blank wait began. It was 3-34. He ought to be on the road now, to make sure of getting his news on the wire. In ten minutes more the chance would be small. In twenty there would be pretty well none. Yet here was news in the making—an archbishop dead, it might be, in trying to bury the great layman. No, he must wait at all costs, see the thing through, and then do what he could. The minutes ebbed fast. Twenty had gone when the parish priest came out and hushed the general hum with an uplifted hand. Thank God, he said, His Grace was in no danger at all. He had fainted, and what wonder at it? But now he was conscious; he would be perfectly well in the morning; so now let them all go quietly to their homes, and at ten o'clock in the morning the funeral would begin. Fane slipped out of the church ahead of the rest and ran to the grocer's yard.

Four o'clock struck as he ran. Night had fairly fallen; the first thing Fane saw in the yard was the lamps of his waiting car shining out on the flicking ears of the homesick horse all ready in the shafts. " Is it possible we can be there before six? " Fane hungrily asked as he jumped to his place.

" Before six! " ejaculated the man, as if scouting a scandalous piece of detraction. " And it a blood horse! " This was a heartener for Fane. And the patrician horse certainly leapt out of the yard and along the high-road like embodied desire. Indeed, the vibration caused by this first burst of speed gave a fantastically dissipated air to the handwriting of Fane as he scrawled on a telegraph form, by the aid of a flash-lamp, the short message he wanted to send to his paper—just the news of the postponement and of its cause—his legs doing unaided, the while, the work of adhesion to the bounding and bumping vehicle under him.

Doubtless blood told while the horse was adding this minor hardship to the career of letters. But Fane's composition was only just finished before it became apparent that six furlongs rather than twenty miles was the racing distance of this particular thoroughbred. After five miles the thought of home seemed to recede from the animal's inconstant mind. Five o'clock came before the half-way village was reached. Two miles more and the beast insisted on walking for a short time on the flat.

The irony of the business stuck pins into Fane—the thought of Morris, Pellatt, and Bute, one after the other, driving back along this road with easy time to send the news, and none to send; and then of him, Fane, trailing home with all the news to himself, only too late to send it. Oh, if the poor weary beast could but do miracles! But how on earth, if any chance did get him to Callow in time, was he to give the others the tip? The "brotherhood of the craft"—last night he had thrilled to the words: it would be scrubby not to act on them now that a chance of giving, and not merely taking, had come to himself in his apprenticeship. Yet, yet—had he not thrilled too at Bute's ideal of never letting his own paper down? Was not his sole ownership of this piece of news a thing that belonged not to him but to his paper, not a thing to be squandered by him for his fine feeling's sake, in standing treat to his friends? Really, it was confoundedly hard—Launcelot Gobbo's case, only with no means of telling which counsellor was conscience and which was the fiend. Well, he would follow both—rush his own message off first of all and then tear round to tell the three others.

Idle dream!—the spent horse was walking again, and Callow was seven miles off, and it was 5-21. He thought he would get out and run; then he put it off for a minute, hearing a cyclist's bell ringing behind; and then a better thought came. He hailed the cyclist, swiftly unfolded the crisis to him, and suggested a deal. The cyclist was open to that. He was a Callow man; he was the man who had done that dispatch-riding duty to-day at Kilmullen. He had had riding enough for one day. On getting security for the bike he was charmed to drive home on the car in Fane's place, howbeit slowly. Fane mounted the bike and plunged into the darkness ahead. But it was almost 5-30 by now, and Callow was still all the seven miles off.

On any strange push-bicycle, well clogged with mud, a pace of fourteen miles an hour on a greasy road at night is harder to attain than many racers on cinder tracks might suppose. Besides, on a patch of slime at the outskirts of Callow Fane made an acrobatic side-slip, was well rolled in the mud, and had to spend four minutes in straightening the handle-bar. That made his lateness a doubly sure thing. It was a quarter past six when he jumped off at the censor's and bounded up, three steps at a time, towards the lair of that dragon upon the first floor. The censor had once or twice given a few minutes' grace. Possibly——

Fane met his fate on the landing. The censor was coming away. He had just locked up for the night. "Could you——?" said Fane, with an agonised look. He held out the pitiful scrawl, like a child's or a drunkard's, that he had produced on the car.

"No *bon*, me boy. *Rien ne va plus*," said the censor, an amiable sportsman really, whom Monte Carlo had educated for the discharge of this delicate duty. He looked at the wild scrawl in Fane's hand and then at the mud on Fane's coat. "'Dad, but you've been at the wake," he concluded with sympathy. "Left at the post be the whole of the field, and you only taking a glass. Tell me now, was the funer'l the great things they tell me?"

Fane gaped at him. "Funeral! Why, it's all off. Put off. Till to-morrow."

The censor gaped now. Then he shut both his mouth and his eyes as a man might pull down the blinds to be quiet and think. At the end of some ruminant seconds he asked: "And what about all the dull thud of the earth on the coffin? Aye, and the women's tears raining into the grave?" He seemed to be mustering reminiscences. "Aye, and one that dropped a spray of winter jasmine in, and she the very spit and moral of Kathleen-ni-Houlihan, that all the English know of now, mourning her son?"

"To-morrow," said Fane; "To-morrow, Ten-thirty a.m."

The censor perceived. Fane was sober. "The three divvils!" muttered the censor. "And not a man buried at all! Begob, their sins have discovered them." There he paused for a moment; then asked, "Was that all you were wishful to wire?"

"Yes," said Fane, hope reviving.

"Mind what I say to you now," said the censor. "We need the most stringent press censorship here. But we don't poke our nose, any more than by way of a form, into any gentleman's private affairs. Now, have you ever a friend in London—a man with a private address? You have—well and good. Does he know your editor's private name—and do you? Well and good. Now, in five minutes from this the post office will close. But it's only two minutes from here, and you're young and you have a good gallop in you. Now, take this"—the censor had been taking out of his pocket a telegraph form and now handed it over and Fane saw it was blank except that it bore at its foot the censor's signed name and his stamp—"and give me your word of honour you'll only write on it, to one private address: 'Archbishop ill. Funeral postponed till to-morrow. Tell O'Flaherty—that, or whatever your editor's name is—at once.' Then your own name."

They shook hands on it. "Off with you now," said the censor. Fane leapt down the stairs with his unhoped-for treasure. An empty side-car was passing the street-door below. He gave the man five shillings to drive like the wind to the inn, not three hundred yards off, and tell the three English gentlemen there, from Fane, that the funeral was off—just "Funeral off. Archbishop ill." Then he pedalled his best to the post office door.

The male clerk of the place was already fingering fondly the steel outer gate, ready to catch the divine sound of a clock striking the liberative half-hour. Within, the female clerk was buzzing off the tail end of some long message—Bute's or Pellatt's, perhaps, Fane reflected—before taking in Fane's. When she read Fane's she turned human and murmured, "Thank God! Now I can be there."

"That's right," Fane humanly said, and official reserve was the more completely suspended because the male clerk had now fastened the outer defences and come in to join them; the three were insensibly leagued together by being alone in a fastness.

The man heard the news. "Who was it at all, then," he asked, "that the archbishop buried to-day?"

"No one," said Fane.

"And wasn't he standing at all," said the man, "with his feet in the slippery yellow clay thrown up from the open grave?"

"And who told you that?" Fane inquired.

"Amn't I just after putting the last of it on to the buzzer for London myself," said the man, "not ten minutes back?"

"Aye, and I at it too," the girl intervened, "till this minute. And earth thudding dull on the coffin and all."

"Wasn't it all written out," the man almost argued, "by two that had seen it happen at twenty to four and the lurid winter dusk going on at the time?"

"And, the queerest of all," said the girl, "was I to be called away from my dinner at twenty to two to wire to London the way the last rites were completed not long after one?"

So at last Fane perceived. One does perceive so. Up to some point or other no evidence, even the strongest, teaches you anything. Then, of a sudden, you see even more of the truth than is proved. In that moment Fane saw all that Pellatt had done at the priest's, and that Bute had done in his bedroom last night, and that Morris had gone home to do. Each brother after his fashion, the brotherhood of the pen had been forging the news. The phrases of last night occurred to him now, framed in derisive inverted commas—"writing history," "don't let your paper down!" How it all stank!

Like other forms of evaporation, that of a faith is chilling. The blank collapse in Fane's face may have refrigerated the clerks, for the deep reserve of their high calling seemed now to constrict them again. "That'll be one and twopence," the girl said with restored professional dryness. The way the man closed the steel outer gate after Fane had a sharply exclusive clang.

As Fane stood on the pavement and tried to pull all this new experience together and make something of it, a quick, dry, rubbing sound approached: Bute, running in slippers, took shape out of the darkness, now turbid with mist. He viewed the locked gate with urbane dismay that seemed to acknowledge its own comic side. He did not strive nor cry, as Pellatt, Fane thought, would have done. "*Dis aliter visum*," Bute said, almost lightly; and then, "You did all that man could do for us. *Unus homo nobis cunctando restituit rem.* But Morris was out, running after vain things, when your messenger came, and Pellatt was in his hot bath. He'll be in hotter water to-morrow—that is, if——" He looked a rather wistful inquiry at Fane.

"Yes," said Fane, "I've wired the news."

"You did quite right," said Bute. "We asked for it. 'The gods are just, and of our pleasant vices Make whips to scourge us.'"

"I'm sorry," said Fane.

As they walked along towards the hotel Bute's arm slipped under Fane's. "I'll tell you," said Bute, "the way I got started on lying. Some silly yarn was going about that a wolf had appeared in the Lakes, and I was sent down by my paper to see. It was my first job; I was on trial. I toiled at the thing for two days, questioning farmers and shepherds until it was perfectly clear that the yarn was a hoax. I was just going back when my editor sent me a wire: 'Time you were seeing that wolf. Cannot afford waste like this.' Well, I had been engaged for three years and was longing to marry. I simply couldn't afford to be sacked. So I saw the wolf—with my little eye, I saw the wolf. That was the start. *Obsta principiis.* But it's devilish hard."

"I'm sorry," said Fane. He too was betrothed, and with him too the date was an affair of finance.

Dinner opened in gloom. Not till after the fish did the good claret do its kind office so far that Morris found tongue: "Stick together, boys—that's all there is to be done. We're all in it."

"I'm not," Fane avowed.

Pellatt glared at the tyro from under storm-laden brows. Morris jeered: "Saved by unpunctuality, eh?"

"I was in time," Fane confessed. Why the deuce had not Bute told the others and saved him, Fane, the beastly job of inflicting these punctures?

Pellatt looked up with his eyes, without raising his head, like a hanging judge asking a question that's sure to damn the accused. "You wired," he asked, "the news of this incredible postponement?"

"Yes," said Fane, with the rails of a dock seeming to sprout up all round him.

"Good God!" said Pellatt—and it sounded like "The Lord have mercy on your soul!"

"I suppose," said Morris, with vitriolic moderation, "loyalty is like gallantry: thank God when you see it, but don't take it hard if there's none."

"Perhaps"—Pellatt austerely ground out the words—"it had never occurred to Fane to consider all that is lost—I mean, of course, national loss—if an accident of the kind that has happened to-day is allowed to shake public faith in the Press—in the value, as I may say, of the authorised minutes of the nation's business as they are kept by the 'Day.'"

Then Fane himself lost hold. "How the deuce," he exclaimed, "could I know you were all playing this rotten trick?"

Pellatt straightened himself. "Trick!" he ejaculated, augustly. Oh, it was far from being their pleasantest evening!

But we are wondrously guided. On Fane's return from the authentic interment next day he found in his room a long telegram from his editor. It was forbearing, but ominous. Due allowance was made for his youth. Still, there was to be no more missing of first-class events, no more rash acceptance of unsifted rumours of postponements. Fortunately the paper had had a good report from the News Agency man to fall back on; otherwise the let-down would have been a disaster. Fane could imagine it all: first, the London evening papers spilling about the streets Morris's tale of the burying, wired before two o'clock; then Fane's own wired message coming roundabout in, over the 'phone, and looking absurd; then, lest there be anything in it, telephone messages flying about, to make sure, and word arriving that all was quite right and the funeral certainly over—the "Day" man and somebody else had sent it in full; and then the pencilled note of Fane's telephoned message going on to the spike in the editor's room, dismissed as the unpromising blunder of a beginner.

What good was it now to report the mere truth? It would not be printed. What paper liked giving the lie to itself? Not Fane's. He knew that, whatever else he did not know. And so he took a day off work, like the rest.

That was their last night in Callow. Fane may have not been elate, but a deep contentment filled two of the others, and Bute never spoiled sport. Pellatt and he both received their editors' felicitations by wire—Pellatt, "Best thanks—first-rate piece of work"; and Bute, "Bravo—the *chose vue* in perfection." All had seen Fane's paper now, and in their relief were prepared, each after his fashion, to let Fane down lightly. "For all the serious purposes of history," Pellatt impressively said in the genial last minutes before they all went to bed, "this fellow Curtayne *was* buried yesterday. Ten years from now he *will have been* buried yesterday."

"I'm not so sure," Morris put in. "There are these God-forsaken Irish papers. They'd say anything."

"Now, do you really often hear," Pellatt impressively asked, "of historians going down to the British Museum to check the file of the 'Day' by that of the 'Skibbereen Eagle'? History *must* have some sense of relative values in evidence."

"No," Bute admitted, "and yet—yet—do you know, I think there may be something in the ways of the Old Journalism after all." Fane felt he knew Bute now. The Butes of every age had been consenting to the stoning of the prophets, out of sheer niceness to the stoners. And yet—and yet all true-born Butes said now and then, while the stoning went merrily on: "Still, there may have been something in what the old buffer was saying." They were as open-minded as that.

"Fane," said Morris, holding up his last whisky before that last one of all which he always tried to carry upstairs in his hand, lest he perish of thirst in those upper wilds, "here's luck and forgiveness. Take care, though, next time. Mean t'shay, *trop de zèle* scuttles the ship. Well, we're none of us too old—mean t'shay, too young to learn. C'rect mishtakes and carry on. Goo'night."

Fane had come to know poor Morris too. But that was easier.

LORD DUNSANY

WHERE THE TIDES EBB AND FLOW

I DREAMT that I had done a horrible thing, so that burial was to be denied me either in soil or sea, neither could there be any hell for me.

I waited for some hours, knowing this. Then my friends came for me, and slew me secretly and with ancient rite, and lit great tapers, and carried me away.

It was all in London that the thing was done, and they went furtively at dead of night along grey streets and among mean houses until they came to the river. And the river and the tide of the sea were grappling with one another between the mud-banks, and both of them were black and full of lights. A sudden wonder came into the eyes of each, as my friends came near to them with their glaring tapers. All these things I saw as they carried me dead and stiffening, for my soul was still among my bones, because there was no hell for it, and because Christian burial was denied me.

They took me down a stairway that was green with slimy things, and so came slowly to the terrible mud. There, in the territory of forsaken things, they dug a shallow grave. When they had finished they laid me in the grave, and suddenly they cast their tapers to the river. And when the water had quenched the flaring lights, the tapers looked pale and small as they bobbed upon the tide, and at once the glamour of the calamity was gone, and I noticed then the approach of the huge dawn; and my friends cast their cloaks over their faces, and the solemn procession was turned into many fugitives that furtively stole away.

Then the mud came back wearily and covered all but my face. There I lay along with quite-forgotten things, with drifting things that the tides will take no farther, with useless things and lost things, and with the horrible, unnatural bricks that are neither stone nor soil. I was rid of feeling, because I had been killed, but perception and thought were in my unhappy soul. The dawn widened, and I saw the desolate houses that crowded the marge of the river, and their dead windows peered into my dead eyes: windows with bales behind them instead of human souls. I grew so weary looking at these forlorn things that I wanted to cry out, but could not, because I was dead. Then I knew, as I had never known before, that for all the years that herd of desolate houses had wanted to cry out too, but, being dead, were dumb. And I knew then that it had yet been well with the forgotten drifting things if they had wept, but they were eyeless and without life: and I, too, tried to weep, but there were no tears in my dead eyes. And I knew then that the river might have cared for us, might have caressed us, might have sung to us, but he swept broadly onwards, thinking of nothing but the princely ships.

At last the tide did what the river would not, and came and covered me over, and my soul had rest in the green water, and rejoiced and believed that it had the Burial of the Sea. But with the ebb the water fell again, and left me alone again with the callous mud among the forgotten things that drift no more, and with the sight of all those desolate houses, and with the knowledge among all of us that each was dead.

In the mournful wall behind me hung with green weeds, forsaken of the sea, dark tunnels appeared, and secret narrow passages that were clamped and barred. From these at last the stealthy rats came down to nibble me away, and my soul rejoiced thereat, and believed that he would be free perforce from the accursed bones to which burial was refused. Very soon the rats ran away a little space and whispered among themselves. They never came any more. When I found that I was accursed even among the rats, I tried to weep again.

Then the tide came swinging back and covered the dreadful mud, and hid the desolate houses, and soothed the forgotten things, and my soul had ease for a while in the sepulture of the sea. And then the tide forsook me again.

To and fro it came about me for many years. Then the County Council found me, and gave me decent burial. It was the first grave that I had ever slept in. That very night my friends came for me. They dug me up and put me back again in the shallow hole in the mud.

Again and again through the years my bones found burial, but always behind the funeral lurked one of those terrible men who, as soon as night fell, came and dug them up and carried them back again to the hole in the mud.

And then one day the last of those men died who once had done to me this terrible thing. I heard his soul go over the river at sunset.

And again I hoped.

A few weeks afterwards I was found once more, and once more taken out of that restless place and given deep burial in sacred ground, where my soul hoped that it should rest.

Almost at once men came with cloaks and tapers to give me back to the mud, for the thing had become a tradition and a rite. And all the forsaken things mocked me in their dumb hearts when they saw me carried back, for they were jealous of me because I had left the mud. It must be remembered that I could not weep.

And the years went by seawards where the black barges go, and the great derelict centuries became lost at sea, and still I lay there without any cause to hope, and daring not to hope without a cause, because of the terrible envy and the anger of the things that could drift no more.

Once a great storm rode up, even as far as London, out of the sea from the South; and he came curving into the river with the fierce East wind. And he was mightier than the dreary tides, and went with great leaps over the listless mud. And all the sad forgotten things rejoiced, and mingled with things that were haughtier than they, and rode once more amongst the lordly shipping that was driven up and down. And out of their hideous home he took my bones, never again, I hoped, to be vexed with the ebb and flow. And with the fall of the tide he went riding down the river and turned to the southwards, and so went to his home. And my bones he scattered among many isles and along the shores of happy alien mainlands. And for a moment, while they were far asunder, my soul was almost free.

Then there arose, at the will of the moon, the assiduous flow of the tide, and it undid at once the work of the ebb, and gathered my bones from the marge of sunny isles, and gleaned them all along the mainland's shores, and went rocking northwards till it came to the mouth of the Thames, and there turned westwards its relentless face, and so went up the river and came to the hole in the mud, and into it dropped my bones; and partly the mud covered them and partly it left them white, for the mud cares not for its forsaken things.

Then the ebb came, and I saw the dead eyes of the houses and the jealousy of the other forgotten things that the storm had not carried thence.

And some more centuries passed over the ebb and flow and over the loneliness of things forgotten. And I lay there all the while in the careless grip of the mud, never wholly covered, yet never able to go free, and I longed for the great caress of the warm Earth or the comfortable lap of the Sea.

Sometimes men found my bones and buried them, but the

tradition never died, and my friends' successors always brought them back. At last the barges went no more, and there were fewer lights; shaped timbers no longer floated down the fairway, and there came instead old wind-uprooted trees in all their natural simplicity.

At last I was aware that somewhere near me a blade of grass was growing, and the moss began to appear all over the dead houses. One day some thistledown went drifting over the river.

For some years I watched these signs attentively, until I became certain that London was passing away. Then I hoped once more, and all along both banks of the river there was anger among the lost things that anything should dare to hope upon the forsaken mud. Gradually the horrible houses crumbled, until the poor dead things that never had had life got decent burial among the weeds and moss. At last the may appeared and the convolvulus. Finally, the wild rose stood up over mounds that had been wharves and warehouses. Then I knew that the cause of Nature had triumphed, and London had passed away.

The last man in London came to the wall by the river, in an ancient cloak that was one of those that once my friends had worn, and peered over the edge to see that I still was there. Then he went, and I never saw men again: they had passed away with London.

A few days after the last man had gone the birds came into London, all the birds that sing. When they first saw me they all looked sideways at me, then they went away a little and spoke among themselves.

"He only sinned against Man," they said; "it is not our quarrel."

"Let us be kind to him," they said.

Then they hopped nearer me and began to sing. It was the time of the rising of the dawn, and from both banks of the river, and from the sky, and from the thickets that were once the streets, hundreds of birds were singing. As the light increased the birds sang more and more; they grew thicker and thicker in the air above my head, till there were thousands of them singing there, and then millions, and at last I could see nothing but a host of flickering wings with the sunlight on them, and little gaps of sky. Then when there was nothing to be heard in London but the myriad notes of that exultant song, my soul rose up from the bones in the hole in the mud and began to climb up the song heavenwards. And it seemed that a laneway opened amongst the wings of the birds, and it went up and up, and one of the smaller gates of Paradise stood ajar at the end of it. And then I knew by a sign that the mud should receive me no more, for suddenly I found that I could weep.

At this moment I opened my eyes in bed in a house in London, and outside some sparrows were twittering in a tree in the light of the radiant morning; and there were tears still wet upon my face, for one's restraint is feeble while one sleeps. But I arose and opened the window wide, and, stretching my hands out over the little garden, I blessed the birds whose song had woken me up from the troubled and terrible centuries of my dream.

LIAM O'FLAHERTY

HIS FIRST FLIGHT

THE young seagull was alone on his ledge. His two brothers and his sister had already flown away the day before. He had been afraid to fly with them. Somehow when he had taken a little run forward to the brink of the ledge and attempted to flap his wings he became afraid. The great expanse of sea stretched down beneath, and it was such a long way down—miles down. He felt certain that his wings would never support him, so he bent his head and ran away back to the little hole under the ledge where he slept at night. Even when each of his brothers and his little sister, whose wings were far shorter than his own, ran to the brink, flapped their wings, and flew away he failed to muster up courage to take that plunge which appeared to him so desperate. His father and mother had come around calling to him shrilly, upbraiding him, threatening to let him starve on his ledge unless he flew away. But for the life of him he could not move.

That was twenty-four hours ago. Since then nobody had come near him. The day before, all day long, he had watched his parents flying about with his brothers and sister, perfecting them in the art of flight, teaching them how to skim the waves and how to dive for fish. He had, in fact, seen his older brother catch his first herring and devour it, standing on a rock, while his parents circled around raising a proud cackle. And all the morning the whole family had walked about on the big plateau midway down the opposite cliff taunting him with his cowardice.

The sun was now ascending the sky, blazing warmly on his ledge that faced the south. He felt the heat because he had not eaten since the previous nightfall. Then he had found a dried piece of mackerel's tail at the far end of his ledge. Now there was not a single scrap of food left. He had searched every inch, rooting among the rough, dirt-caked straw nest where he and his brothers and sister had been hatched. He even gnawed at the dried pieces of spotted eggshell. It was like eating part of himself. He had then trotted back and forth from one end of the ledge to the other, his grey body the colour of the cliff, his long grey legs stepping daintily, trying to find some means of reaching his parents without having to fly. But on each side of him the ledge ended in a sheer fall of precipice, with the sea beneath. And between him and his parents there was a deep, wide chasm. Surely he could reach them without flying if he could only move northwards along the cliff face? But then on what could he walk? There was no ledge, and he was not a fly. And above him he could see nothing. The precipice was sheer, and the top of it was perhaps farther away than the sea beneath him.

He stepped slowly out to the brink of the ledge, and, standing on one leg with the other leg hidden under his wing, he closed one eye, then the other, and pretended to be falling asleep. Still they took no notice of him. He saw his two brothers and his sister lying on the plateau dozing, with their heads sunk into their necks. His father was preening the feathers on his white back. Only his mother was looking at him. She was standing on a little high hump on the plateau, her white breast thrust forward. Now and again she tore at a piece of fish that lay at her feet, and then scraped each side of her beak on the rock. The sight of the food maddened him. How he loved to tear food that way, scraping his beak now and again to whet it! He uttered a low cackle. His mother cackled too, and looked over at him.

"Ga, ga, ga," he cried, begging her to bring him over some food. "Gaw-ool-ah," she screamed back derisively. But he kept calling plaintively, and after a minute or so he uttered a joyful scream. His mother had picked up a piece of the fish and was flying across to him with it. He leaned out eagerly, tapping the rock with his feet, trying to get nearer to her as she flew across. But when she was just opposite to him, abreast of the ledge, she halted, her legs hanging limp, her wings motionless, the piece of fish in her beak almost within reach of his beak. He waited a moment in surprise, wondering why she did not come nearer, and then, maddened by hunger, he dived at the fish. With a loud scream he fell outwards and downwards into space. His mother had swooped upwards. As he passed beneath her he heard the swish of her wings. Then a monstrous terror seized him and his heart stood still. He could hear nothing. But it only lasted a moment. The next moment he felt his wings spread outwards. The wind rushed against his breast feathers, then under his stomach and against his wings. He could feel the tips of his wings cutting through the air. He was not falling headlong now. He was soaring gradually downwards and outwards. He was no longer afraid. He just felt a bit dizzy. Then he flapped his wings once and he soared upwards. He uttered a joyous scream and flapped them again. He soared higher. He raised his breast and banked against the wind. "Ga, ga, ga. Ga, ga, ga. Gaw-ool-ah." His mother swooped past him, her wings making a loud noise. He answered her with another scream. Then his father flew over him screaming. Then he saw his two brothers and his sister flying around him curveting and banking and soaring and diving.

Then he completely forgot that he had not always been able to fly, and commenced himself to dive and soar and curvet, shrieking shrilly.

He was near the sea now, flying straight over it, facing straight out over the ocean. He saw a vast green sea beneath him, with little ridges moving over it, and he turned his beak sideways and crowed amusedly. His parents and his brothers and sister had landed on this green floor in front of him. They were beckoning to him, calling shrilly. He dropped his legs to stand on the green sea. His legs sank into it. He screamed with fright and attempted to rise again, flapping his wings. But he was tired and weak with hunger and he could not rise, exhausted by the strange exercise. His feet sank into the green sea, and then his belly touched it and he sank no farther. He was floating on it. And around him his family was screaming, praising him, and their beaks were offering him scraps of dog-fish.

He had made his first flight.

MULK RAJ ANAND

THE LOST CHILD

IT was the festival of Spring. From the wintry shades of narrow lanes and alleys emerged a gaily clad humanity, thick as a crowd of bright-coloured rabbits issuing from a warren, and entering the flooded sea of sparkling silver sunshine outside the city gates, sped towards the fair. Some walked, some rode on horses, others sat, being carried in bamboo and bullock-carts. One little boy ran between his parent's legs, brimming over with life and laughter, as the joyous, smiling morning, with its open greetings and unashamed invitations to come away into the fields, full of flowers and songs.

" Come, child, come," called his parents, as he lagged behind, arrested by the toys in the shops that lined the way.

He hurried towards his parents, his feet obedient to their call, his eyes still lingering on the receding toys. As he came to where they had stopped to wait for him, he could not suppress the desire of his heart, even though he well knew the old, cold stare of refusal in their eyes.

" I want that toy," he pleaded.

His father looked at him red-eyed in his familiar tyrant's way. His mother, melted by the free spirit of the day, was tender, and giving him her finger to catch, said:

" Look, child, what is before you."

The faint disgust of the child's unfulfilled desire had hardly been quelled in the heavy, pouting sob of a breath, " M—o—th—e—r," when the pleasure of what was before him filled his eager eyes. They had left the dusty road on which they had walked so far to wend its weary way circuitously to the north, and had entered a footpath in a field.

It was a flowering mustard-field, pale, pale, like melting gold, as it swept across miles and miles of even land, a river of yellow light, ebbing and falling with each fresh eddy of wild wind, and straying at places into broad, rich tributary streams, yet running in a constant sunny sweep towards the distant mirage of an ocean of silver light. Where it ended, on a side stood a dense group of low, mudwalled houses put into relief both by the lower forms of a denser crowd of yellow-robed men and women and by high-pitched sequence of whistling, creaking, squeaking, roaring, humming noises that rose from it, across the groves, to the blue-throated sky like the weird, strange sound of Siva's mad laughter.

The child looked up to his father and mother, saturated with the shrill joy and wonder of this vast glory, and feeling that they, too, wore the evidence of this pure delight in their faces, left the footpath and plunged headlong into the field, prancing like a young colt, his small feet chiming with the fitful gusts of wind that came winnowing from the fragrance of more distant fields.

A group of dragon-flies were bustling about on their gauzy, purple wings, intercepting the flight of a lone black bee or butterfly in search of sweet perfume from the hearts of flowers. The child followed them in the air, with his gaze, till one of them would fold its wings and sit down, and he would try to catch it. But it would go, fluttering, flapping, hovering in the air, when he had almost caught it in his hands. One bold black bee, having evaded capture, sought to tempt him by whining round his ear, and nearly settled on his lips, when his mother made a cautionary call:

"Come, child, come; come on the footpath."

He went towards his parents gaily, and walked abreast of them for a while, being, however, soon left behind, attracted by the little insects and worms along the footpath that were coming out teeming from their hiding-places to enjoy the sunshine.

"Come, child, come," his parents called from the shade of a grove where they had seated themselves on the edge of a well. He ran towards them.

An old banyan here outstretched its powerful arms over the blossoming jack and jaman and neem and champak and serisha, and cast its shadows across beds of golden cassis and crimson gulmohur, as an old grandmother spreads her skirts over her young ones. The blushing blossoms freely offered their adoration to the Sun, however, in spite of their protecting chaperon, by half uncovering themselves; and the sweet perfume of their pollen mingled with the soft, cool breeze that came and went in little puffs, only to be wafted aloft by a stronger gush.

A shower of young flowers fell upon the child as he entered the grove, and, forgetting his parents, he began to gather the raining petals in his hands, but lo! he heard the cooing of the doves and ran towards his parents, shouting: "The dove!

The dove!" The raining petals dropped from his forgotten hands. A curious look was in his parents' faces, till a koel struck out a note of love and released their pent-up souls.

"Come, child, come," they called to the child, who had now gone running in a wild caper round the banyan tree and, gathering him, they took the narrow, winding footpath which led to the fair from the mustard-fields.

As they neared the village, the child could see many other footpaths full of throngs, converging to the whirlpool of the fair, and felt at once repelled and fascinated by the confusion of the world he was entering.

A sweetmeat-seller hawked, "Gulab-jaman, rasgula, burfi, jalebi," at the corner of the entrance, and a crowd pressed round his counter at the foot of an architecture of many-coloured sweets, decorated with leaves of silver and gold. The child stared open-eyed, and his mouth watered for the burfi that was his favourite sweet. "I want that burfi," he slowly murmured. But he half knew as he made the request that it would not be heeded, because his parents would say he was greedy. So, without waiting for an answer, he moved on.

A flower-seller hawked, "A garland of gulmohur, a garland of gulmohur." The child seemed irresistibly drawn by the implacable sweetness of the scents that came floating on the wings of the languid air. He went towards the basket where the flowers lay heaped and half murmured, "I want that garland," but he well knew his parents would refuse to buy him these flowers because they would say they were cheap. So, without waiting for an answer, he moved on.

A man stood holding a pole with yellow, red, green and purple balloons flying from it. The child was simply carried away by the rainbow glory of their silken colours, and he was possessed by an overwhelming desire to possess them all. But he well knew his parents would never buy him the balloons, because they would say he was too old to play with such toys. So he walked on farther.

A juggler stood playing a flute to a snake which coiled itself in a basket, its head raised in a graceful bend like the neck of a swan, while the music stole into its invisible ears like the gentle rippling of a miniature water-fall. The child went towards the juggler. But knowing his parents had forbidden him to hear such coarse music as the jugglers play, he proceeded farther.

There was a roundabout in full swing. Men, women and children, carried in a whirling motion, shrieked and cried with dizzy laughter. The child watched them intently going round and round, a pink blush of a smile on his face, his eyes rippling with the same movement, his lips half parted in amaze, till he felt he himself was being carried round. The ring seemed to go fiercely at first, then gradually it began to move less fast. Presently, the child, rapt, his finger in his mouth, beheld it stop. This time, before his over-powering love of his anticipated sensation of movement had been chilled by the fact of his parents' eternal denial, he made a bold request: "I want to go on the roundabout, please, father, mother."

There was no reply. He turned to look at his parents. They were not there, ahead of him. He turned to look on the side. They were not there. He looked behind. There was no sign of them.

A full, deep cry arose within his dry throat, and with a sudden jerk of his body he ran from where he stood, crying in red fear, "Mother, father." Tears rained down from his eyes, heavy and fierce, his flushed face was convulsed with fear. Panic-stricken, he ran to one side first, then to the other, before and aft in all directions, knowing not where to go. "Mother, father," he wailed, with a moist, shrill breath now, his throat being wet with the swallowing of his spittle. His yellow turban came untied, and his clothes, wet with perspiration, became muddy where the dust had mixed with the sweat of his body. His light frame seemed heavy as a mass of lead.

Having run to and fro in a sheer rage of running for a while, he stood defeated, his cries suppressed into sobs. At little distances on the green grass he could see, through his filmy eyes, men and women talking. He tried to look intensively among the patches of bright yellow clothes, but there was no sign of his father and mother among these people, who seemed to laugh and talk just for the sake of laughing and talking. He ran hotly again, this time to a shrine to which people seemed to be crowding. Every little inch of space here was congested with men, but he ran through people's legs, his little sob lingering, "Mother, father." Near the entrance of the temple, however, the crowd became very thick: men jostled each other—heavy men, with flashing, murderous eyes and hefty shoulders. The poor child struggled to carve a way between their feet, but, knocked to and fro by their brutal paws, he might have been trampled underfoot, had he not shrieked at the highest pitch of his voice, "F—ather, mother." A man in the surging crowd heard his groan, and, stooping with very great difficulty, lifted him up in his arms.

"How did you get here, child? Whose baby are you?" the man asked as he steered clear of the mass.

The child wept more bitterly than ever now and only cried, "I want my mother, I want my father."

The man tried to soothe him by taking him up to the round-about. " Will you have a lift on the horses? " he gently asked as he approached the ring.

The child's throat tore into a thousand shrill sobs and he only shouted, " I want my mother, I want my father."

The man headed towards the place where the juggler still played on the flute to the dancing cobra.

" Listen to that nice music, child," he pleaded.

But the child shut his ears with his fingers and shouted his double-pitched strain, " I want my mother, I want my father."

The man took him near the balloons, thinking the bright colours of the balls would distract the child's attention and quieten him. " Would you like a rainbow-coloured balloon? " he persuasively asked.

But the child turned his eyes from the flying balloons and just sobbed, " I want my mother, I want my father."

The man, still importunate in his kindly desire to make the child happy, bore him to the gate where the flower-seller stood. " Look! Can you smell these nice flowers, child? Would you like a garland to put round your neck? "

The child turned his nose away from the basket and reiterated his sob, " I want my mother, I want my father."

Thinking to humour his disconsolate find by a gift of sweets, the man took him to the counter of the sweet-shop. " What sweets would you like, child? " he asked.

The child turned his face from the sweet-shop and only sobbed, " I want my mother, I want my father."

OLIVE SCHREINER

THE BUDDHIST PRIEST'S WIFE

COVER her up! How still it lies! You can see the outline under the white. You would think she was asleep. Let the sunshine come in; it loved it so. She that had travelled so far, in so many lands, and done so much and seen so much, how she must like rest now! Did she ever love anything absolutely, this woman whom so many men loved, and so many women; who gave so much sympathy and never asked for anything in return! did she ever need a love she could not have? Was she never obliged to unclasp her fingers from anything to which they clung? Was she really so strong as she looked? Did she never wake up in the night crying for that which she could not have? Were thought and travel enough for her? Did she go about for long days with a weight that crushed her to earth? Cover her up! I do not think she would have liked us to look at her. In one way she was alone all her life; she would have liked to be alone now! . . . Life must have been very beautiful to her, or she would not look so young now. Cover her up! Let us go!

. . . . . .

Many years ago in a London room, up long flights of stairs, a fire burnt up in a grate. It showed the marks on the walls where pictures had been taken down, and the little blue flowers in the wall-paper and the blue felt carpet on the floor, and a woman sat by the fire in a chair at one side.

Presently the door opened, and the old woman came in who took care of the entrance hall downstairs.

"Do you not want anything to-night?" she said.

"No, I am only waiting for a visitor; when they have been, I shall go."

"Have you got all your things taken away already?"

"Yes, only these I am leaving."

The old woman went down again, but presently came up with a cup of tea in her hand.

"You must drink that; it's good for one. Nothing helps one like tea when one's been packing all day."

The young woman at the fire did not thank her, but she ran her hand over the old woman's from the wrist to the fingers.

"I'll say good-bye to you when I go out."

The woman poked the fire, put the last coals on, and went.

When she had gone the young one did not drink the tea but drew her little silver cigarette-case from her pocket and lighted a cigarette. For a while she sat smoking by the fire; then she stood up and walked the room.

When she had paced for a while she sat down again beside the fire. She threw the end of her cigarette away into the fire, and then began to walk again with her hands behind her. Then she went back to her seat and lit another cigarette, and paced again. Presently she sat down, and looked into the fire; she pressed the palms of her hands together, and then sat quietly staring into it.

Then there was a sound of feet on the stairs and someone knocked at the door.

She rose and threw the end into the fire and said without moving, "Come in."

The door opened and a man stood there in evening dress. He had a great-coat on, open in front.

"May I come in? I couldn't get rid of this downstairs; I didn't see where to leave it!" He took his coat off. "How are you? This is a real bird's nest!"

She motioned to a chair.

"I hope you did not mind my asking you to come?"

"Oh no, I am delighted. I only found your note at my club twenty minutes ago."

He sat down on a chair before the fire.

"So you really are going to India? How delightful! But what are you to do there? I think it was Grey told me six weeks ago you were going, but regarded it as one of those mythical stories which don't deserve credence. Yet I'm sure I don't know! Why, nothing would surprise me."

He looked at her in a half-amused, half-interested way.

"What a long time it is since we met! Six months, eight?"

"Seven," she said.

"I really thought you were trying to avoid me. What have you been doing with yourself all this time?"

"Oh, been busy. Won't you have a cigarette?"

She held out the little case to him.

"Won't you take one yourself? I know you object to smoking with men, but you can make an exception in my case!"

"Thank you." She lit her own and passed him the matches.

"But really, what have you been doing with yourself all this time? You've entirely disappeared from civilised life. When I was down at the Grahams' in the spring, they said you were coming down there, and then at the last moment cried off. We were all quite disappointed. What is taking you to India now? Going to preach the doctrine of social and intellectual equality to the Hindu women and incite them to revolt? Marry some old Buddhist priest, build a little cottage on the top of the Himalayas and live there, discuss philosophy and meditate? I believe that's what you'd like. I really shouldn't wonder if I heard you'd done it!"

She laughed and took out her cigarette-case.

She smoked slowly.

"I've been here a long time, four years, and I want change. I was glad to see how well you succeeded in that election," she said. "You were much interested in it, were you not?"

"Oh, yes. We had a stiff fight. It tells in my favour, you know, though it was not exactly a personal matter. But it was a great worry."

"Don't you think," she said, "you were wrong in sending that letter to the papers? It would have strengthened your position to have remained silent."

"Yes, perhaps so; I think so now, but I did it under advice. However, we've won, so it's all right." He leaned back in the chair.

"Are you pretty fit?"

"Oh, yes; pretty well; bored, you know. One doesn't know what all this working and striving is for sometimes."

"Where are you going for your holiday this year?"

"Oh, Scotland, I suppose; I always do; the old quarters."

"Why don't you go to Norway? It would be more change for you and rest you more. Did you get a book on sport in Norway?"

"Did you send it me? How kind of you! I read it with much interest. I was almost inclined to start off there and then. I suppose it is the kind of *vis inertiæ* that creeps over one as one grows older that sends one back to the old place. A change would be much better."

"There's a list at the end of the book," she said, "of exactly the things one needs to take. I thought it would save trouble; you could just give it to your man, and let him get them all. Have you still got him?"

"Oh, yes. He's as faithful to me as a dog. I think nothing would induce him to leave me. He won't allow me to go out hunting since I sprained my foot last autumn. I have to do it surreptitiously. He thinks I can't keep my seat with a sprained ankle; but he's a very good fellow; takes care of me like a mother." He smoked quietly with the firelight glowing on his black coat. "But what are you going to India for? Do you know anyone there?"

"No," she said. "I think it will be so splendid. I've

always been a great deal interested in the East. It's a complex, interesting life."

He turned and looked at her.

"Going to seek for more experience, you'll say, I suppose. I never knew a woman throw herself away as you do; a woman with your brilliant parts and attractions, to let the whole of life slip through your hands, and make nothing of it. You ought to be the most successful woman in London. Oh, yes; I know what you are going to say: 'You don't care.' That's just it; you don't. You are always going to get experience, going to get everything, and you never do. You are always going to write when you know enough, and you are never satisfied that you do. You ought to be making your two thousand a year, but you don't care. That's just it! Living, burying yourself here with a lot of old frumps. You will never do anything. You could have everything and you let it slip."

"Oh, my life is very full," she said. "There are only two things that are absolute realities, love and knowledge, and you can't escape them."

She had thrown her cigarette-end away and was looking into the fire, smiling.

"I've let these rooms to a woman friend of mine." She glanced round the room, smiling. "She doesn't know I'm going to leave these things here for her. She'll like them because they were mine. The world's very beautiful, I think—delicious."

"Oh, yes. But what do you do with it? What do you make of it? You ought to settle down and marry like other women, not go wandering about the world to India and China and Italy, and God knows where. You are simply making a mess of your life. You're always surrounding yourself with all sorts of extraordinary people. If I hear any man or woman is a great friend of yours, I always say: 'What's the matter? Lost his money? Lost his character? Got an incurable disease?' I believe the only way in which anyone becomes interesting to you is by having some complaint of mind or body. I believe you worship rags. To come and shut yourself up in a place like this away from everybody and everything! It's a mistake; it's idiotic, you know."

"I'm very happy," she said. "You see," she said, leaning towards the fire with her hands on her knees, "what matters is that something should need you. It isn't a question of love. What's the use of being near a thing if other people could serve it as well as you can. If they could serve it better, it's pure selfishness. It's the need of one thing for another that makes the organic bond of union. You love mountains and horses, but they don't need you; so what's the use of saying anything about it! I suppose the most absolutely delicious thing in life is to feel a thing needs you, and to give at the moment it needs. Things that don't need you, you must love from a distance."

"Oh, but a woman like you ought to marry, ought to have children. You go squandering yourself on every old beggar or forlorn female or escaped criminal you meet; it may be very nice for them, but it's a mistake from your point of view."

He touched the ash gently with the tip of his little finger and let it fall.

"I intend to marry. It's a curious thing," he said, resuming his pose with an elbow on one knee and his head bent forward on one side, so that she saw the brown hair with its close curls a little tinged with grey at the sides, "that when a man reaches a certain age he wants to marry. He doesn't fall in love; it's not that he definitely plans anything; but he has a feeling that he ought to have a home and a wife and children. I suppose it is the same kind of feeling that makes a bird build nests at certain times of the year. It's not love; it's something else. When I was a young man I used to despise men for getting married; wondered what they did it for; they had everything to lose and nothing to gain. But when a man gets to be six-and-thirty his feeling changes. It's not love, passion, he wants; it's a home; it's a wife and children. He may have a house and servants; it isn't the same thing. I should have thought a woman would have felt it too."

She was quiet for a minute, holding a cigarette between her fingers; then she said slowly:

"Yes, at times a woman has a curious longing to have a child, especially when she gets near to thirty or over it. It's something distinct from love for any definite person. But it's a thing one has to get over. For a woman, marriage is much more serious than for a man. She might pass her life without meeting a man whom she could possibly love, and, if she met him, it might not be right or possible. Marriage has become very complex now it has become so largely intellectual. Won't you have another?"

She held out the case to him. "You can light it from mine." She bent forward for him to light it.

"You are a man who ought to marry. You've no absorbing mental work with which the woman would interfere; it would complete you." She sat back, smoking serenely.

"Yes," he said, "but life is too busy; I never find time to look for one, and I haven't a fancy for the pink-and-white prettiness so common and that some men like so. I need something else. If I am to have a wife I shall have to go to America to look for one."

"Yes, an American would suit you best."

"Yes," he said, "I don't want a woman to look after; she must be self-sustaining and she mustn't bore you. You know what I mean. Life is too full of cares to have a helpless child added to them."

"Yes," she said, standing up and leaning with her elbow against the fireplace. "The kind of woman you want would be young and strong; she need not be excessively beautiful, but she must be attractive; she must have energy, but not too strongly marked an individuality; she must be largely neutral; she need not give you too passionate or too deep a devotion, but she must second you in a thoroughly rational manner. She must have the same aims and tastes that you have. No woman has the right to marry a man if she has to bend herself out of shape for him. She might wish to, but she could never be to him with all her passionate endeavour what the other woman could be to him without trying. Character will dominate over all and will come out at last."

She looked down into the fire.

"When you marry you mustn't marry a woman who flatters you too much. It is always a sign of falseness somewhere. If a woman absolutely loves you as herself, she will criticise and understand you as herself. Two people who are to live through life together must be able to look into each other's eyes and speak the truth. That helps one through life. You would find many such women in America," she said: "women who would help you to succeed, who would not drag you down."

"Yes, that's my idea. But how am I to obtain the ideal woman?"

"Go and look for her. Go to America instead of Scotland this year. It is perfectly right. A man has a right to look for what he needs. With a woman it is different. That's one of the radical differences between men and women."

She looked downwards into the fire.

"It's a law of her nature and of sex relationship. There's nothing arbitrary or conventional about it any more than there is in her having to bear her child while the male does not. Intellectually we may both be alike. I suppose if fifty men and fifty women had to solve a mathematical problem, they would all do it in the same way; the more abstract and intellectual, the more alike we are. The nearer you approach to the personal and sexual, the more different we are. If I were to represent men's and women's natures," she said, "by a diagram, I would take two circular discs; the right side of each I should paint bright red; then I would shade the red away till in a spot on the left edge it became blue in the one and green in the other. That spot represents sex, and the nearer you come to it, the more the two discs differ in colour. Well then, if you turn them so that the red sides touch, they seem to be exactly alike, but if you turn them so that the green and blue paint form their point of contact, they will seem to be entirely unlike. That's why you notice the brutal, sensual men invariably believe women are entirely different from men, another species of creature; and very cultured, intellectual men sometimes believe we are exactly alike. You see, sex love in its substance may be the same in both of us; in the form of its expression it must differ. It is not man's fault; it is nature's. If a man loves a woman, he has a right to try to make her love him because he can do it openly, directly, without bending. There need be no subtlety, no indirectness. With a woman it's not so; she can take no love that is not laid openly, simply, at her feet. Nature ordains that she should never show what she feels; the woman who had told a man she loved him would have put between them a barrier once and for ever that could not be crossed; and if she subtly drew him towards her, using the woman's means—silence, finesse, the dropped handkerchief, the surprise visit, the gentle assertion she had not thought to see him when she had come a long way to meet him, then she would be damned; she would hold the love, but she would have desecrated it by subtlety; it would have no value. Therefore she must always go with her arms folded sexually; only the love which lays itself down at her feet and implores of her to accept it is love she can ever rightly take up. That is the true difference between a man and a woman. You may seek for love because you can do it openly; we cannot because we must do it subtly. A woman should always walk with her arms folded. Of course friendship is different. You are on a perfect equality with man then; you can ask him to come and see you as I asked you. That's the beauty of the intellect and intellectual life to a woman, that she drops her shackles a little; and that is why she shrinks from sex so. If she were dying perhaps, or doing something equal to death, she might. . . . Death means so much more to a woman than a man; when you knew you were dying, to look round on the world and feel the bond of sex that has broken and crushed you all your life gone, nothing but the human left, no woman any more, to meet everything on perfectly even ground. There's no reason why you shouldn't go to America and look for a wife perfectly deliberately. You will have to tell no lies. Look till you find a woman that you absolutely love, that you have not the smallest doubt suits you apart from love, and then ask her to marry you. You must have children; the life of an old childless man is very sad."

"Yes, I should like to have children. I often feel now, what is it all for, this work, this striving, and no one to leave it to? It's a blank, suppose I succeed . . .?"

"Suppose you get your title?"

"Yes; what is it all worth to me if I've no one to leave it to? That's my feeling. It's really very strange to be sitting and talking like this to you. But you are so different from other women. If all women were like you, all your theories of the equality of men and women would work. You're the only woman with whom I never realise that she is a woman."

"Yes," she said.

She stood looking down into the fire.

"How long will you stay in India?"

"Oh, I'm not coming back."

"Not coming back! That's impossible. You will be breaking the hearts of half the people here if you don't. I never knew a woman who had such power of entrapping men's hearts as you have in spite of that philosophy of yours. I don't know," he smiled, "that I should not have fallen into the snare myself—three years ago I almost thought I should—if you hadn't always attacked me so incontinently and persistently on all and every point and on each and every occasion. A man doesn't like pain. A succession of slaps damps him. But it doesn't seem to have that effect on other men. . . . There was that fellow down in the country when I was there last year, perfectly ridiculous. You know his name . . ."—he moved his fingers to try and remember it—"big, yellow moustache, a major, gone to the east coast of Africa now; the ladies unearthed it that he was always carrying about a photograph of yours in his pocket; and he used to take out little scraps of things you printed and show them to people mysteriously. He almost had a duel with a man one night after dinner because he mentioned you; he seemed to think there was something incongruous between your name and——"

"I do not like to talk of any man who has loved me," she said. "However small and poor his nature may be, he has given me his best. There is nothing ridiculous in love. I think a woman should feel that all the love men have given her which she has not been able to return is a kind of crown set up above her which she is always trying to grow tall enough to wear. I can't bear to think that all the love that has been given me has been wasted on something unworthy of it. Men have been very beautiful and greatly honoured me. I am grateful to them. If a man tells you he loves you," she said, looking into the fire, " with his breast uncovered before you for you to strike him if you will, the least you can do is to put out your hand and cover it up from other people's eyes. If I were a deer," she said, " and a stag got hurt following me, even though I could not have him for a companion, I would stand still and scrape the sand with my foot over the place where his blood had fallen; the rest of the herd should never know he had been hurt there following me. I would cover the blood up, if I were a deer," she said, and then she was silent.

Presently she sat down in her chair and said, with her hand before her: " Yet, you know, I have not the ordinary feeling about love. I think the one who is loved confers the benefit on the one who loves, it's been so great and beautiful that it should be loved. I think the man should be grateful to the woman or the woman to the man whom they have been able to love, whether they have been loved back or whether circumstances have divided them or not." She stroked her knee softly with her hand.

" Well, really, I must go now." He pulled out his watch. " It's so fascinating sitting here talking that I could stay all night, but I've still two engagements." He rose; she rose also and stood before him looking up at him for a moment.

" How well you look! I think you have found the secret of perpetual youth. You don't look a day older than when I first saw you just four years ago. You always look as if you were on fire and being burnt up, but you never are, you know."

He looked down at her with a kind of amused face as one does at an interesting child or a big Newfoundland dog.

" When shall we see you back? "

" Oh, not at all! "

" Not at all! Oh, we must have you back; you belong here, you know. You'll get tired of your Buddhist and come back to us."

" You didn't mind my asking you to come and say good-bye? " she said in a childish manner unlike her determinateness when she discussed anything impersonal. " I wanted to say good-bye to everyone. If one hasn't said good-bye one feels restless and feels one would have to come back. If one has said good-bye to all one's friends, then one knows it is all ended."

" Oh, this isn't a final farewell! You must come in ten years' time and we'll compare notes—you about your Buddhist

Priest, I about my fair ideal American; and we'll see who succeeded best."

She laughed. "I shall always see your movements chronicled in the newspapers, so we shall not be quite sundered; and you will hear of me perhaps."

"Yes, I hope you will be very successful."

She was looking at him, with her eyes wide open, from head to foot. He turned to the chair where his coat hung.

"Can't I help you put it on?"

"Oh, no, thank you."

He put it on.

"Button the throat," she said, "the room is warm."

He turned to her in his great-coat and with his gloves. They were standing near the door.

"Well, good-bye. I hope you will have a very pleasant time."

He stood looking down upon her, wrapped in his great-coat.

She put up one hand a little in the air. "I want to ask you something," she said quickly.

"Well, what is it?"

"Will you please kiss me?"

For a moment he looked down at her, then he bent over her.

In after years he could never tell certainly, but he always thought she put up her hand and rested it on the crown of his head, with a curious soft caress, something like a mother's touch when her child is asleep and she does not want to wake it. Then he looked round, and she was gone. The door had closed noiselessly. For a moment he stood motionless, then he walked to the fireplace and looked down into the fender at a little cigarette-end lying there, then he walked quickly back to the door and opened it. The stairs were in darkness and silence. He rang the bell violently. The old woman came up. He asked her where the lady was. She said she had gone out, she had a cab waiting. He asked when she would be back. The old woman said, "Not at all"; she had left. He asked where she had gone. The woman said she did not know; she had left orders that all her letters should be kept for six or eight months till she wrote and sent her address. He asked whether she had no idea where he might find her. The woman said no. He walked up to a space in the wall where a picture had hung and stood staring at it as though the picture were still hanging there. He drew his mouth as though he were emitting a long whistle, but no sound came. He gave the old woman ten shillings and went downstairs.

That was eight years ago.

How beautiful life must have been to it that it looks so young still!

TAKING THE VEIL

IT seemed impossible that anyone should be unhappy on such a beautiful morning. Nobody was, decided Edna, except herself. The windows were flung wide in the houses. From within there came the sound of pianos, little hands chased after each other and ran away from each other, practising scales. The trees fluttered in the sunny gardens, all bright with spring flowers. Street-boys whistled, a little dog barked; people passed by, walking so lightly, so swiftly, they looked as though they wanted to break into a run. Now she actually saw in the distance a parasol, peach-coloured, the first parasol of the year.

Perhaps even Edna did not look quite as unhappy as she felt. It is not easy to look tragic at eighteen, when you are extremely pretty, with the cheeks and lips and shining eyes of perfect health. Above all, when you are wearing a French blue frock and your new spring hat trimmed with cornflowers. True, she carried under her arm a book bound in horrid black leather. Perhaps the book provided a gloomy note, but only by accident; it was the ordinary Library binding. For Edna had made going to the Library an excuse for getting out of the house to think, to realise what had happened, to decide somehow what was to be done now.

An awful thing had happened. Quite suddenly, at the theatre last night, when she and Jimmy were seated side by side in the dress-circle, without a moment's warning—in fact, she had just finished a chocolate almond and passed the box to him again—she had fallen in love with an actor. But—fallen—in—love . . .

The feeling was unlike anything she had ever imagined before. It wasn't in the least pleasant. It was hardly thrilling. Unless you can call the most dreadful sensation of hopeless misery, despair, agony and wretchedness, thrilling. Combined with the certainty that if that actor met her on the pavement after, while Jimmy was fetching their cab, she would follow him to the ends of the earth, at a nod, at a sign, without giving another thought to Jimmy or her father and mother or her happy home and countless friends again . . .

The play had begun fairly cheerfully. That was at the chocolate-almond stage. Then the hero had gone blind. Terrible moment! Edna had cried so much she had to borrow Jimmy's folded, smooth-feeling handkerchief as well. Not that crying mattered. Whole rows were in tears. Even the men blew their noses with a loud trumpeting noise and tried to peer at the programme instead of looking at the stage. Jimmy, most mercifully dry-eyed—for what would she have done without his handkerchief?—squeezed her free hand, and whispered "Cheer up, darling girl!" And it was then she had taken a last chocolate almond to please him and passed the box again. Then there had been that ghastly scene with the hero alone on the stage in a deserted room at twilight, with a band playing outside and the sound of cheering coming from the street. He had tried—ah! how painfully, how pitifully!—to grope his way to the window. He had succeeded at last. There he stood holding the curtain while one beam of light, just one beam, shone full on his raised, sightless face, and the band faded away into the distance . . .

It was—really, it was absolutely—oh, the most—it was simply—in fact, from that moment Edna knew that life could never be the same. She drew her hand away from Jimmy's, leaned back, and shut the chocolate box for ever. This at last was love!

Edna and Jimmy were engaged. She had had her hair up for a year and a half; they had been publicly engaged for a year. But they had known they were going to marry each other ever since they walked in the Botanical Gardens with their nurses, and sat on the grass with a wine biscuit and a piece of barley-sugar each for their tea. It was so much an accepted thing that Edna had worn a wonderfully good imitation of an engagement-ring out of a cracker all the time she was at school. And up till now they had been devoted to each other.

But now it was over. It was so completely over that Edna found it difficult to believe that Jimmy did not realise it too. She smiled wisely, sadly, as she turned into the gardens of the Convent of the Sacred Heart and mounted the path that led through them to Hill Street. How much better to know it now than to wait until after they were married! Now it was possible that Jimmy would get over it. No, it was no use deceiving herself; he would never get over it! His life was wrecked, was ruined; that was inevitable. But he was young

. . . Time, people always said, Time might make a little, just a little difference. In forty years, when he was an old man, he might be able to think of her calmly—perhaps. But she,—what did the future hold for her?

Edna had reached the top of the path. There under a new-leafed tree, hung with little bunches of white flowers, she sat down on a green bench and looked over the Convent flower-beds. In the one nearest to her there grew tender stocks, with a border of blue, shell-like pansies, with at one corner a clump of creamy freezias, their light spears of green criss-crossed over the flowers. The Convent pigeons were tumbling high in the air, and she could hear the voice of Sister Agnes, who was giving a singing lesson. *Ah-me*, sounded the deep tones of the nun, and, *Ah-me*, they were echoed . . .

If she did not marry Jimmy, of course she would marry nobody. The man she was in love with, the famous actor—Edna had far too much common-sense not to realise that would never be. It was very odd. She didn't even want it to be. Her love was too intense for that. It had to be endured silently: it had to torment her. It was, she supposed, simply that kind of love.

"But, Edna!" cried Jimmy. "Can you never change? Can I never hope again?"

Oh, what sorrow to have to say it, but it must be said. "No, Jimmy, I will never change."

Edna bowed her head: and a little flower fell on her lap, and the voice of Sister Agnes cried suddenly, *Ah-no*, and the echo came, *Ah-no* . . .

At that moment the future was revealed. Edna saw it all. She was astonished; it took her breath away at first. But, after all, what could be more natural? She would go into a convent . . . Her father and mother do everything to dissuade her, in vain. As for Jimmy, his state of mind hardly bears thinking about. Why can't they understand? How can they add to her suffering like this? The world is cruel, terribly cruel! After a last scene, when she gives away her jewellery and so on to her best friends—she so calm, they so broken-hearted—into a convent she goes. No, one moment. The very evening of her going is the act's last evening at Port Willin. He receives by a strange messenger a box. It is full of white flowers. But there is no name, no card. Nothing? Yes, under the roses, wrapped in a white handkerchief, Edna's last photograph with, written underneath:

The world forgetting, by the world forgot.

Edna sat very still under the trees; she clasped the black

book in her fingers as though it were her missal. She takes the name of Sister Angela. Snip! Snip! All her lovely hair is cut off. Will she be allowed to send one curl to Jimmy? It is contrived somehow. And in a blue gown with a white head-band Sister Angela goes from the convent to the chapel, from the chapel to the convent with something unearthly in her look, in her sorrowful eyes, and in the gentle smile with which they greet the little children who run to her. A saint! She hears it whispered as she paces the chill, wax-smelling corridors. A saint! And visitors to the chapel are told of the nun whose voice is heard above the other voices, of her youth, her beauty, of her tragic, tragic love. "There is a man in this town whose life is ruined . . ."

A big bee, a golden furry fellow, crept into a freezia, and the delicate flower leaned over, swung, shook; and when the bee flew away it fluttered still as though it were laughing. Happy, careless flower!

Sister Angela looked at it and said, "Now it is winter." One night, lying in her icy cell, she hears a cry. Some stray animal is out there in the garden, a kitten or a lamb or—well, whatever little animal might be there. Up rises the sleepless nun. All in white, shivering but fearless, she goes and brings it in. But next morning, when the bell rings for matins, she is found tossing in high fever . . . in delirium . . . and she never recovers. In three days all is over. The service has been said in the chapel, and she is buried in the corner of the cemetery reserved for the nuns, where there are plain little crosses of wood. Rest in Peace, Sister Angela . . .

Now it is evening. Two old people leaning on each other come slowly to the grave and kneel down sobbing, "Our daughter! Our only daughter!" Now there comes another. He is all in black; he comes slowly. But when he is there and lifts his black hat, Edna sees, to her horror, his hair is snow-white. Jimmy! Too late, too late! The tears are running down his face; he is crying *now*. Too late, too late! The wind shakes the leafless trees in the churchyard. He gives one awful bitter cry.

Edna's black book fell with a thud to the garden path. She jumped up, her heart beating. My darling! No, it's not too late. It's all been a mistake, a terrible dream. Oh, that white hair! How could she have done it? She has not done it. Oh, heavens! Oh, what happiness! She is free, young, and nobody knows her secret. Everything is still possible for her and Jimmy. The house they have planned may still be built, the little solemn boy with his hands behind his back watching them plant the standard roses may still be born.

His baby sister . . . But when Edna got as far as his baby sister, she stretched out her arms as though the little love came flying through the air to her, and gazing at the garden, at the white sprays on the tree, at those darling pigeons blue against the blue, and the Convent with its narrow windows, she realised that now at last, for the first time in her life—she had never imagined any feeling like it before—she knew what it was to be in love, but—in—love!

SIR CHARLES GEORGE DOUGLAS ROBERTS

THE MOOSE AND RUSTY JONES

NOT within the memory of the oldest settlers had there been a winter so severe. All the country about the Ottanoonsis and Quahdavic waters was buried under an unprecedented depth of snow. Never before, it was said, had such implacable cold fixed its grip upon the land. Storm piled upon the heels of bitter storm till landmarks were all but blotted out, and the little, lonely backwoods cabins were smothered to the eaves. The scattered settlers gave up, before mid-winter had passed, all effort to keep their road open, and all their necessary travelling was done on snowshoes, tramping their trails seven, eight, nine, or ten feet above the hidden ground. The little trees were submerged from sight, forgotten. The taller spruce and fir towered in snowy domes and pinnacles, except where a rough wind had shaken their branches free of the intolerable burden, and left them standing sharply dark against the wide white desolation.

For the wild creatures of the forest it was a prolonged tragedy, except for those which were so fortunate as to be hibernating, sleeping away the bitter time in their deep holes beneath the snow where the fiercest cold could not touch them. Among the chief sufferers were the moose. These heavy animals, accustomed to select a sheltered spot in the woods for their winter home, and tramp out a maze of narrow pathways all about it leading to the thickets of young birch, poplar, and striped maple, whose twigs furnished them their food, early found it difficult to keep their paths open. As the winter progressed, they browsed away all the edible twigs and even the coarser branches of the thickets in their immediate neighbourhood. These consumed, they could only reach further supplies, and these all too scanty, by long and painful flounderings through the smothering depths of the snow. Some of these imprisoned moose families succeeded in getting enough forage to keep them alive, if barely. Others, less fortunately situated, slowly starved to death.

And so that winter wore grimly on towards the late release of spring.

At Brine's Corners, outside Smith's Store—which was also the settlement Post Office—young Rusty Jones, so called from the colour of his bristling shock head, was roping parcels, and an oat-bag, a big stone-ware molasses jug, and a kerosene oil tin, securely upon his toboggan. This done to his satisfaction, he pulled on his thick blue home-knit mittens, slipped his moccasined feet into the moosehide thongs of his snowshoes, waved farewell to the little group of loungers in the store, and set out on his four-mile tramp over the buried road to the farm. It was late, already just on sundown—an hour later than he had expected to be. He had waited to get the mail—for there was a story running in the weekly paper (last week's issue) which he was eager to get on with. Now, he thought of all the chores awaiting him at home, after supper, which would have to be cleared up before he could get to his reading.

Half a mile down the road a new idea came to him. By striking away from the road, across the valley, on his left, he could save nearly a mile. In ordinary seasons this would have meant no saving, the intervening country being an almost impassable tangle of swamps and deadfalls and dense undergrowth. But now, he reflected, it would be as easy travelling as by the road. Silly of him not to have thought of it before! Dragging the loaded toboggan easily behind him, he struck off at a long, loping stride through the forest. Boy though he was, he knew that his woodsman's sense of direction and his familiarity with the lay of the land would guide him straight to his destination.

Threading his way through the silent corridors of towering spruce and hemlock, skirting the dense groups of tall, slim white birches, avoiding the snowy swells and mounds which meant, to his experienced eyes, traps for his snowshoes, Rusty Jones struck on across the valley till he was within less than a mile of his father's lonely little farm. Then, in the cold, blue-grey, ghostly twilight, he checked himself on the brink of a deep hollow in the snow, half overshadowed by a spreading hemlock, and found himself peering down upon a huddled group of moose. He had never imagined there were any moose within a dozen miles of him. Yet here, in the tangled recesses of the valley, a little moose family had chosen to "yard up" for the winter.

In the gloom of the trodden and littered hollow he made out their forms—a gigantic greyish-brown bull, a dark, smallish cow, and two yearling calves. They were all lying down; but one of the calves, stretched awkwardly on its side, was obviously dead and frozen stiff. The others were all staring up at him with pathetic, hopeless eyes, as if too despairing for fear. But presently the great bull staggered to his feet and stood in threatening attitude, ready to defend his charges to the last, even against the most terrible of all enemies, Man. Rusty Jones perceived that he was piteously emaciated, the shaggy hide drooping in creases on his flanks. Rusty's kind grey eyes clouded with sympathy. "Gee," he muttered, "poor beggars, they're starving, that's what they are!"

He dropped the rope of his toboggan and started off on a run up the slope, remembering a thicket of birch saplings which he had passed a few hundred yards back. Here, with the aid of the long sheath-knife which he carried at his belt, he gathered an armful of the aromatic branches, the favourite forage of the moose.

When he threw his burden down into the hollow the great bull grunted eagerly, the cow and calf got to their feet as if new life already flowed in their veins, and all three fell hungrily to the feast. Rusty hastened to fetch them another armful.

"There," he panted, picking up his toboggan rope once more, "I guess that'll do yous fer to-night. I'll bring yous some good hay to-morrow mornin'."

When the boy got home, very late, with his story, he found his father and mother sympathetic enough in regard to the cause of his lateness, but adamant as to his promise of the hay.

"We hain't got more'n enough hay to see our own critters through," said his mother, decidedly. "But maybe father'll let you take some straw. Plenty good enough for them kind."

Bob Jones, a huge, lean backwoodsman, known throughout the settlements, for obvious reasons, as "Red Bob," laughed good-humouredly.

"Reckon ye'll hev to chop birch an' poplar for 'em, Rusty," said he. "That's their natural fodder, anyways. But ye're goin' to hev yer work cut out fer yeh if ye're going to feed all the starvin' critters in the woods *this* winter."

"That's all right," said Rusty, cheerfully, helping himself liberally to molasses on his pile of hot buckwheat pancakes. "I'll take 'em a bundle o' straw in the mornin', an' after that I'll chop for 'em. Don't worry. I'll see 'em through, all right. If you two had *seen* how pitiful them poor beasts looked, you'd feel jest as I do about it. But of course you're right about the hay. We *hain't* got none too much for ourselves."

Thereafter, for the next few weeks, regularly every other day would Rusty Jones betake himself to the hollow under the hemlock, axe in hand and dragging his toboggan, and leave for his sombre protégés a two days' supply of the twigs and branches which they loved. He found that they preferred this rough fodder to the best cat straw, and even to the few wisps of choice timothy hay which he once brought them as an experiment. By his third visit the bull and the leggy yearling had become so tame that they would come up and snatch the fodder from his hand with their long, prehensile muzzles. The dark cow, of a suspicious and jealous disposition, was slower to be won; but when won, showed herself more greedy and familiar than the others, pushing them rudely aside to try and get more than her share of the titbit which Rusty took to bringing them in his capacious pockets. Being something of a naturalist, and a keen reader of all the nature stories he could get hold of, Rusty liked to experiment on the tastes of the moose. He found that they liked bread, the staler and harder the better—and corn-cake—and even soggy, cold buckwheat pancakes; while the most tempting gingerbread was scornfully rejected. Sugar they would have none of, but salt they licked up enthusiastically, following him around for more. He tried them with a handful of grain—oats—on a tin plate; but the bull, after an inquiring sniff, blew into the plate a great, gusty breath from his wide nostrils, and the oats flew in every direction. Oats were scarce and precious, so Rusty did not try that experiment again. But the oats were not wasted; for a pair of saucy, smartly feathered "Whiskey Jacks," or Canada jays—known to Rusty as "Moose-birds"—who frequented the moose-yard, lost no time in picking them up, to the very last grain. Nothing was small enough to escape their bright, confiding, impudent eyes.

Meanwhile the body of the dead calf, rigid and pathetic, had lain ignored in the very centre of the hollow. At last Rusty took notice of it, and decided that it was a blot upon the kindly scene. He decided to get rid of it. Seizing it by the rigid hind legs he started to drag it to the side of the yard, intending to hoist it up over the edge. But the cow, seeming suddenly to remember that this dead thing had been her calf, ran at him with an angry grunt. Startled and indignant, Rusty struck her a sharp blow across the muzzle, and shouted at her with that voice of assured authority which he used with the yoke of oxen on the farm. The stupid cow drew back, puzzled both by the blow and the shout. To add to her bewilderment the sagacious old bull, who had become as devoted to Rusty as a faithful dog, lunged at her so fiercely with his massive, unantlered head that she went sprawling half-way across the hollow. And there she stood, wagging her long ears in puzzled discomfiture, while Rusty laboriously hoisted the awkward weight and pushed it forth upon the upper level of the snow. This accomplished, he dragged it a few yards away and left it behind a white-domed bush, where it would no longer offend his vision. Then he went down again into the hollow and stroked the big bull's muzzle, and scratched his ears, and talked to him, and finally gave him a generous portion of salt as a reward for his fidelity. The calf crowded up appealingly and was granted a small lump; and then the cow, forgetting her resentment, came nosing in to claim her share. But Rusty, still indignant at her, would only allow her to lick the last grain or two from his palm.

"That'll larn yeh," said he severely, "not to be gittin' so fresh."

On Rusty's next visit to the moose-yard, two days later, he was at first surprised to observe the numerous tracks of wild creatures on the surrounding snow. The neat footprints of foxes predominated, and the slender trails of the weasels. But there were also, standing out conspicuously, the broad, spreading pad-marks of a big lynx. Rusty examined them all intently for a few moments, then stepped round behind the shrouded bush to look at the body of the dead calf. The news of a banquet had spread swiftly among the hungry wild folk, and the carcass was half gnawed away. He scratched his red head thoughtfully, and peered about him to see if he could catch sight of any of the banqueters. Some thirty or forty paces away the tops of a buried spruce sapling had been jarred clear of its swathing and stood out sharply against the whiteness. He eyed it piercingly, understandingly—and presently, through the thick green, made out the form of a red fox, crouching motionless.

In a few seconds the fox, perceiving that he was detected, stood up, and stared Rusty in the eyes with a fine assumption of unconcern. He yawned, scratched his ear with his hind paw, flicked his splendid, tawny brush, and trotted away with elaborate deliberation, as much as to say "That, for you!" till he had gained cover. Rusty, who knew foxes, could picture the furry humbug throwing dignity to the winds and running for dear life as soon as he felt himself out of sight.

"Gee," he muttered, "that red beggar's got a fine pelt on him!" He wondered how many dollars it would be worth. He called to mind also those tracks of the big lynx, and wondered what a lynx pelt would fetch. He thought what a scheme it would be to set traps around the dead calf. But this plan he threw overboard promptly with a grunt of distaste. He had always detested the idea of trapping. Then he thought of his gun—which he used chiefly against the marauding hawks when they came after his chickens.

"Easy enough to get a shot at that red varmin, he's so darn bold an' sassy," he mused, still dwelling on the price of that fine pelt. Then his thoughts turned to the owner of the pelt. He had rather liked the audacious insolence of the creature—such a brave piece of camouflage in the face of the enemy!

"After all," he murmured to himself, "I guess I won't bother. It don't seem quite fair, when they're all so starved, an' I've tricked 'em all into comin' round here by puttin' out that there carcass. I better let 'em all have a good time while it lasts. An' besides, if I fired a gun here now it would scare my moose out o' their senses."

Having come to this decision he turned back to the moose-yard, thinking with a deprecating grin: "But *what* a blame fool father would call me, if he knew! An' maybe he'd be right!"

At last, at long last, the grip of that inexorable winter loosened suddenly, and fell away. As the snow shrank, assailed above by warm rains and ardent suns, mysteriously undermined beneath, the tangled undergrowth began to emerge, black and sodden, from its hiding, and the valley became more difficult to traverse. The moose were soon able to forage for themselves, and Rusty's visits to the hollow under the hemlock grew more and more infrequent. They were no longer needed, indeed; but he had become so attached to his charges, and to the sagacious old bull in particular, that he hated to let them slip quite out of his life. It had to be, however; and in this fashion, finally, came it about.

One morning, after an arduous struggle, he arrived, wet and exasperated, at the hollow under the hemlock, to find that the cow and the yearling had gone. But there, all expectant, was the faithful bull, who knew that this was Rusty's usual hour of coming. Rusty had his pockets filled with dry corn-cake and salt, and these the bull devoured appreciatively, stopping now and then to nuzzle the boy lovingly with his long, sensitive upper lip. At last, with a shamefaced grin, Rusty flung his arms about the great animal's neck, and murmured: "Good-bye, you old beggar. Take care o' yerself, an' keep out o' the way o' the hunters when next Fall comes 'round. Gee, what a pair o' horns you must have on that big head o' yourn!"

He turned away rather hurriedly, and started homeward on a longer but less obstructed route than that by which he had come.

He had not gone many paces, however, when he was startled to feel a long muzzle thrust over his shoulder, gently brushing his neck. Noiselessly as a cat the bull had followed him. Deeply touched, but somewhat embarrassed to know what to do with him, Rusty fondled the devoted beast affectionately, and continued his journey. The bull accompanied him right up to the edge of the open, in full view of the farmyard. The farmer was lowering his bucket into the well, and the sharp clanking of the chain rang on the still spring air. The big black and white farm-dog, barking loudly, came capering down the slope to greet Rusty. The bull halted, waving his long ears.

"Better quit now!" said Rusty. "Good-bye, an' take keer o' yerself!"

Not allowing himself to look round he trotted forward to meet the noisy dog; and the gaunt, dark form of the great moose faded back, soundlessly as a shadow, into the trees.

VANCE PALMER

THE BIRTHDAY

DARROW was awakened before the sun, by the twins rushing in and bounding on to his bed, their arms full of the presents he had brought down the night before. They snuggled up on the quilt on either side of him, their shrill cries penetrating the mist of sleepiness that still hung about his brain.

"I knew you'd come," said Tib. "I saw the lights of a car on the window-blind when I woke in the night."

"So did I," chimed in Peter.

"Oh, you fibber!" said Tib. "You didn't see anything. You were asleep—sound as sound."

"I wasn't," asserted Peter; "I heard the door bang and someone talking. . . . Look, Dad! A gun that will really kill things."

"My doll's eyes open and shut without you shoving them with your finger the weeniest bit," said Tib, "and there are lots of other things. We woke in the real dark before you could see."

"I was awake first," said Peter. "Tib didn't know anything till she heard me crackling the brown paper."

They disputed the question of who had been awake first, clutching at each other's pyjamas and rolling over among the tumbled blankets. The doll fell across Darrow's face. From the bed on the other side of the room their mother's voice came with a drowsy petulance:

"That's enough, children! Go back to bed now. You'll be tired to death before the day's out."

"Yes, you little ruffians, go back to bed now!" repeated Darrow. "I've got something else for you at breakfast. Something alive."

"I know," said Tib. "A monkey."

"Rubbish! Where would I get a monkey?"

"A little baby brother, then?"

Darrow laughed, looking across the dimness to the other bed. They swarmed about him with questions, sprawling over his chest, but he turned over on his side and tipped them gently to the floor.

" Back to bed now," he commanded; " I'm not going to tell you anything till breakfast."

After they had pattered back along the veranda he sat up and lit a cigarette, looking out of the window at the blue stretch of water and the yellow sandbank. It was early, but the tops of the ti-trees were splashed with gold. Near the entrance of the passage a man was sitting fishing in a punt, a blob of black on the pale water. A little to the right, a row of gulls were arranged along the sand, still as shapes of glass. Magic!

" I don't think I'll get up for breakfast," said Margaret across the room. " See that the children really eat something. . . . Ugh, those cigarettes, Phil! "

" They're the same as I always smoke," he said, tossing the butt out of the window. " What is it? Queasy? "

" I never feel right till near the end of the morning." she told him.

He remembered that it had been the same before the twins came. No need to worry! She was really well, and there was no reason why she should have a bad passage. Life was flooding through his veins, and he sang as he stripped for the shower-bath he had rigged up under the house. A grey thrush in the scrub at the back was moved by a like impulse, and its notes came fresh and clear as falling water, though the day was for it not a short respite snatched from briefs and conveyancing. From the back porch, where Jessie, the maid-of-all-work, was laying the breakfast, came a rattle of crockery, and then a shriek of joy echoed from the yard:

" It's a dog! A live puppy! . . . He said it was alive."

They had anticipated his surprise. When he dressed and came out, Peter was racing over the buffalo-grass in his bare feet, the retriever-pup after him, and Tib was following in its wake.

" Here! " called out Darrow, " where the deuce did you get that thing? "

" It was in a little box under the house," replied Tib. " You said it was for us. You know you did."

All the other presents were forgotten in their preoccupation with the retriever-pup. Peter's air-rifle lay somewhere among the wet buffalo-grass, and Tib's doll sprawled across the end of the veranda. Nothing like something alive, Darrow reflected, something they could exercise proprietary rights over! The irony of it was that the pup was only an afterthought, fobbed on to him by the man next door, the morning before he left town. And he had spent time and thought on the other presents!

They insisted on having the pup on a chair beside them at breakfast, and fought about who should feed it. Darrow let them wrangle; it was their day. The pup was a shapeless little thing, with flopping ears and a tongue that lolled out like a lump of pink wool, but it was alive! When they went out for a walk to the surfing-beach after breakfast it frolicked beside them, getting between their legs and giving them tumbles in the sand. Darrow watched them tolerantly.

"It's more real to them than I am," he thought, knowing the way they forgot him when the car turned the bend among the ti-trees.

It was a soft, gold morning, and the summer visitors were out on the beach. A party of girls was coming down from the hotel, some in coloured jumpers, and spots of blue and maroon showed on the white sand where children were hunting crabs. Voices came floating clearly over from the sandbank. Someone was calling across to the shore for a boat. By the side of the passage, half a dozen men were fishing silently, all with their pipes lit.

As they rounded the headland, they could see a knot of bathers gathered on the surfing-beach, and men standing at regular intervals in the sea. Peter, who was teaching the pup to dig out sand-crabs, commenced to run, his little round legs twinkling in the sunlight.

"It's the life-savers," he shouted. "They're practising. Come on!"

They were a long way ahead of Darrow before he had covered half the distance, and the dog was panting to keep up with them. Darrow had a sense that something was wrong. Men were hurrying down the beach from all directions, and women were shouting and gesticulating as the dark figure at the end of the line was towed in. A hundred yards out, just beyond the line of surf, two seagulls were hovering.

"Someone's gone out too far," thought Darrow. "Got a cramp, most likely."

He found himself running to keep up to the children, who had joined the crowd that looked like a swarm of ants on the white beach. A couple of young men in coloured jerseys and short pants tore past him.

"What is it?" he called out to them. "Just practising?"

But his voice was carried away on the air. The wet, sagging figure was being carried in, and a big man was waving the crowd back. Darrow heard a babble of high-pitched voices as he drew near. A woman in a green bathing-suit was pointing out to sea.

"There it is!" she screamed; "I saw a black fin."

Darrow's first instinct was to get the children away. He sensed a calamity, and he feared the effect of it on their vivid little brains. Tib was standing on the outskirts with the pup in her arms, but Peter had dived in among a tangle of bare legs, and Darrow could only get a glimpse of his fair hair and red jersey. Fragments of broken talk flew about. A woman had fainted and was lying in the sand, her hair tumbled over her death-white face.

"Stand back!" the big fellow was pleading. "Give us a chance. For the love of God, let the man have some air."

Burrowing in among the crowd, Darrow grabbed Peter by the shoulder and dragged him out. He had a confused impression of seeing a man with dark, curly hair lying on his face in the sand, but all his thoughts were concentrated on getting the children away. If there was horror, they mustn't come in contact with it! This was their birthday.

"Come on," he said, shepherding them doggedly. "We'll go and play in the sand on the other side of the rocks."

They were unwilling to go, and he had to hustle them, picking up the dog and striding ahead. From the way they rattled on he could see they were impressed but not overawed by what had happened.

"It was Con Delaney," said Tib, "I heard a woman say."

"He was bit by a shark," Peter confirmed. "I saw blood. All down the side of his leg."

"Con Delaney, that works at the hotel," chimed in Tib. "He was out on a surf-board."

Darrow selected a warm spot behind the rocks that shut out the bathing-beach and sat down. When he tried to light a cigarette he found his hands were trembling, but from the beginning he had seen the affair through the children's eyes rather than his own. A dark, meaningless smudge on the soft gold of the morning! Con Delaney, he was reflecting. That tall, loose-limbed young fellow who was always hanging round the yard of the hotel. Wasn't he the son of the widow who used to keep the store when Margaret and he had come down there first?

"How's the casualty?" he asked a man who was passing. "Better?"

"No, right out to it," was the response. "They've taken him up to the hotel and rung up the ambulance."

It seemed as if the beach had suddenly become deserted. Tib and Peter were playing life-saving in the sand; Tib was lying flat on her back with her frock rucked up over her knees, and Peter restoring circulation in the way he had seen the men do. They were in dead earnest, and for once their babble had ceased. With its head on one side, the pup watched them curiously, its tongue lolling out of the corner of its mouth.

When it was time to go, Darrow took them over the top of the cliffs, avoiding the surfing-beach.

" They're fishing for the shark," said Peter excitedly, watching a boat out at sea. " Old Corney caught one last week. A man-eater, he said it was! "

" Con Delaney comes round to see Jessie," said Tib. " He took her out once in Old Corney's motor-boat. Jessie says she's going back home after Christmas."

Knots of people were standing round the store and the post-office, talking in a subdued way. Darrow had a sudden feeling that Margaret would get more of a shock than the children. And in her present state——! Before the twins came she had nearly collapsed on seeing a snake go under the veranda.

But when the children began to babble disconnectedly about the disaster at lunch, he found her wrapped in her own protective thoughts as in a cocoon. She had not been outside the door for a fortnight, and nothing had any reality but the life within her.

" Con Delaney? " she said, frowning slightly. " I thought something would happen to that boy. He hasn't done any work for weeks and he's always in the water. Lives in it, nearly."

And she went on to rebuke Peter for taking too much on his fork at a time.

Darrow felt she had some obscure grudge against Delaney, and after lunch, while the youngsters were playing on the lawn, he pursued it to its source. Delaney was a bit of a Lothario, he found out. He had got more than one girl into trouble, and for some time he had been hanging round after Jessie. Waiting at the corner for her when she had her afternoon off!

" She's such a little empty-head, that girl," said Margaret. " I have to look after her like a mother. She stands dreaming, and things come apart in her hands."

It was Darrow's turn to dream. He had a vision of that black mop of wet hair, and bronzed men in bathing-suits, kneeling about the limp figure. Had the boy really been bitten by a shark before they brought him in? Or was the blood just a flash of Peter's imagination? He had a feeling that he ought to go and find out all about the affair, but his strongest impulse was to protect the youngsters from any news that might spoil their birthday. Through the lazy afternoon, as he lolled in his canvas-chair, he heard them disputing on the grass.

" We'll call it Rover."

" No, we won't. That's a he-name. It's a she. Jessie said so."

" Jessie don't know about dogs. They're all ' he.' Jus' like horses."

They were rolling over on the grass, letting the pup try its teeth on their hands. Except for their high-pitched voices, there was silence everywhere, for Jessie had gone out, and Margaret was lying down in her room. Tea was early, and there was a cake with coloured candles, that had to be blown out with ceremony. When it was over, Darrow took his stick and went up the road to the hotel.

There had seemed to be a hush ever since morning, and he had a sense of moving through a dream. On the lawn behind the boarding-house they were playing tennis, and a man and a girl were searching for balls in the dusk. Lights were beginning to appear in the little houses along the beach. Darrow was thinking of the mop of black hair, wet from the sea, and the way the children had played at life-saving in the sand. Had there really been anything between Con Delaney and Jessie? And if so, oughtn't they to have told the girl at once?

At the hotel he made inquiries from a young fellow who was bending over his car in the yard.

" Passed out before they got him in," he was told. " The doctor came out to meet them."

Darrow dulled himself consciously against the shock.

" I thought—— Had he been badly mauled? "

" No, but he'd lost blood," said the young fellow. " Bitten in the thigh and back. There's half a dozen lines out after the brute now."

Darrow stood for a while on the hill, looking at the rising moon across the water. He was in no hurry to go home. There would be questions, and he still had an impulse to protect Margaret and the twins from the shock that was spreading in a queer way through his own body. The lights danced on the water below, rendered pale and fugitive by the moon. There were three boats out, trying to hook that grey shape that hovered somewhere, shadowy and elusive, beyond the line of surf.

" . . . And deliver us from evil," reflected Darrow, visualising the twins mumbling their prayers by the side of the bed.

When he came down the road, Margaret was waiting at the gate, a white apparition in the moonlight. She was distressed and on the verge of hysteria.

" Oh, Phil, what ever kept you? I've been nearly out of my

mind. I thought Tib was going off into one of those convulsions she used to have when she was three."

He felt her quivering beneath his arm.

"Tib?" he said in dismay. "What was the trouble?"

"Both of them have been upset," faltered Margaret. "Horribly so! It was that pup. They took it out to play on the road and it got run over by a car. Such an unspeakable evening I've had! Oh, Phil, you mustn't give them live things, again—ever."

She was shaken and unnerved, and Darrow felt her limp weight against his body as they went up the steps. There was an atmosphere of tragedy about the still house. A night-light was burning in the children's room, and when he went in, he saw their two tousled heads on the one pillow, as if they had drawn close together in sympathy. They were asleep, but their ravaged faces showed signs of an emotion that had worn itself out. Peter's arm was thrown over the quilt with the palm upturned, and Tib's eyelashes seemed glued to her sodden cheeks. As Darrow turned away she gave a little sob in her sleep, and a tear trickled slowly down her nose.

"It's all right now," he said assuringly to Margaret. "They'll have forgotten all about it by the morning."

Later, when he was smoking a cigarette out in the moonlight, his eyes fell on a little dark blotch near the gate. It was the body of the pup, he discovered, bruised and shapeless. Better bury it, he reflected, so that the children would have nothing to remind them of the tragedy in the morning! Picking it up, he carried it to the back, stopping suddenly as he saw a figure by the fence in the shadow of the ti-tree. Jessie, leaning on the rail, with her head in her arms and her body as rigid and motionless as if it had been turned to stone! Moving away, Darrow began to feel emotion rise like a warm, expanding bubble in his brain, till it softly burst.

"Life! . . ." he thought vaguely, feeling for the spade in the darkness of the outhouse.

THE NECKLACE

SHE was one of those pretty and charming girls who, by some freak of destiny, are born into families that have always held subordinate appointments. Possessing neither dowry nor expectations, she had no hope of meeting some man of wealth and distinction, who would understand her, fall in love with her, and wed her. So she consented to marry a small clerk in the Ministry of Public Instruction.

She dressed plainly, because she could not afford to be elegant, but she felt as unhappy as if she had married beneath her. Women are dependent neither on caste nor ancestry. With them, beauty, grace and charm take the place of birth and breeding. In their case, natural delicacy, instinctive refinement and adaptability constitute their claims to aristocracy and raise girls of the lower classes to an equality with the greatest of great ladies. She was eternally restive under the conviction that she had been born to enjoy every refinement and luxury. Depressed by her humble surroundings, the sordid walls of her dwelling, its worn furniture and shabby hangings were a torment to her. Details which another woman of her class would scarcely have noticed, tortured her and filled her with resentment. The sight of her little Breton maid-of-all-work roused in her forlorn repinings and frantic yearnings. She pictured to herself silent antechambers, upholstered with Oriental tapestry, lighted by great bronze standard lamps, while two tall footmen in knee breeches slumbered in huge arm-chairs, overcome by the oppressive heat from the stove. She dreamed of spacious drawing-rooms with hangings of antique silk, and beautiful tables laden with priceless ornaments; of fragrant and coquettish boudoirs, exquisitely adapted for afternoon chats with intimate friends, men of note and distinction, whose attentions are coveted by every woman.

She would sit down to dinner at the round table, its cloth already three days old, while her husband, seated opposite to her, removed the lid from the soup tureen and exclaimed,

"Pot au feu! How splendid! My favourite soup!" But her own thoughts were dallying with the idea of exquisite dinners and shining silver, in rooms whose tapestried walls were gay with antique figures and grotesque birds in fairy forests. She would dream of delicious dishes served on wonderful plate, of soft, whispered nothings, which evoke a sphinx-like smile, while one trifles with the pink flesh of a trout or the wing of a plump pullet.

She had no pretty gowns, no jewels, nothing—and yet she cared for nothing else. She felt that it was for such things as these that she had been born. What joy it would have given her to attract, to charm, to be envied by women, courted by men! She had a wealthy friend, who had been at school at the same convent, but after a time she refused to go and see her, because she suffered so acutely after each visit. She spent whole days in tears of grief, regret, despair and misery.

One evening her husband returned home in triumph with a large envelope in his hand.

"Here is something for you," he cried.

Hastily she tore open the envelope and drew out a printed card with the following inscription:

"The Minister of Public Instruction and Madame George Ramponneau have the honour to request the company of Monsieur and Madame Loisel at an At Home at the Education Office on Monday, January 18th."

Instead of being delighted, as her husband had hoped, she flung the invitation irritably on the table, exclaiming:

"What good is that to me?"

"Why, my dear, I thought you would be pleased. You never go anywhere, and this is a really splendid chance for you. I had no end of trouble in getting it. Everybody is trying to get an invitation. It's very select, and only a few invitations are issued to the clerks. You will see all the officials there."

She looked at him in exasperation, and exclaimed petulantly:

"What do you expect me to wear at a reception like that?"

He had not considered the matter, but he replied hesitatingly:

"Why, that dress you always wear to thc theatre seems to me very nice indeed . . ."

He broke off. To his horror and consternation he saw that his wife was in tears. Two large drops were rolling slowly down her cheeks.

"What on earth is the matter?" he gasped.

With a violent effort she controlled her emotion, and drying her wet cheeks said in a calm voice:

" Nothing. Only I haven't a frock, and so I can't go to the reception. Give your invitation to some friend in your office, whose wife is better dressed than I am."

He was greatly distressed.

" Let us talk it over, Matilda. How much do you think a proper frock would cost, something quite simple that would come in useful for other occasions afterwards? "

She considered the matter for a few moments, busy with her calculations, and wondering how large a sum she might venture to name without shocking the little clerk's instincts of economy and provoking a prompt refusal.

" I hardly know," she said at last, doubtfully, " but I think I could manage with four hundred francs."

He turned a little pale. She had named the exact sum that he had saved for buying a gun and making up Sunday shooting parties the following summer with some friends, who were going to shoot larks in the plain of Nanterre.

But he replied:

" Very well, I'll give you four hundred francs. But mind you buy a really handsome gown."

. . . .

The day of the party drew near. But although her gown was finished, Madame Loisel seemed depressed and dissatisfied.

" What is the matter? " asked her husband one evening. " You haven't been at all yourself the last three days."

She answered: " It vexes me to think that I haven't any jewellery to wear, not even a brooch. I shall feel like a perfect pauper. I would almost rather not go to the party."

" You can wear some fresh flowers. They are very fashionable this year. For ten francs you can get two or three splendid roses."

She was not convinced.

" No, there is nothing more humiliating than to have an air of poverty among a crowd of rich women."

" How silly you are! " exclaimed her husband. " Why don't you ask your friend, Madame Forestier, to lend you some jewellery? You know her quite well enough for that."

She uttered a cry of joy.

" Yes, of course, it never occurred to me."

The next day she paid her friend a visit and explained her predicament.

Madame Forestier went to her wardrobe, took out a large jewel-case and placed it open before her friend.

" Help yourself, my dear."

Madame Loisel saw some bracelets, a pearl necklace, a Venetian cross exquisitely worked in gold and jewels. She tried on these ornaments in front of the mirror and hesitated, reluctant to take them off and give them back.

"Have you nothing else?" she kept asking.

"O yes, look for yourself. I don't know what you would prefer."

At length she discovered a black-satin case containing a superb diamond necklace, and her heart began to beat with frantic desire. With trembling hands she took it out, fastened it over her high-necked gown, and stood gazing at herself in rapture.

Then in an agony of doubt, she said:

"Will you lend me this? I shouldn't want anything else."

"Yes, certainly."

She threw her arms round her friend's neck, kissed her effusively, and then fled with her treasure.

It was the night of the reception. Madame Loisel's triumph was complete. All smiles and graciousness, in her exquisite gown, she was the prettiest woman in the room. Her head was in a whirl of joy. The men stared at her and inquired her name and begged for an introduction, while the junior staff asked her for waltzes. She even attracted the attention of the minister himself.

Carried away by her enjoyment, glorying in her beauty and her success, she threw herself ecstatically into the dance. She moved as in a beatific dream, wherein were mingled all the homage and admiration she had evoked, all the desires she had kindled, all that complete and perfect triumph so dear to a woman's heart.

It was close on four before she could tear herself away. Ever since midnight her husband had been dozing in a little, deserted drawing-room together with three other men, whose wives were enjoying themselves immensely.

He threw her outdoor wraps round her shoulders—unpretentious, everyday garments, whose shabbiness contrasted strangely with the elegance of her ball dress. Conscious of the incongruity, she was eager to be gone, in order to escape the notice of the other women in their luxurious furs. Loisel tried to restrain her.

"Wait here while I fetch a cab. You will catch cold outside."

But she would not listen to him, and hurried down the staircase. They went out into the street, but there was no cab to be seen. They continued their search, vainly hailing drivers, whom they caught sight of in the distance. Shivering with cold and in desperation, they made their way towards the Seine. At last, on the quay, they found one of those old vehicles which are only seen in Paris after nightfall, as if ashamed to display their shabbiness by daylight.

The cab took them to their door in the Rue des Martyrs, and they gloomily climbed the stairs to their dwelling. All was over for her. As for him, he was thinking that he would have to be in the office by ten o'clock.

She took off her wraps in front of the mirror, for the sake of one last glance at herself in all her glory. But suddenly she uttered a cry. The diamonds were no longer round her neck.

" What is the matter? " asked her husband, who was already half undressed.

She turned to him in horror. " I . . . I . . . have lost Madame Forestier's necklace."

He started in dismay. " What? Lost the necklace? Impossible."

They searched the pleats of the gown, the folds of the cloak and all the pockets, but in vain.

" You are sure you had it on when you came away from the ball? "

" Yes, I remember feeling it in the lobby at the Education Office."

" But if you had lost it in the street, we should have heard it drop. It must be in the cab."

" Yes. I expect it is. Did you take the number? "

" No. Did you? "

" No."

They gazed at each other, utterly appalled. In the end, Loisel put on his clothes again.

" I will go over the ground that we covered on foot and see if I cannot find it."

He left the house. Lacking the strength to go to bed, unable to think, she collapsed into a chair and remained there in her evening gown, without a fire.

About seven o'clock her husband returned. He had not found the diamonds.

He applied to the police; advertised a reward in the newspapers, made inquiries of all the hackney-cab offices; he visited every place that seemed to hold out a vestige of hope.

His wife waited all day long in the same distracted condition, overwhelmed by this appalling calamity.

Loisel returned home in the evening, pale and hollow-cheeked. His efforts had been in vain.

" You must write to your friend," he said, " and tell her that you have broken the catch of the necklace and that you are having it mended. That will give us time to think things over."

She wrote a letter to his dictation.

. . . . .

After a week had elapsed, they gave up all hope. Loisel, who looked five years older, said:

"We must take steps to replace the diamonds."

On the following day they took the empty case to the jeweller, whose name was inside the lid. He consulted his books.

"The necklace was not bought here, Madam; I can only have supplied the case."

They went from jeweller to jeweller, in an endeavour to find a necklace exactly like the one they had lost, comparing their recollections. Both of them were ill with grief and despair.

At last in a shop in the Palais Royal they found a diamond necklace, which seemed to them exactly like the other. Its price was forty thousand francs. The jeweller agreed to sell it to them for thirty-six. They begged him not to dispose of it for three days, and they stipulated for the right to sell it back for thirty-four thousand francs, if the original necklace was found before the end of February.

Loisel had eighteen thousand francs left to him by his father. The balance of the sum he proposed to borrow. He raised loans in all quarters, a thousand francs from one man, five hundred from another, five louis here, three louis there. He gave promissory notes, agreed to exorbitant terms, had dealings with usurers, and with all the money-lending hordes. He compromised his whole future, and had to risk his signature, hardly knowing if he would be able to honour it. Overwhelmed by the prospect of future suffering, the black misery which was about to come upon him, the physical privations and moral torments, he went to fetch the new necklace, and laid his thirty-six thousand francs down on the jeweller's counter.

When Madame Loisel brought back the necklace, Madame Forestier said reproachfully:

"You ought to have returned it sooner; I might have wanted to wear it."

To Madame Loisel's relief she did not open the case. Supposing she had noticed the exchange, what would she have thought? What would she have said? Perhaps she would have taken her for a thief.

. . . . .

Madame Loisel now became acquainted with the horrors of extreme poverty. She made up her mind to it, and played her part heroically. This appalling debt had to be paid, and pay it she would. The maid was dismissed; the flat was given up, and they moved to a garret. She undertook all the rough household work and the odious duties of the kitchen. She washed up after meals and ruined her pink finger-nails scrubbing greasy dishes and saucepans. She washed the linen, the shirts and the dusters, and hung them out on the line to dry. Every morning she carried down the sweepings to the street, and brought up the water, pausing for breath at each landing. Dressed like a working woman, she went with her basket on her arm to the greengrocer, the grocer and the butcher, bargaining, wrangling and fighting for every farthing.

Each month some of the promissory notes had to be redeemed, and others renewed, in order to gain time.

Her husband spent his evenings working at some tradesman's accounts, and at night he would often copy papers at five sous a page.

This existence went on for ten years.

At the end of that time they had paid off everything to the last penny, including the usurious rates and the accumulations of interest.

Madame Loisel now looked an old woman. She had become the typical poor man's wife, rough, coarse, hard-bitten. Her hair was neglected; her skirts hung awry; and her hands were red. Her voice was no longer gentle, and she washed down the floors vigorously. But now and then, when her husband was at the office, she would sit by the window, and her thoughts would wander back to that far-away evening, the evening of her beauty and her triumph.

What would have been the end of it if she had not lost the necklace? Who could say? Who could say? How strange, how variable are the chances of life! How small a thing can serve to save or ruin you!

One Sunday she went for a stroll in the Champs Elysées, for the sake of relaxation after the week's work, and she caught sight of a lady with a child. She recognised Madame Forestier, who looked as young, as pretty, and as attractive as ever. Madame Loisel felt a thrill of emotion. Should she speak to her? Why not? Now that the debt was paid, why should she not tell her the whole story? She went up to her.

"Good morning, Jeanne."

Her friend did not recognise her and was surprised at being addressed so familiarly by this homely person.

"I am afraid I do not know you—you must have made a mistake," she said hesitatingly.

"No. I am Matilda Loisel."

Her friend uttered a cry.

"O my poor, dear Matilda, how you have changed!"

"Yes, I have been through a very hard time since I saw you last, no end of trouble, and all through you."

"Through me? What do you mean?"

"You remember the diamond necklace you lent me to wear at the reception at the Education Office?"

"Yes. Well?"

"Well, I lost it."

"I don't understand; you brought it back to me."

"What I brought you back was another one, exactly like it. And for the last ten years we have been paying for it. You will understand that it was not an easy matter for people like us, who hadn't a penny. However, it's all over now. I can't tell you what a relief it is."

Madame Forestier stopped dead.

"You mean to say that you bought a diamond necklace to replace mine?"

"Yes. And you never noticed it? They were certainly very much alike."

She smiled with ingenuous pride and satisfaction.

Madame Forestier seized both her hands in great distress.

"O my poor, dear Matilda. Why, mine were only imitation. At the most they were worth five hundred francs!"

ANATOLE FRANCE

THE PROCURATOR OF JUDÆA

L. ÆLIUS LAMIA, born in Italy of noble parents, was still only a boy when he went to study philosophy in the schools of Athens. Afterwards, in Rome, at his house on the Esquiline, he lived a life of debauchery with a company of young libertines. There he was accused, and found guilty, of illicit intercourse with Lepida, wife of Sulpicius Quirinus, a high consular official, and was exiled by Tiberius Cæsar. He was then barely twenty-four years old.

He was eighteen years in exile, and during this time he travelled in Syria, Cappadocia, Palestine and Armenia, and made long sojourns in Antioch, Cæsarea and Jerusalem. When Tiberius died and Caius became Emperor, Lamia was allowed to come home. He was even able to recover some of his property.

Misfortune had made him wise. He shunned the women of his own class, kept clear of politics and place-seeking and shut himself up in his house on the Esquiline. He spent his time in making a record of his travels, turning (as he put it) past pains into present pleasure. He was engaged quietly in this pursuit, and in reading the works of Epicurus, when one day he realised, with some surprise and not a little sorrow, that he was an old man.

In his sixty-second year, plagued by a cold which he could not shake off, he went to take the waters at Baiæ. This resort, where once the halcyons came to roost, was at that time frequented by wealthy, pleasure-loving Romans. Lamia had been there a week, alone and friendless amid the gay and fashionable throng, when one evening he took it into his head to climb the dunes which, draped with vine-leaves like bacchantes, overlooked the sea. He reached the summit and sat by the pathway in the shade of a terebinth, from thence letting his gaze wander over the beautiful countryside. On his left the bare and livid Phlegræan fields stretched to the ruins of Cumæ; on his right Cape Misenum thrust its sharp spur into the flank of the Tyrrhenian sea. Opulent Baiæ, beneath his feet, stretched westward over the curving coast, offering to his view a rich treasure of villas, gardens, statues, porticos and marble terraces fringed by blue waves in which the dolphins played. Beyond the bay lay Campania, where, painted a rich gold by the setting sun, shone the temples which crowned the laurel-groves of Posilippo. Far away on the horizon, Vesuvius caught the light. Lamia took from his robe a scroll which held the *Treatise Upon Nature* and, reclining at his ease, began to read.

He was not there long before the voice of a slave disturbed him, asking him to make way for a litter which was coming along the narrow pathway between the vines. As it approached, Lamia was able to study the occupant, who had not troubled to close the curtains; he was an aged gentleman of vast corpulence, who reclined indolently upon the cushions, head in hand, and looked out with an air of weariness and disdain. His lips were clamped between a beak-like nose, square chin and powerful jaw. At once Lamia recognised that face, but, for an instant, the name escaped him; then suddenly he started forward with an expression of surprise and delight.

"Pontius Pilate! May the gods be praised that we meet again!"

The other called his slaves to a halt and looked closely up at Lamia.

"Pontius, my generous host!" the latter cried. "Have twenty years so whitened my hair and lined my brow that you no longer remember Ælius Lamia?"

At that name, the portly gentleman clambered, with as much agility as his age and great size allowed, out of his litter.

"My dear friend!" he exclaimed, greeting Lamia with the warmest affection. "How delighted I am to see you! How you bring back to me those days of long ago when I was still in Syria, as Procurator of Judæa! It must be thirty years since we met for the first time; that was in Cæsarea, where you came in exile. I was able to relieve your sufferings a little and, out of friendship, you came with me to that accursed Jerusalem, where the Jews filled my life with bitterness and disgust. Ten years we lived there together, managing to console ourselves with talk of Rome, so that, for a while, I was able to forget my office and you your exile."

Lamia pressed his hand warmly.

"You are forgetting something, Pontius. You do not mention that you spoke well of me to Herod Antipas and loaned me sums of money from time to time."

"We will not discuss the question of money, since, on

your return to Rome, you sent one of your freedmen to me with an amount that repaid all my loans with interest."

"Pontius, my friend, no money could discharge my debt to you. But let us talk about yourself. Have the gods been good to you? Have you all the happiness you so richly deserve? And your family, your health and your affairs—what about them?"

"I have retired now, Lamia, and live on my estate in Sicily; grain-farming occupies most of my time, and my eldest daughter Pontia, who lost her husband not long ago, has come to keep house for me. I must thank the gods that I still have my mind and my strength unimpaired, but old age brings troubles and woes to all of us; in my case gout is the worst of them. It is gout that brings me here—on my way to the Phlegræan fields to try out a remedy. At night, they say, the hot earth there gives off sulphurous vapour which loosens the joints and eases up the system. At least, so the doctors tell me."

"For your sake I hope they speak the truth. But apart from a few twinges of gout, you do not seem a day older than I am, in spite of the fact that I must be ten years your junior. Certainly you seem more vigorous now than I ever was. It is wonderful to see you looking so healthy! What made you give up your governorship? Why leave Judæa to bury yourself in Sicily? What happened to you after I left? As far as I can remember, you were preparing to crush a revolt of the Samaritans when I set out for Cappadocia with a scheme for making some money in breeding mules and horses. Was your expedition successful? Tell me all about it. Everything that concerns you is of interest to me."

Pontius Pilate made a weary movement of the head.

"It is my nature," he said, "in whatever work I am concerned, not only to do it well, but also to make it a labour of love. I have put my heart into all that I have done, but it has availed me nothing. Jealousy and intrigue have dogged my footsteps, and hatred has poisoned the roots of every tree that I have planted.

"You were asking me about the revolt of the Samaritans. Let us sit down here, and I will tell you about it in a few words. It is as fresh in my memory as if it happened yesterday.

"One of those fiery fanatics who spring up all too often from among the common people in Syria had persuaded the Samaritans to muster, fully armed, on Mount Gerizim, which they consider a sacred place in those parts. This fellow promised to reveal to them the sacred relics that one of their tribal gods or mythical heroes, called Moses, had buried there in the times of Evander and our father Æneas. They believed him and started arming. I heard about their little scheme in time, and was able to put a stop to it by drawing a cordon of infantry around the hill and posting outlying pickets of cavalry to keep a watch in the neighbourhood. I had no time for hesitation, since the rebels were already at Tyrathaba at the foot of Mount Gerizim.

"As it was, everything turned out beautifully; the revolt was nipped in the bud and the insurgents dispersed without bloodshed. Just to make an example of them, I had the ring-leaders tortured.

"Now, you know what a millstone around my neck was the proconsul Vitellius; you know how it seemed that he was governing Syria not for, but against Rome, treating the provinces of our mighty Empire as if they were gifts to be given to favourites. Well, the chiefs of the Samaritans went to this man, bemoaning their fate. To listen to them, you would think that nothing was farther from their thoughts than to disobey the laws of Cæsar. I had started the trouble, according to them. They had gathered at Tyrathaba solely to resist my cowardly onslaught on their people. Vitellius heard everything they had to say, then handed over the command in Judæa to his friend Marcellus; me he sent back to Rome to plead my case before the Emperor. I set sail at once, my heart weighed down with grief and resentment and, barely had we reached the shores of Italy when we learned that Tiberius, worn out with age and the cares of the Empire, had just died at Misenum—on that very cape that we can see from here, stretching into the mists of twilight.

"I threw myself on the mercy of Caius, his successor, a man of some intelligence who knew how things were going in Syria. Just as luck would have it, Caius had staying with him in Rome at that moment the Jew Agrippa, a companion of his childhood, his dearest friend. See how fate worked against me! Agrippa favoured Vitellius because Vitellius was an enemy of Antipas, whom Agrippa loathed. Whoever gained the friendship of Agrippa was a friend of Caius. He refused to see me. My luck was out. I had to bear the unmerited disgrace. Broken-hearted, nursing my rancour, I travelled home to Sicily, where shame and sorrow would have killed me had it not been for my dear Pontia, who came to comfort her old father. So now I am a farmer, sowing my wheat and harvesting the best crop in the province. My life is over. Posterity shall judge between Vitellius and I."

"Pontius, I do not need to be told that your dealings with the Samaritans were governed by what you conceived to be the best interest of Rome. But in this instance were you not letting your impetuous nature get the better of you? When I was in Judæa, although younger and more hot-headed than you, it was often my part to counsel calm and gentleness."

"Gentleness towards the Jews!" exclaimed Pilate. "It seems that your years amongst them have not taught you much about their nature. They are the worst enemies of the human race, a mixture of pride and servility, of shameless roguery and mule-like obstinacy. They are too vile for either love or hatred. My conduct, Lamia, is based on the maxims of the divine Augustus. When I was created Procurator of Judæa, the *pax romana* reigned over the whole globe. No longer, as in the Civil Wars, did one see proconsuls feathering their nests at the expense of the luckless provinces they were supposed to govern. I knew my duty. Wisdom and moderation were my watchwords—the gods are my witness to that. But what good came of my gentleness? You were there in the early days of my command, when the first revolt broke out. Do I need to remind you of it? The garrison of Cæsarea had gone into winter quarters at Jerusalem. Each standard of the legion bore a portrait of the Emperor, and, if you please, the Jews disliked the sight of them being carried on high through their city. They would not worship Cæsar as a god, and could not see that, since one must obey, it is better to obey a god than a mere man.

"Their priests came to my headquarters to beg, with mock humility, that the standards should be left outside the walls. Naturally I refused. Out of respect for the Empire and the divinity of Cæsar, I could not do otherwise. When the mob heard this they started getting out of hand. I ordered the troops to pile arms at the Antonine tower and sent them into the rabble armed only with their cudgels, like so many lictors. But, do you know, rather than disperse, those insolent fools howled all the louder, letting themselves be beaten senseless rather than move a foot! You saw how I was humiliated, Lamia. By the order of Vitellius the standards were marched back to Cæsarea. That was something I had not deserved. By the almighty gods I swear that not once in my whole service have I offended against justice and the law. But I am an old man. My enemies and those who spoke evil against me are dead. I shall die unrevenged. Who will defend my memory?"

He sighed deeply and was silent.

Lamia spoke. "You are right to have no hopes nor fears for a future that we cannot know. Does it matter what men will think of us in days to come? We witness our own lives; we are the best judges of them. Be content that you and your friends are assured of the excellence of your intentions. Gentleness, indeed, is no weapon to govern men. The kindliness to our fellows that philosophy teaches has few counterparts in the world of action."

"Let us leave that now, Lamia. These fumes of sulphur that are to cure my gout are more potent when the earth is still warm from the setting sun. I must hurry. But since we have met again, we must not lose sight of each other; this is an occasion to celebrate. Will you dine with me to-morrow? My house is on the cliff, at the edge of the town as you go towards Misenum. You will know it by the painting on the porch of Orpheus charming the beasts with his lyre. I will expect you, then; we will be able to talk of the old days in Judæa. Farewell!"

Pontius Pilate climbed into his litter and was borne away.

. . . .

The next day Lamia arrived at Pilate's house in time for dinner. Places were laid for two, and the meal was modest but satisfying; beccaficos in honey, thrushes, oysters from Lake Lucrine and Sicilian lampreys were the main dishes, all served on silver plate. As they ate, the two old men discoursed upon their various bodily ailments—how, when and where the symptoms occurred and what remedies had been tried or recommended. Then, talking of how lucky a coincidence had been their meeting on the dunes at Baiæ, they praised the scenery of the coast and its invigorating climate. Lamia found particular pleasure in the exotically beautiful courtesans who paraded upon the water-front, bedecked with ornaments of gold and soft, transparent veils of foreign workmanship. But the old procurator could not abide the thought of all that trumpery stuff being paid for in good Roman money, money that, as often as not, went straight into the hands of Rome's worst enemies. Soon they came to speak of the great public-works schemes then being put on foot all over the country, of the monstrous bridge constructed by Caius between Puteoli and Baiæ, and of the canals that Augustus had planned to take water from the sea to Lakes Lucrine and Avernus.

"In my time I too was interested in such works for the good of the commonwealth," Pontius Pilate said. "When, for my sins, I was appointed to Judæa, I mapped out the course of a huge aqueduct that should bring an abundant supply of fresh water to Jerusalem. I had gone into every detail with the engineers: elevation of the levels, capacity of each section, thickness of the brass tanks to which the pipes for distribution should be fixed—all discussed and decided upon;

I had even drawn up regulations for policing the pipe-line so that it should not be tapped at any point by unauthorised individuals. Architects and labourers had been engaged and the work begun; but the moment the Jews saw the preparations we were making to bring the scarce and precious gift of water into their parched city, they set up a howling tumult. The mob charged my workmen and tore up the foundation-stones, cursing their sacrilegious act in building upon hallowed ground. Can you conceive such an ungracious set of barbarians? Believe it or not, Vitellius agreed with their objections and ordered me to stop the work."

"It is a moot point," murmured Lamia, "whether one is entitled to do good to one's fellow-men against their wishes."

Pilate seemed not to hear him. "Refuse a water supply!" he exclaimed. "What madness! But everything that comes from Rome is hateful to the Jews. To them we are unclean; our very presence in Jerusalem they regard as a profanation. You remember how they would not come into my council-chamber for fear of contaminating themselves; I was forced to hold courts of judgment in the open streets among the passers-by.

"They hate us and fear us. But why? Every other nation we have conquered flourishes beneath our care. Peace and liberty have marched with our eagles to the ends of the earth. Wherever Rome rules, the people are treated as Romans, their customs are fostered and their laws respected. Is it not a fact that, since Pompey captured the country, Syria has enjoyed peace and prosperity for the first time in its long history of petty, bickering kings? And when we might fill our coffers by pillaging the temples of the foreign gods, do we do it? To reward ourselves for the trouble we have taken on their behalf, have we touched a single idol? The Mother-Goddess of Pessinus is untouched, the priceless shrines of Jupiter at Morimene and Cilicia have still their treasures, so has the Jewish god at Jerusalem. Antioch, Palmyra and Apamea, prosperous and safe, are no longer haunted by fear of the nomad Arab tribes; they build temples to the genius of Rome and for the worship of Cæsar. Only the Jews stand out against us. The taxes have to be dragged from them, and military service they will not do."

"The Jews," Lamia interposed, "cling to their ancient customs. They suspected you—without reason, I am sure—of wishing to change their way of life and abolish their laws. You must allow me to say, Pontius, that your behaviour there was not always calculated to set their fears at rest. In spite of yourself, I am convinced, you made them uneasy;

you found it difficult to disguise your impatience with their religious ceremonies and beliefs. You particularly vexed them by placing the robes and ceremonial ornaments of the high priest under a guard of legionaries in the Antonine tower. I think we must allow that, although not educated like ourselves to the contemplation of divine truths, the Jews worship a god whose very antiquity deserves respect."

Pilate shrugged his shoulders.

"They have no exact knowledge of the nature of the gods," he said. "They worship Jupiter, but without naming him or building an idol in his likeness. They do not even bow down to him in the form of a stone, as do certain Asiatic peoples. They have never heard of Apollo, Neptune, Mars, Pluto, nor of any goddess. Nevertheless, it is my belief that Venus was once sacred to them, for even to-day their women take doves to the altar for sacrifice, and, as you know, dealers throng the forecourts of their temple offering these birds for sale. I was told on one occasion that some madman had come among them, upsetting their stalls and chasing them out of the building. Their priests treated that as a most serious sacrilege. The sacrifice of turtle-doves would certainly point to the cult of Venus, I think. But what are you laughing at, Lamia?"

"Just a passing thought! It crossed my mind that you would be in trouble if the god of the Hebrews overheard you and were to follow you to Rome for his vengence! But seriously, why should their Jehovah not come here? In Rome they have temples for the cult of Isis, Anubis and many other Asiatic and African gods; the Bona Dea of the Syrians is borne on asses through the streets and into the fair-grounds, and (as I dare say you will have heard) when Tiberius was Emperor, a young rake disguised as the horned deity of the Egyptians used this mask to enjoy the favours of a lady of quality. She was far too pious to refuse anything to a god! Beware, Pontius! One day the god of the Jews may land at Ostia."

A fleeting smile crossed the Procurator's face. The idea that Judæa might produce a god for Rome was too ludicrous for his consideration.

"How could the Jews impose their religion on another people?" he asked. "They themselves cannot agree even on its simplest points. You have seen them yourself, divided into twenty rival sects, cursing and spitting in the public places, shaking their sticks and pulling each other by the beard. You have seen them gathered on the steps of the temple, tearing their filthy robes in sign of desolation as they surround some wretched fellow in prophetic delirium. It never enters their heads that sacred matters, veiled and uncertain as they are, should be discussed in serenity when the mind is at ease. The nature of the Immortals is hidden from us, and we poor humans can only guess at what is true. Nevertheless I believe they wish us well. The Jews, now, permit no diversity of opinion concerning their god, and they would torture to death any of their countrymen who might question one word of the holy writ. Since they have been under Roman rule, all capital sentences pronounced by their tribunal must be ratified by us, with the result that our magistrates are harried all day long with their cries for the death of someone. A hundred times I have seen them, rich and poor, priest and pauper together, reconciled for one instant as they crowded about my chair to ask, to demand, the execution of some unhappy fellow whose crime I was unable to see and whom I thought no better nor worse than his accusers. Yet they would be pulling at my robe and clutching at my sandals in their haste to have away with him. Why do I say a hundred times? It happened, not every day, but every hour of every day. And I was helpless in such matters, since, as Procurator of Judæa, it was my place not to destroy, but to uphold their customs; I had the power of life and death over them, but the power had to be exercised as their laws should direct.

"When I first took office I tried to reason with them, to spare one or two of their miserable victims; but this attempt at clemency infuriated them the more; they shrieked about me like vultures waiting to swoop on their prey. Their priests sent messages to Cæsar that I was violating their laws, and their appeals, backed by Vitellius, brought me a severe reprimand. How many times have I not wished, in the words of the Greeks, to send accused and accusers both together to the crows!

"Do not think that these are the senile mutterings of an impotent old man against a people who have embittered his life and destroyed for ever his peace of mind. I know what I am talking about, and I can see where we will end unless that whole nation is wiped out. Sooner or later, with their endless seditions and revolts, the Jews will rise against us with a fury beside which the wrath of the Numidians and the muttering of the Parthians will seem child's play. Those Hebrews are for ever planning and scheming, intent upon our ruin. How can it be otherwise, since they believe in the coming of a prince of their blood who will reign over the whole world? They are dangerous in the extreme; they must be wiped out. Jerusalem should be razed to the ground. May the gods grant that I see the day when its walls will fall, when fire shall devour its houses and its inhabitants be put to the sword! The day when I see the plough cutting through the earth where once their temple stood, that day I shall feel that justice has been done to Jewry!"

Lamia endeavoured to change the conversation to a more peaceful subject.

"It is easy to understand, Pontius, that your experience of the Jewish people has not endeared them to you; from your standpoint dislike and mistrust were the only possible sentiments. But I lived in Jerusalem as a sightseer, and mixed daily with the common people; I was able to unearth much goodness and virtue in their lives that was necessarily hidden from you. I have known Jews of infinite kindness and charity, with simple minds and open hearts, like the famous sage of Sparta. And yourself, Pontius, you have seen men of the common people who could not write their own names, cudgelled to death by your legionaries for what they considered to be the cause of truth. Such men deserve more than scorn. I mention this because, in all things, we should preserve some sense of proportion. Though I have never felt much enthusiasm for the Jews, I have, on the other hand, the warmest admiration for Jewesses.

"I was a youth in those days, and all the women of Syria made me feel the same. Those warm, full lips those moist, inviting eyes and the long looks they gave one; they were like burning irons to the flesh. Their faces were painted with care and cunning, and rare perfumes were used for heightening their charms. Such women were dishes for an epicure!"

Pontius Pilate did not disguise his impatience with such talk.

"I was not the sort of man to fall into the clutches of such birds of prey," he interrupted. "And since we are on the subject, Lamia, I must say that I have never approved of your incontinent behaviour with women. I did not mention to you before how gravely I viewed the fault for which you were exiled, because you were suffering the full penalty of your sin. Believe me, marriage is a sacred institution—particularly to people of our class, and on us the Roman Empire depends. It does not matter, of course, if you keep your philandering restricted to slaves or foreign women; but even then such voluptuous pleasures should not become a habit. You must not be offended when I say that, in my opinion, you are far too fond of sacrificing to the Venus of the Cross-roads; and your worst fault, in my eyes, is that you have not married and begotten children for the republic, as a man in your position should have done."

But the man whom Tiberius had exiled was deaf to the words of the magistrate. He emptied a glass of Falernian wine and smiled at some secret thought. After a while he roused himself and, in a voice that rose as he spoke, said: "They dance with such langourous grace, the women of Syria! I knew a Jewess once who used to dance in a little drinking-den, lit by one smoky lamp and furnished with one ragged carpet. Her arms moved like snakes as she clashed and tinkled the cymbals; her back arched and her head fell back as if the weight of the long, dark hair was dragging it to the ground; her eyes were liquid fire, and the suppleness of her hips would have made Cleopatra pale with envy. I adored those barbaric dances, her low, hoarse singing-voice, the smell of incense, the half-sleep in which she seemed to live! I followed her wherever she went, mixing with the troopers, cheap-jacks and publicans who were her friends. One day she disappeared, and I never saw her again. I searched all the streets of easy virtue and all the taverns without success. She was more difficult to drive from one's head than the fumes of Grecian wine. After a few months of despair I heard that she had joined a little band of men and women who were following in the train of a young preacher from Galilee called Jesus the Nazarene. He was later crucified for some crime or other. Do you remember anything about him?"

Pontius Pilate searched his memory for a moment, passing a hand wearily across his brow.

"Jesus?" he murmured—"Jesus, the Nazarene? No, I cannot remember him. The name means nothing to me."

COUNT VILLIERS DE L'ISLE ADAM

TORTURE BY HOPE

"Oh for a voice to speak!"—E. A. Poe, *The Pit and the Pendulum.*

FAR beneath the cellars of the *Official* of Saragossa, the venerable Pedro Arbuez d'Espila, sixth prior of the Segovian Dominicans, third Grand Inquisitor of Spain, descended at the close of a day, long since passed. Followed by a *fra redemptor* (master-torturer) and preceded by two familiars of the Holy Office holding lanterns, he made his way towards a hidden dungeon.

The lock of a massive door creaked, and they entered a stifling *in pace* where the grudging light from above just revealed a blood-blackened whipping-horse, a chafing dish and a stone jug. On a heap of mouldering straw, fastened by fetters to the walls with an iron ring about his neck, squatted the figure of a man of uncertain age. He was dressed in rags, and his face was ghastly in its pallor.

The prisoner was none other than the Rabbi Aser Abarbanel, a Jew of Arragon who, accused of usury and of an arrogant lack of charity towards the poor, had been tortured every day for more than a year. Nevertheless, his "stubbornness being as tough as his hide," he had refused to abjure his faith.

Proud of his thousand-fold relationships, glorying in the antiquity of his forbears—for every Jew worthy of the name is jealous of his blood—he was descended, according to the Talmud, from Othniel, and in consequence from Ipsiboe, wife of this last judge of Israel, a circumstance that had sustained his courage against the most awful of his incessant tortures.

It was therefore with tears in his eyes at the thought of so staunch a soul excluded from salvation, that the venerable Pedro Arbuez d'Espila pronounced these words as he approached the trembling rabbi:

"My son, rejoice, for your present trials are nearly at an end. If, in the face of so much obstinacy, I have had, unwillingly, to employ force, my task of brotherly correction has its limits. You are the barren fig-tree, which, being found so often without fruit, is in danger of being withered at the roots . . . but only God can pronounce upon your soul. Perhaps the Infinite Mercy may shine upon you at the supreme instant. We must continue to hope. Your case is not without precedent. . . . So be it. Sleep, then, this evening in peace. To-morrow you will take part in the *auto-da-fè*—that is to say, you will suffer the *quemadero*, the premonitory symbol of the Eternal Flame. Its heat, you know, is distant, my son, and death often takes two, and sometimes three hours to arrive, on account of the wet, frozen cloths with which we take care to wrap the foreheads and breasts of the 'offerings.' There will be only forty-three of you. Bear in mind that, as you will be among the last, you will have enough time to invoke God and to offer up to Him this baptism of fire which is the Holy Spirit. Put your trust, therefore, in the Light, and sleep."

At the end of this speech, Dom Arbuez, who had signed for the unhappy man to be unchained, embraced him tenderly. Then it was the turn of the *fra redemptor*, who begged the Jew in a low voice to forgive him for everything he had had to make him suffer for his redemption; next came the two familiars, whose kiss under their hoods could not be heard. This ceremony completed, the captive was left in the shadows, solitary and doomed.

. . . . .

With his mouth dry and his features ravaged by suffering, the Rabbi Abarbanel pondered on the locked door, at first without serious application. "Locked? . . ." The word awoke a train of thought in the secret, innermost depths of himself, for he had spied for an instant the glimmer of the lantern through the crack between the door and its frame. A crazy hope, born of his weakening brain, shot through his being. He dragged himself towards the incredible thing he had seen. And, very gently, with infinite precautions, slipping a finger into the rebate, he drew the door towards him. Amazing! By some extraordinary chance the familiar who had locked up had turned the key a little before the door was actually closed, so that, the tongue not having entered its groove, the door swung back into the cell.

The rabbi risked a glance outside.

By a sort of pale darkness he was able to distinguish, first of all, a semi-circle of earthy walls hollowed out by spiral staircases, and straight in front of him, commanding a flight of six or seven stone steps, a kind of inky vestibule giving on to a vast corridor, of which it was only possible to glimpse the first few arches from below.

Flattening himself against the wall, he crept to the level of this threshold. Yes, it was a corridor—but immeasurably long! A faint light—a light as in a dream—illumined it: lamps suspended from the vaulted roof cast at intervals a pale blue radiance in the stagnant air. The far distance was lost in shadow. Not a single door in all its length! On one side only, to the left, ventilating holes, covered with grilles set into the depths of the wall, let through a feeble twilight, which must be from the evening sky, for red beams stained the flagstones at long intervals. And what a terrifying silence! . . . Yet there, in the depths of the shadows, might lie a path to liberty. The wavering hopes of the Jew died hard, for they were his last.

Without further hesitation he ventured on to the flagstones, keeping close to the coping of the ventilators, striving to conceal himself as much as possible against the shadowy tones of the walls. He dragged himself along slowly, stifling a cry when a recently opened wound sent a sharp pang through him.

Suddenly the sound of a sandal echoed along the stone passage. A trembling seized him; he choked with anguish; his sight grew dim. This, then, was the end! He squeezed himself into a recess and waited, half dead with terror.

It was a familiar hurrying along. In his hand he was carrying an iron claw for tearing out muscles, and his hood was thrown back. He passed rapidly and disappeared. The shock which the rabbi had just experienced had almost paralysed his powers of motion, and it was nearly an hour before he could move again. Born of a fear of the increased torments if he were caught, the thought came to him of returning to his cell. But the former hope whispered in his soul—that divine *Perhaps* which comforts in the worst distresses. A miracle had taken place. There was no room for further doubt. He began again to crawl towards the possible escape. Worn out by suffering and hunger, trembling with anguish, he went on—and the gloomy corridor seemed mysteriously to expand. But he, never pausing, stared into the darkness in front of him towards where there *must* surely be a way of escape!

Oh, here were footsteps again! But this time, slower and more solemn. The black-and-white shapes of two inquisitors, with their tall hoods with rolled-back edges, emerged into the faint light at the far end. They were talking in low voices, and seemed to be discussing something important, for their hands made gestures.

At the sight of them the Rabbi Aser Abarbanel closed his eyes; his heart throbbed as if it would kill him; his rags were drenched in an icy sweat of agony. Motionless, gasping, he lay in the angle of the wall, under the gleam from a lamp, praying to the God of David.

When they reached him the two inquisitors stopped under the lamp, through a mere chance, no doubt, in their discussion. One of them, while listening to his interlocutor, looked straight at the rabbi! And under this gaze, whose unseeing expression he did not at first realise, the wretched man seemed to feel the hot pincers biting into his poor flesh. Once again he was to become a living wound, a living woe! Fainting, unable to breathe, his eyelids flickering, he shuddered as a cassock brushed him. But—at once strange and natural—the eyes of the inquisitor were those of a man deeply preoccupied by what he was about to reply, absorbed in what he was listening to—they were fixed—and seemed to gaze at the Jew without seeing him!

And in fact, after a few minutes the two sinister conversationalists went slowly on their way, still talking in low tones, towards the direction from which the prisoner had come. *They had not seen him!* For a moment, in the horrible confusion of his senses, the idea flashed across his brain: "Perhaps I am already dead, and so no one can see me?" A hideous impression jerked him from his lethargy. Gazing at the wall exactly opposite his face, he thought he saw two fierce eyes staring into his. He flung back his head in a blind, unreasoning terror . . . but no! His hand felt forward along the stones. What he had seen was the *reflection* of the eyes of the inquisitor still imprinted upon his pupils which he had focused upon two spots on the wall.

Forward! He must hasten towards the end where he imagined (crazily, no doubt) that deliverance might lie; towards those shadows from which he was distant, surely no more than thirty paces. He began again his grievous pilgrimage on hands and knees and stomach, and soon he was in the darkest part of this fearful corridor.

Suddenly the wretch felt the sensation of cold *upon* his hands pressed on the flagstones: it was a strong draught that came from beneath a little door at the very end of the passage. Oh, God! if only this door opened on the outer world! The whole being of the wretched captive whirled round in a sort of hopeful giddiness. He examined the door from top to bottom without being able to distinguish it completely on account of the darkness about him. He felt over it. Not a lock, not a bolt! A latch! . . . He got up: the latch yielded beneath his finger; the door slipped open noiselessly before him!

. . . . .

"Hallelujah!" murmured the rabbi, with a deep-drawn sigh for mercies received, as he gazed before him from the threshold.

The door opened on to gardens, under a starry night—on to spring, liberty, life! The gardens gave access to the neighbouring country that stretched away to the sierras, whose sinuous blue edges were silhouetted on the horizon. There lay liberty! Oh, to escape! He would wander all night under the lemon trees whose perfume he could smell. Once in the mountains, he would be safe. He breathed the good, the blessed air. The breeze refreshed him, his lungs revived. He heard in his expanding heart the "Lazarus, come forth!" and, to give thanks to God Who had granted him this mercy, he stretched out his arms to the firmament in an ecstasy.

And then he thought he saw the shadows of his arms returning upon him; he seemed to feel those shadow arms surround, embrace him, and feel himself pressed tenderly against some breast. A tall figure was indeed opposite to him. Confidently he lowered his gaze upon this figure, and stood gasping, stupefied, with staring eyes and open mouth slavering with terror.

Horror! He was in the arms of the Grand Inquisitor himself, the venerable Pedro Arbuez d'Espila, who was gazing at him with eyes full of great tears, like a good shepherd who has found again his lost sheep.

The solemn priest pressed him against his heart with such a transport of charity that the raw edges of his hair shirt rasped against the chest of the Dominican under his cassock. And while the Rabbi Aser Abarbanel, his eyes turned upwards under his eyelids, shook with anguish in the arms of the ascetic Dom Arbuez with the realisation *that every phase of that dreadful evening had been a deliberate torture, a torture by Hope*, the Grand Inquisitor, with a look of distress and in accents of poignant reproach, murmured in his ear with the burning breath of abstinence:

"What, my child! On the eve, perhaps, of salvation . . . were you thinking of leaving us?"

JACOB WASSERMANN

ADAM URBAS

CHIEF JUSTICE DIESTERWEG, who died recently, was a shrewd, intelligent criminologist of the type of the great Anselm Feuerbach. It was in the papers he left that I came upon the following story:

Late one evening in October a Franconian peasant named Adam Urbas appeared at the police station in Gunzenhausen and declared that on that very day, in his native village of Aha, he had cut the throat of his eighteen-year-old son, Simon. The boy lay dead in his room at home. Adam had brought with him, and produced, the knife with which he had committed the crime. It was still stained with blood.

This confession, made in a calm voice and with the fewest possible details, was duly taken down by the police. Urbas refused to add another word and to answer the questions put by the Commissioner of Police. In the course of the night, an official inspection was made of the scene of the crime, and Urbas's deposition was found to be exact. His wife was at home, half mad with anguish and horror, surrounded by terrified farm-hands and dairymaids.

Adam Urbas was locked up in the Ansbach jail.

I was then almost at the outset of my legal career and had been appointed, a few weeks earlier, to this district seat. I welcomed the occasion to sit as examining magistrate on this case.

In the beginning, the case seemed transparently clear: a peasant, intellectually circumscribed by the ignorance and brutishness of his caste, had quite simply rid himself of a degenerate son who had brought upon him nothing but shame and grief; in this way he had executed just punishment upon the lad and averted the promise of further misery.

The witnesses testified unanimously that Simon had been an altogether worthless fellow, a loafer who would not go to work, and a constant frequenter of all the taverns and fairs of the countryside. His idle, disorderly mode of living had required a good deal of money, and when the money was not forthcoming from his terrorised mother (whether because she would not or could not give it to him), he found other ways to procure it. For example, in August he had gone to a Weissenburg grain merchant, one Kohn, had extracted from the man eight hundred marks in payment of barley delivered by his father, and then dissipated the entire sum. In Nordlingen a prostitute got him into her clutches and announced herself with child by him. One day he lured her into a deserted place and attempted to strangle her. Passers-by heard the woman's screams and rescued her. This affair was still under investigation when Adam Urbas exercised summary justice himself.

The testimony further revealed habits and characteristics of Simon's youth which displayed him in the worst possible light. His childhood was marked by a malicious and evil shrewdness of which no good ever transpired. Another example: one day the housemaid returned from town with six new linen shifts which she showed proudly to the farmer's wife. Vespers sounded, and the maid left the flower-white linen on the kitchen table while she went to church. When she returned, the garments lay there, so smeared with axle-grease as to be forever unwearable. Nobody doubted that it was Simon who had done this, but proof was never forthcoming in this instance any more than in the affair with Scharf, the drayman. Scharf had left his flour-laden wagon standing before the tavern. When he started to drive on, the flour poured in a white stream along the road; some ten or twelve sacks had been slashed with a knife. Everybody knew it must have been Simon Urbas who had done this, yet there was no proof.

To his meanness and thieving, Simon later added cheekiness and brutality. All right-thinking people agreed that a poisonous weed was growing up, so high that no shears could reach its tip, and so firmly rooted, that no hoe was strong enough to dig it up. I did not really need more than a fraction of the evidence offered. There was here no problem at all, no complication, no mystery. So far as the dead lad was concerned, everything was clear, simple, pointing only in one direction.

The last act of this village tragedy opened at Gunzenhausen on a Sunday, during the county fair. Two peasants from Windbach had been sitting in the tavern at Aha, discussing the fact that a warrant had been issued for the arrest of Simon Urbas. They had not observed that Adam Urbas was seated at a neighbouring table. The others in the tap-room, landlord and guests, looked anxiously towards Adam and saw from the fashion in which he set down his glass and stood up from his bench that he had, until that moment, heard nothing of the Nordlingen episode. As a matter of fact, Simon's outrages were always withheld from the old man's knowledge as long as possible. His extraordinary, silent demeanour, his dignified bearing, and not least of all, the great affection in which he was held in the community and indeed in the entire region, had contributed to the erection of a kind of protective wall about him. Moreover, through all these years his wife had managed to intercept the slightest bad news and soften its harshness before it reached his ears. But people were mistaken who imagined that he was ignorant of what went on, or shut his eyes voluntarily to half the truth. He knew just how to leave them in doubt about what he saw and what went on in his mind.

A chattering servant girl had told the farmer's wife, while she was churning butter, of the trouble in the air. When Urbas reached home, he moved over to a window so as not to be obliged to look into his wife's face. Evening had already fallen. Franz Schieferer, a bricklayer, came by. He called out to Urbas's wife that Simon was treating men and women to drink at the Hart Tavern in Gunzenhausen, and throwing money about in reckless fashion. Then he added with an excited laugh: "But they'll clap your bird in a cage soon. The police are on their way now." This, it turned out later, was not so; even the news that a warrant had been issued was merely a rumour.

All the servants had gone to the fair. The farmer's wife let herself sink down upon a bench against the wall. Urbas tramped heavily back and forth in the room. Soon they heard clumsy steps moving in from the road, and the ringing of the door bell. Fists pounded on the massive wood, to the accompaniment of curses. The woman sprang up and started out. Urbas raised his finger and pointed—nothing more. She stopped on the threshold. Now Simon's face appeared at the window, discoloured with drink, an evil light in his eyes. His mother cried out and motioned him to go away. He vanished. There was silence for a time. Then noise in an adjoining room. Simon had come into the house through the farmyard door. It was dark, and he stumbled against the implements in the store-room. Something crashed. His mother tore open the door, and in the flood of lamplight she saw the drunken fellow raise himself heavily from the floor. He stretched out his arms towards his mother and father, and a stream of horrible language poured from his mouth. This was probably a decisive moment in Adam Urbas's life. His wife testified later that at that moment she had seen him shudder from head to foot.

Simon, meantime, had groped his way to his room. Roaring, he slammed the door behind him. There was silence again. Urbas started out into the threshing-shed. His wife stood behind him, her face buried in her apron. They remained thus for about five minutes. Then Urbas emerged and went across to the bedroom. Later, the farmer's wife said that she had realised and felt what was about to happen, but her limbs seemed frozen and she was powerless to stir. Whether Simon was so drunk that he slept from the moment he threw himself across the bed, or whether there was any conversation between father and son, could therefore not be learned. Once she said that all had remained silent, and then again that they had talked together, even for a fairly long time. Both doors, however, were shut, and since by her own statement she was seated in the chimney-corner, the sound of voices—as was proved by numerous tests—could not possibly have reached her. It is to be observed, also, that her evidence concerning the length of time spent by Adam Urbas in his son's room was noticeably uncertain: once she said it could not have been more than fifteen minutes; another time, over an hour. The knife used had not belonged to Urbas but to his son. Whether the boy had carried it on his person, or whether it had been lying in the room was another detail which remained obscure. On this point, Urbas was obdurate in his silence, and, important as the circumstance was, no light was shed on it.

I must say that in the beginning, despite their extraordinary character, these incidents did not greatly interest me. They were the typical accompaniments of such a crime. The father, an inflexibly stubborn man, his peasant sense of honour outraged, his true peasant arrogance recognising no justice higher than himself; the son, a scoundrel whose violent and untimely end one could scarcely deplore; the mother wavering between the two. It was the usual combination, and justice could take its course unhindered by obscurities.

Gradually, however, after careful scrutiny of the past and of Adam Urbas's character, my interest became more keen. Suppose yourself to be walking along a wall which seems like any other wall in the world. Suddenly, you become aware of faint markings on the wall. As the inscriptions grow gradually clearer, the temptation to decipher them becomes more and more irresistible. You begin to make out one group after another until in a flash you have a revelation of the secret realm lying behind that wall. Something of this sort was happening to me.

For thirteen years, Urbas and his wife were childless. She had accepted this fact as ineluctable destiny; Urbas, on the other hand, was rebellious to the decree of nature. He was the last of an ancient line of peasants; the name Urbas appears in Franconian chronicles as early as the fourteenth century; to be without an heir seemed to him disgraceful. What was the good of the working and the saving? What was the good of a house filled with well-laden chests, of the cattle in their stalls, the grain in the barn, the fields, the meadows, the mill, the river, and the woodland?

But Urbas never complained, either to his wife or to others. His expression never changed when conversation turned on this subject. No hard word, no curt question came from him the year round.

But, once each month he would chance to look squarely at his wife, and from his eyes would emanate a force that would grow and wax independently of his will, to no apparent purpose. It might come over him in the fields: he would stop binding a sheaf of grain and gaze at his wife. Or the woman might waken in the night to find him propped up on his elbow, gazing at her. Or on the square before the church: she would stand talking with other women; suddenly she would become dumb, for there, three steps away, he would stand staring at her. Never any anger; never a threat; never a word of reproach; only a man who gazed searchingly at her, gazed long and silently, from under his shaggy eyebrows.

Once in every month it was expected to happen, was certain to happen. In the beginning, the woman remained unperturbed by what she took to be a mere vagary, whose meaning she need not bother to learn. She would laugh and try to say something cheerful. Then came a time when she would turn away, try to dismiss it from her mind. But there came hours, and finally whole days, when she would ponder and wonder; and the question she dared not ask the peasant to his face, she would ask his haunting shadow.

She would brood over it. Can't people speak to one another? Why has he a tongue in his head, if not to speak his mind with? She decided to take the bull by the horns. Yet, when the moment came and she approached him, her courage evaporated. A sense of guilt grew in her; a voice clamoured for speech; the moment for speech did not come. She felt that she was not guilty. Something was guilty, however, and that something was within her. The changing seasons and their varied activities forced the days back into their normal course, but the period of relief grew ever shorter. Dread of the peasant's steady glance paralysed her thoughts, penetrating her as often as her beating blood signalled a deeper sense of guilt. From November to February, the walls and rafters of the house became more and more oppressive. The indoor air grew heavy; the sky came down against the window-panes; the evening clung like a wet sack about her body. Pale linen lay drying on the planks. The cows lay in a rosy stream, while in the path leading between the walls of snow to the byre, a lantern, swinging from the hand of a pregnant maid, sent forth wide rainbow-rings of light.

She was conscious only of two things: her body and her fear. Twenty-eight days and nights passed without distraction. Urbas sat beside the stove, his pipe between his teeth; went to the inn and returned in the evening; sat again beside the stove and studied the newspaper; stood up when the pot of cabbage and dumplings was brought in; said grace; listened quietly while the others spoke. There was nothing secretive in his expression; no hint of gathering ill-will; only silence.

And then the moment would come! Already the woman felt it in her bones; she felt it at the roots of her hair. A door opened, and there he stood. In the morning; late at night. In the parlour; in the threshing-shed. There he stood with that unfathomable look. No clearing of the throat; no gesture; no word; only that look which said: Why not? Why all the others and not you, too? Why does your field lie barren?

Twelve years went by in this way, and then the woman's strength gave out. She became morose. In the night she tossed sleeplessly. Through the darkness burned the eyes of the peasant; though he might be asleep, she felt them on her. During the day, she would creep at the sound of his tread into a corner of the barn and crouch there trembling until calls for her would resound from every side. She relaxed her grip on the household; the servants grew slack.

She denied herself to him. She shuddered in his embrace. To her darkening senses it seemed that if she refused to give herself, the man could not demand anything of her. She grew cold at his touch and her blood ran chill. The woman in her froze. Then Urbas began to woo her, but in a new way, as she had never known him to woo before. Not with words did he woo, but rather with timid offerings. There was often a kind of agitation in his wooing, as if she had hidden herself away and he had to find her; as if he sought and was unable to find her. He was like a suffering animal. For a year or more, this went on. Gradually the woman lost her dread of him as she realised that she was not, in his eyes, a mere down-trodden creature, to be fed and caressed when it has done his bidding, otherwise to be beaten; but that she meant something else to him, was worthy of his respect and esteem. She turned again to him with a willing heart. One month later she was with child.

When there was no further doubt about this, her being underwent a change. She moved about the house with youthful steps, drove the laggards at their work, took a hand in everything that went on, became talkative, gay, and blooming. Everybody was amazed. Even Urbas marvelled. She did not wish to tell him point-blank what was in store; she wanted to make of it a festive occasion, for it was as if she were bringing him a precious gift. On Maundy Thursday, she donned her holiday dress and with it a long black head-dress fastened by silver clasps. Then she called Urbas upstairs into the room where, in their cupboards, stood the old silver and china, the heritage of centuries. She sat down solemnly in an arm-chair, folded her hands in her lap, and told him briefly and simply what there was to tell.

A shudder ran through Urbas's powerful body. When she spoke of this nineteen years later, picturing the scene and describing Urbas's shock, one could see that she was living over again the tremor of that moment. Urbas's earth-brown face became as red as a poppy. He let forth a roar of laughter. Then tears streamed from his eyes. He strode over to her and struck her so roughly on the shoulder that she cried out. Dismayed that she did not take as a caress what had been so intended, he stroked her back tenderly, devoutly, while a melodious growl hummed like an organ-tone in his throat.

He ordered her peremptorily to be careful of herself. He went secretly to the doctor for advice. An extra serving maid was taken on to free his wife from all work. He would watch over her, spring up to remove things from her path. Sometimes, while the baby clothes were being sewn, he would sit by, staring with round eyes and nodding his heavy head. Events proceeded in their natural course, and the hour of birth arrived. For a long time, Urbas held in his arms the new-born babe, gazing at the puny, ill-favoured mass with mingled feelings of joy and apprehension.

Simon grew up as other peasant children do. Nothing was made easier for him. He was not allowed to learn how long and impatiently he had been awaited. What he was worth to his people had to be proved by his industry. Childhood displays of temper were dashed against the unyielding order of things; childhood illnesses were merely trials which served to answer the question: Are you worthy or unworthy? Throughout, a sharp observer might have perceived in Urbas a restless suspense, as though he were listening to the very pulse-beat in the boy's body. This look of strained attentiveness remained in his features. It etched lines into his face. However much he might seem unobservant of Simon's words and movements, such seeming was false. None about him could measure how accurately he saw everything that occurred. Eventually, I learned the truth, learned it in a way never to be forgotten, or, in fact, to be explained in words, which are the only means at my disposal.

An almost exalted conception of the ideal relations between father and son was fused with Urbas's very being. He knew himself a peasant, which is to say a king. The earth was his earth; the farm-hand his farm-hand. The seasons were made for him, for his fields, his harvests. He was lord over the land. His eye fixed its limits to the very boundary stone which had laid undisturbed since ancient times. No blade of grass came up but in his name. Property was of all things most sacred, and property implied a master who would guard it vigilantly and inexorably, down to the last penny, the last grain of wheat. A son took it over from his father; a father passed it on to his son. Through the ages. This was the natural order of things; any other kind of world was unthinkable.

But I am getting ahead of my story and losing its thread.

The formal examination of Urbas, which it was my duty to make, revealed nothing of significance. His answers never varied, and he seemed fatigued and mystified by the need for repetition. He confined himself to the bare fact and would explain nothing. He scorned any defence, refused to hear of legal counsel, and was stubbornly indifferent to my advice and suggestions. When I pointed out that a voluntary declaration of the motive of his crime would result in a considerably mitigated sentence, he answered laconically: "That is beside the point." I made up my mind to give up this fruitless questioning, especially since the testimony of the witnesses, added to what I had learned about the victim and the accused, seemed to me to have forged an unbroken chain of motives.

Nevertheless, there were two details upon which no light had been thrown. One was the coroner's testimony to the effect that the body showed not the slightest trace of violence, either in the position of the stiffened limbs and the state of the clothing, or in the facial expression of the deceased. Had the peasant not accused himself, it would have been difficult to prove murder. The second debatable point concerned the undisputed fact that the knife had belonged to Simon Urbas. The peasant asserted that it had been sticking in Simon's belt, and that he had simply drawn it out. Even to this statement he committed himself only after continued pressure had been exercised. This had so patent an air of improbability that he retracted it the following day, saying the knife had lain open on a table, that Simon had cut bread with it that same morning. When I expressed surprise about his uncertainty on so important a point, he lowered his glance with some embarrassment. It was the only time I thought he seemed disconcerted in any way.

To bring that silent tongue to speak became a compelling urge in me. I thought of him almost uninterruptedly. The patent clarity of the case, and the obstinacy with which it haunted me, perturbed and annoyed me. Over and over a voice in me said: This man is no murderer. This is not the kind of man who cuts a human throat as casually as if he were slaughtering a chicken; who makes himself the horrible, brutal executioner of his own son. Yet, he had confessed the deed! What had really happened? Regarding the length of time spent in the room, he had remained silent, or at most had shrugged his shoulders. It was only during the final examination that he confessed reluctantly that he might have been in the room a half-hour. What took place in that half-hour? He had guessed my thought, and his brow had clouded.

I saw that the only way I could put an end to my intolerable obsession would be to put off my professional attitude and confront him man to man. It seemed to me I had won his confidence in a certain degree. I had tried to deal delicately with such disagreeable points as arose from time to time, and in these moments I had a sense of his gratitude. For a while I hesitated, fearing that his innately suspicious nature would arise to rebuff an intruder from a foreign sphere. I wondered, too, whether there existed a common ground on which our different natures could meet. But the thought of him drove such doubts from my mind. Adam Urbas was no ordinary peasant. He belonged to our peasant aristocracy; his very bearing betrayed intelligence and character. I hoped, therefore, that my approach would not be made in vain. I weighed the matter no longer. One evening in December I walked into the prison and entered Urbas's cell.

I had seen to his comfort during his custody. The cell was a livable place, decently furnished with washstand, bed, and mirror, and adequately heated. He was sitting with an open Bible before him in the light of a lamp. I greeted him, took off my coat, hung it on a peg, seated myself opposite him at the table.

Each time I saw him, his appearance struck me afresh. It did so now. He was as massive as a bull. He had the round, brachycephalic head of the true native Franconian, but the skull, particularly in the formation of the temples, showed signs of ancient breeding; the bones there were strikingly thin, and the skin was bluish-yellow and nearly transparent. His mouth was broad, with thin, firm lips; his nose aquiline and high-bridged. His carefully shaven face might have been that of an old actor. His hands were the hands of a giant. His heavy-lidded eyes rarely opened more than a crack, but when they were wide open their gaze was amazingly piercing and difficult even for me to sustain.

By way of creating an opening, I said that I had long felt the need of coming to see him. However, I had not come in my official capacity, but rather—if he had no objection—as a friend who happened to be privileged to visit him. As a matter of fact, he was my ward, and I was responsible for his well-being.

He looked at me in silence. After a time he said: " Very good of you."

I made a gesture of protest. " That is not how I should like you to receive me," I said. " I hope that you will cease to mistrust me now. One is naturally suspicious of a judge on the bench. You say to yourself: ' If he is not here officially, to complete his depositions, then he is here out of curiosity, to pry into my affairs.' Neither is true. The papers are practically all prepared. We are ready now for the trial. I have little reason to be curious, for it seems to me I have learned all there is to know. Why I have come, I scarcely know myself. I had to come. It seemed to me my duty."

Again Urbas was silent for a long time. At last he spoke: " I believe you."

I grasped at the thread. " If you believe me," I said, " we can talk in peace about what has happened, like two old acquaintances."

Urbas reflected. Then he said: " What is the use of saying anything? Bad enough that it had to happen."

" That is just the question," I exclaimed. " Did it have to happen? Have to? "

He raised his head, but his glance remained lowered. " To doubt that would be sheer foolhardiness," he said.

" Not only does a doubt exist," I persisted, " but society rejects your deed and abhors it. If every man were to mete out justice in these cases according to his own lights, there would be no end of horrors, and we should live surrounded by savage beasts. How you plan to justify your deed to yourself and your highest Judge, I do not know. But you are still answerable to society."

Urbas shook his head. " What can talking do or undo? " he murmured indifferently.

I said: "The slate must be wiped clean between you and society. So long as you continue your obdurate silence, the horror and the confusion remain."

"But what if a man lacks words to explain?"

"Does he lack them, or merely withhold them out of pride and stubbornness?" I retorted. "Look into yourself!"

He said: "My tongue is clumsy. I am unaccustomed to speech." He wrinkled his forehead. I saw that I could press him no further. I waited. At last a rumble awoke in his breast: "I made him." His gaze dropped. "May I not also exterminate him?" he added with a strange, crafty expression. "You may all contest that as much as you like: that which a man has made he may also exterminate, if it was only to do evil that the thing was made. I went after him myself; dug him out of his mother's womb. Other women carry their fruit nine months. Of his mother it is true to say she carried him thirteen years. I insisted that she bear him; I insisted that God send him. I determined everything about him before he was born. He shall be this to me, and this, I said to myself. Like a lump of clay you dig up out of the earth and mould and knead to your liking. Suddenly you see that you are holding mere mud in your hand. You throw it down on the earth out of which it came."

The crafty expression deepened. He scrutinised me through half-closed eyes. "It was only little by little that you learned he was doomed to evil," I suggested.

He interrupted me with an imperious gesture. "Bad from the beginning. Bad blood; I smelt it with my nose. Others, with far worse antecedents, grow up without much looking after and do not turn out wrong. They may bend themselves crooked in the beginning, but time straightens them out. With him, the crooked grew ever crookeder. Then I saw that much wrong would ensue. And so it was. Every day a grain of sand; finally, a mountain. There I stood, asking myself: 'How will this end?' When you rooted it up in one place, it grew twice as high in another. When you sought to grasp it in your hand, it slipped through your fingers. There was no help for it."

"But cannot defective seeds be made to thrive through careful cultivation?" I asked. "Did you try to awaken his conscience? Did you try seriously to teach him?"

For the first time, Urbas raised his heavy lids. He looked dazed. "Sir," he said abruptly, "one cannot command the elements. I said to myself: 'If the eye cannot see, then the tongue cannot help it to sight. If example does not suffice, then neither will the rod.' So far as speech goes, my wife did her duty. Women understand these things better. If he could not hear my voice speaking in hers, what good was it to him? If he could not hear what I, without speaking, gave him to understand, then the words of the prophet, even, would have been vain sounds to him. This I told myself. When I led, he could have followed. When I followed him, he could have turned round. He never saw me; he never heard me. It would go against my grain to seize a person and shout in his ear: 'Man! be decent!' What would be the use, if decency were not in his nature? The man who makes a scornful face while others pray is a lost creature. Punishment avails only where the worm is not already gnawing at the root."

"Were you really certain of all this?" I asked, not without some diffidence, for his words and his voice rang with a sinister conviction. "Were you so firmly convinced of your own infallibility?"

He stretched his arm across the table. His breath came heavily as he answered me. "If my flesh and blood rises up against me can I dispute with it as with a cheating tradesman? If the seed I sowed brings forth a brood of hissing vipers can I, like a schoolmaster, go for them with a rod? There would be neither sense nor dignity in that. If the person on whom you have staked your whole future is a creature of evil, and causes nothing but evil, incessant evil, until house and farm are engulfed in slime, what are you to do? Can you break his bones and hope they'll grow another way? or breathe into him another brain and heart?"

His powerful face trembled and blazed. This man, who for so long—a life-time, no doubt—had confided in no one, was baring his soul before my eyes, finding words, images, and tones with which to awe and silence me. But I had suddenly the unshakable impression that he was talking to me, turning towards me, only in appearance; that in reality he was trying to ward off an unseen assailant, whose questions and reproaches he was not now hearing for the first time. It seemed to me that what he was telling me had long been fermenting in him, and was now gushing forth, pouring itself out; while he, unable to control the rush of his own terribly constrained and oppressive words, stood helplessly by, listening mutely in rage and pain to the sound of his own voice.

With bowed head and squared jaw, he went on, his voice growing more tranquil. "You might ask, 'When did you first realise? When did your hope end?' Ask the leper when he first realised that his skin was beginning to fester. He knew it, of course, on the first day; but he only believed it when his leprosy forced him to take to bed. Night after night, I lay thinking and thinking. Thought about myself; thought about him. Weighed this, and weighed that. Watched and watched the leprosy eating its way in. Tortured my spirit with wondering how to fight this evil. Discipline? Discipline is always one step behind, the misdeed always one step ahead. The club with which I might have beaten him would have splintered in my fist, and the welts on his back would merely have calloused him. Ought I to have laid down rules? What kind of rules? Where are the infallible ones? Should I have chained him up like a dog? Everything in him that I fastened on was myself. I the tree, he the branch; I the wick, he the flame; I the earth, he the spring. How can the tree quarrel with the branch? The same sap runs through them. And the wick with the flame it nourishes? The earth with the spring that gushes forth from it? So much is true; but whence came this evil? There it is, spreading like a prairie-fire. But where does it come from? How cruelly it advances! First the petty lie, then the serious one; first the penny filched, then the pound; first the beast maltreated, then the human being; first the pocket picked, then all honour gone; first a rogue, then a procurer. No respect, no faith, no honesty, no love. Where did it all come from? From me? Obviously. And then I asked myself: Where, Urbas, and when, were your body and soul so scorched in Hell that you should bring forth such stench and foulness into the world? Is it possible that man is merely filth and vileness, reproducing only filth and vileness in his turn?"

He looked at me with his stolid gaze, like a beast of burden panting under its load. There was silence once more. With his coat-sleeve he wiped the moisture from his brow. I sympathised with his anguish; I shared it; but something in me that would not be silenced accused him of exaggeration. "It seems to me that you take upon yourself more responsibility than any man has the right to assume," I began. "When you exaggerate your notion of duty, you are bound to exaggerate your idea of the rights you possess. You have, as man and as father, been thinking only of yourself. But what about the boy's mother, who has an equal, or even a greater, claim on her son? She will not sanction your reasoning, and even less the violent act which tore all family ties asunder."

"That is something we cannot discuss," Urbas answered coldly. "We have gone beyond the realm of reason. Whether she approves of my reasons I do not know. She has lost something, and so have I. Her suffering is great, but my damnation is greater. She has nothing left in life, but my life has been poisoned for many a year. Certainly, she deserves more pity than I. Her body seemed to give forth its fruit reluctantly; it has revenged itself upon my pride and my folly. Men ought merely to seek to understand nature; instead, we defy her, try to improve upon her, and butt like steers against the bolted door. No woman should have only one child; too much depends on it. My mother had nine. To be sure, seven of them died. My grandmother had sixteen, and of them also eight were early taken by death. There is nothing bitter about such death. Not all the seeds sown in the fields bring forth grain. One should never have an only child; the risk is too great. It is a lottery. No; the analogy is bad, for here we are dealing with a scorching flame that is blown back upon us and leaves its scars. A mother is doubtless fearful when her only offering is rejected by God and man, and her soul is filled with sorrow. She is his in time and eternity, so that even if he came towards her with uplifted axe, his life would still seem to her worth more than her own. To her, good and evil are meaningless; blood speaks in a louder voice than they.

"As for me, 'Father!' it cried out to me. What does 'Father!' mean, I have wondered, striving to learn its deepest sense. Had I bedded with a serving-maid and begotten a son, he also would have called me father. Would it have been the same? It would not. He might have been decent, respectful, the son I desired. Why not have begotten him, then? Why the indecent one? But the law forbids, and the law is sacred. And would that servant have been my wife? Let me say this: a man's aspirations are both higher and deeper than a woman's. And I will say this, too, that a father's guilt goes deeper than a mother's. A mother sits at the hem of our Lord's robe, and He will not let harm befall her. A father is called before the Seat and a reckoning demanded from him. He is the central link in the chain of his race, the link between his forebears and his descendants. He may not surrender to tenderness and caresses, for through the eyes of his son, his community, his king, his ancestors, and all who come after him unto the fourth and the fifth generation, are watching him. The son is loaned to him as a kind of pledge, to be given back to the world when the time is ripe. Woe unto him who must come forward with empty hands and says: 'I have betrayed my trust!'"

He looked fixedly into space, rose from his chair, and repeated: "I have betrayed my trust!" Then he sat down again.

I dared not break in upon his absorption. Besides, I was seeking in my mind a way that would lead us farther on. From one moment to the next I felt more sure of my theory, but I was afraid. My certainty was such that conclusions which, until now, had been founded on mere assumption and circumstantial evidence, took on the bright colours of reality. One picture fitted into another with prophetic clearness. Undoubtedly the personal magnetism of the man seated opposite me contributed both to my vision and my fear. Despite a long career as lawyer and judge—or, rather, because of it—I have had too much experience of extraordinary telepathic communication to ridicule the idea of the transference of mental states.

There was something solemnly impressive about this man. To rob him of his secret seemed to me almost dishonourable. I trembled. I could not find the proper opening. Finally, however, breaking the deep silence, I leaned far across the table and asked him: "And did you go into that room intending to end it all?"

He did not answer. The firm lips refused to open. But the obstinate forehead burst open to my gaze. It opened like a book and I was able to read all that lay behind it.

"You went into that room twice," I said suddenly at a venture—or perhaps not at a venture; perhaps my words were dictated by the burning inspiration of the moment. "Twice!" I went on. "And when you left the first time, Simon was still alive. When you went in the second time, he was already lying on the bed, a corpse!"

I should never have thought that this peasant's face, normally as brown as stained wood, could grow so white. The pallor seemed to flow visibly out of his pores, coating his skin with a shimmer as of wet chalk. He stared at me with wide open eyes; his cheeks quivered; he clutched at his throat with both hands. My uncertainty vanished. I forced myself to speak calmly, and continued: "You went in to take him some money. You had none in the house on that Sunday, and borrowed, directly after dinner, two thousand marks from your neighbour, Stephen Buchner. Isn't that so? You were to rid yourself with this money of Simon. He was to reach a seaport that same evening and take ship to America. Isn't that so? You offered him the money; you explained your plan; and you expected him to obey without hesitation. But not only did he refuse to obey; he also refused the money. You questioned him, and then he began to speak. At first, what he said was confused and incoherent, for he was still befuddled with drink. Later, though, his words became clear to you, terribly clear. You stood before him and said not a word. You were not even offended at his lying on the bed and speaking into the air, for you knew if he had to look you in the face, he would never have the courage to speak out. You listened, simply listened, and out of the listening arose all that happened later. Is that so or not?"

Urbas did not take his frightened gaze from my face. "You must have been a ghostly presence in the house," he stammered in his bewilderment.

"No," I said. "There are simple conclusions drawn from verifiable facts. The most insignificant facts often leave behind them the most telling traces. There is no witchery or magic about this. Nature has ruled that a man's actions shall always form links in an unbroken chain. It is as if you threw a stone into a pool: the ripples widen and vanish, but the vibration may still be felt long after the eye has ceased to detect anything. Thus there is really no escape from the net of circumstance, which draws more closely about a man with each step taken, each touch of a finger, each exhalation of a breath. I had one clue to which in the beginning I attached little value; only as time passed did I become aware of its significance. Suddenly it clarified the whole situation. In Eichstadt lives a painter named Kiessling. He was a friend and boon companion of Simon. The fellow is a ne'er-do-well who has come down in the world, but is not without a crude kind of uprightness. He had a number of things to tell me. For instance: you will recall that last winter one of your antique, beautifully painted china jugs disappeared. You and your wife felt certain that Simon had abstracted it and sold it to a dealer in town, for it was a valuable piece. Your wife went so far as to express the suspicion that Kiessling had served as go-between in its disposal. Simon did, as a matter of fact, take the jug. It is also true that Kiessling had a hand in the affair, and that he would not have been above sharing in the proceeds, although he now denies this. But things never went as far as that. Simon smashed the jug before the eyes of his friend. They were in the little shop on the Pleinfeld road. Simon had brought the jug. Kiessling held it in his hands, and was inspecting it expertly with approval, when Simon wrenched it from his grasp and dashed it with all his might to the ground, where, naturally, it broke into a hundred bits. Kiessling remonstrated angrily with him, but Simon, after brooding morosely for a moment, cried out of a sudden: 'I should like to do something that would really hurt him, something he would feel in the very marrow of his bones!' Kiessling could not guess immediately against whom this rage was directed. His acquaintance with Simon was then still fresh. Later, he realised who was meant. He said he had never seen a son possessed of such a hatred for his father.

Similar outbursts succeeded one another from time to time. An impotent bitterness would come over Simon, an urge to destroy. These spells would alternate with a morbid joylessness, a clouded melancholy during which time he would brood silently. Often what he seemed to feel was not hate but fear; often not fear but something more unfathomable. Other people have testified that at various times he had been heard to say something like this: 'I wish I could tell him everything right out to his face, just once; then I'd feel better.' What could he have meant by this? Kiessling was not alone to speak in his favour; there were others who said he was not really wicked, at bottom, and most of these were people who had no reason to speak for him. They described him as weak-willed, easily led astray, unstable, dissipating in order to numb himself, evading work like a man hunted and constantly in flight, vicious through heartsickness, but not fundamentally bad. This is the way I see him now myself. But by whom, exactly, did he feel himself hunted? Whom was he defying? What was he trying to numb within himself? It seems to me, Urbas, that you and I know the answers. Though the whole world cudgel its brains, we two know the truth. But you did not know it until that evening in the bedroom. You learned it then."

Urbas drew a long breath of relief. His face twitched as if he were wincing at blows from within. Apparently he was trying to summon words that would not come. But the lights and shadows in his bony, sensitive, honourable countenance were sufficiently eloquent. The gloomy amazement, the almost superstitious horror he had felt at the unveiling of what he had regarded as his inviolable, eternally buried secret, was gone. Now that he had no longer to guard his secret, his heart was relieved of a heavy burden. And so he sighed deeply with relief.

I felt it my duty to help him through the last remaining difficulties, and went on. "If you look at it properly, you see that men are worse off in these matters than animals. Animals cannot misunderstand one another. Men misunderstand one another continually in deed and in thought; this is true of brothers, of friends, of fathers and sons. Each man dwells at the centre of his own incomprehension as in a black cave, and suffers from the extravagant delusion that his cave is a brilliantly lighted room. And the man who imagines that God has been at particular pains to select him as His mouthpiece on earth soon discovers that he has been the instrument of Satan. For thirteen years your only thought was to have a son, and after he came it took you eighteen years to discover what your son was like; and then it was too late. Is not human wisdom a pretty sad thing? Why then, Urbas, should you go on assuming responsibility for a crime you did not commit? Why call yourself the murderer of him who chose his own way out of the world? Why do you insist upon cheating earthly justice? Why, man! Why?"

"I'll tell you the reason," said Urbas, "now that my game is completely up. But have patience with me; it is difficult." He seemed to be searching within himself; his fingers twitched as if they too were seeking, with his thoughts, the most precise, the briefest word, the most truthworthy explanation. He began fumblingly: "It is true that I went in to give him the money. I had not thought of America. Get him away, I said to myself, as quickly as possible, as far as possible, and be spared, at least, the sight of policemen in the house. I crossed over to the room. It was dark when I entered, and I had to light a candle. There he was, lying on the bed and staring at me. It is true that he did not accept the money. He turned his face to the wall, gritted his teeth, and said that money could no longer help him. I stood beside the bed and said: 'Stand up in your father's presence!' He answered: 'Why should I stand in your presence when it is you who have flung me down?' My fists clenched of themselves and I said: 'What do you mean? How have I flung you down, you scoundrel!' A single word came from his lips: 'You——!' Nothing else. 'You——!' he said. I looked at him; he stared back at me; and after a pause he repeated: 'You——!' In that word was so much spite and fury and venom, such a convulsive threat, that the saliva turned bitter in my mouth. 'What do you mean by *you*?' I cried; 'What do you mean by *you*?' 'Oh . . . you——!' he said again between clenched teeth; 'the weight of you has been crushing down my chest from the day I was born.' I was silent. 'Go on standing there and glaring at me with those eyes of yours,' he went on. 'Is there never to be an end to your staring at me with those eyes? From the very first minute of my life it has been like this; you staring, staring, staring, saying never a word. Sitting at table, knowing everything there is to know about me, and never a word. A fine long road you have driven me with your staring and staring. Why have you never called me by name and spoken to me? Why have I never had a word out of you? Small wonder I went to the dogs! Small wonder I turned to carousing and sought my pals in taverns. At least they speak, they laugh, they have a good word for a fellow. At least they say Whoa and Giddap, and you know where you stand with them. But you! Have I ever known where I stood with you? I used to say to myself: There he is, lying in wait again. He's after you again about something. When I was just a kid, if you came and stood in the doorway, whatever I was eating would stick in my throat. Hundreds and hundreds of times I have wanted to go to you, but I was afraid to take a step in your direction. I used to wonder what I had done that was wrong, and when I did something wrong I was happy, for then at least I knew *that*. And so I would be restless and nervous until I did something irreparable and aroused people's anger. Yes, I am bad, but I don't know that I was born that way. Yes, I am a scoundrel, but that is no reason why you need play the Lord almighty with me. You ought to be worrying about how you failed in your duty towards me. I might have honoured you, as it says in the Ten Commandments; I might have been as tame as a starling. I could have done it; it was in me; but you drove it out. I have become a scoundrel and I am sick of life and I am sick of human beings and boon companions, and nothing gives me pleasure any more.' He went on that way and said several other things which I have forgotten. Then he rolled over on the bed, ground his teeth, and whimpered. He laughed angrily, turned once more to the wall and fell silent again. I said to myself: Urbas, there is a soul gone to perdition, but yours is probably damned, too. But I could not utter a word. I was tongue-tied. What good would it have done to go whining to my Maker? I could not utter a word. I went out. I walked across the farmyard as far as the hedge. Everything was bathed in peace as on spring nights when the roots in the earth run with sap. I looked up to the stars. No help there. I opened the stable door and sniffed the warm acrid air. One of the oxen raised its head and went on chewing its cud. Suddenly I was seized with horror and thought: You must go back into that room; even if words don't come to you, something must be done. I went back. When I entered the room he was already lying in his blood. I stood still a long while. Then I said to myself: If this is what he has come to, then you are his murderer. If this is his charge against you, you must pay it. . . . Now I have told you everything."

He folded his hands over the Bible and then, in a milder tone and with a curiously veiled glance, he went on: "I want to tell you also about a dream I had the night before this happened. A farm-hand stepped into the room and said: 'Farmer, the horses are harnessed. Let us start.' I went out where the horses stood waiting in the deep snow, and got in to drive the wagon. All at once we were off the road and the horses were wading in snow up to their bellies. Suddenly

I turned around and there was the farm burning behind me, casting a red glow over the snow. The horses began to run, dragging me along beside them by the reins. I was losing my breath. I could not loose the reins. They were wound round my hand. We came down towards the old mill by the railway bridge, where the water is sixty ells across and more than ten deep. There the horses ran on still more wildly while the glowing blaze filled the whole sky. The river was frozen over and I wondered fearfully if the ice would bear the weight of wagon and horses. The horses—heavy farm horses—rushed down the bank, but the ice held firm. On the opposite bank stood Simon, and as the horses raced over their frozen course I shouted across to him: 'Help, Simon!' He answered: 'I have to go home; the house is burning; the stable is burning.' I could not swing myself back on to the wagon. The horses were dragging me along. I cried out in great distress: 'Help, Simon! Come and loose the reins!' He answered: 'You will have to loose them yourself. The ice will not hold the two of us.' Then I shouted to him: 'I'll give you everything for your own—horses, wagon, everything; but help, for God's sake!' He turned back towards me, and as he turned the horses stopped. But at the first step Simon took the ice cracked, and as he seized the horses' bridle the ice broke, and wagon, horses, Simon, and I sank into the water. I was sinking when I awoke."

He was silent. He expected no comment from me, and I had none to make. I saw with astonishment how in the course of a few minutes he had aged: his chin was sharp, his eyes were dull, his neck was thin, his hands had grown flabby, and his carriage was that of a feeble old man. The dominating, clear-headed, powerful man who had sat across from me had suddenly shrivelled. When I took my leave he did not look up; he scarcely seemed to notice my going. The silence in which the whole of his former life had been wrapped spread itself once more about him, impenetrable, flowing into death. For, the next morning, when he was to have been arraigned, the jailer found him hanging from the window-beam.

CARL STEPHENSON

LEININGEN *VERSUS* THE ANTS

"UNLESS they alter their course, and there's no reason why they should, they'll reach your plantation in two days at the latest."

Leiningen sucked placidly at a cigar about the size of a corn-cob and for a few seconds gazed without answering at the agitated District Commissioner. Then he took the cob from his lips, and leaned slightly forward. With his bristling grey hair, bulky nose and lucid eyes, he had the look of an ageing and shabby eagle.

"Decent of you," he murmured, "paddling all this way just to give me the tip. But you're pulling my leg, of course, when you say I must do a bunk. Why, even a herd of saurians couldn't drive me from this plantation of mine."

The Brazilian official threw up lean and lanky arms and clawed the air with wildly distended fingers. "Leiningen!" he shouted. "You're insane! They're not creatures you can fight—they're an elemental—an 'act of God'! Ten miles long, two miles wide—ants, nothing but ants! And every single one of them a fiend from hell; before you can spit three times they'll eat a full-grown buffalo to the bones. I tell you if you don't clear out at once there'll be nothing left of you but a skeleton picked as clean as your own plantation."

Leiningen grinned. "Act of God, my eye! Anyway, I'm not an old woman; I'm not going to run for it just because an elemental's on the way. And don't think I'm the kind of fathead who tries to fend off lightning with his fists, either. I use my intelligence, old man. With me, the brain isn't a second blind-gut; I know what it's there for. When I began this model farm and plantation three years ago, I took into account all that could conceivably happen to it. And now I'm ready for anything and everything—including your ants."

The Brazilian rose heavily to his feet. "I've done my best," he gasped. "Your obstinacy endangers not only yourself, but the lives of your four hundred workers. You don't know these ants!"

Leiningen accompanied him down to the river, where the

Government launch was moored. The vessel cast off. As it moved downstream, the exclamation mark neared the rail and began waving its arms frantically. Long after the launch had disappeared round the bend, Leiningen thought he could still hear that dimming, imploring voice. " You don't know them, I tell you! *You don't know them !* "

But the reported enemy was by no means unfamiliar to the planter. Before he started work on his settlement, he had lived long enough in the country to see for himself the fearful devastations sometimes wrought by these ravenous insects in their campaigns for food. But since then he had planned measures of defence accordingly, and these, he was convinced, were in every way adequate to withstand the approaching peril.

Moreover, during his three years as a planter, Leiningen had met and defeated drought, flood, plague and all other " acts of God " which had come against him—unlike his fellow-settlers in the district, who had made little or no resistance. This unbroken success he attributed solely to the observance of his lifelong motto: *The human brain needs only to become fully aware of its powers to conquer even the elements.* Dullards reeled senselessly and aimlessly into the abyss; cranks, however brilliant, lost their heads when circumstances suddenly altered or accelerated and ran into stone walls, sluggards drifted with the current until they were caught in whirlpools and dragged under. But such disasters, Leiningen contended, merely strengthened his argument that intelligence, directed aright, invariably makes man the master of his fate.

Yes, Leiningen had always known how to grapple with life. Even here, in this Brazilian wilderness, his brain had triumphed over every difficulty and danger it had so far encountered. First he had vanquished primal forces by cunning and organisation, then he had enlisted the resources of modern science to increase miraculously the yield of his plantation. And now he was sure he would prove more than a match for the " irresistible " ants.

That same evening, however, Leiningen assembled his workers. He had no intention of waiting till the news reached their ears from other sources. Most of them had been born in the district; the cry " The ants are coming! " was to them an imperative signal for instant, panic-stricken flight, a sprint for life itself. But so great was the Indians' trust in Leiningen, in Leiningen's word, and in Leiningen's wisdom, that they received his curt tidings, and his orders for the imminent struggle, with the calmness with which they were given. They waited, unafraid, alert, as if for the beginning of a new game or hunt which he had just described to them. The ants were indeed mighty, but not so mighty as the boss. Let them come!

They came at noon the second day. Their approach was announced by the wild unrest of the horses, scarcely controllable now either in stall or under rider, scenting from afar a vapour instinct with horror.

It was announced by a stampede of animals, timid and savage, hurtling past each other; jaguars and pumas flashing by nimble stags of the pampas, bulky tapirs, no longer hunters, themselves hunted, outpacing fleet kinkajous, maddened herds of cattle, heads lowered, nostrils snorting, rushing through tribes of loping monkeys, chattering in a dementia of terror; then followed the creeping and springing denizens of bush and steppe, big and little rodents, snakes, and lizards.

Pell-mell the rabble swarmed down the hill to the plantation, scattered right and left before the barrier of the water-filled ditch, then sped onwards to the river, where, again hindered, they fled along its bank out of sight.

. . . . .

This water-filled ditch was one of the defence measures which Leiningen had long since prepared against the advent of the ants. It encompassed three sides of the plantation like a huge horseshoe. Twelve feet across, but not very deep, when dry it could hardly be described as an obstacle to either man or beast. But the ends of the "horseshoe" ran into the river which formed the northern boundary, and fourth side, of the plantation. And at the end nearer the house and outbuildings in the middle of the plantation, Leiningen had constructed a dam by means of which water from the river could be diverted into the ditch.

So now, by opening the dam, he was able to fling an imposing girdle of water, a huge quadrilateral with the river as its base, completely around the plantation, like the moat encircling a medieval city. Unless the ants were clever enough to build rafts, they had no hope of reaching the plantation, Leiningen concluded.

The twelve-foot water-ditch seemed to afford in itself all the security needed. But while awaiting the arrival of the ants, Leiningen made a further improvement. The western section of the ditch ran along the edge of a tamarind wood, and the branches of some great trees reached over the water. Leiningen now had them lopped so that ants could not descend from them within the "moat."

The women and children, then the herds of cattle, were escorted by *peons* on rafts over the river, to remain on the other side in absolute safely until the plunderers had departed. Leiningen gave this instruction, not because he believed the non-combatants were in any danger, but in order to avoid hampering the efficiency of the defenders. " Critical situations first become crises," he explained to his men, " when oxen or women get excited."

Finally, he made a careful inspection of the " inner moat "—a smaller ditch lined with concrete, which extended around the hill on which stood the ranch-house, barns, stables and other buildings. Into this concrete ditch emptied the inflow pipes from three great petrol-tanks. If by some miracle the ants managed to cross the water and reach the plantation, this " rampart of petrol " would be an absolutely impassable protection for the beseiged and their dwellings and stock. Such, at least, was Leiningen's opinion.

He stationed his men at irregular distances along the water-ditch, the first line of defence. Then he lay down in his hammock and puffed drowsily away at his pipe until a *peon* came with the report that the ants had been observed far away in the south.

Leiningen mounted his horse, which at the feel of its master seemed to forget its uneasiness, and rode leisurely in the direction of the threatening offensive. The southern stretch of ditch—the upper side of the quadrilateral—was nearly three miles long; from its centre one could survey the entire countryside. This was destined to be the scene of the outbreak of war between Leiningen's brain and twenty square miles of life-destroying ants.

It was a sight one could never forget. Over the range of hills, as far as eye could see, crept a darkening hem, ever longer and broader, until the shadow spread across the slope from east to west, then downwards, downwards, uncannily swift, and all the green herbage of that wide vista was being mown as by a giant sickle, leaving only the vast moving shadow, extending, deepening, and moving rapidly nearer.

When Leiningen's men, behind their barrier of water, perceived the approach of the long-expected foe, they gave vent to their suspense in screams and imprecations. But as the distance began to lessen between the " sons of hell " and the water-ditch, they relapsed into silence. Before the advance of that awe-inspiring throng, their belief in the powers of the boss began to dwindle.

Even Leiningen himself, who had ridden up just in time to restore their loss of heart by a display of unshakable calm, even he could not free himself from a qualm of *malaise*. Yonder were thousands of millions of voracious jaws bearing down upon him, and only a suddenly insignificant, narrow ditch lay between him and his men and being gnawed to the bones "before you can spit three times."

Hadn't his brain for once taken on more than it could manage? If the blighters decided to rush the ditch, fill it to the brim with their corpses, there'd still be more than enough to destroy every trace of that cranium of his. The planter's chin jutted; they hadn't got him yet, and he'd see to it they never would. While he could think at all, he'd flout both death and the devil.

. . . . .

The hostile army was approaching in perfect formation; no human battalions, however well-drilled, could ever hope to rival the precision of that advance. Along a front that moved forward as uniformly as a straight line, the ants drew nearer and nearer to the water-ditch. Then, when they learned through their scouts the nature of the obstacle, the two outlying wings of the army detached themselves from the main body and marched down the western and eastern sides of the ditch.

This surrounding manœuvre took rather more than an hour to accomplish; no doubt the ants expected that at some point they would find a crossing.

During this outflanking movement by the wings, the army on the centre and southern front remained still. The besieged were therefore able to contemplate at their leisure the thumb-long, reddish-black, long-legged insects; some of the Indians believed they could see, too, intent on them, the brilliant, cold eyes, and the razor-edged mandibles, of this host of infinity.

It is not easy for the average person to imagine that an animal, not to mention an insect, can *think*. But now both the European brains of Leiningen and the primitive brains of the Indians began to stir with the unpleasant foreboding that inside every single one of that deluge of insects dwelt a thought. And that thought was: Ditch or no ditch, we'll get to your flesh!

Not until four o'clock did the wings reach the "horseshoe" ends of the ditch, only to find these ran into the great river. Through some kind of secret telegraphy, the report must then have flashed very swiftly indeed along the entire enemy line. And Leiningen, riding—no longer casually—along his side of the ditch, noticed by energetic and widespread movements of troops that, for some unknown reason, the news of the check had its greatest effect on the southern front, where the main army was massed. Perhaps the failure to find a way over the ditch was persuading the ants to withdraw from the plantation in search of spoils more easily attainable.

He was soon disillusioned. The shouts of outposts made him

put spurs to his horse and ride smartly along the southern bank, until at length he pulled up before a sight that made him catch his breath.

. . . . .

An immense flood of ants, about a hundred yards in width, was pouring in a glimmering black cataract down the far slope of the ditch. Many thousands were already drowning in the sluggish, creeping flow, but they were followed by troop after troop, who clambered over their sinking comrades, and then themselves served as dying bridges to the reserves hurrying on in their rear.

Shoals of ants were being carried away by the current into the middle of the ditch, where gradually they broke asunder and then, exhausted by their struggles, vanished below the surface. Nevertheless, the wavering, floundering hundred-yard front was remorselessly if slowly advancing towards the besieged on the other bank. Leiningen had been wrong when he supposed the enemy would first have to fill the ditch with their bodies before they could cross; instead, they merely needed to act as stepping-stones, as they swam and sank, to the hordes ever pressing onwards from behind.

Near Leiningen a few mounted herdsmen awaited his orders. He sent one to the weir—the river must be dammed more strongly to increase the speed and power of the water coursing through the ditch. A second *peon* was dispatched to the out-houses to bring spades and petrol-sprinklers. A third rode away to summon to the zone of the offensive all the men, except the observation posts, on the nearby sections of the ditch, which were not yet actively threatened.

The ants were getting across far more quickly than Leiningen would have deemed possible. Impelled by the mighty cascade behind them, they struggled nearer and nearer to the inner bank. The momentum of the attack was so great that neither the tardy flow of the stream nor its downward pull could exert its proper force; and into the gap left by every submerging insect hastened forward a dozen more.

When reinforcements reached Leiningen, the invaders were half-way over. The planter had to admit to himself that it was only by a stroke of luck for him that the ants were attempting the crossing on a relatively short front: had they assaulted simultaneously along the entire length of the ditch, the outlook for the defenders would have been black indeed.

Even as it was, it could hardly be described as rosy, though the planter seemed quite unaware that death in a gruesome form was drawing closer and closer. As the war between his brain and the " act of God " reached its climax, the very shadow of annihilation began to pale to Leiningen, who now felt like a champion in a new Olympic game, a gigantic and thrilling contest, from which he was determined to emerge victor. Such, indeed, was his aura of confidence that the Indians forgot their stupefied fear of the peril only a yard or two away; under the planter's supervision, they began fervidly digging up the edge of the bank and throwing clods of earth and spadefuls of sand into the midst of the hostile fleet.

The petrol-sprinklers, hitherto used to destroy pests and blights on the plantation, were also brought into action. Streams of evil-reeking oil now soared and fell over an enemy already in disorder through the bombardment of earth and sand.

The ants responded to these vigorous and successful measures of defence by further developments of their offensive. Entire clumps of huddling insects began to roll down the opposite bank into the water. At the same time, Leiningen noticed that the ants were now attacking along an ever-widening front. As the numbers both of his men and his petrol-sprinklers were severely limited, this rapid extension of the line of battle was becoming an overwhelming danger.

To add to his difficulties, the very clods of earth they flung into that black floating carpet often whirled fragments towards the defenders' side, and here and there dark ribbons were already mounting the inner bank. True, wherever a man saw these they could still be driven back into the water by spadefuls of earth or jets of petrol. But the file of defenders was too sparse and scattered to hold off at all points these landing-parties, and though the *peons* toiled like madmen, their plight became momently more perilous.

One man struck with his spade at an enemy clump, did not draw it back quickly enough from the water; in a trice the wooden haft swarmed with upwards scurrying insects. With a curse, he dropped the spade into the ditch; too late, they were already on his body. They lost no time; wherever they encountered bare flesh they bit deeply; a few, bigger than the rest, carried in their hindquarters a sting which injected a burning and paralysing venom. Screaming, frantic with pain, the *peon* danced and twirled like a dervish.

Realising that another such casualty—yes, perhaps this alone—might plunge his men into confusion and destroy their morale, Leiningen roared in a bellow louder than the yells of the victim: "Into the petrol, idiot! Douse your paws in the petrol!" The dervish ceased his pirouette as if transfixed, then tore off his shirt and plunged his arm and the ants hanging to it up to the shoulder in one of the large open tins of petrol.

But even then the fierce mandibles did not slacken; another *peon* had to help him squash and detach each separate insect.

Distracted by the episode, some defenders had turned away from the ditch. And now cries of fury, a thudding of spades, and a wild trampling to and fro, showed that the ants had made full use of the interval, though luckily only a few had managed to get across. The men set to work again desperately with the barrage of earth and sand. Meanwhile an old Indian, who acted as medicine-man to the plantation workers, gave the bitten *peon* a drink he had prepared some hours before, which, he claimed, possessed the virtue of dissolving and weakening ants' venom.

Leiningen surveyed his position. A dispassionate observer would have estimated the odds against him at a thousand to one. But, then, such an onlooker would have reckoned only by what he saw—the advance of myriad battalions of ants against the futile efforts of a few defenders—and not by the unseen activity that can go on in a man's brain.

For Leiningen had not erred when he decided he would fight elemental with elemental. The water in the ditch was beginning to rise; the stronger damming of the river was making itself apparent. Visibly the swiftness and power of the masses of water increased, swirling into quicker and quicker movement its living black surface, dispersing its pattern, carrying away more and more of it on the hastening current.

. . . . .

Victory had been snatched from the very jaws of defeat. With an hysterical shout of joy, the *peons* feverishly intensified their bombardment of earth-clods and sand.

And now the wide cataract down the opposite bank was thinning and ceasing, as if the ants were becoming aware that they could not attain their aim. They were scurrying back up the slope to safety.

All the troops so far hurled into the ditch had been sacrificed in vain. Drowned and floundering insects eddied in thousands along the flow, while Indians running on the bank destroyed every swimmer that reached the side.

Not until the ditch curved towards the east did the scattered ranks assemble again in a coherent mass. And now, exhausted and half-numbed, they were in no condition to ascend the bank. Fusilades of clods drove them round the bend towards the mouth of the ditch and then into the river, wherein they vanished without leaving a trace.

The news ran swiftly along the entire chain of outposts, and soon a long, scattered line of laughing men could be seen hastening along the ditch towards the scene of victory. For once they seemed to have lost all their native reserve, for it was in wild abandon now they celebrated the triumph—as if there were no longer thousands of millions of merciless, cold and hungry eyes watching them from the opposite bank, watching and waiting.

The sun sank behind the rim of the tamarind wood and twilight deepened into night. It was not only hoped, but expected, that the ants would remain quiet until dawn. But to defeat any forlorn attempt at a crossing, the flow of water through the ditch was powerfully increased by opening the dam still further.

In spite of this impregnable barrier, Leiningen was not yet altogether convinced that the ants would not venture another surprise attack. He ordered his men to camp along the bank over-night. He also detailed parties of them to patrol the ditch in two of his motor-cars and ceaselessly to illuminate the surface of the water with headlights and electric torches.

After having taken all the precautions he deemed necessary, the farmer ate his supper with considerable appetite and went to bed. His slumbers were in no wise disturbed by the memory of the waiting live twenty square miles.

. . . . .

Dawn found a thoroughly refreshed and active Leiningen riding along the edge of the ditch. The planter saw before him a motionless and unaltered throng of besiegers. He studied the wide belt of water between them and the plantation, and for a moment almost regretted that the fight had ended so soon and so simply. In the comforting, matter-of-fact light of morning, it seemed to him now that the ants hadn't the ghost of a chance to cross the ditch. Even if they plunged headlong into it on all three fronts at once, the force of the now powerful current would inevitably sweep them away. He had got quite a thrill out of the fight—a pity it was already over.

He rode along the eastern and southern sections of the ditch and found everything in order. He reached the western section, opposite the tamarind wood, and here, contrary to the other battle-fronts, he found the enemy very busy indeed. The trunks and branches of the trees and the creepers of the lianas, on the far bank of the ditch, fairly swarmed with industrious insects. But instead of eating the leaves there and then, they were merely gnawing through the stalks, so that a thick green shower fell steadily to the ground.

No doubt they were victualling columns sent out to obtain provender for the rest of the army. The discovery did not surprise Leiningen. He did not need to be told that ants are intelligent, that certain species even use others as milch-cows, watchdogs and slaves. He was well aware of their power of adaptation, their sense of discipline, their marvellous talent for organisation.

His belief that a foray to supply the army was in progress was strengthened when he saw the leaves that fell to the ground being dragged to the troops waiting outside the wood. Then all at once he realised the aim that rain of green was intended to serve.

Each single leaf, pulled or pushed by dozens of toiling insects, was borne straight to the edge of the ditch. Even as Macbeth watched the approach of Birnam Wood in the hands of his enemies, Leiningen saw the tamarind wood move nearer and nearer in the mandibles of the ants. Unlike the fey Scot, however, he did not lose his nerve; no witches had prophesied his doom, and if they had he would have slept just as soundly. All the same, he was forced to admit to himself that the situation was now far more ominous than that of the day before.

He had thought it impossible for the ants to build rafts for themselves—well, here they were, coming in thousands, more than enough to bridge the ditch. Leaves after leaves rustled down the slope into the water, where the current drew them away from the bank and carried them into midstream. And every single leaf carried several ants. This time the farmer did not trust to the alacrity of his messengers. He galloped away, leaning from his saddle and yelling orders as he rushed past outpost after outpost: " Bring petrol pumps to the south-west front! Issue spades to every man along the line facing the wood! " And arrived at the eastern and southern sections, he dispatched every man except the observation posts to the menaced west.

Then, as he rode past the stretch where the ants had failed to cross the day before, he witnessed a brief but impressive scene. Down the slope of the distant hill there came towards him a singular being, writhing rather than running, an animal-like, blackened statue with a shapeless head and four quivering feet that knuckled under almost ceaselessly. When the creature reached the far bank of the ditch and collapsed opposite Leiningen, he recognised it as a pampas stag, covered over and over with ants.

It had strayed near the zone of the army. As usual, they had attacked its eyes first. Blinded, it had reeled, in the madness of hideous torment, straight into the ranks of its persecutors, and now the beast swayed to and fro in its death agony.

With a shot from his rifle Leiningen put it out of its misery. Then he pulled out his watch. He hadn't a second to lose, but for life itself he could not have denied his curiosity the satisfaction of knowing how long the ants would take—for personal reasons, so to speak. After six minutes the white, polished bones alone remained. That's how he himself would look before you can—— Leiningen spat once, and put spurs to his horse.

The sporting zest with which the excitement of the novel contest had inspired him the day before had now vanished; in its place was a cold and violent purpose. He would send these vermin back to the hell where they belonged, somehow, anyhow. Yes, but how was indeed the question: as things stood at present it looked as if the devils would raze him and his men from the earth instead. He had under-estimated the might of the enemy; he really would have to bestir himself if he hoped to outwit them.

The biggest danger now, he decided, was at the point where the western section of the ditch curved southwards. And, arrived there, he found his worst expectations justified. The very power of the current had huddled the leaves and their crews of ants so close together at the bend that the bridge was almost ready.

True, streams of petrol and clumps of earth still prevented a landing. But the number of floating leaves was increasing ever more swiftly. It could not be long now before a stretch of water a mile in length was decked by a green pontoon over which the ants could rush in millions.

Leiningen galloped to the weir. The damming of the river was controlled by a wheel on its bank. The planter ordered the man at the wheel first to lower the water in the ditch almost to vanishing point, next to wait a moment, then suddenly to let the river in again. This manœuvre of lowering and raising the surface, of decreasing then increasing the flow of water through the ditch, was to be repeated over and over again until further notice.

This tactic was at first successful. The water in the ditch sank, and with it the film of leaves. The green fleet nearly reached the bed and the troops on the far bank swarmed down the slope to it. Then a violent flow of water at the original depth raced through the ditch, overwhelming leaves and ants, and sweeping them along with it.

This intermittent rapid flushing prevented just in time the almost completed fording of the ditch. But it also flung here and there squads of the enemy vanguard simultaneously up the inner bank. These seemed to know their duty only too well, and lost no time accomplishing it. The air rang with the curses of bitten Indians. They had removed their shirts and pants to detect the quicker the upwards hastening insects;

when they saw one, they crushed it; and fortunately the onslaught as yet was only by skirmishers.

Again and again, the water sank and rose, carrying leaves and drowned ants away with it. It lowered once more nearly to its bed; but this time the exhausted defenders waited in vain for the flush of destruction. Leiningen sensed disaster; something must have gone wrong with the machinery of the dam. Then a sweating *peon* tore up to him—

" They're over! "

. . . . .

While the besieged were concentrating upon the defence of the stretch opposite the wood, the seemingly unaffected line beyond the wood had become the theatre of decisive action. Here the defenders' front was sparse and scattered; everyone who could be spared had hurried away to the south.

Just as the man at the weir had lowered the water almost to the bed of the ditch, the ants on a wide front began another attempt at a direct crossing like that of the preceding day. Into the emptied bed poured an irresistible throng. Rushing across the ditch, they attained the inner bank before the slow-witted Indians fully grasped the situation. Their frantic screams dumbfounded the man at the weir. Before he could direct the river anew into the safeguarding bed he saw himself surrounded by raging ants. He ran like the others, ran for his life.

When Leiningen heard this, he knew the plantation was doomed. He wasted no time bemoaning the inevitable. For as long as there was the slightest chance of success, he had stood his ground, and now any further resistance was both useless and dangerous. He fired three revolver shots into the air—the prearranged signal for his men to retreat instantly within the " inner moat." Then he rode towards the ranch-house.

This was two miles from the point of invasion. There was therefore time enough to prepare the second line of defence against the advent of the ants. Of the three great petrol cisterns near the house, one had already been half emptied by the constant withdrawals needed for the pumps during the fight at the water-ditch. The remaining petrol in it was now drawn off through underground pipes into the concrete trench which encircled the ranch-house and its outbuildings.

And there, drifting in twos and threes, Leiningen's men reached him. Most of them were obviously trying to preserve an air of calm and indifference, belied, however, by their restless glances and knitted brows. One could see their belief in a favourable outcome of the struggle was already considerably shaken. The planter called his *peons* around him.

" Well, lads," he began, " we've lost the first round. But

we'll smash the beggars yet, don't you worry. Anyone who thinks otherwise can draw his pay here and now and push off. There are rafts enough and to spare on the river, and plenty of time still to reach 'em."

Not a man stirred.

Leiningen acknowledged this silent vote of confidence with a laugh that was half a grunt. "That's the stuff, lads. Too bad if you'd missed the rest of the show, eh? Well, the fun won't start till morning. Once these blighters turn tail, there'll be plenty of work for everyone and higher wages all round. And now run along and get something to eat; you've earned it all right."

In the excitement of the fight the greater part of the day had passed without the men once pausing to snatch a bite. Now that the ants were for the time being out of sight, and the "wall of petrol" gave a stronger feeling of security, hungry stomachs began to assert their claims.

The bridges over the concrete ditch were removed. Here and there solitary ants had reached the ditch; they gazed at the petrol meditatively, then scurried back again. Apparently they had little interest at the moment for what lay beyond the evil-reeking barrier; the abundant spoils of the plantation were the main attraction. Soon the trees, shrubs and beds for miles around were hulled with ants zealously gobbling the yield of long, weary months of strenuous toil.

As twilight began to fall, a cordon of ants marched around the petrol trench, but as yet made no move towards its brink. Leiningen posted sentries with headlights and electric torches, then withdrew to his office, and began to reckon up his losses. He estimated these as large, but, in comparison with his bank balance, by no means unbearable. He worked out in some detail a scheme of intensive cultivation which would enable him, before very long, to more than compensate himself for the damage now being wrought to his crops. It was with a contented mind that he finally betook himself to bed, where he slept deeply until dawn, undisturbed by any thought that next day little more might be left of him than a glistening skeleton.

. . . . .

He rose with the sun, and went out on the flat roof of his house. And a scene like one from Dante lay around him; for miles in every direction there was nothing but a black, glittering multitude, a multitude of rested, sated, but none the less voracious ants: yes, look as far as one might, one could see nothing but that rustling black throng, except in the north, where the great river drew a boundary they could not hope to pass. But even the high stone breakwater along the bank of the river, which Leiningen had built as a defence against inundations, was, like the paths, the shorn trees and shrubs, the ground itself, black with ants.

So their greed was not glutted in razing that vast plantation? Not by a long chalk; they were all the more eager now on a rich and certain booty—four hundred men, numerous horses, and bursting granaries.

At first it seemed that the petrol trench would serve its purpose. The besiegers sensed the peril of swimming it, and made no move to plunge blindly over its brink. Instead they devised a better manœuvre; they began to collect shreds of bark, twigs and dried leaves and dropped these into the petrol. Everything green, which could have been similarly used, had long since been eaten. After a time, though, a long procession could be seen bringing from the west the tamarind leaves used as rafts the day before.

Since the petrol, unlike the water in the outer ditch, was perfectly still, the refuse stayed where it was thrown. It was several hours before the ants succeeded in covering an appreciable part of the surface. At length, however, they were ready to proceed to a direct attack.

Their storm-troops swarmed down the concrete side, scrambled over the supporting surface of twigs and leaves, and impelled these over the few remaining streaks of open petrol until they reached the other side. Then they began to climb up this to make straight for the helpless garrison.

During the entire offensive, the planter sat peacefully, watching them with interest, but not stirring a muscle. Moreover, he had ordered his men not to disturb in any way whatever the advancing horde. So they squatted listlessly along the bank of the ditch and waited for a sign from the Boss.

The petrol was now covered with ants. A few had climbed the inner concrete wall and were scurrying towards the defenders.

"Everyone back from the ditch!" roared Leiningen. The men rushed away, without the slightest idea of his plan. He stooped forward and cautiously dropped into the ditch a stone which split the floating carpet and its living freight, to reveal a gleaming patch of petrol. A match spurted, sank down to the oily surface—Leiningen sprang back; in a flash a towering rampart of fire encompassed the garrison.

This spectacular and instant repulse threw the Indians into ecstasy. They applauded, yelled and stamped, like children at a pantomime. Had it not been for the awe in which they held the Boss, they would infallibly have carried him shoulder high.

It was some time before the petrol burned down to the bed of the ditch, and the wall of smoke and flame began to lower. The ants had retreated in a wide circle from the devastation, and innumerable charred fragments along the outer bank showed that the flames had spread from the holocaust in the ditch well into the ranks beyond, where they had wrought havoc far and wide.

Yet the perseverance of the ants was by no means broken; indeed, each setback seemed only to whet it. The concrete cooled, the flicker of the dying flames wavered and vanished, petrol from the second tank poured into the trench—and the ants marched forward anew to the attack.

The foregoing scene repeated itself in every detail, except that on this occasion less time was needed to bridge the ditch, for the petrol was now already filmed by a layer of ash. Once again several thousand ants went up in flames.

Once again they withdrew; once again petrol flowed into the ditch. Would the creatures never learn that their self-sacrifice was utterly senseless? It really was senseless, wasn't it? Yes, of course it was senseless—provided the defenders had an *unlimited* supply of petrol.

When Leiningen reached this stage of reasoning, he felt for the first time since the arrival of the ants that his confidence was deserting him. His skin began to creep; he loosened his collar. Once the devils were over the trench there wasn't a chance in hell for him and his men. God, what a prospect, to be eaten alive like that!

For the third time the flames immolated the attacking troops, and burned down to extinction. Yet the ants were coming on again as if nothing had happened. And meanwhile Leiningen had made a discovery that chilled him to the bone—petrol was no longer flowing into the ditch. Something must be blocking the outflow pipe of the third and last cistern—a snake or a dead rat? Whatever it was, the ants could be held off no longer, unless petrol could by some method be led from the cistern into the ditch.

Then Leiningen remembered that in an outhouse near by were two old disused fire-engines. Spry as never before in their lives, the *peons* dragged them out of the shed, connected their pumps to the cistern, uncoiled and laid the hose. They were just in time to aim a stream of petrol at a column of ants that had already crossed and drive them back down the incline into the ditch. Once more an oily girdle surrounded the garrison, once more it was possible to hold the position—for the moment.

It was obvious, however, that this last resource meant only the postponement of defeat and death. A few of the *peons* fell on their knees and began to pray; others, shrieking insanely, fired their revolvers at the black, advancing masses, as if they felt their despair was pitiful enough to sway fate itself to mercy.

At length two of the men's nerves broke: Leiningen saw a naked Indian leap over the north side of the petrol trench, quickly followed by a second. They sprinted with incredible speed towards the river. But their fleetness did not save them; long before they could attain the rafts, the enemy covered their bodies from head to foot.

In the agony of their torment, both sprang blindly into the wide river, where enemies no less sinister awaited them. Wild screams of mortal anguish informed the breathless onlookers that crocodiles and sword-toothed pirayas were no less ravenous than ants, and even nimbler in reaching their prey.

In spite of this bloody warning, more and more men showed they were making up their minds to run the blockade. Anything, even a fight midstream against alligators, seemed better than powerlessly waiting for death to come and slowly consume their living bodies.

Leiningen flogged his brain till it reeled. Was there nothing on earth could sweep this devils' spawn back into the hell from which it came?

Then out of the inferno of his bewilderment rose a terrifying inspiration. Yes, one hope remained, and one alone. It might be possible to dam the great river completely, so that its waters would fill not only the water-ditch but overflow into the entire gigantic "saucer" of land in which lay the plantation.

The far bank of the river was too high for the waters to escape that way. The stone breakwater ran between the river and the plantation; its only gaps occurred where the "horseshoe" ends of the water-ditch passed into the river. So its waters would not only be forced to inundate into the plantation, they would also be held there by the breakwater until they rose to its own high level. In half an hour, perhaps even earlier, the plantation and its hostile army of occupation would be flooded.

The ranch-house and outbuildings stood upon rising ground. Their foundations were higher than the breakwater, so the flood would not reach them. And any remaining ants trying to ascend the slope could be repulsed by petrol.

It was possible—yes, if one could only get to the dam! A distance of nearly two miles lay between the ranch-house and the weir—two miles of ants. Those two *peons* had managed only a fifth of that distance at the cost of their lives. Was there an Indian daring enough after that to run the gauntlet five times as far? Hardly likely; and if there were, his prospect of getting back was almost nil.

No, there was only one thing for it, he'd have to make the attempt himself; he might just as well be running as sitting still, anyway, when the ants finally got him. Besides, there *was* a bit of a chance. Perhaps the ants weren't so almighty, after all; perhaps he had allowed the mass suggestion of that evil black throng to hypnotise him, just as a snake fascinates and overpowers.

The ants were building their bridges. Leiningen got up on a chair. "Hey, lads, listen to me!" he cried. Slowly and listlessly, from all sides of the trench, the men began to shuffle towards him, the apathy of death already stamped on their faces.

"Listen, lads!" he shouted. "You're frightened of those beggars, but you're a damn sight more frightened of me, and I'm proud of you. There's still a chance to save our lives—by flooding the plantation from the river. Now one of you might manage to get as far as the weir—but he'd never come back. Well, I'm not going to let you try it; if I did, I'd be worse than one of those ants. No, I called the tune, and now I'm going to pay the piper.

"The moment I'm over the ditch, set fire to the petrol. That'll allow time for the flood to do the trick. Then all you have to do is to wait here all snug and quiet till I'm back. Yes, I'm coming back, trust me"—he grinned—"when I've finished my slimming-cure."

He pulled on high leather boots, drew heavy gauntlets over his hands, and stuffed the spaces between breeches and boots, gauntlets and arms, shirt and neck, with rags soaked in petrol. With close-fitting mosquito goggles he shielded his eyes, knowing too well the ants' dodge of first robbing their victim of sight. Finally, he plugged his nostrils and ears with cotton-wool, and let the *peons* drench his clothes with petrol.

He was about to set off, when the old Indian medicine-man came up to him; he had a wondrous salve, he said, prepared from a species of chafer whose odour was intolerable to ants. Yes, this odour protected these chafers from the attacks of even the most murderous ants. The Indian smeared the Boss's boots, his gauntlets, and his face over and over with the extract.

Leiningen then remembered the paralysing effect of ants' venom, and the Indian gave him a gourd full of the medicine he had administered to the bitten *peon* at the water-ditch. The planter drank it down without noticing its bitter taste; his mind was already at the weir.

He started off towards the north-west corner of the trench. With a bound he was over—and among the ants.

The beleagured garrison had no opportunity to watch Leiningen's race against death. The ants were climbing the inner bank again—the lurid ring of petrol blazed aloft. For the fourth time that day the reflection from the fire shone on the sweating faces of the imprisoned men, and on the reddish-black cuirasses of their oppressors. The red and blue, dark-edged flames leaped vividly now, celebrating what? The funeral pyre of the four hundred, or of the hosts of destruction?

. . . . .

Leiningen ran. He ran in long, equal strides, with only one thought, one sensation, in his being—he *must* get through. He dodged all trees and shrubs; except for the split-seconds his soles touched the ground the ants should have no opportunity to alight on him. That they would get to him soon, despite the salve on his boots, the petrol in his clothes, he realised only too well, but he knew even more surely that he must, and would, get to the weir.

Apparently the salve was some use after all; not until he had reached half-way did he feel ants under his clothes, and a few on his face. Mechanically, in his stride, he struck at them, scarcely conscious of their bites. He saw he was drawing appreciably nearer the weir—the distance grew less and less—sank to five hundred—three—two—one hundred yards.

Then he was at the weir and gripping the ant-hulled wheel. Hardly had he seized it when a horde of infuriated ants flowed over his hands, arms and shoulders. He started the wheel—before it turned once on its axis the swarm covered his face. Leiningen strained like a madman, his lips pressed tight; if he opened them to draw breath . . .

He turned and turned; slowly the dam lowered until it reached the bed of the river. Already the water was overflowing the ditch. Another minute, and the river was pouring through the nearby gap in the breakwater. The flooding of the plantation had begun.

Leiningen let go the wheel. Now, for the first time, he realised he was coated from head to foot with a layer of ants. In spite of the petrol, his clothes were full of them, several had got to his body or were clinging to his face. Now that he had completed his task, he felt the smart raging over his flesh from the bites of sawing and piercing insects.

Frantic with pain, he almost plunged into the river. To be ripped and slashed to shreds by pirayas? Already he was running the return journey, knocking ants from his gloves and jacket, brushing them from his bloodied face, squashing them to death under his clothes.

One of the creatures bit him just below the rim of his goggles; he managed to tear it away, but the agony of the bite and its etching acid drilled into the eye-nerves; he saw now through circles of fire into a milky mist, then he ran for a time almost blinded, knowing that if he once tripped and fell . . . The old Indian's brew didn't seem much good; it weakened the poison a bit, but didn't get rid of it. His heart pounded as if it would burst; blood roared in his ears; a giant's fist battered his lungs.

Then he could see again, but the burning girdle of petrol appeared infinitely far away; he could not last half that distance. Swift-changing pictures flashed through his head, episodes in his life, while in another part of his brain a cool and impartial onlooker informed this ant-blurred, gasping, exhausted bundle named Leiningen that such a rushing panorama of scenes from one's past is seen only in the moment before death.

A stone in the path . . . too weak to avoid it . . . the planter stumbled and collapsed. He tried to rise . . . he must be pinned under a rock . . . it was impossible . . . the slightest movement was impossible . . .

Then all at once he saw, starkly clear and huge, and, right before his eyes, furred with ants, towering and swaying in its death-agony, the pampas stag. In six minutes—gnawed to the bones. God, he *couldn't* die like that! And something outside him seemed to drag him to his feet. He tottered. He began to stagger forward again.

Through the blazing ring hurtled an apparition which, as soon as it reached the ground on the inner side, fell full length and did not move. Leiningen, at the moment he made that leap through the flames, lost consciousness for the first time in his life. As he lay there, with glazing eyes and lacerated face, he appeared a man returned from the grave. The *peons* rushed to him, stripped off his clothes, tore away the ants from a body that seemed almost one open wound; in some places the bones were showing. They carried him into the ranch-house.

As the curtain of flames lowered, one could see in place of the illimitable host of ants an extensive vista of water. The thwarted river had swept over the plantation, carrying with it the entire army. The water had collected and mounted in the great "saucer," while the ants had in vain attempted to reach the hill on which stood the ranch-house. The girdle of flames held them back.

And so, imprisoned between water and fire, they had been delivered unto the annihilation that was their god. And near the farther mouth of the water-ditch, where the stone mole had its second gap, the ocean swept the lost battalions into the river, to vanish for ever.

The ring of fire dwindled as the water mounted to the petrol trench, and quenched the dimming flames. The inundation rose higher and higher: because its outflow was impeded by the timber and underbrush it had carried along with it, its surface required some time to reach the top of the high stone breakwater and discharge over it the rest of the shattered army.

It swelled over ant-stippled shrubs and bushes, until it washed against the foot of the knoll whereon the besieged had taken refuge. For a while an alluvial of ants tried again and again to attain this dry land, only to be repulsed by streams of petrol back into the merciless flood.

. . . . .

Leiningen lay on his bed, his body swathed from head to foot in bandages. With fomentations and salves, they had managed to stop the bleeding, and had dressed his many wounds. Now they thronged around him, one question in every face. Would he recover? "He won't die," said the old man who had bandaged him, "if he doesn't want to."

The planter opened his eyes. "Everything in order?" he asked.

"They're gone," said his nurse, "to hell." He held out to his master a gourd full of a powerful sleeping-draught. Leiningen gulped it down.

"I told you I'd come back," he murmured, "even if I am a bit streamlined." He grinned and shut his eyes. He slept.

ARTHUR SCHNITZLER

DEAD GABRIEL

SHE danced past him on the arm of a man whom he did not know, nodded her head very slightly, and smiled. Ferdinand bowed more deeply than usual. So she is here, he thought to himself in surprise, and suddenly felt a new sense of freedom. If Irene, only a month after Gabriel's death, could bring herself to wear a ball dress and glide round a brightly lit room with an agreeable stranger, he felt he might cease reproaching himself for appearing at such a place of public gaiety. For the first time this evening, after a month's quiet seclusion, he had been seized by the desire to go out into the world once more. To his parents' pleasant surprise, who had scarcely been able to understand their son's deep depression over the death of a merely casual acquaintance, he had appeared at dinner in his evening clothes, announced his intention of going to the Law Students' Ball, and soon departed with the comfortable sensation of having given the kind old people a small pleasure without much trouble to himself.

In the cab that drove him to the Sophiensäle he still felt a slight sinking at the heart. He thought of the night when he had looked down from Wilhelmine's window and seen a dark form pacing up and down by the park railings: of the morning when, while still lying in bed, he had found the news of Gabriel's suicide in the paper: of the moment when Wilhelmine had shown him the pathetic letter in which Gabriel, without a word of reproach, had taken eternal leave of her. Even while he was going up the broad staircase, and in the ballroom itself, amid the din of the orchestra, he did not feel more cheerful: only Irene's glance had put him into a brighter mood.

He had known Irene now for several years without having taken any special interest in her, and to him, as to all frequenters of the house, her feelings for Gabriel had remained no secret. One evening when Ferdinand, shortly before Christmas, had been at her parents' house, she had sung a few songs in her pleasant husky voice. Gabriel had accompanied her upon the piano, and Ferdinand particularly remembered asking himself why that worthy young man did not marry that charming, simple creature, instead of hanging on to the magnificent Wilhelmine, who would be sure to betray him very soon. That he himself was designed by fate to fulfil this presentiment, Ferdinand, of course, had then not the least suspicion. So far as his share of the guilt of Gabriel's death was concerned, Anastasius Treuenhof, who understood all things earthly and divine, had at once convinced him that his part in the whole situation had not been that of an individual but of a social force, and that the matter was possibly one for mild regret but in no way an occasion for serious remorse. Still, it had been a painful moment for Ferdinand when he stood with Wilhelmine at Gabriel's grave, on which still lay the withered garlands, and his companion suddenly turned to him, as he stood there with the tears streaming down his cheeks, and, in the tone he had heard so often on the stage, "Yes, you miserable creature, you may well weep now." An hour later, of course, she swore that better men than Gabriel had been willing to die for her sake, and in these last few days it often seemed to Ferdinand as though she had simply forgotten the whole tragic business. Treuenhof was also able to explain this singular circumstance by maintaining that women had more of the elemental in them than men, and from the beginning were created to bear with composure what cannot be changed.

For the second time Irene danced past Ferdinand and again she smiled. But her smile seemed different this time; it was more friendly and more inviting, and her gaze remained fixed on Ferdinand as she glided off again and disappeared with her partner into the crowd. When the waltz had come to an end Ferdinand walked round the room, wondering what had decoyed him to such a place where the dignified melancholy of his existence, to which the passionate hours spent in Wilhelmine's arms now lent but the impress of a mournful charm, was bound to be disturbed by all the clamorous banalities of a public ball. And he was suddenly seized by a longing, not merely to leave the place, but very soon—possibly to-morrow—to leave Vienna and start on a journey to the south, to Sicily or Egypt. He even reflected whether he should say good-bye to Wilhelmine—when Irene suddenly stood before him. She inclined her head slightly and returned his greeting; he offered her his arm, led her through the throng in the ballroom, up the half-dozen steps to the broad daïs, dotted with supper tables, that surrounded the dancing-floor. At that moment the music started again, and as the first chords rang out Irene said softly: "He is dead, and we two are here." Ferdinand felt a little alarmed, unconsciously hastened his step, and remarked: "To-day is the first time I have come into such a large company."

"It is the third time for me," Irene replied in a clear voice. "I have been once to a theatre and once to an evening party."

"Was it amusing?" asked Ferdinand.

"I don't know. Someone played the piano, someone else sang some comic songs, and then we danced."

"Yes, it is always the same," remarked Ferdinand.

They were standing by a door. "I am engaged for the quadrille," said Irene, "but I shall not dance. Let us escape to the gallery."

Ferdinand led Irene up the narrow, chilly, spiral staircase. He noticed a few scattered flecks of powder on Irene's shoulders. She wore her dark hair in a heavy knot low down on her neck. Her arm lay lightly upon his. The door to the gallery stood open, and a waiter, who was sitting in the first box, hastily got up.

"I should like a glass of champagne," said Irene.

"Oh!" thought Ferdinand, "perhaps she is going to be more interesting than I imagined. Or is it affectation?"

He ordered the wine and then moved a chair back for her so that she could not be seen from below.

"You were a friend of his?" asked Irene, and looked him straight in the eyes.

"A friend? I can hardly say that. In any case in the last few years our relations were very slight." And he thought to himself: "How strangely she looks at me. I wonder if she guesses that . . ." But he went on: "Five or six years ago I went to a few lectures with him at the University. As a matter of fact, we were both studying law in a casual sort of way. Then, three years ago, in the autumn, we went on a bicycling tour from Innsbruck, where we had met quite by chance, over the Brenner. We parted again in Verona: I returned to Vienna and he went on to Rome."

Irene nodded several times, as if she had just been listening to somebody that she knew quite well.

"In Rome," Ferdinand continued, "he in fact wrote his first play, or rather his first that was produced."

"Yes," said Irene.

"He did not have much luck," remarked Ferdinand.

The champagne stood on the table, and Ferdinand poured it out. They clinked glasses, and while they were drinking, they looked earnestly into each other's eyes as if the first glass was a toast to the memory of the departed. Then Irene put her glass down and said quietly, "He killed himself over the Bischof woman."

"So people say," Ferdinand replied simply, and with a sense of satisfaction that his expression did not betray him.

The opening bar of the quadrille crashed out so furiously that the champagne glasses trembled.

" Do you know the Bischof personally? " asked Irene.

" Yes," replied Ferdinand. Then she does not suspect, he thought. Of course not. If she did, she would not be drinking champagne with me up here. Or perhaps she might all the more . . . ?

" I saw the Bischof the other day as Medea," said Irene. " I only went to the theatre on her account. Since the first performance of Gabriel's play last winter I had never seen her on the stage. Did the affair begin then? "

Ferdinand shrugged his shoulders; he had no idea. " She is a great artist," he observed.

" That is quite possible," Irene replied; " but I don't think that gives her the right to . . ."

" What right? " asked Ferdinand, as he filled the glasses once more.

" The right to drive a man to his death," said Irene, finishing her sentence and staring into vacancy.

" Yes," said Ferdinand thoughtfully, " where the right begins on the one side and the responsibility on the other it is difficult to decide. And if one does not know the more intimate circumstances of the case, how can one . . . In any case, Fraulein Bischof is one of those beings who—how shall I say? —seem to belong to a more primitive world than ours, and are not to be judged by our measure."

Irene had laid her small old-fashioned ivory fan upon the table; she picked it up and drew it across her cheeks and forehead, as if to cool herself. Then she drank a glass of wine at a gulp, and said: " That she wasn't faithful to him—well, that I can understand. But why wasn't she straightforward with him? Why didn't she say to him: ' It is all over: I love another, let us part.' It would have hurt him very much, but it would not have driven him to his death."

" Who knows? " said Ferdinand slowly.

" Of course it would not," repeated Irene sharply. " It was disgust that drove him to that—simply disgust. He must have thought to himself: the very same words she used to me, the very same endearments . . ." A shiver went through her body, her gaze wandered across the balustrade down into the hall, and she was silent.

Ferdinand looked at her and could not understand how any man on earth could kill himself for Wilhelmine's sake when this girl was in love with him. At this moment he doubted more deeply than ever whether Gabriel had ever had any talent. It was true that he only had the vaguest recollection of the piece in which Wilhelmine had played the leading part the year before, and after the failure of which, as a sort of compensation, she had become Gabriel's mistress. Then, with averted eyes, Irene said softly: " Did you see nothing of him, then, these last few years? "

" Very little," answered Ferdinand. " It was not until last autumn that we met again a few times. I ran into him once in the Ring. He was with the Bischof, and we all had supper together in the Volksgarten. It was a very pleasant evening. One could still sit in the open air although it was already the end of October. Then we met a few times after that evening, once or twice actually in Fräulein Bischof's flat. Yes, it might have seemed to some extent as though we had found each other again after a long interval. But nothing came of it." Ferdinand glanced at Irene and smiled.

" Now I will tell you something," said Irene. " I had intended to call on Fraulein Bischof."

" What! " cried Ferdinand, and looked at Irene's forehead, which was very white, and higher than girls' foreheads usually are.

The quadrille was at an end, and the music stopped. A confused hum of voices surged up from below. A few indifferent words rang out more clearly as though they had been strong enough to force their way through the din.

" I had really quite made up my mind," said Irene, as she snapped her ivory fan to and fro, " but—it was very childish of me, I know—my courage always failed me at the last moment."

" Why did you want to call on her? " asked Ferdinand.

" Why? Surely that is very simple. I wanted to see her face to face, to hear her voice, I wanted to know how she speaks and moves in daily life, and ask her questions about all manner of ordinary things. Can't you understand that? " she added with sudden vehemence, laughed shortly, drank a mouthful of wine, and went on. " It is interesting to know what these women are really like, these secret creatures, that are to be judged by a different measure, in your opinion; these women for whom good men kill themselves, and who then appear on the stage three days later, tall and magnificent, as if nothing in the world were changed."

Two men sauntered past, stopped, turned, and stared at Irene.

Ferdinand was annoyed, and decided, if this insolence lasted a second longer, to get up and call the two men to account. And he saw himself already exchanging cards, receiving seconds, driving through the *Prater* in the grey dawn, wounded in the chest, sinking down on to the damp earth, and last of all Wilhelmine standing with some actor at his graveside. But before the second's grace had elapsed they had ceased to stare and walked on. And Ferdinand again heard Irene's voice.

"I should have the courage now," she said, with a strange half-despairing smile.

"Courage for what?" asked Ferdinand.

"Courage to go and see Fräulein Bischof."

"Go and see Fräulein Bischof . . . now?"

"Yes, now at once. What do you think?" and she swayed her shoulders in time with the music. "Or shall we dance a waltz?"

"After all, it isn't far off," said Ferdinand.

"Isn't it marvellous?" said Irene, with a merry look: "What has changed since we have been sitting in this box and drinking champagne? Nothing. Not the least thing. And suddenly one realises that death is not so dreadful as one had usually imagined. Look: I feel quite prepared to throw myself down from here—or from the top of a tower. I should not mind in the least—really! And how well we have got to know each other! But you must thank Gabriel for that."

"I never imagined . . ." began Ferdinand, with a polite smile, and he noticed that his heart was throbbing slightly.

The merry look had gone from Irene's eyes: they were large, dark, and serious. "And do you know what was in my mind?" she said, without listening to him. "I wanted to introduce myself as a budding actress or simply as an enthusiastic admirer. 'For a long time I've been longing to . . . I've been so terribly anxious . . .' that's how I should have begun. These women are all very vain, aren't they?"

"That is part of their profession," replied Ferdinand.

"Ah, I should have flattered her so that she would have been simply enchanted, and would certainly have asked me to come again. . . . And I would have come many times, we should have become very intimate—friends, in fact; until one day—yes—I should have screamed into her face some time or other: 'Do you know what you did? Do you know what you are? A murderess. That's what you are, Fräulein Bischof.'"

Ferdinand looked at her with astonishment, and again wondered what sort of a fool this Gabriel must have been.

The quadrille was over, a buzz and a clatter rose up from the room, and it all seemed to come from further away than before. Two couples walked by, sat down not far away at a table by the wall, talking and laughing loudly. Then the orchestra crashed out into another dance.

" Supposing I went to see her now? " asked Irene.

" Now? "

" Do you think she would receive me? "

" It would be an odd time to go," said Ferdinand, with a smile.

" Oh, well, it can't be nearly midnight yet, and she was acting to-day."

" How do you know? "

" There's nothing surprising about that, it was in the paper, wasn't it? She will just have come home. It would be the simplest thing in the world. We will send in our names, and tell any story you like, or just simply the truth. Yes; I was coming straight back from a ball—my longing to get to know her got the better of me—I wanted just to kiss her hand once and so on. The carriage will wait for us below, and we shall be back before the interval. No one will have noticed."

" If you really mean to go, Fräulein," said Ferdinand, " then you must let me go with you."

Irene looked at him. There was a tense decided look on her face. " Then you don't think that I really. . ."

" But have you the courage to jump off a tower, Fräulein? "

Irene stared into his eyes and suddenly got up.

" Come along, then," she said, and a dark shadow passed over her forehead.

Ferdinand called the waiter, paid, gave Irene his arm, and led her down the two flights of stairs into the ante-room. Then he helped her into a light grey cloak: she turned up the fur collar and tied a lace scarf round her head. Without a word to each other, they went out through the door into the gateway. A carriage came up and they sped noiselessly to their destination over the snow-covered streets.

From time to time Ferdinand threw a sidelong glance at Irene. She sat motionless, and from her veiled face her eyes stared out into the darkness. When, after a few minutes, the carriage stopped in front of the house in the Park-ring Irene waited until Ferdinand had rung the bell and the door had opened. Ferdinand felt as though he had awakened from a dream, as the familiar parlour-maid stood before him and looked with astonishment at him and his companion.

" Please ask the Fräulein," said Ferdinand, " whether she will be so good as to receive us."

The girl smiled, said nothing, and showed the pair into the drawing-room. Under the light from the candelabra, Ferdinand saw the semblances of himself and Irene hovering like two strange beings in the Venetian mirror that hung out from the wall over the black, gleaming grand piano. A sudden thought came into his head. How if Irene had got him to introduce her so that she might murder Wilhelmine? The idea vanished as soon as it had come: and yet the girl who stood at his side, and slowly unwound the scarf from her head, seemed to him entirely changed—almost like some strange creature whose voice he had never heard before

A door opened, and Wilhelmine entered wearing a soft velvet indoor dress cut away from the neck. She gave a hand to Ferdinand, and looked at him and his companion with an air of welcome rather than of surprise. Ferdinand tried to give some facetious explanation of this nocturnal visit. He told Wilhelmine that during the dance his companion had talked of nothing but her admiration for Fräulein Bischof, and how, he, in a sort of carnival mood, had offered at this unearthly hour to go with her to her idol's house—at the risk of both being bundled downstairs again.

"What nonsense," replied Wilhelmine; "on the contrary I am delighted," and she gave a hand to Irene. "I must only ask you to be kind enough to keep me company at supper—I have just come back from the theatre."

They all went into the next room where under a greenish crystal shade with little frosted lights a table stood, half of which was laid for supper. While Ferdinand took off his fur coat and threw it on to the divan, Wilhelmine herself took Irene's cloak from her shoulders and hung it over the back of a chair. Then she took some glasses from a sideboard, filled them with white wine, and set them before Ferdinand and Irene, after which she herself sat down, calmly helped herself to some cold meat, cut it up, said "Excuse me," and began to eat. From time to time she threw a friendly, faintly smiling glance at Irene and Ferdinand.

"She naturally takes it as a matter of course," thought Ferdinand, a little disappointed; "and if I had brought the Empress of China and announced my appointment as Mandarin, she would not have thought it strange. It is really rather a pity."—'For women who are never surprised never entirely belong to any man.' It was a remark of Treuenhof's which suddenly came into his mind.

"Did you have a good time at the ball?" asked Wilhelmine. Ferdinand answered that the room was too full, the people mostly detestable, and the music poor; and so he went on. Wilhelmine glanced at him good-humouredly, and turning to Irene asked whether her companion were a good dancer. Irene nodded and smiled. Her "Yes" was almost inaudible.

"Did you play Feodora to-day, Fräulein?" asked Ferdinand

so as not to let the conversation drop. " Was there a large audience? "

" Packed," Wilhelmine replied.

Irene then said: " I am sorry to say I have never seen you as Feodora, Fräulein Bischof. But I saw you as Medea not so long ago. It was splendid."

" Thank you very much," answered Wilhelmine.

After a few more words of admiration, Irene asked Wilhelmine which were her favourite parts, and seemed to listen to her answers with interest. Then they came upon the eternal question—whether the greater actor is the one who loses himself in the part he is presenting or the one who stands above it. Ferdinand mentioned that a young comedian he knew had told him that he had played a certain highly amusing part more effectively than ever on the very day of his father's funeral.

" Nice sort of friends you must have," Wilhelmine observed, putting a section of orange into her mouth.

" What on earth is all this? " thought Ferdinand. " Has Fräulein Irene forgotten that she wanted to call Wilhelmine a murderess to her face? . . . And is Wilhelmine still aware that I am her lover, though I have called upon her in the middle of the night with a strange woman? . . ."

" You are so keenly interested in the theatre, Fraulein," remarked Wilhelmine, " I wonder if you have ever thought of taking up acting as a career."

Irene shook her head. " Alas, I have no talent! "

" Well, you may be thankful," said Wilhelmine, " stage life is a sink."

And as she began to talk of all the humiliations that an actress has to endure, Ferdinand noticed that Irene was staring, as though bewitched, at a half-open door, through the crack of which a bluish glow was visible. And he noticed how Irene's face, which had hitherto been motionless, began to stir slightly under its pallor, and how the silent lips began to quiver strangely. And he thought he could see in her wide-open eyes an evil longing to force her way into that bluish room and bury her face in the pillow on which Gabriel's head had once rested. It then occurred to him that although Irene's absence might until now have been unnoticed, if she stayed away any longer it might be awkward for her and for himself: and he pushed back his chair.

Irene turned towards him as though awakening from a dream. Wilhelmine's last words still echoed in their ears, though they had not heard them.

" It is quite time for us to go," said Irene, and got up.

"I am very sorry that you can't stay longer," answered Wilhelmine.

Irene gazed at her with a calm and searching look.

"Well, my child?" asked Wilhelmine.

"It is strange, Fräulein," said Irene, "how you remind me of a picture we have at home of a Croat or Slovak peasant woman praying before a holy image at the side of a snowy country road."

Wilhelmine nodded thoughtfully, as if she clearly remembered the winter day on which she had knelt in the snow in Croatia before that holy image. Then she insisted on putting Irene's cloak round her shoulders and accompanied her guests into the hall. "Well, go back and have some more jolly dances," she said; "that is, if you really are going back to the ball."

Irene became deathly pale—but smiled.

"You need to be careful of him," added Wilhelmine, and threw a glance at Ferdinand—the first that held anything like a recollection of the past night.

Ferdinand did not answer: he only felt how Irene covered Wilhelmine and himself with one and the same dark look.

The maid appeared, Wilhelmine once more held out her hands to her guests, said she hoped the girl would come and see her again soon, and smiled at Ferdinand as though she had won a game against him—a game that they had both agreed to play.

Accompanied by the maid carrying a taper, Ferdinand and Irene went down the stairs in silence. The outer door was soon shut behind them. The driver stood by the carriage, Irene got in, and Ferdinand sat down beside her. The horses trotted through the noiseless snow. Suddenly a ray of light from a street lamp fell on Irene's face. Ferdinand saw that she was staring at him with parted lips.

"So it was you," she said softly, and her voice seemed to quiver with amazement, horror, and hate. And again they were in darkness.

"If she had a dagger with her," thought Ferdinand, "I wonder would she stab me with it? . . . And yet, however you look at the thing, I really shouldn't deserve it. Surely I was a social force, not a . . ." And he fell to meditating whether he should not try and explain the affair to her. Not in the least to justify himself, but because this intelligent creature well deserved to be initiated into the deeper significances of the whole story.

Suddenly he felt arms about him, and Irene's lips on his—savage, hot, and sweet. It was a kiss such as he believed he had never felt before, so fragrant and mysterious, and he wished it might not end. Mouth clung to mouth till the carriage stopped.

Ferdinand got out and gave his hand to Irene.

" You are not to follow me," she said harshly, and disappeared into the hall. Ferdinand stayed outside. It did not for a moment occur to him to disobey her command. He realised quite clearly, and with sudden sorrow, that it was over, and that this kiss could have no sequel.

Three days later he related his adventure to Anastasius Treuenhof, to whom one could tell everything, for discretion in his company would have been as childish as in the presence of the good God.

" It is a pity," said Anastasius, after brief reflection, " that she did not become your mistress. Your child would have interested me. We have enough children of Love, far too many children of Indifference, but of children of Hatred far too few. And yet it is not impossible that from them may come our salvation."

" So you think . . ." began Ferdinand.

" Come now, don't you flatter yourself," answered Anastasius sharply.

Ferdinand hung his head and was silent.

Besides, he had his sleeping-car ticket to Trieste in his pocket, and from there he went on to Alexandria, Cairo, Assouan. . . . Three days ago he too had realised that people may die of hopeless love—other people, of course—other people.

STEFAN ZWEIG

THE INVISIBLE COLLECTION

AT the first junction beyond Dresden, an elderly gentleman entered our compartment, smiled genially to the company, and gave me a special nod, as if to an old acquaintance. Seeing that I was at a loss, he mentioned his name. Of course I knew him! He was one of the most famous connoisseurs and art-dealers in Berlin. Before the war, I had often purchased autographs and rare books at his place. He took the vacant seat opposite me, and for a while we talked of matters not worth relating. Then, changing the conversation, he explained the object of the journey from which he was returning. It had, he said, been one of the strangest of his experiences in the thirty-seven years he had devoted to the occupation of art-pedlar. Enough introduction. I will let him tell the story in his own words, without using quote-marks—to avoid the complication of wheels within wheels.

. . . . .

You know [he said] what has been going on in my trade since the value of money began to diffuse into the void like gas. War-profiteers have developed a taste for old masters (Madonnas and so on), for incunabula, for ancient tapestries. It is difficult to satisfy their craving; and a man like myself, who prefers to keep the best for his own use and enjoyment, is hard put to it not to have his house stripped bare. If I let them, they would buy the cuff-links from my shirt and the lamp from my writing-table. Harder and harder to find wares to sell. I'm afraid the term " wares " may grate upon you in this connection, but you must excuse me. I have picked it up from customers of the new sort. Evil communications . . . Through use and wont I have come to look upon an invaluable book from one of the early Venetian presses much as the philistine looks upon an overcoat that cost so or so many hundred dollars, and upon a sketch by Guercino as animated by nothing more worthy of reverence than the transmigrated soul of a banknote for a few thousand francs.

Impossible to resist the greed of these fellows with money to burn. As I looked round my place the other night, it seemed to me that there was so little left of any real value that I might as well put up the shutters. Here was a fine business which had come down to me from my father and my grandfather; but the shop was stocked with rubbish which, before 1914, a street-trader would have been ashamed to hawk upon a hand-cart.

In this dilemma, it occurred to me to flutter the pages of our old ledgers. Perhaps I should be put on the track of former customers who might be willing to resell what they had bought in prosperous days. True, such a list of sometime purchasers has considerable resemblance to a battlefield laden with the corpses of the slain; and in fact I soon realised that most of those who had purchased from the firm when the sun was shining were dead or would be in such low water that it was probable they must have sold anything of value among their possessions. However, I came across a bundle of letters from a man who was presumably the oldest yet alive —if he was alive. But he was so old that I had forgotten him, since he had bought nothing after the great explosion in the summer of 1914. Yes, very, very old. The earliest letters were dated more than half a century back, when my grandfather was head of the business. Yet I could not recall having had any personal relationships with him during the thirty-seven years in which I had been an active worker in the establishment.

All indications showed that he must have been one of those antediluvian eccentrics, a few of whom survive in German provincial towns. His writing was copperplate, and every item in his orders was underlined in red ink. Each price was given in words as well as figures, so that there could be no mistake. These peculiarities, and his use of torn-out fly-leaves as writing paper, enclosed in a scratch assortment of envelopes, hinted at the penuriousness of a confirmed backwoodsman. His signature was always followed by his style and title in full: "Forest Ranger and Economic Councillor, Retired; Lieutenant, Retired; Holder of the Iron Cross First Class." Since he was obviously a veteran of the war of 1870–1871, he must by now be close on eighty.

For all his cheese-paring and for all his eccentricities, he had manifested exceptional shrewdness, knowledge, and taste as collector of prints and engravings. A careful study of his orders, which had at first totalled very small sums indeed, disclosed that in the days when a taler could still pay for a pile of lovely German woodcuts, this country bumpkin had got together a collection of etchings and the like outrivalling the widely trumpeted acquisitions of war profiteers. Merely those which, in the course of decades, he had bought from us for trifling sums would be worth a large amount of money to-day;

and I had no reason to suppose that he had failed to pick up similar bargains elsewhere. Was his collection dispersed? I was too familiar with what had been going on in the art trade since the date of his last purchase not to feel confident that such a collection could scarcely have changed hands entire without my getting wind of the event. If he was dead, his treasures had probably remained intact in the hands of his heirs.

The affair seemed so interesting that I set forth next day (yesterday evening) on a journey to one of the most out-of-the-way towns in Saxony. When I left the tiny railway station and strolled along the main street, it seemed to me impossible that anyone inhabiting one of these gimcrack houses, furnished in a way with which you are doubtless familiar, could possibly own a full set of magnificent Rembrandt etchings together with an unprecedented number of Dürer woodcuts and a complete collection of Mantegnas. However, I went to the post office to inquire, and was astonished to learn that a sometime Forest Ranger and Economic Councillor of the name I mentioned was still living. They told me how to find his house, and I will admit that my heart beat faster than usual as I made my way thither. It was well before noon.

The connoisseur of whom I was in search lived on the second floor of one of those jerry-built houses which were run up in such numbers by speculators during the sixties of the last century. The first floor was occupied by a master tailor. On the second landing to the left was the name-plate of the manager of the local post office, while the porcelain shield on the right-hand door bore the name of my quarry. I had run him to earth! My ring was promptly answered by a very old, white-haired woman wearing a black lace cap. I handed her my card and asked whether the master was at home. With an air of suspicion she glanced at me, at the card, and then back at my face once more. In this God-forsaken little town a visit from an inhabitant of the metropolis was a disturbing event. However, in as friendly a tone as she could muster, she asked me to be good enough to wait a minute or two in the hall, and vanished through a doorway. I heard whispering, and then a loud, hearty, masculine voice: "Herr Rackner from Berlin, you say, the famous dealer in antiquities? Of course I shall be delighted to see him." Thereupon the old woman reappeared and invited me to enter.

I took off my overcoat, and followed her. In the middle of the cheaply furnished room was a man standing up to receive me. Old but hale, he had a bushy moustache and was wearing a semi-military frogged smoking-jacket. In the most cordial way, he held out both hands towards me. But though this gesture was spontaneous and nowise forced, it was in strange contrast with the stiffness of his attitude. He did not advance to meet me, so that I was compelled (I must confess I was a trifle piqued) to walk right up to him before I could shake. Then I noticed that his hand, too, did not seek mine, but was waiting for mine to clasp it. At length I guessed what was amiss. He was blind.

Ever since I was a child I have been uncomfortable in the presence of the blind. It embarrasses me, produces in me a sense of bewilderment and shame to encounter anyone who is thoroughly alive, and yet has not the full use of his senses. I feel as if I were taking an unfair advantage, and I was keenly conscious of this sensation as I glanced into the fixed and sightless orbs beneath the bristling white eyebrows. The blind man, however, did not leave me time to dwell upon this discomfort. He exclaimed, laughing with boisterous delight:

" A red-letter day, indeed! Seems almost a miracle that one of the big men of Berlin should drop in as you have done. There's need for us provincials to be careful, you know, when a noted dealer such as yourself is on the war-path. We've a saying in this part of the world: ' Shut your doors and button up your pockets if there are gipsies about! ' I can guess why you've taken the trouble to call. Business doesn't thrive, I've gathered. No buyers or very few, so people are looking up their old customers. I'm afraid you'll draw a blank. We pensioners are glad enough to find there's still some dry bread for dinner. I've been a collector in my time, but now I'm out of the game. My buying days are over."

I hastened to tell him he was under a misapprehension, that I had not called with any thought of effecting sales. Happening to be in the neighbourhood I felt loath to miss the chance of paying my respects to a long-standing customer who was at the same time one of the most famous among German collectors. Hardly had the phrase passed my lips when a remarkable change took place in the old man's expression. He stood stiffly in the middle of the room, but his face lighted up and his whole aspect was suffused with pride. He turned in in the direction where he fancied his wife to be, and nodded as if to say, " D'you hear that? " Then, turning back to me, he resumed—having dropped the brusque, drill-sergeant tone he had previously used, and speaking in a gentle, nay, almost tender voice:

" How charming of you. . . . I should be sorry, however, if your visit were to result in nothing more than your making the personal acquaintanceship of an old buffer like myself. At any rate I've something worth while for you to see—more worth while than you could find in Berlin, in the Albertina at Vienna, or even in the Louvre (God's curse on Paris !). A man who has been a diligent collector for fifty years, with taste to guide him, gets hold of treasures that are not to be picked up at every street-corner. Lisbeth, give me the key of the cupboard, please."

Now a strange thing happened. His wife, who had been listening with a pleasant smile, was startled. She raised her hands towards me, clasped them imploringly, and shook her head. What these gestures signified was a puzzle to me. Next she went up to her husband and touched his shoulder, saying:

" Franz, dear, you have forgotten to ask our visitor whether he may not have another appointment; and, anyhow, it is almost dinner-time.—I am sorry," she went on, looking to me, " that we have not enough in the house for an unexpected guest. No doubt you will dine at the inn. If you will take a cup of coffee with us afterwards, my daughter Anna Maria will be here, and she is much better acquainted than I am with the contents of the portfolios."

Once more she glanced piteously at me. It was plain that she wanted me to refuse the proposal to examine the collection there and then. Taking my cue, I said that in fact I had a dinner engagement at the Golden Stag, but should be only too delighted to return at three, when there would be plenty of time to examine anything Herr Kronfeld wanted to show me. I was not leaving before six o'clock.

The veteran was as pettish as a child deprived of a favourite toy.

" Of course," he growled, " I know you mandarins from Berlin have extensive claims on your time. Still, I really think you will do well to spare me a few hours. It is not merely two or three prints I want to show you, but the contents of twenty-seven portfolios, one of each master, and all of them full to bursting. However, if you come at three sharp, I dare say we can get through by six."

The wife saw me out. In the entrance hall, before she opened the front door, she whispered:

" Do you mind if Anna Maria comes to see you at the hotel before you return? It will be better for various reasons which I cannot explain just now."

" Of course, of course, a great pleasure. Really, I am dining alone, and your daughter can come along directly you have finished your meal."

An hour later, when I had removed from the dining-room to the parlour of the Golden Stag, Anna Maria Kronfeld arrived. An old maid, wizened and diffident, plainly dressed, she contemplated me with embarrassment. I did my best to put her at her ease, and expressed my readiness to go back with her at once, if her father was impatient, though it was short of the appointed hour. At this she reddened, grew even more confused, and then stammered a request for a little talk before we set out.

"Please sit down," I answered. "I am entirely at your service."

She found it difficult to begin. Her hands and her lips trembled. At length:

"My mother sent me. We have to ask a favour of you. Directly you get back, Father will want to show you his collection; and the collection . . . the collection. Well, there's very little of it left."

She panted, almost sobbed, and went on breathlessly:

"I must be frank. . . . You know what troublous times we are passing through, and I am sure you will understand. Soon after the war broke out, my father became completely blind. His sight had already been failing. Agitation, perhaps, contributed. Though he was over seventy, he wanted to go to the front, remembering the fight in which he had taken part so long ago. Naturally there was no use for his services. Then, when the advance of our armies was checked, he took the matter very much to heart, and the doctor thought that may have precipitated the oncoming of blindness. In other respects, as you will have noticed, he is vigorous. Down to 1914 he could take long walks, and go out shooting. Since the failure of his eyes, his only pleasure is in his collection. He looks at it every day. 'Looks at it,' I say, though he sees nothing. Each afternoon he has the portfolios on the table, and fingers the prints one by one, in the order which many years have rendered so familiar. Nothing else interests him. He makes me read reports of auctions; and the higher the prices, the more enthusiastic does he become.

"There's the dreadful feature of the situation. Father knows nothing about the inflation; that we are ruined; that his monthly pension would not provide us with a day's food. Then we have others to support. My sister's husband was killed at Verdun, and there are four children. These money troubles have been kept from him. We cut down expenses as much as we can, but it is impossible to make ends meet. We began to sell things, trinkets and so on, without interfering with his beloved collection. There was very little to sell, since Father had always spent whatever he could scrape together upon woodcuts, copperplate engravings, and the like. The collector's mania! Well, at length it was a question whether we were to touch the collection or to let him starve. We didn't ask permission. What would have been the use? He hasn't the ghost of a notion how hard food is to come by, at any price; has never heard that Germany was defeated and surrendered Alsace-Lorraine. We don't read him items of that sort from the newspapers!

"The first piece we sold was a very valuable one, a Rembrandt etching, and the dealer paid us a long price, a good many thousand marks. We thought it would last us for years. But you know how money was melting away in 1922 and 1923. After we had provided for our immediate needs, we put the rest in a bank. In two months it was gone! We had to sell another engraving, and then another. That was during the worst days of inflation, and each time the dealer delayed settlement until the price was not worth a tenth or a hundredth of what he had promised to pay. We tried auction-rooms, and were cheated there too, though the bids were raised by millions. The million- or milliard-mark notes were waste-paper by the time we got them. The collection was scattered to provide daily bread, and little of that.

"That was why Mother was so much alarmed when you turned up to-day. Directly the portfolios are opened, our pious fraud will be disclosed. He knows each item by touch. You see, every print we disposed of was immediately replaced by a sheet of blank cartridge-paper of the same size and thickness, so that he would notice no difference when he handled it. Feeling them one by one, and counting them, he derives almost as much pleasure as if he could actually see them. He never tries to show them to anyone here, where there is no connoisseur, no one worthy to look at them; but he loves each of them so ardently that I think his heart would break if he knew they had been dispersed. The last time he asked someone to look at them, it was the curator of the copperplate engravings in Dresden, who died years ago.

"I beseech you"—her voice broke—"not to shatter his illusion, not to undermine his faith, that the treasures he will describe to you are there for the seeing. He would not survive the knowledge of their loss. Perhaps we have wronged him; yet what could we do? One must live. Orphaned children are more valuable than old prints. Besides, it has been life and happiness to him to spend three hours every afternoon going through his imaginary collection, and talking to each specimen as if it were a friend. To-day may be the most enthralling experience since his sight failed. How he has longed for the chance of exhibiting his treasures to an expert! If you will lend yourself to the deception . . ."

In my cold recital, I cannot convey to you how poignant was this appeal. I have seen many a sordid transaction in my business career; have had to look on supinely while persons ruined by inflation have been diddled out of cherished heirlooms which they were compelled to sacrifice for a crust. But my heart has not been utterly calloused, and this tale touched me to the quick. I need hardly tell you that I promised to play up.

We went to her house together. On the way I was grieved (though not surprised) to learn for what preposterously small amounts these ignorant though kind-hearted women had parted with prints many of which were extremely valuable and some of them unique. This confirmed my resolve to give all the help in my power. As we mounted the stairs we heard a jovial shout: "Come in! Come in!" With the keen hearing of the blind, he had recognised the footsteps for which he had been eagerly waiting.

"Franz usually takes a siesta after dinner, but excitement kept him awake to-day," said the old woman with a smile as she let us in. A glance at her daughter showed her that all was well. The stack of portfolios was on the table. The blind collector seized me by the arm and thrust me into a chair which was placed ready for me.

"Let's begin at once. There's a lot to see, and time presses. The first portfolio contains Durers. Nearly a full set, and you'll think each cut finer than the others. Magnificent specimens. Judge for yourself."

He opened the portfolio as he spoke, saying:

"We start with the Apocalypse series, of course."

Then, tenderly, delicately (as one handles fragile and precious objects), he picked up the first of the blank sheets of cartridge-paper and held it admiringly before my sighted eyes and his blind ones. So enthusiastic was his gaze that it was difficult to believe he could not see. Though I knew it to be fancy, I found it difficult to doubt that there was a glow of recognition in the wrinkled visage.

"Have you ever come across a finer print? How sharp the impression. Every detail crystal-clear. I compared mine with the one at Dresden; a good one, no doubt, but 'fuzzy' in contrast with the specimen you are looking at. Then I have the whole pedigree."

He turned the sheet over and pointed at the back so convincingly that involuntarily I leaned forward to read the non-existing inscriptions.

"The stamp of the Nagler collection, followed by those of Remy and Esdaille. My famous predecessors never thought that their treasure would come to roost in this little room."

I shuddered as the unsuspecting enthusiast extolled the blank sheet of paper; my flesh crept when he placed a finger-nail on the exact spot where the alleged imprints had been made by long-dead collectors. It was as ghostly as if the disembodied spirits of the men he named had risen from the tomb. My tongue clave to the roof of my mouth—until once more I caught the sight of the distraught countenances of Kronfeld's wife and daughter. Then I pulled myself together and resumed my rôle. With forced heartiness, I exclaimed:

" Certainly you are right. This specimen is peerless."

He swelled with triumph.

" But that's nothing," he went on. " Look at these two, the *Melancholia*, and the illuminated print of the *Passion*. The latter, beyond question, has no equal. The freshness of the tints! Your colleagues in Berlin and the custodians of the public galleries would turn green with envy at the sight."

I will not bore you with details. Thus it went on, a pæan, for more than two hours, as he ransacked portfolio after portfolio. An eerie business to watch the handling of these two or three hundred blanks, to chime in at appropriate moments with praise of merits which for the blind collector were so eminently real that again and again (this was my salvation) his faith kindled my own.

Once only did disaster loom. He was " showing " me a first proof of Rembrandt's *Antiope*, which must have been of inestimable value and which had doubtless been sold for a song. Again he dilated on the sharpness of the print, but as he passed his fingers lightly over it the sensitive tips missed some familiar indentation. His face clouded, his mouth trembled, and he said:

" Surely, surely it's the *Antiope*? No one touches the woodcuts and etchings but myself. How can it have got misplaced?"

" Of course it's the *Antiope*, Herr Kronfeld," I said, hastening to take the " print " from his hand and to expatiate upon various details which my own remembrance enabled me to conjure up upon the blank surface.

His bewilderment faded. The more I praised, the more gratified he became, until at last he said exultantly to the two women:

" Here's a man who knows what's what! You have been inclined to grumble at my ' squandering ' money upon the collection. It's true that for half a century and more I denied myself beer, wine, tobacco, travelling, visits to the theatre, books, devoting all I could spare to these purchases you have despised. Well, Herr Rackner confirms my judgment. When I am dead and gone, you'll be richer than anyone in the town, as wealthy as the wealthiest folk in Dresden, and you'll have good reason for congratulating yourself on my 'craze.' But so long as I'm alive, the collection must be kept together. After I've been boxed and buried, this expert or another will help you to sell. You'll have to, since my pension dies with me."

As he spoke, his fingers caressed the despoiled portfolios. It was horrible and touching. Not for years, not since 1914, had I witnessed an expression of such unmitigated happiness on the face of a German. His wife and daughter watched him with tear-dimmed eyes, yet ecstatically, like those women of old who—affrighted and rapturous—found the stone rolled away and the sepulchre empty in the garden outside the wall of Jerusalem. But the man could not have enough of my appreciation. He went on from portfolio to portfolio, from "print" to "print," drinking in my words, until, outwearied, I was glad when the lying blanks were replaced in their cases and room was made to serve coffee on the table.

My host, far from being tired, looked rejuvenated. He had story after story to tell concerning the way he had chanced upon his multifarious treasures, wanting, in this connection, to take out each relevant piece once more. He grew peevish when I insisted, when his wife and daughter insisted, that I should miss my train if he delayed me any longer. . . .

In the end he was reconciled to my going, and we said good-bye. His voice mellowed; he took both my hands in his and fondled them with the tactile appreciation of the blind.

"Your visit has given me immense pleasure," he said with a quaver in his voice. "What a joy to have been able at long last to show my collection to one competent to appreciate it. I can do something to prove my gratitude, to make your visit to a blind old man worth while. A codicil to my will shall stipulate that your firm, whose probity everyone knows, will be entrusted with the auctioning of my collection."

He laid a hand lovingly upon the pile of worthless portfolios. "Promise me they shall have a handsome catalogue. I could ask no better monument."

I glanced at the two women, who were exercising the utmost control, fearful less the sound of their trembling should reach his keen ears. I promised the impossible, and he pressed my hand in response.

Wife and daughter accompanied me to the door. They did not venture to speak, but tears were flowing down their cheeks. I myself was in little better case. An art-dealer, I had come in search of bargains. Instead, as events turned out, I had been a sort of angel of good-luck, lying like a trooper in order to assist in a fraud which kept an old man happy.

Ashamed of lying, I was glad that I had lied. At any rate I had aroused an ectasy which seems foreign to this period of sorrow and gloom.

As I stepped forth into the street, I heard a window open, and my name called. Though the old fellow could not see me, he knew in which direction I should walk, and his sightless eyes were turned thither. He leaned out so far that his anxious relatives put their arms round him lest he should fall. Waving a handkerchief, he shouted:

" A pleasant journey to you, Herr Rackner."

His voice rang like a boy's. Never shall I forget that cheerful face, which contrasted so grimly with the careworn aspect of the passers-by in the street. The illusion I had helped to sustain made life good for him. Was it not Goethe who said: " Collectors are happy creatures "?

KAREL CAPEK, Ph.D.

THE SHIRTS

HE wanted to think about other infinitely more important matters, but, do what he would, the unpleasant thought kept running through his mind: his housekeeper was robbing him. She had been with him so many years, and he had got quite out of the habit of keeping track of his personal belongings. There stood his linen-cupboard: in the morning he would open it and take a clean shirt from the top of the pile. From time to time, at irregular intervals, Mrs. Johanka would come and display before him a torn shirt, declaring that they were all in the same plight, and that master must buy new ones. Very good, master would then go out and buy half a dozen shirts at the first shop he came to, not, however, without a vague idea that he had gone through the same performance not very long before. It was the same with collars and ties, clothes and boots, soap, and the thousand and one other things which a man needs, even when he is a widower. Everything has to be renewed from time to time, but on an old man things all get somehow old and shabby at once, or goodness knows what happens to them; he was continually buying new things, only to be faced, when he opened his wardrobe, with a jumble of worn and faded garments made he could not tell when. But after all there was no need to bother about these things. Mrs. Johanka saw to everything.

Now, for the first time after all these years, it was borne in on him that he was being systematically robbed. It happened like this: he had received that morning an invitation to go to a banquet given by some society or other. For years he had been nowhere at all; the narrow circle of his friends was so small that the unexpected invitation bewildered him altogether; he was delighted beyond measure, but rather scared. First of all, he began searching to see if he had any shirt splendid enough; he pulled them all out of the cupboard, but there was not one which was not frayed at the cuffs or round the collar. He called Johanka and asked her whether he had not some more presentable linen.

Mrs. Johanka gulped, was silent for a moment, and then declared sharply that master must certainly buy new ones; it was useless for her to go on mending the old ones, they were regular cobwebs. He had, however, a vague impression that he had bought some not long before, but not being sure he was silent and at once began to put on his coat to go and buy them. But now, he was once started on tidying up, he pulled some old papers out of his pockets to see if he should keep them or throw them away. Among them was the last bill for shirts, paid on such and such a date. Seven weeks ago. Seven weeks ago, half a dozen new shirts. That was his whole discovery.

He did not go and buy any others, but wandered about the room meditating. He looked back upon years and years of solitude. Since his wife's death Johanka had kept house for him, and never for a moment had he felt the least suspicion or distrust; but now an uneasy feeling came over him that he was being robbed all that time. He glanced about him; he could not say what was missing, but he suddenly perceived that the place was empty and desolate, and he tried to remember whether there used not to be more things about, a more intimate look, more of everything. . . . Full of dismay, he opened the chest in which lay memorials of his wife: dresses, linen. A few shabby articles were there, but all breath of the past was gone from them; heavens! the number of things which his wife had really left! What had become of them all?

He closed the chest and forced himself to think of other things; for instance, the banquet that evening. But those past years returned insistently. They seemed now more desolate, bitter and miserable than when he was living through them; they appeared suddenly as if despoiled, and from them breathed an agony of desolation. Of course, at intervals he had been contented, lulled, as it were, to sleep; but now he was appalled to see the slumber of a lonely man whom strange hands robbed of even the pillow beneath his head; and he felt forlorn, suffering from a keen pain, greater than he had known since the day—the day when he returned from the funeral. He found himself grown old and weary, as one to whom life had been too cruel.

One thing, however, he could not make out: why should she steal my things? What would she do with them? Oh, I see, he remembered suddenly with a certain malicious satisfaction. That's what it is! She has a nephew somewhere whom she loves with the foolish love of an infatuated aunt; have I not had to listen to innumerable babblings about that flower of men? Let me see, not long ago she actually showed me his photo: curly hair, snub nose, and a particularly impertinent moustache; though she, for her part, wiped away tears of pride and emotion. So that's where all my things have strayed, he said to himself. He flew into a terrible rage at the thought; he ran to the kitchen and called out to Johanka something like, " You wretched old hag! " and then bolted away again, leaving her fearfully and tearfully rolling her old goggle sheep's eyes.

He did not speak to her again for the rest of that day; she sighed as though she had been insulted, and clattered things about whenever they came handy, not realising in the least what the cause of the trouble was. In the afternoon he embarked on a complete overhauling of his cupboards and drawers; it was terrible; he remembered first one thing and then another which he had at some time possessed; various family heirlooms, which now seemed to him particularly precious. And now there was nothing left, nothing—not one thing left of it all. It was just as though there had been a great fire. He could have broken down and wept with rage and loneliness.

He was sitting in the midst of open drawers, out of breath, covered with dust, and holding in his hand the one solitary relic which was left—his father's purse, a bead bag with holes now at both ends. For how many years must she have been robbing him to have left nothing at all? He was almost beside himself with rage; if he had come across her at that moment he would have slapped her face. What shall I do with her? he said in emotion. Pack her off at once? Hand her over to the police? But who will cook for me to-morrow? I will go to a restaurant, he decided; but who will heat water and light the fire for me? With a supreme effort he drove these cares away. I will settle the matter to-morrow, he assured himself; something will turn up. The idea that I am dependent upon her! Nevertheless, the problem weighed on him more heavily than he would admit; only the consciousness of wrong suffered and the necessity of punishment kept up his courage.

When it grew dusk he pulled himself together so far as to go to the kitchen and say to Johanka carelessly, " You must go out somewhere or other," and then he gave her some complicated and lengthy errands of a somewhat irrelevant nature, which he said must be done at once, and which he had devised with no small trouble. Mrs. Johanka said nothing, but set about the business with the pained air of a martyr.

At last the door slammed behind her and he was left alone. With beating heart he stole to the kitchen, and then hesitated with his hand on the latch; he was seized with panic as he felt that he would never bring himself to the point of opening her cupboard: it seemed to him the act of a thief. But when he was already thinking of giving it up the thing came of itself; he opened the door and went in.

The kitchen literally shone with cleanliness. There stood Johanka's cupboard; but it was locked and no sign of a key. This discovery confirmed him in his purpose; he tried to force the cupboard with a kitchen knife, but he only hacked it about and did not succeed in opening it. He pulled out every drawer in search of a key, tried every key of his own; but at last, after half an hour of raging, he found that the cupboard was not locked at all, and could be opened with a button-hook.

Neatly arranged and ironed lay the linen on separate shelves. And just on the top were his six new shirts, still tied up with the blue ribbon from the shop. In a cardboard box was his wife's brooch with the dark amethyst; his father's mother-of-pearl cuff-links; his mother's portrait on ivory—goodness, had she a use even for that? He pulled everything out of the cupboard: he found his socks and collars, a box of soap, tooth-brushes, an old silk waistcoat, pillow-cases, an old officer's pistol, and a smoke-stained and quite useless amber mouthpiece. These were indeed portions of his wardrobe; the greater part had evidently been made over long ago to the curly-headed nephew. The heat of passion subsided, but there remained the reproachful distress. So this is how it is. . . . Johanka, Johanka, how have I deserved this from you?

One by one he removed his things to his own room and spread them out on the table; they formed an imposing exhibition of every imaginable article. Those which were Johanka's property he threw back into the cupboard in the kitchen; he even wanted to put them neatly in order, but after some attempts he retreated helplessly, leaving the cupboard gaping open as if after a robbery. And then he began to be afraid that Johanka would return, and that he would have to talk to her seriously. . . . The idea disgusted him so much that he began to dress hurriedly. To-morrow I will take her to task he said to himself; to-day it will be enough for her to realise that I have found out. He picked up one of the new shirts, which was as stiff as paper, so that with all his efforts he could not manage to fasten his stiff collar. And Johanka might come back at any moment.

He dived quickly into his old shirt, regardless of the fact that it was torn, and no sooner was he dressed than he slunk out like a thief, and for an hour loitered about the streets in the rain until it was time to go to the banquet. At the gathering he felt lonely; he tried to fall into intimate talk with old acquaintances; but in some way, he did not know how, the years had come between him and other people; just imagine it, we can hardly understand each other. But he had no grudge against anyone; he stood apart and smiled, dazzled by the glare of lights and the noise and movement . . . until for some unknown reason he was seized with fresh alarm—just think what I must look like! There are threads hanging from my shirt, a stain on my dress coat, and as for my boots, bless me! He wished he could sink into the ground, and looked round for a hiding-place, but on every side there shone brilliant shirt-fronts—where could he slip away unnoticed? He was afraid to take a step towards the door lest every glance should suddenly be turned upon him. He perspired with embarrassment; he pretended to be standing motionless, but all the time he was shuffling with his feet so as to reach the door by inches, without being perceived. As ill-luck would have it an old acquaintance, a fellow-student of his at the High School, accosted him, which added to his embarrassment. He answered him confusedly, and very nearly offended him; he breathed a sigh of relief when he was once more alone, and measured his distance from the door. At length he escaped and fled home; it was not yet midnight.

On the way Johanka came into his mind again. His brain became active with rapid walking, and he planned in his mind what he should say to her. With unaccustomed ease, long, forceful, dignified phrases strung themselves together; a lengthy discourse of severe condemnation and ultimate mercy. Yes, mercy; because in the end he would forgive her. He would not turn her into the street. Johanka would weep and implore, then promise to mend her ways; he would listen in silence, unmoved, and at last would say to her solemnly: "Johanka, I will give you a chance to make amends for your ingratitude; be honest and loyal, I ask no more of you. I am an old man and do not wish to be cruel."

He was so excited that before he realised it he found himself at home and had unlocked the door. A light was burning in Johanka's room. He just peeped through the curtain into the kitchen; good gracious, what was that? Johanka, her face flushed and swollen with weeping, was rushing about the kitchen and throwing her things into a trunk. He was terribly alarmed. Why the trunk? He crept to his room on tiptoe, confused, oppressed, and quite bewildered. Was Johanka going away?

There in front of him on the table lay all the things she had stolen from him. He fingered them, but felt not the smallest pleasure at their recovery. I see, he said to himself, Johanka has discovered that I have found her guilty of thieving and expects to be sent off at once—that is why she is packing up. Very well, I will leave her with that idea—until to-morrow; that will be sufficient punishment for her; yes, I will talk to her in the morning. But perhaps—perhaps, even now she will come and ask my pardon. She will burst into tears before me, fall on her knees, and that sort of thing. That will do, Johanka, I don't want to be harsh; you can stay.

He sat down in his evening clothes to await developments. There was silence, unbroken silence in the house; he heard every step of Johanka's in the kitchen, heard the angry slamming of a trunk lid, then again calm. What was that? He sprang up in alarm and listened: a prolonged, terrible howl, as of some creature not human; then it trailed off into a series of hysterical sobs; there followed the sound of knees sinking heavily to the floor, and subdued moaning. Johanka was weeping. He had certainly been prepared for something, but this was unexpected. With beating heart he stood and listened to what was going on in the kitchen. Nothing, only weeping. Presently Johanka will come to herself and ask for forgiveness.

He paced the room in order to recover his firmness, but still Johanka did not come. At intervals he stopped and listened; her wailing changed into a monotonous series of unabated howls. This dreadful despair was distressing to him. I will go to her, he resolved, and just say: " Now, let this be a lesson to you, Johanka, and stop crying. I will forget all about it, but be honest in future."

Suddenly a violent rush, the door burst open, and there stood Johanka on the threshold, howling; it was dreadful to see her face so swollen with weeping.

" Johanka," he gasped.

" Have—I—deserved this? " broke from Johanka. " Nice thanks this—as if I were a thief—such a shame! "

" But, Johanka," he cried alarmed, " but you have taken my things—all these, do you see? Did you take them or not? "

But Johanka did not hear. " What I have to put up with—such a shame—searching in my cupboard—as if—I was—some pilfering gipsy. To shame me so, me, indeed—you shouldn't have done it, sir—no right to—insult me—never—not to my dying day—would I have expected the like. Am I a thief indeed? I—I a thief, indeed? " She shrieked in passionate distress. " Am I really a thief? I, indeed, considering my family! That—that I never did expect—never deserved such a thing! "

" But, Johanka," he said, somewhat damped, " just have

some sense. How did these things get into your cupboard? Is this yours or mine? Say, my good woman, is this yours?"

"I don't want to hear anything," sobbed Johanka. "Good Lord, what a shame! Just as if—I was a gipsy—search my cupboard!—but this instant," she cried, fearfully excited, "this instant I'll be off. I shall not stop here till the morning. No—no."

"But look here," he protested in alarm, "I don't want to turn you out. You will stay on, Johanka. As fc what has happened, well, heaven save us from anything worse. I have not yet said a word to you about it. So stop crying."

"Engage someone else," said Johanka, choking with tears. "I shall not stay here even till to-morrow morning. As if one were—a dog—to put up with anything—I won't," she ejaculated desperately, "not if you paid me thousands. I would rather spend the night on the pavement."

"But why, Johanka," he argued helplessly. "Have I hurt your feelings, then? But still you cannot deny——"

"No, not hurt my feelings," cried Johanka in a still more wounded tone. "It is not hurting my feelings—searching my cupboard—as if I were a thief. That is nothing at all—that I have to put up with—no one ever did such a thing to me—such a shame. I am not—just a tramp," she shrieked with a convulsive burst of tears and rushed out, slamming the door.

He was immensely perplexed. Instead of repentance, all this scene. What does it mean? She steals like a jackdaw, no doubt of that, and feels insulted because I know about it; not ashamed of being a thief, but terribly hurt in her sensitiveness when put down as one. Is the woman out of her mind?

But gradually he felt more and more sorry for her. You see, he said to himself, everyone has his weak spot, but you never offend him more than by remarking on it. Ah, what an unbounded moral sensitiveness man harbours even amid his faults! How painfully and tenderly susceptible even in his misdeeds! Just put your finger on his secret vice and you hear nothing but a cry of pain and indignation in reply. Do you not see that in judging the offender you are judging the offended?

From the kitchen came the sound of weeping stifled by a feather bed. He wanted to go in, but the door was locked; he stood there trying to reason with her, upbraided her, and then attempted to soothe her; but all the reply he met with was more violent and noisy sobbing. He went back to his room oppressed with helpless pity. There on the table lay the stolen articles: fine new shirts, a quantity of linen, mementos, and what not. He caressed them with his finger, but in the touch there was something sad and forlorn.

JOSEF BARD, LL.D.

THE TALE OF A CHILD

. . . TO-DAY it is very warm and we shall go and bathe in the Danube. We are not allowed to bathe in the Danube because it is dangerous but we know a spot where there is a bad smell because it is near a factory where they make leather from the hide of oxen. There the water is shallow and we can all stand up in the water. Jacob too can stand up though he is small but he is very wise and Andreas can swim and we all cling to the neck of Roka my dog. Jacob holds most of Roka's neck although Roka is my dog but Jacob is very frightened of the Danube and he would be punished if he drowned, because his father told him so. His father is a man with a curly long black beard and apart from that he is also our grocer and he has black rings under his eyes. I don't like Jacob's father because he always pats me on the head and then my hair smells of cheese, and I must wash always although I have washed already. But I like Jacob because he is wise. I don't know how but he is very wise. We all play at marbles after class and we all lose. But Jacob never plays because his father told him so. But he exchanges our bad marbles for better marbles and we buy them from him. Andreas says this is because Jacob is a Jew and his father told him so. I like Andreas but I think he is a liar. He told me the other day there is a dead mason hidden in the walls of every big house. The mason was alive when they walled him in but now he is dead. I don't believe it but I don't like it. Andreas' father is a gentleman who builds houses for others and he told him so.

I am sure Andreas is a liar. Now when we have all come out of the water and were drying ourselves in the grass so that nobody could tell we had been in the Danube and Roka sat down on our clothes and made them wet and we drove Roka away with stones although we all held his neck in the water, now Andreas was chewing a leaf of grass and told us he saw God yesterday early in the afternoon.

"You are a liar," I said to Andreas. Jacob said nothing but he smiled. He is very wise when he smiles. I saw that Jacob also thought that Andreas was a little liar.

"I am not a liar. I came down to the river and I saw a big white cloud in the sky just like a feather-pillow and God flew out, dipped his feet in the water, smiled at me and flew back again."

So we looked up into the sky. We saw white clouds, fluffy like the sheep in the village and not a bit like feather-pillows. I knew Andreas was a liar. And God simply couldn't fly out of such a cloud.

Still I was envious. I shall be ten years old after two years and I haven't seen God yet. I thought maybe Jacob had more luck. So I asked him: "Jacob, have you see God?" But Jacob looked frightened and he said he must not speak of God because his father told him so. Then I turned to Andreas again and said to him: "Andreas, I know you are just lying. Look in my eyes and say again that you saw God!" And Andreas who was lying on his back turned round on his belly and looked at me. Andreas is very beautiful. He has long flaxen locks and his face is very white and his eyes are like brown fruit-drops when you have sucked them and taken them out of your mouth and then hold them in your hand to see how much is left. But I could not look into his eyes as mother looks into mine. His eyes were not in his face they were just like clouds in the sky. So I just said: "Andreas, I believe you are a liar." Still I am not quite sure. And then we all went home, Jacob and Andreas and Roka and I and we never said another word.

. . . . .

. . . to-day Father eats the marrow-bone. When Father is away I eat the marrow-bone, when he is at home he gives me a bit of the marrow, on a bit of bread, salted and peppered. I was waiting for my bit to-day but he forgot me. He often is like that. I said: "Father—" because I am told to call him Father and not Daddie—"Father, Andreas told me he saw God in the afternoon—do you think it is true?" But Father finished the marrow-bone and said I was a donkey. I looked sad and then Mother told Father "don't be rude to the child." Then Father said that Mother spoils me. Then they quarrelled. Then I stopped sulking. I love Mother. All the boys love their Mothers but they respect their Fathers. But my Mother is very beautiful. She has long hair and big eyes and a big mouth and she is soft and plump.

So we were all eating quietly in the garden under the mulberry-tree and the ripe mulberries kept dropping from the tree into my rice-pudding, so wonderful is nature. But still I wanted to know whether Andreas saw God. When Father left the table I asked Mother: "Mother dear—do you think

Andreas really saw God?" But she looked tired because Father had not kissed her when he left the table because they quarrelled and she sighed. She said: "The questions you ask! How should I know?" And then she also left the table and followed Father into the house.

Mother is very beautiful and plump but she never answers my questions. I shall ask Kate, our cook who is plumper than Mother but not so very beautiful. She has already told me where babies come from. She will know whether Andreas, the little liar, saw God or not.

. . . . .

. . . to-day I have not spoken to Andreas in school because I am not sure whether he is a liar or not. This is a warm morning. The sun is shining and we all wanted to laugh but we had no chance because our teacher Prunk spoke only of serious things and had the birch in his hand. Jacob brought some old stamps and we are all collecting stamps because Jacob says it is the best way to learn the map of the world. Slezak sits behind me and he is the son of our washer-woman, but he hates Jacob. But Slezak is very stupid and our teacher Prunk told him so. We are all a little afraid of Slezak because he is very strong and hits us on the jaw. He says the English all hit each other on the jaw which makes them very strong. Jacob has many English stamps because he has an uncle there who sends them to him. His uncle hits nobody on the jaw but publishes books which others have written, and his father told him so. But when Slezak hit Jacob on the jaw, Jacob smiled mildly and asked him "is this what you have learned from your Reverend Father and Jesus Christ?" And Slezak said Jacob crucified Jesus Christ and now he must be hit on the jaw. And we were all very excited and Prunk came in and birched Slezak and told the class we were all Hungarians and we must love each other because anyhow we are only few and our enemies are many. Then he read us a poem which said that the earth is the hat of God and Hungary is a bunch of flowers on the top of the hat. This was written by a great poet called Petöfi, who fell in the battle when the Hungarians were just conquering the Russians. We Hungarians have the habit of winning all the battles but this we lost because we were already tired by conquering the Austrians. The Russians and the Austrians are our enemies and so are others we haven't yet learned about and Prunk says our enemies are many and our friends are few and we must prepare to be proud when the moment arrives when we shall die for Hungary. But we still have time and so we must learn Petöfi's poem by heart and we must not forget that now the Austrians are our friends and our King Francis Joseph rules over them too but he loves only the Hungarians and he only rules over the Austrians because his father told him to. Our King is hanging on the wall and he is very dignified and hairy, and he is now very old but he was young when he began to be a King. When we sing the National Anthem we all look at him and he looks back at us very dignified and hairy.

We all read aloud what is called the poem and it was difficult to remember it because the lines all end the same way, but we were all very proud that we were so few and always conquered our enemies who were many and Slezak wanted to go to the lavatory, which he always wants to do when we must learn something by heart. And Jacob stood up and asked our teacher how could the earth be the hat of God when he told us that the earth was round like a rubber-ball. Jacob is very wise and when we were reading the poem we had quite forgotten that Prunk told us the earth was round. We all looked at Prunk and we all saw clearly he could say just nothing. But he was trying very hard. He said Petofi was a very great poet and very great poets are permitted to say sometimes what is not quite true. But we all thought that Jacob conquered Prunk. But perhaps Prunk told the truth. And perhaps Andreas is not a little liar but only a great poet?

. . . .

. . . to-day grandma arrived from town. Grandma is a much older lady than Mother but this is only natural. She is small and she always smoothes her mouth with her fingers because her teeth are not natural. But she was sad to-day because my Uncle Berti came with her who is also her son and Uncle Berti is ill. I don't know what is wrong with Uncle Berti they only say he is mad. I like Uncle Berti because he is so funny, and he sometimes pushes his spoon under his chin because he can't find his mouth and pours the soup under his collar which is a good joke from a grown-up man but Grandma looks sad and kicks me under the table when I laugh. Uncle Berti worked in town and he was almost a bank-director but not quite but this was before he poured the soup under his collar. Now he lives with Grandma who is also his Mother. And he is very big and very silent but he likes to play with me when I play in the garden building castles from mudpies. And Mother and Grandma sat under the mulberry tree and watched us and we sat on the ground and when I turned round I think Mother and Grandma were blowing their noses and I think they wept although Uncle Berti made much better mudpies than I did. And then they went into the house and I followed them to wash my hands and I heard them talk although I did not want to listen but they had not seen me. And Mother was afraid Uncle Berti would get wild one day and wanted him to go to a place where he could get wild safely. But Grandma only wept and cursed Uncle Berti's wife but he had two wives and this was unhealthy for him especially when they both loved him. And then I went to the kitchen and just heard Kate the cook say to the maid that Uncle Berti had water in his head but when they saw me they said no more.

And so I went back to Uncle Berti and he was all right doing well with mudpies. And I sat down next to Uncle Berti and looked in his eyes and they were blue but they were not there. And I thought he might perhaps know whether Andreas saw God, so I asked him. And he only said: "Very-berry-mulberry" and then he smiled. And then he stood up and was very tall and his hair I saw was white and he said "let us go to Church I would like to pray." So I took him by the hand and we went into the house and I said to Mother "Uncle Berti and I want to go to Church." And Mother looked frightened but Grandma said it was all right. And so we walked out, I holding his hand and I took him to the Chapel although it was three o'clock in the afternoon and God is seldom at home at that hour. And it was very dark and cool in the chapel and candles burnt in the corners and I was not comfortable because Uncle Berti held my hand very tight. And I don't go to Church because Father says he hates all the priests and if there is God there is only one who also hates the priests. But it is beautiful in our chapel it smells good not like near the river where they make leather from the hide of oxen. And the lady-saints were very beautiful and they all had flowers on the altar. We just stood in the middle of the chapel and we were quite alone and it was very silent. And Uncle Berti whispered into my ear whether I could see a gentleman-saint because he would like to pray before a gentleman-saint and not before a lady-saint to-day. And I found him one in the right corner who was tied to a tree and he was very naked but there were arrows in him. And Uncle Berti let my hand go and fell on his knees and began to pray, but it seemed to have little sense and I wondered whether the saint would understand what he was saying. Then Uncle Berti wept and he wept very loud and I was afraid because it was very silent and we were alone and I had heard Mother say Uncle Berti might get wild. But it was not true because he stood up and was very quiet and stroked my hand and thanked me for taking him to the chapel. It was all right what he said, so I told him why did he let himself be called mad. Then he laughed and he laughed just as loud as he wept before, and I got frightened again. But he became quiet again and we walked out of the chapel and he said he wanted to buy me something. So I took him to Jacob's father who is the grocer and I chose a box of green lizards made of rubber-candy. And Jacob's father made big eyes and forgot to pat me on the head which made me grateful. And Uncle Berti shook hands with Jacob's father and forgot to pay and we all went back to Mother and Grandma.

Then Grandma and Uncle Berti went to the station and we accompanied them and Uncle Berti was so big and Grandma very small but she led him by the hand. And Uncle Berti was very pale and when he shook hands with me, my heart hurt because I was now sorry for him. I wished he had something better than water in his head.

. . . . .

. . . to-day we went to swim in the Danube again where it stinks but it is safe and I kept my head out of water because I was afraid water might get into my head through my ears as with Uncle Berti. We are friends again with Andreas and I always like Jacob because he is wise. And we went rather late and we rolled about naked and Jacob was different because he was taken into the bosom of Abraham that way and it happened when he was eight days old and his father told him so. Jacob has very thin legs and thin arms and Andreas is much more beautiful but Andreas rolled very close to me and I told him I didn't like it because we must only love girls and Kate the cook told me so. And so Andreas rolled on his belly and his bottom was turned towards me and it seemed beautiful but it was his bottom and bottoms are ugly because my Mother told me so and you must never show it except when you are alone and the doctor asks you to. I told this to Andreas but he laughed and then he lied again because he must always lie except when he is a great poet. Andreas lied that children are made of marble and rose-leaves and they are beautiful everywhere and we only cover our bottoms because otherwise we would be too beautiful for our parents. So I called him a liar because I know babies are made by mothers and Slezak the son of our washer-woman brought me the cord which came out with him into the world and he found it in a drawer and it was wrapped in a paper and it was brown and horrid. And Jacob said we must not bother about this, but collect stamps in peace and learn the map of the world because his father told him so.

But I still called Andreas a liar because I saw our dog Roka starting to make babies to his wife and Kate, the cook told me father was not different. Andreas did not answer but smelt the daisies in the grass. Then he said he didn't care what we knew but he dreamt babies were made of marbles and rose-leaves. Now I knew he was lying again because I dreamt that uncle Berti came back and I broke a hole in his head with my hatchet and all the water flowed out and our teacher Prunk was drowned in the flood but it was not true because in the morning I saw that Prunk was still alive and teaching history. I wanted Jacob to be on my side against Andreas but Jacob is very wise and he only wants to collect stamps in peace.

So I teased Andreas who was still smelling the daisies which I know have no smell and told him if he knew everything did he know what the stars were. Andreas said he knew but he couldn't say it because he didn't know the words. So I asked him did he know what the moon was. And Andreas said the moon is a pale woman who is looking for a lost world. And then I got frightened just like in the chapel when uncle Berti wept aloud and I thought perhaps water had got into the ears of Andreas because I also see ghosts in the dark but I know they are not there because my Mother told me so. So I asked him what the sun is and Andreas lifted his head and said the sun is an angry flame which wants to burn everything and the earth is running away from him because he is frightened. And Jacob and I were also frightened and it was now dark and Jacob said we must not ask more questions from Andreas because he is perhaps a prophet and we must be happy when prophets are silent because his father told him so. And we all walked home and said no more.

. . . . .

. . . to-day I saw Kate the cook drinking rum in the kitchen but I shall not tell Mother because Kate is my friend and always answers my questions and Mother is more beautiful but she never answers my questions and Father is always angry. And Kate gave some rum to Peti the milkman who always smells of what the cows leave when they don't behave properly and who is waiting on the cows. And Peti the milkman started to be like Roka my dog when he joined his wife but Kate pushed him back and asked him whether he was not ashamed before the child which was me. And then I remembered that Lola had her birthday and she had asked me to come and have some of her birthday cake and I had not asked Mother because now it was after dinner and I had to go to bed. So I asked Kate to let me in through the kitchen door when I came back and then I went into the garden and picked white and red roses which she liked and walked to Lola's house because I think I love Lola and I would like to marry Lola if she could preserve herself till I grow up. Because Lola is already very big and her hair is perfumed when she kisses me and she lives in a big house, with a big orchard where a brook flows through and she has many young men playing the piano with her which is very musical. And when I arrived she was playing but she stopped and kissed me again and her hair was again perfumed. And there were many people and they were eating sandwiches and Lola wore a long white dress and her arms were puffed but this was only her dress and not her arms. And everybody was very nice to me though they laughed and a fat man who played with Lola pinched my cheeks, and I told him I didn't like that and I thought he was stupid. I said this because I saw him breathe down on Lola's neck when she played the piano and I love Lola. And Lola saw that I was angry and she said we two will go out into the garden, and so we went out and we sat down under a cherry tree and we sat on the grass and I put my head on Lola's white neck and kissed it which Lola said I must not do. And Lola was sad and she looked up at the moon and she sighed. And she said "do you see the moon?" And I said "yes, I see the moon she is like a pale woman looking for a lost world." And then I blushed because I remembered that I had heard this from Andreas, that little liar. But Lola did not remember it and she kissed me on the mouth and said that it was very beautiful and asked me whether I could say something else as beautiful. Then I said the sun is an angry flame which wants to burn everything and the earth is running away from him because he is frightened. Then I blushed again because I remembered that I heard this also from Andreas the little liar. But Lola kissed me on the mouth again and she said how poetic children are and I saw she thought of the fat man who was not so poetic and then she said I must come when I had something beautiful to say and that she would always kiss me. So we parted in the garden and I did not go back to the house with her because I didn't like the fat man but Lola went back and I walked to my home. I was very happy and wondered what the stars were but then Father was waiting for me in the kitchen and he said he would break my bones if I left the house without permission at night and he began doing so, but Mother came and told him not to be rude to the child and then they quarrelled and I hurried to my room before they had finished and I thought I hated to be beaten and I would kill whoever dares to beat me, only fathers unfortunately can't be killed because my Mother told me so. So I went to bed and I dreamt of Lola but it was not true because I could not remember it in the morning.

. . . to-day Slezak was late for school because he said his mother had borne him a brother which is curious because Slezak has no father. But we did not ask questions because Prunk told us more about our History and he said we Hungarians were somewhere else a thousand years ago and we had the habit of multiplying ourselves quickly so we went out to find another home so we came to Hungary which is where we now are and we conquered the people we found here because we had the habit of winning all the battles. But it was not easy to find Hungary because it was far from the place where we multiplied ourselves, but our very own Battle-god sent us a bird and he flew ahead of us and when we arrived he flew back to our very own Battle-god and so Prunk said we have been in Hungary now for over a thousand years and had much glory and we have fought against the Turks who also belonged to our enemies but we haven't yet learnt about them and we have suffered much glory because we were only few and our enemies were many. And we were all very proud but then Jacob stood up and asked Prunk why we had so many enemies. Prunk knows much and has a big wart on his forehead but Jacob is wise and Prunk thought a little while and then said we are the bunch of flowers on God's hat and our neighbours are all envious of us. Then we all stood up and sang the National Anthem and our King Francis Joseph hanging on the wall listened to us and he listened to our promise that we would all die here because we couldn't go elsewhere. Then Prunk left us for half an hour to give us time to wash our hands and eat our bread and butter and we all stood round Slezak who was sad because now his mother can't wash for a month and he did not want a brother because they are very poor and his father died when they hit him on the head with a bottle of rum. Slezak said it was Peti the milkman who did it to his mother but he would buy a gun and shoot him. Then Andreas pulled me by the sleeve and we all left Slezak and whispered because Andreas asked us to collect money for Slezak because he is very poor. And we all promised to give him our pocket money for the week and to ask our parents to give him money. Then Slezak had to go to Prunk's room and he came back weeping because Prunk asked him to leave the school. And we all hated Prunk and called him an ugly wart which he had on his forehead. And when Prunk came back to teach history we all stood up and Jacob walked in front of us and asked Prunk in the name of the class to take back Slezak because Slezak is innocent because he did not tell Peti the milkman to do it to his mother. Then Prunk was very angry and told Jacob to go back to his place and said we should not know about such things and that Slezak was a bad influence. Then he taught us more about our glorious past and how we conquered our enemies and how our Kings helped us but I don't remember because we did not listen because we thought of Slezak. And when the class was over Prunk saw that we were all sad and he said he would talk about Slezak to the headmaster. Then we all cheered and were proud again of our glorious past.

. . . .

. . . to-day is Friday evening and I was permitted to go to Jacob's house and have dinner with them because I gave some old stamps to Jacob and he was grateful. And it was very warm in the room and we all kept our hats on our heads because Jacob's God likes that and also we were more than thirteen because otherwise Jacob's God is not present. And Jacob's father was very clean and he had a white stole on his neck and he prayed loud and we all murmured and then we had soup with big dumplings in it and we had roast goose with much stuffings. And Jacob's relatives were there and they had beards but the women were only fat. Jacob has no mother but his aunt cooks for him and she is called Hannah and she is only half-witted but she cooks well. Jacob says Jews are wise, but when they are not they are very stupid. It was very hot and we were not happy because Jacob's God really lives in Palestine and only comes for a short visit to our village. And I said to Jacob now we will go to my garden and eat fruit from the trees.

And then we walked home which is not far because our village is small. And Jacob was sad because he had no mother and Friday night he always remembers her. So I told him stories to amuse him how the Austrian villagers carry ladders sideways through the forest and cut down the trees to make way. But Jacob was still sad and I looked up at the stars and wondered what they were and whether Andreas the little liar had found the words for them. Then I told Jacob about Lola and that I was going to marry her if she can preserve herself until I grow up but Jacob only smiled and he said I would forget her when I grew up. I know Jacob is very wise but I don't believe what he said. But when we turned into my garden we could not eat fruit because we found Kate the cook weeping under the mulberry tree and Father came out and told her she must go away, because she wanted to push the carving knife into Peti the milkman because Peti did it to Slezak's mother and he also did it to Kate, and Peti also had a wife. Peti must be very healthy because now he has three wives and has no water in his head and uncle Berti had only two wives and his head was full of water. But Mother came out and she is very kind and she patted Kate on the cheek and told her to stay and she sent Father back into the house. And then a policeman came because Kate had just scratched Peti with the carving knife and the policeman wanted Kate to go with him but Father said everything was all right and gave a cigar to the policeman and then Peti came with his head bandaged and said it was all a misunderstanding and Kate remained with us but we shall get milk elsewhere. And Father said to Peti that he would break his bones if he ever dared to come to our house again but Mother said don't be rude to the poor fellow and sent Father into the house. Then Kate went to bed weeping and Peti and the policeman left and I took Jacob to the garden gate because it was now late. And Jacob who is so wise said to me it is much better to collect stamps in peace. He said love is very unhappy always because his father told him so.

. . . . .

. . . to-day when Father was eating my marrow-bone I asked him to give me money because we are collecting for Slezak in school. But Father said he had no money to throw away and I looked sad and Mother said to Father don't be rude to the child. And then they quarrelled. And when we were left alone under the mulberry-tree Mother said she would give me money but I must be nicer to Father. And I said I am very nice to him but he never talks to me. Mother said Father works for us and he is tired and we must cheer him up. All fathers must be cheered up. They all work for their wives and children and when they don't they are not happy. So I must not forget to greet Father when I see him in the morning which I always do. So I asked Mother why she married Father and she said the questions children ask and left me alone. Mother is plump and beautiful but I don't understand her. I understand Kate much better who is now very plump. But I love Mother and she gave me money for Slezak. Slezak is now back in school with us and he wanted to give me his cord which is in a tissue paper because he is grateful because I collected for him but I did not want his cord because it is horrid. Slezak is very stupid and he hit Jacob on the jaw because he said it will make him strong because the English all hit each other on the jaw which makes them strong. But Jacob always says he hates violence because his father told him so.

Slezak is also very happy because the brother his mother bore him recently died yesterday and now Slezak is again his mother's only orphan. And he asked us to come and see him because he is now in a coffin over the washing-tub and candles burn.

And in the afternoon we all went to see Slezak's brother, Jacob and Andreas and Roka and I but Roka had to wait outside in the courtyard. And Slezak's brother was in a small white coffin and Slezak's mother who is our washer-woman when she has no babies gave rum to her friends who came to see her and she wanted to give rum to us too but we did not want it. So we just stared at the candles and we were silent and Jacob was sad because he remembered his mother as on Friday evenings and Andreas was very pale and he whispered something but I could not hear it. Then we all coughed because we wanted to go out and Slezak's mother thanked us for coming and thanked us for collecting money for Slezak who is only a silly bully. Then she wept and her cheeks were all very red like apples and when she wiped her tears I saw her hands were all red from washing. So we coughed again and blew our noses and went out into the courtyard because the room opens on a courtyard which is not clean. And Roka was chewing an old bone which he had found on the dustheap and we took it away from him. But Slezak only stood there leaning against the door and he looked on the ground and he forgot to hit Jacob on the jaw to make him strong which he always does.

. . . . .

. . . to-day we are very excited because Aunt Leonie arrived who is also my Mother's sister. And she married an Austrian who lives in Vienna where also lives our King Francis Joseph when he rules over the Austrians. But Aunt Leonie married long ago and now she has children and she brought one called Pamperl which sounds silly but is Austrian because the Viennese are also Austrian. Aunt Leonie married Uncle Pepi because he was beautiful and he sang songs about Vienna which is also beautiful and he was very funny and because she thought Uncle Pepi was almost a bank-director but he was only a great traveller for business and he always was travelling when Aunt Leonie had the babies. So we all sat under the mulberry-tree and Aunt Leonie wept and she had anyhow watery eyes and Father said why did she marry Uncle Pepi and she must go back to Uncle Pepi because now they had four children and then Aunt Leonie finished her cake and wept some more and Mother said to Father don't be rude to my sister and then we were left alone.

Then Mother asked Aunt Leonie what she intended to do and Aunt Leonie said the children should go for a walk. And I took Pamperl by the hand which is very soft and we walked out and Pamperl who has a sallow face and a lace collar talked to me but it was Austrian or Viennese and it sounded funny but I could not understand it. So we walked to the river and I led Pamperl through the dam where the water is very wild and I thought it was a pity the Austrians were our friends now and our King Francis Joseph rules over them also, because otherwise I would push Pamperl into the water and then Uncle Pepi and Aunt Leonie would have only three children and we would all be happier. But I hurried through the dam and I took Pamperl to where we bathe and I wanted Pamperl to bathe in the river because I thought Pamperl might drown without my help and then we should have one enemy less when the Austrians will be our enemies again, because we are only few and our enemies are many. But Pamperl shrieked and so I walked back with him to our house. And there we found Uncle Pepi who is very bald but has a lovely beard and a moustache like our King Francis Joseph but he is not so dignified because he always laughs. And Uncle Pepi followed my Aunt from Vienna because he thought now that he loved her better than Gullash and beer which he loves very much. And he took Pamperl on his knees and gave him beer and he sang a song about a Viennese cab which all Viennese sing and is also loved by our King Francis Joseph when he rules over the Austrians. Mother was sad and told Aunt Leonie that she must go back to Vienna tomorrow. And we went to bed but I slept only little because Uncle Pepi sang about the Viennese cab all night long.

. . . . .

. . . to-day Slezak hit the butcher's son on the jaw who called him a bastard and then Slezak hit him again and Jacob asked Slezak whether he had learnt this from his Reverend Father and Jesus Christ our Saviour because Jacob hates violence and wants us all to collect stamps in peace. Slezak hit Jacob on the jaw but only to make him strong. But I stood up for Slezak because he was called a bastard which was true but not very beautiful. And Slezak wanted to give me his cord again but I did not want it because it is horrid. Then he wanted to give me holy pictures which he got from our Reverend Father because Slezak has very good marks in religion and the Reverend Father calls him a lost sheep who is now back with the flock. And the holy picture was very beautiful and the Virgin Mary on it looked like Lola whom I love only Lola has no baby. But I did not take the holy picture because if there is a God there is only one who hates the priests because my Father told me so. Then Slezak who is very grateful because I have also collected money for him said he would tell me a secret but I must swear not to tell it to anybody else. And he told me there is a house in our village which stands alone in a meadow and which is always shut with green shutters during the day because the ladies who live there always sleep during the day and only wake up at night. And they are all very beautiful because they are all painted and perfumed and he knows one lady called Amanta who looks like the Virgin Mary on the picture only she is not a virgin although she has no baby. And they have many visitors during the night but they are all men who want no babies. And I thought Slezak was lying to me and I told him so but Slezak swore it was all true because his mother is washing for the ladies who sleep during the day and it is all very beautiful and full of mirrors and he went one day with his mother to help with the laundry and his mother told him not to look but he looked very much. And now I remembered I had seen the house with the green shutters alone in the meadow but I did not know ladies lived there who were sleeping during the day just like in the fairy-tales. So when I went home from school I asked mother to come with me for a walk and she was happy because I always go with Jacob and Andreas. And then I wanted to go where the house with the green shutters stood and we saw it standing alone in the meadow. I told Mother to look what a beautiful house it was. But she blushed and said it was an ugly house and I must never go near it. And I said I thought it was the house of the Sleeping Beauty which I read in the tales. But Mother said this was a very bad house and I must promise never to go near it. Mother is plump and very beautiful but she never answers my questions. Kate the cook always answers them. So I went to the kitchen to ask Kate about the fairy castle which stands alone in the meadow because I also dreamt of the fairies but I can't remember. But Peti the milkman was there although my Father will break his bones because he told him so. Peti still smells of cows but Kate our cook loves him again. He also gave me a whistle which he brought for me but I will wash it because Peti made it wet with his mouth. And Kate is now very plump and she weeps but she says she loves Peti again because the baby died which Peti did to Slezak's mother and Peti's wife has also the dry rot and she will die soon and then Peti will marry Kate. And we were all very happy and Kate gave him goose-liver. And I wanted to ask Kate about the house but I thought she would not know because she is only a cook and she cooks well but she never told me a good fairy-tale. I think I shall not ask anyone about the house standing alone in the meadow because all the people I know sleep during the night and they would know nothing about the ladies who sleep during the day.

. . . . .

. . . to-day it is almost summer and now we know already how to add up and subtract and multiply and divide and we have learnt about most of our enemies and of our glorious past and how the Austrians have always swindled us after we have so often conquered them. And we have learned many poems and I think Petofi wrote better poems than the one about God's hat and I have learned some and I have won a prize for reading poetry. And now we sing the anthem in tune to our King who hangs on the wall. And soon school will be over and then Mother and I shall go to the Lake Balaton which is the most beautiful lake in the world where all the Hungarians go and the Jewish Hungarians live on one end and the Roman Catholic Hungarians on the other and scattered in between are the rest. But I am not very happy because Lola whom I love will marry the fat man whom I hate and she will kiss the fat man with the same mouth with which she kissed me and she will not wait for me and preserve herself. And I am sad because Grandma came and told us that Uncle Berti is now very wild and he wants to eat his collar-buttons with his breakfast and he will die because now he has more water in his head. So I went out with Roka and looked for Jacob and then we went to find Andreas to ask him to bathe with us in the Danube. Andreas lives in a big house called a villa and he sat in the garden with his mother who has very soft hands which I like. So we kissed her hands and Roka misbehaved on the flowers and we asked Andreas to come with us. And Andreas was reading a book of poems by a poet called Shelley who was also loved by our poet Petofi. Andreas got the book to-day because he only wants to read poetry and he said Shelley died very young and he was English but very frail, but that was perhaps because they did not hit him on the jaw to make him strong. And the father of Andreas came out into the garden and smiled at us because he is very kind and he builds houses for others and when you do that you can build some for yourself. So we all went to the Danube where it smells but it is safe and we went into the water holding Roka's neck. And I said the Danube was very beautiful this afternoon because the water was blue and green and when the leather did not stink the acacia-trees smelt sweet on the banks. But Andreas says the Danube is not very beautiful and the people who live along the Danube are all very unhappy. Andreas has travelled much already because his father takes him along with him and he has seen high mountains and he told us stories of beautiful lakes in Italy. So I was sad that the Danube was not very beautiful and we scampered back to the riverside to dry in the grass and I told Andreas to move away because we must love only girls because Kate the cook told me so. And Jacob was also very sad because his father has a bad heart and that is why he has rings under his eyes and I thought of Lola who was not faithful to me. And we all ate grass and lay on our bellies and I said when we grow up we shall also have rings under our eyes and bad hearts and perhaps water in our heads like uncle Berti and how nice it would be to preserve ourselves. And Andreas rolled on his back and looked into the clouds which were swimming over the sky and he said everything passes away only the clouds pass and stay and I thought this was very beautiful and I could easily have told it to Lola and she would have kissed me on the mouth but now she has married the fat man who is not so poetic as we are. And I also thought this Danube river comes from Vienna where Uncle Pepi and Pamperl live and where our King Francis Joseph enjoys to hear the song of Uncle Pepi. But I got tired of thinking and I played with Roka who rolled on his back and watched Andreas who always looks into the clouds when he finds some in the sky, and I asked Andreas whether he had seen God fly out again because perhaps he said the truth after all and Andreas said he wanted to fly with the wind and hold the whole world against his heart. And he said he hated to think that one day he must die and he said there were many Gods and most of them hated us and that is why we must die. But Jacob who is very wise said that he must not say such things and there is only one God who punishes those who call him names and we must all collect stamps in peace and learn the map of the world, because his father told him so. But Andreas was not listening to him because he still watched the clouds swimming in the blue sky and I pinched him to wake him up and then he rose and we all walked home very silent and said no more.

LEO TOLSTOY

HOW MUCH LAND DOES A MAN REQUIRE?

AN elder sister came from the town to visit a younger one. The elder one was married to a tradesman, and the younger to a peasant. As the two drank tea and talked the elder sister began to boast and make much of her life in town—how she lived and went about in ease and comfort, dressed her children well, had nice things to eat and drink, and went skating, walking, and to the theatre.

The younger sister was vexed at this, and retorted by running down the life of a tradesman's wife and exalting her own country one.

"For my part, I should not care to exchange my life for yours," she said. "I grant you ours is an uneventful existence and that we know no excitement; yet you, on the other hand, with all your fine living, must either do a very large trade indeed or be ruined. You know the proverb: 'Loss is Gain's elder brother.' Well, you may be rich to-day, but to-morrow you may find yourself in the street. We have a better way than that, here in the country. The peasant's stomach may be thin, but it is long. That is to say, he may never be rich, yet he will always have enough."

The elder sister took her up quickly.

"'Enough,' indeed?" she retorted. "'Enough'—with nothing but your wretched pigs and calves? 'Enough,' with no fine dresses or company? Why, however hard your man may work, you have to live in mud, and will die there—yes, and your children after you."

"Oh, no," replied the younger. "It's like this with us. Though we may live hardly, the land is at least our own, and we have no need to bow and scrape to anyone. But you in town—you live in an atmosphere of scandal. To-day all may be well with you, but to-morrow the evil eye may look upon you, and your husband find himself tempted away by cards or wine, and you and yours find yourselves ruined. Is it not so ? "

Pakhom, the younger sister's husband, had been listening near the stove.

"That is true," he said. "I have been turning over our mother earth since childhood, so have had no time to get any foolishness into my head. Yet I have one grievance—too little land. Only give me land, and I fear no man—no, not even the Devil himself."

The two women finished their tea, chattered a little longer about dress, washed up the crockery, and went to bed.

All this time the Devil had been sitting behind the stove, and had heard everything. He was delighted when the peasant's wife led her husband on to brag—led him on to boast that, once given land, not even the Devil himself should take it from him.

"Splendid!" thought the Devil. "I will try a fall with you. I will give you much land—and then take it away again."

Near these peasants there lived a lady landowner, with a small property of 120 *dessiatins*.[1] Formerly she had got on well with the peasants and in no way abused her rights; but she now took as overseer a retired soldier, who began to persecute the peasants with fines. No matter how careful Pakhom might be, one of his horses would get into the lady's oats, or a cow stray into her garden, or the calves break into her meadows: and for all these things there would be fines levied.

Pakhom paid up, and then beat and abused his household. Much trouble did he get into with the overseer for the doings of the summer, so that he felt devoutly thankful to have got his cattle standing in the straw-yard again. He regretted the cost of their keep there, yet it cost him less anxiety in other ways.

That winter a rumour went abroad that the *Barina*[2] was going to sell her land, and that the overseer was arranging to buy both it and the highway rights attached. This rumour reached the peasants, and they were dismayed.

"If," they thought, "the overseer gets the land he will worry us with fines even worse than he did under the *Barina*. We must get hold of the property somehow, as we all live round it in a circle."

So a deputation from the *Mir*[3] went to see the *Barina*, and besought her not to sell the land to the overseer, but to give them the refusal of it, and they would outbid their rival. To

[1] A *dessiatin* is an area of 2¾ acres.
[2] Great Lady.
[3] Village Commune.

this the *Barina* agreed, and the peasants set about arranging for the *Mir* to purchase the whole of her estate. They held a meeting about it, and yet another one, but the matter did not go through. The fact was that the Unclean One always defeated their object by making them unable to agree. Then the peasants decided to try and buy the land in separate lots, each man as much as he could; and to this also the *Barina* said she was agreeable. Pakhom heard one day that a neighbour had bought twenty *dessiatins*, and that the *Barina* had agreed to let half the purchase money stand over for a year. Pakhom grew envious. "If," he thought, "the others buy up all the land, I shall feel left out in the cold." So he took counsel of his wife. "Everybody is buying some," he said, "so we too had better get hold of ten *dessiatins*. We can't make a living as things are now, for the overseer takes it all out of us in fines." So they took thought how to effect the purchase.

They had 100 roubles laid by; so that by selling a foal and half their bees, in addition to putting out their son to service, they managed to raise half the money.

Pakhom collected it all together, selected fifteen *dessiatins* and a small piece of timber land, and went to the *Barina* to arrange things. The bargain struck, they shook hands upon it, and Pakhom paid a deposit. Then he went to town, completed the conveyance (half the purchase money to be paid now, and half within two years' time)—and lo! Pakhom was a landowner! He also borrowed a small sum of his brother-in-law, wherewith to purchase seed. This he duly sowed in his newly acquired property, and a fine crop came up; so that within a year he had repaid both the *Barina* and his brother-in-law. He was now an absolute proprietor. It was his own land that he sowed, his own hay that he reaped, his own firewood that he cut, and his own cattle that he grazed. Whenever he rode out to his inalienable estate, either to plough or to inspect the crops and meadows, he felt overjoyed. The very grass seemed to him different to other grass, the flowers to bloom differently. Once, when he had ridden over his land, it was just—land; but now, although still land, it was land with a difference.

Thus did Pakhom live for a time, and was happy. Indeed, all would have been well if only the other peasants had left Pakhom's corn and pasture alone. In vain did he make repeated remonstrances. Shepherds would turn their flocks out into his meadows, and horses would somehow get into the corn at night. Again and again Pakhom drove them out and overlooked the matter, but at last he lost his temper and laid a complaint before the district court. He knew that the peasants only did it from lack of land, not maliciously; yet it could not be allowed, since they were eating the place up. He must teach them a lesson.

So he taught first one of them a lesson in court, and then another; had one fined, and then a second. This aroused feeling against him, and his neighbours now began, of set purpose, to steal his crops. One man got into the plantation at night, and stripped the bark off no less than ten linden-trees. When Pakhom next rode that way and saw what had been done he turned pale. He drew nearer, and perceived that bark had been stripped off and thrown about, and trunks uprooted. One tree only had the miscreant left, after lopping all its branches, but the rest he had cleared entirely in his evil progress. Pakhom was furious. "Ah!" he thought, "if only I knew who had done this, I would soon get my own back on him!" He wondered and wondered who it could be. If anyone in particular, it must be Semka. So he went to see Semka, but got nothing out of him except bad language: yet he felt more certain than ever now that it *was* Semka who had done it. He laid a complaint against him, and they were both of them summoned to attend the court. The magistrates sat and sat, and then dismissed the case for want of evidence. This enraged Pakhom still more. He abused both the *starshina* [1] and the magistrates. "You magistrates," he said, "are in league with thieves. If you were honest men you would never have acquitted Semka." Yes, there was no doubt that Pakhom was ill pleased both with the magistrates and with his neighbours. He began to live more and more apart on his land, and to have less and less to do with the *Mir*.

At this time there arose a rumour that some of the peasantry thereabouts were thinking of emigrating. This made Pakhom think to himself: "But there is no reason why I should leave *my* land. If some of the others go, why, it will make all the more room for me. I can buy up their land, and so hedge myself in all round. I should live much more comfortably then. At present I am too cramped."

It happened soon afterwards that Pakhom was sitting at home one day, when a travelling peasant dropped in. Pakhom gave him a night's lodging and a meal, and then questioned him, in the course of conversation, as to whence in the name of God he had come. To this the peasant replied that he had come from lower down the river—from a spot beyond the Volga, where he had been in service. Then he went on to relate how a settlement was being formed there, every settler being enrolled

[1] Village headman.

in the *Mir* and allotted ten *dessiatins* of land. It was *such* land, too, he said, and grew *such* rye! Why, the straw of the rye was tall enough to hide a horse, and thick enough together to make a sheaf per five handfuls! One peasant, he went on, who had arrived there a poor man and had had nothing but his two hands to work with now grew his fifty *dessiatins* of wheat. Indeed, during the past year that man had made 5000 roubles by his wheat alone!

Pakhom's soul was fired by this, and he thought to himself: "Why should I stay here, poor and cramped up, when I might be making such a fine living as that? I will sell out here—both land and homestead—and go and build myself a new house and farm there with the money. Here, in this cramped-up spot, life is one long worry. At any rate, I might take a trip there and make inquiries."

So when the summer came he got himself ready and set out. He took a steamer down the Volga to Samara, and thence tramped 400 versts[1] till he came to the place. It was all as had been described. The peasants lived splendidly, with ten *dessiatins* of free land to each soul, and he was assured of a welcome by the *Mir*. Moreover, he was told that anyone who came there with money could buy additional land—as much as ever he wanted—right out and in perpetuity. For three roubles a *dessiatin* a man could have the very finest land possible, and to any extent.

All this Pakhom learnt, and then returned home in the autumn. He began straightway to sell out, and succeeded in disposing both of land, buildings, and stock at a profit. Then he took his name off the *Mir's* books, waited for the spring, and departed to the new place with his family.

They duly arrived at their destination, and Pakhom was forthwith enrolled in the *Mir* of the great settlement (after moistening the elders' throats, of course, and executing the necessary documents). Then they took him and assigned him fifty *dessiatins* of land—ten for each soul of his family—in different parts of the estate, in addition to common pasturage. Pakhom built himself a homestead and stocked it, his allotted land alone being twice what he had formerly possessed in the old place. It was corn-bearing land, too. Altogether life was ten times better here than where he had come from, for he had at his disposal both arable and pasture land—sufficient of the latter always to keep as many cattle as he cared to have.

At first, while building and stocking, he thought everything splendid. Later, when he had settled down a bit, he began to feel cramped again. He wanted to grow white Turkish

[1] A verst is equal to $1166\frac{2}{3}$ linear yards.

wheat as several others did, but there was hardly any wheat-bearing land among his five allotments. Wheat needed to be grown on grass, new, or fallow land, and such land had to be sown one year and left fallow for two, in order that the grass might grow again. True, he had as much soft land as he wanted, but it would only bear rye. Wheat required hard land, and hard land found many applicants, and there was not enough at all. Moreover, such land gave rise to disputes. The richer peasants sowed their own, but the poorer had to mortgage theirs to merchants. The first year, Pakhom sowed his allotments with wheat, and got splendid crops. Then he wanted to sow them with wheat again, but they were not large enough to admit both of sowing new land and of leaving last year's land to lie fallow. He must get hold of some more. So he went to a merchant, and took a year's lease of some wheat land. He sowed as much of it as he could, and reaped a magnificent crop. Unfortunately, however, the land was a long way from the settlement—in fact, the crop had to be carted fifteen versts; so, as Pakhom had seen merchant farmers living in fine homesteads and growing rich in the district where the land lay, he thought to himself: "How would it be if I took a longer lease of it and built a homestead there the same as they have done? Then I should be right on the land." So he set about arranging to do so.

Thus did Pakhom live for five years, continually taking up land and sowing it with wheat. All the years were good ones, the wheat thrived, and the money came in. Yet just to live and live was rather tedious, and Pakhom began to tire of leasing land every year in a strange district and removing his stock there. Wherever there was a particularly good plot of land there would be a rush made for it by the other peasants, and it would be divided up before he was ready to lease and sow it as a whole. Once he went shares with a merchant in leasing a plot of pasturage of some peasants, and ploughed it up. Then the peasants lost it in a law-suit, and his labour went for nothing. If only it had been his own land, absolutely, he need have given in to no one and been put to no trouble.

So he began to cast about where he could buy an estate outright. In this endeavour he fell in with a certain peasant who had ruined himself and was ready to let him have his property of 500 *dessiatins* cheap. Pakhom entered into negotiations with him, and, after much discussion, closed at 1000 roubles—half down, and half to stand over. One day after they had thus clinched the matter, a merchant drove up to Pakhom's homestead to bait his horses. They drank a tea-pot empty and talked. The merchant said he had come a long,

long way—from the country of the Bashkirs, in fact, where (so he said) he had just purchased 5000 *dessiatins* for only 1000 roubles! Pakhom went on to question him further, and the merchant to answer. " All I did," said the latter, " was to make the elders there a few presents (*khalats*,[1] carpets, and a chest of tea), to distribute about a hundred roubles, and to stand *vodka* to anyone who felt inclined for it. In the result I got the land for twenty copecks[2] a *dessiatin*," and he showed Pakhom the deed. " The property," he concluded, " fronts upon a river, and is all of it open, grass, steppe land." Pakhom questioned him still further.

" You would not," went on the merchant, " find such land as that in a year. The same with all the Bashkir land. Moreover, the people there are as simple as sheep. You can get things out of them absolutely for nothing."

" Well," thought Pakhom, " what is the good of my giving 1000 roubles for only 500 *dessiatins*, and still leaving a debt round my neck, when there I might become a proprietor indeed for the same money? "

Pakhom inquired of the merchant as to how to reach the country of the Bashkirs, and as soon as his informant had departed, got ready for the journey. Leaving his wife at home, and taking with him only his workman, he set out first for the town, where he bought a chest of tea, *vodka*, and other gifts, as the merchant had advised. Then the two drove on and on until they had covered 500 versts, and on the seventh day arrived at the camp of the Bashkirs. Everything turned out to be as the merchant had said. The people there lived in hide-tilted wagons, which were drawn up by the side of a river running through the open steppe. They neither ploughed the land nor ate corn, while over the steppe wandered droves of cattle and Cossack horses, the foals being tied to the backs of the wagons and their dams driven up to them twice a day to give them milk. The chief sustenance of the people was mare's milk, which the women made into a drink called *kumiss*, and then churned the *kumiss* into cheese. In fact, the only drink the Bashkirs knew was either *kumiss* or tea, their only solid food mutton, and their only amusement pipe-playing. Nevertheless they all of them looked sleek and cheerful, and kept holiday the whole year round. In education they were sadly deficient, and knew no Russian, but were kindly and attractive folk for all that.

As soon as they caught sight of Pakhom they came out of their wagons and surrounded the guest. An interpreter was

[1] A *khalat* is a sort of long coat.
[2] Farthings.

found, and Pakhom told him that he had come to buy land. At once the people were delighted, and, embracing Pakhom fervently, escorted him to a well-appointed wagon, where they made him sit down on a pile of rugs topped with soft cushions, and set about getting some tea and *kumiss* ready. A sheep was killed, and a meal served of the mutton, after which Pakhom produced the gifts from his *tarantass*,[1] distributed them round, and shared out also the tea. Then the Bashkirs fell to talking among themselves for a while, and finally bade the interpreter speak.

"I am to tell you," said the interpreter, "that they are greatly taken with you, and that it is our custom to meet the wishes of a guest in every possible way, in return for the presents given us. Since, therefore, you have given us presents, say now what there is of ours which you may desire, so that we may grant it you."

"What I particularly desire," replied Pakhom, "is some of your land. Where I come from," he continued, "there is not enough land, and what there is is ploughed out, whereas you have much land, and good land, such as I have never before beheld."

The interpreter translated, and the Bashkirs talked again among themselves. Although Pakhom could not understand what they were saying, he could see that they kept crying out something in merry tones and then bursting into laughter. At last they stopped and looked at Pakhom, while the interpreter spoke.

"I am to tell you," he said, "that in return for your kindness we are ready to sell you as much land as you may wish. Merely make a gesture with your hand to signify how much, and it shall be yours."

At this point, however, the people began to talk among themselves again, and to dispute about something. On Pakhom asking what it was, the interpreter told him: "Some of them say that the Starshina ought to be asked first about the land, and that nothing should be done without him, while others say that that is not necessary."

Suddenly, while the Bashkirs were thus disputing, there entered the wagon a man in a foxskin cap, at whose entry everyone rose, while the interpreter said to Pakhom: "This is the Starshina himself." At once Pakhom caught up the best *khalat* and offered it to the newcomer, as well as five pounds of tea. The Starshina duly accepted them, and then sat down in the place of honour, while the Bashkirs began to expound to him some matter or another. He listened and listened, then gave a smile, and spoke to Pakhom in Russian.

[1] Light two-wheeled cart.

"Very well," he said, "pray choose your land wheresoever it pleases you. We have much land."

"So I am to take as much as I want!" thought Pakhom to himself. "Still, I must strengthen that bargain somehow. They might say, 'The land is yours,' and then take it away again."

"I thank you," he said aloud, "for your kind speech. As you say, you have much land, whereas I am in need of some. I only desire to know precisely which of it is to be mine; wherefore it might be well to measure it off by some method and duly convey it to me. God only is lord of life and death, and, although you are good people who now give it to me, it might befall that your children would take it away again."

The Starshina smiled.

"The conveyance," he said, "is already executed. This present meeting is our mode of confirming it—and it could not be a surer one."

"But," said Pakhom, "I have been told that a merchant visited you recently, and that you sold him land and gave him a proper deed of conveyance. Pray, therefore, do the same with me."

The Starshina understood now.

"Very well," he replied, "We have a writer here, and will go to a town and procure the necessary seals."

"But what is your price for the land?" asked Pakhom.

"Our price," answered the Starshina, "is only 1000 roubles per day."

Pakhom did not understand this day-rate at all.

"How many *dessiatins* would that include?" he inquired presently.

"We do not reckon in that way," said the Starshina. "We sell only by the day. That is to say, as much land as you can walk round in a day, that much land is yours. That is our measure, and the price is 1000 roubles."

Pakhom was astounded.

"Why, a man might walk round a great deal in a day," he said.

The Starshina smiled again.

"Well, at all events," he said, "it will be yours. *Only*, there is one condition—namely, that if on that same day you do not return to the spot whence you started, your money is forfeited."

"But how do you decide upon that spot?" asked Pakhom.

"We take our stand," replied the Starshina, "upon whatsoever spot you may select. I and my people remain here, while you start off and describe a circle. Behind you will ride some of our young men, to plant stakes wherever you may desire that to be done. Thereafter a plough will be driven round those stakes. Describe what circle you wish; only, by the time of the setting of the sun you must have returned to the place from which you started. As much land as you may circle, that much land will be yours."

So Pakhom accepted these terms, and it was agreed to make an early start on the morrow. Then the company talked again, drank more *kumiss*, and ate more mutton, passing on thence to tea, and the ceremonies being prolonged until nightfall. At length Pakhom was led to a bed of down and the Bashkirs dispersed, after first promising to gather on the morrow beyond the river and ride out to the appointed spot before sunrise.

Pakhom lay on his bed of down, but could not get a wink of sleep for thinking of the land which, as he said, "I am going to farm here."

"For I mean to mark out a very large 'Promised Land' to-morrow," he continued to himself. "I can cover at least fifty versts in the day, and fifty versts should enclose somewhere about 10,000 *dessiatins*. Then I shall be under nobody's thumb, and be able to afford a pair-ox plough and two labourers. I shall plough up the best land, and feed stock on the rest."

All that night Pakhom never closed his eyes, but dozed off for a short while just before dawn. The instant he did so he had a dream. He seemed to be lying in this identical wagon and listening to somebody laughing and talking outside. Wishing to see who it was that was laughing so much, he went outside, and saw the Starshina sitting on the ground and holding his sides as he rolled about in ecstasies of mirth. Then in his dream Pakhom walked up to him and asked him what the joke was—and immediately saw that it was not the Starshina at all, but the merchant who had so lately visited him to tell him about this land. Then again, he had scarcely so much as said to the merchant, "Did I not see you at my home a little while ago?" when the merchant suddenly changed into the peasant from away down the Volga who had called at his farm in the old country. Finally Pakhom perceived that this peasant was not a peasant at all, but the Devil himself, with horns and hoofs, and that he was gazing fixedly at something as he sat there and laughed. Then Pakhom thought to himself: "What is he looking at, and why does he laugh so much?" And in his dream he stepped a little aside to look, and saw a man—barefooted, and clad only in a shirt and breeches—lying flat on his back, with his face as white as a sheet. And presently, looking yet more attentively at the man, Pakhom saw that the man was himself!

He gave a gasp and awoke—awoke feeling as if the dream were real. Then he looked to see if it were getting light yet, and saw that the dawn was near.

"It is time to start," he thought. "I must arouse these good people."

Pakhom arose, awakened his workman in the *tarantass*, and told him to put the horse in and go round to call the Bashkirs, since it was time to go out upon the steppe and measure off the land. So the Bashkirs arose and got themselves ready, and the Starshina also arrived. They breakfasted off *kumiss*, and were for giving Pakhom some tea, but he could not wait. "If we are to go, let us go," he said. "It is fully time." So the Bashkirs harnessed up and set out, some on horseback, and some in carts, while Pakhom drove in his *tarantass* with his workman. They came out upon the steppe just as the dawn was breaking, and proceeded towards a little knoll—called in the Bashkir dialect a *shichan*. There the people in carts alighted, and everyone collected together. The Starshina approached Pakhom and pointed all round with his hand. "Whatsoever land you see from here," he said, "is ours. Choose whichsoever direction you like." Pakhom's eyes glowed, for all the land was grass, level as the palm of his hand, and black beneath the turf as a poppy-head. Only where there was a ravine was there a break in the grass—grass which was everywhere breast-high. The Starshina took off his foxskin cap, and laid it in the exact centre of the knoll. "This," he said, "will be the mark. Lay you your money in it, and your servant shall remain beside it while you are gone. From this mark you will start, and to this mark you will return. As much land as you circle, all of it will be yours."

Pakhom took out his money, and laid it in the cap. Then he divested himself of his cloak, stripped himself to his waistcoat, tightened his belt round his stomach, thrust his wallet with some bread into his bosom, tied a flask of water to his shoulder-strap, pulled up his long boots, and prepared to start. He kept debating within himself which direction it would be best to take, for the land was so good everywhere. "Oh, well, as it is all the same, I will walk towards the rising sun," he decided at length. So he turned his face that way, and kept trying his limbs while waiting for the sun to appear. "I must lose no time," he thought, "for I shall do my best walking while the air is yet cool."

Then the mounted Bashkirs also ascended the knoll, and stationed themselves behind Pakhom. No sooner had the sun shot his first rays above the horizon than Pakhom started forward and walked out into the steppe, the mounted men riding behind them.

He walked neither slowly nor hurriedly. After he had gone about a verst he stopped, and had a stake put in. Then he went on again. He was losing his first stiffness and beginning to lengthen his stride. Presently he stopped again, and had another stake put in. He looked up at the sun—which was now lighting the knoll clearly, with the people standing there—and calculated that he had gone about five versts. He was beginning to grow warm now, so he took off his waistcoat, and then fastened up his belt again. Then he went on another five versts, and stopped. It was growing really hot now. He looked at the sun again, and saw that it was breakfast time. "One stage done!" he thought. "But there are four of them in the day, and it is early yet to change my direction. Nevertheless, I must take my boots off." So he sat down, took them off, and went on again. Walking was easier now. "As soon as I have covered another five versts," he reflected, "I will begin to bend round to the left. That spot was exceedingly well chosen. The farther I go, the better the land is." So he kept straight on, although, when he looked round, the knoll was almost out of sight, and the people on it looked like little black ants.

"Now," he said to himself at length, "I have made the circle large enough, and must bend round." He had sweated a good deal and was thirsty, so he raised the flask and took a drink. Then he had a stake put in at that point, and bent round sharply to the left. On he went and on, through the high grass and the burning heat. He was beginning to tire now, and, glancing at the sun, saw that it was dinner-time. "Now," he thought to himself, "I might venture to take a rest." So he stopped and ate some bread, though without sitting down, since he said to himself: "If I once sat down I should go on to *lying* down, and so end by going off to sleep." He waited a little, therefore, till he felt rested, and then went on again. At first he found walking easy, for the meal had revived his strength, but presently the sun seemed to grow all the hotter as it began to slant towards evening. Pakhom was nearly worn out now, yet he merely thought to himself: "An hour's pain may a century gain."

He had traversed about ten versts of this lap of the circle, and was about to bend inwards again to the left, when he caught sight of an excellent bit of land round a dry ravine. It would be a pity to leave that out. "Flax would grow so splendidly there!" he thought. So he kept straight on until he had taken in the ravine, and, having had a stake planted at the spot, again wheeled inwards. Looking towards the knoll he could see that the people there were almost indistinguishable. They could not be less than fifteen versts away. "Well," he thought, "I have covered the two long laps of the circuit, and must take this last one by the shortest cut possible." So he started upon the last lap, and quickened his pace. Once again he looked at the sun. It was now drawing near to the time of the evening meal, and he had only covered two versts of the distance. The starting point was still thirteen versts away. "I must hurry straight along now," he said to himself, "however rough the country be. I must not take in a single extra piece on the way. I have enclosed sufficient as it is." And Pakhom headed straight for the knoll.

He pressed on straight in its direction, yet found walking very difficult now. His feet were aching badly, for he had chafed and bruised them, and they were beginning to totter under him. He would have given anything to have rested for a while, yet knew that he must not if he was ever to regain the knoll before sunset. The sun at least would not wait. Nay, it was like a driver ever lashing him on. From time to time he staggered. "Surely I have not miscalculated?" he thought to himself. "Surely I have not taken in too much land ever to get back, however much I hurry? There is such a long way to go yet, and I am dead beat. It cannot be that all my money and toil have gone in vain? Ah, well, I must do my best."

Pakhom pulled himself together, and broke into a run. He had torn his feet till they were bleeding, yet he still ran on, ran on, ran further and further. Waistcoat, boots, flask, cap—he flung them all away. "Ah!" was his thought, "I was too pleased with what I saw. Now everything is lost, and I shall never reach the mark before sunset." His fears served to render him only the more breathless, but he still ran on, his shirt and breeches clinging to his limbs with sweat, and his mouth parched. In his breasts there were a pair of blacksmith's bellows working, and in his heart a steam hammer, while his legs seemed to be breaking under him and to be no longer his own. He had lost all thought of the land now. All that he thought of was to avoid dying from exertion. Yet, although he was so afraid of dying, he could not stop. "To have gone so far," he thought, "and then to stop! Why, they would think me a fool!" By this time he could hear the Bashkirs cheering and shouting to him, and their cries stirred his heart with fresh spirit. On, on he ran with his last remaining strength, while the sun was just touching the horizon. Ah, but he was close to the spot now! He could see the people on the knoll waving their hands to him and urging him on. He could see the foxskin cap lying on the ground, the money in it, the Starshina sitting beside it with his hands pressed to his sides. Suddenly Pakhom remembered his dream. " Yet I have much land now," he thought, " if only God should bring me safe to live upon it. But my heart misgives me that I have killed myself." Still he ran on. For the last time he looked at the sun. Large and red, it had touched the earth, and was beginning to sink below the horizon. Pakhom reached the knoll just as it set. " Ah! " he cried in his despair, for he thought that everything was lost. Suddenly, however, he remembered that he could not see from below so well as could the people on the knoll above him, and that to them the sun would still seem not to have set. He rushed at the slope, and could see as he scrambled up it that the cap was still there. Then he stumbled and fell—yet in the very act of falling stretched out his hands towards the cap—and touched it!

" Ah, young man," cried the Starshina, " you have earned much land indeed! "

Pakhom's servant ran to his master and tried to raise him, but blood was running from his mouth. Pakhom lay there dead. The servant cried out in consternation, but the Starshina remained sitting on his haunches—laughing, and holding his hands to his sides.

At length he got up, took a spade from the ground, and threw it to the servant.

" Bury him," was all he said.

The Bashkirs arose and departed. Only the servant remained. He dug a grave of the same length as Pakhom's form from head to heels—three Russian ells—and buried him.

ANTON CHEHOV

THE KISS

AT eight o'clock in the evening of 20th May the six batteries of the " U " reserve artillery on its way to camp stopped for the night in the village of Mestechko. During the bustle, when some officers were busy with the guns and others scattered over the square hearing the reports of the quartermasters, a horseman in civilian clothes appeared from behind the church on a curious, small light bay with a beautiful neck and a clipped tail, which ran sideways rather than straight, and threw out its legs in short frisky movements as though they were being lashed with a whip. The horseman drew up by a group of officers and, raising his hat, said:

" His Excellency General von Rabbek, the squire here, would be glad if you gentlemen would come and take tea with him."

The horse frisked and backed sideways; the horseman once more raised his hat and, turning, disappeared behind the church with his strange-looking animal.

" Damn! " some of the officers grumbled, departing to their quarters. " A fellow wants to sleep, and here comes this von Rabbek with his tea! We know what that means! "

And every officer in the six batteries vividly recalled an incident that had happened to them last year during manœuvres when, together with the officers of a certain Cossack regiment, they were invited to tea in this manner by a certain count and retired officer, and how the cordial, hospitable count had entertained them royally and insisted on their spending the night in his house instead of at their quarters. It was all very nice, of course, and nothing better could have been desired, only the count was overmuch pleased with the society of the young men. Until daybreak he wearied them with episodes of his own happy past, led them from room to room to show them his costly pictures, old engravings and rare pieces of armour; he even read them letters he had received from various celebrities, and the tired officers listened and looked, inwardly longing for their beds and yawning cautiously behind their palms; when at last their host released them it was too late to go to bed.

Was von Rabbek by any chance such another? However, there was nothing to be done. The officers washed and dressed and set off together to find the squire's house. In the square by the church they were told that they could cut down to the river by a path behind the church, and then along the bank till they came to the squire's own garden, and the avenue would bring them to the door, or they could ride along the road that turned off half a verst up by the squire's barns. The officers chose the latter.

"Who is this von Rabbek?" they asked each other on the way. "Is he the man who commanded the 'U' cavalry division in Plevna?"

"No, that was not von Rabbek, but simply Rabbe, without the von."

"What lovely weather it is!"

At the first barn the road divided in two—the one straight ahead vanished into the evening darkness, the other to the right led to the squire's house. The officers turned to the right and lowered their voices. On either side of the road stretched the stone barns with red roofs, massive and sombre, like the barracks of a provincial town.

"A good sign, gentlemen," one of the officers remarked. "Our setter is in front, which means that he scents game!"

Ahead of us all was Lieutenant Lobitko, tall and broad-shouldered, with clean upper lip. He was twenty-five, though his full round face did not show it. He was famous in the brigade for his knack of sensing the presence of women in a place, even at a distance. He turned round and said:

"Yes, I am sure there are women here; I feel it by instinct."

At the door of the house the officers were met by von Rabbek himself, a handsome old man of sixty, in civilian clothes. Shaking hands with his guests, he said that he was pleased and happy to see them, but begged them to excuse him for not having invited them to stay the night; his two sisters and their children had come, as well as his brothers and some neighbours, and in consequence he had not a single spare room.

The general was affability itself, but from the expression of his face it was obvious that he was not quite as overjoyed with his guests as the count of last year, and that he had invited them merely out of a sense of politeness. And this was made quite clear to them as they walked up the carpeted stairs, listening to their host, and saw the footmen hurrying to light the lamps in the hall and on the staircase. They felt that they were a nuisance in the house. Under a roof where two sisters and brothers and neighbours had gathered together, perhaps for the celebration of some family event, how could the family be pleased with the presence of nineteen strangers?

At the drawing-room door the guests were received by a tall, graceful old lady with an oval-shaped face and dark brows, who resembled the Empress Eugénie. With a gracious smile she welcomed them, apologising for not being able to ask them to stay the night. By the smile that disappeared from her face the moment she turned away, it was plain that the lady had seen many officers in her day and that she had no use for them now, and that if she had invited them to her house and was offering her excuses, it was only because her breeding and position demanded it of her.

When the officers entered the dining-room about a dozen men and women, old and young, were sitting at one end of a long table having tea. Behind their chairs, enveloped in cigar smoke, was a group of men, in the midst of whom a thin young man with red mustachios was speaking in English in a loud voice. Behind the group, through a door, was a view of a brightly lighted room with pale blue furniture.

"Gentlemen, there are so many of you that it is impossible to introduce you all!" the general said aloud with an effort at gaiety. "Please introduce yourselves in a homely way."

The officers—some with solemn countenances, others with strained smiles, and all feeling extremely uncomfortable, bowed and seated themselves at the table. There was one among them who felt more uncomfortable than the rest—the staff officer Riabovitch, a round-shouldered little man in spectacles.

At the moment when some of his comrades put on a serious expression and others constrained themselves to smile, his face, lynx-like mustachios, spectacles and all, seemed to say, "I am the shyest, most modest, most colourless officer in the whole brigade!" When he first entered the room and sat down by the table he could not fix his attention on any one particular object or face—faces, garments, cut-glass decanters of cognac, the steam from the glasses, the stucco cornices—all mingled into a single impression that confused Riabovitch and aroused in him a desire to hide his head. Like a lecturer facing his audience for the first time, he saw the objects before his eyes, but seemed to comprehend nothing. (This condition, when a subject sees without comprehending, is known among physiologists as "psychological blindness.") Becoming used to his surroundings after a while, Riabovitch began to look about him. Being a shy man unused to society, he was first of all struck by the unusual courage of his new acquaintance—von Rabbek, his wife, two elderly ladies, a girl in a lilac dress, a young man with red whiskers, that turned out to be Rabbek's youngest son, who had very cleverly, as though they had rehearsed the thing beforehand, distributed themselves among the officers and begun an enthusiastic discussion in which the guests could not help but join. The lilac girl maintained warmly that life in the artillery was much easier than in the cavalry or infantry, while Rabbek and one of the old ladies defended an opposite view. A cross-conversation arose. Riabovitch looked at the lilac girl discussing a subject she knew nothing about and that she was not the least interested in, and watched the artificial smiles playing over her face.

Von Rabbek and his wife cleverly drew the officers into the discussion, keeping a careful eye meanwhile on their guests' glasses and plates to see that all were eating and drinking. The more Riabovitch looked and listened, the more he liked this insincere though excellently disciplined family.

After tea the officers went into the drawing-room. Lieutenant Lobitko's instinct had not failed him; there were many girls and young women in the room. The setter lieutenant stood near a fair young girl in a black dress, bending gallantly towards her as though he were leaning on an invisible sword. He smiled and moved his shoulders coquettishly. He must have been talking some interesting nonsense, no doubt, for the fair girl looked condescendingly at his round face and said indifferently, "Really?" By this apathetic "really" the setter, had he been wise, might have known that she was not very much entertained.

Someone began to play a melancholy valse on the piano; the sad air floating through the wide-open windows made everyone remember that it was May and that the weather was beautiful, and that the scent of lilac and rose and young poplars was in the air.

Riabovitch, who in addition to the music was under the influence of the cognac he had drunk, leant against the window, smiling. He began to follow the movements of the women, and it seemed to him that the scent of rose and lilac and poplar did not come from the garden but from their faces and dresses.

Von Rabbek's son invited a tall, thin girl to dance, and took two or three turns round the room. Lobitko glided over the polished floor to the girl in lilac and whirled her away across the room. The dancing began. . . . Riabovitch stood by the door among the non-dancing men and watched. He had never once danced in his life, nor had it ever fallen to his lot to put his arm around the waist of a respectable woman. The idea that a man in the sight of all should take a strange young girl by the waist and offer his shoulder for her arm to rest on was very pleasing to Riabovitch, but he could never imagine himself in the position of such a man. There had been a time when he had envied the courage and daring of his comrades, and his heart had sickened at the consciousness that he was shy and round-shouldered and colourless and that he had lynx-like mustachios, but with the years he became reconciled; as he now gazed at the dancing couples and at those talking in loud assured voices he no longer envied them, he was affected only by a feeling of sadness.

When the quadrille was about to begin young von Rabbek came up to the non-dancing men and invited a couple of the officers to a game of billiards. The officers followed him out of the drawing-room. Riabovitch, from want of something to do and a desire to participate in some way in the general bustle, went after them. They walked through the drawing-room, then along a narrow glass corridor and into another room, where three sleepy footmen jumped up hastily from a couch at their appearance, and, passing through a host of other rooms, they at last entered the billiard-room. The game began.

Riabovitch, who never played at anything but cards, stood by the table looking indifferently at the players, while they, coats unbuttoned, cues in hand, walked about joking and calling out incomprehensible words. The players took no notice of him, only now and again when someone accidentally hit him with an elbow or a cue they turned with a polite " pardon ! " The first game had scarcely finished when he grew tired of it, and it seemed to him that he was not wanted there and was in the way. Again he was drawn to the ballroom and went out.

On his way back he met with a little adventure. About half-way he observed that he was not going in the right direction. He remembered quite well that he should have passed through a room where there were three sleepy footmen, but he had gone through six rooms and the footmen seemed to have vanished. Seeing his mistake he went back a little way, and turning to the right entered a dimly lighted room which he did not remember to have seen on his way to the billiard-room; standing still for a moment, he resolutely opened the first door that met his gaze and found himself in a dark room. In front of him through the cracks in a door a bright light shone through, and from behind the door came the muffled strains of a sad melody. Here, as in the ballroom, the windows were wide open and there was a scent of poplar, lilac and rose. . . .

Riabovitch stopped in perplexity. At this moment he heard a hurried footstep and the rustle of a dress, a woman's voice full of emotion whispered " At last! " and two soft, fragrant arms, unmistakably a woman's, were put around his neck; a warm cheek was laid against his own, and at the same moment there was the sound of a kiss. But instantly the woman gave a faint cry and, it seemed to Riabovitch, jumped away from him in horror. He, too, nearly cried out and made a rush towards the bright crack in the door. . . .

When he returned to the ballroom his heart beat fast and his hands trembled so visibly that he hastily hid them behind his back. For the first few moments he was torn by shame and terror. It seemed to him that everyone in the room must know that he had just been embraced and kissed by a woman, and he cast an anxious glance around, but being convinced that all were dancing and chatting calmly as before, he abandoned himself to the enjoyment of the sensation experienced for the first time in his life. Something strange had happened to him. . . . His neck, that had only just been encircled by two soft, fresh arms, seemed to him to be anointed with oil; on his cheek near the left ear, where the strange unknown had kissed him, was a pleasant sensation of cold as from peppermint drops, and the more he rubbed the spot the greater this sensation became; from the crown of his head to the soles of his feet he was filled with a new strange feeling that grew and grew. . . . He wanted to dance, to talk, to run out into the garden, to laugh aloud. . . . He had quite forgotten that he was round-shouldered and colourless, that his appearance " was indefinite " (as a lady of his acquaintance had said in a conversation with another woman, a conversation he happened to have overheard). When von Rabbek's wife passed him, he gave her such a broad, kindly smile that she stopped and looked at him in surprise.

" I do like your house! " he said, refixing his spectacles.

The general's wife smiled and remarked that the house had belonged to her father, then she went on to ask him if his parents were alive, and how long he had been in the service, and why he was so thin, and so on. . . . After talking to him for a while she went on further, and Riabovitch began to smile still more broadly and kindly and to imagine that he was surrounded by the kindest of people. . . .

At supper Riabovitch ate and drank mechanically everything that was placed before him. He did not hear a word that was being said and tried to puzzle out his recent adventure. The adventure was both mysterious and romantic, but not difficult to explain. Some girl or a married woman, perhaps, had arranged to meet some man in that dark room, and being in a state of nervous excitement because she had waited a long time, she had mistaken Riabovitch for her hero, particularly as Riabovitch had stopped in uncertainty when he had entered the room, as though he, too, were expecting to meet someone. . . . In this way Riabovitch accounted for the kiss he had received.

"But who is she?" he thought, gazing round at the faces of the women. "She must be young, for old women do not arrange meetings with men. And she must be intellectual; I felt it in the rustle of her dress, in the scent about her, in her voice. . . ."

His gaze alighted on the girl in lilac and she seemed very attractive to him; she had beautiful shoulders and arms, an intelligent face, and a beautiful voice. Looking at her Riabovitch determined that she and none other should be his fair unknown. . . . But she smiled in an artificial way and screwed up her long nose, which made her seem old; then he removed his gaze to the fair girl in the black dress. She was younger and simpler, had beautiful temples and a pretty manner of drinking out of her glass. Riabovitch now wanted her to be his unknown, but soon he found that her features were too flat, and turned his attention to her neighbour.

"One can't tell," he thought musingly. "If one could take the shoulders and arms of the girl in lilac and add the temples of the fair girl and the eyes of the one sitting on Lobitko's left, then . . ."

In imagination he modelled the form of the girl who had kissed him, a form that he desired but could not see at the table.

After supper the guests, satisfied and a little the worse for drink, thanked their hosts and took their leave. Once more the general and his wife apologised for not being able to put them up for the night.

"Very glad to have met you, gentlemen!" the general said, quite sincerely this time. (Departing guests are treated more frankly than arriving ones.) "Very glad! I hope you will come and see us on your way back! Quite simply, you know. Which way are you going? Are you riding? If not, go down by the garden, it is much nearer."

The officers went out into the garden. After the bright light and the noise it seemed to them very dark and still in the garden. They walked to the gate without speaking.

They were half-drunk, merry and contented, but the darkness and stillness made them pensive for a moment. No doubt the same thought had occurred to them as to Riabovitch. Would they, like Rabbek, one day possess a big house, a family, a garden, and would they have the opportunity of entertaining guests, even insincerely, and of making them drunk and contented?

Coming out of the gate, they began to talk all at once and to laugh without any cause. They were now walking along the path that led down to the river and ran along the water's edge, winding round bushes and overhanging willows. The bank and the path were scarcely visible, and the opposite bank was completely enveloped in darkness. Here and there in the dark water were the reflections of stars, and only by the way they trembled and swam asunder could one tell that the river was flowing swiftly. The air was still. Sleepy woodcocks called on the opposite bank, and on a bush a nightingale, disregarding the officers, poured out its song. One of them stopped by the bush and shook it, but the nightingale continued to sing.

"What a brave beggar!" approving voices exclaimed. "Here we are, standing near him, and he takes no notice of us, the rogue!"

Towards the end the path began to ascend, and by the church it led out on to the road. Here the officers, out of breath with their walk uphill, sat down to smoke. A dim red light appeared on the opposite bank, and from want of something to do they spent a long time in speculating whether it was a camp-fire, a light in a window, or something else. . . . Riabovitch also gazed at the light, and it seemed to him that it smiled and winked at him, as though it knew about the kiss.

Reaching his quarters, Riabovitch undressed quickly and went to bed. In the same hut were Lobitko and Lieutenant Mersliakov, the latter a quiet taciturn fellow, who was held to be a cultured man, and who always read *The Messenger of Europe*, which review he carried about with him everywhere. Lobitko undressed and paced the room from end to end with a dissatisfied air, then he sent the orderly for beer. Mersliakov got into bed, at the head of which he placed a candle, then buried himself in the pages of the review.

"I wonder who she was?" Riabovitch thought, gazing at the grimy ceiling.

His neck still seemed to be anointed with oil, and a sensation of cold as of peppermint was still about his mouth. His imagination conjured up images of the shoulders and arms of the girl in lilac, the temples of the fair girl in black, her waist, garments, jewels. He tried to fix his attention on these images, but they danced before his eyes, appearing and disappearing. When, on shutting his eyes the images completely vanished, he could hear hasty footsteps, the rustle of a dress, the sound of a kiss, and a feeling of intense unreasoning joy took possession of him. As he abandoned himself to this feeling he heard the orderly return and say that no beer was to be had. Lobitko was much annoyed and again began to pace the room.

" Isn't he an idiot? " he said, stopping now by Riabovitch's bed, now by Mersliakov's. " A man must be a dolt and a fool not to be able to get beer, what? The rascal! "

" Of course he can't get beer here," Mersliakov remarked, without looking up from the pages of his journal.

" Why do you think so? " Lobitko persisted. " I'll bet you anything I'll find some beer, and women too! I'll go this minute. . . . You can call me any names you like if I don't find them! "

He took a long time in dressing and pulling on his long boots, then he lighted a cigarette and went out without another word.

" Rabbek, Grabbek, Labbek," he mumbled, stopping in the passage. " I don't feel like going alone, damn it! Riabovitch, won't you come for a stroll, eh? "

Receiving no reply, he came back, undressed slowly, and went to bed. Mersliakov sighed, threw his journal aside, and blew out the candle.

" Yes," Lobitko muttered, smoking a cigarette in the darkness.

Riabovitch pulled the bed-clothes over his head, and curling up began piecing together the disconnected images floating about in his brain, but he failed to obtain any result. He soon fell asleep, his last thought being that someone had caressed and made him happy. Some good, joyous thing had come into his life even though it was senseless. This thought did not leave him even in sleep.

When he awoke the feeling of oil on his neck and the sensation of cold as from peppermint around his lips had left him, but as yesterday a feeling of joy filled his heart. In ecstasy he gazed at the window-frames turned golden by the rising sun, and listened to the noise in the street without. A loud conversation was going on under his very window. His battery-commander, Lebedetsky, who had only just caught up the brigade was talking to a sergeant at the top of his voice from force of habit, never speaking in any other tone of voice.

" And what else? " the commander cried.

" Golubushka was hurt when she was shod, your Honour;

the surgeon applied some clay and vinegar. And last night, your Honour, Mechanic Artiemev was drunk, and the lieutenant ordered him to be put on the reserve gun-carriage."

The sergeant informed him also that Karpov had forgotten the new lanyards for the friction-tubes and the pegs for the tents, and that the officers had spent the evening at General von Rabbek's. During the conversation Lebedetsky's red beard appeared at the window. His short-sighted eyes peered at the sleepy faces of the officers; he greeted them.

"Is everything all right?" he asked.

"The saddle-horse galled his withers with the new yoke," Lobitko replied with a yawn.

The commander sighed, deliberated for a while, then said aloud:

"I was thinking of going to Alexandra Evgrafovna—I must pay her a visit. Good-bye. I will catch you up by the evening."

In a quarter of an hour the brigade had started on its way. When they had passed von Rabbek's barns Riabovitch looked at the house. The blinds were still down. The inmates were doubtless asleep. And she, too, slept—the girl who had kissed Riabovitch yesterday. He tried to picture her sleeping. There was the wide-open window of her bedroom, the green branches peeping in, the fresh morning air, the scent of poplar, lilac and rose, the bed, a chair with the dress she had worn yesterday thrown over it, slippers, a watch on the table—all these objects he saw clearly and precisely, but the girl's features, her sweet dreamy smile, the very thing he most desired to see, slipped his imagination as quicksilver slips through the fingers. About half a verst further on he turned round; the yellow church, the house, the river and garden were bathed in light; the river looked beautiful with its bright green banks, reflections of the sky, and silver patches of sunlight. Once more Riabovitch looked at the village, and a feeling of sadness came over him, as though he were leaving something very near and dear to him behind.

On the road, only the familiar scenes, void of interest, met the eye. To the right were fields of young rye and buckwheat and hopping rooks; in front, dust and the napes of human necks; behind, the same dust and faces. Ahead of the column marched four soldiers with guns—the vanguard. Next came the bandsmen. Vanguard and bandsmen, like mutes in a funeral procession, now and then ignoring the regulation intervals, marched too far ahead. Riabovitch with the fifth battery could see four batteries in front of him.

To a civilian, the marching brigade, long and cumbersome, presented a novel, interesting spectacle. It is hard to understand why a single gun needs so many men, or why so many strangely harnessed horses are needed to drag it, but to Riabovitch, who was familiar with all these things, it was extremely dull and uninteresting. He had learned years ago why a solid sergeant-major rides beside the officer in front of each battery and the drivers of leaders and wheelers behind them. Riabovitch knew why the near horses were called saddle-horses and the off horses led-horses, and he found it all intensely boring. On one of the wheelers rode a soldier, his back still covered with yesterday's dust and a clumsy ridiculous guard on his leg. Riabovitch knew the use of this guard and found it in no way ridiculous. The horsemen, every man of them, rode mechanically, with an occasional cry or flourish of the whip. The guns were not beautiful to look at. On the limbers were tarpaulin sacks full of oats, and the guns themselves, hung round with teapots, the soldiers' wallets and bags, looked like some harmless animals surrounded for some reason by horses and men. On the lee side of each gun, brandishing their arms, marched six gunners, and behind came more leaders, wheelers and more guns, each as ugly and uninspiring as the one in front. Behind the second followed a third and then a fourth, by the fourth an officer, and so on. There were six batteries in the brigade, and each battery had four guns. The cavalcade stretched about half a verst along the road. At the end came a train of wagons, near which, with head bent in thought, walked the donkey Ulagar, who had been brought over from Turkey by a battery commander.

Riabovitch gazed indifferently at the necks in front and the faces behind; another day he would have closed his eyes and tried to doze, but now he abandoned himself to his new and pleasant thoughts. When the brigade had first started he tried to convince himself that the incident of the kiss was only a funny little adventure that could not be taken seriously, but he soon waved logic aside and abandoned himself to his dreams. . . . He imagined himself in the Rabbeks' drawing-room, now by the side of a girl resembling the one in lilac and the fair girl in black, now, when he closed his eyes, by the side of a strange girl with vague, elusive features. In thought he spoke to her, caressed her, drew her to his breast. He imagined himself going to the wars and leaving her behind, then the return and the supper with his wife and children.

"To the brakes!" rang the command before the descent of each hill. He too cried, "To the brakes!" dreading each time that the cry would break the spell of his dream and bring him back to reality.

They passed a large country house. Riabovitch looked over the hedge into the garden. An avenue, long and straight as a rule, met the eye, strewn with yellow gravel and planted with young birches. . . . With the ecstasy of a dreamer he pictured tiny feminine feet walking along the yellow path, and unexpected the image of the girl who had kissed him rose before his mind, the girl he had been unable to visualise yesterday at supper. This image became fixed in his brain and never afterwards left him.

At midday a loud command was heard from the rear of the column:

" Attention! Eyes right! Officers! "

In a carriage drawn by a pair of white horses was the brigade general. He stopped by the second battery and called out something that no one understood. Several officers rode up, Riabovitch among them.

" Well, how goes it? " the general asked, blinking his reddened eyes. " Are there any sick? "

Receiving a reply, the little general mused for a moment, then turned to one of the officers:

" The driver of your third gun wheeler has taken off his leg-guard and hung it on the limber, the blackguard. Punish him." He raised his eyes to Riabovitch and continued, " And the breechings of your harness are too long."

After a few more tiresome remarks the general turned to Lobitko with a smile.

" Why so sad to-day, Lieutenant Lobitko? " he asked. " Are you sighing for Madame Lopukhova, eh? Gentlemen, Lobitko is sighing for Madame Lopukhova! "

Madame Lopukhova was a tall, portly lady, well on the wrong side of forty. The general, who had a weakness for large women of any age, suspected his officers of a like taste. The officers smiled respectfully. The general, pleased with his amusing sally, laughed aloud, then touched the coachman's back and saluted. The carriage rolled away.

" Though it seems to me like the wildest if dreams, beyond the range of possibility, it is really a very commonplace thing." Riabovitch mused, gazing at the cloud of dust raised by the general's carriage. " It is very usual and happens to every-one. . . . Take the general, for instance; he must have fallen in love; now he is married and has children of his own. Captain Bachter is also married and loved, no doubt, for all that he has an ugly neck and no waist; and Salmanov is a rough fellow, too much of the Tartar, yet he had a love affair that ended in marriage. I am just as other men, and sooner or later the same fate will befall me. . . ."

And the thought that he was an ordinary man and that his life was ordinary rejoiced and encouraged him. He gave free rein to his imagination and pictured *her* and his future happiness as he would like it to be.

When the brigade reached its destination and the officers rested in the tents, Riabovitch, Mersliakov and Lobitko were seated at supper round a box. Mersliakov ate slowly, reading *The Messenger of Europe* lying on his knee. Lobitko talked incessantly and kept on filling his glass with beer, and Riabovitch, whose head was in a whirl with his long day-dreams, drank silently. After the third glass he grew tipsy and weak; an uncontrollable desire came over him to tell his colleagues of his new emotions.

" A funny incident happened to me at those Rabbeks'," he began, trying to give an indifferent, disdainful tone to his voice. " I went into the billiard-room, you know." . . . And he related the tale of the kiss in detail and was surprised that it took so little time in the telling—not more than a minute at most. It seemed to him that the story of the kiss would have taken at least till the morning in the telling. Lobitko, who was a confirmed liar, and thus believed no one else, looked at Riabovitch with an incredulous smile. Mersliakov raised his brows, and without looking up from his journal said:

" A strange thing, to be sure! to throw herself on a man's neck without a word. The girl must be neurotic, I should think."

" No doubt," Riabovitch agreed.

" A similar incident once happened to me," Lobitko began. " I was travelling to Kovna last year, second class. The carriage was packed with people; to sleep was impossible. I gave the conductor half a rouble and he took up my luggage and led me into a sleeping car. I lay down and covered myself with a blanket. . . . It was quite dark, you know. Suddenly I felt someone touch me on the shoulder and breathe into my face. I put out my hand and felt an elbow. . . . I opened my eyes, and would you believe it—there was a woman! Black eyes, lips as red as a fine salmon, nostrils breathing passion, a bosom like a buffer. . . ."

" I can understand about the bosom," Mersliakov interrupted him calmly, " but how could you see the lips in the dark? "

Lobitko began to hedge and then to laugh at Mersliakov's lack of imagination. Riabovitch was offended; he walked away from the box, lay down and promised himself never to be communicative again.

The life of the camp began. Day followed day, each like every other. Riabovitch the whole time thought and felt and behaved like a man in love. Every morning, when the orderly brought his washing things and he poured the cold water over his head, he remembered that something sweet and precious had come into his life.

Sometimes, when his comrades began to talk of love and women, he drew nearer, listening, his face assuming the expression of a soldier hearing the tale of a battle in which he had fought. And on evenings when the officers, at the instigation of the setter, Lobitko, made Don Juan excursions into the village, Riabovitch, though he participated in them, was miserable and felt himself immeasurably to blame; in thought he asked forgiveness of *her*. . . . In leisure hours, or on sleepless nights, when the desire usually came over him to recall his childhood, his father, mother, all that was near and dear to him, he invariably thought of Mestechko, the curious horse, Rabbek, his wife who looked like the Empress Eugénie, the dark room, the bright crack in the door. . . .

On the 31st of August he returned from camp, not with the whole brigade, but with two batteries only; the whole way he was strangely excited, as though he were going home to his native place. Once more he longed to see the strange horse, the church, Rabbek's affected family, the dark room. An "inner voice" that so often deceives those in love told him that he would see *her*. And he began to wonder how he would greet her, what he would say to her. Had she forgotten about the kiss? If the worst were to happen and he did not see her at all, he would, at any rate, walk through the dark room and remember. . . .

Towards the evening, the familiar church and white barns appeared on the horizon. Riabovitch's heart beat fast. He did not hear what the officer who rode near him was saying, he forgot everything, and with a great longing gazed at the river sparkling in the distance, at the roof of the house, at the dovecot and circling doves, lighted up by the setting sun.

They arrived at the church; he listened to the quartermaster's report, expecting every moment to see the horseman appear who would invite them to the general's to tea, but the quartermaster had finished, the officers hastened to the village and still the horseman did not come. . . .

"Rabbek will soon learn from the peasants that we are here and will send for us," Riabovitch thought, entering the hut and failing to comprehend why his comrades had lighted the candles and why the orderlies were preparing the samovars.

He felt depressed. He lay down, then got up and looked

out of the window to see if the horseman was coming. But no horseman was in sight. Once more he lay down, and unable to bear his anxiety, after a while he went out into the street and made his way to the church. The square by the church fence was dark and deserted. Three soldiers were standing together in silence at the crest of the hill. At sight of Riabovitch they started and gave the salute. He saluted in turn and began to descend the hill along the familiar path.

On the opposite bank the sky was a bright purple; the moon rose; two women, talking loudly, were pulling cabbage leaves in a kitchen-garden: beyond the kitchen-garden were the dark outlines of several huts. . . . On this side it was the same as in May—there was the path, the bushes, the overhanging willows—only the song of the brave little nightingale was missing and the scent of poplar and young grass.

Riabovitch approached the garden and looked through the gate. It was dark and quiet within. The white trunks of the nearest birches were visible and a part of the avenue, the rest was a darkened mass. Riabovitch listened intently and peered into the darkness, but after half an hour of waiting and watching, and hearing no sound and seeing no light, he turned back.

He stopped by the river. Before him, gleaming in the darkness, was the general's bathing-hut and a sheet hanging on the rail of the little bridge. He went on to the bridge and without any reason put out his hand to touch the sheet. . . . He gazed down into the water. . . . The river flowed quickly and made a faint murmur by the stakes of the bathing-hut. The moon, large and red, was reflected near the left bank; tiny waves floated across it, extending the reflection, breaking it to pieces, as though they wished to carry it away. . . .

"How senseless! how senseless!" Riabovitch thought, gazing at the quickly flowing water. "How senseless it all is!"

Now that he no longer expected anything, the story of the kiss, his impatience, his vague hopes and disillusionment appeared to him in a true light. It seemed no longer strange to him that the general's horseman had not appeared and that he would never meet the girl who had kissed him in mistake for someone else; on the contrary it would have been strange if he had met her. . . .

The water flew past him, whither and why no one knew. It had flown past in May. From a little stream it had poured into a great river, then into the sea; from the sea it had risen in mist, then come down in rain, and now perhaps the water flying past him was the very same he had seen in May. Why? Wherefore?

And the whole world and life itself seemed to Riabovitch to be one great, incomprehensible, senseless jest. He raised his eyes from the water and looked up at the sky; once more he remembered how fate, in the form of an unknown women, had unexpectedly caressed him; he recalled his dreams and images of the summer, and his life appeared to him so poor, wretched and colourless. . . .

When he returned to his quarters, not one of his colleagues was there. The orderly informed him that the officers had all gone to General "Fontrabkin," who had sent a horseman for them. . . . A feeling of joy for a moment sprang into Riabovitch's heart, but he instantly smothered it. As though to spite Fate, who had treated him so badly, he did not go to the general's, but went instead to bed.

ALEXANDER SERGIVITCH PUSHKIN

THE PISTOL SHOT

"We fired at each other."—BARATINSKY.

"I swore to kill him by the law of duelling, and I held my shot in reserve for him."—THE BIVOUAC.

WE were stationed in the little town of ——. The life of an army officer is well known. In the morning—drill, the riding-school; dinner with the regimental commander or at an eating-house kept by a Jew; in the evening, punch and cards. In —— there was not a single open house, not one marriageable girl; we used to assemble at each other's quarters, where we set eyes on nothing but our own uniforms.

In our society there was only one fellow who was not a military man. He was about thirty-five years of age, and so we regarded him as practically an old man. Experience gave him many advantages over us, in addition to which his habitual moroseness, severe disposition and caustic tongue had a powerful influence over young men of our turn of mind. Some mystery or other enshrouded his destiny; he appeared to be a Russian, yet he bore a foreign name. At one time he had served in the hussars, and even with distinction. No one knew the reason that had induced him to leave the service and settle in a wretched little place where he lived poorly, though at the same time extravagantly. He invariably went out on foot, in a worn-out black overcoat, yet he kept an open table for all the officers of our regiment. True, his dinner consisted of only two or three courses, prepared by an old soldier, yet for all that there was champagne in abundance. No one knew his means or what his income was, and no one had dared to question him upon the subject. He had a number of books, for the most part military works and novels. He willingly lent them to people, without ever asking for them back; at the same time, he never returned to its owner any book which he had borrowed. His chief recreation was shooting with the pistol. The walls of his room were pitted all over with bullets, and were as full of holes as a honeycomb. A splendid collection of pistols was the sole item of luxury in the poor little plastered cottage in which he lived. The skill to which he had attained was incredible, and if he had offered to shoot off a pear from anybody's forage-cap, there was no one in our regiment who would have hesitated to lend his head for the experiment.

Our conversation often turned upon duels; Silvio (for so I shall call him) never took part in it. On being asked whether he had ever fought, he answered dryly that he had done so, but he would not enter into details, and it was evident that such questions were distasteful to him. We concluded that upon his conscience there lay some unhappy victim of his dreadful skill. However, it never entered our heads to suspect in him anything approaching cowardice. There are people whose external appearance alone repels such suspicions. But something happened unexpectedly which amazed us all.

One evening about ten of our officers were dining with Silvio. We drank as much as usual—that is to say, a great deal. After dinner we began to persuade our host to hold the bank for us. For a long time he refused, for he scarcely ever played, but in the end he ordered cards to be brought, strewed out on the table a hundred and fifty roubles in gold, and sat down to deal. We gathered around him, and play began. Silvio was accustomed to preserve complete silence during play; he never entered into disputes or explanations. If the punter happened to miscount, then he immediately either paid up the difference or noted down the surplus. We were aware of this, and allowed him to keep the reckoning in his own way; but among us there was an officer who had but recently been transferred to our regiment. During the game he absent-mindedly scored one point too many. Silvio took the chalk and corrected the score, according to his custom. Thinking he had made a mistake, the officer began an explanation. Silvio went on dealing in silence. Losing patience, the officer seized the brush and rubbed out what seemed to him to have been marked down wrongly. Silvio picked up the chalk and wrote it down again. The officer, inflamed by wine, play and the laughter of his comrades, considered himself deeply insulted, and snatching up in his rage a brass candlestick from the table, he hurled it at Silvio, who barely managed to stoop and avoid the impact. We were struck with consternation. Silvio rose to his feet, pale with anger, and said with flashing eyes:

"My dear sir, kindly leave, and thank God that this has taken place in my house."

We were in no doubt regarding what would follow, and we looked upon our new comrade as already a dead man. The officer left, saying that he was ready to answer for the insult in whatever way the banker wished. The game continued for a few minutes longer, but, feeling that our host had no further inclination for play, we took our departure one by one and returned to our quarters, discussing the prospective vacancy in our regiment.

Next day, in the riding-school, we were asking whether the poor lieutenant were still alive, when he himself appeared among us, whereupon we put the same question to him. He replied that he had not heard the slightest news of Silvio. This astonished us. We went to see Silvio, and found him in the yard sending bullet after bullet into an ace of spades fastened to the gate. He received us as usual, not uttering a word about the incident of the night before. Three days elapsed, and the lieutenant was still alive. With astonishment we asked, "Could it be that Silvio did not intend to fight?"

Silvio did not fight. He contented himself with a very perfunctory explanation, and made up the quarrel. This looked like injuring him seriously in the opinion of us young fellows. Want of courage is less excusable than anything in the eyes of young men, who in bravery generally see the summit of manly qualities and an excuse for all possible failings. However, gradually all was forgotten, and Silvio once more regained his old ascendency.

I alone could not become intimate with him again. Endowed by nature with a romantic imagination, I had formerly been attracted more strongly than the rest to this man, whose life was an enigma and who seemed to me the hero of some tale of mystery. He was fond of me—at least, it was with me alone that he dropped his habitually sarcastic tone and spoke on different subjects with sincerity and unusual charm. But after that unfortunate evening the thought that his honour had been besmirched and that of his own free will he had suffered the stain to remain—this thought would not leave me, and it prevented me from behaving towards him as I had been wont. I was even ashamed to look at him. Silvio was too astute and experienced not to remark this and divine the reason. It seemed to grieve him—at least, I observed in him once or twice a desire to have an explanation with me, but I would not give him an opportunity, and Silvio retired abashed. Henceforth I visited him only with my comrades, and our former heart-to-heart talks came to an end.

The inhabitants of a capital, who have so many things to distract them, have no idea of the multitude of impressions known only to those who live in villages or small towns—as, for example, waiting for post-day to come round. On Tuesdays and Fridays our regimental office was full of officers, some waiting for money, others for letters or papers. Packets were usually opened on the spot, news spread from mouth to mouth, and the office presented the most lively picture. Silvio used to receive his letters addressed to the care of our regiment, and usually waited for them in the office. One day they handed him a packet from which he tore the seal with an air of the greatest impatience. His eyes glittered as he ran through the letter. The officers, each of whom was occupied with his own letters, noticed nothing. " Gentlemen," said Silvio, " circumstances demand my instant departure. I leave to-night. I hope you will not refuse to dine with me for the last time. I shall expect you, too," he continued, turning to me. " I shall expect you without fail." With these words he hurried off, and, after agreeing to meet at Silvio's, we went our different ways.

I arrived at Silvio's at the appointed time, and found almost the entire regiment assembled there. All his effects were already packed—there remained only the bare, bullet-riddled walls. We sat down at the table. Our host was in exceptionally good spirits, and soon the whole company became infected with his gaiety. Corks popped every minute, the glasses foamed and bubbled over incessantly, and with the greatest goodwill we wished the traveller God-speed and a pleasant journey.

It was already far into the evening when we rose from the table. While we were sorting out our caps, Silvio, who was bidding his guests good-bye, took me by the hand and detained me just as I was making ready to leave. " I have something to say to you," he said in a low voice. I remained behind.

The guests had gone. Left together, we sat down opposite one another and smoked our pipes in silence. Silvio was preoccupied; already all trace of his spasmodic gaiety had vanished. His deadly pallor and glittering eyes and the dense smoke that issued from his mouth gave him the appearance of a veritable demon. After several minutes had passed Silvio broke silence.

" It may be that we shall never see each other again," he said, " and before parting I wished to have an explanation with you. You may have remarked that I have little respect for the opinion of other people, but I have taken a liking to you, and it would be painful to me to leave a wrong impression in your mind."

He paused and began to knock out his pipe; I remained silent, with downcast eyes.

" It appeared strange to you," he proceeded, " that I did not demand satisfaction from that drunken fool R——. You will agree that, since I had the right to choose the weapons, his life was in my hands, while mine was in practically no danger. I could ascribe my forbearance to magnanimity alone, but I have no wish to lie. If I could have punished R—— without exposing my own life at all, then I should not have let him off for the world."

I gazed at Silvio with amazement. Such a confession completely disconcerted me. Silvio continued.

"Quite so; I have no right to expose myself to death. Six years ago I received a slap in the face, and my enemy is still living."

My interest was thoroughly aroused. "You didn't fight him, then?" I queried. "No doubt circumstances kept you apart?"

"Yes, I fought with him," replied Silvio, "and here is a souvenir of our duel."

Silvio rose and took from a cardboard box a red cap trimmed with braid and adorned with a gold tassel (the kind of cap that the French call "bonnet de police"). He put it on. It had been perforated by a bullet nearly two inches from the forehead.

"You are aware," continued Silvio, "that I served in the —— regiment of hussars. My character is known to you. I am accustomed to taking the first place in everything, but in my youth this was a positive passion with me. In our day wildness was in fashion—and I was the wildest blade in the army. We prided ourselves on our drunkenness—and I outdrank the celebrated Bourtsev, whose prowess has been sung by Denis Davidov.[1] In our regiment duels were a constant occurrence—in all of them I was either a second or a principal. My comrades idolised me, while the commanding officers, who were constantly being changed, looked upon me as a necessary evil.

"I was peacefully—or, rather, unpeacefully—enjoying my reputation when there was appointed to our regiment a young man of a rich and illustrious family (I will not mention his name). In all my life I have not met such a dazzlingly lucky fellow! Picture to yourself youth, wit, good looks, the wildest gaiety, the most reckless daring, a celebrated name, wealth the extent of which he did not know himself and which he never even bothered his head about—and imagine what kind of effect he must have produced among us.

"My pre-eminence was shaken. Allured by my reputation, he began to seek my friendship, but I received him coldly, and without any regret he held aloof from me. I grew to hate him. His successes in the regiment and in the society of women reduced me to complete despair. I began to seek a quarrel with him. To my epigrams he replied with others which

[1] A Russian poet contemporary with Pushkin.

always seemed to me more original and more cutting than mine and which were, of course, far more entertaining, for he jested while I indulged in malice.

"At last, at a ball one evening at the Polish ambassador's, seeing him the object of the attention of all the ladies, and particularly of the hostess herself, with whom I had once had an intrigue, I whispered in his ear some trivial insult or other. He flared up and gave me a slap in the face. Our hands flew to our swords. The ladies collapsed in a swoon. We were dragged apart, and that same night we went out to fight.

"Day was breaking. I stood at the appointed place with my three seconds. It was with inexplicable impatience that I awaited my antagonist. The spring sun had risen, and it had already begun to grow hot. I caught sight of him in the distance. He was on foot, with his sword under his military coat, attended by a single second. We went to meet him. He approached, holding his forage-cap full of wild cherries. The seconds measured off twelve paces for us. I was to fire first, but hatred had raised such strong agitation in me that I could not rely upon the steadiness of my hand, and in order to give myself time to grow cool, I offered to let him fire first. My opponent would not agree to this. It was proposed that we should draw lots. The first number fell to him, the constant favourite of fortune. He took aim and sent his bullet through my cap.

"It was now my turn. His life at last was in my hands. I looked at him searchingly, seeking to detect but one shadow of uneasiness. He stood facing my pistol, selecting the ripe cherries out of his cap and spitting out the stones, which flew as far as where I was standing. His indifference maddened me. 'What advantage would it be to me,' I thought, 'to deprive him of his life, when he does not prize it in the least?' A wicked thought flashed through my mind. I lowered my pistol.

"'Apparently, you are not ready for death at the moment,' I said to him. 'You are deigning to have your breakfast. I have no wish to hinder you.'

"'You are not hindering me in the least,' he returned. 'Please be so good as to fire—or rather, do just as you like. The shot remains yours, and I am always at your service.'

"I turned to the seconds, declaring that I did not intend to fire just then, and thereupon the duel came to an end.

"I retired from the service, and withdrew to this little place. From that time not a day has passed but I have not dreamed of revenge. Now my hour has come. . . ."

Silvio took from his pocket the letter he had received in the morning, and gave it to me to read. The writer (apparently his agent) informed him from Moscow that " a certain person " was soon to be lawfully married to a young and beautiful girl.

" You will guess," said Silvio, " who this 'certain person' is. I am going to Moscow. We shall see whether he will embrace death with as much indifference when he is about to be married as when once he awaited it with his cherries! "

With these words Silvio got up, threw his cap on the floor, and began to pace up and down the room like a tiger in its cage. I had listened to him without moving; I was agitated by strange, conflicting feelings.

The servant entered and announced that the horses were ready. Silvio pressed my hand warmly; we embraced. He took his seat in the carriage, in which a couple of valises were reposing, one containing pistols, the other his effects. We said good-bye once more, and the horses broke into a gallop.

Several years passed by, and domestic circumstances obliged me to settle in a wretched little village in the district of N——. Busying myself with agriculture, I did not cease to sigh in secret for my former boisterous and carefree existence. More irksome to me than anything else was getting used to passing the spring and autumn evenings in absolute solitude. I managed somehow or other to spin out the time until dinner, by chatting with the bailiff, riding about to see how the various kinds of work were progressing, or making a tour of the new buildings; but as soon as it began to grow dark I was completely at a loss to know what to do with myself. The few books which I found inside the cupboards and in the store-room, I had come to know by heart. All the stories which my housekeeper Kirilovna managed to call to mind had been related to me again and again. The songs of the peasant women only made me sad. I applied myself to drinking raw spirit, but this made my head ache; and I must confess I was somewhat afraid of becoming a " drunkard from grief,"[1]—that is to say, the most hardened type of drunkard, of which I had seen many examples in our district. Near neighbours I had none, apart from two or three of these same drinkers, whose conversation consisted for the most part of sighs and hiccoughs. My solitude was more endurable than this.

Within four versts of my place there was a wealthy estate belonging to the Countess B——; but only the steward lived there, for the countess had visited her estate only once, in the first year of her marriage, and then she had stayed there no longer than a month. However, in the second spring of my

[1] There is here an untranslatable play upon words—between " goré," grief, and " gorki," sad, bitter, an epithet applied idiomatically to a confirmed drunkard.

seclusion a rumour was spread that the countess and her husband were coming to their estate for the summer. And, sure enough, they arrived at the beginning of June.

The arrival of a wealthy neighbour is an important landmark among those who live in the country. The landowners and their households discuss it for about two months beforehand and for about three years afterwards. As far as I was concerned, I must confess that hearing of the presence of a young and beautiful neighbour had a strong effect upon me; I burned with impatience to see her, and accordingly, the first Sunday of her arrival, I set out after dinner to the village of —— to introduce myself to their excellencies as their nearest neighbour and very humble servant.

A lackey showed me into the Count's cabinet, and then went to announce me. The spacious cabinet was furnished with the greatest luxury. Cases of books stood round the walls, each surmounted by a bronze bust; over the marble mantelpiece there was a large mirror, and the floor was covered with green cloth and spread with rugs. Unaccustomed to luxury in my own poor little place, and not having set eyes on the wealth of others for a long time, I was overcome with timidity, and awaited the Count with some trepidation, just as a petitioner from the provinces awaits the entry of a minister.

The doors were opened, and in came a very handsome man of about thirty-two. The Count came up to me with a frank and cordial air; I strove to pluck up my courage and began to introduce myself, but he forestalled me. We sat down. His conversation, which was unconstrained and genial, soon put to flight my timid shyness; I was already beginning to regain my customary composure, when suddenly the Countess entered, and confusion seized upon me more strongly than before. In very truth, she was a beauty. The Count presented me to her; I wished to appear unconstrained, but the more I tried to assume an appearance of ease, the more awkward I felt. In order to give me time to recover myself and to grow accustomed to my new acquaintances, they began to talk to one another, behaving with me as with a good neighbour and without ceremony.

In the meantime, I began to walk up and down, examining the books and pictures. I am not a connoisseur of pictures, but one of them attracted my attention. It showed some view in Switzerland, but what struck me about it was not the painting, but the fact that the picture had been perforated by two bullets, placed one on top of the other.

"That was a good shot," said I, turning towards the Count.

"Yes," he replied, "an altogether remarkable shot. And do you shoot well?" he continued.

" Tolerably well," I replied, glad that the conversation had touched at last upon a subject with which I was at home. " I can shoot the pips out of a playing-card at thirty paces without once missing—of course, using pistols with which I am familiar."

" Indeed? " said the Countess, with an air of great attentiveness. " And you, my dear, can you hit a card at thirty paces? "

" Some day," replied the Count, " we will try. I was not a bad shot in my time, but it is four years now since I took a pistol in hand."

" Oh," I remarked, " in that case I am prepared to wager that your Excellency will not hit a card even at twenty paces. Pistol-shooting demands daily practice. This I know from experience. I was reckoned one of the best shots in our regiment. It fell out once that for a whole month I did not touch a pistol, for mine had gone to be repaired, and what do you think, Your Excellency? The first time I began to shoot again I missed a bottle four times in succession at twenty-five paces. We had a captain who was a witty fellow and a wag; he happened to come along just then and said to me, ' I'll tell you what it is, brother; your hand won't lift itself against the bottle! ' No, Your Excellency, it doesn't do to disdain practising, or you are sure to lose your skill. The best shot I ever encountered used to shoot every day—at least three times before dinner. It was as customary for him as taking his glass of vodka."

The Count and Countess were pleased that I had found something to talk about.

" And how did he shoot? " the Count asked me.

" I'll tell you, Your Excellency. He would happen to see a fly alight on the wall. You are laughing, Countess? By Jove, it is the truth. Well, he catches sight of the fly and calls out, ' Kouzka! a pistol! ' Kouzka brings him a loaded pistol. He fires, and crushes the fly against the wall! "

" It's amazing! " said the Count. " And what was his name? "

" Silvio, your Excellency."

" Silvio! " cried the Count, jumping up. " You knew Silvio? "

" How could I help knowing him, Your Excellency? I was a friend of his. He was accepted in our regiment like our own brother and comrade; but it is now five years since I had any news of him. Then I suppose Your Excellency knew him, too? "

" Yes, I knew him very well. Did he never tell you about a certain very strange incident? "

" Does Your Excellency mean the slap in the face which he received from some madman at a ball? "

" And did he tell you the name of this madman? "

" No, Your Excellency, he never mentioned it. . . . Ah! Your Excellency," I went on, divining the truth, " forgive me . . . I did not know . . . surely it was not you? "

" Yes, it was I," replied the Count, with an air of extraordinary agitation, " and the bullet-holes in that picture are a souvenir of our last meeting. . . ."

" Ah! my dear," said the Countess, " for God's sake, do not relate that incident. It would be distressing to me to listen to it."

" No," replied the Count, " I will relate everything. He knows how I insulted his friend; let him hear, too, how Silvio took his revenge."

The Count pushed an armchair towards me, and it was with the keenest interest that I listened to the following story.

" Five years ago I got married. The first month—the honeymoon—we spent here, in this village. To this house I am indebted for the best moments of my life, and also for some of the most painful memories.

" One evening we went out together on horseback. My wife's horse became rather restive. She grew frightened, handed over the bridle to me and went home on foot, while I rode on ahead of her. Outside the door I saw a travelling-carriage; they informed me that there was a man waiting for me in my cabinet who had refused to give his name, declaring simply that he had business with me. I entered this room, and in the gloom I saw a man, covered with dust and with a growth of beard. He was standing just here, by the chimney-piece. I went towards him, endeavouring to place his features.

" ' Do you not recognise me, Count? ' he said in a tremulous voice.

" ' Silvio! ' I exclaimed, and I must confess that I felt my hair suddenly stand on end.

" ' Just so,' he proceeded. ' There is a shot owing to me, and I have come to fire off my pistol. Are you ready? '

There was a pistol sticking out of his side-pocket. I measured off twelve paces and stood there in the corner, begging him to hurry up and fire before my wife returned. He delayed—he asked for lights. They brought in the candles. I closed the doors, forbade anybody to enter, and once more begged him to fire. He drew out his pistol and took aim . . . I counted the seconds . . . I thought of her . . . Thus passed a dreadful minute! Silvio lowered his hand.

" ' I regret,' said he, ' that the pistol is not loaded with cherry-stones . . . the bullet is heavy. It seems to me that we have here not a duel, but a murder. I am not used to taking aim at an unarmed man. Let us begin again. We will draw lots to decide who shall fire first.'

"My head was going round. . . . It seems that I would not agree. . . . In the end we loaded another pistol and screwed up two pieces of paper, which he placed in the very cap which had once been pierced by my bullet. Once more I drew the first number.

"'You have the devil's own luck, Count,' said he, with a smile which I shall never forget. I cannot understand what had come over me, and how he could have compelled me to do it, but . . . I fired, and the bullet hit that picture."

The Count pointed with his finger to the bullet-pierced picture. His face was as red as fire; the Countess was whiter than her own handkerchief. I could not repress an exclamation.

"I fired," proceeded the Count, "and, thank God, it was a miss. Then Silvio—at that moment he was truly terrible—Silvio began to take aim at me. Suddenly the door flew open, and Masha ran in and threw herself upon my neck with a shriek. Her presence recalled to me all my courage. 'Do you not see, dear,' I said to her, 'that we are joking? What a fright you have had! Go and drink a glass of water and return to us; I will present to you an old friend and comrade.'

"Masha could not bring herslf to believe me. 'Tell me, is my husband speaking the truth?' she said, turning to the relentless Silvio. 'Is it true that you are both joking?'

"'He is always joking, Countess,' replied Silvio. 'One day, while joking, he gave me a slap in the face; joking still, he sent a bullet through this cap of mine; joking, he has just missed shooting me. And now I have a wish to joke.'

"With these words, he was about to take aim at me—in her presence! Masha threw herself at his feet.

"'Get up, Masha! For shame!' I cried in a rage. 'And you, sir, will you cease making fun of a poor woman? Are you going to fire or not?'

"'No, I'm not,' replied Silvio. 'I am satisfied. I have witnessed your agitation, your dismay. I have forced you to fire at me, and I am satisfied. I leave you to your to own conscience.'

"With that he was about to go, but he stopped in the doorway, glanced at the picture which had been pierced by my bullet, fired at it almost without aiming, and disappeared. My wife lay in a faint. The servants did not dare to detain him, and looked upon him with horror. He went out on the steps, called his driver, and drove away before I had succeeded in recovering myself."

The Count ceased speaking. In this manner I learned the conclusion of the story whose beginning had once so struck me. The hero of it I never encountered again. It is said that Silvio commanded a division of Hetairists during the insurrection of Alexander Ypsilanti and was killed in the battle of Skuliany.

MAXIM GORKY

TWENTY-SIX MEN AND A GIRL

THERE were twenty-six of us fellows—twenty-six living machines shut up in a damp cellar, where from morning till night we kneaded dough and made cracknels. The windows of our cellar looked into a sort of pit that was excavated in front of them and was lined with bricks which had become green with damp; the window-frames were blocked up from the outside with a piece of iron netting, and it was impossible for the sunlight to reach us through the panes, which were covered with a dusting of flour. Our employer had fixed this iron over the windows so as to prevent our giving a morsel of his bread to beggars or to those of our friends who, being out of work, were going hungry in consequence. Our employer used to call us sharpers, and for dinner gave us putrid tripe instead of meat.

It was cramped and stuffy, living in that stone box beneath the low, oppressive ceiling, covered with soot and cobwebs. We felt stifled and sickly between those thick walls, decorated with patches of filth and mould. . . . We got up at five in the morning, without having had enough sleep, and, dull and indifferent, by six were already seated at the bench making cracknels out of the dough that had been prepared for us by our comrades while we were asleep. And all day long, from the morning until ten o'clock at night, a number of us sat at the bench, rolling out the elastic dough with our hands, and now and then giving ourselves a shake so as not to get numb, while at the same time others mixed the flour with water. And all day long, pensively and sadly, the seething water purred in the boiler where the cracknels were simmering, while the baker's shovel scraped swiftly and spitefully over the floor of the oven, tossing the slippery lumps of boiled dough on to the hot bricks. From morning till night the wood burned in one side of the oven, and the crimson glare of the flames danced on the wall of the workshop, as though silently mocking at us. The huge oven resembled the misshapen head of a monster in a fairy-tale—it seemed to thrust itself up from beneath the floor, open its wide jaws, full of glowing fire, and breathe its hot breath over us, contemplating our endless labours with the two black cavities of vent-holes above its mouth. These two deep cavities were like eyes—the pitiless, passionless eyes—of a monster: they watched us always with the same sombre look, as though they had grown tired of looking upon slaves, and, not expecting anything human from them, despised them with the cold contempt of superior knowledge.

Day after day, amid flour dust, amid filth brought in on our feet from the yard, in a dense, reeking atmosphere, we rolled out dough and made cracknels, which became moistened with our sweat. And we hated our work with bitter hatred; we never ate the product of our own hands, preferring black bread to cracknels. Seated opposite one another at the long bench, nine opposite nine, we moved our hands and fingers like machines, hour after hour, and so accustomed were we to our work that we no longer troubled to follow our own movements. And we had studied one another so thoroughly that each of us was acquainted with every wrinkle on the faces of his companions. There was nothing for us to talk about, but we had grown accustomed to this, and observed a perpetual silence—that is, when we were not wrangling, for there is always something to find fault with a man for, especially a comrade. But it was seldom that we wrangled—for how can a man be at fault if he is half-dead, if he has become like a dummy, if his every feeling has been stifled by the severity of his daily work? Yet silence is dreadful and grievous only for those who have already said everything and who have nothing more to utter; for people who have not yet begun to speak, silence is an easy and simple business. . . .

Sometimes we sang, and our song would begin in this manner: suddenly, in the middle of his work, one of us would utter the heavy sigh of a weary horse, and in a low voice would begin to sing one of those long-drawn songs the bitter-sweet refrain of which always lightens the burden that is oppressing the heart of the singer. Thus one of us sings, and we at first listen silently to his solitary song, as it dies away and is extinguished under the heavy roof of the cellar, like a little fire of twigs in the steppe on a damp autumn night, when the grey sky overhangs the earth like a roof of lead. Then another joins in with the singer, and now there are two voices softly and sadly floating in the foul atmosphere of our narrow cell. And suddenly several voices take up the song simultaneously; it surges like a wave, grows stronger, louder, and seems to thrust asunder the damp, heavy walls of our stone prison. . . .

Now all twenty-six of us are singing; our loud voices, attuned through long practice, fill the workroom; our song is stifled there; it beats against the stone walls, groans, weeps, and quickens the heart with a gentle, tantalising ache, irritating old wounds and arousing poignant yearnings. . . . The singers utter deep and heavy sighs; now one of them abruptly breaks off his song and listens long to the voices of his comrades, and then once again his voice flows into the general wave of sound. Another, with a bitter cry of "Ah!", sings with closed eyes, and perhaps the great, broad flood of sound seems to him like a distant road bathed in bright sunshine, a wide road along which he can see himself proceeding. . . .

The flame flickers in the stove, the baker's shovel scrapes against the oven-bricks, the water murmurs in the boiler, and the glare of the fire flickers on the wall with silent laughter. . . . And in the borrowed words of our song we pour out our dull grief, the sorrowful yearning of living beings deprived of the sun, the yearning of slaves. Thus we lived, twenty-six of us, in the cellar of a big stone house, and so burdensome was our life that it seemed as though all the three storeys of this house were resting upon our shoulders. . . .

. . . . . .

However, we had something else that was nice besides songs, something which we loved and which, perhaps, supplied for us the place of the sun. On the second floor of our house was a gold-embroiderer's shop, and there, together with numerous work-girls, lived a sixteen-year-old maidservant called Tanya. Every morning a rosy little face with merry blue eyes appeared behind the glazed door leading into the workroom from the passage, and a sweet, ringing voice called out to us,

"Little prisoners! Give me some cracknels!"

We would all turn round at this clear, familiar sound, and joyously, good-naturedly, gaze at the pure, girlish face smiling so charmingly at us. We were filled with happiness by the familiar spectacle of her nose pressed against the glass and her little white teeth gleaming between her rosy lips, parted in a smile. Jostling one another, we rushed to open the door to her, and in she would come, so gay and pretty, holding out her apron—would stand before us smiling all the time, with her head a little on one side. A long, thick plait of chestnut hair fell over her shoulder and rested on her bosom. And we—a lot of dirty, black, deformed chaps—would look up at her with our heads thrown back (for the threshold of the door was four steps higher than the floor) and bid her good-morning, using words to which we had grown unaccustomed and which we reserved only for her. When we were talking to her, our voices would grow softer and our jokes more restrained. Everything had to be of the best when she was with us. The baker would take out of the oven a shovelful of the crispest, brownest cracknels and toss them deftly into Tanya's apron.

"Mind you don't run into the boss!" we would always warn her. She would give a roguish laugh and, calling merrily "Good-bye, little prisoners!" would vanish swiftly like a little mouse.

And that was all. . . . But long after she had gone we would discuss her happily with one another; we would always repeat the same things that we had said yesterday and the day before, because she and we and all around us remained just the same as we had been yesterday and the day before. . . . It is a very dreary and painful business for a man to go on living while around him nothing changes, and if it does not end by killing his soul, then the stagnation of his surroundings grows more and more insufferable the longer he lives. . . . We were always accustomed to speak about women in such terms that we ourselves were disgusted at times by our coarse and shameless words, and this is not to be wondered at, for such women as we knew were, perhaps, not worth any politer expressions. But we never spoke coarsely about Tanya; she never even heard a broad joke from us, let alone would any of us so much as venture to lay a finger on her. Perhaps this was because she never stayed long with us—she flashed before our eyes like a star falling from heaven, and disappeared; but it may have been because she was small and very pretty, and all beauty inspires respect, even among rough natures. And besides, although the drudgery of our work had reduced us to the condition of doltish oxen, at the same time we were still men and, like all men, could not live without worshipping something or other. We had no one better than she, and no one else had ever paid any attention to us, living as we did in the cellar—no one, although there were dozens of people in the house. And at length—this, indeed, is the chief thing—we all came to regard her as something particularly our own, something whose very existence depended upon our cracknels; we had imposed upon ourselves the duty of providing her with hot cracknels, and this became for us the daily sacrifice to an idol; it was almost a holy rite, and it bound us to her more strongly every day. Besides cracknels, we used to give Tanya a great deal of advice, such as to dress more warmly, not to run rapidly up and down stairs, not to carry heavy bundles of wood. She listened to our advice with a smile, replied to it with a laugh, and never obeyed us; but this did not offend us—all we wanted was to let her see how much care we took of her.

She frequently came to us with various requests—asking us, for example, to open the heavy door of the ice-house or to split some wood for her—and it was with joy and even a kind of pride that we executed these tasks and anything else she wished. But once, when one of us asked her to mend his only shirt for him, she sniffed disdainfully and said, "What next? The idea of it!"

We chaffed the poor fellow a good bit, and never again did we ask her to do anything for us. We loved her—with that word all is said. Man always wants an object upon which to bestow his love, even though that object may be besmirched or crushed thereby; his love may even poison the life of his nearest and dearest, because he loves without respecting his beloved. We had to love Tanya, for there was no one else for us to love.

Now and then, for some reason, one of us would suddenly begin to ruminate thus:

"Why do we spoil the hussy so? What is there about her, eh? Why is it we make such a fuss over her?"

We came down pretty sharply on the man who dared to say such things—we had to have something to love; we had found it and loved it, and what the whole twenty-six of us loved must be steadfast and unalterable for each one of us, like a holy thing, and anyone who went against us in this was our enemy. We loved, and perchance we had not really done wisely, but at any rate there were twenty-six of us concerned, and we intended to see that what was dear to us should also be sacred to others.

Our love is no less burdensome than hatred . . . and it may be that this is just why some proud souls affirm that our hatred is more flattering than our love. . . . But why, then, do they not run away from us, if this is so?

. . . . .

Besides the cracknel factory, our boss also ran a bakery; it was in the same house, and only a wall separated it from our cellar, but the bakery-hands—there were four of them—held aloof from us, regarding their work as cleaner than ours and themselves, consequently, as better than we. They never visited our workroom, and laughed derisively at us when they encountered us in the yard; neither did we visit them, for the boss had forbidden us to do so, for fear we should steal his fancy bread. We did not like the bakery-hands, because we were jealous of them; their work was less arduous than ours, and they were paid more and fed better; also, they had an airy, well-lighted workroom and were all so clean and healthy —in striking contrast to us. We all looked yellow and grey; three of us had syphilis and several suffered from the itch, while one of us was completely doubled up with rheumatism. On holidays and in their leisure time they used to wear jackets and squeaky boots, while a couple of them sported harmonicas, and they all went parading in the public gardens; whereas we were arrayed in filthy rags, with clogs or bast shoes on our feet, and we were not allowed by the police to enter the gardens —so how could we possibly like the bakers?

And then one day we heard that their head-baker had taken to drink and that the boss had sacked him and taken on another, and that this other was a soldier who wore a satin waistcoat and a watch with a gold chain. We were impatient to set eyes on such a dandy, and in the hope of catching a glimpse of him, we were continually running out into the yard, one after another.

However, he appeared of his own accord in our workroom. Kicking open the door with his foot and leaving it open, he stood upon the threshold, smiling, and said to us:

" Lord help us! How are you, mates? "

The frosty air rushed in through the door in great, smoke-like clouds, and whirled round his feet as he stood there on the threshold looking down at us, and behind his fair, neatly twisted moustache there gleamed large, yellow teeth. His waistcoat was indeed out of the ordinary—it was blue and embroidered with flowers and shone resplendently, while the buttons were made of some red stone or other. And it was true about the watch-chain. . . .

He was a handsome fellow, this soldier—tall and healthy-looking, with ruddy cheeks and a clear, friendly expression in his big, bright eyes. He had a stiffly starched white cap upon his head, while the pointed toes of fashionable, highly polished boots peeped out from beneath his immaculately clean apron.

Our foreman politely asked him to shut the door; he did so without showing any haste, and then began to ask us questions about our employer. All talking at once, we hastened to inform him that our boss was a cunning rogue, a sharper, a villain and a tyrant—we told him, in fact, all that we couldn't help telling him about the boss, although it is impossible to write it down here. The soldier listened, twitched his moustache and surveyed us with a bright, friendly gaze.

" Anyway, you've got plenty of girls here," he suddenly remarked.

A few of us tittered deferentially, others gave a smirk, and somebody explained to the soldier that we had nine girls in the place.

" I suppose you make the best of them? " queried the soldier, with a wink.

Again we tittered, but not very loudly and in an embarrassed way. . . . Many of us would have liked to show the soldier that they were just as bold sparks as he was, but none had the courage to do so. One of us admitted as much by remarking in a low voice, " How can we . . .? "

" Well, it certainly would be a bit too much for you," observed the soldier with conviction, as he looked us over closely. " Somehow you don't quite look up to it. There's no . . . bearing about you . . . appearance . . . style, in fact. And a woman loves style in a man. She will have a fellow with a well-set-up frame, with everything about him as it should be. What's more, she's got an eye for strength. She wants a fist like that! "

The soldier drew his right hand out of his pocket and showed it to us; his shirt-sleeve was rolled up, and his arm, bare to the elbow, was white-skinned and powerful and covered with glistening, golden hairs.

" Legs, chest—all must be sturdy. And then, a fellow must be dressed decently, so as to show himself off favourably. Take myself, for instance—all the women fall in love with me. I don't even have to invite them or angle for them—they simply throw themselves on my neck, five at a time! "

He seated himself upon a sack of flour and held forth at length upon the subject of how women loved him and how gallant he was with them. Then he took his departure, and when the door had creaked to behind him we were silent for a long time, thinking of him and of his tales. And then all began to talk at once, and it was obvious immediately that we had all taken to him. He was so artless and charming—he had simply come in, sat down and chatted with us, and usually no one came to see us, no one chatted with us like that, like friends. And we went on talking about him and his future successes with the embroideresses, who, when they encountered us in the yard, either passed us on one side with their lips pursed disdainfully, or looked straight through us as though we had not been there. But we had nothing but admiration for them, whether we met them in the yard or whether they passed by our windows—in winter dressed in fur cloaks and bonnets, in summer wearing hats trimmed with flowers and carrying gaily-coloured parasols. Nevertheless, we used to discuss these girls in a way that, if they could have heard us, would have driven them mad with shame and mortification. . . .

"But he mustn't corrupt little Tanya!" exclaimed the foreman all of a sudden, with anxiety in his voice.

All were silent, dumbfounded by these words. Somehow, we had forgotten about Tanya; the huge, handsome figure of the soldier had, as it were, blotted her out of our minds. Then there began a vigorous debate, some maintaining that Tanya would not lend herself to such a thing, others that she would not be able to withstand the soldier, while a third group proposed eventually that we should bash in his ribs if he should take it into his head to pester Tanya. We all ended by deciding to watch the soldier and Tanya, and to warn the girl to be on her guard against him. . . . This put an end to the debate.

. . . . .

About a month passed by; the soldier baked the bread walked out with the embroideresses, and paid us frequent visits in the workshop, but regarding his conquests among the girls he said not a word, but only twirled his moustache and licked his lips with relish.

Tanya came to us every morning for her "little cracknels," and was as gay, sweet and charming with us as ever. When we introduced the topic of the soldier, she called him a "pop-eyed calf" and other comical nicknames, and this reassured us. Seeing how the embroideresses were carrying on with the soldier, we were proud of our little girl; somehow, Tanya's attitude towards him uplifted us all, and, as though taking a lead from her conduct, we too began to treat him slightingly. And we loved her more dearly than ever, welcomed her in the mornings with still greater kindliness and joy.

But one day the soldier came to us a little drunk, sat down and began to giggle, and when we asked him what he was laughing about, he explained,

"Two of the girls have been fighting on my account . . . Lydka and Grushka. . . . How they have knocked themselves about! Ha! ha! One grabbed the other by the hair, pulled her on to the floor in the passage and got on top of her! Ha! ha! ha! They clawed and scratched each other's faces . . . it was the greatest fun! But why is it that women can't fight fair? Why must they claw one another about, eh?"

He sat there on the bench, so healthy, fresh and merry—sat there and went on laughing. We were silent. For some reason, we found him objectionable on this occasion.

"There's no d-denying I'm devilish lucky with women! What a joke! Eh? One wink from me, and they're ready to eat out of my hand!"

He lifted up his white hands, covered with glossy hair, and brought them down upon his knees again with a resounding slap. And he looked at us with such an air of happy surprise, as though he himself could not understand why he was so fortunate in his affairs with women. His plump, red face beamed with happiness and self-satisfaction, as he licked his lips with eager relish.

Our foreman scraped his shovel violently and angrily over the floor of the oven, and suddenly exclaimed with derision:

"It doesn't take much strength to pull up little fir-trees, but you just try a pine. . . ."

"What do you mean? Are you saying that to me?" queried the soldier.

"Yes, to you."

"What do you mean, then?"

"Nothing . . . it just slipped out."

"No, wait a bit! What are you talking about? What pine-tree?"

Busily plying his shovel in the oven, our foreman made no reply; he threw the boiled cracknels into the oven and took out those that were done, flinging them noisily on to the floor, to the boys who were stringing them on threads of bast. It seemed as though he had forgotten about the soldier and his altercation with him. But the soldier had fallen suddenly into a kind of uneasiness. He rose to his feet and went up to the oven, at the risk of getting a blow in the chest from the handle of the shovel, which was flashing to and fro convulsively in the air.

"No, tell me, you—whom do you mean? You've insulted me. I? . . . There's no woman who could resist me, not one! How dare you say such insulting things to me?"

And, indeed, he seemed genuinely affronted. Evidently he had nothing to respect himself for apart from his skill in seducing women; besides this talent, there was probably nothing alive in him, and it was only that that enabled him to feel himself a living man.

There are people with whom the finest and most precious thing in life takes the form of some disease or other of soul or body. It accompanies them throughout their lives, and, living only by it, suffering from it, they nourish themselves upon it and lament about it to others, and thus they draw upon themselves the attention of their fellow-men. On account of their disease they call forth people's sympathy, and apart from it they have nothing. Take from them this malady, cure them of it, and they will be unhappy, because they have lost their only resource in life—they are empty without it. Sometimes a man's life becomes so poverty-stricken that he is obliged involuntarily to set a price upon his own depravity and live by it; certain it is that men often become depraved from sheer boredom.

The soldier was affronted; he rushed at our foreman and yelled:

"No, tell me, you—who is it?"

"Shall I tell you?" The foreman suddenly turned to him.

"Well?"

"Do you know Tanya?"

"Well?"

"Well, there you are! Just try her!"

"I?"

"Yes, you!"

"Her? That's nothing to me—pooh!"

"We shall see!"

"Yes, you will see! Ha! ha!"

"She'll show you!"

"Only give me a month!"

"You've got some opinion of yourself, soldier!"

"A fortnight! I'll show you! What's Tanka? Pooh!"

"Now clear out! You're in my way!"

"A fortnight, and the thing's done! Ah! you. . . ."

"Get out, I tell you!"

Our foreman suddenly grew furious and began to flourish his shovel. The soldier backed away from him in astonishment, looked at us and was silent a moment; then in a quiet, ominous tone he said, "Very well, then!" and took his departure.

While the quarrel was going on we had all kept silent, absorbed in it. But when the soldier had gone out, a noisy buzz of conversation rose among us. One of us shouted to the foreman:

"It's a bad business you've stirred up, Pavel!"

"Get on with your work!" the foreman retorted savagely.

We realised that the soldier had been stung to the quick, and that danger threatened Tanya. We realised this, and yet at the same time all were seized by a burning, agreeable feeling of curiosity. What would happen? Would Tanya resist the soldier? And nearly all of us cried out confidently: "Little Tanya? She'll resist him all right! You won't take her with your bare hands!"

We were dreadfully anxious to test the strength of this divinity of ours; with ardent enthusiasm we assured one another that it was a strong divinity, and would issue from this encounter victorious. In the end we began to imagine that we had not incited the soldier sufficiently, that he would forget about the quarrel and that we ought to soundly provoke his vanity. From that day onwards we began to lead a peculiar life of nervous tension, such as we had never lived before. For days on end we disputed with one another, and somehow our wits grew sharper and our conversation improved and became more fluent. It seemed to us that we were engaged in a game with the devil, and that the stake on our side was Tanya. And when we heard from the bakery hands that the soldier had begun to " court our Tanya," it gave us a delightfully tormenting thrill, and we became so interested in life that we even failed to notice that our employer had taken advantage of our excitement to increase our work by five hundred pounds of dough a day. Even our work ceased to tire us. All day long Tanya's name never left out lips. And every morning we waited for her with particular impatience. Sometimes we imagined that she came to us not as the old Tanya, but another, a different one.

However, we did not mention a word to her about the quarrel that had taken place. We did not question her, either, and we were just as kind and affectionate towards her as before. But already into our attitude there had crept something new, something alien to our old feelings towards Tanya—and this new element was keen curiosity, as keen and cold as a steel knife. . . .

" Brothers! The time's up to-day! " said the foreman one morning, as he began his work.

We were well aware of this without his reminding us, but all the same we gave a start.

" Let's notice her carefully. She'll be here in a minute," suggested the foreman, whereupon one fellow cried out in an afflicted tone:

" And what do you expect to notice? "

And again there began among us a loud and animated dispute. To-day we should know at last how pure, how incorruptible by filth, was that vessel in which we had enshrined all that was best in us. It was this morning that we realised all at once, and for the first time, how really big was the gamble that we were carrying on—realised that this test of the purity of our goddess might result in destroying her for us. Day after day we had heard that the soldier was obstinately and importunately pursuing Tanya, but why was it none of us had asked her what attitude she was adopting towards him? And she had continued to turn up promptly every morning for her cracknels, and was just the same as ever.

And this morning, too, it was not long before we heard her voice:

" Little prisoners! Here I am! "

We hastened to admit her, but when she had come in,

contrary to our usual custom, we met her with silence. Devouring her with our eyes, we were at a loss what to say to her, what to ask her. And we stood before her in a gloomy, silent crowd. She was plainly astonished at this unusual reception—and suddenly we saw her grow pale and begin to get uneasy and agitated, and in a stifled voice she asked:

" Why are you . . . like this? "

" And you? " the foreman hurled at her sternly, without shifting his eyes from her.

" I . . . what? "

" N . . . nothing. . . ."

" Well, then, hurry up and give me the cracknels. . . ."

Never before had she hurried us. . . .

" You'll have plenty of time! " said the foreman, without stirring and without taking his eyes from her face.

Then suddenly she turned and disappeared through the door.

The foreman took up his shovel and quietly remarked, as he turned towards the oven:

" That means . . . the thing's done! . . . But a soldier! . . . a wretch like that, a scoundrel! . . ."

Jostling one another like a herd of rams, we went up to the table, took our places in silence and lethargically set to work. Presently one of us said:

" Perhaps, after all . . ."

" That's right, jabber away! " shouted the foreman.

We all knew him for a clever man—cleverer than ourselves. And in this cry of his we read confirmation of the soldier's triumph. . . . We felt sorrowful and uneasy. . . .

At twelve o'clock—that is to say, at dinner-time—the soldier appeared. He was as clean and trim as ever, and he looked us straight in the eyes, just as he always did. But we found it embarrassing to look at him.

" Well, good sirs, would you like me to show you what soldierly enterprise means? " said he, with a proud smile. " Then go into the passage and look through the cracks . . . do you understand? "

We went out and, crowding upon one another, pressed up close to the cracks in the plank wall of the passage leading into the yard. We had not long to wait. . . . Soon, with hurried footsteps and a preoccupied expression, across the yard came Tanya, jumping over the puddles of melted snow and mud. She disappeared through the door of the cellar. Afterwards, whistling and not hurrying himself, came the soldier, bound for the same place. His hands were thrust into his pockets, and his moustache was twitching. . . .

The rain was coming down, and we watched the drops fall into the puddles, making ripples all over them. The day was damp and grey—a very dreary sort of day. Snow was still lying on the roofs, but already on the ground could be seen dark blotches of mud. And the snow on the roofs, too, was covered with a layer of brownish mud. The rain fell slowly, with a dreary sound. We felt cold and wretched, waiting there. . . .

The first to come out of the cellar was the soldier; he walked slowly across the yard, twitching his moustache, his hands in his pockets—just the same as ever.

Then Tanya, too, came out. Her eyes . . . her eyes were shining with joy and happiness, and there was a smile upon her lips. And she walked as though in a dream, staggering, with uncertain footsteps. . . .

We could not put up with this quietly. We all rushed to the door, tore out into the yard and—hissed at her, bawled at her, evilly, loudly, wildly.

At the sight of us she shrank back and stood as though rooted in the mud beneath her feet. We surrounded her, and, malevolently and without any restraint, overwhelmed her with foul words, telling her shameless things.

We did this without raising our voices very much and without hurrying ourselves, seeing that she was surrounded by us and could not escape, and we could make sport of her as much as we liked. But we did not strike her—why, I do not know. She stood in the midst of us, turning her head from one side to another as our insults fell upon her ears. And we assailed her more and more violently with the filth and venom of our abuse.

The colour left her face. Her blue eyes, so happy but a moment before, opened wide, her bosom heaved deeply, and her lips trembled.

And, gathered around her in a circle, we took our revenge upon her, for she had robbed us. She had belonged to us, we had lavished our best upon her, and although this consisted only of beggars' crumbs, yet there were twenty-six of us and only one of her, and that was why there was no torment we could inflict upon her that would equal her guilt. How we insulted her! . . . And she was silent all the time, gazing at us with wild eyes, while a shudder ran all over her.

We laughed, roared, yelled. . . . Other people came running up from somewhere to join us. . . . One of us pulled Tanya by the sleeve of her blouse. . . .

Suddenly her eyes flashed; she leisurely put up her hands to her head and, straightening her hair, said loudly but calmly, right in our faces:

"Oh! you miserable jailbirds! . . ."

And she came straight up to us, as simply as though we had not been standing before her, barring her way. And because of this not one of us refused to let her pass.

Walking out of the circle we had formed, without even turning towards us, she repeated loudly and with indescribable contempt:

"Oh! you scum . . . you riff-raff!"

And she went away.

We remained there in the middle of the yard, in the mud, beneath the falling rain and the grey, sunless sky. . . .

Then in silence we returned to our damp stone cellar. The sun, as before, never so much as peeped in through our windows, and Tanya never came any more! . . .

HANS CHRISTIAN ANDERSEN

THE LITTLE MERMAID

FAR out at sea, the water is as blue as the prettiest cornflowers, and as clear as the purest crystal. But it is very deep—so deep, indeed, that no rope can fathom it; and many church steeples need be piled one upon the other to reach from the bottom to the surface. It is there that the sea-folk dwell.

Nor must it be imagined that there is nothing but a bare, white, sandy ground below. No, indeed! The soil produces the most curious trees and flowers, whose leaves and stems are so flexible that the slightest motion of the waters seems to fluster them as if they were living creatures. Fishes, great and small, glide through the branches as birds fly through the trees here upon earth. In the deepest spot of all stands the sea-king's palace; its walls are of coral, and its tall, pointed windows of the clearest amber, while the roof is made of mussel-shells, that open and shut according to the tide. And beautiful they look; for in each shell lies a pearl, any one of which would be worthy to be placed in a queen's crown.

The sea-king had been a widower for many years, so his aged mother kept house for him. She was a very wise woman, but extremely proud of her noble birth, which entitled her to wear twelve oyster-shells on her tail, while other well-born persons might only wear six. In all other respects she was a very praiseworthy sort of body; and especially as regards the care she took of the little princesses her grand-daughters. They were six pretty children; but the youngest was the prettiest of all. Her skin was as clear and delicate as a rose-leaf, and her eyes as blue as the deepest sea; but she had no feet any more than the others, and her body ended in a fish's tail.

They were free to play about all day long in the vast rooms of the palace below water, where live flowers grew upon the walls. The large amber windows were opened, when the fishes would swim inwards to them just as the swallows fly into our houses when we open the windows; only the fishes swam right up to the princesses, and ate out of their hands.

In front of the palace was a large garden with bright red and dark-blue trees, whose fruit glittered like gold, and whose blossoms were like fiery sparks, as both stalks and leaves kept rustling continually. The ground was strewed with the most delicate sand, but blue as the flames of sulphur.

Each of the little princesses had a plot of ground in the garden where she might dig and plant as she pleased. One sowed her flowers so as to come up in the shape of a whale; another preferred the figure of a little mermaid; but the youngest planted hers in a circle to imitate the sun, and chose flowers as red as the sun appeared to her. She was a singular child, both silent and thoughtful; and while her sisters were delighted with all the strange things that they obtained through the wrecks of various ships, she had never claimed anything—with the exception of the red flowers that resembled the sun above—but a pretty statue, representing a handsome youth, and hewn out of pure white marble, that had sunk to the bottom of the sea when a ship ran aground. She planted a bright red weeping-willow beside the statue; and when the tree grew up, its fresh boughs hung over it nearly down to the blue sands, where the shadow looked quite violet and kept dancing about like the branches.

There was nothing she delighted in so much as to hear about the upper world. She was always asking her grandmother to tell her all she knew about ships, towns, people and animals; what struck her as most beautiful was that the flowers of the earth should shed perfumes, which they do not below the sea; that the forests were green; and that the fishes amongst the trees should sing so loud and so exquisitely, that it must be a treat to hear them. It was the little birds that her grandmother called fishes, or else her young listeners would not have understood her, for they had never seen birds.

"When you have accomplished your fifteenth year," said the grandmother, "you shall have leave to rise up out of the sea, and sit on the rocks in the moonshine, and look at the large ships sailing past. And then you will see both forests and towns."

In the following year one of the sisters would reach the age of fifteen; but as all the rest were each a year younger than the other, the youngest would have to wait five years before it would be her turn to come up from the bottom of the ocean and see what our world is like. However, the eldest promised to tell the others what she saw, and what struck her as most beautiful on the first day; for their grandmother did not tell them enough.

But none of them longed for her turn to come so intensely as the youngest, who had to wait the longest, and was so reserved and thoughtful. Many a night did she stand at the open window, and gaze upwards through the dark blue water, and watch the fishes as they lashed the sea with their fins and tails. She could see the moon and stars, that appeared indeed rather pale, though much larger, seen through the water, than they do to us. If something resembling a black cloud glided between the stars and herself, she knew that it was either a whale swimming overhead, or a ship full of human beings, none of whom probably dreamed that a lovely little mermaid was standing below, and stretching forth her white hands towards the keel of their vessel.

The eldest princess was now fifteen, and was allowed to rise up to the surface of the sea.

On her return she had a great deal to relate; but the most delightful thing of all, she said, was to lie upon a sand-bank in the calm sea, and to gaze upon the large city near the coast, where lights were shining like hundreds of stars; to listen to the sounds of music, to the din of carriages, and the busy hum of the crowd; and to see the church steeples, and hear the bells ringing. And she longed after all these things, just because she could not approach them.

O, how attentively her youngest sister listened! And later in the evening, when she stood at the open window, and gazed up through the dark blue water, how she thought about the large city with its din and bustle, and even fancied she could hear the church-bells ringing from below!

In the following year, the second sister obtained leave to rise up to the surface of the water and swim about at her pleasure. She went up just at sunset, which appeared to her the finest sight of all. She said that the whole sky appeared like gold; and as to the clouds, their beauty was beyond all description. Red and violet clouds sailed rapidly above her head, while a flock of wild swans, resembling a long, white scarf, flew still faster than they, across the sea towards the setting sun. She, too, swam towards it, but the sun sank down, and the rosy hues vanished from the surface of the water.

The year after, the third sister went up. She was the boldest of them all; so she swam up a river that fell into the sea. She saw beautiful green hills covered with vines; castles and citadels peeped out from stately woods; she heard the birds singing, and the sun felt so warm that she was frequently obliged to dive down under the water to cool her burning face. In a small creek she met with a whole troop of little human children. They were naked, and dabbling about in the water. She wanted to play with them, but they flew away in great alarm; and there came a little black animal (she meant a dog, only she had never seen one before), who barked at her so tremendously that she was frightened, and sought to reach the open sea. But she should never forget the beautiful forests, the green hills, or the pretty children, who were able to swim in the water although they had no fish's tails.

The fourth sister was less daring. She remained in the midst of the sea, and maintained that it was most beautiful at that point, because from thence one could see for miles around, and the sky looked like a glass bell above one's head. She had seen ships, but only at a distance.

It was now the fifth sister's turn. Her birthday was in the winter, therefore she saw what the others had not seen the first time they went up. The sea looked quite green, and huge icebergs were floating about; each looked like a pearl, she said, only larger than the churches built by human beings. They were of the oddest shapes, and glittered like diamonds. She had placed herself upon the largest of them, and all the vessels scudded past in great alarm, as though fearful of approaching the spot where she was sitting, and letting the wind play with her long hair; but towards evening the sky became overcast, it thundered and lightened, while the dark sea lifted up the huge icebergs on high, so that they were illuminated by the red flashes of the lightning. All the vessels reefed in their sails, and their passengers were panic-struck—while she sat quietly on her floating block of ice, and watched the blue lightning as it zig-zagged along the shining sea.

The first time that each of the sisters had successively risen to the surface of the water, they had been enchanted by the novelty and beauty of all they saw; but being now grown up, and at liberty to go above as often as they pleased, they had grown indifferent to such excursions. They longed to come back into the water, and at the end of a month they had all declared that it was far more beautiful down below, and that it was pleasanter to stay at home.

It frequently happened in the evening that the five sisters would entwine their arms and rise up to the surface of the water all in a row. They had beautiful voices, far finer than any human being's; and when a storm was coming on, and they anticipated that a ship might sink, they swam before the vessel, and sang most sweetly of the delights to be found beneath the water, begging the seafarers not to be afraid of coming down below. But the sailors could not understand what they said, and mistook their words for the howling of the tempest; and they never saw all the fine things below, for if the ship sank, the men were drowned, and their bodies alone reached the sea-king's palace.

When the sisters rose up arm-in-arm through the water, the youngest would stand alone, looking after them, and felt ready to cry; only mermaids have no tears, and therefore suffer all the more.

"How I wish I were fifteen!" said she. "I am sure I shall love the world above, and the beings that inhabit it."

At last she reached the age of fifteen.

"Well! now you are grown up," said her grandmother, the widow to the late king. "So let me dress you like your sisters." And she placed in her hair a wreath of white lilies, every leaf of which was half a pearl; and the old dame ordered eight large oyster-shells to be fastened to the princess's tail, to denote her high rank.

"But they hurt me so," said the little mermaid.

"Pride must suffer pain," said the old lady.

O! how gladly would she have shaken off all this pomp, and laid aside her heavy wreath—the red flowers in her garden adorned her far better—but she could not help herself. "Farewell!" cried she, rising as lightly as a bubble to the surface of the water.

The sun had just sunk as she raised her head above the waves, but the clouds were still pink, and fringed with gold; and through the fast-vanishing rosy tints of the air, beamed the evening in all its beauty. The atmosphere was mild and cool, and the sea quite calm. A large ship with three masts was lying on its surface; only a single sail was hoisted, for not a breeze was stirring, and the sailors were sitting all about in the rigging. There were musical instruments playing, and voices singing; and when the evening grew darker, hundreds of gay-coloured lanterns were lighted, which looked like the flags of all nations streaming through the air. The little mermaid swam close to the cabin-window, and as often as the water lifted her up, she peeped in through the transparent panes, and saw a number of well-dressed persons. But the handsomest of all was the prince, with large black eyes; he could not be above sixteen, and it was his birthday that was being celebrated with such magnificence. The sailors danced upon deck; and when the young prince came up, above a hundred rockets were let off, that lit the air till it was as bright as day, and so frightened the little mermaid that she dived under the water. But she soon popped out her head once more, when all the stars in heaven seemed to be falling down upon her. She had never seen such fireworks before: large suns were throwing out sparks, beautiful fiery fishes were darting through the blue air, and all these wonders were reflected in the calm sea below. The ship itself was thrown into such bright relief, that every little cord was distinctly visible.

It was late. Still the little mermaid could not take her eyes off the ship or the handsome prince. The variegated lanterns were now extinguished, the rockets ceased to be let off, and no more cannons were fired; but there was a rumbling and a grumbling in the depths of the sea. Still she sat rocking up and down in the water, so as to peep into the cabin. But now the ship began to move faster, the sails were unfurled one after another, the waves ran higher, heavy clouds flitted across the sky, and flashes of lightning were seen in the distance. A tremendous storm seemed coming on, so the sailors reefed in the sails once more. The large ship kept pitching to and fro in its rapid course across the raging sea; the billows heaved, like so many gigantic black mountains, threatening to roll over the topmast; but the ship dived down like a swan between the high waves, and then rose again on the towering pinnacle of the waters. The little mermaid fancied this was a right pleasant mode of sailing; but the crew thought differently. The ship kept cracking and cracking, the thick planks gave way beneath the repeated lashings of the waves, a leak was sprung, the mast was broken right in twain like a reed, and the vessel drooped on one side, while the water kept filling the hold. The little mermaid now perceived that the crew were in danger, and she was herself obliged to take care not to be hurt by the beams and planks belonging to the ship, that were dispersed upon the waters. For one moment it was so pitch dark that she could see nothing; but when a flash of lightning illumined the sky, and enabled her to discern distinctly all on board, she looked especially for the young prince, whom she perceived sinking into the water, just as the ship burst asunder. She was then quite pleased at the thought of his coming down to her, till she reflected that human beings cannot live in water, and that he would be dead by the time he reached her father's castle. But die he must not; therefore she swam towards him through the planks and beams that were driven about on the billows, forgetting that they might crush her to atoms. She dived deep under the water, and then, rising again between the waves, she managed at length to reach the young prince, who was scarcely able to buffet any longer with the stormy sea. His arms and legs began to feel powerless, his beautiful eyes were closed, and he would have died had not the little mermaid come to his assistance. She held his head above the water, and then let the waves carry them whither they pleased.

Towards morning the storm had abated; but not a wreck of the vessel was to be seen. The sun rose red and beaming from the water, and seemed to infuse life into the prince's cheeks; but his eyes remained closed. The mermaid kissed his high, polished forehead, and stroked back his wet hair; she fancied he was like the marble statue in her garden, and she kissed him again, and wished that he might live.

They now came in sight of land; and she saw high, blue mountains, on the tops of which the snow looked as dazzling white as though a flock of swans were lying there. Below, near the coast, were beautiful green forests, and in front stood a church or a convent—she did not rightly know which—but, at all events, it was a building. Citrons and China oranges grew in the garden, and tall palm-trees stood in front of the door. The sea formed a small bay at this spot, and the water, though very deep, was quite calm; so she swam with the handsome prince towards the cliff, where the delicate white sands had formed a heap, and here she laid him down.

The bells now pealed from the large white building, and a number of girls came into the garden. The little mermaid then swam farther away, and hid herself behind some high stones that rose out of the water; and covering her head and bosom with foam, so that no one could see her little countenance, she watched whether any one came to the poor prince's assistance.

It was not long before a young maiden approached the spot where he was lying. She appeared frightened at first, but it was only for a moment, and then she fetched a number of persons; and the mermaid saw that the prince came to life again, and that he smiled on all those around him. But he did not send her a smile, neither did he know she had saved him: so she felt quite afflicted; and when he was led into the large building, she dived back into the water with a heavy heart, and returned to her father's castle.

Silent and thoughtful as she had always been, she now grew still more so. Her sisters inquired what she had seen the first time she went above, but she did not tell them.

Many an evening, and many a morning, did she rise up to the spot where she had left the prince. She saw the fruit in the garden grow ripe, and then she saw it gathered; she saw the snow melt away from the summits of the high mountains: but she did not see the prince, and each time she returned home more sorrowful than ever. Her only consolation was to sit in her little garden, and to fling her arm round the beauteous marble statue that was like the prince; but she ceased to tend her flowers, and they grew like a wilderness all over the paths, entwining their long stems and leaves with the branches of the trees, so that it was quite dark beneath their shade.

At length she could resist no longer, and opened her heart to one of her sisters, from whom all the others immediately learned her secret, though they told it to no one else except to a couple of other mermaids, who divulged it to nobody except to their most intimate friends. One of these happened to know who the prince was. She, too, had seen the gala on shipboard, and informed them whence he came, and where his kingdom lay.

"Come, little sister!" said the other princesses; and, entwining their arms, they rose up, in a long row, out of the sea, at the spot where they knew the prince's palace stood.

This was built of bright yellow, shining stone, with a broad flight of marble steps, the last of which reached down into the sea. Magnificent golden cupolas rose above the roof, and marble statues, closely imitating life, were placed between the pillars that surrounded the edifice. One could see, through the transparent panes of the large windows, right into the magnificent rooms, fitted up with costly silk curtains and splendid hangings, and ornamented with large pictures on all the walls; so that it was a pleasure to look at them.

Now that she knew where he lived, she spent many an evening, and many a night, on the neighbouring water. She swam much nearer the shore than any of the others had ventured to do; nay, she even went up the narrow canal, under the handsome marble balcony, that threw its long shadow over the water. Here she would sit, and gaze at the young prince, who thought himself quite alone in the bright moonshine.

Many an evening did she see him sailing in his pretty boat, adorned with flags, and enjoying music: then she would listen from amongst the green reeds; and if the wind happened to seize hold of her long, silvery-white veil, those who saw it took it to be a swan spreading out his wings.

Many a night, too, when fishermen were spreading their nets by torchlight, she heard them speaking highly of the young prince; and she rejoiced that she had saved his life, when he was tossed about, half dead, on the waves.

She soon grew to be more and more fond of human beings, and to long more and more fervently to be able to walk about amongst them, for their world appeared to her far larger and more beautiful than her own. They could fly across the sea upon ships, and scale mountains that towered above the clouds; and the lands they possessed—their fields and their forests—stretched away far beyond the reach of her sight.

There was such a deal that she wanted to learn, but her sisters were not able to answer all her questions; therefore she applied to her old grandmother, who was well acquainted with the upper world, which she called, very correctly, the lands above the sea.

"If human beings do not get drowned," asked the little mermaid, "can they live for ever? Do not they die, as we do here in the sea?"

"Yes," said the ancient dame, "they must die as well as we; and the term of their life is even shorter than ours. We can live to be three hundred years old; but when we cease to be here, we shall only be changed into foam, and are not even buried below among those we love. Our souls are not immortal. We shall never enter upon a new life. We are like the green reed, that can never flourish again when it has once been cut through. Human beings, on the contrary, have a soul that lives eternally—yea, even after the body has been committed to the earth—and that rises up through the clear, pure air, to the bright stars above! Like as we rise out of the water, to look at the haunts of men, so do they rise to unknown and favoured regions, that we shall never be privileged to see."

"And why have we not an immortal soul?" asked the little mermaid, sorrowfully. "I would willingly give all the hundreds of years I may have to live, to be a human being but for one day, and to have the hope of sharing in the joys of the heavenly world."

"You must not think about that," said the old dame. "We feel we are much happier and better than the human race above."

"So I shall die, and be driven about like foam on the sea, and cease to hear the music of the waves, and to see the beautiful flowers, and the red sun? Is there nothing I can do to obtain an immortal soul?"

"No," said the old sea-queen; "unless a human being loved you so dearly that you were more to him than either father or mother; if all his thoughts and his love were centred in you, and he allowed the priest to lay his right hand in yours, promising to be faithful to you here and hereafter: then would his soul glide into your body, and you would obtain a share in the happiness awaiting human beings. He would give you a soul without forfeiting his own. But this will never happen! Your fish's tail, which is a beauty amongst us sea-folk, is thought a deformity on earth, because they know no better,—

it is necessary there to have two stout props, that they call legs, in order to be beautiful!"

The little mermaid sighed as she cast a glance at her fish's tail.

"Let us be merry," said the old dame; "let us jump and hop about during the three hundred years that we have to live—which is really quite enough in all conscience. We shall then be all the more disposed to rest at a later period. To-night, we shall have a court ball."

On these occasions there was a display of magnificence such as we never see upon earth. The walls and the ceiling of the large ballroom were of thick though transparent glass. Hundreds of colossal mussel-shells—some of a deep red, others as green as grass—were hung in rows on each side, and contained blue flames that illuminated the whole room, and shone through the walls, so that the sea was lighted all around. Countless fishes, great and small, were to be seen swimming past the glass walls, some of them flaunting in scarlet scales, while others sparkled like liquid gold or silver.

Through the ballroom flowed a wide stream, on whose surface the mermen and mermaids danced to their own sweet singing. Human beings have no such voices. The little mermaid sang the sweetest of them all, and the whole court applauded with their hands and tails; and for a moment she felt delighted, for she knew that she had the loveliest voice ever heard upon earth or upon the sea. But her thoughts soon turned once more to the upper world, for she could not long forget either the handsome prince, or her grief at not having an immortal soul like his. She therefore stole out of her father's palace, where all within was song and festivity, and sat down sadly in her own little garden. Here she heard a bugle sounding through the water.

"Now," thought she, "he is surely sailing about up above; he who incessantly fills all my thoughts, and to whose hands I would fain entrust the happiness of my existence. I will venture everything to win him, and to obtain an immortal soul. While my sisters are dancing yonder in my father's castle, I will go to the sea-witch, who has always frightened me hitherto, but now, perhaps, she can advise and help me."

The little mermaid then left her garden, and repaired to the rushing whirlpool, behind which the sorceress lived. She had never gone that way before. Neither flowers nor sea-grass grew there; and nothing but bare, gray, sandy ground led to the whirlpool, where the waters kept eddying like waving mill-wheels, dragging everything they clutched hold of into the fathomless depth below. Between these whirlpools, that might have crushed her in their rude grasp, was the mermaid forced to pass to reach the dominions of the sea-witch; and even here, during a good part of the way, there was no other road than across a sheet of warm, bubbling mire, which the witch called her turf-common. At the back of this lay her house, in the midst of a most singular forest: its trees and bushes were polypi—half animal, half plant—they looked like hundred-headed serpents growing out of the ground; the branches were long, slimy arms, with fingers like flexible worms, and they could move every joint from the root to the tip. They laid fast hold of whatever they could snatch from the sea, and never yielded it up again. The little mermaid was so frightened at the sight of them that her heart beat with fear, and she was fain to turn back; but then she thought of the prince, and of the soul that human beings possessed, and she took courage. She knotted up her long, flowing hair, that the polypi might not seize hold of her locks; and crossing her hands over her bosom, she darted along, as a fish shoots through the water, between the ugly polypi, that stretched forth their flexible arms and fingers behind her. She perceived how each of them retained what it had seized, with hundreds of little arms, as strong as iron clasps. Human beings, who had died at sea, and had sunk below, looked like white skeletons in the arms of the polypi. They clutched rudders, too, and chests, and skeletons of animals belonging to the earth, and even a little mermaid, whom they had caught and stifled—and this appeared to her, perhaps, the most shocking of all.

She now approached a vast swamp in the forest where large, fat water-snakes were wallowing in the mire, and displaying their ugly, whitish-yellow bodies. In the midst of this loathsome spot stood a house built of the bones of shipwrecked human beings, and within sat the sea-witch, feeding a toad from her mouth, just as people amongst us give a little canary-bird a lump of sugar to eat. She called the nasty fat water-snakes her little chicks, and let them creep all over her bosom.

"I know what you want!" said the sea-witch. "It is very stupid of you, but you shall have your way, as it will plunge you into misfortune, my fair princess. You want to be rid of your fish's tail, and to have a couple of props like those human beings have to walk about upon, in order that the young prince may fall in love with you, and that you may obtain his hand and an immortal soul into the bargain!" And then the old witch laughed so loud and so repulsively that the toad and the snakes fell to the ground, where they lay wriggling about.

"You come just at the nick of time," added the witch, "for to-morrow, by sunrise, I should no longer be able to help you till another year had flown past. I will prepare you a potion; and you must swim ashore with it to-morrow, before sunrise, and then sit down and drink it. Your tail will then disappear, and shrivel up into what human beings called neat legs—but mind, it will hurt you as much as if a sharp sword were thrust through you. Everybody that sees you will say you are the most beautiful mortal ever seen. You will retain the floating elegance of your gait; no dancer will move so lightly as you, but every step you take will be like treading upon such sharp knives that you would think your blood must flow. If you choose to put up with sufferings like these, I have the power to help you."

"I do," said the little mermaid, in a trembling voice, as she thought of the prince and of an immortal soul.

"But bethink you well," said the witch; "if once you obtain a human form, you can never be a mermaid again! You will never be able to dive down into the water to your sisters, or return to your father's palace; and if you should fail in winning the prince's love to the degree of his forgetting both father and mother for your sake, and loving you with his whole soul, and bidding the priest join your hands in marriage, then you will never obtain an immortal soul! And the very day after he will have married another, your heart will break, and you will dissolve into the foam on the billows."

"I am resolved," said the little mermaid, who had turned as pale as death.

"But you must pay me my dues," said the witch, "and it is no small matter I require. You have the loveliest voice of all the inhabitants of the deep, and you reckon upon its tones to charm him into loving you. Now, you must give me this beautiful voice. I choose to have the best of all you possess in exchange for my valuable potion. For I must mix my own blood with it, that it may prove as sharp as a two-edged sword."

"But if you take away my voice," said the little mermaid, "what have I left?"

"Your lovely form," said the witch; "your aerial step, and your expressive eyes—with these you surely can befool a man's heart. Well? Has your courage melted away? Come put out your little tongue, and let me cut it off for my fee, and you shall have the valuable potion."

"So be it," said the little mermaid; and the witch put her cauldron on the fire to prepare the potion. "Cleanliness is a virtue!" quoth she, scouring the cauldron with the snakes that she had tied into a knot, after which she pricked her own breast and let her black blood trickle down into the vessel. The steam rose up in such fanciful shapes, that no one could have looked at them without a shudder. The witch kept flinging fresh materials into the cauldron every moment; and when it began to simmer it was like the wailings of a crocodile. At length the potion was ready, and it looked like the purest spring water.

"Here it is," said the witch, cutting off the little mermaid's tongue; so now she was dumb, and could neither sing nor speak.

"If the polypi should seize hold of you on your return through my forest," said the witch, "you need only sprinkle a single drop of this potion over them, and their arms and fingers will be shivered to a thousand pieces." But the little mermaid had no need of this talisman; the polypi drew back in alarm from her on perceiving the dazzling potion, that shined in her hand like a twinkling star. So she crossed rapidly through the forest, the swamp, and the raging whirlpool.

She saw her father's palace—the torches were now extinguished in the large ballroom—and she knew the whole family were asleep within, but she did not dare venture to go and seek them, now that she was dumb and was about to leave them for ever. Her heart seemed ready to burst with anguish. She stole into the garden and plucked a flower from each of her sisters' flower-beds, kissed her hand a thousand times to the palace, and then rose up through the blue waters.

The sun had not yet risen when she saw the prince's castle, and reached the magnificent marble steps. The moon shone brightly. The little mermaid drank the sharp and burning potion, and it seemed as if a two-edged sword was run through her delicate frame. She fainted away, and remained apparently lifeless. When the sun rose over the sea, she awoke, and felt a sharp pang; but just before her stood the handsome young prince. He gazed at her so intently with his coal-black eyes that she cast hers to the ground, and now perceived that her fish's tail had disappeared, and that she had a pair of the neatest little white legs that a maiden could desire. Only, having no clothes on, she was obliged to enwrap herself in her long, thick hair. The prince inquired who she was, and how she had come thither; but she could only look at him with her mild but sorrowful deep-blue eyes, for speak she could not. He then took her by the hand, and led her into the palace. Every step she took was, as the witch had warned her it would be, like treading on the points of needles and sharp knives; but she bore it willingly; and, hand in hand with the prince, she glided in as lightly as a soap-bubble, so that he, as well as everybody else, marvelled at her lovely, aerial gait.

She was now dressed in costly robes of silk and muslin, and was the most beautiful of all the inmates of the palace; but she was dumb, and could neither sing nor speak. Handsome female slaves, attired in silk and gold, came and sang before the prince and his royal parents; and one of them happening to sing more beautifully than all the others, the prince clapped his hands and smiled. This afflicted the little mermaid. She knew that she herself had sung much more exquisitely, and thought: "Oh, did he but know that to be near him, I sacrificed my voice to all eternity!"

The female slaves now performed a variety of elegant, aerial-looking dances to the sound of the most delightful music. The little mermaid then raised her beautiful white arms, stood on the tips of her toes, and floated across the floor in such a way as no one had ever danced before. Every motion revealed some fresh beauty, and her eyes appealed still more directly to the heart than the singing of the slaves had done.

Everybody was enchanted, but most of all the prince, who called her his little foundling; and she danced on and on, though every time her foot touched the floor she felt as if she were treading on sharp knives. The prince declared that he would never part with her, and she obtained leave to sleep on a velvet cushion before his door.

He had her dressed in male attire that she might accompany him on horseback. They then rode together through the perfumed forests, where the green boughs touched their shoulders, and the little birds sang amongst the cool leaves. She climbed up mountains by the prince's side; and though her tender feet bled so that others perceived it, she only laughed at her sufferings, and followed him till they could see the clouds rolling beneath them like a flock of birds bound for some distant land.

At night, when others slept throughout the prince's palace, she would go and sit on the broad marble steps, for it cooled her burning feet to bathe them in the sea-water; and then she thought of those below the deep.

One night her sisters rose up arm-in-arm, and sang so mournfully as they glided over the waters! She then made them a sign, when they recognised her, and told her how deeply she had afflicted them all. After that they visited her every night; and once she perceived at a great distance her aged grandmother, who had not come up above the surface of the sea for many years, and the sea-king with his crown on his head. They stretched out their arms to her, but they did not venture so near the shore as her sisters.

Each day she grew to love the prince more fondly; and he loved her just as one loves a dear, good child. But as to choosing her for his queen, such an idea never entered his head; yet, unless she became his wife, she would not obtain an immortal soul, and would melt to foam on the morrow of his wedding another.

"Don't you love me the best of all?" would the little mermaid's eyes seem to ask, when he embraced her, and kissed her fair forehead.

"Yes, I love you best," said the prince, "for you have the best heart of any. You are the most devoted to me, and you resemble a young maiden whom I once saw, but whom I shall never meet again. I was on board a ship that sank; the billows cast me near a holy temple, where several young maids were performing Divine service; the youngest of them found me on the shore and saved my life. I saw her only twice. She would be the only one that I could love in this world; but your features are like hers, and you have almost driven her image out of my soul. She belongs to the holy temple; and, therefore, my good star has sent you to me—and we will never part."

"Alas! he knows not that it was I who saved his life!" thought the little mermaid. "I bore him across the sea to the wood where stands the holy temple, and I sat beneath the foam to watch whether any human beings came to help him. I saw the pretty girl whom he loves better than he does me." And the mermaid fetched a deep sigh; for tears she had none to shed. "He says the maiden belongs to the holy temple, and she will therefore never return to the world. They will not meet again, while I am by his side and see him every day. I will take care of him, and love him, and sacrifice my life to him."

But now came a talk of the prince being about to marry, and to obtain for his wife the beautiful daughter of a neighbouring king; and that was why he was fitting out such a magnificent vessel. The prince was travelling ostensibly on a mere visit to his neighbour's estates, but, in reality, to see the king's daughter. He was to be accompanied by a numerous retinue. The little mermaid shook her head and smiled. She knew the prince's thoughts better than the others did. "I must travel," he had said to her. "I must see this beautiful princess, because my parents require it of me; but they will not force me to bring her home as my bride. I cannot love her. She will not resemble the beautiful maid in the temple whom you are like; and if I were compelled to choose a bride, it should sooner be you, my dumb foundling, with those expressive eyes of yours." And he kissed her rosy mouth, and played with her long hair, and rested his head against her heart, which beat high with hopes of human felicity and of an immortal soul.

"You are not afraid of the sea, my dumb child, are you?" said he, as they stood on the magnificent vessel that was to carry them to the neighbouring king's dominions. And he talked to her about tempests and calm, of the singular fishes to be found in the deep, and of the wonderful things the divers saw below; and she smiled, for she knew, better than any one else, what was in the sea below.

During the moonlit night, when all were asleep on board, not even excepting the helmsman at his rudder, she sat on deck, and gazed through the clear waters, and fancied she saw her father's palace. High above it stood her aged grandmother, with her silver crown on her head, looking up intently at the keel of the ship. Then her sisters rose up to the surface, and gazed at her mournfully, and wrung their white hands. She made a sign to them, smiled, and would fain have told them that she was happy and well off; but the cabin-boy approached, and the sisters dived beneath the waves, leaving him to believe that the white forms he thought he descried were only the foam upon the waters.

Next morning the ship came into port at the neighbouring king's splendid capital. The bells were all set a-ringing, trumpets sounded flourishes from high turrets; and soldiers, with flying colours and shining bayonets, stood ready to welcome the stranger. Every day brought some fresh entertainment: balls and feasts succeeded each other. But the princess was not yet there; for she had been brought up, people said, in a far-distant, holy temple, where she had acquired all manner of royal virtues. At last she came.

The little mermaid was curious to judge of her beauty, and she was obliged to acknowledge to herself that she had never seen a lovelier face. Her skin was delicate and transparent, and beneath her long, dark lashes sparkled a pair of sincere, dark-blue eyes.

"It is you!" cried the prince—"you who saved me, when I lay like a lifeless corpse upon the shore!" And he folded his blushing bride in his arms. "Oh, I am too happy!" said he to the little mermaid: "my fondest dream has come to pass. You will rejoice at my happiness, for you wish me better than any of them." And the little mermaid kissed his hand, and felt already as if her heart was about to break. His wedding-morning would bring her death, and she would be then changed to foam upon the sea.

All the church-bells were ringing, and the heralds rode through the streets, and proclaimed the approaching nuptials. Perfumed oil was burning in costly silver lamps on all the altars. The priests were swinging their censers; while the bride and bridegroom joined their hands, and received the bishop's blessing. The little mermaid, dressed in silk and gold, held up the bride's train; but her ears did not hear the solemn music, neither did her eyes behold the ceremony; she thought of the approaching gloom of death, and of all she had lost in this world.

That same evening the bride and bridegroom went on board. The cannons were roaring, the banners were streaming, and a costly tent of gold and purple, lined with beautiful cushions, had been prepared on deck for the reception of the bridal pair.

The vessel then set sail, with a favourable wind, and glided smoothly along the calm sea.

When it grew dark, a number of variegated lamps were lighted, and the crew danced merrily on deck. The little mermaid could not help remembering her first visit to the earth, when she witnessed similar festivities and magnificence; and she twirled round in the dance, half poised in the air, like a swallow when pursued; and all present cheered her in ecstacies, for never had she danced so enchantingly before. Her tender feet felt the sharp pangs of knives; but she heeded it not, for a sharper pang had shot through her heart. She knew this was the last evening she should ever be able to see him for whom she had left both her relations and her home, sacrificed her beautiful voice, and daily suffered most excruciating pains, without his having even dreamed that such was the case. It was the last night on which she might breathe the same air as he, and gaze on the deep sea and the starry sky. An eternal night, unenlivened by either thoughts or dreams, now awaited her; for she had no soul, and could never now obtain one. Yet all was joy and gaiety on board till long past midnight; and she was fain to laugh and dance, though the thoughts of death were in her heart. The prince kissed his beautiful bride, and she played with his black locks; and then they went, arm-in-arm, to rest beneath the splendid tent.

All was now quiet on board: the steersman only was sitting at the helm, as the little mermaid leaned her white arms on the edge of the vessel, and looked towards the east for the first blush of morning. The very first sunbeam, she knew, must kill her. She then saw her sisters rising out of the flood. They were as pale as herself, and their long and beautiful locks were no longer streaming to the winds, for they had been cut off.

"We gave them to the witch," said they, "to obtain help, that you might not die to-night. She gave us a knife in exchange—and a sharp one it is, as you may see. Now, before sunrise, you must plunge it into the prince's heart; and when his warm blood shall besprinkle your feet, they will again close up into a fish's tail, and you will be a mermaid once more, and can come down to us, and live out your three hundred years, before you turn into inanimate, salt foam. Haste, then! He or you must die before sunrise! Our old grandmother has fretted till her white hair has fallen off, as ours has fallen under the witch's scissors. Haste, then! Do you not perceive those red streaks in the sky? In a few minutes the sun will rise, and then you must die!" And they then fetched a deep, deep sigh, as they sank down into the waves.

The little mermaid lifted the scarlet curtain of the tent, and beheld the fair bride resting her head on the prince's breast; and she bent down and kissed his beautiful forehead, then looked up at the heavens where the rosy dawn grew brighter and brighter—then gazed on the sharp knife, and again turned her eyes towards the prince, who was calling his bride by her name, in his sleep. She alone filled his thoughts, and the mermaid's fingers clutched the knife instinctively—but in another moment she hurled the blade far away into the waves, that gleamed redly where it fell, as though drops of blood were gurgling up from the water. She gave the prince one last, dying look, and then jumped overboard, and felt her body dissolving into foam.

The sun now rose out of the sea; its beams threw a kindly warmth upon the cold foam, and the little mermaid did not experience the pangs of death. She saw the bright sun, and above were floating hundreds of transparent, beautiful creatures; she could still catch a glimpse of the ship's white sails, and of the red clouds in the sky, across the swarms of these lovely beings. Their language was melody, but too ethereal to be heard by human ears, just as no human eye can discern their forms. Though without wings, their lightness poises them in the air. The little mermaid saw that she had a body like theirs, that kept rising higher and higher from out the foam.

"Where am I?" asked she, and her voice sounded like that of her companions, so ethereal, that no earthly music could give an adequate idea of its sweetness.

"Amongst the daughters of the air!" answered they. "A mermaid has not an immortal soul, and cannot obtain one, unless she wins the love of some human being—her eternal welfare depends on the will of another. But the daughters of the air, although not possessing an immortal soul by nature, can obtain one by their good deeds. We fly to warm countries, and fan the burning atmosphere, laden with pestilence, that destroys the sons of man. We diffuse the perfume of flowers through the air to heal and to refresh. When we have striven for three hundred years to do all the good in our power, we then obtain an immortal soul, and share in the eternal happiness of the human race. You, poor little mermaid! have striven with your whole heart like ourselves. You have suffered and endured, and have raised yourself into an aerial spirit, and now your own good works may obtain you an immortal soul after the lapse of three hundred years."

And the little mermaid lifted her brightening eyes to the sun, and for the first time she felt them filled with tears. All was now astir in the ship, and she could see the prince and his beautiful bride looking for her, and then gazing sorrowfully at the pearly foam, as though they knew that she had cast herself into the waves. She then kissed the bride's forehead, and fanned the prince, unseen by either of them, and then mounted, together with the other children of the air, on the rosy cloud that was sailing through the atmosphere.

" Thus shall we glide into the kingdom of heaven, after the lapse of three hundred years," said she.

" We may reach it sooner," whispered one of the daughters of the air. " We enter unseen the dwellings of man, and for each day on which we have met with a good child, who is the joy of his parents, and deserving of their love, the Almighty shortens the time of our trial. The child little thinks, when we fly through the room, and smile for joy at such a discovery, that a year is deducted from the three hundred we have to live. But when we see an ill-behaved or naughty child, we shed tears of sorrow, and every tear adds a day to the time of our probation."

PER HALLSTRÖM, Ph.D.

THE HONEYMOON

THE day before the wedding the young couple had paid a visit to the bridegroom's mother to say good-bye. She had been a widow for many years, and now the last of her children was to leave her altogether, for after the honeymoon he was going to live upon the family estate, which she had vacated for him. He would certainly see her once again, but then amid all the ceremony and excitement of the wedding, so that there would hardly be time for a proper farewell, particularly as the bridal pair wished to disappear as unobtrusively as possible from the company and go straight to the railway-station. They had begged not to be accompanied there, and were already longing with almost nervous eagerness for the time when they could at last be left together in that which really concerned themselves alone, but in which the whole world, with importunate kindness, seemed to wish to intervene with good wishes and advice.

There was therefore no real peace at the mother's either, though no one else disturbed it, and she herself by no means overwhelmed them with her emotions or her words. For the most part she sat and looked at them, and seemed to dream back the hours to something in her memory, something similar, but very far away. Her look was that of one suddenly seized by the familiar yet mysterious conviction: "I have been through this already, this has happened once before." But in her case there was this difference that she obviously knew *when*, and it was easy to guess that it was of her own wedding-trip that she was thinking.

The young people felt themselves embarrassed by this rather too intimate participation in their joy, for they were convinced that it was something entirely apart, and they needed no one to share it. They even found it a trifle absurd that a former generation, so different in every way, and on the whole so decidedly inferior to theirs, should lift up its head and make comparisons. They talked about their plans for the journey, through Switzerland to Italy, and they did it with cheerfulness and decision, and in a tone that discouraged all attempts to stop them on the way by dragging in place-names that were indifferent to them and probably deserved to be so.

The old lady noticed all this, but thought such youthful arrogance excusable and perhaps reasonable enough, as long as it might last. There was only one place which it pained her to have set aside in this fashion: "If you should come to Bevers, in the Engadine"—she repeated, in a tone which seemed to say that there was something more to tell about that place.

"But, mother dear, we shan't be going anywhere near there."

"That is a pity; it is a lovely place, too. I should like to have been remembered to the people at the *Weissen Rössli*, if it is still there."

"What a pretty name!" said the girl with a smile.

"Yes, but it means, not the 'Little White Rose,' as you might think, but the 'Little White Horse.' Such names are not common in the Engadine, but they were German-Swiss folk that christened it. So you will certainly notice if it you go there." And again there was something in the tone which suggested that she had more to say.

But the young people did not notice it, and were not interested in Bevers or its little horse.

"No, unfortunately we shall not be going there."

Thereupon, with a slightly melancholy look in her eyes, she abandoned this and everything else that distracted her, and unselfishly gave her whole attention to all they had to tell her. The atmosphere became untroubled, and the farewell, when it came, was as unsentimental in all its heartiness as the young couple could have desired.

But when they had gone, the dreamy look came back again, and she lost herself in the memory that had been aroused. It was quite a little story, the most noteworthy incident in her life. She would certainly have related it briefly and incompletely if it had had to be told at such an unseasonable hour, but now, when she had it to herself, it took on completeness and colour and was invested with a strangely tangible atmosphere.

She was on her honeymoon at the beginning of the 'eighties, and they had come to Bevers through the Albula pass, between walls of snow even at midsummer, in a diligence with six horses and a postilion blowing his horn—a regular little fairy-tale in itself. As they were the only passengers, they had been able to get the coachman and postilion to slow down a little, and they had jumped out and run about to get warm, throwing snowballs at each other, once or twice full in the face. The snow that was melting could hardly be called cold, so brightly shone the sun, and so quickly was the moisture absorbed in the intoxicatingly thin air. Had they had any troubles in their heads, these, too, would have been driven away as quickly, but they had none, they had never been younger and gayer as far as even she, with her twenty summers, could remember.

At the hospice they had an early dinner and in their merriment they mercilessly chaffed the host, who insisted on speaking French, and could not. There they heard for the first time the name *Weissen Rössli* in his eager recommendation of his colleague at Bevers, but it came in the most amusing travesty—" *l'etablissement le plus superbe, monsieur et madame, le petit cheval rose.*"

" Then you must get us rose-coloured horses to go there," they said, " we won't have any others "—and as a matter of fact they got them, for there was no other colour on anything that day.

When they arrived, they found the place delightful, and as soon as the host perceived what kind of guests they were, he gave them the best room in the house. It was large, with walls and ceiling of soft, light-brown larch-wood, which was gilded by the evening sun when the windows were opened. In one direction could be seen Piz Muraigl and Piz Langard, dark blue and with their snow-covered peaks touched with pink, and right over against them they had the valley of the Inn, whose icy-green waters flowed between fruitful meadows. The whole house, which was white-washed inside and out, except where the larch timbering intervened, had an indescribable smell of milk, but it seemed only clean and countrified. Everything was curiously new and strange, yet at the same time friendly.

They stayed there for several days, and made long excursions in the most wonderful weather without ever feeling any weariness in the rare, cool atmosphere. On the contrary, when they had scaled some height, they would suddenly feel a rush of health and strength flow through them like a passing gust of wind, and blood and nerves were filled with a healthy vigour and enjoyment as of life's own joy on living. Once, when climbing a mountain on the other side of the river, they came upon a valley lying deep down between precipices, which was like a little world in itself with a sparkling stream and sallows in their spring-tide green and thin, light grass—a world which seemed to have been newly created and to be as yet untouched by time. They gazed long upon it and seemed to belong there, and they tried to get down but found the place quite inaccessible, except possibly for the chamois.

When they went on, the memory went with them, and lingered in a way that seemed significant.

Something dream-like could hardly fail to pass into such an existence, however eagerly they might drink in impressions of reality, and when anything came to remind them of their old, familiar world, they welcomed it as an assurance that all this about them was true. Thus the young wife had felt when they went for the first time to Palud Marcha, a track with patches of bog at the bottom of a pine-wood dell; suddenly in some way they felt themselves to be at home, and as they looked around and up at Cresta Mora, they noticed that it was of granite. The mountain itself was as foreign as the name, but the stone or the air from it spoke to them, and they gladly revisited it. Had their feelings expressed themselves in words they would have been: "You and I and happiness, everything is real, and at home we shall live our lives together just as now."

One day, when they were up on Muottas Muraigl, they tried to make their way down to Palud Marcha. On the top they had seen marmots squatting on their hind-legs on blocks of stone, and uttering a mysterious warning whistle to one another ere they sought their hiding-places. After that, they met a herd of goats tended by a lad who had lit a fire to while away the time and have something more to look after. They talked with the goatherd, whose eyes became unnaturally round, and with the goats, who watched them with a calm and mystic gaze from their horizontal slits of pupils. They got much the same answers from both species of creature, but it was at least an experience of strange and primitive life. They gave the boy a coin, and as he seemed by way of thanks to wish them luck upon their journey, they gave him another, so that he too might be really happy.

A little way down the slope they found that he had served them well, since for the first time they saw Alpine roses blooming right below the path. She had wanted them badly, and uttered a cry of delight.

But the place was so steep that she could not pick them herself, but could only receive them one by one, as he passed them up while he held on to the side by one hand.

Suddenly he made a stumbling movement and seized a rose-bush with his free hand. "Don't be frightened," he said, in a low and serious voice. "I'm not standing quite safely, I seem to have missed my foothold and must find a new one, but I daren't move. If I leave go of this bush I don't know if the other will hold." And with an intuition swifter than she had ever known, she grasped his whole position and saw what was the only means of averting the danger. She saw, too, how great the danger was, with a curious icy clearness, which embraced every patch and stone in the precipice below him and right down to the valley far beneath.

"Don't move," she said, "wait a minute, and I'll soon . . ." She had a long shawl over her shoulders and round her waist, which she snatched off and twisted into a rope. Around her grew some dwarf pines, and in a moment she had chosen the one that seemed to be the strongest and most firmly rooted, and tied the shawl fast to it. The other end she wrapped round her left wrist, and gripped it with all her strength. By leaning out in this way and bending over, she could just reach one of his hands.

"Take hold of me," she said, "you will have a better grip."

"I shall be too heavy, I am so badly balanced."

"You must do it very quickly, and just as you leave go of the bush you must find another footing. I think there is one if you swing a little to the right, and you can reach it just as you take hold of me, and pull yourself up. You'll reach further with your foot that way, and I'll help you as you move."

He looked up at her with a smile of admiration on his pale, set face. "You see it all wonderfully clearly; that is a possibility. I had thought something of the kind, but a good many other things, too. It's strange how quickly things pass through my mind. If I give up my one hold, the other may break, and then I shall be hanging with my whole weight on you."

"No matter, I am strong enough."

"But suppose the shawl doesn't hold, or what you have tied it to?"

"It'll hold all right. Come on, now!"

"But don't you see? I mustn't drag you with me?"

"If it must be, why not? What should I do alone if . . ." And now it was she who smiled, so ecstatically and tenderly, with her face shining and close above his, that he felt exactly as she did: they must go together, and whatever happened there was no terror in it, not even on her account.

He seized her hand firmly and found himself quite able to make the movement demanded; his foot reached the place it sought, and there was no longer any danger. A moment afterwards he was able to climb cautiously up, and there they sat side by side, dazed and strangely tired in all their limbs: they knew not whether it was from the strain upon the nerves just now or from the shock of the great joy, which goes deeper than anything else. But suddenly all their stupor passed and they kissed, and fondled one another and whispered happy, disconnected words. It was not the danger past that was in their minds, they thought of nothing at all; they only felt their love, grown somehow different, something entirely new, in a wave of tenderness and joy that flowed over the heart and was physically perceptible there, like a bath from which it would emerge clean and fresh and noble. And the strangest thing was that this feeling was common to both, as though only one heart beat in their united being.

When they went on down the path, their hands sought one another as often as they could, and in the contact the current of feeling came back as strong as ever, though in between whiles there was room for each one's thoughts.

Her own did not go far, they stopped at the marvel: "How is it possible that I can have become still happier?" She troubled little about the answer, and it did not occur to her to seek it in what she had done. That was something simple and obvious which she could not have properly remembered, and still less explained, had she wished. He loved her still more, that was everything.

But the husband thought deeply and remembered every word and look of hers as she rescued him. He was proud of her, and had a feeling of reverence for what she was. He had not really known what he possessed until now. He had fallen in love with her as the prettiest girl he had met, and one made just for him; and his joy, when he had won her, had had something dreamlike remaining in its intimacy. When she had become his wife and comrade for life, his lovely plaything and the solace of his senses, he had thought that he had won all that Fortune had to offer. But now the gift had shown itself to be far greater than he had thought, and that just at the moment when it had been so nearly lost. In her shining eyes and brave and simple words he had caught a glimpse of that infinity in which the soul is conscious of its existence as something more than a dark, uneasy longing. Already in her love he had found it, but now he knew it certainly. It was as though they were now for the first time truly man and wife.

When they reached the hotel, people saw that something had happened, and they had to put on their everyday manners in order to divert attention. It was very difficult, though in themselves they had never felt so easy or so free. It was like appearing incognito with some princely joy, like controlling one's movements in a world where there was no law of gravity.

When they were alone, they could give themselves up undisturbed to that great, intoxicating emotion which had come upon them by the cliff-edge above the roses, but which was still no less new, since the ineffable is ever new.

In the morning he was awakened early by the sunlight coming into the room through a window which had been left ajar. As he flung it wide open to the cool, morning air, he breathed in the heavy scent of the flowers from the meadows, and he seemed to see their colours bathed in a pearly sheen of blue and purple and dewy silver. The blue mountains, too, were watered with a silvery light. All was strangely clear and new, and, notwithstanding its signs of habitation, the whole valley was as untouched and pure as that which they had looked upon from the cliffs up above, in which no human foot had trod. While he dressed, longing for his wife to wake but anxious not to disturb her, his whole thought was: "I have never truly lived before."

He saw that there was something written on the walls by the window, evidently the kind of scrawl that is often left by travellers at places of interest and provokes as much disgust as the insolent pollution of flies. But now he read it, and found more beside it and read that also, for they were all names of men and women, English for the most part, with a date beneath, and he could guess that they were names of young couples who had left this record behind them in the traditional bridal chamber of the house. Here, their childishness seemed natural enough, and before he realised what he was doing he had himself taken out a pencil from his pocket and inscribed upon the brown wood a line which seemed to dominate all the rest and ring like music in his heart.

Then he heard his wife's voice behind him, laughing and surprised.

"Whatever are you doing?"

He was ashamed at being discovered and muttered "Oh! it's something very silly," but when he turned to meet her beaming countenance, he went across and raised her from the bed and bore her to the window. There, when her eyes had grown accustomed to the brightness, she read, written in his well-known hand, the words: "I am happy!"

The line had so engraved itself upon her vision that she saw it just as clearly now, after so many years, as she sat and called up all the circumstances that had led to it.

There was much else that remained almost as clear—the mountains with their snowy tops, the white village with its slated roofs, and the faint smell of milk in the *Weissen Rössli*, all the scents from the variegated mass of flowers in the meadows, and the impressions which the odours seemed to make more real. She saw again the Alpine rose-bushes and the steep leading down to Palud Marcha and the whole scene there, down to herself, young and strong in her well-remembered dress.

That which her memory did not retain as clearly, since it can never do so, was no doubt the most important part of all—the feelings that had filled her mind. She knew indeed *what* they had been, but not—except in a dim, obscure fashion —*how* they had come to be; she could not bring back their whole depth and height, nor the palpitating life, and above all the storming of the young blood in her veins. For such things memory has too weak a hold; they slip away, like the inner meaning of life itself, which no one catches but in passing glimpses. The time when she had come nearest to grasping them was the moment immediately after the danger, when gladness and tenderness flowed in upon her heart along with the immediate perception of another's feelings. That could be retained, because the tenderness still had its object left somewhere, in the unknown, even though the gladness had faded away. And next to that, and almost unchanged, she could recall her joy at his confession of happiness, there in the morning light.

She told herself now, as often before, that he and she had not let their happiness go, though it was not always at such a height as then, nor even for long together, for life is not like that. But at one moment in their lives it had reached its climax for them, and they had felt themselves to belong there. And wherever the road might lead in after days, they could always trace their way back to it more or less exactly, as long as they had one another.

The son and his wife also visited the Engadine, although they had not intended to do so. It came about through the disruption of all their plans by an outbreak of cholera in Italy, and particularly because the epidemic was officially kept secret. So rumour took a hand in it and sported with it: now the disease was here, now it was there; to this place, again, it had never come. The stream of travellers from the north was frightened back from one route, tempted by the most definite denials to try another which was nearer, and was there met by refugees who declared that they had narrowly escaped the danger. Some of them in their confusion looked as though they carried the infection with them and were aware of it, but gave the denials fresh life so as not to be refused admittance to the hotels. There was genuine panic all along the frontier, and none could tell where he might land up by nightfall.

The young Swedish couple were not among the most irresolute, but their very unwillingness to leave Italy kept them back in the stream of tourists and they were carried along with it. At St. Moritz there was such a crowd that there was no room for them; they were directed to the smaller places northwards up the valley, and at last found refuge at Bevers. The name told them nothing, but when the hotel turned out to bear the name of *Weissen Rössli*, they remembered that someone had recommended the place to them. They were rather the worse for their journey, the latter part of which had been undertaken in a sudden burst of cold and a snowstorm, following right upon the fierce heat of summer, and can therefore hardly have looked like a happy bridal pair; but in those parts folk have sharp eyes for such things, and they too were given the traditional room. The apartment pleased them, though it looked old-fashioned with its larch-wood panelling, and they resolved therefore to stay there until the problem of the cholera was decided. That very evening the matter came closer to them than before, for they both felt far from well, and had to leave the dinner-table. Up in the room, as he was going to bed, the husband noticed that he had fever, and naturally the thought suggested itself to both that he might have caught the infection from one of the travellers coming from the south: neither mentioned it, however. It was possible enough, but the worst of it was that the same idea had got about among the people of the house. The host himself stood outside the door, and from a safe distance put forward his request that they would seek another lodging, though he could not tell them where. He realised, however, that he had come too late for such a course to be possible, and he had then nothing to say except that the travellers must not count upon any attendance in their room. He was very sorry, but the lady would no doubt understand that it was impossible.

She agreed with the utmost composure, for she had already thought out the matter fully, as she was dressing again. There was much to agree upon and arrange. "There is no reason yet," said she, "to fear the worst, but we must act as if it were so." The host promised to send a doctor there as soon as possible, though it would probably not be until next day; but he could at once see to the disinfecting that she asked for, and he agreed to everything that she proposed in regard to isolation.

When all this was done, she had the sick man to prevail upon.

"How will you be able to nurse me?" he said. "You look at least as ill as I."

"It is only the journey, and I don't feel tired now that I have something else to think about. You have fever, and I haven't."

She was not so sure of it, but she determined that it should be so, and she felt her will strong enough to drive away every tremor, whatever might be its cause. She soon had so much to see to that he had to be silent, and besides he was himself too tired to talk any more; he began to feel pain, too, and became not quite clear in the head. She sat by him all night, and did whatever she could think of to alleviate his distress, and most of her measures seemed to be successful.

The doctor confirmed this, when he came next day, and he brought still greater comfort with him. There was probably no real danger, and it was perhaps only a peculiar case of mountain sickness; although the elevation was not particularly great, the rapid variations in air-pressure and temperature might have had such a result. It was just possible, however, that it might be something more serious, and it would be better to keep him isolated. The young wife knew that the isolation would be maintained of itself by the terror of the people in the hotel, and when the doctor wished to investigate her own state of health she refused point-blank, for she had simply no leisure to be ill. Whether she really was better or merely drove away her indisposition by sheer force of will had to remain undecided.

Next morning she had no more anxiety in regard to herself, and had a reassuring report from the doctor as to her husband; in a few days all would be well.

They were days of a strangely deep and radiant peace for both of them, which came not merely from their undisturbed existence but out of the tide of Time itself, from a kind of lull in the strain and stress of life. Their love was part of it, and the best part of all, a love no less certain than before, but in process of change towards something at once simpler and more comprehensive. They belonged to a generation which had been taught to speak and reflect more about love than its forbears had done. It had seemed to them that love must be isolated from life, as the only precious thing therein and be brought to perfection independently, as though it were a flower to be refined independently of the plant from which it grew. Actually the flower, as long as it was there, would remain much the same as if it had not been so carefully tended, but its permanence was made more doubtful by anxious care. It became so more especially because it was called in question out of a kind of fanatical honesty, which was essentially the gambler's passion: "I put everything upon this card, and if it loses, all is lost." The whole was really an expression of a lust for pleasure, masked as idealism, and however strong the feelings that were involved, there was a certain egoism beneath them which was not without its possibility of danger.

For these two upon their honeymoon there had been no loss of happiness yet, but there had been no surer foundation for it than this, and once or twice, in weary or unguarded moments, they had felt a cold blast blowing upon it. But now, in the quiet of the sick-room, the atmosphere grew tranquil; there was more directness in their feelings for one another, and when they thought, there was no disturbing factor present. The danger that had threatened them had made life more precious and at the same time greater, by the very prosaic and commonplace nature of the demands which it had put upon them. The young woman had discovered that she had courage and the power of decision to meet the gravest situation, and the husband had found in her something fairer than beauty to admire. As the impression of his illness wore away, it developed into a calm, bright, and solemn joy, an expanse in which they saw both further and more clearly than before.

The first morning when they were both dressed to leave their chamber, the place became especially dear to them and took on a new significance. In the sunlight, which now streamed freely in from the glittering, azure world outside and lit up every corner, they perceived that something had been written on the walls. It was a number of names, and they read them with friendly curiosity, feeling their fates linked with the fates of those who owned them, and who had once had their hour here and then passed away for ever. There was melancholy in the thought, but it was followed closelv by another: "For no one else, surely, can this place mean what it does for us."

Suddenly the young wife exclaimed: "Why, here's a line in Swedish! There is no name or date, but it was done very long ago, you can tell by the other writing near it. Such a funny thing to write!"

"What is it?" asked her husband.

"Read it yourself. It might have been one of us that wrote it."

He read aloud: "Jag är lycklig!" And with a tremor through his whole frame he seemed to recognize the handwriting, and he called to mind clearly where and how he had first heard the name *Weissen Rössli.*

"My father wrote those words," said he gently. "The time fits in exactly. It was here they came upon *their* honeymoon."

"Why, of course! Now I remember, too."

They were both moved almost to tears, although they smiled at one another. They were struck by the thought that he who had written this was dead long ago with his joy, but still more deeply were they penetrated with a sense of the dark and all-embracing mystery of Life—its oneness, its constant recurrence and eternal newness, its beauty and its freshness, its seriousness, and its grandeur.

BJÖRNSTJERNE BJÖRNSON

THE BROTHERS

THE schoolmaster's name was Baard, and he had a brother named Anders. They thought a great deal of each other, enlisted together, lived together in town, went through the war together, served in the same company, and both rose to the rank of corporal. When they came home from the War, people said they were two fine stalwart fellows.

Then their father died. He left much personal property, which it was difficult to divide, and therefore they said to each other that they would not let this come between them, but would put the property up at auction, that each might buy what he wanted, and both share the proceeds. And it was so done.

But the father had owned a large gold watch, which had come to be known far and wide, for it was the only gold watch people in those parts had ever seen. When this watch was put up, there were many wealthy men who wanted it, but when both brothers began to bid, all the others desisted. Now Baard expected that Anders would let him have it, and Anders expected the same of Baard. They bid in turn, each trying the other out, and as they bid they looked hard at each other. When the watch had gone up to twenty dollars, Baard began to feel that this was not kind of his brother, and bid over him until he almost reached thirty. When Anders did not withdraw even then, Baard felt that Anders no longer remembered how good he had often been to him, and that he was furthermore the elder of the two; and the watch went over thirty. Anders still kept on. Baard then raised the price to forty dollars with one bound, and no longer looked at his brother. It grew very still in the auction room; only the bailiff repeated the figures quietly. Anders thought, as he stood there, that if Baard could afford to go to forty dollars, so could he, and if Baard begrudged him the watch, he might as well take it, and bid over him. This to Baard seemed the greatest disgrace that had ever befallen him; he bid fifty dollars in a low voice. There were many people there, and Anders said to himself that he would not let his brother mock him before them all, and again raised the bid. Baard burst out laughing.

"One hundred dollars and my brotherhood into the bargain," he said, as he turned on his heel, and left the room.

A little later, as he stood saddling the horse he had just bought at the auction, a man came out to him.

"The watch is yours; Anders gave in."

The instant he heard the news, there welled up in him a sense of remorse; he thought of his brother and not of the watch. The saddle was already in place, but he paused, his hand on his horse, uncertain whether to mount. Many people came out, Anders among them, and when he saw his brother, with horse saddled, ready to leave, he little knew what Baard was turning over in his mind.

"Thanks for the watch, Baard!" he shouted over to him. "You shall never see the day when your brother shall tread on your heels!"

"Nor you the day I shall darken your doors again!" Baard answered, his face pale, as he swung himself on his horse.

After that day neither of them ever set foot in the home where they had both lived with their father.

Anders married into a crofter's family, not long afterwards, but he did not invite Baard to the wedding. Nor did Baard go to the church. The first year he was married, Anders lost his only cow. It was found dead one morning on the north side of the house, where it had been tethered, and no one could explain what it had died of. Other misfortunes befell him, and he fared from bad to worse. But the heaviest blow came when his hayloft and all it contained burned down one night in the dead of winter. No one knew how the fire had started.

"This has been done by someone who wishes me ill," Anders said, and all that night he wept. He became a poor man, and lost he all inclination to work.

The evening after the fire, Baard appeared at his brother's house. Anders lay on his bed, but sprang up as Baard entered.

"What do you want here?" he asked, then stopped short, and stood staring fixedly at his brother.

Baard waited a little before he answered.

"I want to help you, Anders; you're in a bad way."

"I'm faring no worse than you wished me to fare! Go—else I'm not sure I can master myself."

"You're mistaken, Anders; I regret——"

"Go, Baard, or God have mercy on us both!"

Baard drew back a step.

"If you want the watch," he said in a trembling voice, "you can have it."

"Go, Baard!" shrieked his brother, and Baard, unwilling to stay any longer, left.

In the meanwhile Baard had fared thus. As soon as he heard of his brother's misfortunes, he had suffered a change of heart, but pride held him back. He felt urged to go to church, and there he vowed many a good resolve, but he lacked strength to carry them out. He frequently went so far that he could see the house, but either someone was just coming out, or there were strangers there, or Anders stood chopping wood outside—there was always something in the way.

But one Sunday, late in the winter, he again went to church, and that Sunday Anders too was there. Baard saw him. He had grown pale and thin, and he wore the same clothes he had worn when the brothers were together, although now they were old and patched. All through the service Anders looked steadily at the minister. To Baard it seemed that he was kind and gentle, and he recalled their childhood days, and what a good boy Anders had been. That day Baard even went to communion, and he made a solemn vow to God that he would make up with his brother, come what might. This resolution swept through his soul as he drank the wine, and when he arose he felt an impulse to go over and take a seat beside him, but there was someone in the way, and Anders did not look up. After the service there was still something in the way; there were too many people about; Anders's wife was with him, and her he did not know. He decided it would be better to seek Anders in his home and have a quiet talk with him.

When evening came, he set out. He went right up to the door. Then he paused, and as he stood there listening, he heard his name mentioned; it was the wife speaking.

"He went to communion this morning," she was saying. "I am sure he was thinking of you."

"No, it wasn't of me he was thinking," Anders replied. "I know him; he thinks only of himself."

For a long time nothing was said, and Baard sweat, as he stood there, although it was a cold night. The wife inside was busy with a kettle; the fire on the hearth crackled and hissed; a child cried now and then, and Anders rocked it. At length the wife spoke again.

"I believe you are both thinking of each other though you won't admit it."

"Let us talk of something else," Anders answered.

After a little he got up to go out. Baard had to hide in the woodshed; but then Anders, too, came to the shed to get an armful of wood. From where he stood in the corner Baard could see him clearly. He had taken off his threadbare Sunday clothes, and put on his uniform, just like Baard's own. These they had promised each other never to wear, but to pass on as heirlooms to their children. Anders's was now patched and worn out, so that his strong well-built frame seemed bundled in rags, while at the same time Baard could hear the gold watch ticking in his own pocket. Anders went over to the brushwood, but instead of bending down immediately to gather up his load, he leaned back against a pile of wood, and looked up at the sky glimmering brightly with stars. Then he sighed heavily and muttered to himself, " Well—well—well—oh Lord, oh Lord! "

As long as he lived, Baard never forgot those words. He wanted to step forward then, but the brother coughed, and it seemed so difficult. No more was needed to hold him back. Anders took his armful of faggots, and as he went out, brushed past Baard so close that the twigs struck him in the face.

For fully ten minutes more he stood rooted to the spot, and it is doubtful how much longer he might have stayed, had not a chill, on top of the emotional stress, seized him, and set him shivering through and through. Then he went out. He frankly confessed to himself that he was too cowardly to enter now; wherefore he conceived another plan. From an ash barrel, which stood in the corner he had just left, he selected some bits of charcoal, found a pitch pine splinter, went up into the hayloft, closed the door, and struck a light. When he had lit the torch he searched about for the peg on which Anders hung his lantern when he came out early in the morning to thresh. Baard then took his gold watch and hung it on the peg, put out his light, and left. He felt so relieved in his mind that he raced over the snow like a youngster.

The day following he heard that the hayloft had burned down during the night. Presumably sparks had flown from the torch he had used while hanging up the watch.

This so overwhelmed Baard that all that day he kept to himself as though he were ill, brought out his hymn book, and sang until the people in the house thought something was wrong with him. But in the evening he went out. It was bright moonlight. He went over to his brother's place, dug around in the charred ruins of the fire, and found, sure enough, a little lump of melted gold—all that remained of the watch.

It was with this in his hand that he had gone in to his brother, anxious to explain everything, and to sue for peace. But how he fared that evening has already been told.

A little girl had seen him digging in the ashes; some boys, on their way to a dance, had observed him go down toward his brother's the Sunday evening in question; and the people where he lived explained how strangely he had acted on the Monday following. And inasmuch as everyone knew that he and his brother were bitter enemies, these details were reported to the authorities, and an inquiry instituted. No one could prove anything against him, yet suspicion hovered around him. He could now less than ever approach his brother.

Anders had thought of Baard when the hayloft burned, but had said nothing. When he had seen him enter his house, the following evening, pale and strange, he had forthwith thought: He is smitten with remorse, but for such a terrible outrage against his brother there can be no forgiveness. Since then he heard how people had see Baard go down towards his home the evening of the fire, and although nothing was brought to light at the inquiry, he felt convinced that his brother was the guilty one.

They met at the hearing, Baard in his good clothes, Anders in his worn out rags. Baard looked at his brother as he entered, and Anders was conscious, in his inmost heart, of an anxious pleading in his eyes. He doesn't want me to say anything, thought Anders; and when he was asked whether he suspected his brother of the deed he answered loudly and decisively, "No!"

Anders took to drinking heavily after that day, and it was not long before he was in a bad way. Even worse, however, fared Baard, although he did not drink; he was so changed that people hardly knew him.

Then late one evening a poor woman entered the little room Baard rented and asked him to come with her. He recognized her; it was his brother's wife. Baard understood at once what her errand was, turned deathly pale, dressed himself, and followed her without a word. A pale glimmer shone from Anders's window, now flickering, now vanishing, and this light they followed, for there was no path across the snow. When Baard again stood in the doorway, he was met with a strange odour which almost made him ill. They went in. A little child sat eating charcoal over by the hearth, its face all black, but it looked up and laughed and showed its white teeth. It was his brother's child.

Over on the bed, with all sorts of clothes over him, lay Anders, pale, emaciated, his forehead high and smooth, and stared at his brother with hollow eyes. Baard's knees trembled. He sat down at the foot of the bed and burst into uncontrollable weeping. The sick man looked at him intently and said nothing. At length he asked his wife to go out, but Baard motioned for her to remain. And then the two brothers began to talk to each other. They explained everything, from the day they bid for the watch down through the years to this day when they finally met again. Baard ended by taking out the lump of gold, which he always carried about him, and it came to light in the course of their talk that never for one single day in all these years had they been really happy.

Anders did not say much, for he had little strength, but Baard watched by the bedside as long as Anders was ill.

"Now I am perfectly well," Anders said one morning, on awakening. "Now, brother, we shall live together always, just as in the old days, and never leave each other."

But that day he died.

The widow and the child Baard took home with him, and they were henceforth well taken care of. But what the brothers had talked of at the bedside came out through the walls and the night, and became generally known to all the people in the valley. Baard grew to be the most highly respected man among them. They all honoured him as one who had had a great sorrow and had found peace again, or as one who had returned after a long absence. And Baard grew in strength of mind by reason of all their friendliness. He became a godly man, and wishing to be of some use, as he said, the old corporal turned schoolmaster. What he impressed upon the children, first and last was love, and, himself, he practised it till the children came to love him as a playmate and a father.

SIGRID UNDSET

SIMONSEN

SIMONSEN paused a moment at the gate entrance, and dug out his old grease-worn wallet, in order to put away a testimonial he held in his hand. But before he did so, he smoothed the soiled paper out and read it through, although he knew it by heart already.

" Anton Simonsen has been a warehouse clerk in our employ for three years. During that time he has proved himself a willing, sober, and industrious worker.

" The Hercules Machine Shops,
By N. NIELSEN."

That testimonial—bah!—wouldn't help him very far. It was pretty damn cheap of the manager—confound him! He was surely not so averse ordinarily to cramming his customers full of lies about one thing and another—shipping dates and the like, but when it came to giving a poor fellow a testimonial which might help smooth the way for him and get him something to do,—ah, that was another matter. " Yes, but I can't very well write that your work has been entirely satisfactory," the old sniffler had said. But the word " sober," at any rate, he had forced him to put in. That wasn't in the first draft. He—Simonsen—had insisted that he put it in. " It seems to me, Simonsen," the manager had said, " that you've smelled of liquor at all hours of the day almost." But at that he had opened up on him. " I've taken a drink now and again, it is true, Mr. Manager," he had said, " but that I venture you'd have done too if you had to dig around all day in that clammy warehouse. But there's no one can say that Anton Simonsen has ever been drunk on the job. Not even a bit on edge once." Well, at that the old wind-bag had had to give in, and the girl copyist had had to rewrite the testimonial with the word " sober " in it. So there it was—such as it was! It didn't amount to very much, it is true, and, what was worse, he had none better to show.

"Look out there, you damn fool!"

Simonsen jumped to one side, in towards the wall. A wagon loaded with iron beams swung rattling through the gate. The big horses steamed and sweat as they dug in with all their might to get the load over the stone bridge at the gateway entrance. The driver yelled something after him, but Simonsen could not hear what it was he said, for it was drowned in the rattle and rumble of the iron beams.

He put the testimonial away and stuck the wallet in his breast pocket. He glowered with hostile eyes after the wagon. It had come to a stop up against the warehouse, just opposite a huge crane, which with its pulleys and chains projected out from a dark hole, between barred windows, in the smoky red-brick wall. The flanks of the horses were steaming white, and the hairs on their sides were plastered together in little wet tufts. The driver had not blanketed them; he stood talking with another fellow.

Simonsen buttoned his winter coat, comparatively new and in fair condition, straightened up, and thrust his abdomen out. There rose within him a feeling of bourgeois dignity; he still considered himself a better member of society than this ruffian driver, even though the fellow did berate him. And with this self-consciousness there was vaguely merged another feeling, which had stirred within him at the sight of the two work-horses, as they tugged away and flexed the muscles of their perspiring flanks. He stepped in through the gate.

"It seems to me you ought to blanket your horses. There's certainly no sense in letting the poor creatures stand unprotected this way in the cold—sweaty as they are."

The driver—a tall, lanky brute—faced about and looked down at him.

"Any of your business, fatty?"

"What do you suppose would happen to you if I were to go up to the office and report how you're treating their horses?"

"Pick up your legs and beat it, and be quick about it. What's it to you any way? There's no need of your butting in." And the driver moved threateningly towards him.

Simonsen drew back a bit, but, he reflected, the fellow would hardly dare touch him here, and he thrust his paunch out still more.

"Well, I merely wanted to call to your attention that they can see you from the office window—how you are treating the company's horses."

With that he faced about. The self-assured bourgeois feeling left him almost immediately. For just as he passed through the gate a man rushed down the stairs and swept by him—red-faced and blond and light-haired—dressed in fur cap and coat and swinging a silver headed cane—the same man he had interviewed at the time he had applied for the position.

It was beginning to grow dark outside. It was going towards four o'clock already. Olga, no doubt, would scold a bit when he came home so late for dinner. Oh well, he'd simply have to tell her he'd had to stay the extra hour at the warehouse.

Simonsen trudged rapidly down Torvgaten. He seemed to mince and drag his steps at the same time, and what with his large round paunch and his bowed arms he suggested a rubber ball rolling and bouncing along. Slight of build he was, and short-necked, and his face was fat and flabby, with bleary eyes that lay deeply hid beneath his eyebrows, bloodshot cheeks, and a blueish something of a nose above a drooping greyish-yellow mustache.

It was a wretched Saturday afternoon in the forepart of December, and the air was thick with a cold grey fog, which both smelled and tasted of gas and soot. Out in the street the sleighs skidded over the hard-frozen, rut-worn snow, and on the walks the stream of humanity swept, dark and heavy, past the lighted, frosty shop windows. Every moment, as he trudged along, immersed in his own thoughts, there was someone who ran into him and glowered angrily back at him.

Not that there was much in the way of thoughts stirring in his mind. For he kept pushing them aside. Surely he would find something by that time. So that he'd not have to let Olga know that he had been laid off finally, beginning with the first of the year. Ugh, life certainly was a struggle!

There was no hurry; he still had the better part of a month left before the beginning of the year. But if worse came to worse, he would have to write to Sigurd. Sigurd could easily get him another job. That wasn't too much to ask of a son who was as well established as Sigurd was. It would not be any fun, to be sure; this would be the fourth time. But then it was only four times in eight years. It was eight years ago exactly this coming New Year that Sigurd had got him that place in the office—all because that elegant daughter-in-law—the vixen—had felt he was not swell enough to have around her home in Fredrikstad. It was unfortunate, to be sure, that he had messed up things in all three places, but that wasn't his fault. In the office it had been the women—the jealous hens—who had got it in for him, as though it was any of their business what sort of man he was as long as he minded his work—and that he had done. And he had never tried to become too familiar with any of them. On that score he was clear. They needn't worry—upstart, angular, washed-out hussies they were. Yes, and then there was the lumber warehouse. There certainly he had been proper and orderly in every way, for it was just at the time that he had taken up with Olga. True, he had not been accustomed to work of that kind, but if it had not been for malice on the part of the foreman he would never have lost that job. And after that he had got into the machine shop. Ah, it was no easy matter for a man already well up towards sixty to learn to master all the mysterious intricacies—all new to him—in connection with the selling and the shipping and the storing and what not. The warehouse foreman was a lazy scamp, and always he—Simonsen—had to shoulder the blame. And right from the start they had been disagreeable to him—from the manager and the chief clerk, who were forever reminding him that he was there only temporarily, and kept asking him whether he didn't have something else in view, down to the warehouse foreman and the other foremen and the teamsters—and the lady cashier, always so crabby and sour and cross and irritable every time he came up and asked for part of his pay in advance.

A grey feeling of restlessness and despondency settled over him like a clammy fog. He shuddered when he thought how Olga would fret and stew when he came home, and how extremely disagreeable Sigurd and his wife would be when they learned that he had been laid off, and how he would be starting in again at some new place, where, dazed and fearful and at his wits' end, he would be rushing around at new tasks, which he did not understand and probably never would come to know—in another warehouse or perhaps another office, full of strangers, unfamiliar and hostile—always cowering beneath constant reprimands and complaints, passively awaiting, half expecting another dismissal, just as he had rushed about and humbled himself, sluggish and old and stupid, through all his other jobs.

Simonsen was, in spite of all, however, somewhat adept at keeping unpleasant thoughts at arm's length. In reality he had gone through life that way, had humbled himself, and had come to look upon dismissals and reprimands and cross words and unpleasantnesses as inevitable. So it had been at sea, and so it had been at the docks when he was with Isachsen, and so it had been at home with his wife, as long as she lived. Cross and dour and severe and disagreeable—his daughter-in-law was not altogether unlike her for that matter. Well, Sigurd had been only too well repaid for aspiring to marry Captain Myhre's climbing daughter. Ah, how cosy their home had been those years immediately after Laura died!

The boy had got a good start, and kind he had always been to his old father, had paid royally for his keep and everything. Not that he had been altogether unhappy here either at first, as a bachelor again and a man about town—he had been into things, had had a good time and lots of fun and all that—and later when he took up with Olga he had in reality—he couldn't deny it—been very comfortable—most of the time, at any rate. A little disagreeable, to be sure, it had been at the time Olga became with child, but Olga was not altogether to blame for that, and she had reconciled herself to it immediately when he had promised her marriage. Even yet, of course, she raised a fuss about it at times and insisted he go through with it and marry her. Not that he didn't some time intend to do it—he'd have done it long ago, had it not been for the disagreeable complications he foresaw with Sigurd and his wife. But some day surely an easy respectable job must fall to his lot, which would be his permanently—and when Olga was able to enlarge her dressmaking establishment, and Henry, her boy, got into the office, where he was now running errands—for that he had been promised; the fellow was rounding out quite satisfactorily—well, they might then at last get a cosy little place and be happy together. He could sit in the sofa with his glass of toddy and his pipe, while Olga went about her work in a leisurely way, and Svanhild sat near him and studied her lessons. For Olga was a real genuine soul, and no one should have occasion to say about Svanhild that she was an illegitimate child—when the time came for her to start school.

Simonsen had by now reached Ruselökveien. The fog lay thick and clammy in the narrow street, streaked here and there by yellow-green light from frozen shop windows, and in all of them, wherever the heat from the gas light or the lamp had cleared a space on the frosted windows, could be seen displays of Christmas tree baskets, whether it was a general merchandise shop or a delicatessen or a tobacco shop. The reddish glare from the huge exhibition windows of the two-story bazaar on the other side of the street oozed unctuously out into the fog. The gas lamps up on the Terrace were just barely discernible. But the private dwellings beyond were entirely lost. Not a single ray of light penetrated to the street from them, although they could be sensed vaguely as towering walls in the fog—which, as it were, dwarfed the street below into a mere gutter.

Simonsen trudged along mincingly. The walks in many places, where the ice had not been cut away, were slippery. Children swarmed about on all sides. Out in the street, between vans and sleighs, they attempted to slide, if it were only along an icy rut in the rough, irregular, brown layer of hard frozen snow.

" Svanhild! "

Simonsen called sharply to a little girl in a dirty white cap. She had crawled up on the bank of snow, piled high along the walk, and let herself slide down into the street on her wee tiny skis, which were quite black from the soot and the dirty snow, and had almost no bend left in them.

The child stood stock still in the middle of the street and looked at up Simonsen as he straddled the snow bank and went out to her. Her heaven-blue eyes testified to a guilty conscience, as she brushed her light hair up under her cap, and wiped her little nose with her red-mittened hand.

" And how many times have you been told, Svanhild, that you are not to run out into the street! Why can't you be a good girl and play in the court? "

Svanhild glanced up timidly.

" But I can't very well ski in the court—for there's no hill there, and——"

" Suppose a wagon came along and ran over you, or a drunken man came up and ran away with you—what do you think pappa and mamma would say then? "

Svanhild was ashamed and said nothing. Simonsen helped her on to the walk again, and they tripped away hand in hand, her tiny, strip-like skis clattering down the bare walk.

" Do you think pappa will take you out walking to-night if you're a bad girl, and won't do as you're told to?—I suppose they've already had dinner? "

" Oh, yes, mamma and Henry and I have eaten long ago——"

Hm! Simonsen trudged in through the gate. A white metal sign read: " Mrs. Olga Martinsen, Dressmaking Establishment. Children's and Boys' Clothes. Third Floor Rear." Simonsen crossed the court diagonally, and glanced up towards a lighted window, against which some fashion journals leaned. Then he picked up Svanhild's skis under his arm and led the child up the narrow back stairway.

Outside Olga's hall door a couple of youngsters stood reading a paper-bound book in the glare of a kitchen lamp which had been hung out. Simonsen grumbled something and let himself in.

The hall was dark. At the farther end a streak of light issued through the door from the living-room. Simonsen went into his own room. It was dark there too—and cold. Ugh, she had let the fire go out. He lit the lamp.

" Run in, Svanhild, and tell mamma I am here."

He opened the door to the room adjoining. At the table, overflowing with cut and half-sewed garments and scraps of lining, sat Miss Abrahamsen bent over her sewing. She had fastened a newspaper to one side of the lamp, and all the light fell on her little yellow spinster face and diminutive brown hands. There was a little reflection of light from the two steel sewing machines, and in towards the wall could be seen the white beds of Olga and Svanhild.

" And you're at it harder than ever, Miss Abrahamsen."

" Ah yes—one has to, you know."

" Yes, isn't this Christmas business the funniest thing—it's almost as if the world was coming to an end."

Svanhild slipped in from the living-room.

" Mamma says to say your dinner is in the warming oven."

" Well, I guess I'll stay right here and make myself comfortable, Miss Abrahamsen; it's so cold in my room—and then, too, I'll have pleasant company."

Miss Abrahamsen had quietly cleared a corner of the table while Simonsen brought out the dinner—cabbage soup and sausages.

" Hm! Not so bad. Now if one only had——," Simonsen got up and tapped on the door to the living-room.

" Oh, Olga——"

" Why good evening, Simonsen! And how are you?"

He opened the door and peered in.

" Well, if it isn't Miss Hellum! And you're having another new dress again?"

Olga, her mouth full of pins, was busy fitting Miss Hellum, arranging the folds over her bust before the console mirror.

" About so, I guess."

Olga removed the lamp from the nickel holder on the wall and held it up.

" It seems all right. You're sure it's not crooked in the back, Mrs. Martisen?"

The two girls who sat waiting over on the plush sofa in the twilight laid aside their fashion journal, looked at each other and smiled, looked at Miss Hellum and smiled again to each other. " Heavens!" one of them whispered audibly. They were almost duplicates, in dress and everything, with short jackets, little neck pieces of fur, and nice-looking felt hats with feathers on. Simonsen was still at the door—they embarrassed him a bit.

" Well, what do you think, Simonsen? Is it going to be pretty?"

" Ah, it is remarkable how that colour suits you, Miss

Hellum—but then anything looks well on the beautiful, as the saying goes."

"Oh, you——!" Miss Hellum exclaimed and chuckled.

Lovely girl—this Miss Hellum! Olga cut around the neck, and Miss Hellum bent her head and shuddered a little as the cold scissors touched her skin. A lovely full neck, with yellow curly hair all the way down, and arms that were soft and round.

"Costly stuff too, I imagine," Simonsen remarked, as he touched the silk—and her arm—while Olga worked on the sleeve.

"For shame, Simonsen," Miss Hellum laughed. Olga looked daggers. She pushed him aside, as she tugged at the sleeve.

"Oh yes, that reminds me—Olga, couldn't Henry run down and get a bottle or two of beer?"

"Henry's had to go down to the office again, poor fellow—some estimate or other that had to be copied, he said."

"Poor fellow—he had to go down again, did he?—It seems to me it's getting to be almost every Saturday afternoon. Ah yes, life is a struggle! It was almost four o'clock before I got away from the warehouse. Oh, if one were only young and beautiful, Miss Hellum!"

Svanhild peeped in.

"Come in here, Svanhild! Do you remember my name to-day?"

"Miss Hellum," Svanhild smiled modestly.

"I suppose you'd like some candy to-day too, wouldn't you?" Miss Hellum opened her purse and brought out a little bag.

"Oh ho, and what do you say now, Svanhild? And your hand, Svanhild! And you can curtsy, can't you?"

Svanhild whispered her thanks, offered her hand, and curtsied. And she took to breaking apart the pieces of camphorated candy which had stuck together.

Miss Hellum talked and laughed while she put on her wraps.

"Well, I'll expect it ready for a final fitting Tuesday next then, about this time. And you won't disappoint me, Mrs. Martinsen, will you? Well, good-bye! Good-bye, Simonsen! And good-bye, Svanhild!"

Simonsen gallantly opened the door, and Miss Hellum swept out, the feathers on her hat swaying as she went, her muskrat neck piece flung loosely down over her shoulders.

"Whew!" One of the girls on the sofa giggled. "Not so bad, eh——!"

"Say, she was a regular——"

Simonsen withdrew again to Miss Abrahamsen and his dinner,

which had got cold. Olga came in after a while with the coffee and poured it.

"Really, it's beyond me, Anton—it's perfectly ridiculous the way you carry on! What can you be thinking of—when there are others around, too, listening!"

"Who are those silly gigglers anyway?"

"The minister's hired girl on the Terrace and a friend of hers. It seems to me you have made it difficult enough as it is for me—without carrying on in this way with that Hellum woman. Well, they'll have something to talk about now—as if they didn't have enough already."

"Shucks! I don't imagine it was as bad as all that."

The door bell rang. Miss Abrahamsen went out to answer it.

"It is Miss Larsen."

Olga set aside her cup and picked up a basted dress and threw it over her arm.

"Never a moment's peace!"

Miss Abrahamsen bent forward over her sewing again.

. . . . .

Mrs. Martinsen and Miss Abrahamsen sat and sewed all day Sunday. They put off their dinner till it was too dark to work, and when it was over, Olga lit the lamp, and they took up their sewing again.

"That vestee of Miss Olsen's, weren't you working on it, Miss Abrahamsen, a while ago?"

Miss Abrahamsen set her machine whirring.

"I laid it on the table."

Olga searched the table—and then the floor—for it.

"Svanhild, you haven't seen a little white bib, have you—of lace?"

"No, mamma, I haven't," Svanhild answered from the corner by the window. And she jumped up and began hunting too, but first she settled her doll in the up-turned footstool, which served as a cradle, and covered it carefully.

"Astri is sleeping. She has diphtheria and scarlet fever," she protested, as her mother rummaged around among the doll clothes. But Olga took the patient ruthlessly out of her cradle. The doll was wrapped in a white pleated bit of lace. carefully fastened about with safety pins.

"Really, are you crazy, child! And, if she hasn't torn a hole in it with the pins! You naughty girl!" and she cuffed Svanhild on the ear. "Oh, what shall I do now—this costly lace of Miss Olsen's too!"

Svanhild howled.

"But I thought it was only a rag, mamma!"

"Haven't I told you you're not to touch anything, not even what's on the floor? Ugh, what a naughty girl you are!"

Miss Abrahamsen inspected the vestee.

"I think I can take up the pleats, and then press it and re-pleat it, so as to bring the tear inside one of the folds—I don't think it will show any——"

Svanhild kept right on howling.

"Well, what's the matter now, Svanhild—crying like this when you know pappa is taking a nap?"

Olga was furious as she explained the trouble.

"What a naughty little girl you are, Svanhild—to play such tricks on mamma! For shame—this isn't my little Svanhild!"

"It seems to me you might take her out, Anton. It's not particularly good for you either to be lying around and sleeping all day."

Simonsen scolded the child industriously as he went off with her. But he comforted her when they had reached the hall and he put on her wraps.

"Come, don't cry any more now! Shame on you for crying so! We'll go over in the park and slide. You know it wasn't nice of you. So wipe your nose now. Pappa'll take you sliding—come along, sweetheart—pappa'll take you sliding——"

Olga was perhaps a bit too severe at times with Svanhild. Not, of course, that children were not to be punished—when they had done something wrong. But Svanhild took everything so to heart—she was still hiccoughing on the sled behind him—poor little thing!

The evening sky rose darkly purple high over the towers and spires on the Terrace. The weather had cleared up. There was left only a thin sooty streak of fog in the street, around the lights, as Simonsen trudged along, pulling his daughter on the sled.

The palace park was such a pretty place. The heavy hoar-frost on the trees and the bushes everywhere sparkled in the reflection from the lamps. And such a mass of children everywhere! On every least little incline they were coasting and skiing. The main slide simply swarmed with them. Big naughty boys—sometimes five or six to a sled—hooted and yelled as they sped down over the icy crust, swinging a thin narrow pole, like the tail of a rat, behind them. But Simonsen knew of a quiet little hill, farther in, where he and Svanhild had been in the habit of coasting before in the evenings. And really Svanhild had a grand time. Pappa stood at the top and gave her a good start, and Svanhild yelled "Look out!" so loud that her thin little voice almost cracked, and Simonsen too roared " Look out there! " from way down inside, although apart from themselves there were only two small boys in sport shoes and knitted caps on the whole hill. Simonsen took the initiative and made their acquaintance. They were Alf and Johannes Hauge, and their father was an office manager, and lived in Parkveien. Simonsen started all three of them down; they were to see whose sled was the fastest, but he gave Svanhild the most vigorous push, and she won. And he ran down after them and helped Svanhild up the hill again, for otherwise she would have stuck fast in the snow every time she went through the crust.

But after a while Svanhild began to whimper.

" Pappa, my feet are so cold."

" Well, then you must run—let's go up on the road and run around a bit."

Svanhild ran and cried—her toes hurt her so.

" Oh ho! You must run much faster, Svanhild—let's see if you can catch pappa! "

Simonsen minced along with wee tiny steps like a bouncing rubber ball. And Svanhild ran after him as fast as she could, and caught him, till she grew warm again and cheerful and happy.

But by that time they had lost track of their sled. Simonsen looked for it above the hill and below the hill and in between the bushes—it was nowhere to be found. Alf and Johannes had seen it stand over by a large tree in the road some time back, but that was all they knew. And—oh yes—some big naughty boys had gone by—that Simonsen too remembered. It was most likely they who had taken it.

Svanhild was heartbroken and cried—it really hurt one to see her. Simonsen thought of Olga. Ugh, she wouldn't grow any sweeter, touchy as she was nowadays. What scamps those boys were! To steal a poor little girl's sled! To think that children could be so mean!

" Don't cry, Svanhild sweetheart—we'll find your sled again all right."

Simonsen went about from hill to hill and inquired after a little blue painted sled. Svanhild trudged along with him and cried, and Alf and Johannes followed them, both holding fast to the rope of their sled, while they told, as their eyes bulged, of all they had heard about big naughty boys, who went about stealing sleds, and ran down children, and threw chunks of ice on the slides.

There was no trace of the sled to be found, but up on the main road they met a smartly dressed angry lady, who turned out to be Alf's and Johannes' nurse, and who scolded them for not coming home long ago and promised them they would get theirs from pappa and mamma. She wasn't at all concerned to learn that the little girl was named Svanhild and that she had lost her sled—as she scolded and shuffled away, holding each of the boys in an iron grip. Then Simonsen was almost hit in the eye by a steering pole and in the shins by a sharp sled runner.

"Well, Svanhild, they've apparently made away with your sled—I don't imagine we'll ever see it again," Simonsen sighed, dejected. "But don't cry so now, little sweetheart. Pappa'll get you a new sled for Christmas. Come, let's go down Carl Johan and look at the shop windows—they're so beautiful to-night—perhaps we'll see a nice new sled for you too——" and he brightened up.

Svanhild and her pappa went down and looked at the shops. And when they came up to a window in front of which the stream of people had stopped and formed one dark stationary milling mass of humanity, Simonsen raised her on his arms, and struggled and edged his way through, till they were right in front of the brilliantly lighted window, where they continued to stand as long as there was one single item left to talk about and guess the price of. In some places there were Christmas trees, colourfully arrayed, and lighted with electric bulbs. Svanhild was also to have a Christmas tree on Christmas Eve. In one window there was a regular Christmas party of lady dolls, smartly dressed—as Svanhild would be when she grew up. And in another shop, which dealt in trunks and bags, there was a wee tiny crocodile in a wee tiny water basin. There they had to stand a long time speculating as to whether it was alive. At last it moved one eye just the least bit—just think, it was alive! And this little crocodile, when it grew up, would be so large that it could swallow a whole Svanhild in a single bite.

"But now it can't bite any, can it?"

"No, now it can't hurt you."

Up near Eketorvet there was a cinematograph in a window among moving picture advertisements. Svanhild, who had been to the movies with pappa—three times already—had to remember all they had seen—the two little girls who had been kidnapped by robbers in an automobile, and all the rest. Forgotten was the sled they had lost, and mamma, who sat pursing her lips over her sewing, till she grew tired and cross. Forgotten was everything now—except that Svanhild was pappa's little girl, and that Christmas Eve was only seventeen days off.

Then they passed by a sporting goods shop, with many

sleds, large and small, on display in the window, and the grandest of them all—the one with the fiery red and the roses painted on it and the bronze gilt iron braces—Svanhild was to get from her pappa for Christmas.

After that they had to have something to warm them up a bit. Simonsen knew of a cosy little temperance café, since it was Sunday, and the wine shop was closed. There were no other people present, and the waitress behind the counter was not insusceptible to Simonsen's flirtatious persiflage, while he had his coffee and sandwich and Svanhild had a piece of cake and a sip now and then of pappa's coffee.

"You needn't tell mamma," Simonsen saw fit to caution her, as he winked one eye. But Svanhild knew better than to tell mamma anything, whenever she and pappa on their evening walks dropped into one place or other, and she had a stick of candy, from which—mamma thought—little girls got a toothache, and pappa had something to drink, from which—mamma thought—he got a bad stomach. But mamma always was so busy, and it made her cross. Pappa too was busy when he was at the warehouse, and Henry when he was at the office. When one was grown up one had to work terribly hard, Svanhild had learned.

. . . . .

After Sunday came Monday and five other gray week-days. Svanhild sat on the floor in the sewing room and played by herself, for pappa now came home so late in the evening that he could not take her out walking. Pappa, too, was cross now, Svanhild noticed—whether it was because he had so much to do at the office or because mamma had so much to do that she scarce had time to prepare dinner or get his supper until late in the evening. And Henry, too, was irritable, for lady customers used the room in which he ordinarily slept, for fitting and trying on till late at night, and kept him from getting to bed as he should. But Svanhild comforted herself with the thought of the new sled she was to get for Christmas.

On the fifteenth Anton Simonsen wrote to his son. He was tired of running around looking for jobs—which he didn't get anyway. And having done so he faced the future blithely again. He had time once more to take Svanhild out walking evenings, and to help her ski in the park, and they talked of the new sled she was to get.

On the eighteenth, just as he was nailing up a case of machinery, the warehouse foreman came over and told him he was wanted at the telephone. It was Sigurd, who was in town, and invited him to drop in and have coffee with him at the Café Augustin—couldn't he beg off a couple of hours after dinner—that they might talk things over a bit?

" And how is Mossa—and the kiddies? "

The children were all right, thanks. And Mossa had come in with him—intended to make some purchases for Christmas.

" When I come to think of it, son, it's well-nigh hopeless to expect even an hour off now, busy as we are just before Christmas," Simonsen explained.

Sigurd himself undertook to see the manager about it.

" Well, in that case, all right—you're very kind! ' Hello ' to Mossa."

It was just like her! Of course she wouldn't ask him to have dinner with them—oh no! But—by George!—he'd have beer and even something stronger before he turned up for that bout!

. . . . .

" Do you think that's necessary? " Mrs. Mossa Carling asked her husband, who was in the act of uncorking a bottle of punch.

" It seems to me we ought to have a glass of punch for father anyway."

" Well, all right—as you please, dear! " Mrs. Carling thrust out her double chin as far as she could. She was not pretty. Her eyelids grew thicker out towards the temples, so that her small grey eyes seemed to creep in towards the bridge of the nose; her face was full and fresh in colour, but her mouth was narrow and small and her lips thin, and her chest, finally, was hollow and undersized, while below she was full and broad.

She was sitting in the centre of the plush sofa, directly underneath the electric chandelier, whose three globes lit up the hotel room—the two iron bedsteads, the two mahogany washstands, the two small tables and the wardrobe with the mirror, the two easy chairs in front of the larger table, on which stood an ash-tray on a doily in the centre of a chenille runner.

There was a hesitant knock on the door, and Simonsen entered cautiously. He shook hands with both of them.

" Good afternoon, Sigurd—glad to see you again, son—good afternoon, good afternoon, Mossa—it's nice to see you once again too—and just as young and pretty as ever——"

Mossa rang for the coffee, and poured it, while Sigurd filled the glasses.

Simonsen kept eyeing his daughter-in-law, who sat silent, her mouth tightly drawn, as he talked with Sigurd. Leisurely and with many flourishes the conversation drifted over to the main business.

"You don't mind if we smoke, do you, Mossa? Here, father—a cigar——?

"And now this matter you wrote about. I was up at the office to-day and had a talk with your manager. He seems to be of the same opinion as I. The city's not quite the place for you. The work here is too strenuous for a man of your age—he seemed to think so too. And I can't get you anything else either for that matter——"

Simonsen said nothing. But Mossa took up the thread.

"Sigurd is himself in a subordinate position, you will have to remember—to some extent at least. The board is not likely to relish having Sigurd forever asking the firm's connections to take his father into their business. He has already done so three times—and you've messed up everything. I may as well tell you outright that Sigurd had some very serious difficulties after he had got you this last place, which you have just been let out of, as I understand——"

"That I had, I assure you. As I say, you don't quite fit in here. You're too old, too, to be constantly trying new things. And there is therefore only one way in which I can help you. I can get you a position up at the Menstad plant in Öimark—nice, easy work. To be sure, the wages aren't much—sixty kroner to begin with, if I'm not mistaken. But, as I say, that place I can get for you."

Simonsen said nothing.

"Well—that is the only way I can help you," Sigurd Carling repeated.

"Well—what do you say—shall I get it for you, father?" he asked after a brief pause.

The father cleared his throat a few times before he spoke.

"Well, it's like this, Sigurd—I don't know whether you've heard about it or not—but the fact is I'm engaged to—the woman I've been lodging with these last six years. So I suppose I'll have to talk it over some with Olga first—see what she thinks. Olga—that's her name," he explained, "Mrs. Olga Martinsen; she is a widow."

There was an uncomfortably long pause. Simonsen played with the tassels on the armchair.

"She is a genuine, thorough, good woman in every way, Olga is—and she has a large thriving sewing establishment here in town. So it's a question whether she'd care to move up into that Godforsaken country up there. And her son has an office job in the city too."

"Is this the woman——" Sigurd spoke very deliberately, "that you are said—from what I have heard—to have had a child with——?"

"We have a little girl, yes—Svanhild by name. She will be five years next April."

"So!" It was Mossa speaking. "So you have a daughter with the woman you are lodging with—who is such a good, proper woman in every way!"

"Well, so Olga is! Orderly and proper—and industrious and hard working too. And, furthermore kind."

"It is really strange, father," Mrs. Mossa made herself very sweet as she spoke, "that you haven't married this excellent Mrs. Martinsen before. It seems to me you had ample reason to do so long ago."

"Let me tell you, Mossa dear,"—Simonsen beamed with delight, proud of what he was inventing,—"I did not want to see my wife work and struggle so hard, and so I waited in hopes of finding something better. But marry Olga I have promised on my word of honour I would, and that promise I'll stand by, as long as my name's Anton Simonsen!"

"Ah," Mossa became sweeter and sweeter, "but sixty kroner a month is not a great deal to get married on—and support a wife and child. And any great amount of sewing of course Olga can't figure on up in Öimark."

"The worst of course, father, is that you have this child. But I suppose Mrs. Martinsen could somehow be made to understand the situation—we might perhaps come to some sort of agreement with her."

"One thing you'll have to remember, Sigurd—there's your little sister, Svanhild. I shouldn't want her to suffer because she is an illegitimate child. It seems to me, Sigurd, you're incurring a grave responsibility by interfering in this matter."

Mossa broke in on him almost before he had finished, and now there was not the slightest suggestion of sweetness in her voice.

"When you speak of responsibility, father—for *your* illegitimate child—you really strike me as very funny. Sigurd offers to get you a position—for the fourth time—in Öimark. Here he is unable to get anything. Why, if you don't think you can leave the city because of your private affairs, you are quite at liberty to remain. If you can find a position here and get married on it—why, that's your affair and not ours. But Sigurd can obviously not help you in any other way. Surely he must think first and foremost of his own wife and children."

. . . . .

Mrs. Mossa had arrayed herself in her silk petticoat and draped herself in her new set of furs, when she mounted the stairs the next morning to Mrs. Martinsen's establishment in the rear apartment in Ruselökveien. She pressed the button underneath Simonsen's soiled card with a determined finger.

The woman who let her in was little, plump and dark. She had pretty blue eyes, set in a faded, sun-starved face.

"Is this Mrs. Martinsen? I am Mrs. Carling. I should like to speak with you."

Olga opened a bit hesitantly the door to the nearest room.

"Won't you come in here? I'm sorry there's no fire in here. But we're sewing in the other rooms."

Mrs. Mossa sailed in and seated herself in the only easy chair in the room. It was a room furnished as rooms for rent usually are. On the white dresser scarf stood, conscientiously arranged, photographs of the former Mrs. Simonsen, of Sigurd and herself—their engagement photographs—and two group pictures of the grandchildren.

"Now, my dear Mrs. Martinsen,"—Olga stood over by the dresser observing her—"there are one or two things I'd like very much to talk over with you. Won't you sit down?"

"Thanks—but I am very busy. What was it Madam wished?"

"Well, I won't keep you very long. Simonsen—my husband's father—is apparently, from what we gathered from him yesterday, under certain obligations to you. Now I don't know whether he has fully informed you as to his position?"

"You mean the position in Öimark?—Indeed, he has."

"So! Well, you understand, of course, it's quite a small place. If he should take it, he would temporarily not be in a position to fulfil his obligations to you."

"Thank you!" Olga spoke rapidly and to the point. "But it's not necessary to trouble Madam with these affairs. We have just agreed—Simonsen and I—have decided to get married right away."

"Well, in that case, Mrs. Martinsen, I must call your attention to one thing: Simonsen can expect no support of any kind from my husband—absolutely none. He has a large family himself. And for four people to live on sixty kroner a month. Besides the little girl, which is said to be my father-in-law's, have you another child too?"

"My son will remain here—I have a sister in Trondhjemsveien whom he can stay with. And our plan was to sort of make our home in Fredrikstad. Simonsen would come down Saturdays—and I would run a dressmaking shop in the city."

"I see. Well, that might not seem unreasonable either. But there is this to remember, you see—there are more than enough seamstresses in Fredrikstad already. It is questionable, *Miss* Martinsen, whether it would pay you to give up your business here and try to establish a new one there."

Olga started.

"*Mrs.* Martinsen, I beg your pardon. For that, I see, is how you style yourself. My husband and I, to be sure, have done a bit of investigating. It need not surprise you surely, that we should want to know what sort of person it was he had taken up with."

Olga sniffed scornfully.

"Well, that's all the same to me, Mrs. Simonsen—Mrs. Carling, I mean—pardon me. But the fact is that Simonsen doesn't seem to hold it against me that the man I was to marry deserted me for America and left me to provide for myself and my little baby as best I could. And Simonsen has promised me—time and time again he has said to me, 'Don't worry, I shall never go back on you, Olga!' And then I don't see why it isn't all the same to you, Mrs. Carling. We shan't ever trouble you, or run in on you—and seeing your husband hasn't cared to keep his father's name——"

"My dear Mrs. Martinsen," Mossa waved her hand and thrust out her chin. "Not so hysterical—please! I've surely never dreamed of interfering in your affairs. On the contrary, I came here with the best of intentions. I merely wanted to enlighten you—in case you ever imagined Simonsen would be a good provider. I must confess, I don't think you'll attain anything, if you marry him, except the privilage of supporting him as well as the child. If you recall, my dear father-in-law has really never been what you might call an up-and-coming man. We have no guarantee that he will not be as shiftless in the future as he has been in the past. So there you are! Do you think it will be easy for a man of his age—with a family—always to be getting new positions?

"I am here in all friendliness to make you an offer on behalf of my husband. Why, my dear woman, hitherto you have managed to get along without being married. Now, my husband would offer you something—we had thought of five hundred kroner—to cover any loss you might suffer by reason of your lodger leaving you thus suddenly. It's without any conditions, you understand. If my father-in-law should subsequently attain a position that would enable him to marry, we'd have no desire or occasion to interfere. As you quite rightly said, that is none of our business. And as regards your little girl, my husband and I have talked the matter over and would offer her a home with us."

"Never—as long as I live!" Olga flashed. "Part with

Svanhild! That you may rest assured I'll never, never consent to."

"All right—as you please, of course. And you and my father-in-law will, of course, suit yourselves, if you want to marry on sixty kroner a month—give up your livelihood here, and undertake to start anew in Fredrikstad, which I can promise you will be very difficult. It is so perfectly incomprehensible to me what you want with Simonsen anyway. Heavens, to marry—you already call yourself 'Mrs.' In your circle people aren't so particular about some little affair you may have had with one of your lodgers. That you ever took up with Simonsen—really you must excuse me for saying it—in my opinion it doesn't speak very well for you. In plain language he's really nothing but an old swine!"

Olga interrupted her.

"You might just as well stop right here, Mrs. Carling. But I'll tell you, in plain language, what it was I wanted with Anton Simonsen. One thing and another there may be about him that one might object to. But I noticed one thing very soon, whatever else one might say, he had a kind heart. And there are not too many kind people around let me tell you! And no sooner did he realise that I took pains and wanted to make him comfortable than he began to feel at home, and straightened up and became regular in his habits, as he might have done sooner, in my opinion, had he been made comfortable before. No, you can't deny—Anton's kind-hearted and grateful. And then his fondness for Svanhild—really he goes too far in his love for the child—he is downright spoiling her. I am fond of Simonsen, let me tell you, Mrs. Carling."

Mossa rose and thrust her gloved finger tips in between the lace frills of her muff.

"Of course—if you're in *love* with Simonsen—that's another matter."

She sailed out.

That Mr. Sigurd Carling had a high opinion of his wife's sagacity is true enough. He had so often heard others say—that he had come to believe it himself—that it was Miss Mossa Myhre who had put life into Sigurd Carl Simonsen when he was a mere clerk and had made him the man he was. But he had nevertheless had his doubts as to whether she was the proper person to come to an understanding with Mrs. Martinsen. For there was no denying that she looked at things quite rigorously, and this Olga, it appeared, had had two children a bit irregularly. Mossa could on occasion be rather sharp and disagreeable. He was sorry therefore afterwards—

he had been foolish to let her go. For some kind of understanding had to be arrived at. Should the father come down to Fredrikstad and live, with a wife and child whom he could not provide for—it was as clear as day what the end would be. Never would he feel secure against unexpected, unforeseen demands for assistance—and then all the other aggravations which always trailed his father. And everlasting difficulties with Mossa.

The affair had to be settled—and that immediately, before the old fellow had time to slip one over on them first. He had been up at the Hercules Machine Shops and had ordered the two new turbines, and had had at the same time a few words *en passant* relative to his father. Simonsen—it was now arranged—was to leave Christmas Eve, in order that he might go home with them and spend Christmas with his family.

Later he started off himself to see Mrs. Martinsen.

Olga's eyes were red from much weeping when Simonsen came home to dinner. Carling had been there. He had been very nice for that matter, she said. He had asked to see Svanhild, and he had set her on his knee, and had promised her something for Christmas. Later he had talked with Olga. It was this miserable debt of hers—she was behind in her rent, and had bills at various shops here and there—so she had accepted the money. He had promised her fifteen kroner a month for Svanhild—that was something sure anyway—and she had to consider Henry too—he wouldn't be able to take care of himself entirely for some time yet. Fifteen kroner a month, he had said, for the time being—"until my father becomes self-supporting and can marry you." Olga was sitting on Simonsen's knee, in his cold room, in the easy chair in front of the dresser with the family portraits, and she wept, and he caressed and comforted her.

"Really, Anton, I don't know——! What else was there I could do? If he won't help you—why, there's no other way out. And I understood from the way he talked—he won't help in any other way. If they are so set against us, I don't suppose we could make a go of it in Fredrikstad either, you see——"

She blew her nose and dried away her tears, and then started to cry again.

"One must take what comes—must stand a lot when one is poor."

But persuade Simonsen to go down and spend Christmas with them—that Sigurd and Mossa were unable to do. They held out the prospect of a Christmas tree and the grandchildren and goose and ale and wine and head-cheese all through the Christmas holidays. But the old man was firm—he wanted to spend Christmas with Olga and the children. All they could get him to promise was that he would run down the day after Christmas. For Sigurd had given him twenty-five kroner by way of a Christmas gift. It was best therefore to get him away from the city, lest he go gadding about during the holidays with money in his pockets and nothing to do. It was preferable after all that the old fellow did his Christmas drinking with them—under supervision.

The day before Christmas Eve, when Simonsen came home, he had the sled under one arm. And he hummed in a deep bass as he lit the lamp in his room and undid his packages.

There was something in the way of drinks for the holidays—aquavit and punch and port for Olga. With a little ale now he'd be all set. A pipe for Henry. It didn't cost a great deal—it was mostly to show the lad he hadn't forgotten him—and a manly thing to get too it was for that matter. Otherwise he had been almost niggardly. The waist material for Olga cost only one forty-five, but he had bought her a brooch too for three seventy-five—and really it looked like something worth upwards of ten kroner. Simonsen took it out of the box—ah, wouldn't she be delighted! And for Miss Abrahamsen, too, he would get something—by way of remembrance. Some trifling thing—he could easily afford it.

And then the sled! Simonsen after removing the table cloth from the table, unwrapped it and placed it on exhibition.

"Oh, Olga dear, can you come here for a second?" he called out into the sewing room.

"Well, what is it? I'm very busy——"

Simonsen moved the lamp over to the table.

"And what do you suppose Svanhild'll say to that, Olga?"

"But the veneer, Anton!" And Olga placed newspapers underneath the sled and lamp. "Yes—a beautiful—lovely—sled——"

"And see here," and Simonsen unbuckled the cushion and showed her the painted roses. "The cushion was extra, of course, you understand."

"Hm! It cost quite a bit, I imagine?"

"Five kroner and twenty-five öre—with the cushion," Simonsen proclaimed proudly.

"So! That seems a lot of money to put into a thing like that, Anton. She's still so young—she might have been satisfied, even if it had not been quite so grand." And Olga sighed.

"Oh, well, seeing we have a few pennies to spend, we might

as well do it. It's only fun, it seems to me, to give a little liberally. And now that you'll be rid of your debt—— I've not forgotten my sweetheart either, you'll see," and he nudged her playfully. "Can you get me a couple of glasses, Olga? I've bought some port—we'll see how you like it—it was mostly for your sake, you see, that I bought it."

Olga glanced at the row of bottles on the dresser. She sighed again. Then she brought in the glasses.

It was late Christmas Eve before Mrs. Martinsen had finished her work. But finally everything was in order. Henry had delivered the last of the dresses as soon as they were done, and Olga and Miss Abrahamsen had straightened up and gathered everything in bundles on the chairs and the table in the sewing room. Miss Abrahamsen had had her coffee and cake, and had received a bottle of eau de cologne from Simonsen before she left.

After that Olga went into the living-room. She cleared the table of the fashion journals and the chairs of dress goods and materials for lining, and gathered up the buttons and pins on the console in glass trays. Then she lit the Christmas tree, which she had trimmed the evening before.

Svanhild and Henry and Simonsen came in. The elders sat down in the plush chairs. But Svanhild danced about and was happy, greatly captivated by all the lights—caught sight of the sled—and shouted for joy—ran back to the tree and scarcely knew what to do with herself for joy. Simonsen beamed and Olga smiled, although her eyes were annoyingly red. Simonsen had noticed them several times during the afternoon. Ugh, it would be just his luck to have her start crying to-night—when he so wanted them all to be happy.

He brought in his gifts, and he smiled mischievously; no doubt she thought the waist material a meagre gift. Then he brought out a bottle of eau de cologne—he had given in to the desire to be extravagant when he was in the fifty öre shop getting something for Miss Abrahamsen. And there was even a sewing basket for Olga, and a little match box, which looked like silver, for Henry. The boy thanked him as a matter of course, and laid the pipe and the box in the window, where he sprawled lazily in a chair.

Then finally the brooch!

"These other things, you see, are kind of practical—I wanted you to have something else too, Olga——"

Olga opened the box, and tears came into her eyes.

"But so many things, Anton!"

Simonsen gave a grand flourish of the hand.

" I hope you'll keep me in mind when you wear it, Olga, dear."

" I certainly shall, Anton ! "

" And, say—what about the box that came this evening for Svanhild ? "

Olga brought it in.

It was addressed " Little Miss Svanhild, care of Mrs. Martinsen's Dressmaking Establishment." Olga opened it. On a card inside was written " A Merry Christmas." It was from Sigurd Carling, and it was a doll—but oh, what a doll !

It had yellow curly hair and eyes that opened and closed, and it was dressed in a white coat with a white fur cap and muff, and there was a tiny pair of skates hung over one arm—that was the grandest of all. Svanhild was struck speechless—but Simonsen prated. He and Svanhild were equally delighted with the doll.

" Well, I suppose mamma had better put this away for you—it wouldn't do, you see, to play with it except on Sundays——"

" After all, Sigurd is kind," he said to Olga, who came in with the glasses and a pitcher of hot water. " That's what I've always said– Sigurd is really kind at heart—it's that confounded wife of his that winds him round her finger, for he is really kind——"

Simonsen brewed himself a hot toddy, and Olga had some port. Svanhild, too, was given a little port in a glass by herself as she sat on pappa's knee.

" Won't you come over here too, Henry, and brew yourself a toddy—you're 'most a grown man now, you know."

Henry rose somewhat reluctantly. He avoided looking at Simonsen. He had a pale freckled face and hard light-coloured eyes. He looked thin and slight in the man-sized clothes he wore.

" Well, skaal then, all three !—This is what I call having a cosy time ! Aren't we having a cosy time, Olga ? "

" Yes, indeed ! " She sat biting her lips for the, tears came into her eyes. " If only one could know where we'd be next Christmas——! "

Simonsen lit his cigar. He seemed a bit annoyed.

" Don't you want to try your pipe, Henry ? There's some tobacco on my dresser—if you don't happen to have any yourself."

" No thanks ! " was Henry's only reply.

" Ah yes—next Christmas——" Olga sighed and struggled to keep from crying.

" It's not easy to know what one doesn't know," Simonsen remarked, and leaned back in the sofa. " This certainly was a good cigar! Well, skaal, Olga! Who knows—perhaps we'll all be celebrating next Christmas with the peasants in the country! They celebrate Christmas royally up in Öimark, I am told. I really think you'd like living in the country, Olga—I really do. It wouldn't be so bad—all you'd have to do would be to step outside and chop down your own Christmas tree. How would you like that, Svanhild,—go with pappa into the woods and get a Christmas tree, and haul it home on your sled?"

Svanhild beamed ecstatically.

"And Henry'd have to beg off a few days at the office and come and celebrate Christmas with us."

Henry smiled—a bit scornfully.

"Wouldn't that be fun, Svanhild, go down to the station and meet Henry at the train? How would you like living with pappa and mamma on a big gaard in the country—with cows and horses and pigs and chickens and everything? And nice Sigurd, who gave you your doll, he has a little girl about your age too, and a boy a bit larger, and a wee tiny baby, you could go down and play with them in the city."

"And I'd go down and drink tea with that swell daughter-in-law of yours, if that's what you mean, Anton!"

"I don't see why *that* should follow."

"How you can sit and talk such nonsense!" Olga laughed, and then began to cry.

"But, Olga, what are you crying for now, my girl? Why must you always take it that way——?"

"Well, how do you want me to take it? I ought to be grateful to boot, I suppose, that this swell daughter-in-law of yours flung in my face that Henry's father once deserted me, and that now you're leaving me. And we'll be left here with our shame—my children and I—my unfathered children! You think, as they do, I suppose, I am only fit to slave away for ever, sewing for these fancy females you carry on with so scandalously. But I 'spose it's natural that all you people think you can treat me just as you please! Well, that's what I get; I should have known what sort you men were—when you've had what you want from a poor woman—why off you go and leave her sitting with the bag."

"But Olga!"

"Ah, it's easy enough for you. I should say so! All you need do is to move up into the country, and then take to drink and women again and all the rest, and run around wallowing in mire, as you were when I first took hold of you——Oh God, how simple and foolish I was to believe you and let you do with me as you pleased!"

" But, Olga, for heaven's sake, think of the children! "

" Oh, don't worry, they hear it, you may rest assured—in the yard and on the stairs. They might just as well hear it from me too."

" But—it's Christmas Eve to-night—surely you ought to remember that," Simonsen protested paternally.

Olga wept quietly, her head on the table. Simonsen placed his hand over on her shoulder.

" But, Olga—surely you know—you know very well that I am fond of you. And Svanhild? Do you think perhaps I shall ever forget my little innocent child? On that score you may rest assured, Olga. I shan't ever betray you or leave you—what I've promised I'll keep! "

" The poor thing! " Olga sat up and blew her nose. " It won't be you, I'm afraid, who'll say as to that, Anton."

" One thing there is, Olga, you must remember," he put one arm about her neck and held Svanhild with the other, and he straightened up and thrust his stomach out, " there's one greater than either Sigurd or Mossa who presides over that—and over all of us.

" But isn't it time to sing some Christmas songs? " he asked after a bit. He took a sip of his toddy and cleared his throat. " ' Oh, blessed aye is Christmas Eve '—shall we sing that? Svanhild knows that, I'm sure. All right, Svanhild, sweetheart."

Svanhild sang whole-heartedly, and Simonsen hobbled along, falling by the wayside at the high notes, but always starting afresh at the beginning of each verse. After a little Olga too joined them with her tear-broken voice. Only Henry did not sing.

And after Olga had gone out to tend to the cream pudding and the spare ribs, Simonsen and Svanhild still went on singing.

. . . . . .

And then finally the last morning came. The alarm clock in Olga's room sounded, but Simonsen merely rolled over, half-dozing in the dark—it was so cold to get up. Everything was grey and gloomy. Especially the prospect of having to get up and go out in the cold—away from everything.

Such a bed—with feather ticks on top and underneath—he had never experienced in any of the many places he had lived in before.

Olga opened the door, and in the light from her own room she set down the tray she was carrying, lit the lamp, and moved the tray over on the bed. There was coffee and cake.

" You'll have to hurry, I guess, Anton."

" I suppose so."

Simonsen sighed. He drew her over to him and patted her, in the intervals of dipping his cakes and drinking his coffee.

" Ah, what excellent coffee you have to-day, Olga dear, can't you sit down and have some with me? "

" I'm afraid I must get busy and start breakfast——"

Simonsen crawled out of bed and got his clothes on. He thrust the last few items into his hand-bag and locked both bags. Then he went into Olga's room.

He crossed over to the bed where Svanhild lay sleeping. He stood there for some time, his hands in his pockets, looking at her. Dear little Svanhild!

He peered into the living-room too. It was pitch dark and icy cold. Henry had gone off to Nordmarken early Christmas morning with some friends of his. He fussed about in there awhile—came up against Svanhild's Christmas tree in the dark and set the tinsel trimmings tinkling. Ah—he sighed—when —if ever—would he see the place again!

And he returned to Olga's room. It was warm and comfortable. The lower end of the table had been cleared, where Olga and Miss Abrahamsen sat all day sewing; a white table cloth had been laid, and breakfast all ready—head-cheese and ale and dram and everything—and the lamp glowed peacefully and hummed softly as it burned. A bit of light fell upon Svanhild, asleep in her little bed, her pretty hair down over her forehead. His poor little girl!

There was a warmth and cosiness in the room. Ah, how comfortable he had been here—with her—Olga—and Svanhild. His eyes filled with tears—he let the tears run—did not wipe them away in order that Olga might see them. His flabby blue-red cheeks were quite wet when Olga came in with the coffee.

" Well, we'd better eat," she said.

" Yes, we may as well. And Svanhild——? Don't you think she might have liked to go to the train with us—have a ride in the sleigh? "

" I had thought of it, Anton, but it's so dark and cold outside—— Perhaps I'd better wake her, anyway—she can have a drop of coffee with us."

She went over to the bed—shook the child gently.

" Svanhild, don't you want to get up and have coffee with pappa and mamma? "

Svanhild blinked her eyes as she sat in her night dress on Simonsen's knee. The coffee wakened her a bit, but she was quite still and spiritless—since the grown ups were so quiet——

" Where are you going, pappa? "

" To Fredrikstad, of course."

" But when are you coming back? "

" Oh, I imagine you'll be coming down to me first."

" In the country—you told about? "

" Why, yes——"

" There you can go sliding with me again, pappa—can't you? "

" There we can go sliding—I should say so! "

The door bell rang. Olga looked out. The sleigh had arrived. The carrier's boy came and took Simonsen's bags down.

Simonsen kissed Svanhild and got up, and stood a moment with her in his arms.

" And now, Svanhild, you must be a nice good little girl—while pappa is away."

" I'll be good," Svanhild answered.

Olga went out into the kitchen and turned off the gas—since Svanhild was to be home alone—and came in again, and stood ready, her finger on the wick of the lamp.

" Well Anton——"

He gave Svanhild a resounding kiss, put her in her bed, and covered her up.

" Well, good-bye, Svanhild dear! "

Olga put out the light, and they went out. In the hall he put his arms about her and pressed her close to him, and they kissed each other.

They sat silent in the sleigh as they shuffled down the streets in the dark morning. Nor had they anything to say to each other as they strolled about in the cold uninviting station hall. But she was ever at his heels—when he bought his ticket, when he checked his baggage—stood right behind him, small and dressed in black and looking short and square in her wraps.

They made their way leisurely into the waiting-room and sat looking up at the station clock.

" We got here early enough surely," Olga remarked.

" We did that, and that's always best when one is travelling. It was a shame, Olga, that you had to get up so early—now in the holidays."

" Oh——! " Olga replied. " But perhaps we'd better go out and make sure of a seat on the train."

Simonsen got himself and his belongings stowed away in a smoking coupé. And he stood at the window and Olga below on the station platform.

" Well, take care of yourself, Olga—and write often—how you're getting on——"

" And you do the same, Anton."

They began to close the doors down the line. Olga stepped up on the runboard, and they kissed each other again.

" Well, Olga, you've been mighty good to me."

" No more than you to me, Anton. And have a good trip! "

The locomotive whistled—a jerk ran down the length of the train—and it began to move forward. Olga and Simonsen got out their handkerchiefs, and waved to each other, as long as they could see anything.

The train thundered away at the first grey sign of dawn—past the homes at Bækkelaget—at Norstrand—at Ljan. Some of the windows were already lit up. The icy grey of the fjord was just visible, on the lower side of the track, with islands scattered about.

Ugh, uncomfortable! Simonsen was alone in the coupé, sucked his cigar, and looked out the window. Gaards and forests swept by—swam by—greyish brown fields with strips of snow in the furrows—black woods—

Well—Olga was probably home by now. He wondered what she might be doing. Dressing Svanhild perhaps. She intended to sew to-day—she had said. So Svanhild would have to sit on the floor over by the window and play with her doll rags. There was no pappa now to take her out coasting in the park.

Ah, that cosy room with the two warm beds in—and the lamp, and the sewing all spread out, and the bits of rag on the floor, which one was forever wading around in—and Svanhild over by the window—ah, his blessed little child!

He could see her sitting quiet all by herself. Now and then a Miss Hellum or some other Miss went over and offered her some candy. Svanhild would surely miss her pappa a lot!

It was not as it should be—not as it should be!

For a moment he was about to explode within—because it was not as it should be. His heart—what life had left him of it—fairly burned within him.

" Svanilla, Svanilla dear," he muttered to himself.

But he pushed the thoughts aside.

The little innocent child—so good—so good—would she not fare all right!

He wiped away his tears. There was, after all, some one mightier than they who ruled such things. Yes—one had to console oneself with the thought that there was after all a higher destiny that ruled everything.

MAARTEN MAARTENS

THE FAIR-LOVER

ANNEKE PETERS stood before the cottage door. She had finished the drudgery of the day for the day. To-morrow morning she would begin the whole thing over again, as she had begun it yesterday, patiently. Anneke Peters was a good girl. She knew it. That was the one bright spot in her life of monotonous doing-your-best.

For seven years, ever since her father died, she had lived with her widowed uncle, old Pete Peters; Pete the miser, as the village called him, " Mammie's Grave Pete." Her own mother she could not remember: her father, she remembered, drank. She was fourteen when she came to keep house for Uncle Pete; she had never done anything else, excepting, before that, keep house for her father. The latter had frequently abused, and occasionally fondled her: Uncle Pete had never done either, but he grumbled from morning till night. He was a respectable man in his way: born amongst a pauper set, he had worked himself up a few steps in the world, as a pedlar, by sheer industry and lies. He had a talent for commercial mendacity, the lie that pays; he was the cleverest liar for miles around. He would swear himself black in the face, while describing his goods, " by the grave of his sister "; his excuse to himself, and to God, being this, that he never had had any sister to swear by. But when he substituted " mother's " for " sister's " he could always be relied on. Those who had frequent doings with him found him out, and that is how he got his nickname. In middle life he had married, and soon after lost, a childless widow with a competency. He then gave up his little business, and henceforward did nothing, living poorly, and lying for diversion, as he had formerly lied for gain. His other amusement was grumbling. He grumbled at everything and everybody, the Government, the weather, and Anneke, from morning till night. And he told stories all over the village, inventing complications, embroiling neighbours, keeping up a sort of perpetual April fooling and finding it excellent sport.

Anneke worked from morning till night to make all things go so well there should be no cause for grumbling, but that undertaking is hopeless where the grumbler needs no cause. She was very ignorant, she could barely read and write, but she had a natural liking for refinement of the outer kind—for pretty things and pleasantness; she put a couple of geraniums upon the window-sill, though "Mammie's Grave Pete" complained they kept you from seeing the girls go by.

"Boys go by," he corrected himself, with a leer. "They don't stop to look in, Anneke—much less, cross the threshold." He had few jokes, but frequent. "There's none come to fetch you for the Kermesse," he said. He said it over and over again.

He had grumbled over it on this summer evening, complaining that no man would ever come to take her off his hands. Here was Truda engaged to the handsomest ne'er-do-well that had ever left black children behind him in India, and nobody to give Anneke as much as a look, unless it be the blind beggar, Jan Siemen.

Anneke had not replied that she saved her uncle a servant, nor had she pointed out that Jan Siemen never came near their uncharitable door. She had simply gone and stood outside in the early summer twilight, and thought how clear and still the sky was in the soft blue evening shades.

Yes, Truda was engaged. To handsome Harmen Reys, the Indian corporal. Truda, the child of Aunt Peters's prosperous sister, the wealthy innkeeper's only daughter, whose father jingled his keys and talked of his "iron safe"; Truda, who wore clothes to church on Sunday such as no other girl could have got at honestly. Truda Batsy had always scorned her low-born uncle's lower niece. She had been taught to do so, and had gladly learnt the lesson. "We must be decent to 'Mammie's Grave,'" said Juffrouw Batsy. "It'll be all the better when he steps into his own."

"Then I wish to God he would," said the innkeeper.

"But, as for Anneke Peters, she's of no account at all," said Juffrouw Batsy. She had slapped Truda as a child for asking if Anneke was a cousin of theirs.

And now Truda was engaged, and more aggressively scornful than ever. For years, from the days of their meeting at the infant school, the bigger girl, two years younger, but florid and healthy, had pinched, bullied, insulted the weakling creature with the plaintive eyes. Many and many a time she had gibed at her in the streets. Now she was triumphant, and, indeed, why should it not be so? She had always triumphed from the first. All success and comfort and delight had always been hers. She even drove in her father's chaise on week-days.

As for being engaged—that is, formally engaged to be

married—such grandeur unachievable formed no part of Anneke Peters's wildest dreams. But certainly she would have felt pleased had she received those more casual attentions which fall to the lot of most country girls. Nobody ever offered to keep company with Anneke; nobody suggested a walk, or stopped for a chat by her window. She was plain; she was poor; she was modest; people did not even feel absolutely sure that her father and mother had " been to the mayor's." Luckily for her, the chief proof on her behalf was furnished by Pete's persistent denial of the fact.

Yes, she would have liked a sweetheart—especially a Kermesse sweetheart—once in a way; a young man who would have taken her, as all the other girls got taken, sooner or later, to the annual fair at Overstad. That fair was the event of the year to all the peasants for miles around. The fair at Overstad, the splendid, riotous, ruinous fair; everybody went there in couples; it was a monstrosity to remain away. She only wanted to go one year. She only wanted to see, to have seen, to be able to talk about the thing with the others, who talked of it all through the year. Her uncle unwilling to accompany her, had always refused to let her go unattended. " If you want to see it," he said, " get a lover—like the others. Ha! "

As she stood before the cottage door, this summer evening, Truda Batsy came by on her way to her own home, the tavern two hundred yards off. Harmen Reys was with her, looking bored. Perhaps the two had been quarrelling? Anneke's little heart gave a little leap of pleasure, instantly checked.

" Well? " said Truda, stopping short. She was vexed with her ne'er-do-well lover, and her heart was full of spite. " Anneke, are you going to the fair this year? They say it's quite unusually fine."

" Perhaps," replied Anneke boldly.

" Really? And whom are you going with? "

" Wouldn't you just like to know? "

" I shouldn't. I don't care tuppence who goes with whom, as long as I go with Harmen. But you'll want a sweetheart, Anneke, unless you take your Uncle Pete."

" Good-night, Truda," said Anneke, turning away.

" Or you might take Beggar Siemen. Anneke, if I were you, I'd rather *hire* a sweetheart than never go at all! " She passed on with a laugh her lover trailing in her wake. Anneke stood looking after her.

" What a brute you are! " said Harmen, and twirled his light moustache.

Truda Batsy laughed again. " Why shouldn't she go with a hired lover? " said Truda. " Better people 'n she have done it a hundred times. But Uncle Pete'd never give her the money: that's why."

"You're a brute," replied Harmen, still more sulkily. "It'd almost be better to go with a meek little brown-eyed thing like that than with such a vixen as you."

"Smooth words, please," said the girl, angrily. "Why don't you go with her yourself, then? Don't overcharge, she ain't got much. None but the lowest of the low let themselves out at the fair."

"You're a brute," he said again. He was a man of few ideas.

She turned round suddenly and struck him a sounding slap on the cheek.

The quondam corporal straightened himself; a pink flush spread round the red mark on his fair skin. "I never strike a woman," he said, and, saluting, left her.

. . . . .

Anneke had gone back into the house. She walked slowly, meditating. She did not hate the innkeeper's daughter, for she could not honestly have wished her ill, but if there was anyone on earth she loathed and dreaded, that person was Truda Batsy.

"Truda, eh?—with her lover?" said old Pete. "I thought so, but I couldn't make sure because of your damned geraniums." She went to mix her uncle his evening glass of brandy and water—cold from June to September, hot from September to June: she had done that nightly now for half a dozen years. He always grumbled over the mixture, yet once, on the single occasion when she had spent a few days in bed, he had told her, grumbling, that no one could prepare it as well as she.

"What a good-looking man he is," pursued old Pete. "No wonder that, out in the Indies, he could bring down sweethearts like coco-nuts!"

"Was he very bad?" asked Anneke, with an innocent thrill.

"Bad? What a fool-girl's question! Is it bad when you potter about your stupid bit of a garden, if you smell at the stocks and wallflowers and things? What are they for else? Though, depend upon it, *he* didn't smell at wallflowers. You're a wallflower, Anneke."

She made no reply, but helped him to bed. He was an unpleasant old man, and this part of her daily task was especially distasteful to her. She went up to her own little white attic—every year she did the whitewashing herself—and lingeringly undressed. "What folly!" she said at last, endeavouring to cast off the thought which returned in the night and next morning. After all, the folly was possible. Other girls had committed it.

In the afternoon, when she ran out with a big tub of washing-water to the reedy canal that creeps along by the village, she saw Truda sitting idle, with a couple of others, under the big chestnut in front of the inn. They were laughing heartily. The "Ho! ho! ho!" of Truda's booby cousin Tony rose above the cackle of the girls. Harmen was there again also. "Do you forgive me?" Truda had asked that morning, a little shamefacedly, for her. "No," he had answered, "let's talk of something else."

"Anneke!" called Truda across the blazing sunlight.

Anneke turned paler than usual. "It is the sign!" she thought. For, in her foolishness, she had told herself that never would she venture to question Truda about girls who had hired their squires, but if Truda began, well, then——

She came away from the waterside, with her tub held out before her, hot from her work, through the lazy heat, to the shadow of the chestnut tree. The others were cool and merry; a great basket of cherries stood in the middle of the group.

"Well, have you got him already?" questioned Truda. "I was telling Corry and Suzy you were going to pay for a sweetheart."

"Will she advertise for one?" said Corry, who had from childhood been Truda's principal friend, and who now was being courted by the red-faced farmer lad, Tony.

"Nonsense," said Truda. "All she need do is to go to old Nell Trops in the Weavers Street at Overstad. That's where the girls apply who can't get a lover for themselves." The big innkeeper's daughter folded her fat pink arms, and looked triumphantly from Anneke to Harmen. "You go to Nell Trops in the Weavers Street," she said.

"It isn't true! You're chaffing me!" said Anneke; but some of them saw the flash in her eyes as Truda gave the address.

"It's true enough," remarked lumbering Tony Dunder. "We had a cow-girl at our place two years ago that got one cost her a florin. A florin he took, and everything free—the shows, and merry-go-rounds, and the waffles."

"And he treated her decent?" questioned Anneke, eagerly. "He—he just kept her company, and let her go home when she liked?"

"Oh, I dare say he treated her just as she wanted him to," replied Tony, laughing clumsily. Corry laughed also. Suzy sat eating cherries, and shying the stones into Anneke's tub.

"I don't believe a word of it!" cried Anneke. "It's all chaff and rubbish!" The girls jeered back at her.

Harmen Reys bent forward, and, taking a big handful of cherries, threw them into the washing-tub. "Have some?" he said. "They're very good."

Anneke's heart was too full for any sort of answer. She crept back to her house and her work.

"Do you know, she intends to do it," announced Truda, and pursed up her lips.

"Nonsense!" cried the other girls.

"I tell you she does. And, look here, we must have a lark. Of course, she will do it on Farmers' Thursday, when all the countryside is there. Harmen, you must go to Mother Trops, and get her to give you to Anneke."

"What!" cried Harmen Reys. "No, thank you; I'm going with you."

"So you shall, you dunderhead! But, first, you must fetch the fair Anneke. You will take her to the circus, and seat yourselves on one side; then we shall come in afterwards—a lot of us—the whole village—and seat ourselves opposite; then, presently, you'll think of some pretext to escape and come over to the empty seat beside me, and Anneke, who's paid for her lover——"

"Ho! ho! ho!" burst in Tony. The others all shook and cried out with laughing.

"What fun it'll be!" screamed Truda.

"*I* think it's rather low," said Harmen.

"Don't be a fool," remonstrated Tony.

"No," retorted Harmen, "I won't so long as I couldn't, anyhow, be as big a fool as you."

"Hush! hush!" interposed Truda. "Let's think the plot out. We must arrange about it all in a day or two."

"It'll keep till to-morrow," said Harmen, rising and stretching his long limbs. "The cherries are all eaten. I'm going home. I've got something to do." A loud laugh went up from them all, for it was well known that Harmen lived and loafed on his Indian corporal's pension.

"I'm coming with you," ejaculated Tony, stumbling to his feet.

"Something to do means gin," said Truda, scornfully. "Why don't you go in and drink father's?"

"Because it comes too expensive," retorted Harmen.

"But if I give it you it costs you nothing."

"It couldn't be dearer than when you give it me," said Harmen with a smirking sneer.

He slung off with a jerk of annoyance. She jarred on him,

especially of late. He wasn't a good man; he didn't mind a bad woman, but the worst man wants a woman to be tender.

"Truda isn't the sort of girl *I* should care to marry," said Tony, slouching along beside the other's army step.

"Nor is Corry," replied Harmen sharply.

The bumpkin grinned, a sudden break of white along his crimson face. "Who talks of marrying Corry?" he replied. "Marrying's one thing, and courting's another. Kermesse comes once in a year, and marriage comes once in a lifetime."

"Yes," said Harmen meditatively, his pale eyes dreamy with reminiscence of a sunny country where the wedding knot is more easily untied.

"And she hasn't got the money either that people say she has."

"What?" cried the other, suddenly attentive, all the dreaminess gone from his gaze.

"No, she hasn't," said Tony with malicious alacrity, "if everybody knew what *we* know! But then, luckily, they don't."

"Tony, let's go and have a drink."

"I'm agreeable, if you pay. You just take the train to Overstad and ask the registrar of mortgages there on whose property he registered a mortgage last Thursday. 'No, thank you, not I,' says father when Uncle Batsy came to him. 'I don't go lending o' my money to chaps as speculate in corn!'"

"Phew!" said the corporal between his teeth.

"But there's old Pete Peters, Tony: all his dead wife's money'll be Truda's some day."

"If he leaves it her. But he always says he is going to leave it to Anneke."

"That don't prove anything, coming from such a born liar. I wonder if he's really free to leave it as he chooses?"

"Let's take him for a drink, and make him tell us on his mother's bones! We shall find him under the beeches by the church."

They marched off in that direction.

"What's Truda done to you?" asked Harmen presently.

"Done to me? Nothing. What should she have done to me? We'll see whether she can always get as many Kermesse sweethearts as she chooses! A lubber may only be a lubber, but he's better than nothing at all."

"I see," said Harmen, scornfully. "That was last year, I suppose."

They found old Pete filling his pipe with newly purchased tobacco. "She's a very good girl," said Pete; his little eyes twinkled, disappeared.

"I shall leave her every penny I have," he said presently, comfortably ensconced in his favourite corner, in his favourite public-house. "I shall. By my sister's grave, I shall." He saw suitors on the horizon. He wanted to have suitors, that he might enjoy dismissing them. The young men gave him a couple more glasses of gin.

"I shall leave her every penny, every penny," he said, nodding over his glass. "Yes, I swear it, every penny. By my mother's grave, I shall."

"Oh, hang your idiotic mother's grave," said Harmen, getting up to go.

. . . . .

Meanwhile Anneke, standing over the washtub, slowly thought the matter out. She felt she could no longer bear the public ignominy, not so much of never having possessed an accredited sweetheart, as of never having found a swain to take her to the fair. She knew that many a maid in her position would have started boldly for the Kermesse, and waited there until some honest fellow invited her to spend the evening with him, as in more exalted circles men came up to claim a waltz. But when she thought of such indelicacy her heart bumped. To hire a cavalier, to pay honourably for honourable companionship, that seemed a very different matter. "Nell Trops in the Weavers Street," she repeated to herself. "Overstad is such a big city, nobody will ever find out." She flattered herself that she had admirably kept her own counsel before her tormentors. It would be best to go on "Farmers' Thursday," when all the villagers, for miles around, trooped in to make high holiday. On that day, following his invariable custom, Uncle Pete would go across to Rotterdam to fetch his quarter's income, getting back at midnight with the money, sober as a judge. That was *his* Kermesse treat, he always used to say.

Yes, she would go, and, taking two tickets for the circus, would sit revealed to all beholders—especially to the young folks of her own village, most especially to Truda—revealed as a girl who can keep Kermesse, if she chooses, and keep it with better men than those she left at home. Her heart glowed as she pictured the hour of triumph to herself. For the twentieth time she counted the few florins in her purse. She believed she had enough.

Two days later, on the morning of the momentous Thursday, Anneke, up betimes from a sleepless couch, hurried through her work as if she had not the whole long day before her. Presently she laid out her uncle's rusty Sunday clothes: she dropped from her trembling hands the fuzzy black hat she was brushing.

"Stupid!" growled Pete; he rarely said anything more, but, then, he was always saying this. There were times when she almost regretted her father's volleys of oaths.

"I shan't be back till midnight," said Uncle Pete. She knew that. These quarterly trips to the bank were the supreme satisfaction of the old man's life. She watched him depart, a tottery old scarecrow with an abnormal umbrella, along the poplar-bordered road.

In the afternoon, having nothing left to do, she sat down to sew at some of the numerous clothes in which her soul delighted. It seemed astonishing, to her accustomed activity, how slow the hot hours passed. She dressed carefully, in her dark green gown, and fastened her mother's great gold ear-pins into the snowy, tightly fitting cap. Then, at seven o'clock, in the full glory of the solemn July evening, she crept forth, locked the cottage door behind her, and hastened away.

The station was a mile off, along open road. But Anneke, trembling like a guilty thing lest the village cronies should observe her, made a circuit of two miles under cover of brushwood, along ditches and fields. The platform, when she reached it, was deserted. All the others had gone in the morning, making a day of it. She had watched them passing the window in excitable groups.

At Overstad Station there was plenty of commotion. The roar of the Kermesse seemed to rush out and welcome the trains. Over the whole city hung an atmosphere of burning grease; in the distance, about the vast Cattle Market, rose a yellow flare of dirty light against the tranquil sunset and the solitary evening star.

Anneke, avoiding that quarter, crept round to the Weavers Street, and studied the names inscribed on the doors, according to a custom very general in Holland.

The street was a side one, short, uncanny in its stillness. Before one of the tall houses a little child was playing on the doorstep. Anneke hoped it would go in.

"Well, my dear, and what are you doing here? Surely you ought to be at the Kermesse," said a pleasant voice behind her. She turned in alarm. The speaker was a tall man, with a somewhat gruff appearance, and a beard that looked as if it would better have fitted somebody else's face.

"Well," he continued, as she did not answer, "what do you say to going there with me?"

The idea of thus accompanying an unknown, unrecommended person struck horror into her breast. "Oh, no, no," she said anxiously. " Please go away. I have come here to see a friend." He fell back, laughing.

" Perhaps your friend lives *there* ! " he cried, pointing to a little house that hung twisted into a corner, half hidden between two tall neighbours—a little house, with a slouching doorway and a window that winked. She watched him turn the corner; she waited until he must be definitely gone. For a moment she desired to return to the station; she was miserable, she was alarmed; she took a few steps towards the road. Then a sort of bravado came over her—the dogged resolve to go through with it. She walked straight up to the little house and boldly rang the bell. An old woman opened the door.

" Do you know where Nell Trops lives? " asked Anneke.

" Nell Trops lives here, my pretty," said the old woman. " Come in."

Anneke followed the creature into a back room. Of procuresses, evil houses, dangers to the innocent, she knew nothing. The vices she had heard of were the vices of the fields.

" And what do you want of Nell Trops, my dear? " The old woman cast a sidelong glance all over the shrinking figure; her expression grew indifferent. Nothing worth much.

" I—I—I," stammered Anneke, her pale face a dusky red; " I had heard—I thought that here——"

" Then you had heard wrong," said the old woman sharply. She held the door open. There was a musty smell in the little dingy room.

" But there was a girl from our village got one," cried Anneke, emboldened by necessity.

" I dare say," replied Nell Trops, drily. Then, suddenly, a light seemed to break in upon her. " You want a sweetheart to go a-fairing with? " she said, with a cunning glance.

Anneke hung her head.

" Is that all? " went on the woman briskly. " Quite right, my dear, quite right. Yes, this is the correct address. Now, what sort would you like to have, my dear—town or country? Do you like 'em fair or dark?—and what are you going to pay for him? "

" Oh, don't! " said Anneke.

" *My* charge," said the old woman with precision, " is fifty cents. With an umbrella, seventy-five."

Anneke lifted her glance. " Why with an umbrella? " she asked in sudden curiosity.

" It has always been so," replied Nell Trops, snappishly. " In my mother's time, and her mother's before her. An umbrella looks respectable; it means a better class. Every one knows that; it's a recognized fact, like the cathedral. Nothing's changed but the prices—they're lowered. Times are bad in everything. And the girls have got so bold, they find sweethearts for themselves!"

"Please, I'll take an umbrella," said Anneke. Nell Trops went out, and locked the door behind her—from habit. The girl started up with a shriek. That dim consciousness of the world's evil which is the torment and the safeguard of every innocent creature fluttered her whole heart with an agony of fear. "Let me out!" she cried, "let me out!"

Instantly the old hag stood before her. "You fool," said Nell Trops, with vast scorn, "how pretty do you think you are, pray?" The words, dimly understood, struck the girl's heart like a foul missile, leaving an indelible stain.

"Would you like a sweetheart with a nice black beard?" continued Nell more gently, for her visitor's expression alarmed her. "Beards are extra respectable. You'd have to pay a quarter more for a beard."

"No, not a beard," replied Anneke, suddenly reminiscent of the stranger in the street.

"Well, I haven't got 'em in boxes like tin soldiers," said the woman, put out. "You should have let me know this morning, and you could have had half a dozen to choose amongst. Beards are *my* taste. A big beard and a bald head for me."

"Yes, yes, a bald head!" exclaimed Anneke, who now only wanted not to have the stranger.

Again the old woman went out, this time without closing the door. She returned immediately, ushering in the man from the street.

"Not—not this gentleman," was what Anneke tried to say. But she dared not. And, whilst the words still struggled in her throat—"There now, my dears," said Nell Trops, "you just go a-fairing together! A pretty couple you make," said Nell Trops. She almost pushed Anneke into the passage. "The florin, my dear, if you please. Yes, that's right. Come and tell me to-morrow how much you've enjoyed yourself!" The door closed behind Anneke. The room had been dark; the street did not seem much lighter.

"Now, let's hurry up and enjoy ourselves," said the stranger gruffly. "You'll find me a good sort. Good as gold, honour bright!"

Somewhat reassured, she walked on beside him in silence, towards the increasing tumult of the Market. As yet this excursion was not very enjoyable: she had pictured it altogether different. In fact, she was miserable.

But the Cattle Market—the central glory of the Kermesse—that certainly was a sight to be seen. Far away it shone into the deep blue silence, a yellow lake of many thousand oil lamps, with—high in air, obtrusive—the white electric glare. The uninterrupted bellow of sound—bands, singing, yells, cat-cries, calls of salesmen and showmen, pistol-shots, merry-go-rounds, organs—formed the music of a Pandemonium. Between the long alleys of flaring booths and stalls of every sort rocked a crowd of red-faced peasants, many of them jumping, hustling, shouting—all excited, and a large percentage drunk. Uniforms were everywhere in quantities, especially about the pipe-hung shooting galleries: men and women massed together—sombre clothes and muslin caps and golden ornaments—whirled, insensate, to the weary jingle of the merry-go-round. Before canvas walls, ablaze with kings and lions, stood acrobats and actors, gorgeously bedizened, hoarsely mouthing their offers of entertainment. And above it all, above the steam of the fritter-shops, the sputter of the fat little grease cakes or "puffers," the big drums, the street songs, the somersaults, the jostlings, the vice and the vulgarity—above it all, and beneath the serenely solemn sky, everywhere, in a hundred medallions and paintings, the pure face, no less serenely unconscious, of the little girl-Queen of the Netherlands.

A great deal of it came back to Anneke now from memories of stray visits with her father when she was quite a child. But it was not at all as she had remembered it: it was noisy and common. Where possibly could be the wild delight of the others? No wonder no one ever cared to take her. No wonder they said she was not like other girls.

There were plenty of gingerbread stalls in all directions; there was plenty of gilt on the gingerbread; but to some people gingerbread is quite unattractive, even when all the gilt is still on.

"Now, what would you like to see first?" courteously inquired her companion. "There's a calf with two heads, of which one is a pig's, and there are some capital fighting fleas."

"Let's go to the circus at once," replied Anneke.

"Just as you like, it *is* rather late. And we can go to some of the shows when the circus is over."

They passed in—she paying for the tickets—and through a long, dimly lit corridor reached their seats. The first thing she noticed on entering was that Truda sat just opposite with her party, and that next to Truda there was a vacant place. Almost simultaneously, as she turned to sit down, a muffled cry escaped her. Her companion had lost his beard, and, with it, his beetling eyebrows. Handsome Harmen stood laughing behind her. "Hush," he said, "it's all right. It's only a joke!"

She had never seen a disguise before: she did not know that beards could be stuck on. As for jokes, she had small experience of those also. *They* knew, then—they would all know—that she had come to Overstad to hire a companion! She sat down in her seat and quietly cried.

"Don't," he whispered presently, "the others will notice." She stopped crying at once. "And, besides, I can't bear to see you do it. Let's be pleasant and enjoy ourselves. Look, they're going to begin!" A couple of clowns came leaping and laughing into the ring. Harmen settled down to the delights of the performance. Anneke tried to turn her eyes from the gay party opposite, who were evidently discussing and deriding her. She knew Harmen Reys but little: he was not of her village. She had always admired him from a distance: he was dashing, good-looking, his gaze was a caress. In these clothes he appeared different, almost a gentleman. She wondered what he wanted, what he intended to do.

The performance proceeded, and the people opposite grew restless. Truda, especially, began to make signs to her lover. In the first interval of ten minutes, when the circus half emptied, these appeals grew obstreperous. Tony came across and said something to Harmen. "You be hanged!" was the audible answer, the only one he got.

Innocent as Anneke might be—and she remained a woman, with all womanly instincts—she could not help realising that Truda was claiming her lover.

"Truda wants you," she said softly.

"Let her want," was his reply.

"But—I think you ought to go to her."

"I so seldom do what I ought to."

"You might begin now."

"Do you know, I almost think I am beginning."

"Oh, what a leap that horse gave!"

"Did it frighten you?"

"No; only startled. I'm not soon afraid of horses."

"I thought you were such a coward. Truda says so."

"P'rhaps I am. I'm afraid of what wants to hurt me.

"Nod away, Truda, nod away. You nod back to her, little Anneke; enjoy your triumph while you can!"

"What triumph?" asked Anneke.

He laughed at her. "Can't you really guess?" he said.

Yes, she could guess. She could see that, for some reason or other, Harmen, remaining beside her—Harmen, the Don Juan of the moment—openly flouted his sweetheart before her friends. He was noticeably amiable to Anneke; he got her a glass of lemonade and refused to let her pay for it. Other girls looked up at him as he bent over her, twirling his moustache. Certainly, for the moment, her success was complete. She smiled; she thought him delightful. He gave her his arm when the performance was over; and, ignoring the now utterly annihilated Truda, led out the lady of his choice.

They went into some of the shows together, Anneke selecting a menagerie and a collection of stereoscopic views. Harmen yawned, but acquiesced.

"And now," he said, "we must go and eat waffles." He conducted her to a white-and-gold pavilion, gay with the movements of immaculate cooks. He was making for a cabinet at the back.

"Not there, please," said Anneke. "Here in front we can see the people passing."

"But we want to be alone, do we not?"

"No."

A long silence followed the answer. They ate their waffles among the smells and the uproar.

"You're not the best of company to go Kermessing with," said Harmen. But a moment later he entirely changed his tone. He was very gentle and sympathetic, full of friendly interest. He told her how often he had pitied and admired her; how Truda's coarseness had long disgusted him—he had never been actually engaged to Truda; how this evening's *ruse* had simply been a means of approaching the better woman, Anneke, just the kind and tender helpmate for a scapegrace anxious to reform. All this music he poured into her unreluctant ears, amidst the clash of cymbals and the caterwaulings, and the ceaseless "By your leave!" of the white-clad waiters, who, the waffles being eaten, now wanted these customers to depart. But the heads of the couple bent lower and their murmurs grew softer, and people respect that sort of thing at fairtime, especially the caterers, who know it to be the corner-stone on which the whole erection rests.

When she lifted her eyes at last, there was a happiness in them such as comes to no woman twice. She believed in him, purely, implicitly.

"I want to go home," she said.

"What now? Why, the fun is only just beginning."

"I want to go to the station"—she detained him. "Alone."

An oath escaped from his lips. It hurt her, but not disagreeably. It reminded her of the only man who had loved her before, and sworn at her.

"Why, what a fool you are!" he said. "Come along with me, and we——"

"I am going to the station," she interrupted him. "Good-night."

She ran off into the darkness, thinking of nothing but joy. Her triumph of the evening she had entirely forgotten. On reaching the railway she asked for the train. They laughed at her: it had left twenty minutes ago. Then first since leaving home she glanced at a clock.

The only train now available did not stop at her village. She would have to walk six miles in the middle of the night. Worse than that, she would get home, with the key in her pocket, an hour after Uncle Pete. She dimly wondered whether Harmen had known about the time? No, he was a good man. She knew already that she would get to love him. He must go to Uncle Pete, and obtain the old man's leave to court her. Uncle Pete was anxious she should marry: there would be no objection on his part. How nobly Harmen had spoken! Already she admired him from the bottom of her heart.

She got out at the other station and flew along the road. How glorious was the stillness around her, the mild light of the great yellow moon among the poplars and across the broad fields, where the cattle occasionally moved. All about her was softness, and sweetness, and silence: the roar of the evening seemed centuries away. And Harmen had truthfully told her he cared for her! Were this little soul of ours less infinite than heaven, how could it contain the whole of heaven for an hour?

As she approached the cottage, she saw that the old man was pacing up and down in front of it. She had known that he would be there, infuriate. But somehow, timid as she usually was, she had not found time to think of him.

"Hussy!" he shouted, as soon as she was near enough. And then he used a yet uglier word. He looked a grotesque figure in the moonlight, with his round umbrella and tall hat.

She hurried to open the door, that she might the sooner conceal his shouting. She was glad when they were safe in the cottage together, and the storm of his wrath broke loose over her alone. She listened, shrinking back, but calmly inattentive. He had never abused her thus before, only grumbled. But then, she had never given him cause.

"Gad, I have found you out!" he cried, "with your smooth white face and soft church manners! Go your ways, as much as you choose: only don't bring the brats to me!"

In an instant the brutal words turned her heart to stone.

She faced her uncle, upright, by the flaring tallow candle. "I am sorry I missed my train," she said.

"And he let you come back by yourself?" asked Pete, more soberly, but with a sneer.

"I went alone. I met Harmen Reys. He was alone too. So we went to the circus together."

"Really? And that was all?"

"No." Her voice and manner again grew gentle. "He told me—uncle—he was fond of me"—very softly. "It seems he has thought—thought so for some time. He is going to ask you about it." Her head sank on her breast.

Old Pete sat down, and laughed till he shook.

"He's been in a mighty hurry about it!" chuckled old Pete. "Lor', it can't be more than three days ago that I told him about my money."

Anneke looked up, suddenly anxious. "What?" she said. "What do you mean?"

"He was mighty inquisitive about my money, he was. Who was I going to leave it to? I told him, you! Lor', what fools men are! I told him, you! By my mother's grave, I did."

"Uncle!" her voice wavered between gratitude and distress.

"And so I shall; it's true enough! Aren't you my natural, lawful heir? Only—I ain't got any money to leave, not a hundred florins, I ain't. The money was your dead aunt's, and she left it all to Truda. The notary's got it, in the city. And whatever I saved—though that ain't much—was to go to Truda also; that was what she made me agree to, and sign at the notary's. 'The saving's is my money; I won't have it go to your beggarly family,' she says. But I ain't saved much, I'm a poor man, a poor man, Anneke. And, besides, I ain't going to die yet awhile!" He sat gloomily staring at the candle, in his big tattered armchair.

"Lor', what a lark!" he said, brightening up again. "He's a cool chap, that Reys. I hadn't never meant to tell you, till after I was dead. But it's greater fun telling you now, and you deserve it for letting me stand about in the dark for two mortal hours. And me that tired!"

"I don't believe it," she said bitterly. She had never spoken so to him before. "Nobody can ever believe you," she went on. "Nobody does. You can't have waited more than one hour, for instance. You always tell lies."

His pimpled face grew black with thunder. He pushed back the old tall hat, and leant forward on the umbrella. "I can tell truth when I choose," he said slowly, "as well as anybody.

You'll never have a halfpenny of mine, you slut. All of it goes to Truda."

She flung herself forward, suddenly, desperately; the candle streamed against her cheek. "Swear it to me," she cried hoarsely. "Swear it. Say you swear it by your mother's grave."

"Lor'," he answered, "have you found that out? Well, every man has his weakness. I'll swear it, if you like, by my sister's grave, and by my mother's, too."

She turned her back on him. "Good-night," she said, and went upstairs with her candle.

The old man, left in the dark, holloaed to her in vain; then, striking a light for himself, he went and banged against her door. He got no answer. Worn out, he stumbled and tumbled into bed, immediately falling asleep.

Next morning, at the usual hour, Anneke, with drawn features and red-rimmed eyes, came down and went about her work. To her uncle she spoke when necessary. Frequently she looked out of window. Her geranium-pots lay smashed outside—old Pete had done that in his rage last night, before the fastened door. She cleared up the mess and hurried in again. She was ashamed to show her face outside the door, until she knew how matters would come to stand between her and her last night's lover. She had always been a good girl—hitherto that had been her one satisfaction and solace.

Towards noon Harmen Reys came lounging along the canal and across the open space between the inn and the clump of cottages. Anneke laid down the pan she was scouring, and walked out to him at once in the laughing summer sunshine.

"Harmen Reys," she began, ignoring his pleasant greeting, "first of all I want to tell you this. What my uncle said to you was a lie, or as good as a lie. When he comes to die, all his money will go to Truda. I shall not have a penny. His money was all his wife's."

Harmen Reys' fair face flushed with swift annoyance. "Oh, nonsense. That can't be true," he said. "It's a lie of the old man's, Anneke." Truda had come out of the inn, and advanced halfway towards them. She stood irresolute—her eyes aflame.

"No, Harmen, it is true. He will leave me what he has, but then he has nothing to leave me. I thought you ought to know." Her tones were wistful, though her face was firm. "I know it's true. I am sure. But—Harmen——" She checked herself.

The handsome corporal slowly lifted his cap, and slightly bent his head. Then, leaving her standing there, he walked straight across to Truda.

"Well," he said, extending his hand, "confess that I've paid you out for that slap in the face you gave me!"

LOUIS COUPERUS

TWO PAIRS OF TWINS

FOR I knew all four of them. Their names were Jan and Hendrik Ruysdonck, and Lizzy and Marjory Leliekamp; the boys were the two sons of the Amsterdam Ruysdoncks, and the two Leliekamp girls belonged to the American branch, who in New York spell their name Lilycamp, but who descend authentically from the Dutch Leliekamps. It was amusing to see them; when the four went for walks or sat in a café or a theatre, even in Paris and London, everyone's eyes turned towards them. The Ruysdoncks were two sturdy Dutch boys, of distinguished appearance, with that solemn, ultra-respectable, almost Calvanistic demeanour, virtuous and dignified in spite of their age—twenty-six—which characterised them at once as sons of a universally esteemed lowland patrician family. Papa's influence had from the outset imparted to the boys something solid: they were sober and simple in all they had—clothes, motor-cars, valet or cigarette-case—but all they had was strong, expensive, lasting, characterised by moderation, good taste and style. Nice boys they were, Jan and Hendrick Ruysdonck; I never quite knew which of them I really preferred, for they were as like as two drops of water. Their hair was equally fair and identically cut. Their clean-shaven faces had the same healthy, fresh and manly complexion. They wore the same signet-ring on the same finger. They had their clothes made by the same tailor. Really, whether you saw Jan or Hendrik, it was exactly the same, only . . . Jan, the elder of the twins, was a fraction of an inch taller than Hendrik, which infinitesimal difference was noticeable only when they stood shoulder to shoulder. Only then you saw which was Jan and which Hendrik, especially as it seemed that the whole of Jan's figure, in height, width and circumference, was a fraction of an inch bigger than Hendrik's. When they walked away together, the similarity was most perplexing.

Father Ruysdonck was a sensible fellow. He did not like the idea that Jan and Hendrik should lead an easy life at the office of the bank in Amsterdam as the sons of a rich father; therefore he had sent them to America to become acquainted with foreign trade. Jan had gone to New York, Hendrik to Baltimore, and in New York Jan had quickly fallen in love with Lizzy Leliekamp, whom he had met in New York society. The fair-headed Lizzy was indeed a delightful girl, pretty, charming, refined, a little free-and-easy after the American fashion, but not too much to shock Jan's propriety; in addition to this, she was rich, for father Lilykamp was king, I really forget of what metal or article of food, and so Jan and Lizzy had married; there was no reason why they should not, and in a few years they would go to Holland, though they would retain a house in New York. That is very convenient when money is no object, and Lizzy wanted to cross regularly every three months from America to " dear old Europe," which she already knew thoroughly, from the Rue de la Paix in Paris to the Wagner Theatre at Bayreuth. However, as chance would have it in this true history, Hendrik at Baltimore fell in love with Marjory Lilycamp, Lizzy's fair-haired twin-sister, also a delightful girl, pretty, charming, refined and witty. They married as Jan and Lizzy had done, for apparently there were no more objections to marriage between Hendrik and Marjory than there had been to marriage between Jan and Lizzy. Only when they stood side by side it was perplexing, to a spectator certainly, and perhaps even to themselves. For, if Hendrik and Jan were as like as two drops of water, the fair-haired Lizzy and the fair-haired Marjory were as like as two drops of dew.

For reasons of no account—I believe that Lizzy had a cold and Hendrik had fallen from his bicycle, or something equally unimportant—neither had been present at the other's wedding. It had been a remarkable coincidence, and had spoilt a great deal of fun—and so, when they saw each other again, they were married, and arranged a nice trip to dear old Europe, the four of them. After the first meeting, however, Jan and Hendrik had turned a shade pale, and their solemn faces looked more respectable and sedate than ever, while the two sisters sat giggling together like mad, appearing to admire each other's rings.

" Hendrik," said Jan gravely to his twin brother, whom he loved very much, " I want to say something to you which is worrying me."

" What is that, Jan? " said Hendrik, the younger, only a fraction of an inch smaller in size, but not in soul, you may be sure of that.

" Hendrik, your wife is indeed remarkably like mine."

"So she is, Jan," said Hendrik; "but there is a difference: Marjory is a little shorter than Lizzy; you can only see it when they stand shoulder to shoulder; it is the same as with us."

"Yes, that is true, old man," said Jan, worried; "all the same, this strong resemblance is something that makes me think. . . . Anyway, my dear fellow, now that we have a moment to ourselves before we cross over to Europe and return to America, let us promise each other to be . . . very, very careful."

And slightly moved, good, honest, high-minded Jan held out his hand to his brother Hendrik. The latter, of a more careless disposition, laughed heartily, and offered his brother a hand of which the fingers showed, or rather did not show, a fractional difference in length from those of Jan.

To be sure, Hendrik, a little shorter in size, was also a little more careless in disposition than Jan, but, like Jan, he had always been a marvellously staid and sober boy. They had always been like that. They had never, not even as schoolboys, played practical jokes still more to perplex mankind, already bewildered as it was. When an uncle or an aunt made a mistake, and said to Jan, "Good morning, Hendrik," the answer had always been very properly: "You are mistaken, uncle or aunt, I am Jan," and conversely. However, I do not believe that this had been the same with the Lilycamp girls. The two darlings had had no end of fun exchanging their identity-ribbons, and each pretending to be the other. American twin-sisters are, after all, more frolicsome than staid Dutch twin-brothers. And thus, with their two pairs of striking resemblances, and infinitesimal differences in body and soul, they booked state rooms on the *Oceanic*.

The sea-voyage was very pleasant, and took place before the War. Before the two Ruysdonck brothers went to introduce their wives to the relations in Amsterdam, a short stay in Paris and a visit to the Rue de la Paix were a matter of course. Young American wives think Parisian shops are ideal: Redfern and Worth have wonderful dresses, Doucet's is excellent for its fine linen, and beautiful jewellery is practically everywhere. Then there are large shops with furs, elegant leather—in short, for well-filled purses there is no lack of anything—and the young wives revelled in it, and Jan and Hendrik thought that, although their American spouses were just a little different from their American cousins—extraordinarily nice girls, the Ruysdonck cousins—they would not be too conspicuous by extravagant and American luxury. The two marriages promised, indeed, to turn out very happy.

Then followed a flying visit to Brussels, and ah! it was all before that terrible War. More shopping, then the opera, then the hotel. The hotel was very full, the day had been very busy. And the supper was excellent and very pleasant. Hendrik stayed for a few minutes in the writing-room of the hotel to write a letter, and then found the room which he shared with Marjory.

It was always his custom to knock at the door correctly and discreetly before he entered his wife's room. He did so now. But there was no answer. He knocked again.

"What on earth is the matter?" growled an angry voice.

Hendrick Ruysdonck, before the door of his conjugal hotel-bedroom, had such a shock as he had never before experienced in his life. He had recognised the firm and self-confident voice of his dear brother Jan. Yes, it was his room: that of Hendrik and Marjory. And Jan growled at him from that room as if he had the right, as if he was certain of having the right, *not* to be disturbed at an hour when most of the hotel guests—who have no urgent letters to write—have retired to rest. Likewise the staff of the hotel. A nocturnally silent, perfectly noiseless hotel atmosphere sang round the shivering Hendrik. A thousand thoughts whirled in kaleidoscopic fashion through his brain in a second. That voice, the voice of Jan, his dear brother . . . the number of the room . . the champagne at supper . . . Lizzy and Marjory . . . the American cousins . . . the time he had taken to write his letters in the writing-room of the hotel . . . during half-past one till half-past two in these noiseless hotel spaces—all this whirled, seethed, raged and roared through the brain of poor Hendrik. If he had not been writing letters for an hour, indeed, he might have taken courage at this moment—now, however, that courage oozed away from him. In spite of his just a trifle more careless nature, he thought, trembling with a sudden fever of anxiety, of his high-minded brother Jan, who had moved him almost to tears by his apprehension, and had so solemnly promised to be careful. Damn those long corridors of a big hotel! . . . It is difficult to find one's way in them . . . the champagne had been very excellent . . . one cannot *always* remember whether a number is one hundred and thirty-one or simply thirty-one. . . . Poor Jan! . . .

Hendrik, too, was an honest boy. He was even a virtuous boy. He would never cause his dear brother Jan the smallest grief, reproach him for anything, or find any fault with him. The upshot of all the whirling, seething, raging, roaring thoughts in the honest brain of poor Hendrik was . . . that he slunk away silently . . . *one floor* higher up, to the room of which the number differed only a hundred from his.

He knocked at the door. A voice called: "Come in."

And added: "Where on earth have you been? You were to come at once, and now I have been waiting an hour for you."

"I also had to write letters, Lizzy, like Jan," said the honest Hendrik.

He heard the funereal sound in his voice. Solemn Dutch voices of sober and staid boys *do* sound funereally on occasion in very particular circumstances. Here was the opportunity which makes a thief, even of the man who does not intend to steal, but who has to steal in order to save that greatest of all things—the pure conscience of a beloved twin-brother, and one, at that, who had been full of apprehension and had given his hand on a promise to be careful. Occasion and circumstances were both very opportune. Great prudence was needed, almost as much as for a financial crisis. The circumstances constituted a crisis, if not a financial one. Honest Hendrik deliberated, you may be sure of that. He knew that his twin-brother was wont to rise at six, before his wife had woken up. This morning he rose at six. He was fortunate enough to be able to slink down one flight of stairs in time to see Jan, matutinal as ever, leaving number thirty-one on his way to the bathroom. In the drowsy morning twilight of the corridors and staircase of a large hotel—damn these corridors! —the two pyjama'd outlines of the brothers Ruysdonck were faintly visible, one peeping from behind the wall of a staircase, the other sure and self-confident, closing a frost-glass door, and locking it carefully on the inside. When shortly after that, Jan meant to enter his room, he found it bolted. And his brother Hendrik called to him through a bolted door in a voice of pretended anger.

"What's the matter?"

"Goodness!" called Jan. "Is this not my room?"

Hendrik appeared at the door magnanimously.

"Is it you, Jan?" he asked gently, and feigning astonishment. "Is it you? What do you want at six in the morning?"

"But, Hendrik," said Jan. "I thought——"

"What?"

"That this was *my* room. *Our* room, Lizzy's and mine. . . ."

"You are mistaken, dear boy," said Hendrik, stretching and yawning sleepily, with a decided talent for dissimulation.

"This is *our* room, one hundred and thirty-one. Marjory's and mine; you have mistaken the floor."

"But I did not come down any stairs!" Jan cried in confusion.

"Of course you did. You must have been dozing. Go

upstairs now: number thirty-one is your room, yours and Lizzy's. As you see, here I am with Marjory."

"Oh!!!" said Jan. And he went upstairs, and indeed found Lizzy in bed, and in a glorious slumber.

Beyond this there was nothing, except that since that day Hendrik carries a dreadful secret about with him. He carries it alone, for neither Jan nor the two sisters—who only giggled about their identical husbands, but who are, for the rest, exemplary little wives—noticed any difference in that almost tragic night at Brussels. A difference of a fraction of an inch is, after all, an infinitesimal one. Only Hendrik, with the secret in his heart, which his sound and adjustable philosophy prevents him from being too much oppressed by, manages things in such a way nowadays that they never travel or stay at hotels together. But when I happen to be with the couples in a café, restaurant or theatre, believe me, everyone's eyes are drawn towards the two pairs of twins.

How do I know this true history? you will ask. I will tell you, reader. I only guessed it, because Hendrik invariably opposes travelling and residing at hotels together. I guessed it, and after a series of delicate psychological experiments on Hendrik, I am now certain of it.

As soon as I was certain of it, I made the true history into a short sketch, as I do with all true histories.

VICENTE BLASCO IBAÑEZ

A SERBIAN NIGHT

ELEVEN o'clock at night. It was the hour at which the theatres of Paris close their doors. Half an hour earlier the cafes and restaurants had sent their patrons to the street.

Our group stood undecided on the edge of the boulevard, while the crowds coming out of the amusement places slipped by in the shadows. The occasional hooded street lamps shed a ghostly light that was quickly absorbed in the darkness. The black sky with its starry blinkings of light drew uneasy glances. Once upon a time the night had only stars; now the sudden yellow expanse of a search-light might show the amber cigar of a Zeppelin.

We felt a desire to prolong our vigil. We were four: a French writer, two Serbian captains, and I. Where could we go in this gloomy Paris that had all its doors closed? . . . One of the Serbians spoke of the grill of a certain fashionable hotel which kept open all night to its guests. All the officers who wished to stay up slipped in there as though they belonged to the house. It was a secret that brothers-in-arms of the different nations communicated to each other when they came to Paris to spend a few days. We cautiously entered the brilliantly lighted salon. It was an abrupt contrast to the dark street. That room was like the inside of a huge lighthouse, with its innumerable mirrors reflecting clusters of electric poppies. It seemed as though we had stepped back two years. Fashionable and painted women, champagne, violins sighing a negro dance with the sentimental quaver of a heart-breaking ballad—it was all a spectacle of the days before the War. But among the men there was not a single one in evening clothes. All—French, Belgian, English, Russian, Serbian—were in uniforms that were dusty and worn. Some British soldiers were playing the violin, acknowledging the applause of the crowd with glittering smiles as cold as marble. They had taken the place of the former red-jacketed gypsies. The women pointed to one of them, whispering the name of his father, Lord ——, famous for his lineage and his millions. "Let us be merry, brothers, for to-morrow we die."

And all these men who had offered their lives on the altar of the pale goddess drank down life in great gulps, laughing, singing, loving, with the reckless enthusiasm of sailors who pass the night on shore to go forth once more at break of day to brave the hurricane.

The two Serbians were young, and seemed satisfied that the fortunes of their country had carried them to Paris, the dream city that had so often filled their thoughts during the horrible monotony of life in a provincial garrison town.

Both of them knew how to tell a story, an ordinary gift in a land where almost all are poets. Lamartine, when he passed through the then Turkish province of Serbia three-quarters of a century ago, was astonished at the importance of poetry in that country of shepherds and warriors. It was through verse that ideas and memories were handed down in a land where few could read or write. The *guzleros* were the national historians, and they all prolonged the life of the Serbian Iliad, by improvising new songs.

As the two captains drank their champagne they recalled the miseries of their retreat several months before: the struggle against hunger and cold; the battles in the snow, one against ten; the flight of the multitudes of human beings and animals in frightful confusion, while at the rear of the column the machine guns and rifles were cracking incessantly; the burning villages; the wounded and the stragglers howling among the flames; the mutilated women, and the crows hovering above them; the flight of old King Peter, crippled with rheumatism, without other support than a gnarled stick, continuing with his Calvary across the white precipices, stooped, silent, defying Fate like one of Shakespeare's kings.

I watched my two Serbs as they talked. They were sturdy lads, slender and sinewy, with extremely aquiline noses, like eagles' beaks. They had sharply pointed moustaches. From beneath their caps, like little houses with inverted roofs, there escaped heroic manes of hair. They were the type of artist that sentimental young ladies used to dream of forty years ago, but in mustard-coloured uniform, and with the bold tranquil air of men who continually brush elbows with death.

They went on talking. They told of things that had happened a few months before, and it seemed as though they were telling of the exploits of Marko Krailovitch, the Serbian Cid, armed with a serpent for a lance, who fought with the *Wilas*, the vampires of the woods. Until very recently these men, now relating their experiences in a Parisian grill, had led the fierce pitiless existence of humanity in its cruel infancy.

Our French friend departed. One of the captains kept interrupting his narrative with glances at the next table. Two shadowy black eyes, framed by the brim of a huge plumed hat and the silky feathers of a white boa, had been fixed on him. They had caught his attention, beyond a doubt. Finally, as though drawn by an irresistible impulse, he moved from our table to the next. A little later he disappeared, and with him vanished the hat and the boa.

I was left alone with the younger of the two captains, the one who had talked least. He took a drink, looked at the clock over the bar. He took another drink. He looked at me with one of those glances which always precedes a serious confidence. I divined his need for communicating to me something of a painful nature which was torturing his memory. He looked at the clock again. It was one o'clock.

"It was just at this time"—he began abruptly, putting his silent monologue into words—"four months ago to-day."

And as he talked I saw the dark night, the snow-filled valley, the white mountains covered with beech and pine trees, from the branches of which the wind was shaking the cotton-like flakes. I saw the ruins of a village, and among the ruins the remnants of a Serbian division in retreat towards the Adriatic.

My friend commanded the rear of this guard, a mass of men, that had once been a company, and now was a mob. The military unit there had been increased by peasants so stupefied by suffering and fear that they moved like automatons, and had to be driven forward like animals; women moaning as they dragged along groups of little ones; and other women, dark, tall, sinewy, who walked along in tragic silence, bending over the dead as they passed to remove their guns and cartridge belts.

The darkness was coloured by the flickering red gleam of shells rising from the ruins. Out of the depths of the night came the response of other mortal flashes. In the black air the bullets hummed, invisible insects of the night.

With the morning would come the crushing, overwhelming attack. They did not know which enemy it was that was lining up against them in the darkness. Were they Germans, Austrians, Bulgarians, or Turks? . . . They had to face so many.

"We had to retreat," continued the Serb, "leaving behind those who delayed us. We had to make the mountains before daybreak."

The long columns of women, children, and old people intermingled with the pack animals, had been swallowed up in the night. There remained in the village only the able-bodied men who were firing from the shelter of the ruins. Part of these in turn began to retreat. Suddenly a cruel recollection seized the captain.

" The wounded! What shall we do with them? "

Stretched out on the straw in a barn whose roof was pierced by shells, there were more than fifty human beings, sunken in the stupor of pain or tossing fretfully about. They were men who had been wounded days before and who had managed to drag themselves that far; men who had been wounded that very night and who staunched the fresh blood with makeshift bandages; women who had been struck by bits of bursting shell.

The captain entered this refuge, which reeked of decaying flesh, dried blood, dirty clothes, and foul breath. At his first words all those who still had any strength left moved restlessly under the smoky light of the solitary lantern. The groans ceased. There was a silence of surprise, of terror, as though those dying men feared something more dreadful than death.

On hearing that they were to be abandoned to the mercy of the enemy, all tried to get up; but most of them fell back again.

A chorus of desperate entreaties, of pathetic prayers rose toward the captain and the soldiers that were with him.

" Brothers, don't desert us. Brothers, for Jesus' sake——"

Then they slowly comprehended the necessity for abandoning them, and accepted their fate with resignation. But to fall into the hands of the enemy! To remain at the mercy of the Bulgarians or the Turks, centuries-old enemies! Their eyes added what their lips dared not say. To be a Serb is a curse when one is taken prisoner. Many who were at the threshold of death trembled at the idea of losing their liberty. The vengeance of the Balkans is more to be feared than death.

" Brother, brother——"

The captain, divining the desires hidden in these cries, turned his eyes away.

" You want me to? " he asked several times.

All moved their heads affirmatively. Since this desertion was inevitable he ought not to go away leaving behind him a living Serbian.

Would he not have asked for the same thing if he were in their place?

The scarcity of munitions caused by the retreat made the

soldiers guard their cartridges jealously. The captain unsheathed his sword. Some of the soldiers had already begun their task, using the bayonet, but their work was faltering, clumsy and rough, slashes at random, interminable agony, torrents of blood. All the wounded dragged themselves toward the captain, attracted by his rank, which made death at his hands an honour, and, through his skilful dexterity, less terrible.

"Take me, brother, take me . . ."

With the blade of his sword turned outward, he thrust the point into their throats, seeking to cut the jugular vein with one stroke.

"*Tac*, *Tac*," marked the captain, evoking the scene of horror before my eyes.

They came, crawling on all fours; they emerged like larvæ from the shadows; they swarmed about his feet. At first he had tried to turn his head away, not to see what he was doing; his eyes had filled with tears. But the result of this weakness was that he struck clumsily, having to repeat the blows and prolonging the suffering. Be calm, then! A steady hand and a firm heart! *Tac—Tac.*

"Brother, take me! . . . Take me!"

They disputed about their turns as though they feared the enemy might arrive before the brotherly sacrifice was completed. They had instinctively learned what was the best position. Each one turned his head to one side, so that the neck might be tense, and the artery rigid and visible for the mortal prick.

"Brother, take me!" And as the stream of blood gushed forth, one more fell back against the other bodies that were slowly emptying like red wine bags.

. . . . .

The grill began to empty. Women leaning on uniformed arms passed, leaving behind them a wake of perfume and powder. The violins of the British breathed forth their last sighs, amid peals of light-hearted laughter.

The Serb had in his hand a small cream-coloured knife, and with the gesture of a man who cannot forget, who never will forget, he went on pounding mechanically on the table . . . Tac! . . . Tac!

MIGUEL DE CERVANTES SAAVEDRA

THE HISTORY OF ISABELLA CASTRUCCIO

LUCCA is a small town but fair, which under the protection of the Empire and Spain conserveth her liberty. There the Spaniards are better entertained than in any place of the world: the cause whereof is this; that they command not there, but entreat: and because they tarry not there above a day, they give no leisure to the inhabitants to know their natural disposition, which everywhere is esteemed arrogant. . . .

The inns of Lucca are able to lodge a company of soldiers; in one of which our pilgrims lodged, being conducted by the warder of the gate, who delivered them to the host by tale, to the end he might deliver them again unto him in like manner in the morning when they should depart.

At the gate Ruperta [1] saw a physician who talked to the mistress of the inn, saying unto her:

" I am not yet certain whether this maid be out of her wits, or possessed of an evil spirit; and lest I should fail, I believe she is both. But yet I have hope she shall recover her health, so that her uncle do not hasten to depart from this place."

" Jesus! " then said Ruperta, " are we come hither to alight at the lodging of demoniacs? "

Unto whom the hostess answered:

" You may come in without scrupulosity, Madam; and if you knew what is within, you would come hither a hundred leagues."

Then they all alighted; and Auristela and Constance, which had heard the words of the hostess, asked her what it was that might be seen in this house, to induce them to come so far.

" Come with me," answered the hostess, " and you shall see as much as I tell you."

And in so saying she brought them into a chamber, where

[1] One of the pilgrims.

they saw on a bed a very fair maid, seeming to be sixteen or seventeen years of age. She had her arms tied to the posts at the bed's head, and two women looked for her legs to fasten them in like manner; to whom the sick woman said that it was sufficient to tie her arms.

And turning to the pilgrims:

"Figures of heaven," said she, "angels of flesh! without doubt I believe you are come to restore me to health; for other thing cannot be hoped for from so fair a company and so Christian a visitation. I conjure you by your beauty, cause me to be loosed; for with four or five bites which I will give myself on my arm, I shall be satisfied, because I am not so mad as I seem to be; and he that tormenteth me is not so cruel but he will suffer me to bite myself."

"My poor niece," said an old man who was come into the chamber. "And who is he that tormenteth thee, and whom thou sayest will permit thee to bite thyself? Commend thyself to God, Isabel; and strive to eat, not thy own flesh, but that which thy uncle will give thee; who loves thee so dearly that that which liveth in the air, that which is maintained in the water, and that which is nourished in the earth I will give thee; for I have both means and will."

Whereto the maid answered:

"Leave me alone with these angels; it may be that the enemy, the devil, will fly from me, because he will not be with them."

And making a sign with her head that the pilgrims Auristela, Constance, Flora, and Ruperta should remain, all the others withdrew themselves at the old man's request. . . .

When she saw herself shut in, she prayed them to look if there were any one besides the four which she had chosen; and after they had assured her that there was no person else, she sat up in her bed; and making a sign that she would speak, her voice was interrupted with so great a sigh, that it seemed her soul should therewith have been plucked away. The end whereof was, to lie down again in her bed, and continue in a swoon with so many signs of death, that the ladies whom she kept with her were constrained to call for water to bathe Isabel's face, who was ready to give up the ghost.

The miserable uncle came again into the chamber, carrying in one hand a cross; and in the other a bunch of hyssop and holy water. With him came in two priests, who, believing that the devil possessed her, did go from her but seldom. The hostess also came in with water, which they threw upon her face.

She came again to herself, and said unto them:

"These preparations are now altogether unprofitable. I will quickly come forth, not when you please, but when I will; which shall be at the coming of Andrew Marulo, the son of John Baptist Marulo, a gentleman of this city, who is now a student at Salamanca."

Upon these words, all of them were fully confirmed in the opinion which they had, that Isabel was possessed of a devil. For they could not imagine how she knew who was John Baptist, nor his son Andrew; and some of them went to tell him what the fair demoniac spake of his son.

Again she prayed them to leave her alone with the four above said. The priests having said the gospels, went forth with all the rest; and Flora, having searched the chamber again and shut the door, said unto her:

"We are alone now; tell us, madam, what you would have."

"That which I would have," said she, "is that you take away these bonds from me, for though they are gentle, they put me to pain because they hinder me."

Which done, she sat up in her bed; and taking Auristela with one hand and Ruperta with the other, she made Constance and Flora sit down on the same bed next unto them; and with a low voice and her eyes full of tears spake unto them in this manner:

"Ladies, I am the unhappy Isabel Castruccio, to whom my parents gave nobility, fortune, and riches; and heaven, beauty, though it be but little. My parents were born in Capua, but they got me in Spain; where I was born, and brought up in the house of this mine uncle here being, who then abode at the Emperor's Court. O God! wherefore do I fetch so far off the stream of my adventures! Being then in my uncle's house, and left an orphan by my parents under this man's tuition, there came to the Court a young man whom I saw in a church; and I marked him in such sort, that I could not be at home in the house but I beheld him, for his favour and comely proportion were so well engraven in my soul, that I could not put them out of my remembrance.

"Finally, I wanted not means to know his name, his birth, his business at the Court, and the cause of his coming. And that which I learned, was, that his name was Andrew Marulo, the son of John Baptist Marulo, a gentleman of this city more noble than rich; and that he went to study at Salamanca. Now in six days that he stayed there, I gave him to understand who I was, what riches I had; and as concerning my beauty, he might see it at the church. I wrote also, that my uncle would marry me with my cousin, to the end my goods might remain in our family (a man, as indeed the truth is, unfitting to my birth and humour), telling him that occasion in me offered unto him her hairy forehead, whereof he should lay hold without giving place to repentance, and that my facility should not give him any subject to despise me.

"After he had seen me I know not how often in the church, he answered me that only for my person, without the ornaments of nobility and riches, he would make me lady of the world if he could; and he besought me to continue firm in this resolution, until he had brought to Salamanca a friend of his of this town, with whom he was going to follow his studies. I promised him so to do; for that my love is none of these violent affections, which are soon engendered and quickly die. He left me for that time, because he would not disappoint his friend; and with tears which I saw him shed in passing by the street the day that he went thence, he departed without leaving me, and I followed him without parting from my house.

"The next morning (who can believe this? that misfortunes have snares so quickly to entangle such as are unhappy), the next morning, I say, my uncle concluded upon his return to Italy; neither did it avail me to any purpose to feign myself sick, because my pulses and colour declared that I was in health, and my uncle would not believe my feigned infirmity; but rather in truth, that my being discontented at the marriage, made me seek devices that I might not depart.

"In this time I had means to write to Andrew what was befallen me, and the necessity of my parting. Nevertheless, that I would labour to pass by this city, where I meant to feign that I was possessed of a devil; and by this invention give him means to leave Salamanca and come back to Lucca, where, in despite of my uncle and all the world, he may espouse me because his fortune and mine rely upon his diligence, if he will show himself mindful of the same. If the letters be come to his hands (as I believe they are, because the post bid me make no doubt) he may be here within these three days. For my part I have done what I can. I have a legion of devils in my body, having an ounce of love in my soul; for they are both all one when hope is far away.

"Behold, ladies, the history of my madness, and the cause which makes me sick; my amorous thoughts are the devils which torment me. I suffer hunger in hope to be satisfied, but my mistrust pursueth me; for as they say in Castille: 'To them that are unhappy, the crumbs freeze betwixt the mouth and the hand.' [1] Order the matter so, my dear friends, that my lie may be believed. Fortify my discourse, and deal so with my uncle, that he may not carry me hence certain days. It may be heaven will permit that with Andrew's coming my contentment shall accompany him."

[1] *A los desdichados se les suelen helar las migas entre la boca y a mano.*

You need not ask if the company were astonished at this discourse, which of itself carried with it admiration and astonishment to put into their minds which heard them. Auristela, Ruperta, Constance, and Flora offered to fortify her designs; and not to part from this place before they had seen the end, because that in reason it could not be long delayed.

The fair Isabel very strongly constrained herself to counterfeit the demoniac; and her four new friends did no less to fortify the opinion of her disease, assuring by all the reasons they could that in truth the devil spake in her; to the end that so it may appear what love is, which makes the amorous seem to be possessed with devils.

Being in these terms, the physician returned in the evening to make his second visitation, and by chance brought with him John Baptist Marulo, the father of Andrew the amorous, unto whom he said in entering into the chamber:

"Mark, Señor Marulo, the pain of this poor maid, if she deserve that in her angel-like body the devil should have his walking place. Nevertheless, one hope comforteth us, which is that he hath told us he will quickly depart thence; and that the token of his going out should be the coming of Senor Andrew your son, whom he hath looked on for every hour."

"I have been so informed," answered Senor Baptist, "and I would be glad that my son were the bringer of so good news."

"Thanks be to God, and my diligence," said Isabel; "for without me he should be at Salamanca, doing God knows what. And let Senor Baptist, who is there present, believe that he hath a son who is more fair than holy, and not so good a student as a gallant. And ill may fare the braveries of young people which do so much wrong to the commonwealth; cursed be the spurs which have no points, and the mules let to hire which go not well in post."

With these last words she intermeddled others equivocal, of double sense, which her secretaries [1] understood one way and the rest of the standers-by another; those interpreted them aright, and these as extravagant follies.

"Gentlewoman," then said Marulo, "where saw you my son Andrew? Was it in Madrid, or Salamanca?"

"It was in Illescas," said Isabel, "in gathering cherries on St. John's day:

Early one morning,
Just as the sun was rising.[2]

---

[1] *i.e.*, the pilgrims.

[2] Isabel quotes the old Spanish ballad of how news of the capture of Antequera was brought to the King of Granada:

La mañana de San Juan,
al tiempo que alboreaba . . .

But I speak the truth (which is a miracle when I speak it), I see him always and carry him always in my soul."

"Yet better was it," replied Marulo, "that my son was found in gathering of cherries than in seeking for fleas, which is sometimes proper to scholars."

"Scholars that are gentlemen," answered Isabel, "seldom spend their time about such a search, but they scratch and rub themselves often; for these creatures do not spare any, and they are so bold that they as soon enter into a prince's breeches as into the bedding of the hospitals."

"Thou knowest all, wicked spirit! It well appears that thou art old," said the physician, speaking to the devil which he supposed to be in the body of Isabel.

Upon this discourse, as if Satan himself had appointed it, came in old Castruccio her uncle, who with a merry countenance said unto her:

"Niece, you shall give me a reward for the good news I bring you, and shall accomplish the hope you have given us to be free at the sight of Señor Andrew Marulo, the son of Senor Baptist who is here present. Ah, my sweet hope, mayst thou fulfil that which thou hast promised, that she shall be free in seeing him! Ah, cursed demon, *Vade retro, exi foras!* Think not to return to this habitation, however swept and garnished thou mayst find it."

"Let him come, let him come," answered Isabel, "this presumptuous Ganymede, this feigned Adonis, and give me his hand in the name of marriage, of his own free will; for I have stayed here more firmly than a rock amongst the waves, which beat thereupon without removing it."

Then entered the young Marulo, who in his house had been told of the sickness of Isabel, and how she expected his coming as a token of the devil's departure. The young man who had been instructed by letters from Isabel what he should do if he found her at Lucca, ran to her lodging; and entering hastily into her chamber began to cry out like a madman:

"Out! Out! Out! Place for the valorous Andrew, sergeant-major of all hell, if a squadron be not sufficient!" [1]

At this noise, even those were astonished who knew the truth of the matter. But the physician and his own father said that he was as much possessed with a devil as Isabel, and they were not deceived.

[1] A reminiscence of the ballad quoted by Pérez de Hita, in his novelesque account of the civil wars of Granada:

¡Afuera, afuera, afuera!
¡aparta, aparta, aparta!
Que entra el valeroso Muza,
cuadrillero de unas cañas . . .

"We hoped," said the old Castruccio, "this young man's coming should be for our good, and I believe that it will prove to our hurt."

"Peace, my son, peace," said the father, "they will think you mad."

"Shall he not be so, if he see me?" answered Isabel. "Am I not the centre where his thoughts rest? Am I not the White[1] where his desires do aim?"

"It is true, my fair," answered Andrew. "You are the mistress of my will, the repose of my travail, and the life of my death. Give me your hand as your spouse, and draw me from the bondage wherein I am into the liberty to be under your subjection. Give me your hand, I say it once again, O my bliss, and advance me from the baseness of Andrew Marulo to the greatness to be the husband of Isabella Castruccio. Let the devils which would alter so sweet a bond be packing from this place, nor let men attempt to separate that which God hath joined together!"

"You say true, Senor Andrew," replied Isabel; "and without interposition of any invention or deceit, give me your hand as my spouse and receive me for your own."

Andrew stretched forth his hand, and in that instant Auristela lifted up her voice and said:

"Well may he give it, for the twain shall be one flesh."

The uncle of Isabel being past himself and almost in a swoon with astonishment, took Andrew's hands and began to say:

"What means this, my masters? Is this the custom of this country, for one devil to marry another?"

"No," said the physician. "It must be in jest to the intent the devil may go hence; for it is not possible that this action could have been premeditated by any wit of man."

"But withal," said her uncle, "I will know from both their mouths what name we shall give this marriage, whether of truth or leasing."

"Of truth," answered Isabel, "for that neither Andrew Marulo is mad, nor I possessed with a devil. I will choose him for my husband, so that he accept and choose me for his wife; not as being frantic or possessed, but with all the judgment which it hath pleased God to give me."

And saying this, she took the hand of Andrew, and gave him hers in the name of marriage. And so with their yea, yea, they were indubitably married one to another.

"What means this?" Castruccio said again. "Is there

[1] *i.e.*, the bull's-eye of the target.

anything here done in God's name? How is it possible that my old white hairs should be here dishonoured?"

"Nothing that is belonging to me can dishonour you," said Andrew's father. "I am noble, though not exceeding rich; yet withal I am not so poor that I stand in need of any. I neither began nor made an end of this business; these two young folks are married without my counsel. Yet let us see if that which is here done may proceed any farther; for if it may be defeated, the riches of Isabel shall not be a cause that I would procure my son's benefit."

Two priests were present who said the marriage was good, presupposing that if they had begun it as fools, they had confirmed it as wise.

"And we confirm it again," said Andrew; and the like said Isabel.

Which her uncle hearing, he let his head fall on his breast; and turning up the whites of his eyes, with a great sigh he fell into a deadly swoon and gave signs that the pains of death were come upon him.

His servants carried him to his bed, Isabel rose from hers; Andrew brought her to his father's house as his wife, and two days after to the church to solemnise the marriage, baptise his young brother, and bury his wife's uncle; to the end we may see how strange are the events of this life: one baptised, others married, and another buried at one and the same time. Isabel nevertheless put on mourning apparel; for death intermeddleth the marriage-beds with graves, and funerals with weddings.

Our pilgrims abode four days at Lucca with the other passengers, during which time they were feasted by the married couple, and by the noble John Baptist Marulo.

GIOVANNI BOCCACCIO

THE POT OF BASIL

THERE were at Messina three young men, that were brothers and merchants, who were left very rich on the death of their father, who was of San Gimignano; and they had a sister, Lisabetta by name, a girl fair enough, and no less debonair, but whom, for some reason or another, they had not as yet bestowed in marriage. The three brothers had also in their shop a young Pisan, Lorenzo by name, who managed all their affairs, and who was so goodly of person and gallant, that Lisabetta bestowed many a glance upon him, and began to regard him with extraordinary favour; which Lorenzo marking from time to time, gave up all his other amours, and in like manner began to affect her, and so, their loves being equal, 'twas not long before they took heart of grace, and did that which each most desired. Wherein continuing to their no small mutual solace and delight, they neglected to order it with due secrecy, whereby one night as Lisabetta was going to Lorenzo's room, she, all unwitting, was observed by the eldest of the brothers, who, albeit much distressed by what he had learnt, yet, being a young man of discretion, was swayed by considerations more seemly, and, allowing no word to escape him, spent the night in turning the affair over in his mind in divers ways. On the morrow he told his brothers that which, touching Lisabetta and Lorenzo, he had observed in the night, which, that no shame might thence ensue either to them or to their sister, they after long consultation determined to pass over in silence, making as if they had seen or heard nought thereof, until such time as they in a safe and convenient manner might banish this disgrace from their sight before it could go further. Adhering to which purpose, they jested and laughed with Lorenzo as they had been wont; and after a while pretending that they were all three going forth of the city on pleasure, they took Lorenzo with them; and being come to a remote and very lone spot, seeing that 'twas apt for their design, they took Lorenzo, who was completely off his guard, and slew him, and buried him on such wise that none was ware of it. On their return to Messina they gave out that they had sent him away on business; which was readily believed, because 'twas what they had been frequently used to do. But as Lorenzo did not return, and Lisabetta questioned the brothers about him with great frequency and urgency, being sorely grieved by his long absence, it so befell that one day, when she was very pressing in her inquiries, one of the brothers said:—"What means this? What hast thou to do with Lorenzo, that thou shouldst ask about him so often? Ask us no more, or we will give thee such answer as thou deservest." So the girl, sick at heart and sorrowful, fearing she knew not what, asked no questions; but many a time at night she called piteously to him, and besought him to come to her, and bewailed his long tarrying with many a tear, and ever yearning for his return, languished in total dejection.

But so it was that one night, when, after long weeping that her Lorenzo came not back, she had at last fallen asleep, Lorenzo appeared to her in a dream, wan and in utter disarray, his clothes torn to shreds and sodden; and thus, as she thought, he spoke:—"Lisabetta, thou dost nought but call me, and vex thyself for my long tarrying, and bitterly upbraid me with thy tears; wherefore be it known to thee that return to thee I may not, because the last day that thou didst see me thy brothers slew me." After which, he described the place where they had buried him, told her to call and expect him no more, and vanished. The girl then awoke, and doubting not that the vision was true, wept bitterly. And when morning came, and she was risen, not daring to say aught to her brothers, she resolved to go to the place indicated in the vision and see if what she had dreamed were even as it had appeared to her. So, having leave to go a little way out of the city for recreation in company with a maid that had at one time lived with them and knew all that she did, she hied her thither with all speed; and having removed the dry leaves that were strewn about the place, she began to dig where the earth seemed least hard. Nor had she dug long, before she found the body of her hapless lover, whereon as yet there was no trace of corruption or decay; and thus she saw without any manner of doubt that her vision was true. And so, saddest of women, knowing that she might not bewail him there, she would gladly, if she could, have carried away the body and given it more honourable sepulture elsewhere; but as she might not so do, she took a knife, and, as best she could, severed the head from the trunk, and wrapped it in a napkin and laid it in the lap of her maid; and having covered the rest of the corpse with earth, she left the spot, having been seen by none, and went home. There she shut herself up in her room, with the head, and kissed it a thousand times in every part, and wept long and bitterly over it, till she had bathed it in her tears. She then wrapped it in a piece of fine cloth, and set it in a large and beautiful pot of the sort in which marjoram or basil is planted, and covered it with earth, and therein planted some roots of the goodliest basil of Salerno, and drenched them only with her tears, or water perfumed with roses or orange-blossoms. And 'twas her wont ever to sit beside this pot, and, all her soul one yearning, to pore upon it, as that which enshrined her Lorenzo, and when long time she had so done, she would bend over it, and weep a great while, until the basil was quite bathed in her tears.

Fostered with such constant, unremitting care, and nourished by the richness given to the soil by the decaying head that lay therein, the basil burgeoned out in exceeding great beauty and fragrance. And, the girl persevering ever in this way to life, the neighbours from time to time took note of it, and when her brothers marvelled to see her beauty ruined, and her eyes as it were evanished from her head, they told them of it, saying:—"We have observed that such is her daily wont." Whereupon the brothers, marking her behaviour, chid her therefore once or twice, and as she heeded them not, caused the pot to be taken privily from her. Which, so soon as she missed it, she demanded with the utmost instance and insistence, and, as they gave it not back to her, ceased not to wail and weep, insomuch that she fell sick; nor in her sickness craved she aught but the pot of basil. Whereat the young men, marvelling mightily, resolved to see what the pot might contain; and having removed the earth they espied the cloth, and therein the head, which was not yet so decayed, but that by the curled locks they knew it for Lorenzo's head. Passing strange they found it, and fearing lest it should be bruited abroad, they buried the head, and, with as little said as might be, took order for their privy departure from Messina, and hied them thence to Naples. The girl ceased not to weep and crave her pot, and, so weeping, died.

LUIGI PIRANDELLO

CLOSE FRIENDS

GIGI MEAR muffled up in an old Inverness cape that morning (when one is over forty a north wind's no joke), his neckerchief turned up to his nose, his hands in a pair of thick English gloves, his person well fed, smooth, and ruddy, was waiting on the Lungo Tevere de' Mellini for the tram which would drop him, as it did each day, in Via Pastrengo in front of the *Corte dei Conti* where he was employed.

A Count by birth but now alas! only too well without either county or the wherewithal to count, Gigi Mear had, in the blissful unconsciousness of childhood, made known to his father the noble plan of entering this office of the State believing then, in his innocence, that the *Corte dei Conti* was a Court for Counts, to which every count had right of entrance.

Now everyone knows that trams never by any chance come when you are waiting for them. Rather they stop half-way because the current has been cut off, or they choose to run over a cart or even crush some unfortunate man. They are a wonderful asset, nevertheless, all things taken into consideration. The morning in question, there was a north wind blowing, icy and keen, and Gigi Mear stamped his feet as he watched the grey river, which looked as though it, too, poor thing, felt very cold, there in its shirt sleeves, so to speak, between the colourless walls of the new embankment.

At last din-dinning up came the tram, and Gigi Mear was getting ready to jump on without it stopping when from the new bridge, the Ponte Cavour, he heard someone shout his name after him:

"Gigi, old man! Gigi!"

And he saw a gentleman running after him and gesticulating with arms flying like a telegraph post. The tram slipped away. In return Gigi Mear had the consolation of finding himself in the arms of a stranger who, to judge by the violence with which he embraced Gigi, twice, full on the silk handkerchief which covered his mouth, was an intimate friend.

" Do you know, I knew you at once, Gigi, old man! At once! But what is this I see?—Getting old already? All these white hairs; aren't you ashamed? Give us a kiss, Gigione, my dear old fellow, for your sainted old age. You stood there looking just as though you were waiting for me. When I saw you put up your arm to get on that demon of a tram I said to myself, ' That's treachery, sheer treachery.' "

" Yes," said Mear, with a forced smile, " I was going to the office."

" Do me the favour not to mention such disgusting things just now."

" What? "

" I mean it. In fact, I insist."

" You're a queer johnny, do you know? "

" Yes, I know I am. But tell me, you weren't expecting to see me, now were you? I see you weren't, judging from your face."

" Well, no . . . to tell the truth——"

" I arrived yesterday evening. Your brother sends his greetings. He, by the way—I can see I shall make you laugh—wanted to give me a letter of introduction to you! . . . ' What,' I said, ' A letter of introduction to Gigione? Do you know, I knew him before you did, so to speak. Friends from boyhood, bless my soul. We've come to blows many a time. Fellow students at the University together.' Famous old Padua, Gigione, do you remember? That huge bell that you never heard: you slept like a—what shall we say?—a dormouse, eh? I think I ought to say like a pig, though. Well . . . Then when you *did* hear it—which was only once—you thought it was the fire-alarm. . . . Good old times, those were! . . . Your brother's very well, thank God. We've embarked together on a certain little affair, and I'm here for that. But whatever's up with you? You look like a funeral. Are you married? "

" No, my dear! " exclaimed Gigi Mear, with energy.

" Going to be? "

" Are you mad? After forty? Good heavens, no. Wouldn't dream of it."

" Forty! It's more likely turned fifty, Gigione. But why not? Still, I was forgetting . . . it's a peculiarity of yours never to hear anything go—bells or years. Fifty, my dear man, fifty, I assure you, and well turned, too. We may well sigh. The business begins to be a bit serious. You were born—let's see . . . in the April of 1851, is that so or is it not? April the twelfth."

"Pardon me, May; and pardon me, eighteen-hundred-and-fifty-two," Mear corrected him, dwelling on each syllable somewhat irritated. "Must you know better than I do? The twelfth of May, 1852. And therefore 49 years and a few months up to present day."

"And no wife! That's fine! I have, you know. Ah, yes, a tragedy. I'll make you burst your sides with laughing. In the meantime, of course, we'll take it that you've invited me to lunch. Where do you feed these days? Still at the old *Barba*?"

"My conscience!" exclaimed Gigi Mear, with growing astonishment. "D'you know even about the *Barba*? You've been there, too, I suppose."

"I at the *Barba*? How could I have been, when I'm at Padua? I was told so. I heard about the goings-on there with you and the other men who go to that old—ought I to call it a pub, a slaughter- or an eating-house?"

"Call it a pub, a low-down pub," replied Mear. "But if you're going to lunch with me, now, we must let the maid at home know."

"Young, is she?"

"Oh, no, old, my boy, old. What's more I don't go to the *Barba* any more now, you know. No goings-on for three years, now. At a certain age. . . ."

"After forty——"

"After forty, you have to have the courage to turn your back on the path which will bring you to a precipice if you follow it. Go down it—h'm well, that's alright, so long as you go ve-ry, ve-ry slowly and gently and don't roll over or come toppling down. Well now, come on up; here we are. I'm going to show what a good little job I've made of that little home of mine."

"Ve-ry, ve-ry slowly and gently . . . good little job . . . little home of yours," began Gigi Mear's friend as he climbed the steps after him. "A big hulking superlative creature like you with mincing diminutives! Poor Gigi! What have they done to you? Singed your tail? Do you want to bring the tears to my eyes?"

"Well. . . ." said Mear as they waited on the landing for the maid to come to open the door, "at this stage, you have to be on good terms with this accursed existence of ours; fondle it, wheedle it with diminutives, or it will diminutive you. I don't at all want to bring myself to a four-foot grave yet, not I."

"So you believe in man as a biped?" broke out the other at this point. "Don't say you do, Gigione. I know what efforts

I make at times to keep standing on two legs only. Believe me, friend; if we leave Nature her course we should all be quadrupeds if we had our way. The best thing out! Nothing more comfortable, a good poise, always well-balanced. The times I could throw myself down to crawl like that with my hands on the ground! This accursed civilisation is ruining us. If I were a quadruped I should be a fine wild beast. I should land you out a couple of kicks for all the beastly things you've said. I should have no wife, no debts, no anxieties. Do you want to make me cry? I'm off."

Stupefied by the queerly jocular talk of this friend of his dropped from the clouds, Gigi Mear watched him and racked his brains to think what the devil his name was and how and when he had known him, at Padua whether as a boy or in his student days at the University. He passed and repassed in review all the intimate friends he had had in those days but without success; not one of them answered to the features of this man. Nevertheless, he did not dare to ask to be enlightened on the subject, for the intimacy which the man showed him was so great and of such a kind that he feared to offend him. He determined that he would get at the truth by cunning.

The maid was a long time before answering the door; she had not expected her master to be back so soon. Gigi Mear rang a second time and she came at last, shuffling her feet.

" Here I am, old girl," Mear said to her. " Back again, and with company. Set for two to-day and look sharp about it. Be careful, for there's no trifling with my friend here who has got a curious name."

" Anthropophagus Goat's Beardhornfoot," said the other with a joke which left the old woman in doubt as to whether she should smile at it or cross herself. " And no one ever wants to know any more about that fine name of mine. Old girl! It makes bank directors pull a wry face and staggers the money-lenders. My wife's the exception; *she* was glad enough to take it. It was only the name that I let her take, though, not me, oh no, not me. I'm too handsome a fellow, by all the devils and their souls! Get along, Gigi, since you have this weakness and let me see your poor things. As for you, old girl, get a move on. Fodder for the beasts."

Mear, discomfited at the failure of his stratagem, took him the round of the five small rooms of the tiny flat all furnished with the loving care of the man who wants nothing to wish for, no needs which cannot be satisfied within his own house, when once he has decided to make it his snail-shell. There was a little sitting-room, a bedroom, a minute bathroom, a dining-room and a study.

In the little sitting-room his amazement and his torture were increased when he heard this friend chatting of the most intimate and private things in his family, as he surveyed the photographs displayed on the mantelpiece.

" Gigione, I wish I had a brother-in-law like yours. If you knew what a rascal mine is ! "

" Does he treat your sister badly, then ? "

" No, he treats *me* badly. It would be such an easy thing to him to help in these straits ! But, oh no, not he."

" Forgive me," said Mear. " I can't just remember your brother-in-law's name."

" Never mind, you *can't* remember it—you don't know him. He's been at Padua barely two years. Do you know what he did to me ? Your brother who's been so kind to me had promised me help, if that wretch would have taken my bills of exchange—but would you believe it ? He refused me the signature. And then your brother, who, when all is said and done, although most friendly, is an outsider, was so indignant that he took it into his own hands. Our affair is a sure enough thing. . . . But if I were to tell you the reason for my brother-in-law's refusal ! . . . I'm still a handsome dog, you can't deny it, a taking sort of fellow, I'll make no bones about saying so. Well, my brother-in-law's sister had the unfortunate idea of falling in love with me, poor girl. Jolly good taste, but not much tact. Just imagine whether I would. . . . Well, she poisoned herself."

" Dead ? " said Mear, pausing.

" No. She vomited a bit, and that cured her. But you can see that it was impossible to me to set foot in my brother-in-law's house after that tragedy. Good heavens, are we going to have anything to eat or not ? I can scarcely see for hunger. I'm as famished as a wolf ! "

Later on at table, Gigi Mear, irked by the affectionate confidences of his friend who pelted him with bad words and for a wonder did not touch him, began to ask news of him of Padua and of this and that acquaintance, hoping to get him to let slip his own name by some chance, or at least (in his exasperation, which was growing stronger every minute) to find distraction, himself, from the obsession to get at it by talking of other things.

" Come now, give me a bit of news—what about that Valverde chap, the director of the Bank of Italy, with the lovely wife and that great lump of a sister who squinted, if I'm not mistaken. Are they still at Padua ? "

His friend burst into a roar of laughter at the question.

" What's the matter? " said Mear, his curiosity awakened. " Doesn't she squint? "

" Stop a moment, for heaven's sake stop! " begged the other, unable to restrain his laughter, which shook him in convulsive spasms. " Squint? I should just think she does! And her nose is so wide that you can see up to her brains! That's *the* woman."

" What woman? "

" My wife! "

Gigi Mear, stunned by the shock, had just sufficient force to mumble something more or less foolish by way of an excuse. But the other man began to laugh even harder and longer than at first. At length he quietened down, frowned, and gave a deep sigh.

" My dear man," he said, " there are unknown heroisms in life which the most unskilled fancy of the poet could never conceive."

" Yes, indeed! " sighed Mear. " You're right . . . I know what you mean."

" You don't, at all," came the other's contradiction, an immediate reply. " Do you believe that I'm alluding to myself? I, the hero, when at most I'm only the victim? Scarcely. The heroism was my sister-in-law's—the wife of Lucio Valverde. Listen to me a bit—heavens! What a blind stupid idiot of a man."

" I? "

" No, I. I! To manage to deceive myself that Lucio Valverde's wife was in love with me up to the point of marrying her husband, who, in all conscience, and this you may believe, Gigione—would have deserved it. But goodness—what do you think happened instead? Example of disinterested spirit of sacrifice, as you'll hear. Valverde goes off, or rather pretends to go off as usual (she being in the know). She then lets me into the house. When the tragic moment of being surprised together comes, she hides me in the sister-in-law's room —the lady with the squint, who, receiving me in a duly chaste and trembling fashion, appeared to be sacrificing herself, too, for the peace and honour of her brother. I scarcely had the time to shout ' But, my dear lady, wait a minute, how can Lucio possibly believe in earnest . . .'—I hadn't finished when in burst Lucio, raging with fury, and you can imagine the rest."

" What! " exclaimed Gigi Mear, " you with all your brains."

" And my notes of credit? " bellowed the other, " my notes of credit on sufferance for which Valverde was allowing me the renewal by the pretended good graces of his wife? He'd have rejected them then at once—d'you see?—and ruined me. Low down trick! Don't let's say any more about it, please. . . . After all the fact being that I haven't a halfpenny of my own and that I'm not ever likely to have; taking into consideration, too, that I've no intention of marrying. . . ."

"What!" Gigi Mear interrupted at this juncture. "You married her!"

"Oh no, I promise you. She married *me*: *she* only was married. I told her beforehand. Straight dealing and part friends. 'Young lady, you want my name. Well then, you take it; I scarcely know what to do with it, upon my word.' But that's enough, eh?"

"Then," ventured Mear, pausing triumphant, "there was nothing more to it. Then her name was Valverde, and now it's——"

"Exactly," laughed the other, rising from table.

"No, listen!" exclaimed Gigi Mear, able to bear it no longer and taking his courage in both hands, "you've made me pass a delightful morning; I've treated you as if you were my brother. Now you must do me a favour."

"Perhaps you'd like my wife as a loan?"

"No, thanks. I want you to tell me your name."

"I? My name?" asked his friend, astonished, tapping his chest with his forefinger as though he did not believe in his own existence. "What do you mean? Don't you know; can't you remember?"

"No," confessed Mear, abashed. "Forgive me, call me the most forgetful man on earth, but I could almost swear to it that I've never seen you."

"Oh? Very good, very good! . . ." replied the other. "My dear Gigione, put your hand here. Thank you with all my heart for your lunch and your company—and I'm off without telling you. And that's that!"

"You shall tell me, damn you!" burst out Gigi Mear, jumping to his feet. "I've racked my brains for a whole morning and I shan't let you go before you tell me."

"Murder me," replied his friend, calmly and nonplussed. "Cut me in pieces! But I shan't tell you."

"Go on, be a good fellow," Mear began again, changing his tone. "I've never had an experience like this before—this loss of memory, you know; and I swear to you that it's a most painful sensation, you're an obsession with me now. Tell me your name, for heaven's sake."

"Go and find out."

"Look here. My forgetfulness hasn't hindered me from

giving you a place at my table and as a matter of fact, even if I have never known you, you've become most dear to me, believe me. I've a very brotherly feeling for you; I admire you; I should like you always with me. So tell me your name."

"It's no good, you know," said the other positively, "you don't miss me ever. Just be reasonable. Do you want to deprive me now of the unexpected pleasure of letting you be duped not knowing who's been your guest? No, go away; you want too much and I can see well enough that you've no recollection of me. If you don't want me to be hurt that you've forgotten me like this let me go away as I am doing."

"Go off then, quickly, that's all I ask," snapped Mear pettishly. "I can't bear to see you in front of me any longer."

"Alright, I'm going. But first, one little kiss, Gigi; I'm off again to-morrow."

"I won't," bawled Mear, "unless you tell me——"

"No, no: that's all. And now, good-bye——" said the other cutting him short.

And he went off laughing, turning again at the top of the stairs to blow him a kiss.

(From the 1st volume of "Novelle per un Anno."
Firenze Bemporad, Publishers.)

NIZĀMĪ

LAYLA AND MAJNÚN

LAYLÁ, Pearl of the Night!

She was beautiful as the moon on the horizon, graceful as the cypress that sways in the night wind and glistens in the sheen of a myriad stars. Her hair was bright with the depths of darkness; her eyes were dark with excess of light; her glance was shadowed by excess of light. Her smile and the parting of her lips were like the coming of the rosy dawn, and, when love came to her—as he did with a load of sorrow hidden in his sack—she was as a rose plucked from Paradise to be crushed against her lover's breast; a rose to wither, droop, and die as Ormazd snatched it from the hand of Ahriman.

Out of the night came Laylá, clothed with all its wondrous beauties; into the light she returned, and, while the wind told the tale of her love to the cypress above her grave, the stars, with an added lustre, looked down as if to say, "Laylá is not lost: she was born of us; she hath returned to us. Look up! look up! there is brightness in the night where Laylá sits; there is splendour in the sphere where Laylá sits."

As the moon looks down on all rivers, though they reflect but one moon, so the beauty of Laylá, which smote all hearts to love. Her father was a great chief, and even the wealthiest princes of other lands visited him, attracted by the fame of Laylá's loveliness. But none could win her heart. Wealth and royal splendour could not claim it, yet it was given to the young Qays, son of the mighty chief of Yemen. Freely was it given to Qays, son of the chief of Yemen.

Now, Laylá's father was not friendly to the chief of Yemen. Indeed, the only path that led from the one to the other was a well-worn war-path; for long, long ago their ancestors had quarrelled, and, though there were rare occasions when the two peoples met at great festivals and waived their differences for a time, it may truly be said that there was always hate in their eyes when they saluted. Always? Not always: there was one exception. It was at one of these festivals that

Qays first saw Laylá. Their eyes met, and, though no word was spoken, love thrilled along a single glance.

From that moment Qays was a changed youth. He avoided the delights of the chase; his tongue was silent at feast and in council; he sat apart with a strange light in his eyes; no youth of his tribe could entice him to sport, no maiden could comfort him. His heart was in another house, and that was not the house of his fathers.

And Layla—she sat silent among her maidens with eyes downcast. Once, when a damsel, divining rightly, took her lute and sang a song of the fountain in the forest, where lovers met beneath the silver moon, she raised her head at the close of the song and bade the girl sing it again—and again. And, after this, in the evenings when the sun was setting, she would wander unattended in the gardens about her father's palace, roaming night by night in ever-widening circles, until, on a night when the moon was brightest, she came to the confines of the gardens where they adjoined the deep forest beyond; but ever and ever the moonlight beyond. And here, as she gazed adown the spaces between the tree trunks, she saw, in an open space where the moonbeams fell, a sparkling fountain, and knew it for that which had been immortalised in the sweet song sung by her damsel with the lute. There, from time immemorial, lovers had met and plighted their vows. A thrill shot through her at the thought that she had wandered hither in search of it. Her cheeks grew hot, and, with a wildly beating heart, she turned and ran back to her father's palace. Ran back, ashamed.

Now, in a high chamber of the palace—it was as wondrous as that of a Sultan—where Laylá was wont to recline at the window looking out above the tree-tops, there were two beautiful white doves; these had long been her companions, perching on her shoulder and pecking gently at her cheek with "Coo, coo, coo;"—preeking and preening on her shoulder with "Coo, coo, coo." They would come at her call and feed from her hand; and, when she threw one from the window, retaining the other against her breast, the liberated one seemed to understand that it might fly to yonder tree; and there it would sit cooing for its mate until Laylá, having held her fluttering bird close for a time, would set it free. "Ah!" she would sigh to herself, as the bird flew swiftly to its mate, "when love hath wings it flies to the loved one, but alas! I have no wings." And yet it was by the wings of a dove that her lover sent her a passionate message, which threw her into joy and fear, and finally led her footsteps to the place of lovers' meeting.

Qays, in the lonely musings which had beset him of late, recalled the story—well known among the people—of Laylá's two white doves. As he recalled it, he raised himself upon his elbow on his couch and said to himself, " If I went to her father, saying, ' Give me thy daughter to wife! ' how should I be met? If I sent a messenger, how would *he* be met? But the doves—if all tales be true, they fly in at her window and nestle to her bosom."

With his thought suddenly intent upon the doves, he called his servant Zeyd, who came quickly, for he loved his master.

" Thou knowest, Zeyd," said Qays, " that in the palace of the chief of Basráh there are two white doves, one of which flies forth at its mistress's bidding, and cooes and cooes and cooes until its mate is permitted to fly to it."

" I know it well, my master. They are tame birds, and they come to their mistress's hand."

" Would they come, thinkest thou, to *thy* hand? "

Zeyd, who was in his master's confidence, and knew what troubled him, answered the question with another.

" Dost thou desire these doves, O my master? My father was a woodman, and I was brought up in the forests. Many a wilder bird than a dove have I snared in the trees. I even know the secret art of taking a bird with my hand."

" Then bring me one of these doves, but be careful not to injure it—not even one feather of its plumage."

Zeyd was as clever as his word. On the third evening thereafter he brought one of Laylá's white doves to Qays and placed it in his hand. Then Qays stroked the bird and calmed its fears, and, bidding Zeyd hold it, he carefully wrapped and tied round its leg a small soft parchment on which were written the following verses:—

Thy heart is as a pure white dove,
   And it hath come to me;
And it hath brought me all thy love,
   Flying from yonder tree.

Thou shalt not have thy heart again,
   For it shall stay with me;
Yet thou shalt hear my own heart's pain
   Sobbing in yonder tree.

There is a fount where lovers meet:
   To-night I wait for thee.
Fly to me, love, as flies the dove
   To dove in yonder tree.

Now, Laylá, who had sent her dove into the warm night, sat listening at her window to hear it coo to its mate held close in her bosom. But it cooed not from its accustomed bough on yonder tree. Holding the fluttering mate to her, she leaned forth from the window, straining her ears to catch the well-known note, but, hearing nothing, she said to herself, "What can have happened? Whither has it flown? Never was such a thing before. Perchance the bird is sleeping on the bough."

Then, as the moon rose higher and higher above the tree-tops, shedding a glistening radiance over everything, she waited and waited, but there came no doling of the dove, no coo from yonder tree. At last, unable to account for it, she took the bird from her bosom and stroked it and spoke to it; then she threw it gently in the air as if to send it in search of its lost mate to bring it back.

The bird flew straight to the tree, and, perching there, cooed again and again, but there was no answering coo of its mate. Finally Laylá saw it rise from the tree and circle round the palace. Many times she saw it flash by, and heard the beating of its wings, until at last it flew in at the window; and when she took it and pressed it to her, she felt that it was trembling. For sure, it was distressed and trembling.

"Alas! poor bird!" she said, stroking it gently. "It is hard to lose one's lover, but it is harder still never to have found him."

But lo, as she was comforting the bird, the other dove suddenly fluttered in and perched upon her shoulder. She gave a cry of delight, and, taking it, held them both together in her arms. In fondling them her fingers felt something rough on the leg of the one that had just returned. Quickly she untied the fastenings, and, with beating heart, unfolded the parchment and read the writing thereon. It was the message from her lover. She knew not what to do. Should she go to the fountain where lovers meet beneath the moon? In her doubt she snatched first one dove and then the other, kissing each in turn. Then, setting them down, she rose and swiftly clothed herself in a long cloak, and stole quietly down the stairs and out of the palace by a side door. Love found the way to the path through the forest that led to the fountain where lovers meet. Like a shadow flitting across the bars of moonlight that fell among the trees, she sped on, and at last arrived at the edge of the open space where the fountain played, its silvery, high-flung column sparkling like jewelled silver ere it fell in tinkling spray upon the shining moss.

Laylá paused irresolute in the shadows, telling herself that if her heart was beating so hard it was because she had been running. Where was he who had stolen her dove and returned it with a message?

Wherever he was he had quick eyes, for he had discovered her in the shadows, and now came past the fountain, hastening towards her.

She darted into the light of the moon.

"Who art thou?"

Their eyes met. The moonlight fell on their faces. No other word was spoken, for they recognised each other in one glance.

"Laylá! thou hast come to me. I love thee."

"And I thee!"

And none but the old moon, who has looked down on many such things before, saw their sudden embrace; and none but the spirit of the fountain, who had recorded the words of lovers ever since the first gush of the waters, heard what they said to one another.

And so Laylá and Qays met many times by the fountain and plighted their vows there in the depths of the forest. And once, as they lingered over their farewells, Qays said to Laylá, "And oh! my beloved, if the desert were my home, and thou and I were free, even in the wilderness, eating the herbs that grow in the waste, or a loaf of thine own baking from the wild corn; drinking the water of the brook, and reposing beneath the bough—then would I let the world go by, and, with no hate of thy people, live with thee and love thee for ever."

"And I thee, beloved."

"Then let us leave all, and fly to the wilderness——"

"Now?"

"No, not now. Thou must prepare. To-morrow, beloved, I will await thee here at this hour with two fleet steeds; and then, as they spurn the dust from their feet, so will we spurn the world—you and I."

That night Laylá dreamed that she was in the wilderness with her lover, sitting beneath the bough, drinking from the waters of the brook, eating a loaf of her own making from the wild corn, and, in her lover's presence, happy to lose the luxury of palaces.

But alas! the dream was never to be realised. Someone at the palace—someone with more than two ears, and with eyes both back and front—someone, moreover, in the pay of Ibn Salám, a handsome young chief who greatly desired Laylá in marriage, breathed a word into the ear of Laylá's father. The following day the palace was deserted. The old chief, with Laylá and the whole of his retinue, had departed to his estate in the mountains, where it was hoped that the keen, pure air would be better for Laylá's health—at least, so her father said, though none could understand why, seeing that she had never looked better in her life.

Qays, knowing nothing of this sudden departure for several days, waited at the fountain at the appointed hour. At last one day, being already sad at heart, he learned—for Ibn Salám had not been idle in the matter—that Laylá had gone to the mountains of her own accord with her father's household, and that Ibn Salám, the favoured one, had gone with her also. Believing this to be true—for lovers are prone to credit what they fear—Qays ran forth from his abode like a man distraught. In the agony of his despair, he thought of nothing but to search for, and find, Laylá. Setting his face towards the distant mountains, he plunged into the desert, calling "Laylá! Laylá!" Every rock of the wilderness, every tree and thorny waste soon knew her name, for it echoed there among all that day and the following night, until at dawn he sank exhausted on a barren stretch of sand.

And here it was that his servant Zeyd and a party of his master's friends found him as the sun was rising. He was distracted. Worn out with fatigue and hunger and thirst, he wandered in his mind as he had wandered in the desert. They took him back to his father's abode and sought to restore him, but, when at last he was well, he still called continually for his lost love Laylá, so that they thought his reason was unhinged, and spoke of him as "Majnún"—that is to say, "mad with love"; and by this name he was called ever afterwards.

His father came and pleaded with him to put away his infatuation for the daughter of a chief no friend of his; but, finding him reasonable in all things save his mad love, the chief said within himself: "If he can be healed of this one thing, he will be whole." Then, being willing further to cement enmity or establish a bond with the chief of Basráh, he decided to set the matter to the test. Collecting a splendid retinue, he journeyed to the mountains on a mission to the chief, his enemy, leaving Majnún in the care of the faithful Zeyd.

When, after many days' journey, he at last arrived at the estate of Layla's father, he stood before that chief and haughtily demanded the hand of his daughter in marriage with his son, setting forth the clear meaning of consent on the one hand and refusal on the other. His proposal was rejected as haughtily as it had been made. "News travels far," said the chief of Basráh. "Thy son is mad: cure him of his madness first, and then seek my consent."

Cyd, the chief of Yemen, was a proud man and fierce. He could not brook this answer. He had proposed a bond of friendship, and it had been turned into a barbed shaft of war.

He withdrew from Basráh's presence with the cloud of battle lowering on his brows. He returned to his own place to come again in war, vowing vengeance on Basráh.

But Yemen's chief delayed his plans, for, on his return, he discovered that his son, accompanied by the faithful Zeyd, had set out on the yearly pilgrimage to Mecca, there to kneel before the holy shrine and drink of the sacred well in the Kaaba.

"Surely," said he, "that sacred well of water which sprang from the parched desert to save Hagar and her son will restore my own son to his health of mind. I will follow him and pray with him at the holy shrine; I will drink also at the sacred well, and so, perchance, he will be restored to me."

But it so chanced that, when the chief, followed by a splendid retinue, was but two days on his journey towards Mecca, he was met by a lordly chief of the desert named Noufal, who, with a small band of warriors, rode in advance of a cloud of dust to greet him in friendly fashion.

"I know thee," said Noufal, reining in his magnificent horse so suddenly that the sand and gravel scattered wide; "thou art the chief of Yemen and the father of Majnún, whom I have met in the desert. Greetings to thee! I have succoured thy son, whom I found in sore straits and nigh unto death. I have heard his story, and I will aid him and thee against the chief of Basráh, if it be thy will, O chief of Yemen."

"Greetings to thee, O Noufal! I know thy name; thou art a wanderer of the desert, but I have heard many brave tales of thy prowess and thy generosity. Thou hast my son in thy keeping? But how comes it that he failed of his pilgrimage to Mecca, whither I was following to join him at the holy shrine?"

"Alas! he fell by the wayside in sight of my warriors; and, when they came to him, his only cry was, 'Laylá! Laylá!' They brought him to me, and from his broken story and this oft-repeated cry of 'Laylá,' I knew him for Majnún, thy son; for the tale of beauty and love, O chief of Yemen, travels far in the silent desert."

"What wouldst thou, then, Noufal?"

"I would that thou and I, for the sake of thy son, go up against the chief of Basráh and demand his daughter. If he consent not, and we conquer, I will extend thine interests and protect them through the desert and beyond. If he consent, thou and I and he will be for ever at peace, and will combine our territories on just terms of thine own choosing."

"Thou hast spoken well, O Noufal, and I trust thee. Go thou up against the chief of Basráh and demand Laylá in my name, I will follow thy path, and, if thou returnest to meet me with Laylá in thy protection, all is well; but, if not, then we will proceed against Basráh together, and thy terms shall be my terms. For the rest, thou hast swift messengers, as have I."

At the word Noufal wheeled his horse and gave commands to some of his warriors, and presently six fleet-footed chargers were speeding towards the horizon in six different directions to call the warriors of the desert to converge on a point at the foot of the mountains. Meanwhile similar messengers were hastening back to Yemen with orders from their chief. Noufal and his band of warriors set out for the rendezvous, but the chief of Yemen waited for the return of his messengers.

. . . . .

Meanwhile Laylá, on her father's estate among the mountains, lived in the depths of misery. The young chief Ibn Salám, well favoured of her father, was continually pleading for her hand in marriage, but Laylá's protestations and tears so moved her father that he was fain to say to the handsome and wealthy suitor, "She is not yet of age; wait a little while and all will be well." For Basráh looked with a calculating eye on this young chief, who had splendid possessions and many thousands of warriors. As for Layla, she immured herself from the light of day, communing only with the stars by night and saying within her heart, "I will die a maiden rather than marry any but Majnún, who is now, alas! distracted, even as I."

Now Laylá, well knowing that her doves were nesting in "yonder tree," had left them to the care of the attendants at the palace. They had always been a solace to her, especially since one had been Love's messenger, and she missed that solace now. A young tiger, obedient only to an Ethiopian slave, could not speak to her of love as the doves had done! But one day a slave-girl brought her a bird of paradise, saying, "My boy lover caught this in the forests of the hills, and bade me offer it to thee for thy kindness to me."

Layla treasured the bird in her solitude, and soon discovered that it could imitate the sounds of her voice. On this she straightway taught it one word, and one word only. Then she would sit for hours, with the bird perched on the back of her hand, listening to its soft intonation of that one word: "Majnun." Again and again and again the bird would speak softly in her ear that sweetest name in all the world: "Majnún, Majnún, Majnún," and her heart would leave her bosom and range through the desolation of the desert, seeking always Majnun.

The affair of her heart stood in such case when, one day at dawn, Noufal, with a large band of warriors, smote with his sword upon the gates and demanded to see the chief of Basráh.

It was a short and pointed exchange of few words between Noufal and Basráh as the broadening band of sunlight crept slowly down the background of mountains; and, when it smote upon the gates as the sun burst up, the talk was finished, and Noufal and his band were galloping towards the desert to meet the oncoming hosts of Yemen. The chief of Basrah gazed upon the cloud of dust that rose between him and the sun, and in it read the signs of sudden war.

Now Basráh's mountain estate adjoined the territory of Ibn Salám, and, as soon as the latter learned that the chief had flouted Noufal in favour of his own suit, and that the thunder-cloud of battle was arising against the wind, he offered the aid of a thousand of his warriors—an offer which was eagerly accepted. But the thousand he offered were not a third part of the warriors at his call.

The way of war was paved. Before noon a host of Ibn Salám's warriors came riding in. Laylá, from her window, noted their brave array. Then, looking far out on to the desert, she saw the dust-cloud rising from the hoofs of an advancing host.

"Alas!" she cried, "the heart that beats in my bosom is the cause of this. I love my father; I love Majnún: Destiny must choose between them."

Destiny hath strange reversals. The shock and clash of battle dinned on her ears till near nightfall, when, with a heart divided between hope and fear, she saw clearly that Ibn's hosts could not hold their ground. The onslaughts of her father's foe were forcing them back. They scattered, and rallied and scattered again. Those that were left retreated within the gates. The gates were battered down, and all was lost—or won. A herald advanced, offering terms of surrender. Laylá leaned from her window, listening. No word could she hear until her father, still defiant in the face of defeat, spoke in ringing tones.

"And, if I deliver not up my daughter, you will take her. Yea, but you will not take her alive. I have but to raise my hand, and she will be slain. I have lost all, but my servants will still obey me: if I give the word, her dead body is yours for the asking."

At this the chief of Yemen bade him hold his hand from committing this terrible deed.

"O chief of Basráh," he said, "I give thee one day to think

about this matter. There are two sides to it: the one is that thou deliver up thy daughter to be given to my son to wife, so that there may be a bond of friendship between us; the other is that thou keep thy daughter and surrender thy sovereignty, retaining thy territories only in vassalage to me."

With that the chief of Yemen and his ally, Noufal, withdrew, leaving Basráh to decide before dawn the following day.

Now, among Ibn Salám's messengers that he had sent out was one whose orders were to ride back, as if from Yemen, bringing word that he had discovered Majnún, who, having fled from his attendants in the night, was lying dead in the desert. This was not truth, but Ibn had reason to believe that it soon would be, for he had sent out others to find him and kill him. It was to his purpose that the false news should arrive quickly, for, on that, and the offer of a further host of warriors at his command, he hoped to gain Laylá's promise and strengthen her father's hand in the matter.

The victors had scarcely withdrawn when the messenger rode in, shouting the news to victors and vanquished alike. The chief of Yemen heard it and wept for his son. Noufal heard it and said, "Laylá is nothing to us now; at dawn we shall dictate our own terms." Ibn Salám and Laylá's father heard the news without grief, and Ibn said, "Now there can be no obstacle to thy daughter's consent, for she is a woman, and must know that the living is more desirable than the dead. I have already helped thee, O Chief, and we have failed. But thy daughter has only to speak the word and a further host of my warriors—more than treble the number that fought to-day—will come out of the desert at my call. Half will come to aid our defence, and half will attack the hosts of Yemen from the desert. Thus your foes will be scattered like chaff in the wind. Go to thy daughter and show her now how a word from her will save thee from destruction and make thee great."

The chief of Basrah went to his daughter, and, when Ibn heard sounds of a woman wailing, he knew that the false news of Majnun's death was believed. Long time the chief pleaded with Laylá, urging the uselessness of weeping for Majnún when, by accepting Ibn in marriage, she could save Basráh and make it a great kingdom. Then he spoke of her duty to him, her father, in this terrible plight, from which her word alone could save him; and Laylá saw, through her tears, that for her father's sake the sacrifice must be made; and through duty, not love, she mournfully pledged herself to Ibn Salám.

As soon as Ibn knew this, he called some of his warriors and questioned them on the matter of his hosts in reserve.

"Four thousand," he said, when he had heard their replies. "The foe is but three thousand, and we are little more than one thousand."

Then he gave orders to some chosen messengers and bade them steal forth secretly and deliver them to his generals. Half the four thousand was to arrive by night under cover of the mountains and be ready for battle at sunrise. The other half was to make a circuit of the desert and fall upon the foe from behind when the battle was at its hottest. On this sudden stroke he relied for complete victory.

And he was not wrong. When dawn broke over the desert, and the mountain peaks were flushed with sunrise fire, the dark shadows at the base were two thousand strong. There they waited hidden from the foe while as the sun rose, a herald came to the gates. In the name of Yemen, he dictated the terms of surrender without any condition in regard to Laylá.

The chief of Basráh laughed him to scorn. "Go tell the chief of Yemen and his robber friend of the desert," he said, "that if they desire my domains they must take them by force of arms. Tell them that Basráh never surrenders: he prefers to live free, or to die fighting."

The herald took back this proud answer of defiance. On hearing it Yemen wondered and questioned, but Noufal, who was a man of the desert, sudden in temper and quick to act, counselled an immediate attack.

The battle was joined. At the first shock came Ibn's two thousand warriors from their concealment, and the invaders fell back in astonishment. Yet they rallied again, and fiercely raged the fight between the opposing hosts, now equally matched in numbers. Layla looked from her window in horror. She noted how the battle swayed this way, then that. And now it seemed that the foe was steadily gaining the mastery. But what was that in the distance of the desert? What was that, thrust forward from the desert? A great cloud of dust, quickly approaching. It drew near, its cause quickly outstripping it. A mighty host of warriors now shook the earth with the thunder of their horses' feet. They drew nearer. Now like a whirlwind they hurled themselves upon the invaders and bore them down like trodden wheat—sweeping the flying remainder of them like chaff to the four winds.

Yemen was slain. Noufal, flying from numbers on swifter steeds than his, laughed back at his pursuers, then slew himself, dying, as he had lived, at full gallop.

Basráh was victorious. That night Layla was given by her father to Ibn Salám. That night, too, the chief of Basráh having been previously wounded in the battle, died. Ibn ruled now over three vast territories welded into one. And, where he was king, Laylá was queen.

. . . .

Years passed by, and Ibn and Laylá reigned in peace. The palace of her fathers was their abode, and the bird of paradise and the two white doves were often her companions, recalling to her heart a lost, but never-to-be-forgotten, love. The faithful Zeyd, who had wandered long in the desert searching in vain for his master, was now her servant.

One day news came secretly to Zeyd that Majnún, long mourned as dead, had returned disguised as a merchant from distant parts, and would be waiting for him at a certain spot on the outskirts of the desert at sunset. Zeyd said nothing of this to his mistress, but unknown to her, he caught one of the doves and took it away with him to the meeting-place, for he reasoned that what had happened once would happen again with like result. Full of joy was the meeting between Majnun and Zeyd on the edge of the desert as the sun went down.

Now, Laylá, when she repaired to her high chamber that evening, was astonished to find one of her doves missing. She sent the other forth to the great tree, thinking the two might return together, but presently it returned alone. Then wondering greatly, she sat by the window, musing on the past: how, three years ago, the dove had returned after an absence, bearing a love-messge from Majnún, and how she had met him again and again at the lovers' fountain in the forest. Alas! all was changed: Majnún was dead, and she was the wife of another. Her eyes filled with tears, and, bowing her head on her arms upon the window-sill, she wept silently.

For a long time she remained like this. Then, suddenly, she was aroused from her weeping by a sound. It was the "coo, coo, coo" of the missing dove, and it came from the great tree. Immediately the other dove fanned her hair as it sped past her to its mate. It made her long for wings that she too might fly away and away to her lover.

Presently the two birds fluttered in at the window and came to her. What strange thing was this? There, wrapped round the leg of one was a small strip of soft parchment as on that night long ago. With trembling fingers she unfastened and read what was written thereon. It was from Majnún. He was alive and well! As before, the writing begged her to come that very night to the lovers' fountain at moonrise.

In her sudden joy at learning that her lover was alive and near at hand, Laylá forgot all, and, as the gibbous moon was already brightening the horizon, she arose and cloaked herself and stole down the stairway of the palace. She reached the side door unobserved. She passed out and closed it behind her. Her heart flew before her to Majnun, but suddenly, as she hastened, it rebounded swiftly and almost stopped beating. Her footsteps faltered and she clutched at a bough of a tree for support. Her husband! Her duty! Once she had given all for duty's sake: should she take it back now, and in this way? What would it mean? With Majnún's arms around her she would forget all—husband, duty, her people: all, all would be forgotten, and the step once taken could not be retraced. Alas! this was not the act of a wife! It was not the act of a queen! She groaned as she grasped the bough, and her body swayed with her spirit's woe as she then and there rejected her purpose and accepted her sorrow.

Slowly Laylá strengthened herself; then, like one in a dream, she turned and retraced her steps to the palace, no sigh, no sob escaping her. All that night she refused sleep or comfort, dry-eyed; and it was only when the dawn came that tears came too, to save her reason on its throne.

Majnun waited long by the lovers' fountain, and, at last, learnin from Zeyd that his mistress had ventured forth and had returned, he went away, treasuring to his heart a love that could not give one glance without giving all; for, from Zeyd's story, he knew this to be so. As Laylá had gone back to the palace, silent and strong, so Majnún set his face towards distant cities, praying ever that the years might bring surcease of woe, if not the rapture of the love of Laylá.

Two years passed by, and Fate stepped in. Ibn Salám fell stricken with a fever and died. The news spread far, and one day Majnun, in a distant city, looked up and heard that Laylá, the queen of Yemen and Basráh, was free. Swift, then, were the steeds that bore him to Yemen. But, remembering how she had twice sacrificed herself for duty, he forbore to approach her until the expiration of the prescribed term of widowhood—four moons and half a moon. This period he spent, alone and unknown, in an abode from which he could see the lights of Layla's palace. His longing ate into his heart, and it was harder to bear than his former distraction, by which he had earned his name of Majnun ('mad with love'). But, as in the first instance, his reason had borne the strain, so now it bore the stress of all this weary waiting at the gates of Paradise.

Zeyd bore tidings of Laylá to Majnún, but from Majnún to Layla no message passed until, on a day when the prescribed term had passed, Zeyd took word to her that Majnún would come to her at the palace at noon, or, according to her choice, wait for her at the lovers' fountain at two hours after sunset.

Zeyd brought back the delayed message: " Noon has passed

but noon will come again—after this eventide." Which was not unlike the answer Majnún had expected.

The saddest part of the history of these ill-destined lovers is yet to be told. Two hours after sunset Majnún kept the tryst. Two hours after sunset Laylá, her eyes smouldering with a pent-up fire, cloaked herself as of old and went out by the side door of the palace. There was no moon, but the stars shed a soft light upon the gardens. She passed among the trees; her heart beat fast and her breath came quick. The whole of her life seemed wrapped up in her two feet, which ran a hot race with each other. She reached the edge of the forest and paused, clasping her hands over her bosom. She must regain her breath to show Majnún how little she had hastened. Then, before she had regained it, she ran on, losing it the more. There was the fountain—the fountain where lovers had always met—she saw it sparkling in the starlight through the trees. Now she stood on the edge of the open space, the folds of her cloak parted, her masses of raven hair fallen loose, her breast heaving.

A figure darted from the fountain's side. She faltered forward, swaying. A moaning cry escaped her as Majnún caught her in a wild embrace.

Who knows if it was but a moment or a thousand years? Love has no dial. But that time-moment two hours after sunset was their swift undoing. At the touch of her lips upon his, Majnún's reason was wrenched away. At the touch of his lips upon hers, she swooned in his arms. He let her fall, and ran, shrieking, out of the forest and into the desert; shrieking her name, far into the desert.

"Laylá! Laylá! Laylá"—his maniac cries echoed on and on until, in the hopeless waste of wildnerness, he fell exhausted. But Zeyd, who had followed his voice, at last found him. Many a day and night he tended his master, but to no purpose. Joy had done what grief had failed to do: he was mad!

Laylá awoke from her swoon, and, hearing her own name repeated again and again—that wild cry coming from farther and farther in the desert—divined the truth and returned, slowly and wringing her hands, to the palace.

From time to time Zeyd sent news of Majnún and his undying love, which even his madness had failed to touch.

Day by day, and week by week, Laylá's eyes grew brighter and her cheeks paler. Slowly she pined away, and then she died of a broken heart. Her last words were a message to Majnún—a message of love that could not die, though it must quit the beautiful, unhappy house of clay in which it had suffered so much.

" And tell him," she said, " that my body shall be buried by the side of the fountain where he first clasped me in his arms. And tell him, too, these very words: ' Majnún, lift thine eyes! See, yonder are the Fields of Light, and a fountain springing in the sunshine—yonder—a fountain of eternal waters, where lovers meet, never to part again; thou shalt find me there! ' " And with that she died, and her spirit sped on her parting thought to that place of lovers' meeting; the immortal font of lovers' meeting.

. . . . .

Dawn was breaking on the desert when two figures came running. Each held the other by the hand, and on the face of one was that look which told how he had been driven mad by love. Majnún, outstripping Zeyd, left him to follow, and plunged into the forest. Soon he came to the open space in which the fountain played. Well he knew the spot where he had first clasped Laylá in his arms. There was now a newly made grave. Exhausted, not with running, but with love, madness, and grief, he flung himself upon it.

" Laylá! Laylá! " he moaned, with a heart-bursting pang. " I will come soon—ah, soon! Hold thy shroud of night about thee! Hide thy beauty in the Fields of Light—until I find thee there! "

And, as the sun rose, Zeyd came and stood by the grave, gazing down upon his master through tears of grief;—gazing down upon the dead through bitter tears of grief.

THE ARABIAN NIGHTS' ENTERTAINMENTS

THE STORY OF THE MAGIC HORSE

THERE was, in ancient times, in the country of the Persians, a mighty King, of great dignity, who had three daughters, like shining full moons and flowery gardens; and he had a male child, like the moon. He observed two annual festivals, that of the New Years' Day, and that of the Autumnal Equinox; and it was his custom, on these occasions, to open his palaces, and give his gifts, and make proclamation of safety and security, and promote the chamberlains and lieutenants: the people of his dominions also used to go in to him and salute him, and congratulate him on the festival, offering him presents and servants; and he loved philosophy and geometry. And while the King was sitting on the throne of his dominions, on a certain day, during one of these festivals, there came in to him three sages: with one of them was a peacock of gold; and with the second, a trumpet of brass; and with the third, a horse of ivory and ebony: whereupon the King said to them, What are these things, and what is their use? The owner of the peacock answered, The use of this peacock is, that whenever an hour of the night or day passeth, it will flap its wings, and utter a cry. And the owner of the trumpet said, If this trumpet be placed at the gate of the city, it will be as a defender of it; for if an enemy enter the city, this trumpet will send forth a sound against him; so he will be known and arrested. And the owner of the horse said, O my Lord, the use of this horse is, that if a man mount it, it will convey him to whatever country he desireth. Upon this the King said, I will not bestow any favour upon you until I make trial of the uses of these things. Then he made trial of the peacock, and found it to be as its owner had said. And he made trial of the trumpet, and found it as its owner had said. He therefore said to the two sages (the owners of the peacock and the trumpet), Request of me what ye will. And they replied, We request of thee that thou marry to each of us one of thy daughters. Whereupon the King bestowed upon them two of his daughters. Then the third sage, the owner of the horse, advanced, and, having kissed the ground before the King, said to him, O King of the age, bestow upon me like as thou hast bestowed upon my companions. The King replied, When I shall have made trial of that which thou hast brought. And upon this the King's son advanced and said, O my father, I will mount this horse, and make trial of it, and obtain proof of its use. So the King replied, O my son, try it as thou desirest.

The King's son accordingly arose, and mounted the horse, and urged it with his feet; but it moved not from its place. He therefore said, O sage, where is its rapidity of pace of which thou boastedst? And on hearing this, the sage came to him, and shewed him a turning pin, by which to make it ascend; saying to him, Turn this pin. And the King's son turned it, and lo, the horse moved, and soared with him towards the upper region of the sky, and ceased not its flight with him until he was out of sight of the people; whereupon the prince was perplexed at his case, and repented of his having mounted the horse. He said, The sage hath made use of a stratagem to destroy me, and there is no strength nor power but in God, the High, the Great! Then he began to examine all the members of the horse; and while he was doing so, he saw a thing like the head of a cock, on the horse's right shoulder, and the like on the left shoulder: so he said, I see not any indication excepting these two buttons. And he turned the button that was on the right shoulder; upon which the horse bore him up with increased velocity into the sky: so he took off his hand from that button, and, looking at the left shoulder, and seeing the button that was there, he turned it; and the movements of the horse became lessened in velocity, and changed from ascending to descending.

Now when he had obtained what he desired with respect to the horse, he proceeded on it towards the earth, and began to look at its countries and cities, which he knew not; for he had never seen them before during the whole of his life. And among the objects that he beheld was a city constructed in the most excellent manner, in the midst of a land beautifully verdant, with trees and rivers; upon which he meditated in his mind, and said, Would that I knew what is the name of this city, and in what region it is. He then made a circuit round the city, viewing it attentively, right and left. The day had nearly departed, and the sun was about to set: so he said within himself, I have not found any place in which to pass the night better than this city: I will therefore pass this night in it and in the morning I will return to my family and my royal residence, and acquaint my family and my father with that which hath happened to me, and inform him of the things that mine eyes have seen. Accordingly he began to search for a place in which he might feel secure of the safety of himself and his horse, and where no one might see him; and while he was thus engaged, lo, he beheld, in the midst of the city, a palace rising high into the air, surrounded by a large wall with high battlements; whereupon he said within himself, This place is agreeable.

He turned the button that caused the horse to descend, and ceased not to be carried downwards on it until he descended steadily on the flat roof of the palace, when he alighted from the horse, praising God (whose name be exalted!), and began to go round about the horse, and to examine it, and said, By Allah, he who made thee thus was an expert sage; and if God (whose name be exalted!) extend the term of my life, and restore me to my country and my family in safety, and reunite me with my father, I will assuredly bestow every favour upon this sage, and treat him with the utmost beneficence. He then sat upon the roof of the palace until he knew that the inmates had betaken themselves to sleep. Hunger and thirst pained him; for since he had parted from his father he had not eaten food; and he said within himself, Verily such a palace as this is not devoid of the necessaries of life. He therefore left the horse in a place alone, and walked down to see for something to eat; and finding a flight of steps, he descended by them to the lower part of the building, where he found a court paved with marble; and he wondered at this palace, and at the beauty of its construction; but he heard not in the palace any sound, nor the cheering voice of an inhabitant. So he paused in perplexity, and looked to the right and left, not knowing whither to go. Then he said within himself, There is no better course for me than to return to the place in which is my horse, and to pass the night by it; and when the morning cometh, I mount and depart.

But while he was addressing himself with these words, he beheld a light approaching the place where he stood, and, looking attentively at that light, he found that it was a party of female slaves, among whom was a beautiful damsel, of a stature like the letter Alif, resembling the splendid full moon. That damsel was the daughter of the King of this city; and her father loved her with so great an affection that he built for her this palace; and whenever her heart was contracted, she used to come hither, together with her female slaves, and to remain here a day, or two days, or more; after which she returned to the palace where she generally resided. It happened that she came that night for the sake of diversion and dilatation of the mind, and she walked among the female slaves, attended by a eunuch armed with a sword; and when they entered the palace, they spread the furniture, and gave vent to the odours from the perfuming vessels, and sported and rejoiced. Now while they were thus engaged, the King's son rushed upon that eunuch, struck him a blow which laid him prostrate, and, taking the sword from his hand, ran upon the female slaves who were with the King's daughter, and dispersed them to the right and left. And when the King's daughter saw his beauty and loveliness, she said, Perhaps thou art he who demanded me in marriage yesterday of my father, and whom he rejected, and whom he asserted to be of hideous aspect. By Allah, my father lied in saying those words; for thou art none other than a handsome person.

Now the son of the King of India had requested her of her father, and he had rejected him, because he was disagreeable in aspect; and she imagined that the prince now before her was he who had demanded her in marriage. She then came to him, and embraced and kissed him, and seated herself with him. The female slaves, however, said to her, O our mistress, this is not the person who demanded thee in marriage of thy father; for that person was hideous, and this is handsome; and he who demanded thee of thy father, and whom he rejected, is not fit to be a servant to this person: but, O my mistress, verily this young man is one of high dignity. And after this, the female slaves went to the prostrated eunuch, and roused him; whereupon he sprang up in alarm, and searched for his sword, not finding it in his hand. So the female slaves said to him, He who took thy sword, and laid thee prostrate, is sitting with the King's daughter.—Now the King had charged this eunuch with the office of guarding his daughter, in his fear for her from misfortune and evil accidents.—The eunuch therefore arose, and went to the curtain, and when he raised it, he saw the King's daughter sitting with the King's son, and they were conversing together; and as soon as he beheld them, he said to the King's son, O my master, art thou a human being or a Jinnee? To which the King's son replied, Wo to thee, O most ill-omened of slaves! How is it that thou regardest the sons of the royal Kisras as of the unbelieving devils?—Then, taking the sword in his hand, he said to him, I am the son-in-law of the King, and he hath married me to his daughter, and commanded me to introduce myself to her.

The eunuch then went shrieking to the King; and he had rent his clothes, and thrown dust upon his head. And when the King heard his crying, he said to him, What hath befallen thee; for thou hast agitated my heart? Acquaint me quickly, and be brief in thy words.—He therefore answered him, O King, go to the assistance of thy daughter; for a devil of the Jinn, in the garb of human beings, and having the form of the sons of the Kings, hath got possession of her: therefore seize him. And when the King heard these words from him, he thought to slay him, and said to him, How came it to pass that thou wast neglectful of my daughter, so that this event befell her? He then went to the palace wherein was his daughter, and on his arrival he found the female slaves standing there, and said to them, What is it that hath happened to my daughter? They answered him, O King, while we were sitting with her, suddenly there rushed upon us this young man, who resembleth the full moon, and than whom we have never seen any one more handsome in countenance, with a drawn sword in his hand; and we inquired of him respecting his business, and he asserted that thou hadst married to him thy daughter; we know nothing more than this.

The King could not control himself through his jealousy for his daughter. He therefore raised the curtain and entered, with a drawn sword in his hand, and rushed upon him as though he were a Ghool. The King's son, on seeing him, said to her, Is this thy father? She answered, Yes. And upon this, he sprang upon his feet, and, taking his sword in his hand, shouted at the King with an amazing cry, which terrified him, and was about to attack him with the sword; but the King, perceiving that the prince was stronger than he, sheathed his sword, and stood until the King's son came up to him, when he met him with courtesy, and said to him, O young man, art thou a human being or a Jinnee? The King's son replied, Were it not that I respect thy right and the honour of thy daughter, I had shed thy blood. How is it that thou derivest me from the devils, when I am of the sons of the royal Kisras, who, if they desired to take thy kingdom, would make thee totter from thy glory and dominion, and despoil thee of all that is in thy dwellings?—So the King, on hearing these words, dreaded and feared him; but said to him, If thou be of the sons of the Kings, as thou hast asserted, how is it that thou hast entered my palace without my permission, and dishonoured me, and come unto my daughter, asserting that thou art her husband, and pretending that I had married thee to her, when I have killed the Kings and the sons of the Kings on their demanding her of me in marriage?

The King's son, however, when he heard these words from him, said to the King, Verily, I wonder at thee, and at the smallness of thy penetration. Dost thou covet for thy daughter a husband better than myself; and hast thou seen any one more firm of heart, and superior in requital, and more glorious in authority and troops and guards than I am?—The King answered him, No, by Allah: but I would, O young man, that thou demand her in marriage publicly, that I may marry her to thee; for if I marry her to thee privately, thou wilt disgrace me by so taking her. And the King's son replied, Thou hast said well: but, O King, if thy slaves and servants and troops were to assemble against me and slay me, as thou hast imagined, thou wouldst disgrace thyself, and the people would be divided with respect to thee, some believing, and others accusing thee of falsehood. It is my opinion that thou shouldst relinquish this idea, and adopt the course that I will point out to thee.—So the King said, Propose what thou wilt. And the King's son rejoined, What I propose to thee is this: either that thou meet me in single combat, and he who killeth the other shall be more deserving and worthy of the kingdom; or else, that thou leave me this night, and when the morning cometh, that thou send forth to me thy soldiers and troops and young men, and acquaint me with their number. The King replied, Their number is forty thousand horsemen, besides the slaves belonging to me, and their followers, who are equal in number. And the King's son said, When the day beginneth, send them forth to me, and say to them, This person hath demanded of me my daughter in marriage on the condition that he will meet you all in combat; and he hath pretended that he will overcome and subdue you, and that ye cannot prevail against him. Then leave me with them to combat them; and if they kill me, the result will be more proper for the concealment of thy secret and the preserving of thine honour; but if I overcome and subdue them, then am I such a person as the King should desire for his son-in-law.—And when the King heard his words, he approved of his advice and accepted it, notwithstanding that he wondered at his saying, and was struck with terror at his determination to meet in combat all his army that he had described unto him.

And after this, the King called the eunuch, and commanded him to go forth immediately to his Wezeer, and to desire him to collect all the troops, and order them to equip themselves with their arms, and to mount their horses. So the eunuch went to the Wezeer, and acquainted him with that which the King had commanded. And upon this the Wezeer summoned the chiefs of the army, and the grandees of the empire, and ordered them to mount their horses, and to go forth equipped with the weapons of war.—Meanwhile, the King continued to converse with the young man, being pleased with his conversation and sense and good breeding; and as they were talking together, the morning arrived. The King therefore arose, and went to his throne, ordered his troops to mount, and caused an excellent horse, one of the best that he possessed, to be brought before the King's son, commanding that it should be equipped for him with handsome saddle and trappings. But the young man said to him, O King, I will not mount until I take a view of the troops, and observe them. And the King replied, It shall be as thou desirest. Then the King proceeded, with the young man before him, until they arrived at the horse-course, when the young man looked at the troops and their number. And the King called out, O companies of men, a young man hath come unto me demanding in marriage my daughter, and I have never beheld any handsomer than he, nor any stronger in heart, nor any greater in intrepedity than he: and he hath asserted that he alone will overcome you and subdue you, and pretendeth that ye, even if your number amounted to a hundred thousand, would be in his estimation but few. But when he cometh forth to combat you, receive him upon the points of your spears, and the edges of your swords; for he hath undertaken a great enterprise.

The King then said to the young man, O my son, do as thou desirest with them. But he replied, O King, thou hast not treated me equitably. How shall I go forth to combat them when I am on foot and thy people are mounted on horses? So the King said to him, I desired thee to mount, and thou refusedst. Take then of the horses and choose of them that which thou wilt.—He replied, None of thy horses pleaseth me, and I will mount none but the horse on which I came. The King therefore said to him, And where is thy horse? He answered him, It is on the top of thy palace.—In what place in my palace? asked the King. He answered, On the roof of the palace. And when the King heard his words, he said to him, This is the first instance that hath appeared of thine insanity. O, wo to thee! How can the horse be upon the roof? But now will thy veracity be distinguished from thy lying.—Then the King looked towards one of his chief officers, and said to him, Go to my palace, and bring what thou shalt find upon the roof. Now the person whom the King had sent to the palace ascended to its roof, and beheld the horse standing there; and he had seen none more handsome than it; and he approached it and examined it, and found it to be of ebony and ivory. Some others of the chief officers of the King also went up with this person; and when they beheld the horse, they laughed together, and said, Did the young man speak of such a horse as this? We imagine that he is no other than a madman: but his case will soon appear to us; and perhaps he may be a person of great importance.—They then raised the horse upon their hands, and carried it without stopping until they came before the King, when they placed it before him; and the people assembled around it, gazing at it, and wondering at the beauty of its make, and at the beauty of its saddle and bridle. The King also admired it, and wondered at it extremely; and he said to the King's son, O young man, is this thy horse? He answered, Yes, O King, this is my horse, and thou shalt see a wonder performed by it. The King said to him, Take thy horse and mount it. But he replied, I will not mount it unless the troops retire to a distance from it. So the King commanded the troops that were around him to retire from it as far as an arrow might be shot.

Then said the young man, O King, I am going to mount my horse, and charge upon thine army, and disperse them to the right and left, and split their hearts. The King replied, Do what thou desirest, and pity them not; for they will not pity thee. And the King's son went to the horse and mounted.

When the King's son had seated himself upon his horse, he turned the pin of ascent. The eyes of the spectators were strained to see what he would do; and his horse bestirred himself, and moved about with violent action, until it had performed the most extraordinary of the motions of horses, and its body became filled with air. Then it rose, and ascended into the sky. So when the King saw that he had risen, and ascended aloft, he called out to his troops, and said, Wo to you! Take him before he escape from you.—But his Wezeer and Lieutenants replied, O King, can any one catch the flying bird? This is none other than a great enchanter. God hath saved thee from him: therefore praise God (whose name be exalted!) for thine escape from his hand.

The King therefore returned to his palace, after he had witnessed these acts of the King's son; and when he arrived at his palace, he went to his daughter, and acquainted her with that which had happened to him with the King's son in the horse-course; but he found her greatly lamenting for him, and for her separation from him, and she fell into a violent sickness, and took to the pillow. So when her father saw her in this state he pressed her to his bosom, kissed her between the eyes, and said to her, O my daughter, praise God (whose name be exalted!) and thank Him for our escape from this crafty enchanter. He began to repeat to her the account of the deeds of the King's son that he had witnessed, describing to her how he had ascended into the air. But she listened to nought of her father's words; her weeping and wailing increased in violence, and afterwards she said within herself, By Allah, I will not eat food, nor drink any beverage, until God reunite me with him. Therefore exceeding anxiety overcame her father the King on account of this; the state of his daughter afflicted him, and he mourned in heart for her.

Now, as to the King's son, when he had ascended into the sky, being alone, he reflected upon the beauty of the damsel, and her loveliness. He had inquired of the King's people respecting the name of the city, and the name of the King, and that of his daughter: and that city was the city of San'a. He then prosecuted his journey with diligence until he came in sight of the city of his father; and after he had made a circuit around the city, he bent his course to his father's palace, and descended upon the roof. Having left his horse there, he descended to his father, and went in to him; and he found him mourning and afflicted on account of his separation: therefore, when his father saw him, he rose to him and embraced him, pressing him to his bosom, and rejoicing exceedingly at his return. And the Prince inquired of his father respecting the sage who made the horse, saying, O my father, what hath fortune done with him? His father answered him, May God not bless the sage nor the hour in which I beheld him; for he was the cause of thy separation from us, and he hath been imprisoned, O my son, since thou absentedst thyself from us. He gave orders, however, to relieve him, and take him forth from the prison, and bring him before him; and when he came before him, he invested him with an honorary dress in token of satisfaction, and treated him with the utmost beneficence: but would not marry his daughter to him. So the sage was violently enraged at this, and repented of that which he had done, knowing that the King's son had become acquainted with the secret of the horse and the mode of its motion. Then the King said to his son, It is my opinion that thou shouldst not approach this horse henceforth, nor mount it after this day; for thou knowest not its properties, and thou art deceived respecting it. The King's son had related to his father what had happened to him with the daughter of the King, the lord of the city, and what had happened to him with her father; and his father said to him, Had the King desired to slay thee, he had slain thee; but the end of thy life was delayed.

After this, they ate and drank and were merry; and there was with the King a handsome slave-girl, who played upon the lute; and she took the lute, and began to play upon it, singing of absence, before the King and his son. Then anxious thoughts were aroused in the mind of the King's son by his love of the damsel, the daughter of the King of San'a: so he rose and went to the horse and mounted it, and turned the pin of ascent; whereupon it soared with him into the air, and rose with him towards the upper region of the sky. And in the morning, his father missed him, and found him not: he therefore went up to the top of the palace, in a state of affliction, and he beheld his son mounting into the air; and upon this he grieved for his separation, and repented extremely that he had not taken the horse and concealed it. He said within himself, By Allah, if my son return to me, I will not preserve this horse, that my heart may be at rest respecting my son. And he resumed his weeping and wailing.—But as to his son, he ceased not his course through the sky until he came to the city of San'a, when he descended in the place where he descended the first time, and he walked down stealthily until he came to the chamber of the King's daughter; but he found neither her nor her female slaves, nor the eunuch who was her guard; and the event greatly afflicted him. Then he went about searching for her through the palace, and at last he found her in a different chamber from that in which he had been with her. She had taken to the pillow, and around her were the female slaves and nurses. And he went in to them and saluted them; and when the damsel heard his speech, she rose to him and embraced him, and began to kiss him between his eyes, and to press him to her bosom. He said to her, O my mistress, thou hast rendered me desolate during this period. And she replied, Thou hast rendered *me* desolate, and had thine absence from me continued longer, I had perished without doubt.—O my mistress, he rejoined, what thoughtest thou of my conduct with thy father, and his actions to me? Were it not for my love of thee, O temptation to all creatures, I had slain him, and made him an example to beholders: but I love him for thy sake.—And she said to him, How could thou absent thyself from me? Can my life be pleasant after thy departure?—He then said to her, Wilt thou comply with my desire, and listen to my words? She answered him, Say what thou wilt; for I will consent to that which thou requirest me to do, and will not oppose thee in anything. And he said to her, Journey with me to my country and my kingdom. She replied, Most willingly.

So when the King's son heard her words, he rejoiced exceedingly, and, taking her by her hand, he made her swear by God (whose name be exalted!) that she would do so.

Then he led her up to the roof of the palace, mounted his horse, and placed her on it behind him, and after he had bound her firmly, he turned the pin of ascent in the shoulder of the horse, and it ascended with them into the sky. Upon this the female slaves cried out, and acquainted the King her father, and her mother, who thereupon came up in haste to the roof of the palace; and the King, looking up into the sky, beheld the ebony horse soaring with them in the air. The King was agitated, and his agitation increased, and he called out and said, O son of the King, I conjure thee by Allah that thou have mercy upon me, and have mercy upon my wife, and that thou make not a separation between us and our daughter! The King's son, however, answered him not; but he imagined that the damsel repented of parting from her mother and her father; so he said to her, O temptation of the age, dost thou desire that I restore thee to thy mother and thy father?— O my master, she answered, by Allah that is not my desire: my desire is rather to be with thee wherever thou shalt be; for I am drawn off by my love of thee from everything else, even from my father and my mother. And when the King's son heard her reply, he rejoiced exceedingly. He proceeded with her, and ceased not in his course through the air until he arrived at the city of his father. His joy thereat was great; and he desired to shew to the damsel the seat of his power and the dominion of his father, and to acquaint her that the dominion of his father was greater than that of her father. He therefore deposited her in one of the gardens in which his father diverted himself, put her in a private chamber that was furnished for his father, and placed the ebony horse at the door of that chamber, charging the damsel to guard it, and saying to her, Sit here until I send to thee my messenger; for I am going to my father, to prepare for thee a palace.

So the King's son left her, and proceeded until he arrived at the city, and went in to his father; and when his father saw him, he rejoiced at his coming, and met him and welcomed him; and the King's son said to his father, Know that I have brought the King's daughter of whom I informed thee, and I have left her without the city, in one of the gardens, and come to acquaint thee with her arrival, that thou mayest prepare the procession of state, and go forth to meet her, and display to her thy dominion and thy troops and guards. The King replied, Most willingly. And immediately he commanded the people of the city to decorate the city in the most handsome manner, and rode forth in a procession equipped in the most perfect manner and with the most magnificent decorations, with all his soldiers and the grandees of his empire, and all his memlooks and servants. The King's son also took forth, from his palace, ornaments and apparel and such things as Kings treasure up, and prepared for the damsel a camel-litter of green and red and yellow brocade, in which he seated Indian and Greek and Abyssinian female slaves, and he displayed wonderful treasures. Then he left the camel-litter, with the persons that were in it, and went on before to the garden; and he entered the private chamber in which he had left the damsel, and searched for her; but found her not, nor did he find the horse. Upon this he slapped his face and rent his clothes, and began to go round about through the garden, with a mind confounded; after which, he returned to his reason, and said within himself, How did she learn the secret of this horse when I did not acquaint her with aught of it? But perhaps the Persian sage who made the horse hath found her, and taken her, as a requital for that which my father hath done unto him.—Then the King's son sought the keepers of the garden, and asked them who had passed by them, saying, Have ye seen anyone pass by you and enter this garden? And they answered, We have not seen anyone enter this garden except the Persian sage.

Now it happened, in accordance with destiny, that, when the King's son left the damsel in the private chamber that was in the garden, and repaired to the palace of his father to make his preparations, the Persian sage entered the garden to collect some useful herbs, and smelt the odour of musk and other perfumes with which the air was impregnated; and this sweet scent was from the odour of the King's daughter. The sage therefore proceeded in the direction of this odour until he came to the private chamber, when he saw the horse that he had made with his hand standing at the door of the chamber. So when the sage saw the horse, his heart was filled with joy and happiness; for he had mourned after it greatly since it had gone from his possession. He approached it, and examined all its members, and found it sound, but when he was about to mount it and depart, he said within himself, I must see what the King's son hath brought and left here with the horse. Accordingly he entered the private chamber, and found the damsel sitting there resembling the shining sun in the clear sky. As soon as he beheld her, he knew that she was a damsel of high dignity, and that the King's son had taken her, and brought her upon the horse, and left her in that private chamber while he repaired to the city to prepare for her a stately procession, and to conduct her into the city with respect and honour. The sage therefore went in to her, and kissed the ground before her; and she raised her eyes towards him, and, looking at him, found him to be of most hideous aspect and disagreeable form; and she said to him, Who art thou? He answered her, O my mistress, I am the messenger of the King's son, who hath sent me to thee, and commanded me to remove thee to another garden, near unto the city. And when the damsel heard from him these words, she said to him, And where is the King's son? He answered her, He is in the city, with his father, and he will come to thee immediately with a grand procession. But she said to him, O thou! Could not the King's son find anyone to send to me but thee?—And the sage laughed at her words, and replied, O my mistress, let not the hideousness of my face, and the disagreeableness of my aspect deceive thee; for hadst thou experienced of me what the King's son hath, thou wouldst approve of me.

So when the damsel heard his reply, it appeared reasonable to her, and she believed it, and arose and went with him, putting her hand in his. She then said to him, O my father, what hast thou brought with thee for me to ride?—O my mistress, he answered, the horse on which thou camest thou shalt ride. She replied, I cannot ride it by myself. And when he heard this reply from her, the sage smiled, and knew that he had got possession of her; and he said to her, I myself will ride with thee. Then he mounted, and mounted the damsel behind him, and, pressing her to him, bound her tightly, while she knew not what he desired to do with her. And after this, he turned the pin of ascent, whereupon the body of the horse became filled with air, and it moved and bestirred itself, and ascended into the sky, and continued incessantly bearing them along until it was out of sight of the city. So the damsel said to him, O thou! What meant that which thou saidst respecting the King's son, when thou assertest that he sent thee to me?—The sage replied, May Allah keep the King's son from everything good; for he is base and vile!—O, wo to thee! she exclaimed; how is it that thou disobeyest thy lord in that which he hath commanded thee to do? He replied, He is not my lord. And knowest thou, he added, who I am? She answered him, I know thee not but as thou hast informed me of thyself. And he said to her, Verily my telling thee this was a stratagem that I made use of against thee and against the King's son. I was lamenting constantly for this horse that is beneath thee, for it is of my making, and he had made himself master of it; but now I have obtained possession of it and of thee also, and have tortured his heart as he hath tortured mine, and he will never have it in his power henceforth. But be of good heart and cheerful eye; for I shall be more useful to thee than he.—And when the damsel heard his words, she slapped her face, and cried out, O my grief: I have neither obtained my beloved nor remained with my father and my mother!—And she wept violently for that which had befallen her, while the sage incessantly proceeded with her to the country of the Greeks, until he descended with her in a verdant meadow.

This meadow was near unto a city, in which was a king of great dignity; and it happened on that day that the King of the city went forth to hunt, and to divert himself, and, passing by that meadow, he saw the sage standing there, with the horse and the damsel by his side. And the sage was not aware of their approach when the slaves of the King rushed upon him, and took him, together with the damsel and the horse, and placed all before the King who, when he beheld the hideousness of his aspect and the disagreeableness of his appearance, and beheld the beauty of the damsel, and her loveliness, said to her, O my mistress, what relation is this sheikh to thee? The sage hastily answered and said, She is my wife, and the daughter of my paternal uncle. But the damsel declared that he was a liar, as soon as she heard his words, and said, O King, by Allah I know him not, and he is not my husband; but he took me away by force and stratagem. And when the King heard what she said, he gave orders to beat the sage; and they beat him until he almost died. Then the King commanded that they should carry him to the city, and cast him into the prison; and so they did with him; and the King took the damsel and the horse from him; but he knew not the property of the horse, nor the mode of its motion.—Thus did it befall the sage and the damsel.

As to the King's son, he put on the apparel of travel, and, having taken what money he required, journeyed forth in a most evil state, and quickly endeavoured to trace them, seeking them from town to town and from city to city, and inquiring respecting the ebony horse; and every one who heard his mention of the ebony horse wondered at it, and was greatly astonished at his words. Thus he continued to do for a long period; but notwithstanding his frequent questions and his searching for them, he met with no tidings of them. Then he journeyed to the city of the damsel's father, and there inquired for her, but he heard no tidings of her, and he found her father mourning for her loss. So he returned, and repaired to the country of the Greeks, endeavouring to trace them, and inquiring respecting them. And it happened that he alighted at one of the Khans, and saw a party of the merchants sitting conversing; and he seated himself near them, and heard one of them say, O my companions, I have met with a wonderful thing.—And what was it? they asked. He answered, I was in a certain district, in such a city (and he mentioned the name of the city in which was the damsel), and I heard its inhabitants talking of a strange story, which was this.—The King of the city went forth one day to hunt, attended by a party of his associates and the grandees of his empire, and when they went forth into the desert, they passed by a verdant meadow, and found there a man standing, and by his side a woman sitting, and with him a horse of ebony. As to the man, he was of hideous aspect, very horrible in form; and as to the woman, she was a damsel endowed with beauty and loveliness, and elegance and perfect grace, and justness of stature; and as to the ebony horse, it was a wonderful thing; eyes have not beheld its superior in beauty or in comeliness of make.—The persons present said to him, And what did the King with them? He answered, As to the man, the King took him, and asking him respecting the damsel, and he pretended that she was his wife, and the daughter of his paternal uncle. But as to the damsel, she declared that he lied in his assertion. So the King took him from her, and gave orders to beat him, and to cast him into the prison. And as to the ebony horse, I know not what became of it.—When the King's son therefore heard these words from the merchant, he approached him, and proceeded to question him with mildness and courtesy until he acquainted him with the name of the city and the name of its King; and when he knew the name of the city and that of its King, he passed the night happy.

He ceased not to prosecute his journey until he arrived at that city; but when he desired to enter it, the gate-keepers took him, and would have conducted him into the presence of the King, that he might inquire of him respecting his condition, and of the cause of his coming into that city, and as to what art or trade he was skilled in; for so was the King's custom to question the strangers respecting their conditions and their arts or trades. But the arrival of the King's son at that city happened to be at eventide; and that was a time at which it was not possible to go in to the King or to consult respecting him. So the gate-keepers took him and conducted him to the prison, to put him in it. When the jailers, however, saw his beauty and loveliness, they could not bear to put him into the prison; on the contrary, they seated him with themselves, outside the prison; and when the food was brought to them, he ate with them until he was satisfied; and after they had finished eating, they sat conversing, and, addressing the King's son, they said to him, From what country art thou? He answered, I am from the country of Persia, the country of the Kisras. And when they heard his answer, they laughed, and one of them said to him, O Kisrawee, I have heard the sayings of men, and their histories, and have observed their conditions;

but I have neither seen, nor heard of, a greater liar than this Kisrawee who is with us in the prison.

So the King's son said to them, What instance of his lying hath appeared unto you? They answered, He pretendeth that he is a sage, and the King saw him as he was going to hunt, and with him a woman of surpassing beauty and loveliness, and elegance and perfect grace, and justness of stature, and there was with him also a horse of black ebony, than which we have never seen any more handsome. As to the damsel, she is with the King, and he loveth her; but the woman is mad; and if that man were a sage as he pretendeth, he had cured her; for the King is striving to find her remedy, desiring to recover her of her malady. As to the ebony horse, it is in the King's treasury; and as to the man of hideous aspect, who was with it, he is with us in the prison. When the keepers of the prison acquainted the King's son with these circumstances, it occurred to his mind that he might contrive a plan by means of which to attain his desire. And when the gate-keepers desired to sleep they put him into the prison, and closed the door upon him; and he heard the sage weeping and lamenting for himself in the Persian language, and saying in his lamentation, Wo unto me for the injustice that I have committed against myself and against the King's son.

Then, when the morning came, the gate-keepers took the King's son and conducted him to the King, and informed him that he had arrived at the city on the preceding day, at a time when it was impossible to go in unto the King. So the King questioned him, and said to him, From what country art thou, and what is thy name, and what thy art or trade, and what the reason of thy coming unto this city? And the King's son answered, As to my name, it is, in the Persian language, Harjeh; and as to my country, it is the country of Persia; and I am of the men of science, especially the science of medicine; for I cure the sick and the mad; and for this purpose I travel about through the regions and cities, to profit myself by adding science to my science; and when I see a sick person, I cure him. This is my occupation.—And when the King heard his words, he rejoiced at them exceedingly, and said to him, O excellent sage, thou hast come to us at a time when we need thee. Then he acquainted him with the case of the damsel, and said to him, If thou cure her, and recover her of her madness, thou shalt receive from me all that thou shalt desire. And the King's son, on hearing this, replied, May God confirm the power of the King! Describe to me everything that thou hast observed of her madness, and inform me how many days ago this madness attacked her, and how thou tookest her and the horse and the sage.—He therefore acquainted him with the matter from beginning to end, and said to him, The sage is in the prison. And the King's son said, O happy King, and what hast thou done with the horse that was with them? The King answered him, It remaineth with me to the present time, preserved in one of the private chambers. So the King's son said within himself, It is my opinion that I should examine the horse before everything else, and if it be sound, and no accident have happened to it, all that I desire is accomplished; but if I see that its motions are destroyed, I will yet devise some stratagem to save my life. Then looking towards the King, he said to him, O King, it is requisite that I see the horse which thou hast mentioned. Perhaps I may find in it something that will aid me to recover the damsel.—The King replied, Most willingly. And he arose, and, taking him by the hand, led him in to the horse; whereupon the King's son began to go round about the horse, and to examine it and observe its condition; and he found it sound without any defect. He therefore rejoiced at it exceedingly, and said, May God confirm the power of the King! I desire to go in to the damsel, that I may see how she will act.

He gave orders to take care of the horse, and the King conducted him to the chamber in which was the damsel. And when the King's son went in to her, he found her beating herself, and falling down prostrate as usual; but she was affected by no madness, and only did thus that no one might approach her. So the King's son, on seeing her in this state, said to her, No harm shall befall thee, O temptation to all creatures; Then he began to address her gently and courteously until he acquainted her with himself; and when she knew him, she uttered a great cry, and fell down in a fit through the violence of the joy that she experienced; and the King imagined that this fit was occasioned by her fear of him. And the King's son put his mouth to her ear, and said to her, O temptation to all creatures, spare my life and thine, and be patient and firm; for this is the place wherein we stand in need of patience and good management in devising stratagems to make our escape from this tyrannical King. A part of my stratagem shall be, that I go forth to him and say to him, The disease that she suffereth ariseth from her being possessed by a Jinnee, and I promise thee her recovery. And I will make a condition with him that he shall loose thy bonds, and will assure him that this Jinnee which hath afflicted thee will be dispelled from thee. Therefore if he come in to thee, address him with pleasant words, that he may see that thou hast recovered through my means, and so shall all that we desire be accomplished.—And she replied,

I hear and obey.—He then went forth from her, and, returning to the King, full of joy and happiness, said, O fortunate King, I have discovered, through thy good fortune, her remedy and cure, and I have cured her for thee. Arise then and go in to her, and speak gently and mildly to her, and promise her that which shall rejoice her; for all that thou desirest of her shall be accomplished for thee.—The King therefore arose and went in to her; and when she saw him, she rose to him, and kissed the ground before him, and welcomed him.

Then they attired her in royal apparel, put upon her neck a necklace of jewels, conducted her to the bath, served her, and brought her out from the bath, resembling the full moon. And when she came to the King, she saluted him, and kissed the ground before him.

The King therefore was greatly rejoiced at seeing her thus, and said to the King's son, All this is occasioned by the blessings attendant upon thee! May God increase to us thy benefactions! —And the King's son replied, O King, the perfection of her recovery and the completion of her affair must be effected by thy going forth with all thy guards and thy soldiers to the place where thou foundest her, and the ebony horse that was with her must be taken with thee, that I may there confine from her the Jinnee that hath afflicted her, and imprison him and kill him, so that he may never return to her. The King said, Most willingly. Accordingly he sent forth the ebony horse to the meadow in which he had found the damsel with the horse and the Persian sage, and the King mounted with his troops, taking the damsel with him; and they knew not what he desired to do. And when they arrived at that meadow, the King's son who feigned himself a sage, ordered that the damsel and the horse should be placed as far from the King and the troops as the eye could reach, and said to the King, With thy permission and leave, I desire to burn perfumes, and to recite a form of exorcism, and imprison the Jinnee here, that he may never return to her. After which I will mount the ebony horse, and mount the damsel behind me; and when I have done that, the horse will move about with violent action, and walk forward until he cometh to thee, when the affair will be finished, and thou shalt do with her what thou wilt.—Then the King's son mounted the horse, and placed the damsel behind him, while the King and all his troops looked at him. And he pressed her to him, and bound her firmly, and turned the pin of ascent; whereupon the horse rose with them in the air.

But as to the King's son, he bent his course to the city of his father, full of joy and happiness, and ceased not in his journey until he descended upon his palace, when he took down the damsel into the palace, and felt secure of her. He then repaired to his father and his mother, and saluted them, and acquainted them with the arrival of the damsel; whereat they rejoiced exceedingly. Meanwhile, the King of the Greeks, when he returned to his city, secluded himself in his palace, mourning and afflicted. So his Wezeers went in to him, and began to console him, saying to him, Verily he who took the damsel is an enchanter; and praise be to God who hath saved thee from his enchantment and craftiness. And as to the King's son, he made magnificent banquets for the people of the city, and they continued the rejoicings for a whole month; after which, he took the damsel as his wife, and they were delighted with each other exceedingly. And his father broke the ebony horse, and destroyed its motions. Then the King's son wrote a letter to the father of the damsel, and in it described to him his state informing him that he had married the damsel, and that she was with him in the most happy condition. He sent it to him by a messenger, bearing precious presents and rarities; and when the messenger arrived at the city of the damsel's father, which was San'a of El-Yemen, he transmitted the letter, with the presents, to that King, who, on reading the letter, rejoiced exceedingly, accepted the presents, and treated the messenger with honour.

Thus they continued until the King, the father of the young man, was taken from the world; and the young man reigned after him over his dominions. He ruled his subjects with equity, and conducted himself among them in a laudable manner; the country was subject to him, and the people obeyed him; and thus they remained, passing the most delightful and most agreeable and most comfortable and most pleasant life.

P'U SUNG-LING

THE PRINCESS LILY

ONCE upon a time at Chiao-chow there lived a man called Tou Hsün. One day, as he lay sleeping in the heat of the day, he suddenly saw standing by his bedside a man dressed in serge clothes who indicated that he had a message to deliver.

Tou inquired of him what was his business, and the man replied that he was the bearer of an invitation from his master.

"And who is your master?" asked Tou.

The messenger would not reply directly, but begged Tou to accompany him saying, "He doesn't live very far away."

So they went away together, and after a while Tou saw countless white houses rising one above the other and shaded by dense groves of lemon-tree. His guide led him past countless doors of a curious and unusual shape, and he saw many official-looking men and women all of whom asked his guide: "Has Tou Hsün come?" and his guide would nod toward Tou with a smile.

At length his guide led him up to one person whom Tou saw to be a mandarin of high degree. And the mandarin, having greeted Tou ceremoniously, escorted him into a wondrous palace.

But now Tou hesitated:

"Deeply as I appreciate your courtesy," he said, "I haven't the honour of knowing you, and I feel diffident of thrusting my presence upon you."

"Our prince," replied the mandarin, "has long heard of you as a man of noble qualities and exulted family. He desires to become better acquainted with you."

"But who is your Prince?" inquired Tou again.

"In a few moments you shall behold him yourself," replied

the mandarin; and as he spoke, two beautiful maidens appeared carrying ceremonial banners, and guided Tou through many doors and halls, until at length they came to a throne upon which sat the Prince.

When the Prince beheld Tou he descended from the throne, and himself led his guest to the seat of honour. Then he ordered that the banquet should be served, and the most delicious food and wine was immediately placed before them.

Then, still bewildered, Tou, casting his eyes round him, beheld a scroll which bore the words *The Cassia Court*, but that did not enlighten him any further as to who was his courteous host. The Prince, noticing his puzzled looks, said:

"The honour of having you for a neighbour is, as it were, a bond of affinity between us. Let us, then, give ourselves up to enjoyment, and put away suspicion and fear."

After this Tou resolved to bother no more about the strange circumstances in which he found himself, but gave himself up to the enjoyment of the feast. When the wine had gone round several times, Tou heard music in the distance: the sound of pipes and voices singing, but unaccompanied by the usual drums. Then said the Prince, "We are going to set a verse for you gentlemen to cap. This is it: 'Genius seeks the Cassia Court.'"

While all the gentlemen of the Court were engaged in thinking of some appropriate antithesis,[1] Tou said, "Refinement loves the Lily flower."

"But this is indeed a strange chance that puts such words into your mouth," exclaimed the Prince, amid murmurs of admiration, "for my daughter's name is Lily. Now you shall behold her for yourself."

He gave an order, and a few moments later a tinkling of ornaments and wafts of delicate perfume announced the arrival of the Princess.

She came in attended by her maidens, a girl between sixteen and seventeen years, and of such surpassing beauty that Tou was rendered speechless, and could only gaze at her. The Prince bade her make an obeisance to Tou, and as soon as she had performed the ceremony, she retired again.

The Prince, seeing that Tou had already fallen deeply in love with his daughter, began to talk of how he had been attempting to find a suitable husband for her, but so great was the ecstasy of the young man, he heard not a word the

[1] In this favourite game of the cultured Chinese Courts, the important point is that each word in the second line should be a due and proper antithesis of the word in the first line to which it corresponds. This play on words is naturally lost somewhat in translation.

Prince was saying, and was oblivious to all that was going on around him, until one of the courtiers touched him on the arm and told him the Prince was addressing him. Thereupon Tou started, and recovering himself a little, stammered his apologies and begged to be allowed to depart.

"I am delighted to have welcomed you to my Court," replied the Prince, "and only regret that your stay must be so short. If you do not forget all about us, I shall hope to see you among us again."

He then gave orders that Tou should be escorted to his home. The courtier who accompanied him asked him why he had said nothing when the Prince had so obviously suggested that he should marry the Princess Lily. The dazed young man was just realising how great was the opportunity he had missed when they reached his home, and he awoke.

The sun had set, and Tou sat in the gloom, bemoaning his lost chance, and thinking of the Princess. Later that evening, when he retired again to rest, he put out his candle, hoping that the thread of his dream would be renewed.

But it was not until some nights later, when he was sleeping at a friend's house, that an officer of the Court suddenly appeared and summoned him to the presence of the Prince.

Once more Tou found himself in that strange palace of halls and countless doors. He prostrated himself before the Prince, who welcomed him again with every kindness.

He told the delighted Tou that he was aware that he had fallen deeply in love with the Princess Lily, and suggested that if the young man were agreeable, the nuptials should be performed immediately. Naturally the young man made no objections, and the banquet was immediately spread before them.

At last came the moment when it was announced that the Princess had completed her toilet, and she came in accompanied by her maidens, the red bridal veil covering her head, and her tiny footsteps sounding like rippling water as they led her up to her bridegroom.

"In your presence, Princess," Tou said, bowing before her, "it would be easy to forget death itself; but, tell me, is not this all a dream?"

"How can it be a dream, beloved," she replied in a low voice, "when you and I are here together?"

The next morning Tou assisted in the ceremonial painting of the face of the Princess, and then, seizing a girdle, began to measure the size of her waist and the length of her fingers and feet.

"Are you mad?" she cried, laughing.

"I have been deceived so often," Tou replied, "that I am going to make a careful record. If this is all just a dream, I shall still have something as a souvenir of you."

Even as they talked together, one of the maidens rushed in crying: "Alas! alas! a great monster has got into the palace. The Prince is fled into a side chamber. Destruction is upon us!"

Tou immediately sought out the Prince, who, with tears in his eyes, begged him not to desert them.

"Our relationship," cried he, "was cemented when Heaven sent this calamity upon us; and now my kingdom will be overthrown. What shall I do?"

Tou begged to know what was the matter; and then the Prince laid a despatch upon the table, telling Tou to open it and make himself acquainted with its contents. This despatch ran as follows:

"The Grand Secretary of State, Black Wings, to His Royal Highness, announcing the arrival of an extraordinary monster, and advising the immediate removal of the Court in order to preserve the vitality of the empire. A report has just been received from the officer in charge of the Yellow Gate stating that, ever since the 6th of the 5th moon, a huge monster, 10,000 feet in length, has been lying coiled up outside the entrance to the palace, and that it has already devoured 13,800 and odd of your Highness's subjects, and is spreading desolation far and wide. On receipt of this information your servant proceeded to make a reconnaissance, and there beheld a venomous reptile with a head as big as a mountain and eyes like vast sheets of water. Every time it raised its head, whole buildings disappeared down its throat; and, on stretching itself out, walls and houses were alike laid in ruins. In all antiquity there is no record of such a scourge. The fate of our temples and ancestral halls is now a mere question of hours; we therefore pray your Royal Highness to depart at once with the Royal Family and seek somewhere else a happier abode."[1]

Just as Tou had finished reading the despatch a messenger rushed in crying: "The Monster!"

The whole Court was immediately thrown into a panic, and Tou heard the sound of wailing and lamentation on all sides.

The Prince, himself, was pale and agitated, and begged Tou to look to his own safety without regarding the wife through whom he was involved in such misfortune. But the Princess,

[1] The language in which this fanciful document is couched is precisely such as would be used by an officer of the Government in announcing some national calamity.

who was standing by wringing her hands, flung herself at his feet and begged him not to desert her.

Tou gently raised her up, and then, bowing before the Prince and begging that his presumption should be excused, he offered his own poor home as a shelter, if they would deign to come.

"We cannot talk of deigning at such a moment as this," cried the princess: "I beg you take us there as quickly as possible."

So Tou conducted her to his own home with all speed, and the Princess, despite his apologies for its humble appointments, professed herself delighted, declaring that it was a charming place of residence—better even than their former kingdom.

"Now I must ask you," she said to Tou, "to make arrangements to receive my father and mother and the whole Court, that the old order may be maintained here."

At this Tou was thunderstruck, for he did not see how he could possibly accommodate her father's entire Court. But at first hint of opposition, the Princess fell into a violent temper, declaring that a man who would not help her in her hour of need was not worthy to be called her husband. Her screams grew louder and louder, and as the distracted Tou was trying to calm her, he awoke, and found it was all a dream!

Yet in his ears he still heard a buzzing, and, on looking round carefully, he noticed two or three bees had settled on his pillow and refused to be dislodged even when he attempted to brush them away.

He called his friend, and together they found several more bees on various parts of his dress and in the room. Tou was greatly astonished, but his friend advised him to get a hive for them at once. He did so, and not only did the bees in his room go quickly to the hive, but a whole swarm of bees came flying over the garden wall and immediately filled it.

Tou and his friend set to work to trace from where the swarm had come. They found it belonging to an old man who lived not far off, and on breaking open the deserted hive, they found in it a huge snake—the "monster" of Tou's dream.

As for the bees, they stayed with Tou, increasing in numbers every year.

THE TONGUE-CUT SPARROW

ONCE upon a time there was an old man who lived with his wife, high up among the mountains of Japan. Not very happily, however, because his wife was older than he, and very bad-tempered. You should have heard her shout and scold at her husband! And jealous, too! Why, the poor man hadn't a single friend in the world except a tame sparrow, and she abused and ill-treated even that.

It happened one day that the old man was off to the fields, and left his wife at her wash-tub. Her temper was always worse on washing day, because of the scrubbing and rinsing that strained her back. She had made some starch, and set it in a red wooden bowl to cool, and when she came for it at last, what did she see but the pet sparrow perched on the rim making a hearty meal. In a rage she caught him and cut off the tip of his tongue with a pair of scissors.

"That will teach you to steal!" she screamed. "Now, be off with you—and never come back!"

And she flung the poor bird, all bleeding, into the air, where it circled round once or twice and then flew mournfully away.

When the old man returned he was very sad and angry at what she had done, and the two of them shouted and quarrelled far into the night. But it was all to no purpose. The sparrow with only half a tongue was gone, and the old man had to settle down to a lonely existence without chick nor child, and only his nagging wife for company.

Then, one day long months afterwards, he was up in the mountains when a small voice chirped "Good morning!" and there was his sparrow. But a different bird now, for the cutting of his tongue had enabled him to speak as humans do.

The old man and his friend bowed and greeted each other in polite Japanese fashion, and then the sparrow begged him to come and visit his wife and daughters.

It was not very far away. The sparrow and his family lived in the most enchanting little bamboo house you could wish for, with a miniature landscape-garden, complete with waterfall, stepping-stones and all. Mrs. Sparrow did the honours of her house and brought out slices of sweet jelly, rock candy, custard and bowls of cornstarch. She did not forget a pair of superbly lacquered chopsticks for her guest, and afterwards the elder Miss Sparrow prepared the ceremonial tea, serving it most gracefully kneeling, as was proper.

"I'm afraid it's a very poor meal we have offered you," said Mrs. Sparrow. "You must excuse us on the grounds that we had no time to make adequate preparations."

The old man was quite dizzy with surprise and delight at his friendly reception. He drank several cups of tea and, when they pressed him, consented at last to spend the night. There was so much to see and do that he extended his visit for nearly a week. Never before had he received so much kindness, and his heart warmed towards his kind little hosts. They pursued an idyllic existence. During the day the old man examined the nice proportions of the garden or played draughts with the younger Miss Sparrow. In the evening Mrs. Sparrow would serve food and wine in the garden while she played on the tsamsein. Mr. Sparrow and his daughters would dance and sing while the old man looked on and forgot his cares.

But on the fifth day he suddenly realised how long he had stayed with them, and said that he simply must go. Mr. Sparrow seemed very sorry, and insisted on him taking a parting gift. He brought out two woven fibre travelling-baskets, one heavy, the other light.

"Choose one of these," he said, "as a small memento of your visit."

The old man was not at all greedy—and besides, he had been well brought up. So he chose the light one, and with many thanks and bows and good-byes he took his leave.

You might have imagined that his wife would have been anxious about her husband's absence and glad to see him back. Not a bit of it! He had hardly got inside his gate before she began scolding him for neglecting her. The old man managed to get her to hold her tongue while he recounted his strange adventures; and at the end he showed her the basket, and they lifted the lid together.

What a marvellous sight! It was simply crammed with gold and silver and jewels and coral and amber and crystal! There was a hat that made one invisible; there were books of spells to get one whatever one desired; and there was even a purse that was always full of money, no matter how much one spent!

You should have seen the old woman alter her frowns to a

greedy grin. " I'm off to get a present from the sparrows as well," she cried.

Her husband tried in vain to stop her. He pointed out that they had quite as much as they wanted already, and that it would be both rude and greedy to ask for more. But she would not be gainsaid. On went her straw pattens, up went her paper umbrella and off she went to Mr. Sparrow's house.

The old man had told her how he went, so she had no difficulty in following the way. When she arrived, she tried to be as polite as she could be, but it was a bit of a strain. Mr. Sparrow was not very pleased to see her, but he invited her in for a cup of tea, just the same. Mrs. Sparrow and her daughters did not appear. They probably knew what she was after.

She finished her tea at length, and as there seemed to be no sign of presents appearing, she actually asked for one, right out! Mr. Sparrow looked down his beak. He said nothing, but went inside and returned with two baskets identical with those he had offered to the old man. You may imagine the greedy old woman seized the heavier one and hurried off almost without saying " Thank you " or " Good-bye " or anything.

She carried her basket back in triumph, and arrived panting, for it was *very* heavy.

" What a fool you were," she said to her husband, " not to choose the heavy basket. There must be twice as much in it."

And then she tore off the lid.

But, goodness me! There was a rustling and a hissing, and instead of a shower of gold and jewels, the most awful cuttlefish reared itself up out of the basket, and a host of demons buzzed out like wasps, while a dreadful hairy snake with a dragon's head—lolling tongue and all—coiled itself round her and squeezed tighter and tighter until she died.

The fearful beasts did not attempt to hurt the old man, who was now left a very wealthy widower. He bought himself a splendid house and adopted a son to comfort him in his old age, to whom he was never tired of pointing out the dangers of greed and the practical advantages of being always polite.

EDITH WHARTON

POMEGRANATE SEED

CHARLOTTE ASHBY paused on her doorstep. Dark had descended on the brilliancy of the March afternoon, and the grinding, rasping street life of the city was at its highest. She turned her back on it, standing for a moment in the old-fashioned, marble-flagged vestibule before she inserted her key in the lock. The sash curtains drawn across the panes of the inner door softened the light within to a warm blur through which no details showed. It was the hour when, in the first months of her marriage to Kenneth Ashby, she had most liked to return to that quiet house in a street long since deserted by business and fashion. The contrast between the soulless roar of New York, its devouring blaze of lights, the oppression of its congested traffic, congested houses, lives, minds and this veiled sanctuary she called home, always stirred her profoundly. In the very heart of the hurricane she had found her tiny islet—or thought she had. And now, in the last months, everything was changed, and she always wavered on the doorstep and had to force herself to enter.

While she stood there she called up the scene within: the hall hung with old prints, the ladderlike stairs, and on the left her husband's long shabby library, full of books and pipes and worn armchairs inviting to meditation. How she had loved that room! Then, upstairs, her own drawing-room, in which, since the death of Kenneth's first wife, neither furniture nor hangings had been changed, because there had never been money enough, but which Charlotte had made her own by moving furniture about and adding more books, another lamp, a table for the new reviews. Even on the occasion of her only visit to the first Mrs. Ashby—a distant, self-centred woman, whom she had known very slightly—she had looked about her with an innocent envy, feeling it to be exactly the drawing-room she would have liked for herself; and now for more than a year it had been hers to deal with as she chose —the room to which she hastened back at dusk on winter days, where she sat reading by the fire, or answering notes at the pleasant roomy desk, or going over her stepchildren's copy books, till she heard her husband's step.

Sometimes friends dropped in; sometimes—oftener—she was alone; and she liked that best, since it was another way of being with Kenneth, thinking over what he had said when they parted in the morning, imagining what he would say when he sprang up the stairs, found her by herself and caught her to him.

Now, instead of this, she thought of one thing only—the letter she might or might not find on the hall table. Until she had made sure whether or not it was there, her mind had no room for anything else. The letter was always the same —a square greyish envelope with "Kenneth Ashby, Esquire," written on it in bold but faint characters. From the first it had struck Charlotte as peculiar that anyone who wrote such a firm hand should trace the letters so lightly; the address was always written as though there were not enough ink in the pen, or the writer's wrist were too weak to bear upon it. Another curious thing was that, in spite of its masculine curves, the writing was so visibly feminine. Some hands are sexless, some masculine, at first glance; the writing on the grey envelope, for all its strength and assurance, was without doubt a woman's. The envelope never bore anything but the recipient's name; no stamp, no address. The letter was presumably delivered by hand—but by whose? No doubt it was slipped into the letter box, whence the parlour-maid, when she closed the shutters and lit the lights, probably extracted it. At any rate, it was always in the evening, after dark, that Charlotte saw it lying there. She thought of the letter in the singular, as "it," because, though there had been several since her marriage—seven, to be exact—they were so alike in appearance that they had become merged in one another in her mind, become one letter, become "it."

The first had come the day after their return from their honeymoon—a journey prolonged to the West Indies, from which they had returned to New York after an absence of more than two months. Re-entering the house with her husband, late on that first evening—they had dined at his mother's—she had seen, alone on the hall table, the grey envelope. Her eye fell on it before Kenneth's, and her first thought was: "Why, I've seen that writing before"; but where she could not recall. The memory was just definite enough for her to identify the script whenever it looked up at her faintly from the same pale envelope; but on that first day she would have thought no more of the letter if, when her husband's glance lit on it, she had not chanced to be looking at him. It all happened in a flash—his seeing the letter, putting out his hand for it, raising it to his short-sighted eyes to decipher the faint writing, and then abruptly withdrawing the arm he had slipped through Charlotte's, and moving away to the hanging light, his back turned to her. She had waited—waited for a sound, an exclamation; waited for him to open the letter; but he had slipped it into his pocket without a word and followed her into the library. And there they had sat down by the fire and lit their cigarettes, and he had remained silent, his head thrown back broodingly against the armchair, his eyes fixed on the hearth, and presently had passed his hand over his forehead and said: "Wasn't it unusually hot at my mother's to-night? I've got a splitting head. Mind if I take myself off to bed?"

That was the first time. Since then Charlotte had never been present when he had received the letter. It usually came before he got home from his office, and she had to go upstairs and leave it lying there. But even if she had not seen it, she would have known it had come by the change in his face when he joined her—which, on those evenings, he seldom did before they met for dinner. Evidently, whatever the letter contained, he wanted to be by himself to deal with it; and when he reappeared he looked years older, looked emptied of life and courage, and hardly conscious of her presence. Sometimes he was silent for the rest of the evening; and if he spoke, it was usually to hint some criticism of her household arrangements, suggest some change in the domestic administration, to ask, a little nervously, if she didn't think Joyce's nursery governess was rather young and flighty, or if she herself always saw to it that Peter—whose throat was delicate—was properly wrapped up when he went to school. At such times Charlotte would remember the friendly warnings she had received when she became engaged to Kenneth Ashby: "Marrying a heart-broken widower! Isn't that rather risky? You know Elsie Ashby absolutely dominated him"; and how she had jokingly replied: "He may be glad of a little liberty for a change." And in this respect she had been right. She had needed no one to tell her, during the first months, that her husband was perfectly happy with her. When they came back from their protracted honeymoon the same friends said: "What have you done to Kenneth? He looks twenty years younger"; and this time she answered with careless joy: "I suppose I've got him out of his groove."

But what she noticed after the grey letters began to come was not so much his nervous tentative fault-finding—which always seemed to be uttered against his will—as the look in his eyes when he joined her after receiving one of the letters. The look was not unloving, not even indifferent; it was the look of a man who had been so far away from ordinary events that when he returns to familiar things they seem strange. She minded that more than the fault-finding.

Though she had been sure from the first that the handwriting on the grey envelope was a woman's, it was long before she associated the mysterious letters with any sentimental secret. She was too sure of her husband's love, too confident of filling his life, for such an idea to occur to her. It seemed far more likely that the letters—which certainly did not appear to cause him any sentimental pleasure—were addressed to the busy lawyer than to the private person. Probably they were from some tiresome client—women, he had often told her, were nearly always tiresome as clients—who did not want her letters opened by his secretary and therefore had them carried to his house. Yes; but in that case the unknown female must be unusually troublesome, judging from the effect her letters produced. Then again, though his professional discretion was exemplary, it was odd that he had never uttered an impatient comment, never remarked to Charlotte, in a moment of expansion, that there was a nuisance of a woman who kept badgering him about a case that had gone against her. He had made more than one semi-confidence of the kind—of course without giving names or details; but concerning this mysterious correspondent his lips were sealed.

There was another possibility; what is euphemistically called an "old entanglement." Charlotte Ashby was a sophisticated woman. She had few illusions about the intricacies of the human heart; she knew that there were often old entanglements. But when she had married Kenneth Ashby, her friends, instead of hinting at such a possibility, had said: "You've got your work cut out for you. Marrying a Don Juan is a sinecure to it. Kenneth's never looked at another woman since he first saw Elsie Corder. During all the years of their marriage he was more like an unhappy lover than a comfortably contented husband. He'll never let you move an armchair or change the place of a lamp; and whatever you venture to do, he'll mentally compare with what Elsie would have done in your place."

Except for an occasional nervous mistrust as to her ability to manage the children—a mistrust gradually dispelled by her good humour and the children's obvious fondness for her—none of these forebodings had come true. The desolate widower, of whom his nearest friends said that only his absorbing professional interests had kept him from suicide after his first wife's death, had fallen in love, two years later, with Charlotte Gorse, and after an impetuous wooing had married her and carried her off on a tropical honeymoon. And ever since he had been as tender and loverlike as during those first radiant weeks. Before asking her to marry him he had spoken to her frankly of his great love for his first wife and his despair after her sudden death; but even then he had assumed no stricken attitude, or implied that life offered no possibility of renewal. He had been perfectly simple and natural, and had confessed to Charlotte that from the beginning he had hoped the future held new gifts for him. And when, after their marriage, they returned to the house where his twelve years with his first wife had been spent, he had told Charlotte at once that he was sorry he couldn't afford to do the place over for her, but that he knew every woman had her own views about furniture and all sorts of household arrangements a man would never notice, and had begged her to make any changes she saw fit without bothering to consult him. As a result, she made as few as possible; but his way of beginning their new life in the old setting was so frank and unembarrassed that it put her immediately at her ease, and she was almost sorry to find that the portrait of Elsie Ashby, which used to hang over the desk in his library, had been transferred in their absence to the children's nursery. Knowing herself to be the indirect cause of this banishment, she spoke of it to her husband; but he answered: " Oh, I thought they ought to grow up with her looking down on them." The answer moved Charlotte, and satisfied her; and as time went by she had to confess that she felt more at home in her house, more at ease and in confidence with her husband, since that long coldly beautiful face on the library wall no longer followed her with guarded eyes. It was as if Kenneth's love had penetrated to the secret she hardly acknowledged to her own heart—her passionate need to feel herself the sovereign even of his past.

With all this stored-up happiness to sustain her, it was curious that she had lately found herself yielding to a nervous apprehension. But there the apprehension was; and on this particular afternoon—perhaps because she was more tired than usual, or because of the trouble of finding a new cook or, for some other ridiculously trivial reason, moral or physical —she found herself unable to react against the feeling. Latch-key in hand, she looked back down the silent street to the whirl and illumination of the great thoroughfare beyond, and up at the sky already aflare with the city's nocturnal life. " Outside there," she thought, " sky-scrapers, advertisements, telephones, wireless, aeroplanes, movies, motors, and all the rest of the twentieth century; and on the other side of the door something I can't explain, can't relate to them. Something as old as the world, as mysterious as life.... Nonsense! What am I worrying about? There hasn't been a letter for three months now—not since the day we came back from the country after Christmas. ... Queer that they always seem to come after our holidays!... Why should I imagine there's going to be one to-night!"

No reason why, but that was the worst of it—one of the worsts!—that there were days when she would stand there cold and shivering with the premonition of something inexplicable, intolerable, to be faced on the other side of the curtained panes; and when she opened the door and went in, there would be nothing; and on other days when she felt the same premonitory chill, it was justified by the sight of the grey envelope. So that ever since the last had come she had taken to feeling cold and premonitory every evening, because she never opened the door without thinking the letter might be there.

Well, she'd had enough of it; that was certain. She couldn't go on like that. If her husband turned white and had a headache on the days when the letter came, he seemed to recover afterward; but she couldn't. With her the strain had become chronic, and the reason was not far to seek. Her husband knew from whom the letter came and what was in it; he was prepared beforehand for whatever he had to deal with, and master of the situation, however bad; whereas she was shut out in the dark with her conjectures.

"I can't stand it! I can't stand it another day!" she exclaimed aloud, as she put her key in the lock. She turned the key and went in; and there, on the table, lay the letter.

II

She was almost glad of the sight. It seemed to justify everything, to put a seal of definiteness on the whole blurred business. A letter for her husband; a letter from a woman —no doubt another vulgar case of "old entanglement." What a fool she had been ever to doubt it, to rack her brains for less obvious explanations! She took up the envelope with a steady contemptuous hand, looked closely at the faint letters, held it against the light and just discerned the outline of the folded sheet within. She knew that now she would have no peace till she found out what was written on that sheet.

Her husband had not come in; he seldom got back from his office before half-past six or seven, and it was not yet six. She would have time to take the letter up to the drawing-room, hold it over the tea-kettle which at that hour always simmered by the fire in expectation of her return, solve the mystery and replace the letter where she had found it. No one would be the wiser, and her gnawing uncertainty would be over. The alternative, of course, was to question her husband; but to do that seemed even more difficult. She weighed the letter between thumb and finger, looked at it again under the light, started up the stairs with the envelope —and came down again and laid it on the table.

"No, I evidently can't," she said, disappointed.

What should she do, then? She couldn't go up alone to that warm welcoming room, pour out her tea, look over her correspondence, glance at a book or review—not with that letter lying below and the knowledge that in a little while her husband would come in, open it and turn into the library alone, as he always did on the days when the grey envelope came.

Suddenly she decided. She would wait in the library and see for herself; see what happened between him and the letter when they thought themselves unobserved. She wondered the idea had never occurred to her before. By leaving the door ajar, and sitting in the corner behind it, she could watch him unseen. . . . Well, then, she would watch him! She drew a chair into the corner, sat down, her eyes on the crack, and waited.

As far as she could remember, it was the first time she had ever tried to surprise another person's secret, but she was conscious of no compunction. She simply felt as if she were fighting her way through a stifling fog that she must at all costs get out of.

At length she heard Kenneth's latchkey and jumped up. The impulse to rush out and meet him had nearly made her forget why she was there; but she remembered in time and sat down again. From her post she covered the whole range of his movements—saw him enter the hall, draw the key from the door and take off his hat and overcoat. Then he turned to throw his gloves on the hall table, and at that moment he saw the envelope. The light was full on his face, and what Charlotte first noted there was a look of surprise. Evidently he had not expected the letter—had not thought of the possibility of its being there that day. But though he had not expected it, now that he saw it he knew well enough what it contained. He did not open it immediately, but stood motionless, the colour slowly ebbing from his face. Apparently he could not make up his mind to touch it; but at length he put out his hand, opened the envelope, and moved with it to the light. In doing so he turned his back on Charlotte, and she saw only his bent head and slightly stooping shoulders. Apparently all the writing was on one page, for he did not turn the sheet but continued to stare at it for so long that he must have re-read it a dozen times—or so it seemed to the woman breathlessly watching him. At length she saw him move; he raised the letter still closer to his eyes, as though he had not fully deciphered it. Then he lowered his head, and she saw his lips touch the sheet.

"Kenneth!" she exclaimed, and went out into the hall.

The letter clutched in his hand, her husband turned and looked at her. "Where were you?" he said, in a low bewildered voice, like a man waked out of his sleep.

"In the library, waiting for you." She tried to steady her voice: "What's the matter! What's in that letter? You look ghastly."

Her agitation seemed to calm him, and he instantly put the envelope into his pocket with a slight laugh. "Ghastly? I'm sorry. I've had a hard day in the office—one or two complicated cases. I look dog-tired, I suppose."

"You didn't look tired when you came in. It was only when you opened that letter——"

He had followed her into the library, and they stood gazing at each other. Charlotte noticed how quickly he had regained his self-control; his profession had trained him to rapid mastery of face and voice. She saw at once that she would be at a disadvantage in any attempt to surprise his secret, but at the same moment she lost all desire to manœuvre, to trick him into betraying anything he wanted to conceal. Her wish was still to penetrate the mystery, but only that she might help him to bear the burden it implied. "Even if it *is* another woman," she thought.

"Kenneth," she said, her heart beating excitedly, "I waited here on purpose to see you come in. I wanted to watch you while you opened that letter."

His face, which had paled, turned to dark red; then it paled again. "That letter? Why especially that letter?"

"Because I've noticed that whenever one of those letters comes it seems to have such a strange effect on you."

A line of anger she had never seen before came out between his eyes, and she said to herself: "The upper part of his face is too narrow; this is the first time I ever noticed it."

She heard him continue, in the cool and faintly ironic tone of the prosecuting lawyer making a point: "Ah; so you're in the habit of watching people open their letters when they don't know you're there?"

"Not in the habit. I never did such a thing before. But I had to find out what she writes to you, at regular intervals, in those grey envelopes."

He weighed this for a moment; then: "The intervals have not been regular," he said.

"Oh, I daresay you've kept a better account of the dates than I have," she retorted, her magnanimity vanishing at his tone. "All I know is that every time that woman writes to you——"

"Why do you assume it's a woman?"

"It's a woman's writing. Do you deny it?"

He smiled. "No, I don't deny it. I asked only because the writing is generally supposed to look more like a man's."

Charlotte passed this over impatiently. "And this woman—what does she write to you about?"

Again he seemed to consider a moment. "About business."

"Legal business?"

"In a way, yes. Business in general."

"You look after her affairs for her?"

"Yes."

"You've looked after them for a long time?"

"Yes. A very long time."

"Kenneth, dearest, won't you tell me who she is?"

"No. I can't." He paused, and brought out, as if with a certain hesitation: "Professional secrecy."

The blood rushed from Charlotte's heart to her temples. "Don't say that—don't!"

"Why not?"

"Because I saw you kiss the letter."

The effect of the words was so disconcerting that she instantly repented having spoken them. Her husband, who had submitted to her cross-questioning with a sort of contemptuous composure, as though he were humouring an unreasonable child, turned on her a face of terror and distress. For a minute he seemed unable to speak; then, collecting himself with an effort, he stammered out: "The writing is very faint; you must have seen me holding the letter close to my eyes to try to decipher it."

"No; I saw you kissing it." He was silent. "Didn't I see you kissing it?"

He sank back into indifference. "Perhaps."

"Kenneth! You stand there and say that—to me?"

"What possible difference can it make to you? The letter is on business, as I told you. Do you suppose I'd lie about it? The writer is a very old friend whom I haven't seen for a long time."

"Men don't kiss business letters, even from women who are very old friends, unless they have been their lovers, and still regret them."

He shrugged his shoulders slightly and turned away, as if he considered the discussion at an end and were faintly disgusted at the turn it had taken.

"Kenneth!" Charlotte moved towards him and caught hold of his arm.

He paused with a look of weariness and laid his hand over hers. "Won't you believe me?" he asked gently.

"How can I? I've watched these letters come to you—for months now they've been coming. Ever since we came back from the West Indies—one of them greeted me the very day we arrived. And after each one of them I see their mysterious effect on you, I see you disturbed, unhappy, as if someone were trying to estrange you from me."

"No, dear; not that. Never!"

She drew back and looked at him with passionate entreaty. "Well, then, prove it to me, darling. It's so easy!"

He forced a smile. "It's not easy to prove anything to a woman who's once taken an idea into her head."

"You've only got to show me the letter."

His hand slipped from hers and he drew back and shook his head.

"You won't?"

"I can't."

"Then the woman who wrote it is your mistress."

"No, dear. No."

"Not now, perhaps. I suppose she's trying to get you back, and you're struggling, out of pity for me. My poor Kenneth!"

"I swear to you she never was my mistress."

Charlotte felt the tears rushing to her eyes. "Ah, that's worse, then—that's hopeless! The prudent ones are the kind that keep their hold on a man. We all know that." She lifted her hands and hid her face in them.

Her husband remained silent; he offered neither consolation nor denial, and at length, wiping away her tears, she raised her eyes almost timidly to his.

"Kenneth, think! We've been married such a short time. Imagine what you're making me suffer. You say you can't show me this letter. You refuse even to explain it."

"I've told you the letter is on business. I will swear to that too."

"A man will swear to anything to screen a woman. If you want me to believe you, at least tell me her name. If you'll do that, I promise you I won't ask to see the letter."

There was a long interval of suspense, during which she felt her heart beating against her ribs in quick admonitory knocks, as if warning her of the danger she was incurring.

"I can't," he said at length.

"Not even her name?"

"No."

"You can't tell me anything more?"

"No."

Again a pause; this time they seemed both to have reached the end of their arguments and to be helplessly facing each other across a baffling waste of incomprehension.

Charlotte stood breathing rapidly, her hands against her breast. She felt as if she had run a hard race and missed the goal. She had meant to move her husband and had succeeded only in irritating him; and this error of reckoning seemed to change him into a stranger, a mysterious incomprehensible being whom no argument or entreaty of hers could reach. The curious thing was that she was aware in him of no hostility or even impatience, but only of a remoteness, an inaccessibility, far more difficult to overcome. She felt herself excluded, ignored, blotted out of his life. But after a moment or two, looking at him more calmly, she saw that he was suffering as much as she was. His distant guarded face was drawn with pain; the coming of the grey envelope, though it always cast a shadow, had never marked him as deeply as this discussion with his wife.

Charlotte took heart; perhaps, after all, she had not spent her last shaft. She drew nearer and once more laid her hand on his arm. "Poor Kenneth! If you knew how sorry I am for you——"

She thought he winced slightly at this expression of sympathy, but he took her hand and pressed it.

"I can think of nothing worse than to be incapable of loving long," she continued; "to feel the beauty of a great love and to be too unstable to bear its burden."

He turned on her a look of wistful reproach. "Oh, don't say that of me. Unstable!"

She felt herself at last on the right tack, and her voice trembled with excitement as she went on: "Then what about me and this other woman? Haven't you already forgotten Elsie twice within a year?"

She seldom pronounced his first wife's name; it did not come naturally to her tongue. She flung it out now as if she were flinging some dangerous explosive into the open space between them, and drew back a step, waiting to hear the mine go off.

Her husband did not move; his expression grew sadder, but showed no resentment. "I have never forgotten Elsie," he said.

Charlotte could not repress a faint laugh. "Then, you poor dear, between the three of us——"

"There are not——" he began; and then broke off and put his hand to his forehead.

"Not what?"

"I'm sorry; I don't believe I know what I'm saying. I've got a blinding headache." He looked wan and furrowed enough for the statement to be true, but she was exasperated by his evasion.

"Ah, yes! the grey-envelope headache!"

She saw the surprise in his eyes. "I'd forgotten how closely I've been watched," he said coldly. "If you'll excuse me, I think I'll go up and try an hour in the dark, to see if I can get rid of this neuralgia."

She wavered: then she said, with desperate resolution: "I'm sorry your head aches. But before you go I want to say that sooner or later this question must be settled between us. Someone is trying to separate us, and I don't care what it costs me to find out who it is." She looked him steadily in the eyes. "If it costs me your love, I don't care! If I can't have your confidence I don't want anything from you."

He still looked at her wistfully. "Give me time."

"Time for what? It's only a word to say."

"Time to show you that you haven't lost my love or my confidence."

"Well, I'm waiting."

He turned towards the door, and then glanced back hesitatingly. "Oh, do wait, my love," he said, and went out of the room.

She heard his tired step on the stairs and the closing of his bedroom door above. Then she dropped into a chair and buried her face in her folded arms. Her first movement was one of compunction: she seemed to herself to have been hard, unhuman, unimaginative. "Think of telling him that I didn't care if my insistence cost me his love! The lying rubbish!" She started up to follow him and unsay the meaningless words. But she was checked by a reflection. He had had his way, after all; he had eluded all attacks on his secret, and now he was shut up alone in his room, reading that other woman's letter.

III

She was still reflecting on this when the surprised parlourmaid came in and found her. No, Charlotte said, she wasn't going to dress for dinner; Mr. Ashby didn't want to dine. He was very tired and had gone up to his room to rest; later she would have something brought on a tray to the drawing-room. She mounted the stairs to her bedroom. Her dinner dress was lying on the bed, and at the sight the quiet routine of her daily life took hold of her and she began to feel as if the strange talk she had just had with her husband must have taken place in another world, between two beings who were not Charlotte Gorse and Kenneth Ashby, but phantoms projected by her fevered imagination. She recalled the year since her marriage—her husband's constant devotion; his persistent, almost too insistent tenderness; the feeling he had given her at times of being too eagerly dependent on her, too searchingly close to her, as if there were not air enough between her soul and his. It seemed preposterous, as she recalled all this, that a few moments ago she should have been accusing him of an intrigue with another woman! But, then, what——

Again she was moved by the impulse to go up to him, beg his pardon and try to laugh away the misunderstanding. But she was restrained by the fear of forcing herself upon his privacy. He was troubled and unhappy, oppressed by some grief or fear; and he had shown her that he wanted to fight out his battle alone. It would be wiser, as well as more generous, to respect his wish. Only, how strange, how unbearable, to be there, in the next room to his, and feel herself at the other end of the world! In her nervous agitation she almost regretted not having had the courage to open the letter and put it back on the hall table before he came in. At least she would have known what his secret was, and the bogy might have been laid. For she was beginning now to think of the mystery as something conscious, malevolent: a secret persecution before which he quailed, yet from which he could not free himself. Once or twice in his evasive eyes she thought she had detected a desire for help, an impulse of confession, instantly restrained and suppressed. It was as if he felt she could have helped him if she had known, and yet had been unable to tell her!

There flashed through her mind the idea of going to his mother. She was very fond of old Mrs. Ashby, a firm-fleshed clear-eyed old lady, with an astringent bluntness of speech which responded to the forthright and simple in Charlotte's own nature. There had been a tacit bond between them ever since the day when Mrs. Ashby senior, coming to lunch for the first time with her new daughter-in-law, had been received by Charlotte downstairs in the library, and glancing up at the empty wall above her son's desk, had remarked laconically: "Elsie gone, eh?" adding, at Charlotte's murmured explanation: "Nonsense. Don't have her back. Two's company." Charlotte, at this reading of her thoughts, could hardly refrain from exchanging a smile of complicity with her mother-in-law; and it seemed to her now that Mrs. Ashby's almost uncanny directness might pierce to the core of this new mystery. But here again she hesitated, for the idea almost suggested a betrayal. What right had she to call in any one, even so close a relation, to surprise a secret which her husband was trying to keep from her? "Perhaps, by and by, he'll talk to his mother of his own accord," she thought, and then ended: "But what does it matter? He and I must settle it between us."

She was still brooding over the problem when there was a knock on the door and her husband came in. He was dressed for dinner and seemed surprised to see her sitting there, with her evening dress lying unheeded on the bed.

"Aren't you coming down?"

"I thought you were not well and had gone to bed," she faltered.

He forced a smile. "I'm not particularly well, but we'd better go down." His face, though still drawn, looked calmer than when he had fled upstairs an hour earlier.

"There it is; he knows what's in the letter and has fought his battle out again, whatever it is," she reflected, "while I'm still in darkness." She rang and gave a hurried order that dinner should be served as soon as possible—just a short meal, whatever could be got ready quickly, as both she and Mr. Ashby were rather tired and not very hungry.

Dinner was announced, and they sat down to it. At first neither seemed able to find a word to say; then Ashby began to make conversation with an assumption of ease that was more oppressive than his silence. "How tired he is! How terribly over-tired!" Charlotte said to herself, pursuing her own thoughts while he rambled on about municipal politics, aviation, an exhibition of modern French painting, the health of an old aunt and the installing of the automatic telephone. "Good heavens, how tired he is!"

When they dined alone they usually went into the library after dinner, and Charlotte curled herself up on the divan with her knitting while he settled down in his armchair under the lamp and lit a pipe. But this evening, by tacit agreement, they avoided the room in which their strange talk had taken place, and went up to Charlotte's drawing-room.

They sat down near the fire, and Charlotte said: "Your pipe?" after he had put down his hardly tasted coffee.

He shook his head. "No, not to-night."

"You must go to bed early; you look terribly tired. I'm sure they overwork you at the office."

"I suppose we all overwork at times."

She rose and stood before him with sudden resolution. "Well, I'm not going to have you use up your strength slaving in that way. It's absurd. I can see you're ill." She bent over him and laid her hand on his forehead. "My poor old Kenneth. Prepare to be taken away soon on a long holiday."

He looked up at her, startled. "A holiday?"

"Certainly. Didn't you know I was going to carry you off at Easter? We're going to start in a fortnight on a month's voyage to somewhere or other. On any one of the big cruising steamers." She paused and bent closer, touching his forehead with her lips. "I'm tired, too, Kenneth."

He seemed to pay no heed to her last words, but sat, his hands on his knees, his head drawn back a little from her caress, and looked up at her with a stare of apprehension. "Again? My dear, we can't; I can't possibly go away."

"I don't know why you say 'again,' Kenneth; we haven't taken a real holiday this year."

"At Christmas we spent a week with the children in the country."

"Yes, but this time I mean away from the children, from servants, from the house. From everything that's familiar and fatiguing. Your mother will love to have Joyce and Peter with her."

He frowned and slowly shook his head. "No, dear; I can't leave them with my mother."

"Why, Kenneth, how absurd! She adores them. You didn't hesitate to leave them with her for over two months when we went to the West Indies."

He drew a deep breath and stood up uneasily. "That was different."

"Different? Why?"

"I mean, at that time I didn't realise——" He broke off as if to choose his words and then went on: "My mother adores the children, as you say. But she isn't always very judicious. Grandmothers always spoil children. And she sometimes talks before them without thinking." He turned to his wife with an almost pitiful gesture of entreaty. "Don't ask me to, dear."

Charlotte mused. It was true that the elder Mrs. Ashby had a fearless tongue, but she was the last woman in the world to say or hint anything before her grandchildren at which the most scrupulous parent could take offence. Charlotte looked at her husband in perplexity.

"I don't understand."

He continued to turn on her the same troubled and entreating gaze. "Don't try to," he muttered.

"Not try to?"

"Not now—not yet." He put up his hands and pressed them against his temples. "Can't you see that there's no use in insisting? I can't go away, no matter how much I might want to."

Charlotte still scrutinised him gravely. "The question is, *do* you want to?"

He returned her gaze for a moment; then his lips began to tremble, and he said, hardly above his breath: "I want—anything you want."

"And yet——"

"Don't ask me. I can't leave—I can't!"

"You mean that you can't go away out of reach of those letters!"

Her husband had been standing before her in an uneasy half-hesitating attitude; now he turned abruptly away and walked once or twice up and down the length of the room, his head bent, his eyes fixed on the carpet.

Charlotte felt her resentfulness rising with her fears. "It's that," she persisted. "Why not admit it? You can't live without them."

He continued his troubled pacing of the room; then he stopped short, dropped into a chair and covered his face with his hands. From the shaking of his shoulders, Charlotte saw that he was weeping. She had never seen a man cry, except her father after her mother's death, when she was a little girl; and she remembered still how the sight had frightened her. She was frightened now; she felt that her husband was being dragged away from her into some mysterious bondage, and that she must use up her last atom of strength in the struggle for his freedom, and for hers.

"Kenneth—Kenneth!" she pleaded, kneeling down beside him. "Won't you listen to me? Won't you try to see what I'm suffering? I'm not unreasonable, darling; really not. I don't suppose I should ever have noticed the letters if it hadn't been for their effect on you. It's not my way to pry into other people's affairs; and even if the effect had been different—yes, yes; listen to me—if I'd seen that the letters made you happy, that you were watching eagerly for them, counting the days between their coming, that you wanted them, that they gave you something I haven't known how to give—why, Kenneth, I don't say I shouldn't have suffered from that, too; but it would have been in a different way, and I should have had the courage to hide what I felt, and the hope that some day you'd come to feel about me as you did about the writer of the letters. But what I can't bear is to see how you dread them, how they make you suffer, and yet how you can't live without them and won't go away lest you should miss one during your absence. Or perhaps," she added—her voice breaking into a cry of accusation—" perhaps it's because she's actually forbidden you to leave. Kenneth, you must answer me! Is that the reason? Is it because she's forbidden you that you won't go away with me?"

She continued to kneel at his side, and raising her hands, she drew his gently down. She was ashamed of her persistence, ashamed of uncovering that baffled disordered face, yet resolved that no such scruples should arrest her. His eyes were lowered, the muscles of his face quivered; she w[illegible] making him suffer even more than she suffered herself. [illegible] this no longer restrained her.

" Kenneth, is it that? She won't let us go away together?"

Still he did not speak or turn his eyes to her; and a sense of defeat swept over her. After all, she thought, the struggle was a losing one. " You needn't answer. I see I'm right," she said.

Suddenly, as she rose, he turned and drew her down again. His hands caught hers and pressed them so tightly that she felt her rings cutting into her flesh. There was something frightened, convulsive in his hold; it was the clutch of a man who felt himself slipping over a precipice. He was staring up at her now as if salvation lay in the face she bent above him. " Of course we'll go away together. We'll go wherever you want," he said in a low confused voice; and putting his arm about her, he drew her close and pressed his lips on hers.

IV

Charlotte had said to herself: " I shall sleep to-night," but instead she sat before her fire into the small hours, listening for any sound that came from her husband's room. But he, at any rate, seemed to be resting after the tumult of the evening. Once or twice she stole to the door and in the faint light that came in from the street through his open window she saw him stretched out in heavy sleep—the sleep of weakness and exhaustion. "He's ill," she thought, "he's undoubtedly ill. And it's not overwork; it's this mysterious persecution."

She drew a breath of relief. She had fought through the weary fight and the victory was hers—at least for the moment. If only they could have started at once—started for anywhere! She knew it would be useless to ask him to leave before the holidays; and meanwhile the secret influence—as to which she was still so completely in the dark—would continue to work against her, and she would have to renew the struggle day after day till they started on their journey. But after that everything would be different. If once she could get her husband away under other skies, and all to herself, she never doubted her power to release him from the evil spell he was under. Lulled to quiet by the thought, she too slept at last.

When she woke, it was long past her usual hour, and she sat up in bed surprised and vexed at having overslept herself. She always liked to be down to share her husband's breakfast by the library fire; but a glance at the clock made it clear that he must have started long since for his office. To make sure, she jumped out of bed and went into his room; but it was empty. No doubt he had looked in on her before leaving, seen that she still slept, and gone downstairs without disturbing her; and their relations were sufficiently loverlike for her to regret having missed their morning hour.

She rang and asked if Mr. Ashby had already gone. Yes, nearly an hour ago, the maid said. He had given orders that Mrs. Ashby should not be waked and that the children should not come to her till she sent for them. . . . Yes, he had gone up to the nursery himself to give the order. All this sounded usual enough; and Charlotte hardly knew why she asked: "And did Mr. Ashby leave no other message?"

Yes, the maid said, he did; she was so sorry she'd forgotten. He'd told her, just as he was leaving, to say to Mrs. Ashby that he was going to see about their passages, and would she please be ready to sail to-morrow?

Charlotte echoed the woman's "To-morrow," and sat staring at her incredulously. "To-morrow—you're sure he said to sail to-morrow?"

"Oh, ever so sure, ma'am. I don't know how I could have forgotten to mention it."

"Well, it doesn't matter. Draw my bath, please." Charlotte sprang up, dashed through her dressing, and caught herself singing at her image in the glass as she sat brushing her hair. It made her feel young again to have scored such a victory. The other woman vanished to a speck on the horizon, as this one, who ruled the foreground, smiled back at the reflection of her lips and eyes. He loved her, then—he loved her as passionately as ever. He had divined what she had suffered, had understood that their happiness depended on their getting away at once, and finding each other again after yesterday's desperate groping in the fog. The nature of the influence that had come between them did not much matter to Charlotte now; she had faced the phantom and dispelled it. "Courage—that's the secret! If only people who are in love weren't always so afraid of risking their happiness by looking it in the eyes." As she brushed back her light abundant hair it waved electrically above her head, like the palms of victory. Ah, well, some women knew how to manage men, and some didn't—and only the fair—she gaily paraphrased—deserve the brave! Certainly she was looking very pretty.

The morning danced along like a cockleshell on a bright sea—such a sea as they would soon be speeding over. She ordered a particularly good dinner, saw the children off to their classes, had her trunks brought down, consulted with the maid about getting out summer clothes—for of course they would be heading for heat and sunshine—and wondered if she oughtn't to take Kenneth's flannel suits out of camphor. "But how absurd," she reflected, "that I don't yet know where we're going!" She looked at the clock, saw that it was close on noon, and decided to call him up at his office. There was a slight delay; then she heard his secretary's voice saying that Mr. Ashby had looked in for a moment early, and left again almost immediately. . . . Oh, very well; Charlotte would ring up later. How soon was he likely to be back? The secretary answered that she couldn't tell; all they knew in the office was that when he left he had said he was in a hurry because he had to go out of town.

Out of town! Charlotte hung up the receiver and sat blankly gazing into new darkness. Why had he gone out of town? And where had he gone? And of all days, why should he have chosen the eve of their suddenly planned departure? She felt a faint shiver of apprehension. Of course he had gone to see that woman—no doubt to get her permission to leave. He was as completely in bondage as that; and Charlotte had been fatuous enough to see the palms of victory on her forehead. She burst into a laugh and, walking across the room, sat down again before her mirror. What a different face she saw! The smile on her pale lips seemed to mock the rosy vision of the other Charlotte. But gradually her colour crept back. After all, she had a right to claim the victory, since her husband was doing what she wanted, not what the other woman exacted of him. It was natural enough, in view of his abrupt decision to leave the next day, that he should have arrangements to make, business matters to wind up; it was not even necessary to suppose that his mysterious trip was a visit to the writer of the letters. He might simply have gone to see a client who lived out of town. Of course they would not tell Charlotte at the office; the secretary had hesitated before imparting even such meagre information as the fact of Mr. Ashby's absence. Meanwhile she would go on with her joyful preparations, content to learn later in the day to what particular island of the blest she was to be carried.

The hours wore on, or rather were swept forward on a rush of eager preparations. At last the entrance of the maid who came to draw the curtains roused Charlotte from her labours, and she saw to her surprise that the clock marked five. And she did not yet know where they were going the next day! She rang up her husband's office and was told that Mr. Ashby had not been there since the early morning. She asked for his partner, but the partner could add nothing to her information, for he himself, his suburban train having been behind time, had reached the office after Ashby had come and gone. Charlotte stood perplexed; then she decided to telephone to her mother-in-law. Of course Kenneth, on the eve of a month's absence, must have gone to see his mother. The mere fact that the children—in spite of his vague objections—would certainly have to be left with old Mrs. Ashby, made it obvious that he would have all sorts of matters to decide with her. At another time Charlotte might have felt a little hurt at being excluded from their conference, but nothing mattered now but that she had won the day, that her husband was still hers and not another woman's. Gaily she called up Mrs. Ashby, heard her friendly voice, and began: "Well, did Kenneth's news surprise you? What do you think of our elopement?"

Almost instantly, before Mrs. Ashby could answer, Charlotte knew what her reply would be. Mrs. Ashby had not seen her son, she had had no word from him and did not know what her daughter-in-law meant. Charlotte stood silent in the intensity of her surprise. "But then, where *has* he been?" she thought. Then, recovering herself, she explained their sudden decision to Mrs. Ashby, and in doing so, gradually regained her own self-confidence, her conviction that nothing could ever again come between Kenneth and herself. Mrs. Ashby took the news calmly and approvingly. She, too, had thought that Kenneth looked worried and overtired, and she agreed with her daughter-in-law that in such cases change was the surest remedy. "I'm always so glad when he gets away. Elsie hated travelling; she was always finding pretexts to prevent his going anywhere. With you, thank goodness, it's different." Nor was Mrs. Ashby surprised at his not having had time to let her know of his departure. He must have been in a rush from the moment the decision was taken; but no doubt he'd drop in before dinner. Five minutes' talk was really all they needed. "I hope you'll gradually cure Kenneth of his mania for going over and over a question that could be settled in a dozen words. He never used to be like that, and if he carried the habit into his professional work he'd soon lose all his clients. . . . Yes, do come in for a minute, dear, if you have time; no doubt he'll turn up while you're here." The tonic ring of Mrs. Ashby's voice echoed on reassuringly in the silent room while Charlotte continued her preparations.

Towards seven the telephone rang, and she darted to it. Now she would know! But it was only from the conscientious secretary, to say that Mr. Ashby hadn't been back, or sent any word, and before the office closed she thought she ought to let Mrs. Ashby know. "Oh, that's all right. Thanks a lot!" Charlotte called out cheerfully, and hung up the receiver with a trembling hand. But perhaps by this time, she reflected, he was at his mother's. She shut her drawers and cupboards, put on her hat and coat and called up to the nursery that she was going out for a minute to see the children's grandmother.

Mrs. Ashby lived near by, and during her brief walk through the cold spring dusk Charlotte imagined that every advancing figure was her husband's. But she did not meet him on the way, and when she entered the house she found her mother-in-law alone. Kenneth had neither telephoned nor come. Old Mrs. Ashby sat by her bright fire, her knitting needles flashing steadily through her active old hands, and her mere bodily presence gave reassurance to Charlotte. Yes, it was certainly odd that Kenneth had gone off for the whole day without letting any of them know; but, after all, it was to be expected. A busy lawyer held so many threads in his hands that any sudden change of plan would oblige him to make all sorts of unforeseen arrangements and adjustments. He might have gone to see some client in the suburbs and been detained there; his mother remembered his telling her that he had charge of the legal business of a queer old recluse somewhere in New Jersey, who was immensely rich but too mean to have a telephone. Very likely Kenneth had been stranded there.

But Charlotte felt her nervousness gaining on her. When Mrs. Ashby asked her at what hour they were sailing the next day and she had to say she didn't know—that Kenneth had simply sent her word he was going to take their passages—the uttering of the words again brought home to her the strangeness of the situation. Even Mrs. Ashby conceded that it was odd; but she immediately added that it only showed what a rush he was in.

"But, mother, it's nearly eight o'clock! He must realise that I've got to know when we're starting to-morrow."

"Oh, the boat probably doesn't sail till evening. Sometimes they have to wait till midnight for the tide. Kenneth's probably counting on that. After all, he has a level head."

Charlotte stood up. "It's not that. Something has happened to him."

Mrs. Ashby took off her spectacles and rolled up her knitting. "If you begin to let yourself imagine things——"

"Aren't you in the least anxious?"

"I never am till I have to be. I wish you'd ring for dinner, my dear. You'll stay and dine? He's sure to drop in here on his way home."

Charlotte called up her own house. No, the maid said, Mr. Ashby hadn't come in and hadn't telephoned. She would tell him as soon as he came that Mrs. Ashby was dining at his mother's. Charlotte followed her mother-in-law into the dining-room and sat with parched throat before her empty plate, while Mrs. Ashby dealt calmly and efficiently with a short but carefully prepared repast. "You'd better eat something, child, or you'll be as bad as Kenneth. . . . Yes, a little more asparagus, please, Jane."

She insisted on Charlotte drinking a glass of sherry and nibbling a bit of toast; then they returned to the drawing-room, where the fire had been made up, and the cushions in Mrs. Ashby's armchair shaken out and smoothed. How safe and familiar it all looked; and out there, somewhere in the uncertainty and mystery of the night, lurked the answer to the two women's conjectures, like an indistinguishable figure prowling on the threshold.

At last Charlotte got up and said: "I'd better go back. At this hour Kenneth will certainly go straight home."

Mrs. Ashby smiled indulgently. "It's not very late, my dear. It doesn't take two sparrows long to dine."

"It's after nine." Charlotte bent down to kiss her. "The fact is, I can't keep still."

Mrs. Ashby pushed aside her work and rested her two hands on the arms of her chair. "I'm going with you," she said, helping herself up.

Charlotte protested that it was too late, that it was not

necessary, that she would call up as soon as Kenneth came in, but Mrs. Ashby had already rung for her maid. She was slightly lame, and stood resting on her stick while her wraps were brought. "If Mr. Kenneth turns up, tell him he'll find me at his own house," she instructed the maid as the two women got into the taxi which had been summoned. During the short drive Charlotte gave thanks that she was not returning home alone. There was something warm and substantial in the mere fact of Mrs. Ashby's nearness, something that corresponded with the clearness of her eyes and the texture of her fresh firm complexion. As the taxi drew up she laid her hand encouragingly on Charlotte's. "You'll see; there'll be a message."

The door opened at Charlotte's ring and the two entered. Charlotte's heart beat excitedly; the stimulus of her mother-in-law's confidence was beginning to flow through her veins.

"You'll see—you'll see," Mrs. Ashby repeated.

The maid who opened the door said no, Mr. Ashby had not come in, and there had been no message from him.

"You're sure the telephone's not out of order?" his mother suggested; and the maid said, well, it certainly wasn't half an hour ago; but she'd just go and ring up to make sure. She disappeared, and Charlotte turned to take off her hat and cloak. As she did so her eyes lit on the hall table, and there lay a grey envelope, her husband's name faintly traced on it. "Oh!" she cried out, suddenly aware that for the first time in months she had entered her house without wondering if one of the grey letters would be there.

"What is it, my dear?" Mrs. Ashby asked with a glance of surprise.

Charlotte did not answer. She took up the envelope and stood staring at it as if she could force her gaze to penetrate to what was within. Then an idea occurred to her. She turned and held out the envelope to her mother-in-law.

"Do you know that writing?" she asked.

Mrs. Ashby took the letter. She had to feel with her other hand for her eyeglasses, and when she had adjusted them she lifted the envelope to the light. "Why!" she exclaimed; and then stopped. Charlotte noticed that the letter shook in her usually firm hand. "But this is addressed to Kenneth," Mrs. Ashby said at length, in a low voice. Her tone seemed to imply that she felt her daughter-in-law's question to be slightly indiscreet.

"Yes, but no matter," Charlotte spoke with sudden deci-
"I want to know—do you know the writing?"

Mrs. Ashby handed back the letter. "No," she said distinctly.

The two women had turned into the library. Charlotte switched on the electric light and shut the door. She still held the envelope in her hand.

"I'm going to open it," she announced.

She caught her mother-in-law's startled glance. "But, dearest—a letter not addressed to you? My dear, you can't!"

"As if I cared about that—now!" She continued to look intently at Mrs. Ashby. "This letter may tell me where Kenneth is."

Mrs. Ashby's glossy bloom was effaced by a quick pallor; her firm cheeks seemed to shrink and wither. "Why should it? What makes you believe—— It can't possibly——"

Charlotte held her eyes steadily on that altered face. "Ah, then you *do* know the writing?" she flashed back.

"Know the writing? How should I? With all my son's correspondents. . . . What I do know is——" Mrs. Ashby broke off and looked at her daughter-in-law entreatingly, almost timidly.

Charlotte caught her by the wrist. "Mother! What do you know? Tell me! You must!"

"That I don't believe any good ever came of a woman's opening her husband's letters behind his back."

The words sounded to Charlotte's irritated ears as flat as a phrase culled from a book of moral axioms. She laughed impatiently and dropped her mother-in-law's wrist. "Is that all? No good can come of this letter, opened or unopened. I know that well enough. But whatever ill comes, I mean to find out what's in it." Her hands had been trembling as they held the envelope, but now they grew firm, and her voice also. She still gazed intently at Mrs. Ashby. "This is the ninth letter addressed in the same hand that has come for Kenneth since we've been married. Always these same grey envelopes. I've kept count of them because after each one he has been like a man who has had some dreadful shock. It takes him hours to shake off their effect. I've told him so. I've told him I must know from whom they come, because I can see they're killing him. He won't answer my questions; he says he can't tell me anything about the letters; but last night he promised to go away with me—to get away from them."

Mrs. Ashby, with shaking steps, had gone to one of the armchairs and sat down in it, her head drooping forward on her breast. "Ah," she murmured.

"So now you understand——"

" Did he tell you it was to get away from them? "

" He said, to get away—to get away. He was sobbing so that he could hardly speak. But I told him I knew that was why."

" And what did he say? "

" He took me in his arms and said he'd go wherever I wanted."

" Ah, thank God! " said Mrs. Ashby. There was a silence, during which she continued to sit with bowed head, and eyes averted from her daughter-in-law. At last she looked up and spoke. " Are you sure there have been as many as nine? "

" Perfectly. This is the ninth. I've kept count."

" And he has absolutely refused to explain? "

" Absolutely."

Mrs. Ashby spoke through pale contracted lips. " When did they begin to come? Do you remember? "

Charlotte laughed again. " Remember? The first one came the night we got back from our honeymoon."

" All that time? " Mrs. Ashby lifted her head and spoke with sudden energy. " Then—— Yes, open it."

The words were so unexpected that Charlotte felt the blood in her temples, and her hands began to tremble again. She tried to slip her finger under the flap of the envelope, but it was so tightly stuck that she had to hunt on her husband's writing table for his ivory letter-opener. As she pushed about the familiar objects his own hands had so lately touched, they sent through her the icy chill emanating from the little personal effects of someone newly dead. In the deep silence of the room the tearing of the paper as she slit the envelope sounded like a human cry. She drew out the sheet and carried it to the lamp.

" Well? " Mrs. Ashby asked below her breath.

Charlotte did not move or answer. She was bending over the page with wrinkled brows, holding it nearer and nearer to the light. Her sight must be blurred, or else dazzled by the reflection of the lamplight on the smooth surface of the paper, for, strain her eyes as she would, she could discern only a few faint strokes, so faint and faltering as to be nearly undecipherable.

" I can't make it out," she said.

" What do you mean, dear? "

" The writing's too indistinct. . . . Wait."

She went back to the table and, sitting down close to Kenneth's reading lamp, slipped the letter under a magnifying glass. All this time she was aware that her mother-in-law was watching her intently.

"Well?" Mrs. Ashby breathed.

"Well, it's no clearer. I can't read it."

"You mean the paper is an absolute blank?"

"No, not quite. There is writing on it. I can make out something like 'mine'—oh, and 'come.' It might be 'come.'"

Mrs. Ashby stood up abruptly. Her face was even paler than before. She advanced to the table and, resting her two hands on it, drew a deep breath. "Let me see," she said, as if forcing herself to a hateful effort.

Charlotte felt the contagion of her whiteness. "She knows," she thought. She pushed the letter across the table. Her mother-in-law lowered her head over it in silence, but without touching it with her pale wrinkled hands.

Charlotte stood watching her as she herself, when she had tried to read the letter, had been watched by Mrs. Ashby. The latter fumbled for her glasses, held them to her eyes, and bent still closer to the outspread page, in order, as it seemed, to avoid touching it. The light of the lamp fell directly on her old face, and Charlotte reflected what depths of the unknown may lurk under the clearest and most candid lineaments. She had never seen her mother-in-law's features express any but simple and sound emotions—cordiality, amusement, a kindly sympathy; now and again a flash of wholesome anger. Now they seemed to wear a look of fear and hatred, of incredulous dismay and almost cringing defiance. It was as if the spirits warring within her had distorted her face to their own likeness. At length she raised her head. "I can't—I can't," she said in a voice of childish distress.

"You can't make it out either?"

She shook her head, and Charlotte saw two tears roll down her cheeks.

"Familiar as the writing is to you?" Charlotte insisted with twitching lips.

Mrs. Ashby did not take up the challenge. "I can make out nothing—nothing."

"But you do know the writing?"

Mrs. Ashby lifted her head timidly; her anxious eyes stole with a glance of apprehension around the quiet familiar room. "How can I tell? I was startled at first. . . ."

"Startled by the resemblance?"

"Well. I thought——"

"You'd better say it out, mother! You knew at once it was *her* writing?"

"Oh, wait, my dear—wait."

"Wait for what?"

Mrs. Ashby looked up; her eyes, travelling slowly past Charlotte, were lifted to the blank wall behind her son's writing table.

Charlotte, following the glance, burst into a shrill laugh of accusation. "I needn't wait any longer! You've answered me now! You're looking straight at the wall where her picture used to hang!"

Mrs. Ashby lifted her hand with a murmur of warning. "Sh-h."

"Oh, you needn't imagine that anything can ever frighten me again!" Charlotte cried.

Her mother-in-law still leaned against the table. Her lips moved plaintively. "But we're going mad—we're both going mad. We both know such things are impossible."

Her daughter-in-law looked at her with a pitying stare. "I've known for a long time now that everything was possible."

"Even this?"

"Yes, exactly this."

"But this letter—after all, there's nothing in this letter——"

"Perhaps there would be to him. How can I tell? I remember his saying to me once that if you were used to a handwriting the faintest stroke of it became legible. Now I see what he meant. He *was* used to it."

"But the few strokes that I can make out are so pale. No one could possibly read that letter."

Charlotte laughed again. "I suppose everything's pale about a ghost," she said stridently.

"Oh, my child—my child—don't say it!"

"Why shouldn't I say it, when even the bare walls cry it out? What difference does it make if her letters are illegible to you and me? If even you can see her face on that blank wall, why shouldn't he read her writing on this blank paper? Don't you see that she's everywhere in this house, and the closer to him because to everyone else she's become invisible?" Charlotte dropped into a chair and covered her face with her hands. A turmoil of sobbing shook her from head to foot. At length a touch on her shoulder made her look up, and she saw her mother-in-law bending over her. Mrs. Ashby's face seemed to have grown still smaller and more wasted, but it had resumed its usual quiet look. Through all her tossing anguish, Charlotte felt the impact of that resolute spirit.

"To-morrow—to-morrow. You'll see. There'll be some explanation to-morrow."

Charlotte cut her short. "An explanation? Who's going to give it, I wonder?"

Mrs. Ashby drew back and straightened herself heroically.

"Kenneth himself will," she cried out in a strong voice. Charlotte said nothing, and the old woman went on: "But meanwhile we must act; we must notify the police. Now, without a moment's delay. We must do everything—everything."

Charlotte stood up slowly and stiffly; her joints felt as cramped as an old woman's. "Exactly as if we thought it could do any good to do anything?"

Resolutely Mrs. Ashby cried: "Yes!" and Charlotte went up to the telephone and unhooked the receiver.

EDNA FERBER

PERFECTLY INDEPENDENT

MRS. HANAUER and Mrs. Grimm were perfectly independent. Frequently they reminded one another of the fact, and always with pride. They boasted of it to their friends. In hoity-toity moments Mrs. Hanauer said to her daughter and son-in-law (as did Mrs. Grimm to her son and daughter-in-law), "You don't have to look after me. Nobody has to bother about me. I'm perfectly independent."

This precious independence was not the only tie that bound these two in friendship. True, they were sufficiently unlike to prevent boredom. But their lives held much in common. Both were widows. Each dwelt alone, comfortably, occupying two rooms and bath in an expensive family hotel overlooking (to quote the ad.) Central Park. In years both could see the sixties receding as the seventies loomed near. They enjoyed mah jong and bridge, commenting on each other's play with an insulting frankness that, in a professional game of chance, could have been wiped out only with blood. Each used the other as a safety valve. Alternately Mrs. Hanauer bragged and complained to Mrs. Grimm of her daughter and son-in-law. Mrs. Grimm's son and daughter-in-law came in for the same treatment.

In moments of triumph: "You'd think they couldn't do anything without me. It's Mother, what do you think of this, and, Mother, what do you think of that. . . . I told them they didn't want an old woman like me along. But they said, 'All right. If you don't go, then we won't.' . . . Ed sent me two tickets for the matinee. I just happened to say I would like to see that Leonore Ulric. It's got so I can't even mention a thing. The next minute I have it. . . . Bernice brought me these handkerchiefs from Atlantic City. If I've got one I've got a hundred. I said, 'Can't you and Jo even go away over the week-end without thinking you have to bring me something!' She said, 'Why, Mother, it isn't that we think we have to. We love to.' They spoil me. Honestly, you'd think I was . . ."

In other moments: "I told them! If I don't tell them the truth, who will? I said I'd like to know what young married people are thinking of nowadays. I'm not a person to make trouble between husband and wife. And Stella can't say that I ever said a word to turn Ed against her. I hope I'm too modern a mother-in-law for that. But I said to Ed yesterday, I said, 'Ed, mark my words . . .' Of course they're spoiling these children, but you can't make them see that. . . . Well, I didn't say another word. I didn't even dispute her. I turned and marched right out of the house. I had hardly got into the room when the telephone rang and there she was, saying she was sorry, and that she had spoken hastily because she was worried. I told her it was all right, but that I wouldn't take that kind of thing from anybody, daughter or no daughter. I don't have to. I'm perfectly independent."

Characteristically, though each might deplore a shortcoming in one of her own family, no criticism of that family was tolerated in the other. "Oh, that's because you don't really know Bernice. She never was one to make a fuss in public. But she doesn't select a piece of chintz for a bedroom curtain that she doesn't want me to go along to give my opinion."

Side by side, then, with their favourite boast of their own independence was the mythical belief in their families' dependence on them. "The children say it's all right for me to live here alone in the hotel during the winter, if I insist. But in the summer nothing will do but that I've got to be with them, wherever they are." For years, Mrs. Hanauer declared, her daughter's family had gone to the mountains because she, Mrs. Hanauer, could not stand the sea air. Mrs. Grimm, with her son's family, spent the summer months at the seashore because the mountains were bad for her heart.

The hotel apartments of the two women were in the same tier, though Mrs. Grimm's was five floors higher than Mrs. Hanauer's, and costlier. She was the more moneyed. Sitting-room and bedroom of each presented a bewildering diversity of tastes and periods. Some hotel furniture, some saved from their own housekeeping days, some selected by the smartly modern daughter or daughter-in-law. Before their widowhood each had lived in one of those narrow high-stooped houses that line New York's side streets. From these days each had cherished certain pieces of furniture or bric-a-brac grimly Victorian in mould. Relics, Mrs. Hanauer's daughter called them, of the brown stone age.

These were likely to be fat armchairs once dressed like portly dowagers in plush, now rejuvenated and simpering in the flowered ruffles of gay-patterned chintz. A gloomy and hideous lamp-base of the gnarled nineties was topped by a silk shade palpably representing the Madison Avenue taste of a young matron. The whole gave the effect of an old hag tricked out in a garden hat.

There were pert pillows, gay hangings, colourful book-ends quarrelling with dyspeptic old vases and disgruntled desks. A costly and beautiful toilet set of enamel reposed on the broad bosom of a hopelessly old-style bureau. All these odds and ends mingled in a kind of discordant harmony, through which ran the motif of comfort. A Vernis-Martin cabinet, curtained in green, displayed when opened an array of china and silver rather surprising when one remembered that these were non-housekeeping hotel apartments. Mrs. Hanauer or Mrs. Grimm would hasten to explain.

"I never do any cooking in my room. I wouldn't bother. I'm at the children's two nights a week. They'd make me come every night if I would, but I won't. I have these things because I like to feel that I can make myself a cup of tea, without sending downstairs for it. Besides, the stuff they send up! Boiled straw, my daughter-in-law calls it."

The visitor, surveying the chop plates and vegetable dishes and saucers, said of course.

On the dresser in the bedroom and on the mantel in the sitting-room were silver-framed photographs of infants. Mrs. Hanauer and Mrs. Grimm always called attention to these.

"My grandchildren!"

"How lovely! How old are they?"

"Let's see. Junior is fifteen and Sister is going on twelve——"

"But then these pictures must have been taken years ago! They're babies!"

"Oh, yes. They're old pictures. But I like them better than the new ones. I always think of them as babies. They were the cutest babies I ever saw, if I do say so."

"Cuter than your own were?"

"Oh, Ed was the ugliest, blackest little thing you ever saw, and cried day and night. Time I was a bride they didn't know all about babies before they were married. Nowadays girls of sixteen know things a midwife wouldn't talk about."

This last speech could have been uttered only by Mrs. Grimm. She prided herself on her modern outlook, but the truth was that her attitude toward that much-discussed menace known as the younger generation bristled with indignation.

In this, as in many other points, she differed from Mrs. Hanauer. Tiny, dark, nervous, you thought of an intelligent little simian as you saw her quick movements, heard her scolding chatter, watched the darting venom of her deep-set black eyes. Despite her years Mrs. Grimm's hair had remained stubbornly black, except for a reluctant strand here and there at the temples. Her eyebrows, too, were dark and vigorous. This, with her sallow colouring, gave to her a formidable look at variance with the almost childlike smallness of her frame. Quick-tempered, arrogant, she was like a little black-and-tan terrier as she snapped her disapproval.

" Look at that girl! I'll wager she hasn't a stitch on except that flimsy dress and her step-ins. It's disgusting! "

" I think it's grand," Mrs. Hanauer would say.

" What's grand about it, I'd like to know! "

" Oh, healthy—and kind of cute." Helplessly.

" Honestly, Sophy Hanauer, sometimes I think you're not quite bright."

Mrs. Hanauer did not resent this. In fact, her next remark might have been considered quite irrelevant. Certainly the bristling Mrs. Grimm so considered it. What Mrs. Hanauer said was, " I don't like being an old woman any more than you do."

Sophy Hanauer was what is known as easy-going; a delightful quality. Though slightly older than her friend, she actually looked younger by ten years. This, paradoxically enough, in spite of her white hair. Plump cushions of fat, comfortably upholstered her generous old frame. Her skin had been lovely in her girlhood and still was fine and soft. She was not above using a dash of rouge to heighten the effect of her white hair, of which she was very proud. She was quite finicking about the bluing in the rinsing water when she had her hair shampooed, at the Beth Beautye Shoppe on Broadway, near Seventy-fourth.

Her son-in-law called her the Sport. He was fond of telling his friends a characteristic story. Mrs. Hanauer, one winter, repaid social obligations by giving a dinner for eight at her hotel. The guests were women of her own age, widowed, many of them, well dressed, priding themselves on their modernness. " Tell you what, Sophy," her genial son-in-law had said, " I'll mix a bunch of cocktails and send them over before dinner, see. Start the girls off right." Mrs. Hanauer liked a cocktail with the best of them.

" Oh, they! " she now said, with infinite scorn. " It's no use passing cocktails to them. They've all got high blood-pressure." Jo had roared at this.

" Listen, Sophy," he would often say, to her infinite delight,

" if this daughter of yours was half the sport that you are I'd look forward to old age without a quiver."

Mrs. Hanauer and Mrs. Grimm were but two of many well-to-do elderly women living their days in the comfortable, care-free atmosphere of the hotel, with its red-carpeted corridors, its liver-coloured marble lobby, its flat-footed old waiters, its reluctant lifts. They enjoyed complaining about the food in the dining-room. Yearly they announced their decision not to renew the lease. Often they spoke of going abroad for a year or more " only the children need me." On rainy days, and during the raw winter months, it was pleasant not to be obliged to go out for company or recreation. Almost any afternoon or evening the quiet of the wide bright corridors was broken by the rattle and clack of mah jong tiles. Through open transoms you heard spoken the poetic or absurd terms of the game. One bam! West wind! Four flowers!

They called each other on the telephone, often addressing one another by the last name only. Coming from them, it produced a racy and piquant effect most startling, and faintly flavoured with rowdyism. " Hello! That you, Hanauer? What are you doing? "

" Oh, I've got some mending——"

" Let it wait. Mrs. Renner is here. I thought we'd have a game if you don't mind playing three-handed."

Their days were very full. They were meticulously manicured at the Beth Beautye Shoppe. They went to the matinée. They went to the theatre occasionally in the evening. They attended symphony concerts. They heard the lectures given under the auspices of the League for Sociological Instruction, of which organisation they were members. Here, English novelists and English university professors and English editors spoke with bright insultingness and an Oxford accent on the subject of money-mad, materialistic America, following which speech they hurriedly collected their fee and scurried on to Chicago, there to eject another mouthful of cultural spittle into the eager faces of the members of the Pantheon Club. They read the new books and discussed them. Theirs was the sprightly intelligence of the American middle-class old lady, alert, eager, curious. A strangely youthful buoyancy was expressed in terms of beige silk stockings and smart hats and modish jewellery and jersey sport costumes. They were dignified but snappy.

Twice a week they dined with the children. They endeavoured not to criticise what they considered the extravagance of the household of which they were guests. Yet sometimes they could not resist it.

Strawberries, h'm? In January! My goodness! Somebody must get an awfully big housekeeping allowance. They said, as Ed or Jo carved generous portions of the roast, " If that's for me I only want half of that."

They invited the children to dinner. " But, Mother, how foolish! We're housekeeping. It's so much easier for you to come here."

" I am here twice a week. You haven't had dinner with me in over a month now."

" But there's four of us, and only one of you."

" A person would think I was a beggar. I wouldn't ask you if I couldn't afford it. I'm perfectly independent."

And so they were. Financially independent. Physically active. Socially interested. Equipped to provide themselves with entertainment, stimulus, companionship, a home, clothes, food. Dependent on their children and grandchildren only for that one thing without which they could not live. Love. Human affection.

It was, curiously enough, after one of these family dinners that both Mrs. Hanauer and Mrs. Grimm learned of a change in the children's usual plans for the summer. Perhaps it was not, after all, so strange. Their grandchildren were tall, slim athletic boys and girls. They thought of them still as babies. Their children were nearing middle age, with greying hair, and with little sudden fans of wrinkles at the corners of the eyes when they smiled.

They regarded them as children, not nearly grown up and needing advice and guidance still. And these children, perhaps because of that very independence of which they so often heard the boast, failed to realise that old age, after all, had really overtaken this courageous, keen, and dominating figure whose presence so often brought discord into the household.

They talked it over, husband and wife. It isn't fair to the children. After all, she's as strong as any of us. Twice the energy I've got, if you ask me. Last summer Junior and Sister couldn't stir from one to three because she was lying down. Almost grown-up now, really. Little parties—their friends over in the evening. You can't expect them to act like babies any more. Entitled to their freedom. After all, we're attentive all winter. No one can say we're not. But we've got to consider the children first, I should think.

So then, summer in the offing. The handsome houses in the East Fifties and Sixties began to be boarded up. You sought the shady side of the street. The English culturists took their American dollars home to idealistic Europe. The plays by Molnar and Shaw and Ibsen and Werfel and O'Neill melted before the hot sun and in their place came the cool vapidness of the musical shows.

"Mother"—Mrs. Grimm's daughter-in-law speaking rather hurriedly, and not looking at her husband—"Ed's hay fever was simply terrible last year, and the cold that Junior had all through August, that hung on so, wasn't a cold at all, but hay fever, too. I suppose he's inherited it."

"Fiddlesticks!" said Mrs. Grimm.

Her daughter-in-law compressed her lips. Then she opened them and spoke still more quickly. "Doctor Borsch said that the pine air is what they both need. In fact, he insists upon it. I'm afraid we'll simply have to go to the mountains this year. Now, you know perfectly well we'd be delighted to have you come along, if you think it would agree with you. We're going quite high up. To Kendall's. The cottage is small, but perhaps you wouldn't mind a day-bed in the . . . or maybe a room at the inn near by, and your meals with us. Cook has promised to go along. . . . Joan has asked two of her friends for July. . . ."

"Nobody," replied Mrs. Grimm, with terrible distinctness, "nobody has to put themselves out for me. Nobody ever has and nobody ever will. A person would think I was a child. I don't know what I may do this summer. I may go abroad."

From Ed, quickly, "I wouldn't hear of your going to Europe alone."

"Who said I was going alone! I can always hire somebody, for that matter. I'm perfectly independent."

"Now, Mother, don't talk like that. You know how Ed and I——"

"Yes; I know," said Mrs. Grimm.

Mrs. Hanauer's daughter wore the double frown of worry between her eyes. "You know how pale and listless Dorothy was all last summer. Well, Borsch says that what she needs is the ocean air and salt bathing. It's only two hours from New York. It'll be wonderful for Jo. He can come out every Friday and stay till Monday. During August, when it's slack, he might even make it on Thursday. Just think, after all these years of having to take a sleeper overnight to get to us in the Adirondacks. I know the sea air doesn't agree with your bronchitis, but I've just got to consider the children, and Jo."

"Nobody," said Mrs. Hanauer, not unkindly, "has got to consider me." One fore-finger was making little circles, round and round, on the arm of her chair; round and round. "A person would think I was a child."

"Don't say that, Mother. It isn't fair. You know we've

always loved having you with us, summers. There's room for you. Dorothy can share——"

"I don't know what I shall do this summer. I may go to Europe."

"I wouldn't hear of your going alone."

"Did I say I was going alone? I have plenty of friends, goodness knows, who go every year and who've begged me to come with them, time and again. For that matter, I could hire a companion. I'm perfectly independent."

Neither would confess to the other the true state of affairs. Mrs. Hanauer lied grandly to Mrs. Grimm. Mrs. Grimm was bristlingly off-hand to Mrs. Hanauer. I'm sick of the seashore. I'm tired of the mountains. The same people you see all winter in the city. What's the change! A little air. What's that!

"Why don't you try the mountains, for a change?" asked Mrs. Hanauer.

"They don't agree with me. My heart. Why don't you go to the seashore?"

"The doctor forbids it. My bronchial tubes."

They eyed each other for a moment with wary unconcern. Mrs. Grimm spoke first, her tone casual to the point of airiness. "I'd go to Europe, only I don't want to go alone, and there are very few people I'd travel with."

"How about me?" suggested Mrs. Hanauer, with heavy jocularity.

"Are you joking, Hanauer?"

It was arranged. They had both been abroad before, in the days of the defunct Grimm and Hanauer; Mrs. Hanauer only once, Mrs. Grimm many times. Grimm, big, blond, personable, had been an importer; and she had accompanied her husband on his frequent foreign trips with a persistence that savoured more of suspicion than of fidelity. He had, in fact, been known to come home at five with the announcement that he was sailing next morning at ten. Whereupon Mrs. Grimm, looking strangely like Rosa Dartle, would pack a hurried trunk, leave the boy Ed in care of the capable *fraulein*, and steam triumphantly away with him, for all the world like an impish little gnome who has a dejected giant in her power. "I have crossed," Mrs. Grimm would tell you on the slightest provocation, "thirty-six times. In fact, I feel as much at home in Paris or London as I do in New York."

She was inclined to patronise the less cosmopolitan Mrs. Hanauer. For that matter; her manner toward her friend frequently was tinged with some spaciousness. Mrs. Grimm had always had money. She was inclined, therefore, to be prudent to the point of parsimony. Mrs. Hanauer, on the other hand, had the gay lavishness of a child with a bag of lollipops. She had known struggle. Hanauer had bought real estate, but it was as though his name on a deed of sale brought blight to that property. Did he buy east the dwellers fled west, as though from a pestilence. He bought north, and progress marched south.

Suddenly, after his death, tumble-down buildings and vacant lots near the East River, left by him to his widow, a source of no revenue, bloomed Aladdin-like into twenty-two storey studio buildings, with ninety-nine-year leases, and Mrs. Hanauer began buying her hats in Fifty-seventh Street. Struggle and disappointment had not embittered her. They had, on the contrary, given her a racy sweetness and tolerance. "What's the diff!" she used to say. "You only live once." As though she had discovered a great truth.

"'At a girl!" her son-in-law would shout. "'At a good sport!"

Their preparations for the journey were simple. In their well-ordered lives there was no need for sudden rush and flurry. Mrs. Grimm was full of travel maxims. "Go with empty trunks and come back with full ones. . . . Take enough American silk stockings. Those over there you can't wear once, even. . . . Comfortable shoes, if you don't take another thing. . . . Your own coffee. This stuff on the boat is like licorice. . . . Sunny side of the deck—heavy coat—American money. . . ."

They had two cabins, with a bath between, at a really outrageous cost. "Travelling like a couple of prima donnas, that's what you girls are," Mrs. Hanauer's son-in-law said jovially. Certainly the appearance of those cabins, at departure, verified his remark. Flowers, books, candy, fruit, telegrams.

"Why do people do it!" Mrs. Grimm exclaimed, making a little sound of disapproval between tongue and teeth. "What a waste! Look at this enormous basket from Mr. Grimm's ex-partner." She surveyed Mrs. Hanauer's less imposing floral edifices with a patronising eye. A small buttons staggered in with a structure of fruit that might have lasted the Noah family their voyage. "Grimm?" inquired the lady of that name.

"Hanner or Hanor or——"

"Hanauer," said the genial Sophy, not without a tinge of complacency. "My, look at the size of those pears! A meal in itself."

"Those big pears are generally hard. I don't know why

people do it. I always said to Mr. Grimm, the thirty-six times we crossed, if people would only send telegrams, and that's all, how much more sensible."

"I like it," said Mrs. Hanauer. Her voice held a little excited note, like a child's. "I think it's grand. It makes me feel so popular."

"It's an old story to me," remarked Mrs. Grimm.

They stood at the ship's rail as she drew warily out into the bay. Waving up at them from the dock were daughter, son, daughter-in-law, son-in-law, grandchildren. Their faces were round white disks turned towards them in space. To the two at the rail those disks were their world; their solar system; their symbol of achievement in life; their living connection with Life itself.

Write, now! Cable as soon as you land. Don't forget! Take care of yourself! Final futile clutchings into the space that was widening between them. Suddenly the little sallow, black-eyed face at the rail and the plump, pink, blue-eyed face at the rail, side by side, broke into grimaces that were absurd and yet not funny. The white disks swam in a blue.

Mrs. Hanauer's daughter, Bernice, clutched her husband's arm. The fingers of the other hand were closed over her mouth, in a tight fist, like that of a child who is fearful. "Oh, Jo, she's crying! Look! I don't think we should have let her go. I don't know—she looks so—so kind of——"

"Oh, now, Bernie, she's all right," said Mrs. Hanauer's son-in-law briskly. "She's a good sport. She'll have a swell time. Person'd think you were the mother and she the daughter, the way you carry on."

Mrs. Grimm's son, Ed, his face turned up toward that wizened dark face so strangely contorted at the rail, suddenly set his teeth so that a white-ridge sprang out along either side of his jaw. He fumbled foolishly with his hat in his hand.

"Look, Stell! She's crying. I don't know. Do you think we ought've let her go like that, alone? She looks so—so——"

"She isn't alone, stupe! What's the matter with you! You know, Jo, I've always said that you had a mother complex. You spoil her."

They were splendid sailors, both of them. Three meals a day—four for Mrs. Hanauer, who liked her tea and cakes in the afternoon.

"I never touch tea on board," Mrs. Grimm declared, bristling, as though there were some special virtue in this abstinence.

Close as their friendship had been, they had never known

the irritating intimacy that comes with travel. Mrs. Hanauer was the kind of person who does not screw the top tight on the tube of tooth paste. A sticky white worm usually ornamented the wash-bowl. Mrs. Grimm was the sort of person whom this infuriates. Both women awoke early and had their breakfast in their rooms, but while Mrs. Hanauer rose, dressed, and went out on deck, Mrs. Grimm remained in bed until noon.

"The day's long enough," she said. "Besides, what a chance to rest. Nobody who's used to travel goes galloping around a boat at this hour of the morning."

Their breakfast trays were a startling point of contrast. In one bright little cabin you saw the plump and ruddy Mrs. Hanauer propped comfortably among her pillows, protected by a baby-blue challis bed jacket, a dish-laden tray on her knees, blandly consuming a meal such as that with which a Kansas farm-hand starts his day. The least of its items were the two cups of coffee, with excellent cream from the private stock which had been one of the many boat gifts sent them. Mrs. Grimm, hearing her give the order to the somewhat astounded stewardess, would sniff with disapproval. She would state her order in a tone whose every shade was a reproach. Coffee, hot water, dry toast.

"My!" called Mrs. Hanauer from her room, as she deftly applied a quarter of a cube of butter to a hot roll, embellished this with an amber crown of orange marmalade, and popped the whole between her lips, "my goodness, Grimm! No wonder you're so skinny."

The swart little Mrs. Grimm, in bed, was a fly-speck in a pan of milk. The sound of Mrs. Hanauer's bath annoyed her. Mrs. Hanauer was one of those musical bathers. "Will you kindly shut the door, Mrs. Hanauer! I didn't close my eyes all night. I might get a few minutes' sleep this morning if I had the chance."

As they sat on deck side by side, swathed in rugs, relaxed, contemplative, they could not but betray in their conversation something of the hurt which son and daughter had dealt them. Little vague remarks, spoken almost unconsciously, after a long silence, as though the speaker were thinking aloud; phrased incompletely. Well, I suppose that's life. . . . You spend your life bringing them up, and then when they don't need you. . . . A daughter is a daughter all her life, but a son is your son only until he marries. . . . Oh, I don't know about that. I sometimes think my son-in-law, Jo, is more considerate of me than my own. . . . They need me a whole lot worse than I need them, I can tell you.

They would catch themselves, and eye each other warily, stiffening. They would fall to commenting jocosely on their fellow passengers tramping the decks in parade. There was a certain type of old lady encountered on the boat and later in their continental travels, that aroused their mirth and contempt. These were the frumpy genteel type, the old conservative American family type, or the English gentlewoman in historic hats, black, cloth-topped, buttoned high shoes, black garments of excellent material and bunchy cut. These were attended, usually, by a defeated-looking maiden daughter or a crushed companion. They walked timorously, under sunshades. The sight of them seemed to release something impish in Mrs. Hanauer and Mrs. Grimm.

" I think I'll have my hair bobbed when I get to Paris," Mrs. Hanauer would announce. " Bernice says she thinks it'll be becoming."

" Don't be a fool! Look at that woman, will you! June, and she's wearing black spats. Black spats always make me think of undertakers. I'll bet she's old family, all right." Mrs. Grimm would survey her own small trim foot in its smart patent-leather slippers and cut-steel buckle. She was vain of the size of her foot for some obscure reason, that people have for being proud of a member which is built merely in proportion to the rest of the body.

London, Paris, Deauville, Frankfort, Brussels, Lucerne. Theirs was a terrific energy. It was as though, now that the sands were running so fast, so fast, they begrudged the time lost in sleep, in repose. They would sleep long enough, they thought, secretly, and pushed the thought from their minds. They seldom retired until after midnight, read in bed, were wide awake at six. They lay there, thinking, Mrs. Grimm in her room, Mrs. Hanauer in hers. More than threescore years of life lay behind them. They thought of yesterday, and of to-day, but never of to-morrow.

And they quarrelled. Their bickering was almost constant. Perhaps, in the closeness of their companionship, each saw herself constantly reflected in the face of the other. To each other they would not confess to being tired, sleepy, nervous, lonely, travel weary—to any of the quite natural sufferings of sight-seeing. They found fault with one another. They complained of each other, privately, to chance friends or acquaintances encountered in hotel lobbies, on trains, in the parks or shops.

Mrs. Hanauer's magnificent appetite was a source of increasing annoyance to the bird-like Mrs. Grimm. Certainly Mrs. Hanauer, large, placid, amiable, liked to eat. She ate lobster, sweets, cucumbers, acids; liked a glass of mild white wine at dinner. She consumed the four or five courses of the European midday lunch, topping it off with cheese and fruit. Always you heard the crackle of a surreptitious paper bag in her room, after she had gone to bed.

Mrs. Grimm would regard her bristling, tight-lipped with disapproval. "You know you can't eat lobster. Why do you order veal when you can't digest it! Nobody can digest it. My daughter-in-law won't have it in the house. Mark my words, you'll be sick. Don't come to me complaining if you are. If you do get sick who'll have to suffer for it!" A rhetorical question, certainly.

Mrs. Hanauer would survey her in mild surprise. "Why, I will."

"You! No!" Mrs. Grimm would retort. "I will! I'll have to take care of you."

"Nobody has to take care of me, Mrs. Grimm. I'm perfectly independent."

Now that each leaned so hard on the memory of the children in America, they perforce denied their dependence on each other.

They confided in such friends as they met on their journeyings. "I hope I can stand it until September," Mrs. Grimm would say to a chance New York friend. "But my patience is nearly exhausted. It has taught me a lesson, I can tell you. My son and daughter-in-law begged me to come to the mountains with them this summer, but I thought a change would do me good. Well, live and learn."

The easy-going Mrs. Hanauer complained in gentle wonderment. "She makes such a fuss about everything. She quarrels with everybody; porters and waiters and chambermaids and people at the railway stations. I honestly am looking forward to the day we sail in September. We'll be home September tenth. I wish it was to-morrow. My daughter insisted that I come with them to the seashore, but I thought I'd come to Europe for a change. It was a mistake. You never know a person till you travel with them, I always say."

Mrs. Grimm's cosmopolitan knowledge was always being flaunted in Mrs. Hanauer's mildly resentful face. "You overtip. They're not used to it. Anybody who has ever travelled wouldn't tip like a drunken sailor. They only take your money and despise you for it."

"What do I care if they despise me! I want my comfort. If an extra few cents at the end of the week means I get hot water with my tea and an extra pillow and two clean bath towels, what do I care what they say about me in the back hall! I don't want to live with them."

" They only laugh at you."

" Let them laugh, poor things. If they can laugh for fifteen cents I'm glad to furnish the money."

" It isn't the money. It's the principle of the thing."

Sometimes you saw them returning from an afternoon's sight-seeing, walking not together but one behind the other, sulkily, like naughty children.

True to the nickname bestowed upon her by her son-in-law, Mrs. Hanauer, the Sport, loved to gamble. She rarely won, but her glee when she did was out of all proportion to her winnings. In the French watering places, nightly, after dinner, she would scurry to the Casino, there to throw her francs into the omnivorous green maw of the roulette table. She shivered delightfully with the curious tension of excitement that hovers, almost a palpable form, above and around the gaming board. She became quite chummy with the weird, exotic creatures manacled from wrist to elbow with incredible diamond bracelets. Sometimes these borrowed money of her—pathetic sums—fifty francs—twenty—ten, even. The light from the huge crystal chandeliers that hung like frozen fountains above them sent a hundred glorious ruby and amber and blue and orange lights, darting from these jewels as the white arms were thrust forward to place a disk on the red, on the black, on the seven, on the eleven.

Mrs. Grimm rarely played. " I've seen too much of it in my life," she said, boredly. " It doesn't interest me. Mr. Grimm used to win five hundred francs one minute and lose it the next. That was when five hundred francs meant something." Sometimes she refused even to accompany Mrs. Hanauer on her night's revelry. " Do you know who that woman was you were talking to last night at the Casino, next to you? A woman I met in the lobby just told me. That was that Madame Bey Khan, or whatever her name is—that Frenchwoman who married the Turk, or something, and murdered him in a London hotel. The papers were full of it."

" I thought she looked sad for a woman so young," said Mrs. Hanauer, pityingly.

" Well, I've got something better to do than run to casinos and talk to murderesses."

" What? " inquired Mrs. Hanauer, bluntly.

" What what? " demanded Mrs. Grimm, bewildered.

" What better to do? "

" Oh, all right. Only when you get sick from nervous indigestion, eating all kinds of things a horse couldn't stand, and then working yourself up over winning a few francs, who'll have to pay for it, I'd like to know! "

Pathetically enough, it turned out to be Mrs. Grimm who first fell ill. There had been some mistake about the train from Frankfort to Brussels. At the last minute they found themselves on the ten-twenty-six, which was not their train, instead of on the ten-thirty-six, which was. Their trunks, too, and innumerable bags were aboard. They discovered this in one panic-stricken minute before the train would have carried them heaven knows where.

There followed the cacophony which attends the making of a mistake in a foreign railway station. Porters, passengers, station agents; shouts, screams, arms waving, luggage hurled, imprecations shouted. Cologne! But we thought it stopped at Cologne. That's the border. We have to change at the border. Which one is it, then? Where is it? We have to get off. Let us off. We're American citizens.

They were off the wrong train and on the right one. Their faces were dully red, with a thick purplish colour. Their foreheads were damp. They were trembling. At last they found seats in a first-class compartment and sank down, spent, their eyes looking strained.

An hour later they could joke about it, feebly. They could even go into the dining-car and eat some of the hot and steaming meal with which the European train bombards its passengers. Thick bilious soup. Veal. Greasy potatoes. Stewed and mysterious greens. Salad. Cheese. Fruit. Mrs. Grimm essayed to eat the salad, the cheese; the fruit; wherein she made her mistake. The terror and excitement of the past hour had set all the nerves a jangle in the little frame. Arrived at the hotel, their journey's end reached, she was seized at midnight with the stabbing, jagged pains of ptomaine.

" I won't have a doctor. I wouldn't have one of these foreign doctors near me. They almost killed Mr. Grimm, once. In Vienna, too. Of all places."

" Now, Fanny, don't be silly. You've got to take something."

" Castor oil and bismuth. That's all they give for ptomaine. That's what it is. Ptomaine. I told you I didn't want to eat on that train, and you nagged me and nagged me, and so I ate something. Oh! " The little face on the pillow was wizened, green.

" I'll send a boy for it. There must be somebody awake in this hotel. It's only a little after twelve."

" Your bare feet. You're walking around in your bare feet. You'll catch your—oh! " She drew herself into a knot of agony.

Finally at the door, a red-eyed waiter ridiculously formal in a dress suit. No, he could not go. No, there was no one to send. It was after midnight. The chemists' shops were closed, naturally. He did not know. He did not know. He did not know. The dark eyes in the face on the pillow were glazed with pain.

"I'll go," said Mrs. Hanauer. "I'll get somebody up. My Lord, when you think of all we did for them in the war." A skirt over her nightgown. A coat over this.

"Your hat," gasped Mrs. Grimm, the stickler. "Hat!"

"Hat hell!" said Mrs. Hanauer; and returned twenty minutes later with a bottle of castor oil, an orange, a spoon, a packet of bismuth. Hold your nose while you swallow it. Now wipe out your mouth with this towel. Suck a piece of orange. Bismuth now, and again in the morning. Mrs. Hanauer was up most of the night, thudding across the floor fearfully to gaze at the shrunken and wattled face turned so gratefully, so wistfully up to hers. Yes, you've got a little bit of fever, maybe. But by morning you'll never know you were sick.

"Put on your shoes," moaned Mrs. Grimm, outraged. "Go back to bed."

But twenty times during the night the bare feet thudded anxiously across the floor.

Next morning Mrs. Grimm was weak, but had only occasional and slight pain. By afternoon she was sipping warm milk. Her eyes were sunk deep in her head, but the black lines which pain had etched deep in her face had vanished. By evening Mrs. Hanauer was sniffling suspiciously. Next day Mrs. Grimm was crawling about, feebly, to administer hot-water bags and aspirin and hot lemonades to the bronchial and wheezy Mrs. Hanauer.

There followed a week of a sort of happy wretchedness, in which each ministered tenderly, unselfishly, to the other.

"You don't need to do anything for me, Fanny. I'm all right."

"Honestly, Sophy, sometimes I think you're not quite bright. If your cold turns into pneumonia who'll have to suffer for it?"

"You will," retorted Mrs. Hanauer unexpectedly, and cackled a hoarse bronchial laugh.

They were sailing from Cherbourg. By the time they reached Paris they were a markedly changed pair, these two who had started out so blithe and independent. Yet still so unchanged. For though they leaned heavily on each other for support, both spiritual and physical, how consistently they refused to admit it.

"You're not fit to go shopping alone. Look at yesterday!

If I hadn't pulled you back, that taxi would have run over you the next minute."

" A person would think I was a farmer to hear you talk. I guess if I can get around in New York I can get around in Paris. I knew Paris before you ever heard of it."

The city's bewildering, frantic street life swirled and eddied all about them. They leaped from curb to curb like harried hares. Oh, well, I'm sick of shopping, anyway. I've got the dress for Bernice, and the handkerchiefs for Jo, and the bracelet for Sister and the field-glasses for Junior. I guess they'll have to be satisfied with that.

Weary, but undefeated. Heads bloody, but unbowed.

The children were on the dock to meet them. Son and daughter-in-law, daughter and son-in-law, they kissed these with a happy perfunctoriness. But the grandchildren they kissed with rapturous devouring kisses, folding them hungrily in their arms.

Please don't stand around me like that while the inspector looks over my things. It makes me nervous. No, Ed, don't give him a cigar. It makes them suspicious. No, I have declared everything, I tell you. But anyway, I get nervous.

" What do you mean, I don't look well! " demanded Mrs. Grimm of her daughter-in-law. " I had a touch of ptomaine, but everybody has that in Europe."

" Just the same," declared her son Ed stoutly, " next summer you'll stay with us. I don't want you running around alone in Europe. I don't like it."

" I'd like to know why not! " blazed Mrs. Grimm, the indomitable. " Nobody has to look out for me. I'm perfectly independent."

" Mother! " exclaimed Mrs. Hanauer's daughter, Bernice, " you look thin! You've lost weight! Have you been sick? "

" A touch of my old bronchial trouble. Anyway, I was too fat."

" Well, the next time you'll have your bronchitis right with us, at home. I don't like your running around Europe alone."

" Fiddlesticks! " said Mrs. Hanauer. She eyed her daughter with loving severity. " For pity's sake, where did you get that hat! Nobody's wearing turned-up brims. Everything turns down this year in Paris."

STEPHEN VINCENT BENET, M.A.

A STORY BY ANGELA POE

I WAS a very young man in the publishing business at the time—even younger, I think, than most young men are nowadays, for this was before the war. Dianna poised her bow at the sky above a Madison Square Garden that was actually on Madison Square—and some of the older men in our New York office still wore the paper sleeve-protectors and worn alpaca coats of an older day. There are young offices and old ones: brisk, shiny, bumptious new offices that positively buzz with expert inefficiency; and resigned, rather wistful little offices that have come to know they will never do well in the world. But the prevailing atmosphere of Thrushwood, Collins, and Co. was that of substantial tradition and solid worth. The faded carpet in the reception-room had been trodden by any number of famous feet—perhaps by not quite so many as I avouched to the young men of other publishers, but still the legends were there. Legends of Henry James and William Dean Howells and a young man from India named Kipling who was taken for a boy from the printer's and sent off with a flea in his ear. New authors were always greatly impressed by our atmosphere—until they looked over their contracts and discovered that even their Australian rights had, somehow or other, become the inalienable property of Thrushwood, Collins, and Co. But then they had only to see Mr. Thrushwood to be convinced that their most successful works were being published from a rigid sense of duty as a distinct financial loss.

I had the desk that was farthest away from both radiators and window in the front office, so I broiled in summer and froze in winter and was perfectly happy. I was in New York, I was part of the making of books, I saw celebrities, and every Sunday I wrote home about it to my family. True, some of the celebrities were not nearly so impressive in the flesh as in the print; but that made me feel I was seeing Real Life at last. And there was always Mr. Thrushwood, with his thin, worn, cameo face and his white plume of hair, to restore my faith in mankind. When he put his hand on my shoulder and said: " You're coming along nicely, Robbins," I felt an accolade. I did not discover until later that I was doing three men's work, but, if I had known it then, I would not have cared. And when Randall Day, of Harper's, irreverently alluded to us as " The Holy Burglars," I flung the insinuation back in his teeth, with an apt quotation about Philistines. For we talked about Philistines, then.

As a matter of fact, we had an excellent list, on the whole—for, though Mr. Thrushwood, like most successful publishers, hardly ever read a book, he had a remarkable nose for the promising and the solid. On the other hand, there were names which, as an idealist, I boggled over—and the first and foremost of these was Angela Poe. I could tolerate Caspar Breed and his lean-jawed, stern-muscled cowboys with the hearts of little children. I could stomach Jeremy Jason, the homespun philosopher, whose small green ooze-leather booklets: *A Wayfarer's Creed*, *A Wayfarer's Vow*, *A Wayfarer's Hearthstone*, produced much the same sensation in me as running a torn finger nail over heavy plush. Publishers must live, and other publishers had their Breeds and their Jasons. But Angela Poe was not merely an author—she was something like breakfast-food or chewing-gum, an American institution, untidy, inescapable, and vast. I could have forgiven her—and Thrushwood, Collins—if she had sold moderately well. But long ago, the *New York Times* had ceased to say anything about her except: " Another Angela Poe . . . sure to appeal to her huge audience . . ." before its painstaking resumé of the plot. I often wondered what unhappy reviewer wrote those resumés. For he must have had to read the books, from *Wanda of the Marshes* to *Ashes of Roses*, and I did not see how that was possible for any one man.

The settings of the novels ranged from the fjords of Norway to the coasts of Tasmania, and every page betrayed that intimate knowledge of a foreign country which can only be acquired by a thorough study of the chattier sort of guide-books. But though the scene might shift, the puppets remained defiantly the same. Even in Tasmania, the wild roses in the heroine's cheeks remained quite unaffected by the climate and the malign but singularly unintelligent snares of the cynical villain in riding-clothes. The villains almost always wore riding-clothes, as I remember it, and were usually militant atheists, though of high social position. The heroines were *petite*, unworldly, and given to calling the native flora pet names. And over all, insipid, lingering, and sweet as the taste of a giant marshmallow, there brooded the inimitable style of Angela Poe. Occasionally, this style would goad some fledgling reviewer to fury and he would write the sort of scarifying review that only very young reviewers write. Then the girl at our reception desk would be warned and Mr. Thrushwood would put off all other appointments for the day. For Angela Poe read all her reviews with passion.

It was on such an occasion that I saw her for the first time. I was passing Mr. Thrushwood's private office, when Mr. Collins popped out of it with a worried look on his face. A dumpy little man who haunted the business department, he left all personal contacts with authors to Mr. Thrushwood, as a rule. But this time, Angela Poe had descended in Mr. Thrushwood's absence and caught him unprepared.

" Look here, Robbins," he said, with no more preface than a drowning man, " have we got any really magnificent reviews on the last Poe? You know the kind I mean—all honey and butter. The *Washoe Gazette* has just called her a purveyor of literary lollipops—and if I could get hold of her clipping-agency, there'd be blood on the moon."

" Why," I said, " I'm afraid I——" and then I remembered. Randall Day had the pestilent habit of sending me all the most fulsome reviews of Angela Poe that he could find—and one had arrived only that morning, with a neat border of hearts and flowers drawn around it.

" As a matter of fact, I have," I said, " but——"

" Thank God! " said Mr. Collins fervently and, taking me by the hand, he fairly ran me into the room.

But at first I could see no reason for the odd, tense look on his face—and on that of Mr. Catherwood, our art director, who was also there. The plump, demure, little old lady with the face of a faded pansy who sat in the big chair opposite them had nothing terrifying about her. She was Angela Poe, of course, though ten years older than her oldest publicity-pictures. And then she began to talk.

It was a sweet, tinkling voice, monotonous and constant. And as it went on, about Mr. Thrushwood and all her kind friends in Thrushwood, Collins, and then—I could not mark the transition—about how her flowers in her wee garden were also her friends, I began to realise the secret of the look on Mr. Collins's face. It was boredom, pure and simple, but boredom raised to a fine art. For when Angela Poe was angry she did not fly into a temper any more. She merely talked in her low, sweet voice—and, as she talked, she bored, relentlessly and persistently, like a drill boring into a shell.

It was no use trying to interrupt her or change the conversation—you cannot change a conversation that has no real subject to change. And yet, as she continued, and each moment seemed longer than the last until the brute flesh could hardly be restrained from breaking into a veritable whimper of tedium, I began to realise that she knew exactly what she was about. For somehow or other, we always came back to Angela Poe and the fact that she was waiting for Mr. Thrushwood. Till I began to feel, myself, that Mr. Thrushwood's absence was a grave calamity of nature and that, if he did not come soon, I, too, might burst into tears.

. . . .

Fortunately, he arrived in time, and saved us, as only Mr. Thrushwood could. Fortunately or unfortunately, for he came while I was showing her the review that Day had sent me. It mollified her greatly, though she said, in a serious voice, that of course she never read reviews. They broke the wings of the butterfly. I didn't know what she meant by that, but I must have made some appropriate response. For Mr. Thrushwood, with one of his Napoleonic gestures, informed me at five o'clock that afternoon that henceforth my salary was raised ten dollars a month.

"And, by the way, Robbins," he said, "I don't want to put too much on you—but Miss Poe liked your looks to-day. Well, Miss Poe is just beginning a new novel—I think this one is to be about Iceland, or possibly Finland—not that it matters greatly——" and he gave me a smile of complicity. "But, as you know, we always get her reference books for her and send them out every week-end—and she will have them brought by some member of the staff. It's on the west shore of the Hudson—and I'm afraid she calls her house 'The Eyrie,'" he went on, with a chuckle, "but she's really a very sensible little woman—quite a head for business, yes, indeed, quite a head," and his face held unwilling respect. "So, if you wouldn't mind? Then that's all settled. How jolly of you, Robbins!" he said, with his boyish laugh.

I had meant to tell him I would do nothing of the sort, but, while you were with him you were under his spell. Nevertheless, it was with internal revolt that I got on the ferry that week-end, with my bag of books in my hand. And then, when I got to "The Eyrie," I met a nice old lady who reminded me of my aunts. She put me at ease at once, she fed me enormously, she fussed over me with just the right amount of fussiness. The tea was solid and bountiful—I was sent to the station in a carriage and pair. To my despair, in the train going back, I discovered that I had enjoyed myself. And through my mind still ran the small, tinkling monotonous voice of Angela Poe—saying nothing, and yet, remembered. I tried very hard to place her; she was like any dozen ladies I knew in

Central City, ladies with little gold watches pinned over their bosoms, who fussily but efficiently presided over strawberry festivals and sales at the Woman's Exchange. And she was not—there was something else about her, some quality I could not place. It had made her Angela Poe—and yet, what was it? Her servants, I had noticed, were perfectly trained and civil and the dog got up from the hearth-rug when she told it to get up. And yet, instinctively, you gave her your arm, when she came down a staircase. I could not make it out, but I knew, rather shamefacedly, that I was looking forward to returning to "The Eyrie." Young men are apt to be hungry—and the tea was superb.

And then, as I told Randall Day, "The Eyrie" alone was worth the price of admission. It was one of those big wooden houses with wide verandas that the eighties built on the cliffs of the Hudson—houses that, somehow or other, remind you of grandiose cuckoo-clocks. There were the lawns and the shrubbery, the big cupolaed stable and the gravelled drive; the hardwood floors and the heavily framed oil-paintings. It might all have come out of an Angela Poe novel—she had done it perfectly, down to the last gas-bracket. And through it all wandered Mr. Everard De Lacey, the man one must never address as Mr. Angela Poe.

. . . .

It was my first experience with the husband of a celebrated authoress, and he still remains unique in my memory. You do not meet them now as often as you did—those men with the large, mobile mouths, the Hamlet eyes, and the skin that has known the grease-paint of a thousand small-town dressing-rooms. The new actors are another breed. Mr. De Lacey was not merely an actor, he was a Thespian—and it makes a difference. He must have been very handsome in his youth—handsome in the old barn-storming tradition of black, flashing eyes and Hyacinthine curls—and his voice still had the rich, portentous boom of Michael Strogoff, the Courier of the Czar. When he fixed me with his Hamlet eyes and quoted—it was The Bard—I felt ashamed of myself for not being a larger audience. But he was really very considerate about it, and I liked the way he treated Miss Poe.

For they were obviously and deeply attached to each other, those two ageing people, and one sensed the bond the moment one saw them together. They deferred to each other ceremoniously, with a Victorian civility that I found rather touching. And Everard was by no means the harmless, necessary husband such husbands often are. It was agreed that he was "resting" from a modern and sin-struck stage unworthy of his talents, but it was also agreed that at any moment, he might return to the boards, amid the plaudits of welcoming multitudes. Later on I discovered that he had been " resting " for almost thirty years, or since Angela Poe first started to sell by the carload. But that made no difference to either of them.

" I could never have done what I have done without Mr. De Lacey," she would say in her sweet, tinkling voice and Everard would boom in return: " My dear, it was but given me to water and tend the rose. The flowers are all your own." Such things, if said, are oftener said than meant. But you felt that the Poes, I mean the De Laceys, meant them. Then a look would pass between them, the look of two souls who are linked by a deeper tie than the crass world knows.

I seem to be writing a little like Angela Poe myself, in describing them. But it was difficult, in that setting, not to become infected with Poe-ishness. If a beautiful girl in a simple muslin frock had met me accidentally in the garden and flitted away with flushed cheeks and a startled cry, I would have been embarrassed but not in the least surprised. And there were times when I fully expected to meet a little lame boy, his pale, courageous face radiant for once with the sunset glow, at almost any corner of the drive. But the De Laceys had no children, though they were extremely kind to the innumerable offspring of Mr. De Lacey's relatives. And that seemed to me rather a shame.

. . . . .

I had come to scoff, you see. But I remained, if not to pray, well, to be rather fascinated. They fed me well, they treated me with ceremonious politeness, they were sentimental, but generous as well. I had to listen a good deal to the tinkling, incessant flow of Angela Poe's words—but, as time wore on, I even became used to that. It was as Mr. Thrushwood had said; she could be extremely sensible, even pungent, when she wished. And she could take criticism, too, which surprised me. At least she could take it from Everard De Lacey. Now and then he would say, in his rich boom, as she sketched a scene or a character for us: " No, my dear, that will not do."

" But, Everard, how is Zepha to escape from the insane asylum, then?"

" That, my dear, I have to leave to your genius. But this passage will not do. I sense it. I feel it. It is not Angela Poe."

" Very well, my dear," she would say, submissively and turn to me with: " Mr. De Lacey is always right, you know." And he would say at the same moment: " Young Man, I am not always right. But such poor gifts as I possess are always at Mrs. De Lacey's service——"

"The fruits of a richly stored mind, Everard——"

"Well, my dear, perhaps some slight acquaintance with the classics of our tongue—some trifling practical experience in interpreting The Bard——"

Then each would make the other a little bob, and again I would be irresistibly reminded, not of a cuckoo-clock but of one of those wooden weather-prophets where an old woman comes out for fine weather, an old man for rain. Only, here, the old man and the old woman were coming out at the same time.

I hope I have given the impression that they gave me—that of two ageing people, a trifle quaint, more than a trifle ridiculous, but, beyond all that, essential to each other. For that is an important thing for a young man to see, now and then; it restores his faith in the cosmos, though he may not realise it at the time. The first taste of real life, for the young, has its frightening moments: one suddenly discovers that actual people, not in books, commit suicide in gas-filled bedrooms because they would rather die than live; one discovers that others really enjoy being vicious and make a success of it. Then, instinctively, one clings to the first security at hand, like a swimmer to an overturned boat. I wouldn't have thought it possible when I first met them, but one of the things I clung to was the De Laceys.

And as I became more and more drawn into the endless spider-web of the work of Angela Poe, I began to realise how much she owed to her husband. Oh, he could never have written anything—be sure of that. But he knew the well-worn paths of stock-melodrama in all their spurious vitality, he knew when a thing would "go." I know because, inevitably, I followed one book of Angela Poe's from conception to delivery. It was not any better, speaking from the point of view of letters, for his suggestions; for it was perfectly terrible. But it worked; it was Angela Poe; the sun rose over the cardboard mountains at precisely the right instant. And every one of his criticisms helped it on.

Then one day, when I came to "The Eyrie," she had a touch of influenza and was in bed. He was obviously worried about her, but insisted on my staying to tea because I always had. I had my own worries at the moment and was glad for a breath of serenity. All his courtliness came into play and he told me a couple of mild theatrical jokes, but you could feel his eyes wandering, his ears listening for any sound from upstairs. If he had not been worried, I wonder—but worry makes people confidential. I thought it a good chance to congratulate him on his part in her work. He listened abstractedly, but I could see he was pleased.

"Glad you think so, my dear fellow, glad you think so," he said. "Often I have said to myself: 'No! This time old boy, let genius burn unhampered! Who are you to profane the—um—the sacred flame?' But genius—even genius—must have its trammels to bring it down to the level of us workaday folk. And, as the—er—appreciative trammel, perhaps I have played my part. I hope so," he said, quite simply. "She means a great deal to me."

"I know that, sir," I said, but he wasn't listening.

"Yes," he said, "we mean a great deal to each other. I hope she's taking those drops; you know, she hates drops. Yes, indeed, my dear fellow. Our first meeting was like a flash of lightning." He stared at me solemnly. "I wish that Mr. Wedge, her first husband, could have understood it better. But he was an earthbound soul. He could not comprehend a marriage of true minds."

"Mrs. De Lacey was married before?" I said, and I could not keep the shrillness of surprise from my voice.

"My dear boy," said Mr. De Lacey, looking surprised in his turn, "I forgot that you did not know. She was Mrs. Marvin Wedge when we first met," he said, reflectively, "and beautiful as a just-unfolding rose."

A thousand unphrasable questions rose to my lips and died there. For Mr. De Lacey continued.

"I used to call her the Rose of Goshen," he said. "Goshen, Indiana, dear boy—I was—er—resting there at the time, after my tour with Barrett. I played both grave-diggers and Charles, the wrestler. Charles, the wrestler, is not a large part, but one can make it tell. It was hard to return to Goshen, after that, but there are financial necessities. But as soon as I met Angela, I knew that I had been led. Wedge was—um—proprietor of our hay-and-feed store—rather older than I am; he used to chase me and call me Slats when I was a boy. But I had not known Angela before. She came from Zook Springs."

. . . . .

He paused and stared at me with his Hamlet eyes. I could see the whole scene so plainly—the dusty streets of the small town and the young, down-at-heels actor, back home discouraged, after his trial flight. I could see Angela Poe, forty years ago, in the simple gingham dress of one of her heroines. It must have been all so innocent and high-minded—innocent and unreal as a stage melodrama, even to the cynical figure of the burly hay-and-feed merchant. I could see him, somehow, in his shirt sleeves, roaring with laughter at the timid respectful speeches of—but the boy could not have been called Everard De Lacey, then. And yet, Romance had triumphed in Goshen. I wondered how.

"So Miss Poe was divorced—divorced Mr. Wedge. I mean," I said.

My companion looked curiously shocked. "Dear boy," he said, with dignity, "never once, in any of her books, has Angela Poe drawn a divorced woman."

"I know," I said feebly, though I didn't. "But in real life——"

"The books of Angela Poe are real life," said Mr. De Lacey, crushingly. Then he relented. "No," he said, "Mr. Wedge is not living. He passed over."

"Passed over?"

"Within a year of my return to Goshen. As a matter of fact, he was murdered," he said, with his Hamlet eyes fixed upon me so sternly that, for an instant, I had the horrific idea that I was about to listen to an incredible confession. But I was not. "By a tramp," he said at last. "In his feed store. For purposes of robbery. It was very upsetting for Angela."

I opened and shut my mouth, but no words came forth.

"Yes, really very upsetting. I was glad I could be with her," he said naively. "Though, naturally, we were not married till later. She was married in a tailored dress, but she held a bouquet of orange-blossoms and lilies-of-the-valley. I insisted upon that," he said with some pride.

"And the tramp?" I said, with youth's delight in horrors. "Was he——"

"Oh, he was never found," boomed Mr. De Lacey abstractedly, as a small sound came from upstairs, "but Angela bore up wonderfully. She is a wonderful woman." He rose. "If you'll just excuse me one moment, my dear fellow——"

"I must catch my train," I said. "But thank you, Mr. De Lacey. And be assured I shall respect your confidence," I said, trying to equal his manner.

He nodded seriously. "Yes, yes," he said. "Perhaps I should have said nothing—but, well, my dear boy, we have grown to know you and value you, in your visits to 'The Eyrie.' And they must not cease with this book—my dear fellow, no. Only, I would not bring up the matter in talking with Miss Poe. She does not like to dwell upon those days; they were not happy ones for her. Mr. Wedge was really——" Words failed him. "Mr. Wedge was really not a very sensitive man," he said.

I assured him of my entire understanding and took my leave. But, all the way home, certain thoughts kept revolving in my mind. I was not surprised that Providence, in the shape of a burglarious tramp, had seen fit to remove the insensitive Mr. Wedge. That was just the sort of thing that happened to Angela Poes. But why had she ever married him, in the first place, and how, having touched real life in her own person, had she been able to forget it so completely in her books? But those were the sorts of questions one could not ask.

. . . . .

And yet in the end I asked them, with youth's temerity. I asked them because I had come to like her—to like them both. And when you like people, you are apt to be more honest with them—that is the trouble.

We had planned to have a little celebration—the three of us —when the book was actually published. But it was not I who put the first copy in her hands. I brought out the dummy and the jacket. That particular Saturday Mr. De Lacey had made one of his rare excursions to New York. I was glad to find her alone, as a matter of fact, for I thought I had noticed a slight constraint between us since my conversation with him. At least, I was conscious that I knew a secret—and kept wondering if she knew that I knew. And I meant to tell her, in all honesty, how much the security and peace of "The Eyrie" had meant to me through the year. I was only waiting a good opening. But, naturally, we started by talking publishing. Her comments were shrewd and I enjoyed them—though the influenza had left its mark, and she looked frailer than before. And then suddenly she startled me by asking what I really thought of her work.

Six months before, I would merely have buttered her, buttered her with a trowel, for the good of Thrushwood, Collins, and let it go at that. But now I had come to like her—and, after all, one has one's convictions. It wasn't the best butter, and she knew it. And monotonously, relentlessly, in her small, gracious voice, she kept pressing the point. That should have warned me, but it didn't. If authors were not megalomaniacs, no books would ever get written. But I forgot that first rule of publishing and floundered on.

"And yet, Mr. Robbins, I can feel that you don't really believe in me—you don't really believe in Angela Poe," she would say, gently and maddeningly, till at last with the rashness of youth I took my courage in both hands.

"It isn't that, Miss Poe," I stammered, "but if you'd only once—why don't you? It mightn't please your audience, but a woman of your experience—of your life——"

" My life?" she said, with dignity. " And what do you know of my life, young man?"

" Oh, nothing," I said, blundering from bad to worse, " but Mr. De Lacey said you both came from small towns—well, now, a *real* novel about an American small town——"

" So Everard has been telling tales—naughty boy! I must scold him," said Angela Poe brightly. But the brightness was all in the voice. I suddenly had the impression that she thought me a tedious young fool and wished me away. I began to long for Mr. De Lacey's return. But though I strained my ears I heard no echo of his rich boom from any corner of the house.

" Oh," I said, " please don't. They were *such* delightful stories. He—he told me you were married in a travelling dress."

" Dear Everard!" said Angela Poe. " He remembers everything. A dove-silk grey, with white collar and cuffs. I looked very pretty in it. And you think I might make a story of that, Mr. Robbins?"

" We have always hoped—your memoirs—the readers of Angela Poe——" I said.

She shook her head, decisively. " I shall never write my memoirs," she said. " Authors' memoirs never sell, you know—not really. The publishers think they are going to, but they don't. And then, it would lift the veil. Do you know who I am, young man? Do you know that people write me from all over the country, every day? They write me asking me what to do with their lives. And I tell them," she said sitting up very straight. " I tell them. Very often they do it, too. Because I'm Angela Poe—and they know my picture and my books. So they can write as they might to Another," and she bowed her head for an instant. " And that is not bad for a woman who writes what you think trash, Mr. Robbins! But I always knew I could do it," she ended, unexpectedly. " I always knew I could do it. But things were put in my way."

. . . . .

I could not leave, for it was not my train-time yet, but I began to feel more and more uncomfortable. There was something odd in the sweet, tinkling voice—the note of a fanatic egoism almost religious in its sincerity. I was used to the egosim of authors, but this was in another key.

She passed a handkerchief across her lips for a moment. " Dear, dear, I forget so many things since my illness," she said. " What were we talking about? Oh, yes, you were suggesting an idea to me—a story about an American small town. Do you know them, Mr. Robbins?"

She asked the question so suddenly and fiercely that I almost said no instead of yes. Then she relaxed.

"But of course," she said, a trifle primly, "you do know them. You know how cramped one's cultural opportunities are. And how one is mocked, perhaps, for striving after them? Or perhaps you do not know that?"

It was a rhetorical question, obviously. So I nodded hoping against hope for the sound of Mr. De Lacey's footfall in the hall.

"Even so," she said sweetly, "you are not a member of the female sex. And they are more easily wounded than gentlemen think. Even Everard has wounded me now and then—oh, not intentionally and I soon forgave him," she said with a regal gesture. "Still, he has wounded." She was evidently talking more to herself than to me, now, but this fact did not increase my comfort.

"I could have forgiven Marvin everything else," she said, "his drinking, his unbridled passions, his coarse jests. That is woman's mission—to submit and forgive. He made jokes about my housekeeping, too. And it would have cost him only eighty dollars to publish my poems. I had the sweetest wreath of field daisies for the cover. I thought he would be a way to higher things; after all, one has so little opportunity in a small town and the feed store was quite successful, financially. But I was mistaken," and she sighed, gently. I was now past wishing for Mr. De Lacey's appearance; I only wished for my train to roar into the room and bear me away. But such things do not happen, unfortunately.

"But I never thought of divorce," the mild, tinkling voice went on. "Never. It crossed my mind, once or twice, but I firmly put it aside. I have always been glad of that. I don't think he really *cared*," she said, opening her pansy eyes widely. "But he might have hurt Everard badly—he was such a very strong man. Sometimes, in the early days of our marriage, he used to carry me around the room on one arm. It frightened me, rather, but I always submitted and forgave. It was always so dusty in the store, too. It used to make me sneeze and then he would laugh. He laughed when Everard read Shakespeare to me. I sneezed that evening, as I was wiping the handle of the hatchet, but no one heard me."

"As you were what?" I said, and my voice was thin and high.

"I suppose it wasn't necessary," she said thoughtfully. "It would be, now, with the fingerprints, but they were quite stupid people and we knew little of fingerprints then. But it seemed tidier—I'd let it fall on the floor and the floor was dirty. They never really swept the store. He was sitting with his back to me, reading my poems and laughing. I'd hidden the new ones, but he'd found them and broken open the drawer. The hatchet was an old one—they used to cut the wire on the feed bales with it. You know, he didn't say anything at all. He was still laughing and trying to get out of the chair. But he wasn't quick enough. I burned the money in the stove and nobody even asked me about the dress. They say salts of lemon will take out blood stains *immediately*," she murmured. "But it seemed better not to try though it was quite a nice dress."

"But weren't you ever—didn't they ever——" I babbled.

"Why, Mr. Robbins, of course," she said, with perfect placidity, "you have no *idea* of the petty malice and gossip of a small town. But I was in bed, you know, when they came to tell me—in bed with a bad cold. Any emotional strain always gives me a very bad cold—I had quite a bad one the day Everard and I were married. And everybody knew he used to sit up in the feed store till all hours, drinking and reading vile atheist books like that horrid Colonel Ingersoll's. The old cats said it was because he was afraid to go home. Afraid of me!" she said with perfect ingenuousness. "There's no limit to what people will say. Why, they even talked about Everard, though everybody knew he was driving a load of vegetables to market with his father. I thought of that before I went to the store."

"And yet," I said, "you lived in Goshen—you didn't marry Mr. De Lacey till a year later——"

"A year and a day," she corrected. "That seemed more fitting. But I went into half-mourning at the end of six months. It's rather soon, I know, but I thought I might. As long as I was to be engaged to Everard," and a faint blush coloured her cheeks. "I told him I could discuss nothing of the sort while I was still in full mourning and he appreciated my wishes—Everard has always been so considerate. At first, I thought the time would hang very heavy on my hands. But, as a matter of fact, it passed quite quickly. I was writing my first novel," she said, in a hushed voice.

. . . . .

I do not know yet how I got out of the house—I hope with decency. But I had left "The Eyrie" behind and was well along on my two-mile tramp to the station before I really came to myself. It was her last words—and the picture they gave me—that sent the cold, authentic shudder down my spine.

I kept wondering wildly how many successful authors were murderers or murderesses and why the police did not arrest them all. For I could see the whole story and fill in every detail. It was fatally plausible, even to Angela Poe's primness. I could even believe that if the unfortunate Mr. Wedge had paid a printer eighty dollars, he might have lived. For there are eogisms which it is not safe to mock or dam up—if you do, you are tempting the explosion of primal forces.

And then, when I had almost reached the station, I suddenly began to laugh—the healing laughter of sanity. For the whole thing was ridiculous and Angela Poe had taken an impeccable revenge. I had told her what I thought of her work—and subtly, tinklingly, convincingly, she had made me swallow the most preposterous farrago of nonsense she could think of; swallow it whole. And, in doing so, she had proved her powers as a story-teller past cavil. But, once away from the monotonous spell of her voice, it was merely impossible to think of her as a murderess, and yet more impossible to think of Everard De Lacey as an accomplice. For accomplice he must have been—after the fact if not before it. Or else, she had hidden the truth from him all these years—and that was impossible too.

For a second, I even thought of turning back to "The Eyrie" and humbly admitting to its mistress my folly and my defeat. But my train, after all, was due in fifteen minutes, and I had a dinner engagement in New York. I would write her a letter instead—she would like a letter. I walked up and down the station platform, composing orotund phrases in my mind.

The late afternoon train from New York arrived some six minutes before my own, and I was pleased to see it disgorge the statuesque form of Everard De Lacey. He shook hands with me and boomed apologies for missing my visit. "And how did you leave Miss Poe?" he said, anxiously. "I have been away since early morning."

"Oh, she was perfectly splendid—I never saw her looking better," I said, warmed by a glow of secret laughter. "We talked for hours—she'll tell you."

"That's good—that's good, my dear fellow—you relieve me greatly," he said, while his eyes roved for the carriage that had not yet arrived. "Jenks is tardy to-day," he said. Then he gave a me quick look. "You didn't happen to mention what you told me in our little chat when she was so ill?" he said.

"Mention it?" I said with a broad grin. "Oh, yes, indeed."

He seemed curiously relieved. "I am much indebted,"

he said. " Then you really do feel—and it means something coming from you—that I am of some genuine help to her? To her books, I mean—her career? "

" I do, indeed," I said, though I was now puzzled.

" Excellent," he boomed. " Excellent." He took me by the lapel with the old actor's gesture. " You see," he said, " oh, it's foolish of me, I know—and we are old now, of course. But every now and then I have the feeling that I may not really be indispensable to her. And it worries me greatly."

For the instant, as he said it, I saw fear look out of his eyes. It was not an ignoble fear, but he must have lived with it a long time.

. . . . .

I did not go back to " The Eryie "; indeed, I did not go back to Thrushwood, Collins. To do the latter without doing the former would have required explanations and I did not feel like giving them. Instead, I changed my boarding-house, and went to work as a salesman of aluminium-ware. And, after six months of that, I went back to Central City and the place in my father's cement business that had been waiting for me. For I had come to the decision that I was not made for New York, nor the life of letters; I did not have the self-confidence of Angela Poe.

Once, during the six months, I thought I saw Mr. De Lacey on the street, but he did not seee me and I fled him. And, naturally, though I tried to escape them, I saw advertisements of the last completed novel of Angela Poe. She died when I had been three months in Central City, and when I read that she was survived by her husband, the actor, Everard De Lacey, I felt as if a weight had been lifted from my breast. But he only survived her a few months. He missed her too much, I suppose, and some ties are enduring. I should like to have asked him one question, only one, and now I shall never know. He certainly played Shakespearian roles—and there must have been quite a period, after they left Goshen, when he was playing. In fact the obituary mentions Othello and Hamlet. But there is another role—and I wonder if he ever played it and what he made of it. I think you know the one I mean.

O. HENRY

SCHOOLS AND SCHOOLS

OLD Jerome Warren lived in a hundred-thousand-dollar house at 35 East Fifty-Soforth Street. He was a downtown broker, so rich that he could afford to walk for his health a few blocks in the direction of his office every morning and then call a cab.

He had an adopted son, the son of an old friend named Gilbert—Cyril Scott could play him nicely—who was becoming a successful painter as fast as he could squeeze the paint out of his tubes. Another member of the household was Barbara Ross, a step-niece. Man is born to trouble; so, as old Jerome had no family of his own, he took up the burdens of others.

Gilbert and Barbara got along swimmingly. There was a tacit and tactical understanding all round that the two would stand up under a floral bell some high noon, and promise the minister to keep old Jerome's money in a state of high commotion. But at this point complications must be introduced.

Thirty years before, when old Jerome was young Jerome, there was a brother of his named Dick. Dick went West to seek his or somebody else's fortune. Nothing was heard of him until one day old Jerome had a letter from his brother. It was badly written on ruled paper that smelled of salt bacon and coffee-grounds. The writing was asthmatic and the spelling St. Vitusy.

It appeared that instead of Dick having forced Fortune to stand and deliver, he had been held up himself, and made to give hostages to the enemy. That is, as his letter disclosed, he was on the point of pegging out with a complication of disorders that even whisky had failed to check. All that his thirty years of prospecting had netted him was one daughter, nineteen years old, as per invoice, whom he was shipping East, charges prepaid, for Jerome to clothe, feed, educate, comfort, and cherish for the rest of her natural life or until matrimony should them part.

Old Jerome was a board-walk. Everybody knows that the world is supported by the shoulders of Atlas; and that Atlas stands on a rail-fence; and that the rail-fence is built on a turtle's back. Now, the turtle has to stand on something; and that is a board-walk made of men like old Jerome.

I do not know whether immortality should accrue to man; but if not so, I would like to know when men like old Jerome get what is due them?

They met Nevada Warren at the station. She was a little girl, deeply sunburned and wholesomely good-looking, with a manner that was frankly unsophisticated, yet one that not even a cigar-drummer would intrude upon without thinking twice. Looking at her, somehow you would expect to see her in a short skirt and leather leggings, shooting glass balls or taming mustangs. But in her plain white waist and black skirt she sent you guessing again. With an easy exhibition of strength she swung along a heavy valise, which the uniformed porters tried in vain to wrest from her.

"I am sure we shall be the best of friends," said Barbara, pecking at the firm, sunburned cheek.

"I hope so," said Nevada.

"Dear little niece," said old Jerome, "you are as welcome to my house as if it were your father's own."

"Thanks," said Nevada.

"And I am going to call you 'cousin,'" said Gilbert, with his charming smile.

"Take the valise, please," said Nevada. "It weighs a million pounds. It's got samples from six of dad's old mines in it," she explained to Barbara. "I calculate they'd assay about nine cents to the thousand tons, but I promised him to bring them along."

It is a common custom to refer to the usual complication between one man and two ladies, or one lady and two men, or a lady and a man and a nobleman, or—well, any of those problems—as the triangle. But they are never unqualified triangles. They are always isosceles—never equilateral. So, upon the coming of Nevada Warren, she and Gilbert and Barbara Ross lined up into such a figurative triangle; and of that triangle Barbara formed the hypotenuse.

One morning old Jerome was lingering long after breakfast over the dullest morning paper in the city before setting forth to his down-town fly-trap. He had become quite fond of Nevada, finding in her much of his dead brother's quiet independence and unsuspicious frankness.

A maid brought in a note for Miss Nevada Warren.

"A messenger-boy delivered it at the door, please," she said. "He's waiting for an answer."

Nevada, who was whistling a Spanish waltz between her teeth, and watching the carriages and autos roll by in the street, took the envelope. She knew it was from Gilbert, before she opened it, by the little gold palette in the upper left-hand corner.

After tearing it open she pored over the contents for a while, absorbedly. Then, with a serious face, she went and stood at her uncle's elbow.

"Uncle Jerome, Gilbert is a nice boy, isn't he?"

"Why, bless the child!" said old Jerome, crackling his paper loudly; "of course he is. I raised him myself."

"He wouldn't write anything to anybody that wasn't exactly—I mean that everybody couldn't know and read, would he?"

"I'd just like to see him try it," said uncle, tearing a handful from his newspaper. "Why, what——"

"Read this note he just sent me, uncle, and see if you think it's all right and proper. You see, I don't know much about city people and their ways."

Old Jerome threw his paper down and set both his feet upon it. He took Gilbert's note and fiercely perused it twice, and then a third time.

"Why, child," said he, "you had me almost excited, although I was sure of that boy. He's a duplicate of his father, and he was a gilt-edged diamond. He only asks if you and Barbara will be ready at four o'clock this afternoon for an automobile drive over to Long Island. I don't see anything to criticise in it except the stationery. I always did hate that shade of blue."

"Would it be all right to go?" asked Nevada, eagerly.

"Yes, yes, yes, child; of course. Why not? Still, it pleases me to see you so careful and candid. Go, by all means."

"I didn't know," said Nevada demurely. "I thought I'd ask you. Couldn't you go with us, uncle?"

"I? No, no, no, no! I've ridden once in a car that boy was driving. Never again! But it's entirely proper for you and Barbara to go. Yes, yes. But I will not. No, no, no, no!"

Nevada flew to the door, and said to the maid:

"You bet we'll go. I'll answer for Miss Barbara. Tell the boy to say to Mr. Warren, 'You bet we'll go.'"

"Nevada," called old Jerome, "pardon me, my dear, but

wouldn't it be as well to send him a note in reply? Just a line would do."

"No, I won't bother about that," said Nevada, gaily. "Gilbert will understand—he always does. I never rode in an automobile in my life; but I've paddled a canoe down Little Devil River through the Lost Horse Cañon, and if it's any livelier than that I'd like to know!"

Two months are supposed to have elapsed.

Barbara sat in the study of the hundred-thousand-dollar house. It was a good place for her. Many places are provided in the world where men and women may repair for the purpose of extricating themselves from divers difficulties. There are cloisters, wailing-places, watering-places, confessionals, hermitages, lawyers' offices, beauty-parlours, airships, and studies; and the greatest of these are studies.

It usually takes a hypotenuse a long time to discover that it is the longest side of a triangle. But it's a long line that has no turning.

Barbara was alone. Uncle Jerome and Nevada had gone to the theatre. Barbara had not cared to go. She wanted to stay at home and study in the study. If you, miss, were a stunning New York girl, and saw every day that a brown, ingenuous Western witch was getting hobbles and a lasso on the young man you wanted for yourself, you, too, would lose taste for the oxidised silver setting of a musical comedy.

Barbara sat by the quartered-oak library table. Her right arm rested upon the table, and her dextral fingers nervously manipulated a sealed letter. The letter was addressed to Nevada Warren; and in the upper left-hand corner of the envelope was Gilbert's little gold palette. It had been delivered at nine o'clock, after Nevada had left.

Barbara would have given her pearl necklace to know what the letter contained; but she could not open and read it by the aid of steam, or a pen-handle, or a hairpin, or any of the generally approved methods because her position in society forbade such an act. She had tried to read some of the lines of the letter by holding the envelope up to a strong light and pressing it hard against the paper, but Gilbert had too good a taste in stationery to make that possible.

At eleven-thirty the theatre-goers returned. It was a delicious winter night. Even so far as from the cab to the door they were powdered thickly with the big flakes downpouring diagonally from the east. Old Jerome growled good-naturedly about villainous cab service and blockaded streets. Nevada, coloured like a rose, with sapphire eyes, babbled of the stormy nights in the mountains around dad's cabin.

During all these wintry apostrophes, Barbara, cold at heart, sawed wood—the only appropriate thing she could think of to do.

Old Jerome went immediately upstairs to hot-water bottles and quinine. Nevada fluttered into the study, the only cheerful lighted room, subsided into an arm-chair, and while at the interminable task of unbuttoning her elbow gloves, gave oral testimony as to the demerits of the "show."

"Yes, I think Mr. Fields is really amusing—sometimes," said Barbara. "Here is a letter for you, dear, that came by special delivery just after you had gone."

"Who is it from?" asked Nevada, tugging at a button.

"Well, really," said Barbara, with a smile, "I can only guess. The envelope has that queer little thing in one corner that Gilbert calls a palette, but which looks to me rather like a gilt heart on a schoolgirl's valentine."

"I wonder what he's writing to me about," remarked Nevada listlessly.

"We're all alike," said Barbara; "all women. We try to find out what is in a letter by studying the postmark. As a last resort we use scissors, and read it from the bottom upward. Here it is."

She made a motion as if to toss the letter across the table to Nevada.

"Great catamounts!" exclaimed Nevada. "These centre-fire buttons are a nuisance. I'd rather wear buckskins. Oh, Barbara, please shuck the hide off that letter and read it. It'll be midnight before I get these gloves off!"

"Why, dear, you don't want me to open Gilbert's letter to you? It's for you, and you wouldn't wish anyone else to read it, of course!"

Nevada raised her steady, calm, sapphire eyes from her gloves.

"Nobody writes me anything that everybody mightn't read," she said. "Go on, Barbara. Maybe Gilbert wants us to go out in his car again to-morrow."

Curiosity can do more things than kill a cat; and if emotions, well recognised as feminine, are inimical to feline life, then jealousy would soon leave the whole world catless. Barbara opened the letter, with an indulgent, slightly bored air.

"Well, dear," she said, "I'll read it if you want me to."

She slit the envelope, and read the missive with swift-travelling eyes; read it again, and cast a quick, shrewd glance at Nevada, who, for the time, seemed to consider gloves as the world of her interest, and letters from rising artists as no more than messages from Mars.

For a quarter of a minute Barbara looked at Nevada with a strange steadfastness; and then a smile so small that it widened her mouth only the sixteenth part of an inch, and narrowed her eyes no more than a twentieth flashed like an inspired thought across her face.

Since the beginning no woman has been a mystery to another woman. Swift as light travels, each penetrates the chart and mind of another, sifts her sister's words of their cunningest disguises, reads her most hidden desires, and plucks the sophistry from her wiliest talk like hairs from a comb, twiddling them sardonically between her thumb and fingers before letting them float away on the breezes of fundamental doubt. Long ago Eve's son rang the door-bell of the family residence in Paradise Park, bearing a strange lady on his arm, whom he introduced. Eve took her daughter-in-law aside and lifted a classic eyebrow.

"The Land of Nod," said the bride, languidly flirting the leaf of a palm. "I suppose you've been there, of course?"

"Not lately," said Eve, absolutely unstaggered. "Don't you think the apple-sauce they serve over there is execrable? I rather like that mulberry-leaf tunic effect, dear; but, of course, the real fig goods are not to be had over there. Come over behind this lilac-bush while the gentlemen split a celery tonic. I think the caterpillar-holes have made your dress open a little in the back."

So, then and there—according to the records—was the alliance formed by the only two who's-who ladies in the world. Then it was agreed that women should for ever remain as clear as a pane of glass—though glass was yet to be discovered—to other women, and that she should palm herself off on man as a mystery.

Barbara seemed to hesitate.

"Really, Nevada," she said, with a little show of embarrassment, "you shouldn't have insisted on my opening this. I—I'm sure it wasn't meant for anyone else to know."

Nevada forgot her gloves for a moment.

"Then read it aloud," she said. "Since you've already read it, what's the difference? If Mr. Warren has written to me something that anyone else oughtn't to know, that is all the more reason why everybody should know it."

"Well," said Barbara, "this is what it says: 'Dearest Nevada—Come to my studio at twelve o'clock to-night. Do not fail.'" Barbara rose and dropped the note in Nevada's lap. "I'm awfully sorry," she said, "that I knew. It isn't like Gilbert. There must be some mistake. Just consider that I am ignorant of it, will you, dear? I must go upstairs now, I have such a headache. I'm sure I don't understand the note. Perhaps Gilbert has been dining too well, and will explain. Good night!"

Nevada tiptoed to the hall, and heard Barbara's door close upstairs. The bronze block in the study told the hour of twelve was fifteen minutes away. She ran swiftly to the front door, and let herself out into the snowstorm. Gilbert Warren's studio was six squares away.

By aerial ferry the white silent forces of the storm attacked the city from beyond the sullen East River. Already the snow lay a foot deep on the pavements, the drifts heaping themselves like scaling-ladders against the walls of the besieged town. The Avenue was as quiet as a street in Pompeii. Cabs now and then skimmed past like white-winged gulls over a moonlit ocean; and less frequent motor-cars—sustaining the comparison—hissed through the foaming waves like submarine boats on their jocund, perilous journeys.

Nevada plunged like a wind-driven storm-petrel on her way. She looked up at the ragged sierras of cloud-capped buildings that rose above the streets, shaded by the night lights and the congealed vapours to grey, drab ashen, lavender, dun, and cerulean tints. They were so like the wintry mountains of her Western home that she felt a satisfaction such as the hundred-thousand-dollar house had seldom brought her.

A policeman caused her to waver on a corner just by his eye and weight.

"Hello, Mabel!" said he. "Kind of late for you to be out, ain't it?"

"I—I am just going to the drug store," said Nevada, hurrying past him.

The excuse serves as a passport for the most sophisticated. Does it prove that woman never progresses, or that she sprang from Adam's rib, full-fledged in intellect and wiles?

Turning eastward, the direct blast cut down Nevada's speed one half. She made zigzag tracks in the snow; but she was as tough as a pinon sapling, and bowed to it as gracefully. Suddenly the studio-building loomed before her, a familiar landmark, like a cliff above some well-remembered cañon. The haunt of business and its hostile neighbour, art, was darkened and silent. The elevator stopped at ten.

Up eight flights of Stygian stairs Nevada climbed, and rapped firmly at the door numbered "89." She had been there many times before, with Barbara and Uncle Jerome.

Gilbert opened the door. He had a crayon pencil in one

hand, a green shade over his eyes, and a pipe in his mouth. The pipe dropped to the floor.

"Am I late?" asked Nevada. "I came as quick as I could. Uncle and me were at the theatre this evening. Here I am, Gilbert!"

Gilbert did a Pygmalion-and-Galatea act. He changed from a statue of stupefaction to a young man with a problem to tackle. He admitted Nevada, got a whisk-broom, and began to brush the snow from her clothes. A great lamp, with a green shade, hung over an easel, where the artist had been sketching in crayon.

"You wanted me," said Nevada simply, "and I came. You said so in your letter. What did you send for me for?"

"You read my letter?" inquired Gilbert, sparring for wind.

"Barbara read it to me. I saw it afterward. It said: 'Come to my studio at twelve to-night, and do not fail.' I thought you were sick, of course, but you don't seem to be."

"Aha!" said Gilbert irrelevantly. "I'll tell you why I asked you to come, Nevada. I want you to marry me immediately—to-night. What's a little snowstorm? Will you do it?"

"You might have noticed that I would long ago," said Nevada. "And I'm rather stuck on the snowstorm idea myself. I surely would hate one of these flowery church noon-weddings. Gilbert, I didn't know you had grit enough to propose it this way. Let's shock 'em—it's our funeral, ain't it?"

"You bet!" said Gilbert. "Where did I hear that expression?" he added to himself. "Wait a minute, Nevada; I want to do a little 'phoning."

He shut himself in a little dressing-room, and called upon the lightnings of the heavens—condensed into unromantic numbers and districts.

"That you, Jack? You confounded sleepy-head! Yes, wake up; this is me—or I—oh, bother the difference in grammar! I'm going to be married right away. Yes! Wake up your sister—don't answer me back; bring her along, too—you *must*. Remind Agnes of the time I saved her from drowning in Lake Ronkonkoma—I know it's caddish to refer to it, but she *must* come with you. Yes! Nevada is here, waiting. We've been engaged quite a while. Some opposition among the relatives, you know, and we have to pull it off this way. We're waiting here for you. Don't let Agnes out-talk you—bring her! You will? Good old boy!

I'll order a carriage to call for you, double-quick time. Confound you, Jack, you're all right!"

Gilbert returned to the room where Nevada waited.

"My old friend, Jack Peyton, and his sister were to have been here at a quarter to twelve," he explained; "but Jack is so confoundedly slow. I've just 'phoned them to hurry. They'll be here in a few minutes. I'm the happiest man in the world, Nevada! What did you do with the letter I sent you to-day?"

"I've got it cinched here," said Nevada, pulling it out from beneath her opera-cloak.

Gilbert drew the letter from the envelope and looked it over carefully. Then he looked at Nevada thoughtfully.

"Didn't you think it rather queer that I should ask you to come to my studio at midnight?" he asked.

"Why, no," said Nevada, rounding her eyes. "Not if you needed me. Out West, when a pal sends you a hurry call—ain't that what you say here?—we get there first and talk about it after the row is over. And it's usually snowing there, too, when things happen. So I didn't mind."

Gilbert rushed into another room, and came back burdened with overcoats warranted to turn wind, rain, or snow.

"Put this raincoat on," he said, holding it for her. "We have a quarter of a mile to go. Old Jack and his sister will be here in a few minutes." He began to struggle into a heavy coat. "Oh, Nevada," he said, "just look at the headlines on the front page of that evening paper on the table, will you? It's about your section of the West, and I know it will interest you."

He waited a full minute, pretending to find trouble in the getting on of his overcoat and then turned. Nevada had not moved. She was looking at him with strange and pensive directness. Her cheeks had a flush on them beyond the colour that had been contributed by the wind and snow; but her eyes were steady.

"I was going to tell you," she said, "anyhow, before—you—before we—before—well, before anything. Dad never gave me a day of schooling. I never learned to read or write a darned word. Now if——"

Pounding their uncertain way upstairs, the feet of Jack, the somnolent, and Agnes, the grateful, were heard.

When Mr. and Mrs. Gilbert Warren were spinning softly homeward in a closed carriage, after the ceremony, Gilbert said:

"Nevada, would you really like to know what I wrote you in the letter that you received to-night?"

"Fire away!" said his bride.

"Word for word," said Gilbert, "it was this: 'My dear Miss Warren—You were right about the flower. It was a hydrangea, and not a lilac.'"

"All right," said Nevada. "But let's forget it. The joke's on Barbara, anyway!"

EDGAR ALLAN POF

THE MYSTERY OF MARIE ROGET

WHEN, in an article entitled "The Murders in the Rue Morgue," I endeavoured, about a year ago, to depict some very remarkable features in the mental character of my friend, the Chevalier C. Auguste Dupin, it did not occur to me that I should ever resume the subject. This depicting of character constituted my design; and this design was thoroughly fulfilled in the wild train of circumstances brought to instance Dupin's idiosyncrasy. I might have adduced other examples, but I should have proven no more. Late events, however, in their surprising development, have startled me into some further details, which will carry with them the air of extorted confession. Hearing what I have lately heard, it would be indeed strange should I remain silent in regard to what I both heard and saw so long ago.

It may readily be supposed that the part played by my friend, in the drama at the Rue Morgue, had not failed of its impression upon the fancies of the Parisian police. With its emissaries, the name of Dupin had grown into a household word. The simple character of those inductions by which he had disentangled the mystery never having been explained even to the Prefect, or to any other individual than myself, of course it is not surprising that the affair was regarded as little less than miraculous, or that the Chevalier's analytical abilities acquired for him the credit of intuition. His frankness would have led him to disabuse every inquirer of such prejudice; but his indolent humour forbade all further agitation of a topic whose interest to himself had long ceased. It thus happened that he found himself the cynosure of the policial eyes; and the cases were not few in which attempt was made to engage his services at the Prefecture. One of the most remarkable instances was that of the murder of a young girl named Marie Rogêt.

This event occurred about two years after the atrocity

in the Rue Morgue. Marie, whose Christian and family name will at once arrest attention from their resemblance to those of the unfortunate " cigar-girl," was the only daughter of the widow Estelle Rogêt. The father had died during the child's infancy, and from the period of his death, until within eighteen months before the assassination which forms the subject of our narrative, the mother and daughter had dwelt together in the Rue Pavée Saint Andrée; Madame there keeping a *pension*, assisted by Marie. Affairs went on thus until the latter had attained her twenty-second year, when her great beauty attracted the notice of a perfumer, who occupied one of the shops in the basement of the Palais Royal, and whose custom lay chiefly among the desperate adventurers infesting that neighbourhood. Monsieur Le Blanc was not unaware of the advantages to be derived from the attendance of the fair Marie in his perfumery; and his liberal proposals were accepted eagerly by the girl, although with somewhat more of hesitation by Madame.

The anticipations of the shopkeeper were realised, and his rooms soon became notorious through the charms of the sprightly *grisette*. She had been in his employ about a year, when her admirers were thrown into confusion by her sudden disappearance from the shop. Monsieur Le Blanc was unable to account for her absence, and Madame Roget was distracted with anxiety and terror. The public papers immediately took up the theme, and the police were upon the point of making serious investigations, when, one fine morning, after the lapse of a week, Marie, in good health, but with a somewhat saddened air, made her re-appearance at her usual counter in the perfumery. All inquiry, except that of a private character, was of course immediately hushed. Monsieur Le Blanc professed total ignorance, as before. Marie, with Madame, replied to all questions, that the last week had been spent at the house of a relation in the country. Thus the affair died away, and was generally forgotten; for the girl, ostensibly to relieve herself from the impertinence of curiosity, soon bade a final adieu to the perfumer, and sought the shelter of her mother's residence in the Rue Pavée Saint Andrée.

It was about five months after this return home, that her friends were alarmed by her sudden disappearance for the second time. Three days elapsed, and nothing was heard of her. On the fourth her corpse was found floating in the Seine, near the shore which is opposite the Quartier of the Rue Saint Andrée, and at a point not very far distant from the secluded neighbourhood of the Barriere du Roule.

Upon the first discovery of the corpse, it was not supposed that the murderer would be able to elude, for more than a very brief period, the inquisition which was immediately set on foot. It was not until the expiration of a week that it was deemed necessary to offer a reward; and even then this reward was limited to a thousand francs. In the meantime the investigation proceeded with vigour, if not always with judgment, and numerous individuals were examined to no purpose; while, owing to the continual absence of all clue to the mystery, the popular excitement greatly increased. At the end of the tenth day it was thought advisable to double the sum originally proposed; and, at length, the second week having elapsed without leading to any discoveries, and the prejudice which always exists in Paris against the police having given vent to itself in several serious *émeutes*, the Prefect took it upon himself to offer the sum of twenty thousand francs "for the conviction of the assassin," or, if more than one should prove to have been implicated, "for the conviction of any one of the assassins." In the proclamation setting forth this reward, a full pardon was promised to any accomplice who should come forward in evidence against his fellow; and to the whole was appended, wherever it appeared, the private placard of a committee of citizens, offering ten thousand francs, in addition to the amount proposed by the Prefecture. The entire reward thus stood at no less than thirty thousand francs, which will be regarded as an extraordinary sum when we consider the humble condition of the girl, and the great frequency, in large cities, of such atrocities as the one described.

No one doubted now that the mystery of this murder would be immediately brought to light. But although, in one or two instances, arrests were made which promised elucidation, yet nothing was elicited which could implicate the parties suspected; and they were discharged forthwith. Strange as it may appear, the third week from the discovery of the body had passed, and passed without any light being thrown upon the subject, before even a rumour of the events which had so agitated the public mind reached the ears of Dupin and myself. Engaged in researches which had absorbed our whole attention, it had been nearly a month since either of us had gone abroad, or received a visitor, or more than glanced at the leading political articles in one of the daily papers. The first intelligence of the murder was brought us by G——, in person. He called upon us early in the afternoon of the 13th of July 18—, and remained with us until late in the night. He had been piqued by the failure of all his endeavours to ferret the assassins. His reputation—so he said, with a peculiarly Parisian air—was at stake. Even his honour was concerned. The eyes of the public were upon him; and there was really no sacrifice which he would not be willing to make for the development of the mystery. He concluded a somewhat droll speech with a compliment upon what he was pleased to term the *tact* of Dupin, and made him a direct, and certainly a liberal proposition, the precise nature of which I do not feel at liberty to disclose, but which has no bearing upon the proper subject of my narrative.

The compliment my friend rebutted as best he could, but the proposition he accepted at once, although its advantages were altogether provisional. This point being settled, the Prefect broke forth at once into explanations of his own views, interspersing them with long comments upon the evidence; of which latter we were not yet in possession. He discoursed much, and beyond doubt learnedly; while I hazarded an occasional suggestion as the night wore drowsily away. Dupin, sitting steadily in his accustomed arm-chair, was the embodiment of respectful attention. He wore spectacles during the whole interview; and an occasional glance beneath their green glasses sufficed to convince me that he slept not the less soundly, because silently, throughout the seven or eight leaden-footed hours which immediately preceded the departure of the Prefect.

In the morning I procured, at the Prefecture, a full report of all the evidence elicited, and, at the various newspaper offices, a copy of every paper in which, from first to last, had been published any decisive information in regard to this sad affair. Freed from all that was positively disproved, this mass of information stood thus :—

Marie Rogêt left the residence of her mother, in the Rue Pavee Saint Andrée, about nine o'clock in the morning of Sunday, June the 22nd, 18—. In going out she gave notice to a Monsieur Jacques St. Eustache, and to him only, of her intention to spend the day with an aunt who resided in the Rue des Drômes. The Rue des Dromes is a short and narrow but populous thoroughfare, not far from the banks of the river, and at a distance of some two miles in the most direct course possible from the *pension* of Madame Rogêt. St. Eustache was the accepted suitor of Marie, and lodged, as well as took his meals, at the *pension*. He was to have gone for his betrothed at dusk, and to have escorted her home. In the afternoon, however, it came on to rain heavily; and, supposing that she would remain all night at her aunt's (as she had done under similar circumstances before), he did not think it necessary to keep his promise. As night drew on, Madame

Rogêt (who was an infirm old lady, seventy years of age) was heard to express a fear " that she should never see Marie again "; but this observation attracted little attention at the time.

On Monday, it was ascertained that the girl had not been to the Rue des Drômes; and when the day elapsed without tidings of her, a tardy search was instituted at several points in the city and its environs. It was not, however, until the fourth day from the period of her disappearance that anything satisfactory was ascertained respecting her. On this day (Wednesday, the 25th of June), a Monsieur Beauvais, who, with a friend, had been making inquiries for Marie near the Barrière du Roule, on the shore of the Seine which is opposite the Rue Pavée Saint Andrée, was informed that a corpse had just been towed ashore by some fishermen, who had found it floating in the river. Upon seeing the body, Beauvais, after some hesitation, identified it as that of the perfumery girl. His friend recognised it more promptly.

The face was suffused with dark blood, some of which issued from the mouth. No foam was seen, as in the case of the merely drowned. There was no discoloration in the cellular tissue. About the throat were bruises and impressions of fingers. The arms were bent over on the chest, and were rigid. The right hand was clenched; the left partially open. On the left wrist were two circular excoriations, apparently the effect of ropes, or of a rope in more than one volution. A part of the right wrist, also, was much chafed, as well as the back throughout its extent, but more especially at the shoulder-blades. In bringing the body to the shore the fishermen had attached to it a rope, but none of the excoriations had been effected by this. The flesh of the neck was much swollen. There were no cuts apparent, or bruises which appeared the effect of blows. A piece of lace was found tied so tightly around the neck as to be hidden from sight; it was completely buried in the flesh, and was fastened by a knot which lay just under the left ear. This alone would have sufficed to produce death. The medical testimony spoke confidently of the virtuous character of the deceased. She had been subjected, it said, to brutal violence. The corpse was in such condition when found that there could have been no difficulty in its recognition by friends.

The dress was much torn and otherwise disordered. In the outer garment, a slip, about a foot wide, had been torn upward from the bottom hem to the waist, but not torn off. It was wound three times around the waist, and secured by a sort of hitch in the back. The dress immediately beneath the frock was of fine muslin; and from this a slip eighteen inches wide had been torn entirely out—torn very evenly and with great care. It was found around her neck, fitting loosely, and secured with a hard knot. Over this muslin slip and the slip of lace, the strings of a bonnet were attached, the bonnet being appended. The knot by which the strings of the bonnet were fastened, was not a lady's, but a slip or sailor's knot.

After the recognition of the corpse, it was not, as usual, taken to the Morgue (this formality being superfluous), but hastily interred not far from the spot at which it was brought ashore. Through the exertions of Beauvais the matter was industriously hushed up, as far as possible; and several days had elapsed before any public emotion resulted. A weekly paper, however, at length took up the theme; the corpse was disinterred, and a re-examination instituted; but nothing was elicited beyond what has been already noted. The clothes, however, were now submitted to the mother and friends of the deceased, and fully identified as those worn by the girl upon leaving home.

Meantime, the excitement increased hourly. Several individuals were arrested and discharged. St. Eustache fell especially under suspicion; and he failed, at first, to give an intelligible account of his whereabouts during the Sunday on which Marie left home. Subsequently, however, he submitted to Monsieur G——, affidavits, accounting satisfactorily for every hour of the day in question. As time passed and no discovery ensued, a thousand contradictory rumours were circulated, and journalists busied themselves in *suggestions*. Among these, the one which attracted the most notice, was the idea that Marie Rogêt still lived—that the corpse found in the Seine was that of some other unfortunate. It will be proper that I submit to the reader some passages which embody the suggestion alluded to. These passages are *literal* translations from *L'Etoile*, a paper conducted, in general, with much ability:—

"Mademoiselle Rogêt left her mother's house on Sunday morning, June the 22nd, 18—, with the ostensible purpose of going to see her aunt, or some other connection, in the Rue des Drômes. From that hour nobody is proved to have seen her. There is no trace or tidings of her at all. . . . There has no person, whatever, come forward, so far, who saw her at all, on that day, after she left her mother's door. . . . Now, though we have no evidence that Marie Rogêt was in the land of the living after nine o'clock on Sunday, June the 22nd, we have proof that, up to that hour, she was alive. On Wednesday noon, at twelve, a female body was discovered afloat on the shore of the Barrière du Roule. This was, even if we presume that Marie Rogêt was thrown into the river within three hours after she left her mother's house, only three days from the time she left her home—three days to an hour. But it is folly to suppose that the murder, if murder was committed on her body, could have been consummated soon enough to have enabled her murderers to throw the body into the river before midnight. Those who are guilty of such horrid crimes, chose darkness rather than light. . . . Thus we see that if the body found in the river *was* that of Marie Rogêt, it could only have been in the water two and a half days, or three at the outside. All experience has shown that drowned bodies, or bodies thrown into the water immediately after death by violence, require from six to ten days for sufficient decomposition to take place to bring them to the top of the water. Even where a cannon is fired over a corpse, and it rises before at least five or six days' immersion, it sinks again, if let alone. Now, we ask, what was there in this case to cause a departure from the ordinary course of nature? . . . If the body had been kept in its mangled state on shore until Tuesday night, some trace would be found on shore of the murderers. It is a doubtful point, also, whether the body would be so soon afloat, even were it thrown in after having been dead two days. And, furthermore, it is exceedingly improbable that any villains who had committed such a murder as is here supposed, would have thrown the body in without weight to sink it, when such a precaution could have so easily been taken."

The editor here proceeds to argue that the body must have been in the water " not three days merely, but, at least, five times three days," because it was so far decomposed that Beauvais had great difficulty in recognising it. This latter point, however was fully disproved. I continue the translation :—

" What, then, are the facts on which M. Beauvais says that he has no doubt the body was that of Marie Rogêt? He ripped up the gown sleeve, and says he found marks which satisfied him of the identity. The public generally supposed those marks to have consisted of some description of scars. He rubbed the arm and found *hair* upon it—something as indefinite, we think, as can readily be imagined—as little conclusive as finding an arm in the sleeve. M. Beauvais did not return that night, but sent word to Madame Rogêt, at seven o'clock on Wednesday evening, that an investigation was still in progress respecting her daughter. If we allow that Madame Rogêt, from her age and grief, could not go over (which is allowing a great deal), there certainly must have been some one who would have thought it worth while to go over and attend the investigation, if they thought the body was that of Marie. Nobody went over. There was nothing said or heard about the matter in the Rue Pavée Saint Andrée, that reached even the occupants of the same building. M. St. Eustache, the lover and intended husband of Marie, who boarded in her mother's house, deposes that he did not hear of the discovery of the body of his intended until the next morning, when M. Beauvais came into his chamber and told him of it. For an item of news like this, it strikes us it was very coolly received."

In this way the journal endeavoured to create the impression of an apathy on the part of the relatives of Marie, inconsistent with the supposition that these relatives believed the corpse to be hers. Its insinuations amount to this—that Marie, with the connivance of her friends, had absented herself from the city for reasons involving a charge against her chastity; and that these friends, upon the discovery of a corpse in the Seine, somewhat resembling that of the girl, had availed themselves of the opportunity to impress the public with the belief of her death. In a subsequent number of the paper, an attempt was made to throw suspicion upon Beauvais himself. The editor says:—

" Now, then, a change comes over the matter. We are told that, on one occasion, while a Madame B—— was at Madame Rogêt's house, M. Beauvais, who was going out, told her that a gendarme was expected there, and that she, Madame B., must not say anything to the gendarme until he returned, but let the matter be for him. . . . In the present posture of affairs, M. Beauvais appears to have the whole matter locked up in his head. A single step cannot be taken without M. Beauvais; for, go which way you will, you run against him. . . . For some reason, he determined that nobody shall have anything to do with the proceedings but himself, and he has elbowed the male relatives out of the way, according to their representations, in a very singular manner. He seems to have been very much averse to permitting the relatives to see the body."

By the following fact, some colour was given to the suspicion thus thrown upon Beauvais. A visitor at his office, a few days prior to the girl's disappearance, and during the absence of its occupant, had observed a *rose* in the keyhole of the door, and the name "*Marie*" inscribed upon a slate which hung near at hand.

The general impression, so far as we were enabled to glean it from the newspapers, seemed to be, that Marie had been the victim of *a gang* of desperadoes—that by these she had been borne across the river, maltreated and murdered. *Le Commerciel*, however, a print of extensive influence, was earnest in combating this popular idea. I quote a passage or two from its columns:—

"We are persuaded that pursuit has hitherto been on a false scent, so far as it has been directed to the Barrière du Roule. It is impossible that a person so well known to thousands as this young woman was, should have passed three blocks without some one having seen her; and any one who saw her would have remembered it, for she interested all who knew her. It was when the streets were full of people, when she went out. . . . It is impossible that she could have gone to the Barrière du Roule, or to the Rue des Drômes, without being recognised by a dozen persons; yet no one has come forward who saw her outside of her mother's door, and there is no evidence, except the testimony concerning her expressed intentions, that she did go out at all. Her gown was torn, bound round her, and tied; and by that the body was carried as a bundle. If the murder had been committed at the Barrière du Roule, there would have been no necessity for any such arrangement. The fact that the body was found floating near the Barrière, is no proof as to where it was thrown into the water. . . . A piece of one of the unfortunate girl's petticoats two feet long and one foot wide, was torn out and tied under her chin around the back of her head, probably to prevent screams. This was done by fellows who had no pocket-handkerchiefs."

A day or two before the Prefect called upon us, however, some important information reached the police, which seemed to overthrow, at least, the chief portion of *Le Commerciel's* argument. Two small boys, sons of a Madame Deluc, while roaming among the woods near the Barrière du Roue, chanced to penetrate a close thicket, within which were three or four large stones, forming a kind of seat, with a back and footstool. On the upper stone lay a white petticoat; on the second a silk scarf. A parasol, gloves, and a pocket-handkerchief were also here found. The handkerchief bore the name "Marie Rogêt." Fragments of dress were discovered on the brambles around. The earth was trampled, the bushes were broken, and there was every evidence of a struggle. Between the thicket and the river, the fences were found taken down, and the ground bore evidence of some heavy burden having been dragged along it.

Consequent upon this discovery, new evidence appeared. Madame Deluc testified that she keeps a roadside inn not far from the bank of the river, opposite the Barrière du Roule. The neighbourhood is secluded—particularly so. It is the usual Sunday resort of blackguards from the city, who cross the river in boats. About three o'clock, in the afternoon of the Sunday in question, a young girl arrived at the inn, accompanied by a young man of dark complexion. The two remained here for some time. On their departure, they took the road to some thick woods in the vicinity. Madame Deluc's attention was called to the dress worn by the girl on account of its resemblance to one worn by a deceased relative. A scarf was particularly noticed. Soon after the departure of the couple, a gang of miscreants made their appearance, behaved boisterously, ate and drank without making payment, followed in the route of the young man and girl, returned to the inn about dusk, and recrossed the river as if in great haste.

It was soon after dark, upon this same evening, that Madame Deluc, as well as her eldest son, heard the screams of a female in the vicinity of the inn. The screams were violent but brief. Madame D. recognised not only the scarf which was found in the thicket, but the dress which was discovered upon the corpse. An omnibus-driver, Valence, now also testified that he saw Marie Rogêt cross a ferry on the Seine, on the Sunday in question, in company with a young man of dark complexion. He, Valence, knew Marie, and could not be mistaken in her identity. The articles found in the thicket were fully identified by the relatives of Marie.

The items of evidence and information thus collected by myself, from the newspapers, at the suggestion of Dupin, embraced only one more point—but this was a point of seemingly vast consequence. It appears that, immediately after the discovery of the clothes as above described, the lifeless, or nearly lifeless body of St. Eustache, Marie's betrothed, was found in the vicinity of what all now supposed the scene of the outrage. A phial labelled "laudanum," and emptied, was found near him. His breath gave evidence of the poison. He died without speaking. Upon his person was found a letter, briefly stating his love for Marie, with his design of self-destruction.

"I need scarcely tell you," said Dupin, as he finished the perusal of my notes, "that this is a far more intricate case than that of the Rue Morgue; from which it differs in one important respect. This is an *ordinary*, although an atrocious instance of crime. There is nothing peculiarly *outré* about it. You will observe that, for this reason, the mystery has been considered easy, when, for this reason, it should have been considered difficult of solution. Thus, at first, it was thought unnecessary to offer a reward. The myrmidons of G—— were able at once to comprehend how and why such an atrocity *might have been* committed. They could picture to their imaginations a mode—many modes—and a motive—many motives; and because it was not impossible that either of these numerous modes and motives *could* have been the actual one, they have taken it for granted that one of them *must*. But the ease with which these variable fancies were entertained, and the very plausibility which each assumed, should have been understood as indicative rather of the difficulties than of the facilities which must attend elucidation. I have before observed that it is by prominences above the plane of the ordinary, that reason feels her way, if at all, in her search for the true, and that the proper question in cases such as this, is not so much 'what has occurred?' as 'what has occurred that has never occurred before?' In the investigations at the house of Madame L'Espanaye, the agents of G—— were discouraged and confounded by that very *unusualness* which, to a properly regulated intellect, would have afforded the surest omen of success; while this same intellect might have been plunged in despair at the ordinary character of all that met the eye in the case of the perfumery girl, and yet told of nothing but easy triumph to the functionaries of the Prefecture.

"With the public the arguments of *L'Etoile* have had weight; and that the journal itself is convinced of their importance would appear from the manner in which it commences one of its essays upon the subject: 'Several of the morning papers of the day,' it says, 'speak of the *conclusive* article in Monday's *Etoile*.' To me, this article appears conclusive of little beyond the zeal of its inditer. We should bear in mind that, in general, it is the object of our newspapers rather to create a sensation—to make a point—than to further the cause of truth. The latter end is only pursued when it seems coincident with the former. The print which merely falls in with ordinary opinion (however well-founded this opinion may be) earns for itself no credit with the mob. The mass of the people regard as profound only him who suggests *pungent contradictions* of the general idea. In ratiocination, not less than in literature, it is the *epigram* which is the most immediately and the most universally appreciated. In both, it is of the lowest order of merit.

"What I mean to say is, that it is the mingled epigram and melodrama of the idea that Marie Rogêt still lives, rather than any true plausibility in this idea, which have suggested it to *L'Etoile*, and secured it a favourable reception with the public. Let us examine the heads of this journal's argument; endeavouring to avoid the incoherence with which it is originally set forth.

"The first aim of the writer is to show, from the brevity of the interval between Marie's disappearance and the finding of the floating corpse, that this corpse cannot be that of Marie. The reduction of this interval to its smallest possible dimension, becomes thus, at once, an object with the reasoner. In the rash pursuit of this object, he rushes into mere assumption at the outset. 'It is folly to suppose,' he says, 'that the murder, if murder was committed on her body, could have been consummated soon enough to have enabled her murderers to throw the body into the river before midnight.' We demand at once, and very naturally, *why*? Why is it folly to suppose that the murder was committed *within five minutes* after the girl's quitting her mother's house? Why is it folly to suppose that the murder was committed at any given period of the day? There have been assassinations at all hours. But, had the murder taken place at any moment between nine o'clock in the morning of Sunday, and a quarter before midnight, there would still have been time enough 'to throw the body into the river before midnight.' This assumption, then, amounts precisely to this—that the murder was not committed on Sunday at all—and, if we allow *L'Etoile* to assume this, we may permit it any liberties whatever. The paragraph beginning 'It is folly to suppose that the murder,' etc., however it appears as printed in *L'Etoile*, may be imagined to have existed actually *thus* in the brain of its inditer: 'It is folly to suppose that the murder, if murder was committed on the body, could have been committed soon enough to have enabled her murderers to throw the body into the river before midnight; it is folly, we say, to suppose all this, and to suppose at the same time (as we are resolved to suppose), that the body was *not* thrown in until *after* midnight'—a sentence sufficiently inconsequential in itself, but not so utterly preposterous as the one printed.

"Were it my purpose," continued Dupin, "merely to *make out a case* against this passage of *L'Etoile's* argument,

I might safety leave it where it is. It is not, however, with *L'Etoile* that we have to do, but with the truth. The sentence in question has but one meaning, as it stands; and this meaning I have fairly stated: but it is material that we go behind the mere words for an idea which these words have obviously intended, and failed to convey. It was the design of the journalist to say that, at whatever period of the day or night of Sunday this murder was committed, it was improbable that the assassins would have ventured to bear the corpse to the river before midnight. And herein lies, really, the assumption of which I complain. It is assumed that the murder was committed at such a position, and under such circumstances that *the bearing it* to the river became necessary. Now, the assassination might have taken place upon the river's brink, or on the river itself; and, thus, the throwing the corpse in the water might have been resorted to, at any period of the day or night, as the most obvious and most immediate mode of disposal. You will understand that I suggest nothing here as probable, or as coincident with my own opinion. My design, so far, has no reference to the facts of the case. I wish merely to caution you against the whole tone of *L'Etoile's suggestion,* by calling your attention to its *ex parte* character at the outset.

"Having prescribed thus a limit to suit its own preconceived notions; having assumed that, if this were the body of Marie, it could have been in the water but a very brief time; the journal goes on to say:—

"'All experience has shown that drowned bodies, or bodies thrown into the water immediately after death by violence, require from six to ten days for sufficient decomposition to take place to bring them to the top of the water. Even when a cannon is fired over a corpse, and it rises before at least five or six days' immersion, it sinks again if let alone.'

"These assertions have been tacitly received by every paper in Paris, with the exception of *Le Moniteur.* This latter print endeavours to combat that portion of the paragraph which has reference to 'drowned bodies' only, by citing some five or six instances in which the bodies of individuals known to be drowned were found floating after the lapse of less time than is insisted upon by *L'Etoile.* But there is something excessively unphilosophical in the attempt on the part of *Le Moniteur,* to rebut the general assertion of *L'Etoile,* by a citation of particular instances militating against that assertion. Had it been possible to adduce fifty instead of five examples of bodies found floating at the end of two or three days, these fifty examples could still have been properly regarded only as exceptions to *L'Etoile's* rule, until such time as the rule itself should be confuted. Admitting the rule (and this *Le Moniteur* does not deny, insisting merely upon its exceptions), the argument of *L'Etoile* is suffered to remain in full force; for this argument does not pretend to involve more than a question of the *probability* of the body having risen to the surface in less than three days; and this probability will be in favour of *L'Etoile's* position until the instances so childishly adduced shall be sufficient in number to establish an antagonistical rule.

"You will see at once that all argument upon this head should be urged, if at all, against the rule itself, and for this end we must examine the *rationale* of the rule. Now the human body, in general, is neither much lighter nor much heavier than the water of the Seine; that is to say, the specific gravity of the human body, in its natural condition, is about equal to the bulk of fresh water which it displaces. Now, in the struggles of one unused to swimming, the arms are invariably thrown upwards, while an attempt is made to keep the head in its usual perpendicular position. The result is the immersion of the mouth and nostrils, and the inception, during efforts to breathe while beneath the surface, of water into the lungs. Much is also received into the stomach, and the whole body becomes heavier by the difference between the weight of the air originally distending these cavities, and that of the fluid which now fills them. This difference is sufficient to cause the body to sink, as a general rule; but it is insufficient in the cases of individuals with small bones and an abnormal quantity of flaccid or fatty matter. Such individuals float even after drowning.

"The corpse, being supposed at the bottom of the river, will there remain until, by some means, its specific gravity again becomes less than that of the bulk of water which it displaces. This effect is brought about by decomposition, or otherwise. But decomposition is modified by innumerable circumstances—is hastened or retarded by innumerable agencies; for example, by the heat or cold of the season, by the mineral impregnation or purity of the water, by its depth or shallowness, by its currency or stagnation, by the temperament of the body, by its infection or freedom from disease before death. Thus it is evident that we can assign no period, with anything like accuracy, at which the corpse shall rise through decomposition. Under certain conditions this result would be brought about within an hour; under others, it might not take place at all.

"The whole of this paragraph must now appear a tissue of inconsequence and incoherence. All experience does *not* show that 'drowned bodies' *require* from six to ten days for sufficient decomposition to take place to bring them to the surface. Both science and experience show that the period of their rising is, and necessarily must be, indeterminate.

"And now what are we to make of the argument, that the body found could not be that of Marie Rogêt, because three days only having elapsed, the body was found floating? If drowned, being a woman, she might never have sunk; or having sunk, might have reappeared in twenty-four hours, or less. But no one supposes her to have been drowned; and, dying before being thrown into the river, she might have been found floating at any period afterwards whatever.

"'But,' says *L'Etoile*, 'if the body had been kept in its mangled state on shore until Tuesday night, some trace would be found on shore of the murderers.' Here it is at first difficult to perceive the intension of the reasoner. He means to anticipate what he imagines would be an objection to his theory—viz., that the body was kept on shore two days, suffering rapid decomposition—*more* rapid than if immersed in water. He supposes that, had this been the case, it *might* have appeared at the surface on the Wednesday, and thinks that *only* under such circumstances it could so have appeared. He is accordingly in haste to show that it *was not* kept on shore; for, if so, 'some trace would be found on shore of the murderers.' I presume you smile at the *sequitur*. You cannot be made to see how the mere *duration* of the corpse on the shore could operate to *multiply traces* of the assassins. Nor can I.

"'And furthermore, it is exceedingly improbable,' continues our journal, 'that any villains who had committed such a murder as is here supposed, would have thrown the body in without weight to sink it, when such a precaution could have so easily been taken.' Observe, here, the laughable confusion of thought! No one—not even *L'Etoile*—disputes the murder committed *on the body found*. The marks of violence are too obvious. It is our reasoner's object merely to show that this body is not Marie's. He wishes to prove that *Marie* is not assassinated—not that the corpse was not. Yet his observation proves only the latter point. Here is a corpse without weight attached. Murderers, casting it in, would not have failed to attach a weight. Therefore it was not thrown in by murderers. This is all which is proved, if anything is. The question of identity is not even approached, and *L'Etoile* has been at great pains merely to gainsay now what it has admitted only a moment before. 'We are perfectly convinced,' it says, 'that the body found was that of the murdered female.'

"Nor is this the sole instance, even in this division of his subject, where our reasoner unwittingly reasons against himself. His evident object, I have already said, is to reduce, as much as possible, the interval between Marie's disappearance and the finding of the corpse. Yet we find him *urging* the point that no person saw the girl from the moment of her leaving her mother's house. 'We have no evidence,' he says, 'that Marie Rogêt was in the land of the living after nine o'clock on Sunday, June the 22nd.' As his argument is obviously an *ex parte* one, he should, at least, have left this matter out of sight; for had any one been known to see Marie, say on Monday, or on Tuesday, the interval in question would have been much reduced, and, by his own ratiocination, the probability much diminished of the corpse being that of the *grisette*. It is, nevertheless, amusing to observe that *L'Etoile* insists upon its point in the full belief of its furthering its general argument.

"Reperuse now that portion of this argument which has reference to the identification of the corpse by Beauvais. In regard to the *hair* upon the arm, *L'Etoile* has been obviously disingenuous. M. Beauvais, not being an idiot, could never have urged, in identification of the corpse, simply *hair upon its arm*. No arm is *without* hair. The *generality* of the expression of *L'Etoile* is a mere perversion of the witness's phraseology. He must have spoke of some *pecularity* in this hair. It must have been a peculiarity of colour, of quantity, of length, or of situation.

"In respect to the insinuations levelled at Beauvais, you will be willing to dismiss them in a breath. You have already fathomed the true character of this good gentleman. He is a *busybody*, with much of romance and little of wit. Any one so constituted will readily so conduct himself, upon occasion of *real* excitement, as to render himself liable to suspicion on the part of the over-acute, or the ill-disposed.

"The suspicious circumstances which invest him will be found to tally much better with my hypothesis of *romantic busybodyism*, than with the reasoner's suggestion of guilt. Once adopting the more charitable interpretation, we shall find no difficulty in comprehending the rose in the keyhole; the 'Marie' upon the slate; the 'elbowing the male relatives out of the way'; the 'aversion to permitting them to see the body'; the caution given to Madame B——, that she must hold no conversation with the gendarme until his return (Beauvais'); and, lastly, his apparent determination 'that nobody should have anything to do with the proceedings except himself.' It seems to me unquestionable that Beauvais was a suitor of Marie's; that she coquetted with him; and that he was ambitious of being thought to enjoy her fullest intimacy and confidence. I shall say nothing more upon this point; and, as the evidence fully rebuts the assertion of *L'Etoile*, touching the matter of *apathy* on the part of the mother and other relatives—an apathy inconsistent with the supposition of their believing the corpse to be that of the perfumery girl—we shall now proceed as if the question of *identity* were settled to our perfect satisfaction."

"And what," I here demanded, "do you think of the opinions of *Le Commerciel*?"

"That, in spirit, they are far more worthy of attention than any which have been promulgated upon the subject. The deductions from the premises are philosophical and acute; but the premises, in two instances at least, are founded in imperfect observation. *Le Commerciel* wishes to intimate that Marie was seized by some gang of low ruffians not far from her mother's door. 'It is impossible,' it urges, 'that a person so well known to thousands as this young woman was, should have passed three blocks without someone having seen her.' This is the idea of a man long resident in Paris—a public man—and one whose walks to and fro in the city have been mostly limited to the vicinity of the public offices. He is aware that *he* seldom passes so far as a dozen blocks from his own *bureau*, without being recognised and accosted. And, knowing the extent of his personal acquaintance with others, and of others with him, he compares his notoriety with that of the perfumery girl, finds no great difference between them, and reaches at once the conclusion that she, in her walks, would be equally liable to recognition with himself in his. This could only be the case were her walks of the same unvarying, methodical character, and within the same *species* of limited region as are his own. He passes to and fro, at regular intervals, within a confined periphery, abounding in individuals who are led to observation of his person through interest in the kindred nature of his occupation with their own. But the walks of Marie may, in general, be supposed discursive. In this particular instance, it will be understood as most probable that she proceeded upon a route of more than average diversity from her accustomed ones.

"But whatever force there may still appear to be in the suggestion of *Le Commerciel*, will be much diminished when we take into consideration *the hour* at which the girl went abroad. 'It was when the streets were full of people,' says *Le Commerciel*, 'that she went out.' But not so. It was at nine o'clock in the morning. Now at nine o'clock of every morning in the week, *with the exception of Sunday*, the streets of the city are, it is true, thronged with people. At nine on Sunday, the populace are chiefly within doors *preparing for church.* No observing person can have failed to notice the peculiarly deserted air of the town, from about eight until ten on the morning of every Sabbath. Between ten and eleven the streets are thronged, but not at so early a period as that designated.

"There is another point at which there seems a deficiency of *observation* on the part of *Le Commerciel.* 'A piece,' it says, 'of one of the unfortunate girl's petticoats, two feet long, and one foot wide, was torn out and tied under her chin, and around the back of her head, probably to prevent screams. This was done by fellows who had no pocket-handkerchiefs.' Whether this idea is, or is not well founded, we will endeavour to see hereafter; but by 'fellows who have no pocket-handkerchiefs,' the editor intends the lowest class of ruffians. These, however, are the very description of people who will always be found to have handkerchiefs even when destitute of shirts. You must have had occasion to observe how absolutely indispensable, of late years, to the thorough blackguard, has become the pocket-handkerchief.

"At present we must occupy ourselves with other investigations. You cannot fail to have remarked the extreme laxity of the examination of the corpse. To be sure the question of identity was readily determined, or should have been; but there were other points to be ascertained. Had the body been in any respect *despoiled*? Had the deceased any articles of jewellery about her person upon leaving home? if so, had she any when found? These are important questions utterly untouched by the evidence; and there are others of equal moment, which have met with no attention. We must endeavour to satisfy ourselves by personal inquiry. The case of St. Eustache must be re-examined. I have no suspicion of this person; but let us proceed methodically. We will ascertain beyond a doubt the validity of the affidavits in regard to his whereabouts on the Sunday. Affidavits of this character are readily made matter of mystification. Should there be nothing wrong here, however, we will dismiss St. Eustache from our investigations. His suicide, however corroborative of suspicion, were there found to be deceit in the affidavits, is, without such deceit, in no respect an unaccountable circumstance, or one which need cause us to deflect from the line of ordinary analysis.

"In that which I now propose, we will discard the interior points of this tragedy, and concentrate our attention upon its outskirts. Not the least usual error, in investigations such as this, is the limiting of inquiry to the immediate, with total disregard of the collateral or circumstantial events. It is the malpractice of the courts to confine evidence and discussion to the bounds of apparent relevancy. Yet experience has shown, and a true philosophy will always show, that a vast, perhaps the larger portion of truth, arises from the seemingly irrelevant. It is through the spirit of this principle, if not precisely through its letter, that modern science resolved to *calculate upon the unforeseen*. But perhaps you do not comprehend me. The history of human knowledge has so uninterruptedly shown that to collateral, or incidental, or accidental events we are indebted for the most numerous and most valuable discoveries, that it has at length become necessary, in any prospective view of improvement, to make not only large, but the largest allowances for inventions that shall arise by chance, and quite out of the range of ordinary expectation. It is no longer philosophical to base, upon what has been, a vision of what is to be. *Accident* is admitted as a portion of the substructure. We make chance a matter of absolute calculation. We subject the unlooked-for and unimagined, to the mathematical formulæ of the schools.

"I repeat that it is no more than fact, that the *larger* portion of all truth has sprung from the collateral; and it is but in accordance with the spirit of the principle involved in this fact, that I would divert inquiry, in the present case, from the trodden and hitherto unfruitful ground of the event itself, to the contemporary circumstances which surround it. While you ascertain the validity of the affidavits, I will examine the newspapers more generally than you have as yet done. So far, we have only reconnoitred the field of investigation; but it will be strange indeed if a comprehensive survey, such as I propose, of the public prints, will not afford us some minute points which shall establish a *direction* for inquiry."

In pursuance of Dupin's suggestions, I made scrupulous examination of the affair of the affidavits. The result was a firm conviction of their validity, and of the consequent innocence of St. Eustache. In the meantime my friend occupied himself, with what seemed to me a minuteness altogether objectless, in a scrutiny of the various newspaper files. At the end of a week he placed before me the following extracts:—

"About three years and a half ago, a disturbance very similar to the present was caused by the disappearance of this same Marie Rogêt, from the *parfumerie* of Monsieur Le Blanc in the Palais Royal. At the end of a week, however, she reappeared at her customary *comptoir*, as well as ever, with the exception of a slight paleness not altogether usual. It was given out by Monsieur Le Blanc and her mother, that she had merely been on a visit to some friend in the country; and the affair was speedily hushed up. We presume that the present absence is a freak of the same nature, and that, at the expiration of a week, or perhaps a month, we shall have her among us again."—*Evening Paper*, Monday, June 23.

"An evening journal of yesterday, refers to a former mysterious disappearance of Mademoiselle Rogêt. It is well known that, during the week of her absence from Le Blanc's *parfumerie*, she was in the company of a young naval officer, much noted for his debaucheries. A quarrel, it is supposed, providentially led to her return home. We have the name of the Lothario in question, who is, at present, stationed in Paris, but, for obvious reasons, forbear to make it public."—*Le Mercurie*, Tuesday Morning, June 24.

"An outrage of the most atrocious character was perpetrated near this city the day before yesterday. A gentleman with his wife and daughter, engaged about dusk the services of six young men, who were idly rowing a boat to and fro near the banks of the Seine, to convey him across the river. Upon reaching the opposite shore, the three passengers stepped out and had proceeded so far as to be beyond the view of the boat, when the daughter discovered that she had left in it her parasol. She returned for it, was seized by the gang, carried out into the stream, gagged, brutally treated, and finally taken to the shore at a point not far from that at which she had originally entered the boat with her parents. The villains have escaped for the time, but the police are upon their trail, and some of them will soon be taken."—*Morning Paper*, June 25.

"We have received one or two communications, the object of which is to fasten the crime of the late atrocity upon Mennais; but as this gentleman has been fully exonerated by a legal inquiry, and as the arguments of our several correspondents appear to be more zealous than profound, we do not think it advisable to make them public."—*Morning Paper*, June 28.

"We have received several forcibly written communications, apparently from various sources, and which go far to render it a matter of certainty that the unfortunate Marie Rogêt has become a victim of one of the numerous bands of blackguards which infest the vicinity of the city upon Sunday. Our own opinion is decidedly in favour of this supposition. We shall endeavour to make room for some of these arguments hereafter."—*Evening Paper*, June 30.

"On Monday, one of the bargemen connected with the revenue service, saw an empty boat floating down the Seine.

Sails were lying in the bottom of the boat. The bargemen towed it under the barge office. The next morning it was taken from thence, without the knowledge of any of the officers. The rudder is now at the barge office."—*Le Diligence*, Thursday, June 26.

Upon reading these various extracts, they not only seemed to be irrelevant, but I could perceive no mode in which any one of them could be brought to bear upon the matter in hand. I waited for some explanation from Dupin.

"It is not my present design," he said, "to *dwell* upon the first and second of these extracts. I have copied them chiefly to show you the extreme remissness of the police, who, so far as I can understand from the Prefect, have not troubled themselves, in any respect, with an examination of the naval officer alluded to. Yet it is mere folly to say that between the first and second disappearance of Marie, there is no *supposable* connection. Let us admit the first elopement to have resulted in a quarrel between the lovers, and the return home of the betrayed. We are now prepared to view a second *elopement* (if we *know* that an elopement has again taken place) as indicating a renewal of the betrayer's advances, rather than as the result of new proposals by a second individual—we are prepared to regard it as a 'making up' of the old amour, rather than as the commencement of a new one. The chances are ten to one, that he who had once eloped with Marie, would again propose an elopement, rather than that she to whom proposals of elopement had been made by one individual should have them made to her by another. And here let me call your attention to the fact, that the time elapsing between the first ascertained and the second supposed elopement, is a few months more than the general period of the cruises of our men-of-war. Had the lover been interrupted in his first villainy by the necessity of departure to sea, and had he seized the first moment of his return to renew the base designs not yet altogether accomplished—or not yet altogether accomplished *by him*? Of all these things we know nothing.

"You will say, however, that, in the second instance, there was *no* elopement as imagined. Certainly not—but are we prepared to say that there was not the frustrated design? Beyond St. Eustache, and perhaps Beauvais, we find no recognised, no open, no honourable suitors of Marie. Of none other is there anything said. Who, then, is the secret lover, of whom the relatives (*at least most of them*) know nothing, but whom Marie meets upon the morning of Sunday, and who is so deeply in her confidence, that she hesitates not to remain with him until the shades of the evening descend, amid the solitary groves of the Barrière du Roule? Who is that secret lover, I ask, of whom, at least, *most* of the relatives know nothing? And what means the singular prophecy of Madame Rogêt on the morning of Marie's departure—'I fear that I shall never see Marie again'?

"But if we cannot imagine Madame Rogêt privy to the design of elopement, may we not at least suppose this design entertained by the girl? Upon quitting home, she gave it to be understood that she was about to visit her aunt in the Rue des Drômes, and St. Eustache was requested to call for her at dark. Now, at first glance, this fact strongly militates against my suggestion; but let us reflect. That she *did* meet some companion, and proceed with him across the river, reaching the Barrière du Roule at so late an hour as three o'clock in the afternoon, is known. But in consenting so to accompany this individual (*for whatever purpose—to her mother known or unknown*), she must have thought of her expressed intention when leaving home, and of the surprise and suspicion aroused in the bosom of her affianced suitor, St. Eustache, when, calling for her at the hour appointed, in the Rue des Drômes, he should find that she had not been there, and when, moreover, upon returning to the *pension* with this alarming intelligence, he should become aware of her continued absence from home. She must have thought of these things, I say. She must have foreseen the chagrin of St. Eustache, the suspicion of all. She could not have thought of returning to brave this suspicion; but the suspicion becomes a point of trivial importance to her, if we suppose her *not* intending to return.

"We may imagine her thinking thus—'I am to meet a certain person for the purpose of elopement, or for certain other purposes known only to myself. It is necessary that there be no chance of interruption—there must be sufficient time given us to elude pursuit—I will give it to be understood that I shall visit and spend the day with my aunt at the Rue des Drômes—I will tell St. Eustache not to call for me until dark—in this way, my absence from home for the longest possible period, without causing suspicion or anxiety, will be accounted for, and I shall gain more time than in any other manner. If I bid St. Eustache call for me at dark, he will be sure not to call before; but, if I wholly neglect to bid him call, my time for escape will be diminished, since it will be expected that I return the earlier, and my absence will the sooner excite anxiety. Now, if it were my design to return *at all*—if I had in contemplation merely a stroll with the individual in question—it would not be my policy to bid St. Eustache call; for calling he will be *sure* to ascertain that I have played him false—

a fact of which I might keep him for ever in ignorance, by leaving home without notifying him of my intention, by returning before dark, and by then stating that I had been to visit my aunt in the Rue des Drômes. But, as it is my design *never* to return—or not for some weeks—or not until certain concealments are effected—the gaining of time is the only point about which I need give myself any concern.'

"You have observed, in your notes, that the most general opinion in relation to this sad affair is, and was from the first, that the girl had been the victim of *a gang* of blackguards. Now, the popular opinion, under certain conditions, is not to be disregarded. When arising of itself—when manifesting itself in a strictly spontaneous manner—we should look upon it as analogous with that *intuition* which is the idiosyncrasy of the individual man of genius. In ninety-nine cases from the hundred I would abide by its decision. But it is important that we find no palpable traces of *suggestion*. The opinion must be rigorously *the public's own*; and the distinction is often exceedingly difficult to perceive and to maintain. In the present instance, it appears to me that this 'public opinion,' in respect to *a gang*, has been superinduced by the collateral event which is detailed in the third of my extracts. All Paris is excited by the discovered corpse of Marie, a girl young, beautiful, and notorious. This corpse is found, bearing marks of violence, and floating in the river. But it is now made known that, at the very period, or about the very period, in which it is supposed that the girl was assassinated, an outrage similar in nature to that endured by the deceased, although less in extent, was perpetrated, by a gang of young ruffians, upon the person of a second young female. Is it wonderful that the one known atrocity should influence the popular judgment in regard to the other unknown? This judgment awaited direction, and the known outrage seemed so opportunely to afford it. Marie, too, was found in the river; and upon this very river was this known outrage committed. The connection of the two events had about it so much of the palpable, that the true wonder would have been a *failure* of the populace to appreciate and to seize it. But, in fact, the one atrocity, known to be so committed, is, if anything, evidence that the other, committed at a time nearly coincident, was *not* so committed. It would have been a miracle indeed, if, while a gang of ruffians were perpetrating, at a given locality, a most unheard-of wrong, there should have been another similar gang, in a similar locality, in the same city, under the same circumstances, with the same means and appliances, engaged in a wrong of precisely the same aspect, at precisely the same period of time!

Yet in what, if not in this marvellous train of coincidence, does the accidentally *suggested* opinion of the populace call upon us to believe?

"Before proceeding farther, let us consider the supposed scene of the assassination, in the thicket at the Barriere du Roule. This thicket, although dense, was in the close vicinity of a public road. Within were three or four large stones, forming a kind of seat, with a back and footstool. On the upper stone was discovered a white petticoat; on the second, a silk scarf. A parasol, gloves, and a pocket-handkerchief, were also here found. The handkerchief bore the name, 'Marie Rogêt.' Fragments of dress were seen on the branches around. The earth was trampled, the bushes were broken, and there was every evidence of a violent struggle.

"Notwithstanding the acclamation with which the discovery of this thicket was received by the press, and the unanimity with which it was supposed to indicate the precise scene of the outrage, it must be admitted that there was some very good reason for doubt. That it *was* the scene, I may or I may not believe—but there was excellent reason for doubt. Had the *true* scene been, as *Le Commerciel* suggested, in the neighbourhood of the Rue Pavée Saint Andrée, the perpetrators of the crime, supposing them still resident in Paris, would naturally have been stricken with terror at the public attention thus acutely directed into the proper channel; and, in certain classes of minds, there would have arisen, at once, a sense of the necessity of some exertion to redivert this attention. And thus, the thicket of the Barrière du Roule having been already suspected, the idea of placing the articles where they were found, might have been naturally entertained. There is no real evidence, although *Le Soleil* so supposes, that the articles discovered had been more than a very few days in the thicket; while there is much circumstantial proof that they could not have remained there, without attracting attention, during the twenty days elapsing between the fatal Sunday and the afternoon upon which they were found by the boys. 'They were all *mildewed* down hard,' says *Le Soleil*, adopting the opinions of its predecessors, 'with the action of the rain, and stuck together from *mildew*. The grass had grown around and over some of them. The silk of the parasol was strong, but the threads of it were run together within. The upper part, where it had been doubled and folded, was all *mildewed* and rotten, and tore on being opened.' In respect to the grass having 'grown around and over some of them,' it is obvious that the fact could only have been ascertained from the words, and thus from the recollections, of two small boys; for these boys removed the articles and took them home before they had been seen by a third party. But grass will grow, especially in warm and damp weather (such as was that of the period of the murder), as much as two or three inches in a single day. A parasol lying upon the newly turfed ground, might, in a single week, be entirely concealed from sight by the upspringing grass. And touching that *mildew* upon which the editor of *Le Soleil* so pertinaciously insists that he employs the word no less than three times in the brief paragraph just quoted, is he really unaware of the nature of this *mildew*? Is he to be told that it is one of the many classes of fungus, of which the most ordinary feature is its upspringing and decadence within twenty-four hours?

"Thus we see, at a glance, that what has been most triumphantly adduced in support of the idea that the articles had been 'for at least three or four weeks' in the thicket, is most absurdly null as regards any evidence of that fact. On the other hand, it is exceedingly difficult to believe that these articles could have remained in the thicket specified, for a longer period than a single week—for a longer period than from one Sunday to the next. Those who know anything of the vicinity of Paris, know the extreme difficulty of finding *seclusion* unless at a great distance from its suburbs. Such a thing as an unexplored, or even an unfrequently visited recess, amid its woods or groves, is not for a moment to be imagined. Let any one who, being at heart a lover of nature, is yet chained by duty to the dust and heat of this great metropolis—let any such one attempt, even during the week-days, to slake his thirst for solitude amid the scenes of natural loveliness which immediately surround us. At every second step, he will find the growing charm dispelled by the voice and personal intrusion of some ruffian or party of carousing blackguards. He will seek privacy amid the densest foliage, all in vain. Here are the very nooks where the unwashed most abound—here are the temples most desecrate. With sickness of the heart the wanderer will flee back to the polluted Paris as to a less odious because less incongruous sink of pollution. But if the vicinity of the city is so beset during the working days of the week, how much more so on the Sabbath! It is now especially that, released from the claims of labour, or deprived of the customary opportunities of crime, the town blackguard seeks the precincts of the town, not through love of the rural, which in his heart he despises, but by way of escape from the restraints and conventionalities of society. He desires less the fresh air and the green trees, than the utter *licence* of the country. Here, at the roadside inn, or beneath the foliage of the woods, he indulges, unchecked by any eye except those of his boon companions, in all the mad excess of a counterfeit hilarity—the joint off-spring of liberty and of rum. I say nothing more than what must be obvious to every dispassionate observer, when I repeat that the circumstance of the articles in question having remained undiscovered, for a longer period than from one Sunday to another, in *any* thicket in the immediate neighbourhood of Paris, is to be looked up as little less than miraculous.

"But there are not wanting other grounds for the suspicion that the articles were placed in the thicket with the view of diverting attention from the real scene of the outrage. And first, let me direct your notice to the *date* of the discovery of the articles. Collate this with the date of the fifth extract made by myself from the newspapers. You will find that the discovery followed, almost immediately, the urgent communications sent to the evening paper. These communications, although various, and apparently from various sources, tended all to the same point—viz., the directing of attention to *a gang* as the perpetrators of the outrage, and to the neighbourhood of the Barriere du Roule as its scene. Now here, of course, the suspicion is not that, in consequence of these communications, or of the public attention by them directed, the articles were found by the boys; but the suspicion might and may well have been, that the articles were not *before* found by the boys, for the reason that the articles had not before been in the thicket; having been deposited there only at so late a period as at the date, or shortly prior to the date of the communications, by the guilty authors of these communications themselves.

"This thicket was a singular—an exceedingly singular one. It was unusually dense. Within its naturally walled enclosure were three extraordinary stones, *forming a seat with a back and footstool.* And this thicket, so full of a natural art, was in the immediate vicinity, *within a few rods*, of the dwelling of Madame Deluc, whose boys were in the habit of closely examining the shrubberies about them in search of the bark of the sassafras. Would it be a rash wager—a wager of one thousand to one—that *a day* never passed over the heads of these boys without finding at least one of them ensconced in the umbrageous hall, and enthroned upon its natural throne? Those who would hesitate at such a wager, have either never been boys themselves, or have forgotten the boyish nature. I repeat—it is exceedingly hard to comprehend how the articles could have remained in this thicket, undiscovered, for a longer period than one or two days; and that this there is good ground for suspicion, in spite of the dogmatic ignorance of *Le Soleil*, that they were, at a comparatively late date, deposited where found.

" But there are still other and stronger reasons for believing them so deposited, than any which I have as yet urged. And now, let me beg your notice to the highly artificial arrangement of the articles. On the *upper* stone lay a white petticoat; on the *second* a silk scarf; scattered around, were a parasol, gloves, and a pocket-handkerchief bearing the name, ' Marie Rogêt.' Here is just such an arrangement as would *naturally* be made by a not over acute person wishing to dispose the articles *naturally*. But it is by no means a *really* natural arrangement. I should rather have looked to see the things *all* lying on the ground and trampled under foot. In the narrow limits of that bower, it would have been scarcely possible that the petticoat and scarf should have retained a position upon the stones, when subjected to the brushing to and fro of many struggling persons. ' There was evidence,' it is said, ' of a struggle; and the earth was trampled, the bushes were broken '—but the petticoat and scarf are found deposited as if upon shelves. ' The pieces of the frock torn out by the bushes were about three inches wide and six inches long. One part was the hem of the frock, and it had been mended. They *looked like strips torn off*.' Here, inadvertently, *Le Soleil* has employed an exceedingly suspicious phrase. The pieces, as described, do indeed ' look like strips torn off ' ; but purposely and by hand. It is one of the rarest of accidents that a piece is ' torn off,' from any garment such as is now in question, by the agency *of a thorn*. From the very nature of such fabrics, a thorn or nail becoming entangled in them, tears them rectangularly—divides them into two longitudinal rents, at right angles with each other, and meeting at an apex where the thorn enters—but it is scarcely possible to conceive the piece ' torn off.' I never so knew it, nor did you. To tear a piece *off* from such fabric, two distinct forces, in different directions, will be, in almost every case, required. If there be two edges to the fabric—if, for example, it be a pocket-handkerchief, and it is desired to tear from it a slip, then, and then only will the one force serve the purpose. But in the present case the question is of a dress, presenting but one edge. To tear a piece from the interior, where no edge is presented, could only be effected by a miracle through the agency of thorns, and no *one* thorn could accomplish it. But, even where an edge is presented, two thorns will be necessary, operating, the one in two distinct directions, and the other in one. And this in the supposition that the edge is unhemmed. If hemmed, the matter is nearly out of the question. We thus see the numerous and great obstacles in the way of pieces being ' torn off ' through the simple agency of ' thorns ' ; yet we are required to believe not only that one piece but that many have been so torn. 'And one part,' too, '*was the hem of the frock*'! Another piece was '*part of the skirt, not the hem*'—that is to say, was torn completely out through the agency of thorns, from the unedged interior of the dress! These, I say, are things which one may well be pardoned for disbelieving; yet, taken collectedly, they form, perhaps, less of reasonable ground for suspicion, than the one startling circumstance of the articles having been left in this thicket at all, by any *murderers* who had enough precaution to think of removing the corpse. You will not have apprehended me rightly, however, if you suppose it my design to *deny* this thicket as the scene of the outrage. There might have been a wrong *here*, or, more possibly, an accident at Madame Deluc's. But, in fact, this is a part of minor importance. We are not engaged in an attempt to discover the scene, but to produce the perpetrators of the murder. What I have adduced, notwithstanding the minuteness with which I have adduced it, has been with the view, first, to show the folly of the positive and headlong assertions of *Le Soleil*, but secondly and chiefly, to bring you, by the most natural route, to a further contemplation of the doubt whether this assassination has, or has not, been the work of a *gang*.

"We will resume this question by mere allusion to the revolting details of the surgeon examined at the inquest. It is only necessary to say that his published *inferences*, in regard to the number of the ruffians, have been properly ridiculed as unjust and totally baseless, by all the reputable anatomists of Paris. Not that the matter *might not* have been as inferred, but that there was no ground for the inference—was there not much for another?

"Let us reflect now upon 'the traces of a struggle'; and let me ask what these traces have been supposed to demonstrate. A gang. But do they not rather demonstrate the absence of a gang? What *struggle* could have taken place—what struggle so violent and so enduring as to have left its 'traces' in all directions—between a weak and defenceless girl and the *gang* of ruffians imagined? If we imagine but one violator, we can conceive, and thus only conceive, the struggle of so violent and so obstinate a nature as to have left the 'traces' apparent.

"And again. I have already mentioned the suspicion to be excited by the fact that the articles in question were suffered to remain *at all* in the thicket where discovered. It seems almost impossible that these evidences of guilt should have been accidentally left where found. There was sufficient presence of mind (it is supposed) to remove the corpse; and yet a more positive evidence than the corpse itself (whose features might have been quickly obliterated by decay), is allowed to lie conspicuously in the scene of the outrage—I allude to the handkerchief with the *name* of the deceased. If this was accident, it was not the accident *of a gang*. We can imagine it only the accident of an individual. Let us see. An individual has committed the murder. He is alone with the ghost of the departed. He is appalled by what lies motionless before him. The fury of his passion is over, and there is abundant room in his heart for the natural awe of the deed. His is none of that confidence which the presence of numbers inevitably inspires. He is *alone* with the dead. He trembles and is bewildered. Yet there is a necessity for disposing of the corpse. He bears it to the river, but leaves behind him the other evidences of guilt; for it is difficult, if not impossible to carry all the burden at once, and it will be easy to return for what is left. But in his toilsome journey to the water his fears redouble within him. His sole thought is immediate escape. He turns his back *for ever* upon those dreadful shrubberies, and flees as from the wrath to come.

" But how with a gang? Their number would have inspired them with confidence; if, indeed, confidence is ever wanting in the breast of the arrant blackguard; and of arrant blackguards alone are the supposed *gangs* ever constituted. Their number, I say, would have prevented the bewildering and unreasoning terror which I have imagined to paralyse the single man. Could we suppose an oversight in one, or two, or three, this oversight would have been remedied by a fourth. They would have left nothing behind them.

" Consider now the circumstance that, in the outer garment of the corpse when found, ' a slip, about a foot wide, had been torn upward from the bottom hem to the waist, wound three times round the waist, and secured by a sort of hitch in the back.' This was done with the obvious design of affording *a handle* by which the carry the body. But would any *number* of men have dreamed of resorting to such an expedient? To three or four the limbs of the corpse would have afforded not only a sufficient, but the best possible hold. The device is that of a single individual; and this brings us to the fact that ' between the thicket and the river, the rails of the fences were found taken down, and the ground bore evident traces of some heavy burden having been dragged along it '! But would a *number* of men have put themselves to the superfluous trouble of taking down a fence, for the purpose of dragging through it a corpse which they might have *lifted over* any fence in an instant?

Would a *number* of men have so *dragged* a corpse at all as to have left evident *traces* of the dragging?

"And here we must refer to an observation of *Le Commerciel*; an observation upon which I have already, in some measure, commented. 'A piece,' says this journal, 'of one of the unfortunate girl's petticoats was torn out and tied under her chin, and around the back of her head, probably to prevent screams. This was done by fellows who had no pocket-handkerchiefs.'

"I have before suggested that a genuine blackguard is never *without* a pocket-handkerchief. But is is not to this fact that I now especially advert. That it was not through want of a handkerchief for the purpose imagined by *Le Commerciel*, that this bandage was employed, is rendered apparent by the handkerchief left in the thicket; and that the object was not 'to prevent screams' appears, also, from the bandage having been employed in preference to what would so much better have answered the purpose. But the language of the evidence speaks of the strip in question as 'found around the neck, fitting loosely, and secured with a hard knot.' These words are sufficiently vague, but differ materially from those of *Le Commerciel*. The slip was eighteen inches wide, and therefore, although of muslin, would form a strong band when folded or rumpled longitudinally. And thus rumpled it was discovered. My inference is this. The solitary murderer, having borne the corpse for some distance (whether from the thicket or elsewhere), by means of the bandage *hitched* around its middle, found the weight, in this mode of procedure, too much for his strength. He resolved to drag the burthen—the evidence goes to show that it was dragged. With this object in view, it became necessary to attach something like a rope to one of the extremities. It could be best attached about the neck, where the head would prevent it slipping off. And now the murderer bethought him, unquestionably, of the bandage about the loins. He would have used this, but for its volution about the corpse, the *hitch* which embarrassed it, and the reflection that it had not been 'torn off' from the garment. It was easier to tear a new slip from the petticoat. He tore it, made it fast about the neck, and so *dragged* his victim to the brink of the river. That this 'bandage,' only attainable with trouble and delay, and but imperfectly answering its purpose—that this bandage was employed *at all*, demonstrates that the necessity for its employment sprang from circumstances arising at a period when the handkerchief was no longer attainable—that is to say, arising, as we have imagined, after quitting the thicket (if the thicket it was), and on the road between the thicket and the river.

"But the evidence, you will say, of Madame Deluc(!) points especially to the presence of *a gang*, in the vicinity of the thicket, at or about the epoch of the murder. This I grant. I doubt if there was not a *dozen* gangs, such as described by Madame Deluc, in and about the vicinity of the Barrière du Roule at *or about* the period of this tragedy. But the gang which has drawn upon itself the pointed animadversion, although the somewhat tardy and very suspicious evidence of Madame Deluc, is the *only* gang which is represented by that honest and scrupulous old lady as having eaten her cakes and swallowed her brandy, without putting themselves to the trouble of making her payment. *Et hinc illæ iræ?*

"But what *is* the precise evidence of Madame Deluc? 'A gang of miscreants made their appearance, behaved boisterously, ate and drank without making payment, followed in the route of the young man and girl, returned to the inn, *about dusk*, and recrossed the river as if in great haste.'

"Now this 'great haste' very possibly seemed *greater* haste in the eyes of Madame Deluc, since she dwelt lingeringly and lamentingly upon her violated cakes and ale—cakes and ale for which she might still have entertained a faint hope of compensation. Why, otherwise, since it was *about dusk*, should she make a point of the *haste*? It is no cause for wonder, surely, that even a gang of blackguards should make *haste* to get home, when a wide river is to be crossed in small boats, when storm impends, and when night *approaches*.

"I say *approaches*; for the night had *not yet arrived*. It was only *about dusk* that the indecent haste of these 'miscreants' offended the sober eyes of Madame Deluc. But we are told that it was upon this very evening that Madame Deluc, as well as her eldest son, 'heard the screams of a female in the vicinity of the inn.' And in what words does Madame Deluc designate the period of the evening at which these screams were heard? It was '*soon after dark*,' she says. But 'soon *after* dark,' is at least *dark*; and '*about dusk*' is as certainly daylight. Thus it is abundantly clear that the gang quitted the Barrière du Roule *prior* to the screams overheard (?) by Madame Deluc. And although, in all the many reports of the evidence, the relative expressions in question are distinctly and invariably employed just as I have employed them in this conversation with yourself, no notice whatever of the gross discrepancy has, as yet, been taken by any of the public journals, or by any of the myrmidons of police.

"I shall add but one to the arguments against *a gang*; but this *one* has, to my own understanding at least, a weight altogether irresistible. Under the circumstances of large reward offered, and full pardon to any king's evidence, it is not to be imagined, for a moment, that some member of *a gang* of low ruffians, or of any body of men, would not long ago have betrayed his accomplices. Each one of a gang so placed is not so much greedy of reward, or anxious for escape, as *fearful of betrayal.* He betrays eagerly and early that *he may not himself be betrayed.* That the secret has not been divulged, is the very best of proof that it is, in fact, a secret. The horrors of this dark deed are known only to *one*, or two, living human beings, and to God.

"Let us sum up now the meagre yet certain fruits of our long analysis. We have attained the idea either of a fatal accident under the roof of Madame Deluc, or of a murder perpetrated, in the thicket at the Barriere du Roule, by a lover, or at least by an intimate and secret associate of the deceased. This associate is of swarthy complexion. This complexion, the 'hitch' in the bandage, and the 'sailor's knot' with which the bonnet-ribbon is tied, point to a seaman. His companionship with the deceased, a gay, but not an abject young girl, designates him as above the grade of the common sailor. Here the well-written and urgent communications to the journals are much in the way of corroboration. The circumstance of the first elopement, as mentioned by *Le Mercurie*, tends to blend the idea of this seaman with that of the 'naval officer' who is first known to have led the unfortunate into crime.

"And here, most fitly, comes the consideration of the continued absence of him of the dark complexion. Let me pause to observe that the complexion of this man is dark and swarthy; it was no common swarthiness which constituted the *sole* point of remembrance, both as regards Valence and Madame Deluc. But why is this man absent? Was he murdered by the *gang*? If so, why are there only *traces* of the assassinated *girl*? The scene of the two outrages will naturally be supposed identical. And where is his corpse? The assassins would most probably have disposed of both in the same way. But it may be said that this man lives, and is deterred from making himself known, through dread of being charged with the murder. This consideration might be supposed to operate upon him now—at this late period—since it has been given in evidence that he was seen with Marie—but it would have had no force at the period of the deed. The first impulse of an innocent man would have been to announce the outrage, and to aid in identifying the ruffians. This *policy* would have suggested. He had been seen with the girl. He had crossed the river with her in an open ferry-boat. The denouncing of the assassins would have appeared, even to an idiot, the surest and sole means of relieving himself from suspicion. We cannot suppose him, on the night of the fatal Sunday, both innocent himself and incognisant of an outrage committed. Yet only under such circumstances is it possible to imagine that he would have failed, if alive, in the denouncement of the assassins.

"And what means are ours of attaining the truth? We shall find these means multiplying and gathering distinctness as we proceed. Let us sift to the bottom this affair of the first elopement. Let us know the full history of 'the officer,' with his present circumstances, and his whereabouts at the precise period of the murder. Let us carefully compare with each other the various communications sent to the evening paper, in which the object was to inculpate *a gang*. This done, let us compare these communications, both as regards style and MS., with those sent to the morning paper, at a previous period, and insisting so vehemently upon the guilt of Mennais. And, all this done, let us again compare these various communications with the known MSS. of the officer. Let us endeavour to ascertain, by repeated questionings of Madame Deluc and her boys, as well as of the omnibus-driver, Valence, something more of the personal appearance and bearing of the 'man of dark complexion.' Queries, skilfully directed, will not fail to elicit, from some of these parties, information on this particular point (or upon others)—information which the parties themselves may not even be aware of possessing. And let us now trace *the boat* picked up by the bargeman on the morning of Monday, the 23rd of June, and which was removed from the barge-office, without the cognisance of the officer in attendance, and *without the rudder*, at some period prior to the discovery of the corpse. With a proper caution and perseverance we shall infallibly trace this boat; for not only can the bargeman who picked it up identify it, but the *rudder is at hand*. The rudder *of a sail-boat* would not have been abandoned, without inquiry, by one altogether at ease in heart. And here let me pause to insinuate a question. There was no *advertisement* of the picking up of this boat. It was silently taken to the barge-office, and as silently removed. But its owner or employer—how *happened* he, at so early a period as Tuesday morning, to be informed, without the agency of advertisement, of the locality of the boat taken up on Monday, unless we imagine some connection with the *navy*—some personal permanent connection leading to cognisance of its minute interests—its petty local news?

"In speaking of the lonely assassin dragging his burden to the shore, I have already suggested the probability of his availing himself *of a boat.* Now we are to understand that Marie Rogêt *was* precipitated from a boat. This would naturally have been the case. The corpse could not have been trusted to the shallow waters of the shore. The peculiar marks on the back and shoulders of the victim tell of the bottom ribs of a boat. That the body was found without weight is also corroborative of the idea. If thrown from the shore a weight would have been attached. We can only account for its absence by supposing the murderer to have neglected the precaution of supplying himself with it before pushing off. In the act of consigning the corpse to the water, he would unquestionably have noticed his oversight; but then no remedy would have been at hand. Any risk would have been preferred to a return to that accursed shore. Having rid himself of his ghastly charge, the murderer would have hastened to the city. There, at some obscure wharf, he would have leaped on land. But the boat—would he have secured it? He would have been in too great haste for such things as securing a boat. Moreover, in fastening it to the wharf, he would have felt as in securing evidence against himself. His natural thought would have been to cast from him, as far as possible, all that had held connection with his crime. He would not only have fled from the wharf, but he would not have permitted *the boat* to remain. Assuredly he would have cast it adrift. Let us pursue our fancies. In the morning, the wretch is stricken with unutterable horror at finding that the boat has been picked up and detained at a locality which he is in the daily habit of frequenting—at a locality, perhaps, which his duty compels him to frequent. The next night, *without daring to ask for the rudder,* he removes it. Now *where* is that rudderless boat? Let it be one of our first purposes to discover. With the first glimpse we obtain of it, the dawn of our success shall begin. This boat shall guide us, with a rapidity which will surprise even ourselves, to him who employed it in the midnight of the fatal Sabbath. Corroboration will rise upon corroboration, and the murderer will be traced."

[For reasons which we shall not specify, but which to many readers will appear obvious, we have taken the liberty of here omitting, from the MSS. placed in our hands, such portion as details the *following up* of the apparently slight clue obtained by Dupin. We feel it advisable only to state, in brief, that the result desired was brought to pass; and that the Prefect fulfilled punctually, although with reluctance, the terms of his compact with the Chevalier. Mr. Poe's article concludes with the following words.—*Eds.*]

It will be understood that I speak of coincidence *and no more*. What I have said above upon this topic must suffice. In my own heart there dwells no faith in præternature. That Nature and its God are two, no man who thinks will deny. That the latter, creating the former, can, at will, control or modify it, is all unquestionable. I say "at will"; for the question is of will, and not, as the insanity of logic has assumed, of power. It is not that the Deity *cannot* modify His laws, but that we insult Him in imagining a possible necessity for modification. In their origin these laws were fashioned to embrace *all* contingencies which *could* lie in the Future. With God all is *Now*.

I repeat, then, that I speak of these things only as of coincidences. And further: in what I relate it will be seen that between the fate of the unhappy Marie Cecilia Rogers, so far as that fate is known, and the fate of one Marie Rogêt up to a certain epoch in her history, there has existed a parallel in the contemplation of whose wonderful exactitude the reason becomes embarrassed. I say all this will be seen. But let it not for a moment be supposed that, in proceeding with the sad narrative of Marie from the epoch just mentioned, and in tracing to its *dénouement* the mystery which enshrouded her, it is my covert design to hint at an extension of the parallel, or even to suggest that the measures adopted in Paris for the discovery of the assassin of a *grisette*, or measures founded in any similar ratiocination, would produce any similar result.

For, in respect to the latter branch of the supposition, it should be considered that the most trifling variation in the facts of the two cases might give rise to the most important miscalculations, by diverting thoroughly the two courses of events; very much, as in arithmetic, an error which, in its own individuality, may be inappreciable, produces, at length, by dint of multiplication at all points of the process, a result enormously at variance with truth. And, in regard to the former branch, we must not fail to hold in view that the very Calculus of Probabilities to which I have referred, forbids all idea of the extension of the parallel—forbids it with a positiveness strong and decided just in proportion as this parallel has already been long-drawn and exact. This is one of those anomalous propositions which, seemingly appealing to thought altogether apart from the mathematical, is yet one which only the mathematician can fully entertain. Nothing, for example, is more difficult than to convince the merely general reader that the fact of sixes having been thrown twice in succession by a player at dice, is sufficient cause for betting the largest odds that sixes will not be thrown in the third attempt. A suggestion to this effect is usually rejected by the intellect at once. It does not appear that the two throws which have been completed, and which lie now absolutely in the Past, can have influence upon the throw which exists only in the Future. The chance for throwing sixes seems to be precisely as it was at any ordinary time—that is to say, subject only to the influence of the various other throws which may be made by the dice. And this is a reflection which appears so exceedingly obvious that attempts to controvert it are received more frequently with a derisive smile than with anything like respectful attention. The error here involved—a gross error redolent of mischief—I cannot pretend to expose within the limits assigned me at present; and with the philosophical it needs no exposure. It may be sufficient here to say that it forms one of an infinite series of mistakes which arise in the path of Reason through her propensity for seeking truth *in detail.*

ERNEST HEMINGWAY

IN ANOTHER COUNTRY

IN the fall the war was always there, but we did not go to it any more. It was cold in the fall in Milan and the dark came very early. Then the electric lights came on, and it was pleasant along the streets looking in the windows. There was much game hanging outside the shops, and the snow powdered in the fur of the foxes and the wind blew their tails. The deer hung stiff and heavy and empty, and small birds blew in the wind and the wind turned their feathers. It was a cold fall and the wind came down from the mountains.

We were all at the hospital every afternoon, and there were different ways of walking across the town through the dusk to the hospital. Two of the ways were alongside canals, but they were long. Always, though, you crossed a bridge across a canal to enter the hospital. There was a choice of three bridges. On one of them a woman sold roasted chestnuts. It was warm, standing in front of her charcoal fire, and the chestnuts were warm afterwards in your pocket. The hospital was very old and very beautiful, and you entered through a gate and walked across a courtyard and out of a gate on the other side. There were usually funerals starting from the courtyard. Beyond the old hospital were the new brick pavilions, and there we met every afternoon and were all very polite and interested in what was the matter, and sat in the machines that were to make so much difference.

The doctor came up to the machine where I was sitting and said: " What did you like best to do before the war? Did you practise a sport? "

I said: " Yes, football."

" Good," he said. " You will be able to play football again better than ever."

My knee did not bend and the leg dropped straight from the knee to the ankle without a calf, and the machine was to bend the knee and make it move as in riding a tricycle. But it did not bend yet, and instead the machine lurched when it came to the bending part. The doctor said: " That will all pass. You are a fortunate young man. You will play football again like a champion."

In the next machine was a major who had a little hand like a baby's. He winked at me when the doctor examined his hand, which was between two leather straps that bounced up and down and flapped the stiff fingers, and said: " And will I too play football, captain-doctor? " He had been a very great fencer and, before the war, the greatest fencer in Italy.

The doctor went to his office in the back room and brought a photograph which showed a hand that had been withered almost as small as the major's, before it had taken a machine course, and after was a little larger. The major held the photograph with his good hand and looked at it very carefully. " A wound? " he asked.

" An industrial accident," the doctor said.

" Very interesting, very interesting," the major said, and handed it back to the doctor.

" You have confidence? "

" No," said the major.

There were three boys who came each day who were about the same age I was. They were all three from Milan, and one of them was to be a lawyer, and one was to be a painter, and one had intended to be a soldier, and after we were finished with the machines, sometimes we walked back together to the Café Cova, which was next door to the Scala. We walked the short way through the communist quarter because we were four together. The people hated us because we were officers, and from a wine-shop someone would call out, " A basso gli ufficiali! " as we passed. Another boy, who walked with us sometimes and made us five, wore a black silk handkerchief across his face because he had no nose then and his face was to be rebuilt. He had gone out to the front from the military academy and been wounded within an hour after he had gone into the front line for the first time. They rebuilt his face, but he came from a very old family and they could never get the nose exactly right. He went to South America and worked in a bank. But this was a long time ago, and then we did not any of us know how it was going to be afterwards. We only knew then that there was always the war, but that we were not going to it any more.

We all had the same medals, except the boy with the black silk bandage across his face, and he had not been at the front long enough to get any medals. The tall boy with a very pale face who was to be a lawyer had been a lieutenant of Arditi and had three medals of the sort we each had only one of.

He had lived a very long time with death and was a little detached. We were all a little detached, and there was nothing that held us together except that we met every afternoon at the hospital. Although, as we walked to the Cova through the tough part of the town, walking in the dark, with light and singing coming out of the wine-shops, and sometimes having to walk into the street when the men and women would crowd together on the sidewalk so that we would have had to jostle them to get by, we felt held together by there being something that had happened that they, the people who disliked us, did not understand.

We ourselves all understood the Cova, where it was rich and warm and not too brightly lighted, and noisy and smoky at certain hours, and there were always girls at the tables and the illustrated papers on a rack on the wall. The girls at the Cova were very patriotic, and I found that the most patriotic people in Italy were the café girls—and I believe they are still patriotic.

The boys at first were very polite about my medals and asked me what I had done to get them. I showed them the papers, which were written in very beautiful language and full of *fratellanza* and *abnegazione*, but which really said, with the adjectives removed, that I had been given the medals because I was an American. After that their manner changed a little towards me, although I was their friend against outsiders. I was a friend, but I was never really one of them after they had read the citations, because it had been different with them and they had done very different things to get their medals. I had been wounded, it was true; but we all knew that being wounded, after all, was really an accident. I was never ashamed of the ribbons, though, and sometimes, after the cocktail hour, I would imagine myself having done all the things they had done to get their medals; but walking home at night through the empty streets with the cold wind and all the shops closed, trying to keep near the street lights, I knew that I would never have done such things, and I was very much afraid to die, and often lay in bed at night by myself, afraid to die and wondering how I would be when I went back to the front again.

The three with the medals were like hunting-hawks; and I was not a hawk, although I might seem a hawk to those who had never hunted; they, the three, knew better and so we drifted apart. But I stayed good friends with the boy who had been wounded his first day at the front, because he would never know now how he would have turned out; so he could never be accepted either, and I liked him because I thought perhaps he would not have turned out to be a hawk either.

The major, who had been the great fencer, did not believe in bravery, and spent much time while we sat in the machines correcting my grammar. He had complimented me on how I spoke Italian, and we talked together very easily. One day I had said that Italian seemed such an easy language to me that I could not take a great interest in it; everything was so easy to say. " Ah, yes," the major said. " Why, then, do you not take up the use of grammar? " Se we took up the use of grammar, and soon Italian was such a difficult language that I was afraid to talk to him until I had the grammar straight in my mind.

The major came very regularly to the hospital. I do not think he ever missed a day, although I am sure he did not believe in the machines. There was a time when none of us believed in the machines, and one day the major said it was all nonsense. The machines were new then and it was we who were to prove them. It was an idiotic idea, he said, " a theory, like another." I had not learned my grammar, and he said I was a stupid impossible disgrace, and he was a fool to have bothered with me. He was a small man and he sat straight up in his chair with his right hand thrust into the machine and looked straight ahead at the wall while the straps thumped up and down with his fingers in them.

" What will you do when the war is over if it is over? " he asked me. " Speak grammatically! "

" I will go to the States."

" Are you married? "

" No, but I hope to be."

" The more of a fool you are," he said. He seemed very angry. " A man must not marry."

" Why, Signor Maggiore? "

" Don't call me ' Signor Maggiore.' "

" Why must not a man marry? "

" He cannot marry. He cannot marry," he said angrily. " If he is to lose everything, he should not place himself in a position to lose that. He should not place himself in a position to lose. He should find things he cannot lose."

He spoke very angrily and bitterly, and looked straight ahead while he talked.

" But why should he necessarily lose it? "

" He'll lose it," the major said. He was looking at the wall. Then he looked down at the machine and jerked his little hand out from between the straps and slapped it hard against his thigh. " He'll lose it," he almost shouted. " Don't argue with me! " Then he called to the attendant who ran the machines. " Come and turn this damned thing off."

He went back into the other room for the light treatment and the massage. Then I heard him ask the doctor if he might use his telephone and he shut the door. When he came back into the room, I was sitting in another machine. He was wearing his cape and had his cap on, and he came directly toward my machine and put his arm on my shoulder.

" I am so sorry," he said, and patted me on the shoulder with his good hand. " I would not be rude. My wife has just died. You must forgive me."

" Oh——" I said, feeling sick for him. " I am *so* sorry."

He stood there biting his lower lip. " It is very difficult," he said. " I cannot resign myself."

He looked straight past me and out through the window. Then he began to cry. " I am utterly unable to resign myself," he said and choked. And then crying, his head up, looking at nothing, carrying himself straight and soldierly, with tears on both his cheeks and biting his lips, he walked past the machines and out of the door.

The doctor told me that the major's wife, who was very young and whom he had not married until he was definitely invalided out of the war, had died of pneumonia. She had been sick only a few days. No one expected her to die. The major did not come to the hospital for three days. Then he came at the usual hour, wearing a black band on the sleeve of his uniform. When he came back, there were large framed photographs around the wall, of all sorts of wounds before and after they had been cured by the machines. In front of the machine the major used were three photographs of hands like his that were completely restored. I do not know where the doctor got them. I always understood we were the first to use the machines. The photographs did not make much difference to the major because he only looked out of the window.